*Look for These Terrifying and Terrific Bestsellers*
*Written by John Saul and Published by Wings Books*

JOHN SAUL: THREE COMPLETE NOVELS

**Brainchild**
**Nathaniel**
**The God Project**

JOHN SAUL: THREE COMPLETE NOVELS

**Hellfire**
**The Unwanted**
**Sleepwalk**

# JOHN SAUL

**THREE TERRIFYING BESTSELLING NOVELS**

# JOHN SAUL

## THREE TERRIFYING BESTSELLING NOVELS

# SUFFER THE CHILDREN
# PUNISH THE SINNERS
# CRY FOR THE STRANGERS

**WINGS BOOKS**

New York ● Avenel, New Jersey

This omnibus was originally published in separate volumes under the titles:

*Suffer the Children,* copyright © 1977 by John Saul
*Punish the Sinners,* copyright © 1978 by John Saul
*Cry For the Strangers,* copyright © 1979 by John Saul

This edition contains the complete and unabridged texts of the original editions. They have been completely reset for this volume.

This 1996 edition is published by Wings Books,
a division of Random House Value Publishing, Inc.,
201 East 50th Street, New York, New York 10022,
by arrangement with Dell Publishing,
a division of Bantam Doubleday Dell Publishing Group, Inc.

Wings Books and colophon are trademarks of Random House Value Publishing, Inc.

Random House
New York • Toronto • London • Sydney • Auckland
http://www.randomhouse.com/

Printed and bound in the United States of America

Library of Congress Cataloging-in-Publication Data

Saul, John.
   [Novels. Selections]
   Three terrifying bestselling novels / John Saul.
      p.    cm.
   Contents: Suffer the children—Punish the sinners—Cry for the strangers.
   ISBN 0-517-18246-7
   1. Horror tales, American.  I. Title.
PS3569.A787A3   1996
813'54—dc20
                                              96-29214
                                                CIP

8 7 6 5

# CONTENTS

SUFFER THE CHILDREN

1

PUNISH THE SINNERS

221

CRY FOR THE STRANGERS

455

# SUFFER
# THE CHILDREN

For Michael Sack,
without whom this book would
not have been written

# PROLOGUE

# ONE HUNDRED YEARS AGO

T HE SURF WAS HIGH THAT DAY, ADDING A backdrop of sound to the late summer afternoon. High above the sea, the same wind that built the waves seemed only to stroke the grass in which the child played.

She was a pretty thing, eleven years old, the cornflower blue of her dress matching her eyes, and the blond hair that only children possess cascading down her back and over her shoulders as she bent to examine one of the tiny creatures that shared her world. She poked at it with one small finger, then pulled the finger away almost before she heard the tiny snap that signaled the beetle's ascent into the air. She watched it fall back to earth, and before it could scuttle away into the grass she poked it again. Again it snapped, rose into the air, and fell back to earth. She smiled to herself, then picked up the beetle and put it in her pocket. Through the heavy material she could just feel the movement of the struggling insect; its snapping sounds were completely muffled.

She glanced toward the house a hundred yards away, then toward the road that wound down the hill and out of sight. She half expected to see a carriage coming up the hill, and her mother waiting expectantly on the porch. But it was too early, much too early. She wondered what her grandmother would bring. She hoped it would be a pet. The child liked pets.

Her attention changed as a gust of wind hit her, and she turned to face the stand of woods that separated the field from the high bank of the ocean beyond. For a long time she stared into the wood, almost as though she saw something there, something that was almost within her range of vision, yet hovered just beyond the edge of sight. She felt an urge to go to the woods, to step in among the trees and ferns and lose herself from the house behind her. She knew she shouldn't. She knew the woods were beyond the limits, that there was danger there. But still, it would be nice to wander in the trees . . .

Perhaps that was why she began to follow the rabbit.

Within the forest, hidden by the foliage and the shadows of the trees above, a man sat staring out into the field. His eyes never left the child, never glanced to the side or farther out to the house that loomed across the field. It was as if he were hypnotized, part of the scene, yet somehow separated from it.

He watched in silence as the child looked first toward the house, then to the road, and finally turned to look directly toward him. For a long moment, as she seemed to examine him, seemed to look into his soul, he was afraid she was going to turn and run. His muscles tensed, but he felt nothing as he stared out of the darkness. Then the moment was over. The girl turned away, and the man relaxed. His hand reached for the bottle propped against a rock next to him, and he took a long drink.

It was a small rabbit, and the child knew it couldn't have been more than a few months old. It peered at her from beneath a bush, as if it knew that it was visible but hoped that maybe no one would notice. For a long time it held very still as the child approached it, but when she was still ten feet away she saw it begin to twitch its nose. She knew that it was about to bolt. Still, if she held herself completely motionless, maybe it would relax again, and then she could creep a little closer. She waited until the rabbit's nose stopped moving, then inched closer. Another foot. The nose began twitching again. She stopped. The rabbit sat up and cocked its ears. The child held still. Carefully, the rabbit eased back down to all fours, and it laid its ears back, as if to disappear entirely into the brush.

The child moved forward once again, and the rabbit bolted. Startled, the child jumped a little too, but her eyes never left the rabbit.

She saw that it was crippled.

One of its hind legs was much weaker than the other, so that when it leaped, it veered a bit to the left. And it seemed to be slow.

Maybe she could help it.

She began following, creeping as close to the rabbit as she could get, then watching in disappointment as it evaded her. The rabbit seemed to have no plan in mind, and for a long time it darted back and forth across the field, hiding first under one bush, then under another.

In the woods, the man watched the chase, his eyes never leaving the child. Occasionally he would see a grayish blur out of the corner of his eye, and he was half aware that it was a rabbit. But it didn't matter to him.

What mattered was the child.

He raised the bottle to his mouth again, and then it was empty.

Suddenly the rabbit seemed to develop a plan. It began making its way toward the woods, still not in a straight line, but with a series of leftward-veering hops that was drawing it directly toward the spot where the man waited.

The child, now conscious only of the rabbit, followed along, quickening her pace. She was beginning to be able to anticipate the rabbit, to correct for its error even before it made its jump. As it leaped into the woods, the girl was only a few feet behind.

The man rose out of the bushes, the bottle held aloft, the knuckles of his right hand white as they gripped its neck. He brought the bottle down hard, crushing the rabbit's skull just as it came to light at his feet. He straightened up in time to see the child step from the light of the field into the shadows of the forest. The wind seemed to pick up, and the roar of the surf grew louder.

She didn't see the rabbit die.

Rather, her mind held impressions:

The rabbit bouncing out of the field into the woods.

A shape looming before her that hadn't been there a second before.

A sound, not a crashing, but a sort of a dull crunching, and then the rabbit, the small animal that she had hoped to help, lying twitching at the feet of the man.

She looked up into his face.

The eyes were bloodshot, and a stubble of beard showed on his chin. His eyes, which might once have been the sparkling blue of an autumn sky, had gone dull, and the hair was a colorless tangle that made his features almost unrecognizable. A flicker of recognition crossed the child's face, but disappeared as the beginning of a cry built in her throat when the man dropped the bottle and reached for her.

One arm snaked around her small body, and the hand that had held the bottle moved to cover her mouth before the cry could be sounded. Her tongue touched his hand, and recoiled from the taste of whiskey.

He picked her up effortlessly and swung around to carry her deeper into the wood. As she struggled in his arms, his grip tightened, and he began to feel a heat in his groin not caused by the liquor in his blood.

He did it silently.

Silently he set her down in a small clearing, and silently he pulled at his belt.

When it was free, he used it to bind her wrists, and when she broke the silence with her cries, he slapped her, hard. Her cries died away to a moan, and she stared up at him with the fear of a trapped animal. The sun disappeared behind a cloud.

He dressed slowly, then removed the belt from the girl's wrists and replaced it around his waist. Then he rearranged the child's torn garments as best he could, and picked her up as gently as he knew how. He cradled her head against his shoulder as he carried her on through the woods, and then he was out of the woods once more, standing on the high bank, holding his child out to the sea, almost as an offering.

It began to rain.

For long moments he stood, as if waiting for a sign of some kind. Then, adjusting the child in his arms so that he would have one hand free, he began picking his way down the embankment, skirting the rocks with a sure step, his free hand steadying himself only when his weight tilted a loose stone.

When he was still fifty feet above the surf he began to make his way around a large boulder. Behind it, hidden from all but the most careful eye, the solid wall of the embankment was broken by a small opening. He pushed the limp form of the child into the opening; then he disappeared after it.

The sky seemed to open up as he emerged, alone, from the opening in the embankment, and the wind whipped rain and sea-spray into his face. The waters mixed, and a strange bittersweetness crossed his tongue. Without looking back at the cave entrance, he began making his way back up the embankment.

The rocks had grown slippery with the wetness of the storm, and the wind seemed to be trying to pluck him from his perch. Each time his foot slipped, his hands bled a little more, but he didn't feel it. He felt only the firmness of the earth below him, and the fury of the elements around him.

Then he had gained the top of the embankment, and he plunged back into the woods as if the sea would reach up to take him if he hesitated for even a second. When the forest closed behind him, he began to relax.

He walked purposefully through the woods now, past the trampled ground where he had so recently lain with the child, to the spot where the empty bottle still lay where he had dropped it.

And the rabbit.

He stopped then, and stared down at the rabbit, whose rain-soaked body lay pitifully still.

He picked it up, cradling it in his arms like a baby, and began to make his way across the field to the house beyond.

He didn't pause in the field, didn't take even a moment to look once more at the place where she had played. Instead he kept his eyes on the house, with the same hypnotic concentration with which he had earlier watched the child.

He left the field, crossed the lawn, and entered the house through the wide front door.

No one was there to watch him as he bore the body of the rabbit down the hall and into his study, nor were the gaslights yet casting the shadows he feared to see.

He closed the door to his study, then went to sit in a chair in front of the fireplace, the dead rabbit in his lap.

He sat there for a long time, huddled forward as if to draw warmth from the cold hearth in front of him, his hands stroking the rabbit's wet fur. Now and then he glanced up at the portrait of the beautiful child in the cornflower silk dress that hung above the mantel.

He didn't hear the carriage arrive, or the sound of the knocker as it fell against the front door.

He didn't hear the light tapping at his own door; didn't hear the slight click of the door opening, or the soft step of the maid who came into his study. She waited quietly by his chair until at last he noticed her.

"Yes?" The word was strange-sounding on his ear, as if someone else had uttered it.

"I'm sorry, Mr. John," the maid said softly. "I'm looking for Miss Beth. Her grandmother's asking for her."

"Miss Beth? Isn't she in the house? She was in the field."

"No, sir," the maid replied. "She doesn't seem to be in the house at all. I thought perhaps—"

He held up a hand wearily. "No," he said. "She isn't with me. Not any more."

The maid turned to go, then turned back.

"Mr. John?" He looked up at her. "What's that in your lap?"

The man looked down, and for the first time seemed to be conscious of the small creature on his lap.

"It's a rabbit," he said slowly.

"But what's wrong with it?" the maid asked.

"It's dead," he said. "It was so innocent, and now it's dead."

The maid left the room.

He sat there for a few more minutes, then he stood up. Carefully, he placed the rabbit on the chair, then glanced once more at the portrait above the mantel.

He left the study, closing the door after himself once more, and retraced his steps down the hallway.

He passed through the front door, then turned to follow a walkway around the corner of the house.

He followed the walkway until it ended, then followed the path that picked up from the end of the walk.

At the end of the path, a cliff fell away to the sea below.

He stood for a moment, staring at the sea that battered far below him, and his lips moved almost silently. And over the wind, lost in the noise of the surf, a word drifted soundlessly away.

"Beth," he whispered. Then he repeated the name, and as the sound fell away from him, he flung himself into the waiting sea.

For him, it was over.

# BOOK ONE

# FIFTEEN YEARS AGO

# ONE

PORT ARBELLO PERCHED SNUGLY ON THE bluffs above the ocean, its trees flourishing the last of their fall finery with a bravado that belied the nakedness soon to come. The breeze off the Atlantic signaled an end to Indian summer, and Ray Norton smelled the first signs of winter in the air as he turned the town's only police car onto Conger's Point Road.

Ray had grown up in Port Arbello, and now, in his mid-fifties, he was beginning to feel old. He had watched himself change and grow older as Port Arbello stayed the same. He tried to remember what changes had come to the town since he had been born, and realized that there just weren't enough to make much of a difference.

There was the new motel, doing its best to act as if it had been there since the beginning of time. It hadn't been, and as he passed it Ray wondered what would become of it when the losses finally became too great for even its management to tolerate. Maybe the town could buy it and turn it into a country club. Get rid of the neon sign. Put in a golf course.

Then he remembered that Port Arbello had already tried a country club, or at least a building near the old golf course. That had failed too, and the building now stood vacant and dying, serving only as a shelter for the few people who still used the golf course. There weren't more than forty or fifty of them, and it was all they could do to keep raising the funds to pay the greenskeeper each year.

All in all, other than the new motel (which was already fifteen years old), there wasn't much that was new in Port Arbello. A store occasionally changed hands, a house came on the market now and then, and once in a while a new family came to town. For the most part, though, the town kept to itself, passing its homes and its businesses from one generation to the next. Its small farms remained small farms, and its small fishing fleet continued to support a small group of fishermen.

But that was the way they liked it, Ray realized. They had grown up with it, and they were used to it. They had no intention of changing it. He remembered a few years back—how many he was no longer sure, but it must have been right after the War—when a real-estate developer had bought up a lot of acreage outside the town limits. He was going to turn Port Arbello into a summer town, filled with A-frames and summer natives.

The town had caught wind of the plan, and for the first time in its history, Port Arbello had moved quickly. In a single town meeting, with the support of everybody except the farmer who had sold his property, Port Arbello had passed zoning ordinances to prohibit such projects, then annexed the property that was to be developed. The developer fought it through the courts, but Port Arbello won. In the end, the developer had been unable to sell the property, and the farmer, a couple of hundred thousand dollars richer, had foreclosed on the mortgage, bought himself all the newest equipment he could find, and was still happily working his land at the age of eighty-six. Ray grinned to himself. That was the way of things in Port Arbello.

He tooted his horn as he passed the old farmer, but didn't wave. He didn't have to, for the farmer, intent on what he was doing, didn't look up from his field. But Ray knew that the next time he saw him in town, the old man would touch the brim of his hat and say, "Nice to see you the other day, Ray." That, too, was the way things were done in Port Arbello.

A mile out of town the Conger's Point Road made the left turn that would take it partway out to the Point before it cut back inland on its way south. Ray supposed that this, too, was something new, though the road had been extended far beyond Conger's Point long before he was born. But in the old days, the really old days, it had probably ended at the Congers' front door, a direct pipeline from the heart of the town to the residence of its leading citizens.

The Conger family, though not the founders of Port Arbello, had been at the top of the social heap there for so long that it was now a tenet of faith with the people that not much could go on in Port Arbello without the approval of the Congers. It was also a tenet of faith that the Congers were rich. Not as rich, perhaps, as the Rockefellers and the Carnegies, but close enough so that, to Port Arbello, it didn't make any difference. They still remembered the days when the railroad had built a special spur into Port Arbello to accommodate the needs of the Admiral's private car. They still remembered the days when the staff at Conger's Point was twice the size of the Conger family (which, until recently, had never been small). They assumed that the Congers, being people of taste and sensitivity, had let the staff go not because they could no longer afford them, but because large staffs had come to be considered ostentatious.

Ray Norton, who lived on the Point Road himself, and had grown up with Jack Conger's father, knew better. Ray had been of an age that fell between Conger generations, and felt himself privileged to be on warm social terms with two generations of Congers, even though the older one was now dead. Ray had been seventeen years younger than Jack Conger's father, and was fifteen years older than Jack. That, plus the fact that he was a neighbor and the chief of police, had put him in a position of being close to power. He enjoyed that position. And he was careful not to undermine it by talking about what he knew of the Congers.

He pulled the car off the road and into the Congers' driveway. You could see the house even before you turned into the drive. Indeed, you could see it from the moment the road passed the end of the forest that flourished along the north bank of the Point, and began flanking the field that separated the house from the woods. But Ray was always careful not to look at the house until he had reached the end of the driveway. From there, he could absorb it, could enjoy the grandeur with which it sat at the end of its lane, its full veranda staring austerely through the double row of ancient oaks that lined the drive. It was a saltbox, nearly two hundred years old, but its simple square lines seemed to fit with the bleakness of the lonely point on which it stood. It had a pride to it, as if it were challenging the sea to reach up and sweep it away. So far, the sea had not met the challenge, and Ray Norton doubted that it ever would.

He parked the car and crossed the porch to the great oaken door. As always, he was tempted to raise the antique brass door knocker and let it crash against its plate to cause the resounding boom in the house that always brought visions of times past into his head. But, as always, he resisted the impulse and pressed the button that would sound the door chimes in the main hall within.

"Newfangled gimcrack," he muttered to himself, parodying his New England background.

Rose Conger opened the door herself, and her face broke into a pleased smile at the sight of Ray Norton.

"Ray! If you're looking for Jack, you're in the wrong place. He really does work these days, you know."

"I'll get to him later," Ray said. "Right now I need to talk to you. Have you got any coffee on?"

Rose stepped back to let him in.

"I don't, but I'm sure Mrs. Goodrich does. If anything ever happens to her, I don't know what we'll all do. Is this a social visit, or are we talking seriously? It makes a difference, you know. When this place was built, they had separate rooms for all kinds of conversations. Take your pick.''

"How about the back study? I always liked that room. But only when a fire's lit.''

Rose smiled. "It's laid, but it's not lit. Let's go fix that. Why don't you get the fire started while I find Mrs. Goodrich?'' Without waiting for an answer, she started toward the back of the house, but turned toward the kitchen, leaving Ray to continue into the back study.

He lit the fire, then seated himself in the old leather wing chair just to the right of the fireplace. He glanced around the room, and realized how comfortable he was here. Often he wished the house were his.

When Rose Conger joined him, Ray was staring at the picture above the mantel.

"That's new, isn't it?'' he said.

"Only for us,'' Rose replied. "I haven't any idea how old it is. We found it in the attic a year ago, but just got around to having it cleaned last month.'' She shuddered slightly. "Have you any idea how much it costs to have a portrait cleaned?''

"I don't have any ancestors worth cleaning. Who was she?''

"I haven't the vaguest idea. From the way she's dressed, I'd say the portrait must be just about ninety years old. We can't figure out who she was. There's no one in any of the family albums who looks like that, or who might have looked like that when she was young.''

Ray looked at the picture carefully. "Well, it's obvious who she looks like. She looks like Elizabeth.''

Rose nodded her head. "She does, doesn't she? She definitely has Elizabeth's eyes, and the hair seems to be the same color, too. But she looks like she's two or three years younger than Elizabeth.''

They looked at the portrait together, and were still staring at it when Mrs. Goodrich appeared with their coffee.

"How children were expected to play dressed like that,'' she said, following their eyes to the painting, "absolutely beats me. No wonder there were so many servants around here. It'd take one girl all week just to wash that child's clothes. And with no machines.'' She shook her head. "All I can say is, I'm glad times have changed.'' She set the coffee down, nodded to Ray, and left the room.

"And if she had her way,'' Rose said as she poured the coffee, "she'd have Elizabeth and Sarah dressed that way all the time. And she'd keep the clothes clean, even if she had to beat them on a rock to do it. Times may change, but not Mrs. Goodrich.''

Ray grinned. "I know. If I didn't know better, I'd swear she hasn't changed at all since I was a kid. I always wondered if there was ever a Mr. Goodrich.''

"Who knows?'' Rose shrugged. "One simply doesn't ask Mrs. Goodrich such questions.'' She settled down on the sofa opposite Ray and sipped the coffee. "So what brings you out here in the middle of the day? Run out of crooks in Port Arbello?''

"I wish we had. Have you heard about Anne Forager?''

"Anne? Has something happened to her?"

"We don't know. Her mother called us this morning, very early. Apparently Anne came in late last night, long after she should have been home, and she was a mess. Her dress was torn, she was covered with mud, and she had a few scratches."

Rose paled. "Good God, Ray, what happened to her?"

"So far, we aren't sure. She says she was on her way home from school and that something happened to her. But she won't say what. She keeps saying that she doesn't remember. That all she remembers is that she was walking home from school, and then she was walking toward town along the Point Road, covered with mud."

"What time was that?"

"She got home around eleven."

"My God, Ray, and you mean her parents didn't call you? I mean, Anne Forager can't be more than seven or eight years old—"

"She's nine."

"All right, so she's nine! You can bet that if Sarah or even Elizabeth were missing that late at night, you'd have already been out looking for her for two or three hours."

"That's you, Rose. But these people are different. Around here, nobody thinks anything bad can happen. Marty and Marge just assumed that Anne was with some friend, and that was that. Until she came home. Now we're trying to find out what happened."

"Has a doctor seen her?"

"She's there now. I should find out what he has to say later this afternoon. What I need to know from you is if you were home yesterday afternoon."

"Not until five or five thirty. Why?"

"I was hoping you might have seen something. Anne says she walked back to town from here, or very close to here. From the mud, it looks like she must have been near the embankment."

"Or the quarry."

Ray's eyebrows rose. "Of course. The quarry. I'd forgotten all about it."

"I wish I could," Rose said. "I wish I could fill it in. Someone's going to get killed out there someday, and I don't care what Jack says, it's going to be our fault."

"Oh, come on, Rose. That old quarry has been there forever and nobody's ever come to grief there yet. Besides, the fishing is the best in town. Fill that old quarry in and half the kids in Port Arbello would be on your back."

"We could consider building them a swimming pool and letting them do their fishing in the stream," Rose said acidly. "I don't think anyone realizes how dangerous that place is."

"Well, be that as it may, we don't know where Anne was. She could have been at the quarry, she could have been on the embankment, or she could have been anywhere else. We won't know until she starts talking."

"If she starts talking . . ." Rose mused, wondering immediately if it had been wise to voice the thought. She glanced at Ray and saw compassion in his eyes. Well, they were old friends, and he had long been aware of the Congers' private torments.

"If?" Ray inquired gently.

Rose shrugged. "She may not, you know. If something happened to her, something she doesn't want to remember, she might simply block it out of her mind."

"Unless the doctor determines she's been raped," Ray said, "I can't imagine what it could be. And, frankly, I just don't think she's been raped. Not here. Not in Port Arbello."

Rose smiled thinly. "Things like that do happen a lot more often than anyone hears about."

Ray shook his head doubtfully. "If you want my opinion, I think Anne stayed out a lot later than she was supposed to, and has thought up a nice story to get herself out of the punishment she deserves. If she were my child . . ."

"Which she's not," Rose pointed out.

Ray chuckled. "No, she isn't, is she? But I am the chief of police, and I have a job to do. Is that what you're saying?"

"That's what I'm saying." Rose smiled. "Let me call Elizabeth. Maybe she'll know something you don't."

She went to the door of the study and called her daughter. She was pouring them both a second cup of coffee when Elizabeth Conger came into the room.

She was about thirteen, but had none of the awkwardness of most children of that age. Ray noted that the resemblance to the old portrait was remarkable indeed. The same eyes, the same silky blond hair, and, if the hair had been combed differently to flow freely over her shoulders, the same features. Elizabeth wore a ponytail, with bangs in front, the blond hair almost blending into the pale skin that was set off by her incredible sky-blue eyes.

Behind Elizabeth another child, Sarah, hovered silently. Two years younger than Elizabeth, Sarah provided an odd contrast to the older girl. She was dark, and her eyes seemed to sink deeply inside her, as if she lived in another world. Her hair was cropped short, and was as dark as Elizabeth's was blond. And, while Elizabeth was dressed in a neatly pressed mini-skirt and ruffled blouse, Sarah wore blue jeans and a plaid flannel shirt.

Elizabeth came into the room and smiled at Ray.

"Hello, Mr. Norton. Did you finally catch up with Mother? She's been overparking again. If you want to take her now, I can have Mrs. Goodrich pack a bag for her." She sat down, enjoying the laughter of her mother and the police chief.

"Sorry, Elizabeth," Rose said. "He can't prove a thing." Then her voice took on a serious tone, and Elizabeth's smile faded as she was asked if she had seen Anne Forager near the house the previous afternoon. She thought carefully before she answered. When she finally spoke, there was a maturity in her voice that belied her age.

"I don't think so. The last I remember seeing Anne yesterday, she was walking toward Fulton Street, by herself. It looked like she was going home.''

Ray nodded. "That's what Anne says, too. She was walking along Fulton Stret, and then she doesn't remember a thing until she was out this way.''

"This way?'' Elizabeth asked.

"Anne says she doesn't know what happened. But she says she walked home along the Point Road about eleven.''

"Then that lets me out,'' Elizabeth said. "I go to bed at nine every night.''

"Well, then,'' Rose said, standing up. "I guess that's that. I'm sorry, Ray, but it doesn't look like we can help you. Your trip's been wasted.''

Ray, too, rose, and all four of them walked together the length of the hall. Ray waited while Elizabeth led her sister up the stairs, then looked at Rose. There was concern in his eyes, and Rose was able to anticipate his question.

"I think she's getting better, Ray. I really do. She still doesn't talk, but she seems a little more animated than she did a year ago.'' Then some of the brightness left her voice. "Of course, I may be kidding myself. The school says that they don't think anything's changed, that she's the same as ever. But, on the other hand, Elizabeth seems to think she's better. And God knows, Sarah spends more time with Elizabeth than with any of the rest of us. I don't know what I'd do without her. I really don't.''

They said their good-byes, and Rose stood on the porch and watched as Ray drove down to the Point Road. Then she turned and stared speculatively across the field to the woods that hid the embankment from her view. Finally she turned back to the house, and went upstairs to find her children.

They were in the playroom, and the door stood open. Rose stayed silently in the hall for a moment, watching as Elizabeth patiently built a tower, then rebuilt it after Sarah knocked it down. Rose once more was impressed with Elizabeth's patience with her strange younger sister.

Elizabeth looked up as her mother came into the room, and smiled.

"One of these days the tower is going to stand,'' she said. "And on that day I'm going to tell Sarah that it's time for a new toy. Until then, I build and she knocks over.'' Elizabeth immediately noticed the pain in her mother's face, and tried to reassure her. "I don't mind, Mother. I'd rather have her knock them over than not do anything at all.''

Rose relaxed, but only a little. In her mind she blessed Elizabeth once more. Aloud she said, "Elizabeth, you don't go near the embankment or the woods, do you?''

"Of course not, Mother,'' Elizabeth said, not looking up from the new construction she was building for Sarah. "You've already told me how dangerous it is. Why would I want to go there?''

She put the last block in place, and watched as Sarah's arm came out to knock it over.

## TWO

**J**ACK CONGER REACHED INSTINCTIVELY TO adjust the mirror as he turned off the Point Road into the long driveway. He was a fraction of a second too late, and the glint of the setting sun caught him in the eyes just before it moved off his face to settle in a harmless rectangle in his lap. He blinked reflexively, and once more cursed his ancestor who had so conscientiously laid this road out on its perfect east-west axis. New England neatness, he thought. God, they were all so—he groped for the right word, then made his choice as he looked down the driveway at his home—severe. That was it, all right. They were severe. An absolutely straight drive leading to an absolutely plain house. He wondered just which of his forebears had had the temerity to break the line of the house with the wide porch. The porch, he had always felt, didn't really fit the house, though without it the house would have been totally lacking in any kind of warmth. Jack parked the car in front of the converted carriage house, now the garage, and went around the corner of the house to go in the front door. The Congers, he had been taught since birth, always used the front door. The side door was for children, and the rear for servants and merchants. Jack knew it was silly, but habit was habit, and besides, it was about the last of the old traditions that he could still keep up. The squire to the end, he thought as he closed the front door behind him.

No butler waited to take his coat, and no maid scurried out of his study as he entered it. He supposed, wryly, that he could pull the old bell cord and ask Mrs. Goodrich to bring him a drink, but he knew he would only be told once more that "grown men can mix their own drinks. Things aren't the way they used to be, you know." Then dinner would be slightly burned, just to remind him that he'd overstepped his bounds. He mixed his drink himself.

He had settled himself in front of the fireplace, and was weighing the pros and cons of stoking up the fire when he heard his wife's footstep in the hall.

"Rose?" he called, almost as if he hoped it wasn't. "Is that you?"

Rose came into the room, crossed the floor to her husband, and gave him one of those kisses usually classified as a peck. She sniffed at his glass.

"Is there another one of those?"

Jack's eyebrows lifted slightly. "So early?"

"It's been one of those days. Will you do the honors, or do I have to fix it myself?"

Jack smiled, but it wasn't a comfortable smile. "Since you didn't make any cracks about 'practice makes perfect,' I'll do it for you. Aren't you home a little early?" he asked as he moved to the bar.

"I've been here since lunch," Rose replied, settling herself on the couch. "All my work this afternoon was on paper, and the office was just too busy. I close three deals tomorrow, making us fifteen thousand dollars richer. Shall we drink to that?" She took the glass from his hand and raised it toward him. "To the recouping of the Conger fortune."

Jack raised his own glass halfheartedly, and settled back into his wing chair.

"You don't seem too thrilled about it," Rose said carefully.

"The Conger fortune," Jack said, "should be recouped by a Conger, if it to be recouped at all. Not a Conger wife."

"Well," Rose said shortly, "I guess we don't need to talk about that any more. I had a visitor this afternoon."

"Is that unusual?"

Rose stared at her husband for a moment, fighting the urge to rise to the bait. When she was sure she had herself under control, she spoke again. "Jack, let's not fight," she said. "Let's spend a quiet, comfortable evening at home, just like we used to."

Jack looked at her carefully, trying to see if he could spot a trap. After a moment, he relaxed, his shoulders dropping slightly and his breath, which he hadn't realized he'd been holding, coming deeply. Now, for the first time since she'd come into the room, his smile was warm.

"I'm sorry," he said. "I guess I'm just learning to be defensive all the time. Who came by? You made it sound important."

"I'm not sure if it was or not. It was Ray Norton, and he was here on business."

"That," Jack said speculatively, "would have to do with Anne Forager, right?"

"You already know?"

"You forget, my love, that I'm the editor of the only paper in town. Granted, it isn't much, but it is mine own. And in my illustrious position, there isn't much that goes on in this town that I don't hear about. The Port Arbello *Courier* may not be a major paper, but it is a fine gossip center. In short, yes, I've heard about Anne. Probably a lot more than you, since my sources, unlike Ray Norton's, are not sworn to stick to the facts, ma'am. What would you like to know?"

"What happened to her," Rose said.

"Ah, now that complicates things," he said, growing somber. "Anne Forager, at various times of the day, has been reported to be missing, to be dead, to have been raped and decapitated, to have been raped but not decapitated, and to have been decapitated but not raped. Also, she has been reported as having been severely beaten and now hovering between life and death. Or she deserves to be spanked, depending on who you listen to. In other words, you probably know a lot more about it than I do, since you talked to Ray, and everybody else talked to me." He drained his glass and stood up. "Would you like me to fix that for you, or are you going to nurse it along?"

"I'll nurse it," Rose said. She continued talking while Jack fixed his second drink. She noted that it was a double, but decided not to mention it. Instead, she occupied herself with recounting Ray Norton's visit that afternoon.

"—And that's about it," she finished. "Ray didn't go down to see you this afternoon?" Jack shook his head. "That's funny. I had the distinct impression he was planning to go directly from here to your office."

"If I know Ray," Jack said drily, "he went from here directly to the quarry, to have a look around. Probably complete with a pipe and a magnifying glass. Was he wearing his deerstalker hat?"

Rose grinned in spite of herself. "Jack, that isn't fair. Ray isn't like that, and you know it."

"How do I know it?" Jack shrugged. "Ray hasn't had a real case to work on since the day he went to work for Port Arbello. I'll bet he was more happy than concerned that something has finally happened here, wasn't he?"

"No, he wasn't. He seemed to be very concerned. And why are you being so hard on him? I thought you were good friends."

"Ray and I? I suppose we are. But we also know each other's limitations. I don't think he's Sherlock Holmes, and he doesn't think I'm Horace Greeley. But we like to act like we are. It makes us feel important."

"And you have to feel important?"

Jack's guard went up immediately. "What's that supposed to mean?"

"Forget it," Rose said quickly. "It wasn't supposed to mean anything. What do you suppose really did happen to Anne Forager?"

"Anne? Probably nothing. I tend to go along with the idea that she stayed out too late and came up with a good story to avoid her punishment. Children are like that."

"Not ours," Rose said quietly.

"No," Jack said. "Not ours." He stared into his drink for a moment. "Where are they?"

"Upstairs. Elizabeth's playing with Sarah. Oh, God, Jack, what if the same thing happened to Anne that happened to Sarah?"

Jack recoiled as if he'd been slapped.

"It didn't Rose. If something like that had happened, she wouldn't be talking about it at all. She wouldn't be talking. She'd be sitting—staring at the walls—just . . . sitting." He broke off for a moment, as if it was too painful to continue. Then he forced himself to speak again.

"She's going to get better. She'll be back in school next year . . ."

"She's in school," Rose said gently.

"I mean regular school, where she belongs. Not that other place." The bitterness in his voice hung in the air.

Rose bit her lip for a minute, trying to choose the right words.

"It's a good school, Jack. Really it is. And Sarah's doing well there. You know she isn't well enough to go to public school. Think what would happen to her. Why, the children alone . . ." She trailed off.

"We should keep her at home," Jack said. "She belongs at home, with people who love her."

Rose shook her head. "It isn't love she needs, right now. She needs to have people around her who understand her problem, who can help her. God knows, I don't have the time or the skills to devote to her."

"It isn't right," Jack insisted. "That school. That's for crazy kids, and retarded kids. Not for Sarah. Not for my daughter. All she needs is to be around normal kids, kids like Elizabeth. Look how well she does with Elizabeth . . ."

Rose nodded. "Of course I know how well she does with Elizabeth. But do you think all children are like Elizabeth? How many other children would have her patience? Children can be cruel, Jack. What do you think would happen to Sarah if she were back in public school? Do you think they'd all play with her the way Elizabeth does? Because if you do, you're crazy. They'd tease her, and taunt her. They'd play with her, all right, but she wouldn't be a playmate; she'd be a toy. It would only make her worse, Jack."

He finished his drink and rose to fix a third. Rose watched him go to the bar, and a wave of pity swept over her. He suddenly seemed unsure of himself, his step wary, as if something were waiting to trip him. As he tilted the bottle to pour the liquor into his glass, she spoke again.

"Do you think you ought to?"

"Ought to?" Jack glanced back at her over his shoulder. "No, I don't think I ought to. But I'm going to. There's a difference, you know."

The scream came before Rose could reply. Jack froze where he stood, the liquor streaming out of the bottle, overflowing the glass as the terrified shriek filled the house. It seemed to root him to the spot, and it wasn't until it had finally died away that he was able to let go of the bottle. Rose was already in the hall by the time the bottle broke on the floor, and if she heard it, she didn't turn around. Jack glanced at the mess at his feet; then he too ran from the room.

The awful sound had come from the floor above. Rose and Mrs. Goodrich met at the bottom of the stairs, and Rose came close to toppling the housekeeper as she scrambled up the single flight. Mrs. Goodrich recovered, and made her way up the stairs as quickly as her age and arthritis would allow. Jack passed her halfway up.

"What was it?" he asked as he passed.

"Sarah," Mrs. Goodrich panted. "It was Miss Sarah's voice. God Almight, hurry!"

Jack was at the top of the stairs when he saw his wife disappear into the children's playroom. By the time he got to the door, he realized that whatever had happened, it was over.

Rose stood just inside the door, a slightly dazed look on her face. In one corner, Sarah sat huddled against the wall, her knees drawn up under her chin, her arms wrapped around herself. She wore a flannel nightgown, whose folds spread around her and seemed to give her extra protection. Her eyes, unnaturally wide, stared vacantly outward, and she was whimpering to herself.

In the center of the room, Elizabeth sat cross-legged on the floor, her fingers on the indicator of a Ouija board, her eyes closed tight. She seemed oblivious of her sister's terror, as if she had not even heard the piercing scream of a moment before. As Jack came into the room, Elizabeth opened her eyes and smiled up at her parents.

"Is something wrong?" she asked.

"Wrong? Didn't you *hear* it?" Jack demanded.

Comprehension dawned on Elizabeth's face. "You mean the scream?" she asked.

Rose swallowed hard. "Elizabeth, what happened?"

"Nothing, really," Elizabeth replied. "We were just in here playing with the Ouija board."

"Where did you find—" Jack started to say, but Rose cut him off.

"Never mind that now. What happened?"

"Nothing happened, Mother. We were just playing with the Ouija board, and nothing much was happening. Then Cecil brushed up against Sarah, and she screamed."

"That's all?" Jack asked, disbelief sounding in his voice. "But look at her. She's terrified." Rose was moving toward Sarah now, and the little girl shrank farther into her corner.

"Well, of course she's terrified," Rose said. "If that cat had brushed up against me, I would have jumped too."

"But that scream," Jack said.

"I guess it was kind of awful," Elizabeth admitted. "But you have to get used to it."

"She's right," Rose said, stooping over Sarah. "Sarah doesn't react the way the rest of us do. Mrs. Montgomery tells me it isn't anything to worry about. It's just that Sarah doesn't react to very much, and when she does react, she tends to overreact. Mrs. Montgomery says the best thing to do is simply act as if nothing happened at all. For instance, if Cecil brushed up against me and I jumped, would you make a big fuss about it? Of course not. And that's what we should try to do with Sarah. If we stay calm, she'll be all right. If we make too much of a fuss, it will only scare her more."

"Can you do it?" Jack asked. "Can you get used to her being this way?"

"I'll never get used to screams like that," Rose muttered as she gathered Sarah into her arms. For a moment Sarah seemed to shrink away from her mother, but then, as if she suddenly realized where she was, her arms went around Rose's neck, and she buried her face in the warm breast. Rose, totally immersed in calming her child, carried Sarah from the room.

Jack, still standing at the door, moved aside to let his wife pass. He made a small gesture, as if to put a comforting hand on Sarah, but Rose was already through the door by the time he had made up his mind to complete it. His hand wavered uncertainly in the air for a moment, then disappeared into his pocket. He stared at the Ouija board.

"Where did you get that thing?" he asked.

Elizabeth glanced up. "It was in the storeroom. You know, the one where we found the old picture. How old do you think it is?"

"Not that old. Probably thirty, forty years. Those things were popular in the twenties. Everybody had one, and everybody was holding séances. I seem to remember my parents and their friends playing with one. Probably that one."

"Want to try it with me?" Elizabeth asked. "Maybe we could find out who the girl in the picture is."

Jack smiled at her. "We know who it is," he said. "It's obviously you. Same eyes, same hair. Only I don't understand why you never wear that dress any more."

"Oh, it's so old," Elizabeth said, her eyes twinkling as she joined the game. "I've had it for at least a hundred years. It's really just a rag now." She sighed. "I suppose I'll have to throw it out."

"Don't. I can't afford to buy you a new one. Maybe that Ouija board can tell me where the money goes."

"Maybe so," Elizabeth said, a note of eagerness in her voice. "Want to try it?"

For a moment Jack was tempted. Then he remembered Sarah, and shook his head. "I'd better get downstairs and see if I can help your mother with Sarah."

Elizabeth nodded. "Okay. I'll be down after a while." She watched her father leave the room, then glanced down at the Ouija board. Then she remembered the cat.

"Cecil," she called. "Cecil? Where are you?" She held still for a minute or two, listening, then called to the cat again.

"Cecil? I'll find you, you know, so you might as well come out now."

There was no telltale scuffling to tell her where the cat was hiding, so she began a search of the room. Eventually she discovered the cat, clinging to the inside of the draperies, halfway up from the floor. She pulled a chair over and stood on it while she disengaged the cat's claws from the thick material.

"Did Sarah frighten you?" she said. "Well, you frightened her first. If you don't want her to scream, you mustn't brush up against her like that. But it isn't your fault, is it? How would you know it would scare her? All you wanted was a little attention. So you let go of that curtain and come down here with me. Come on, let go. It's all right now."

She freed the last of the claws and, holding the cat close, stepped down from the chair. She carried the cat to the Ouija board and sank back to her cross-legged position, placing Cecil in her lap. She sat for a long time, stroking the cat, talking softly to him, waiting for him to calm down. When at last Cecil closed his eyes and began to purr, Elizabeth stopped stroking him and put her fingers back on the indicator of the Ouija board.

An hour later, still carrying the sleeping Cecil, Elizabeth came downstairs for dinner.

# THREE

SHE WATCHED THE MOON CREEP UP FROM the horizon, watched the silvery road shoot across the sea toward the base of the cliff that supported the house high above the surf. She listened for a moment, as if expecting the pounding surf to lessen its dull roar in the new brightness of the full moon. But the noise did not abate. The end of the silver road appeared, just short of the horizon, and she felt depressed as the gap between the moon and its reflection widened. As the moon climbed out of the sea, it seemed to shrink.

"It always seems to get smaller as it gets higher," Rose said, more to herself than to Jack. He glanced up from the book he was reading, and adjusted his sprawling position as Rose came over to the bed.

"What does?"

"The moon. It always looks so huge when it starts to rise, then gets smaller."

"It's an illusion," Jack said. "Something to do with the proximity to the horizon."

She cuddled close to him, and tried to ignore the slight drawing away she felt in his body. "That's my Jack, literal to the core. Can't you try to imagine it as really shrinking? As though somebody was letting some of the air out?" She ran her fingers through the hair on his chest, feeling the ripple of muscles just below the skin. She reached across his stomach and snatched the book away from him. He rolled over and scowled at her.

"Hey," he said. "I was reading that book."

She grinned at him.

"Not any more. I'm tired of you keeping your nose in that book. I want to play." She sat up and slipped the book behind her.

"Oh? Okay, we'll play. Give me back the book before I count to ten." As he reached nine, Rose slipped the book into the bodice of her nightgown. Jack's eyebrows rose a notch. "So that's what you want to play?"

Rose lay back, striking a seductive pose. "If you want it, come and get it." Her eyes danced as she challenged him.

Jack made a grab at the book, and as he came close to her, Rose tossed the book aside and slid her arms around his neck. His hand, caught between them, was pressed against her breast.

"Touch me, darling," she whispered into his ear. "Please touch me." Jack hesitated for a moment, then began moving his hand over his wife's breast, feeling the nipple harden under his touch. Rose moved her face around and began kissing him, her tongue lightly probing between his lips, trying to find an entry. She pulled him down till he was lying on top of her, and her hands began to move over his back, caressing him, stroking him. For a moment—just a moment—she thought he was going to respond. As she felt his body go limp, felt the weight of him lying inertly above her, her fingers turned into claws, and she scratched at him violently. Reacting to the pain, Jack leaped from the bed.

"God damn you," Rose snarled. "God damn you to hell for the no-good man you are!" There was no laughter in her eyes now, only a blinding rage that frightened Jack.

"Rose—" he began. But she got up swiftly, her sudden movement cutting off his plea, and stood opposite him as though the bed had suddenly become a battlefield.

"Don't 'Rose' me, you bastard. Do you think that's what I need?"

"I'm sorry," Jack began again.

"You're always sorry. That's all I've heard for a year now. Did you know it's been a year? I've been keeping track!"

"You didn't have to do that."

"Didn't I? Why not? So you'd never have to know how long it's been since you made love to your wife? So you wouldn't have to know how long it's been since you acted like a man?"

"That's enough, Rose," Jack said.

"It's not enough," she shot back, her voice rising. "It won't be enough till you get through this thing, whatever it is. Look at me. Aren't I attractive any more?" She stripped the nightgown off and stood before him, naked, the moonlight streaming through the window to bathe her pale form in an almost metallic hue, the high breasts jutting out above the narrow waist, the full hips tapering into her long, lithe legs.

"Well," she demanded as Jack stared at her. "What about it? Have I turned into some sort of pig?" Jack shook his head, saying nothing. "Well then, what is it? What's happened to you? If it isn't me, it must be you. What's wrong with you, Jack?"

Again he shook his head. "I—I can't tell you, Rose. I'm not sure I know."

"Then shall I tell you?" There was a note of malevolence in her voice that frightened him. He moved back a step, then sank into a chair, waiting. Rose began pacing the room, her eyes wild. She seemed to be casting about, wondering where to start, and for a second Jack waited, trying to fathom the direction from which the attack would come.

"It's the money, isn't it?" she demanded. Safe, he thought. "You just can't stand the idea that the fortune's gone, can you? That you, the last of the Congers, actually has to work, not for the fun of it, but for the money?" She stared at him as if waiting for a defense, then plunged on. "Well, when are you going to learn that it doesn't matter? There's enough left to pay the taxes on this place, though God knows why we even need it, and between us we certainly make enough to pay for whatever we need. It's not as if we were poor, for God's sake. And even if we were, so what? You don't have to be rich to be a man, damn it!"

He sat silently, knowing what was coming next. Rose didn't disappoint him.

"Or is it me? Do you feel like I've cut your balls off by making more money than you do? I happen to be good at my job, Jack, and you should be proud of that. But not you! Oh, no! You take it as some kind of personal threat to your manhood. Christ, I begin to understand what all those liberationists are talking about. You *do* resent a successful woman. Well, let me tell you something. Do you want to know why I went to work in the first place? I was bored, Jack, just plain bored."

"Rose, we've been all through this—"

"And we'll go through it again." Suddenly she sank onto the bed, her rage spent. "We'll go through it till we get to the bottom of it." The tears started, and Rose buried her face in her hands. "I don't know how much more I can stand, Jack. I really don't. I'm sorry I said I was bored. It wasn't that. I was really just frustrated." She looked up, as if imploring him to understand. "Jack, it's terrible to love a man who doesn't love you."

"That's not it, Rose," he said softly. "I love you very much. I always have."

She sighed. "Well, it's a strange way you show it. I don't know what to do. Sometimes I think it would help if I quit my job. But it's too late for that now." She smiled thinly. "Do you know what it's like to be successful? It's intoxicating. You want more, and more. And I'm going to have more, Jack. I don't get anything at home any more, so I have to have some fulfillment somewhere else."

"If it's that bad," Jack said dully, "why are you still here?"

She stared at him, and there was a hardness in her eyes that frightened him. "Someone," she said slowly, "has to protect the children. Since you don't qualify, that leaves me, doesn't it?"

His blow fell so fast that she had no time to move with it. His fist struck her hard on the cheek, and the force of the blow knocked her flat out on the bed, but she didn't cry out. Instead, she touched the bruise gently and stared up at him. "At least I'm fairly close to your size," she said softly.

He stared at her, then at his hand, and it seemed like an eternity before he realized what he had done. "My God," he breathed. He went to the bathroom and ran the water until it was cold. Then he soaked a washcloth and brought it to her, handing it to Rose to press against her cheek, knowing that she wouldn't let him touch her now.

"I didn't mean to do that."

"Didn't you?" Her voice was listless, as if nothing mattered. "I suppose you don't mean to do a lot of things you do."

"Rose, that isn't fair."

"Life isn't fair, Jack. Leave me alone."

He got up to leave the room. "Maybe it's the curse," he said, trying to keep his voice light. "Maybe the old family curse has finally caught up with me."

"Maybe it's caught up with both of us," Rose said miserably. She watched him leave the bedroom, and wanted to call him back, wanted to hold him and be held by him. But she couldn't. She turned off the light, rolled over, and tried to sleep.

Jack sank into his chair in the study and took a sip of the drink in his hand. He stared moodily out the window, watching the play of moonlight and shadows on the branches of the maple trees that broke the clean sweep of lawn from the house to the edge of the cliff beyond. The cliff looked inviting, but Jack knew that that was not one of the things that happened when he drank. Often he wished it were.

The memory was still not clear. Perhaps it never would be, sodden as it was in alcohol.

Rose was right; it was just about a year. It had been a Sunday, and it must have been a little over a year ago, for the leaves were still on the trees, glowing gold and red. Rose had gone off for a game of golf—who with? He couldn't remember. There was so much of that day he couldn't remember. He had been drinking, which wasn't unusual for a Sunday, and in the afternoon he had decided to go for a walk. With Sarah.

And then it was foggy. They had started off across the field, and Sarah had run ahead, calling to him to hurry. But he hadn't hurried, and she had waited for him. They had talked, there in the field, but he couldn't remember what they had talked about. And then Sarah had asked him to take her to the woods. There were so many things in the woods she wanted to see, and she never got to go there. And so they had gone to the woods.

He remembered carrying her out of the woods, but that was all.

He listened to the clock strike, and watched the shadows dance on the window. It was an ugly dance, and he didn't want to watch it. He looked at his drink, and tried to force himself not to refill it.

Sarah slept restlessly, and the dream swept over her again, as it did every night, over and over, never ending.

She was in a room, and the room was big. There was nothing in the room except Sarah and her toys. But she didn't want to play with them. Then Daddy was there, and they were going out of the house together and into the field. She ran ahead of him and stopped to look at a flower. There was an ant on the flower, and she picked the flower to take back to her daddy. But she knew that if she tried to carry it, the ant would fall off. So she called him.

"Daddy! Hurry!"

But he hadn't hurried, and she had waited for him. When he was finally there, the ant was gone, and the flower too, blown out of her hand on a gust of wind. It had gone to the forest, and she wanted to find it.

"The flower's in the woods, Daddy. Take me to the woods."

And so they went to the woods, and her daddy was holding her hand. She felt safe.

They stepped out of the sunlight of the field into the deep shadow of the trees, and Sarah held her father's hand even tighter. She looked around for the flower, and saw a bush. The flower was in the bush. She was sure the flower was in the bush, and the ant would be there too.

She pulled her father toward the bush.

"Hurry, Daddy, hurry. We're almost there."

And then she was there, crawling under the bush, its branches catching at her hair, thorns reaching out to scratch at her. Then she felt something grab at her ankle. A vine. It must have been a vine. She tried to shake loose, but the thing held tighter to her ankle and began pulling her from the bush. She couldn't find the flower. Wait! There it was. If she could only grab it!

But she couldn't, and the thing was pulling her out of the bush. She cried out.

"Daddy! Help! Make it let go, Daddy!"

She twisted around, and the thing was Daddy. But it wasn't Daddy. It was someone else, and he looked like Daddy, but it couldn't be Daddy. Not this man with his wild look. This man who was going to hit her.

She felt the blow, and tried to cry out to her father to help her, but she had no voice. Her father would help her.

Her father hit her.

She wanted her father to pull the man off her.

She wanted her father to stop hitting her.

She wanted her father.

The hand moved up and down through the air, and then Sarah couldn't hear anything any more. She watched herself being beaten, but she felt no pain. She tried to get away, but she couldn't move. As Daddy hit her again and again, she watched herself fade away. And then there was only the gray, the gray that she lived in, and in a far corner of the gray a girl—a blond, blue-eyed girl who would take care of her.

Elizabeth. Elizabeth knew what had happened, and would take care of her. As the gray closed around her, she reached out to Elizabeth.

Sarah woke up, and the hands that were outstretched moved slowly back, and she held herself. When she slept, she dreamed the dream again.

Elizabeth lay in her bed, staring at the ceiling, watching the progress of the moonlight as it moved slowly toward the far wall. She listened to the silence.

She had tried not to hear it; tried to bury her head under her pillow as her parents fought. But the sounds came through the walls, under the door, into the bed, and she listened. Finally she heard her father as he went down the stairs. Now she waited, and watched the moonlight. She would wait until she heard him come back up the stairs, until she heard the click of her parents' door finally closing for the night. Then she would sleep.

Didn't her mother know what had happened in the woods that day? Elizabeth knew that she could tell her mother, but that she wouldn't. Elizabeth knew that she shouldn't know what had happened. And she also knew she couldn't forget it, either.

She had been watching them from the house, and had decided to go with them. She had called to them, but the wind had blown her words the wrong way and they hadn't heard. So she had followed them across the field. Then, just as she had been about to catch up with them, she had decided to play a game with them instead.

She had veered off to the left, toward the road, and cut into the woods about fifty feet from them. Then she had begun making her way back, moving from tree to tree, keeping herself hidden. At the last minute, when she was so close that they would have to see her, she would jump out at them.

She had heard a scuffling noise, and peeped around the tree to see Sarah crawling under a bush. She used the opportunity to dart closer and hide behind a fallen log, watching her sister through the tangle of rotting roots that thrust skyward. Sarah had pushed farther under the bush, and Elizabeth thought her father was about to crawl after her.

But instead he grasped her ankle and began pulling her back toward him.

She heard Sarah cry out, and watched as her father lifted his fist into the air. Suddenly, yanking Sarah free of the bush, he brought his fist down on her. Sarah screamed then, and turned to look up at her father.

Elizabeth stayed hidden behind the log, watching the scene before her with a strange detachment. Suddenly it had all seemed to be far away from her, not connected to her. She suddenly no longer saw her sister and her father, but two strangers, a little girl and a man, and the man was beating the child. And it seemed to have no effect on Elizabeth at all. She simply crouched there, watching it unfold before her.

When Sarah finally lay still, Elizabeth saw her father straighten up, and she could barely recognize him. There was a vacant look in his face, and his black hair, usually so neatly brushed, hung in damp strings around his face. He looked around wildly, then down at the child at his feet. She heard a sob wrack his body, then watched as he picked Sarah up and began carrying her across the field toward the house. She stayed perfectly still until her father, still carrying her sister, had disappeared through the front door. Then she stood up and moved slowly to the spot where her sister had lain. She looked once more toward the house, then turned and began making her way through the woods toward the embankment.

When she had returned to the house an hour later, the doctors were there, and they had taken Sarah away. Her father was nowhere to be seen, and her mother was hysterical. Mrs. Goodrich had finally noticed her, and asked her where she had been. She said she had been for a walk. Down by the quarry. It was the only thing she had ever said about that afternoon, and it was the only thing she would ever say about it.

Elizabeth continued to stare at the ceiling, and when, much later, she heard the click of her parents' door, she slept.

Jack lay in bed, but he still didn't sleep. He remembered what he could remember.

He remembered the doctors coming, and he remembered them putting Sarah in the ambulance. He remembered Rose coming home, and he remembered that someone had given him a shot.

They had flown Sarah to a hospital, a hospital far enough from Port Arbello that no one would ever have known what had happened to Sarah. She had been there for three months, and the doctors had been able to repair her body. The ribs had healed and there were no longer any scars on her face.

But they had not been able to repair her mind. When she had come home from the hospital, she had been changed. She was no longer the bright elfin child she had always been. She no longer laughed, or ran through the house. She no longer shouted, or played in the field.

She was quiet. She neither spoke nor laughed, and when she moved she moved slowly, as if something were holding her back.

Occasionally, she screamed.

She seemed to be frightened, but she learned to tolerate the presence of her mother. She was never left alone with her father.

She responded only to Elizabeth. She would follow Elizabeth whenever she could, and if Elizabeth could not be with her, she would sit quietly and wait. But that wasn't often.

Elizabeth was usually with her. Except when they were in school, Elizabeth spent most of her time with Sarah—reading to her, talking to her, not seeming to notice that Sarah never talked back. Elizabeth played with Sarah, never losing her patience when Sarah's interest wandered, always finding something new to distract Sarah from whatever was going on in her mind.

The doctors said that Sarah could recover someday, but they didn't know when it would be. Since they didn't know exactly what had happened to Sarah, and nobody seemed able to tell them, they weren't entirely sure how to treat her. But someday, they were sure, Sarah would be able to remember what had happened to her that day, and face it. When that day came, Sarah would be all right again. But until that day, Sarah might do anything. Schizophrenia, they said, was unpredictable.

## FOUR

ROSE CONGER STARED ACROSS THE BREAKfast table and wondered for the twentieth time how her husband could drink so much and never show the effects of it.

Had he been less engrossed in his morning paper, Jack would have noticed the look of annoyance on Rose's face as she studied his own. At forty, he looked ten years younger, and where the lines of character, or age, should have begun their march from his forehead to his jowls, only the smooth skin of youth was present, still unaffected by the years of drinking. It isn't right, Rose thought. Any other man would have veins standing on his nose, and the awful pallor would make him look skeletal. But not Jack.

"What time did you come to bed?" she asked.

He looked up, then went back to his paper. "One thirty. Two. I don't know."

"Would you like some more coffee?"

He put down the paper, and a twisted smile crossed his face.

"Do I look like I need it?"

"I wish you did," Rose said bitterly. "Maybe if it showed on your face you wouldn't drink so much."

"Oh, come on, Rose. Let's let it alone, shall we? The kids will be down in a minute." He glanced at his watch, as if the gesture would bring the girls into the room and rescue him from what he knew was coming.

"They'll be ten minutes yet," Rose replied. "Jack, what we were talking about last night . . ."

"Is it going to be the drinking this morning? Why is it, Rose, that it's always the money at night and the drinking in the morning? Why don't you, just for the sake of variety, talk about the drinking at night and the money in the morning? Then maybe we could both think of something new to say."

Rose glowered down at her plate and tried to keep her voice even. "I suppose I harbor the vain hope that maybe, if I don't talk about it at night, you won't do it. You'd think I'd learn, wouldn't you?"

"Yes," Jack said, "you would." He folded the paper noisily and tried to concentrate on the print. He read a paragraph, then reread it as he realized that he hadn't any idea of what it was about. He was on his third reading when Rose spoke again.

"How long can we go on like this?"

He put the paper aside and stared across at her. For a long time he was silent, and when he spoke his voice was hard.

"What do you mean, 'like this'? If you mean how long until I can get it up for you again, I don't know. If you mean how long before I'm going to stop drinking, I don't know. If you mean how long before you stop harping at me all the time, that's up to you. I have a strange feeling that I will stop drinking, and start screwing, when you decide to let the whole thing alone and give me some peace. There are reasons, you know, why I have problems, and your nagging doesn't help at all. So why don't you just leave it alone, Rose? Just leave it alone." He stood up and left the room, and Rose was amazed to hear the warmth with which he greeted his daughters before he left the house. His failure to slam the door as he left only increased her annoyance. She poured herself some coffee, and tried to match Jack's warmth as the girls came into the room.

"You have your choice this morning," she said. "Mrs. Goodrich says waffles and pancakes are equally easy, so you can have either one."

"We'll have waffles," Elizabeth said. She kissed her mother good morning and seated herself. Sarah pulled her father's recently vacated chair around and sat beside Elizabeth.

"Sarah? Don't you want to sit in your own chair?"

There was no response from the little girl. She sat quietly with her hands in her lap until Elizabeth poured her some orange juice. She picked it up, dutifully drained the glass, and set it down again. Her hand went back to her lap. Rose watched in silence, feeling helpless.

"Sarah," she repeated. "Are you sure you don't want to sit in your own chair?"

Sarah's head turned toward Rose, and she stared at her mother for a moment. Rose looked vainly into the tiny, dark face, trying to see if Sarah had understood her. It was like trying to fathom the feeling of a mask. After a few seconds, Sarah turned her face away again. A knot formed in Rose's stomach.

"Maybe she'd rather have pancakes," she said pensively. "But how can I know?"

Elizabeth smiled at her mother. "The waffles will do fine," she said. "She likes them. How come Daddy left so early?"

"I guess he had a lot to do at the office," Rose answered distractedly, her eyes still on her younger daughter. She felt that there was something she ought to do, something she ought to say to Sarah, but she didn't know what it was. She felt confused. Hurriedly, she put her napkin on the table and stood up.

"I have a lot to do myself," she said. "Can you manage by yourself, Elizabeth?"

"Sure," Elizabeth said. "If I have to leave before the van gets here, shall I leave Sarah with Mrs. Goodrich?"

"If you think it would be—" "All right" was what she was about to say, but it struck her that she was the mother, not Elizabeth, and that even if she did feel all at sea where Sarah was concerned, it was still her duty to be a mother. She should not defer to a thirteen-year-old child, even one as mature as Elizabeth.

"That will be fine," she corrected herself. "I'll be in my office. Come in before you leave."

She started to leave the room, then, on an impulse, leaned down to kiss Sarah. Sarah didn't respond at all, and, the knot in her stomach tightening, Rose left the room. As she made her way into the little parlor at the front of the house that she had converted into an office for herself, she heard Elizabeth chattering brightly to Sarah, never pausing to give Sarah a chance to say anything, never sounding annoyed at Sarah's—"Dumbness" was the word that came to mind, but Rose couldn't bring herself to use it. She avoided the issue completely by turning her mind to her work.

She pulled out the files she had been working on the previous afternoon and began checking her figures once more. She found two errors, and corrected them. She prided herself on her attention to detail, and had become even more careful as time went on. Since her first day in the real-estate business she had not turned in any paperwork that was less than perfect, and she knew that the men in her office resented it. It had become an unspoken game, good-natured on her part but played with a slight edge of envy by the others involved, to give Rose wrong figures and see how long it would take her to find them. She suspected there was a pot building that would eventually go to the person who succeeded in catching her in a mistake. She intended for that pot to keep on growing till they finally gave it up and either split it up among themselves or handed it all over to her. She finished the files just as Elizabeth came in.

"That time already?" she said.

"I told Kathy Burton I'd meet her before school. Sarah's in the kitchen with Mrs. G."

"Will you be home right after school?"

"Aren't I always?"

Rose smiled at her daughter appreciatively, and held out her arms. Elizabeth came to her mother and hugged her.

"You're a great help to me, you know," Rose whispered to her.

Elizabeth nodded her head briefly and freed herself. "See you tonight," she said. Rose watched as she pulled the door closed behind her, and turned to gaze out the window. In a moment she heard the front door open and close, then saw Elizabeth, pulling a coat on, skip down the steps and start the walk to the Point Road.

Rose went back to her work, thumbing through her listings and mentally pairing off houses with clients. She had discovered that she had a knack for picking the right house for the right person, and her reputation was spreading. She made it a practice to spend at least a couple of hours with each client, talking about everything but houses. Then, when she felt she knew something about her client, she would pull out her listings and give them a couple to look over. Finally she would pull out her own choice for them, and she was usually right. More and more, lately, people had begun to come to her, not so much to see what she had available as to ask her what she thought they ought to have. It was making her work much easier, and her volume much larger.

One more year, she thought, and I'll get my broker's license. Then, watch out, Port Arbello. Another Conger is on the rise.

She was only half aware that the little Ford van that served as a school bus had arrived to take Sarah to White Oaks School, and didn't look up from her work until she heard the tapping at her door.

"Come in," she called.

The door opened, and Mrs. Goodrich, looking resentful at having to intrude on Rose, stuck her head in.

"Sorry to bother you," she said, the deep Yankee voice rumbling from her immense bosom. "Mr. Diller wonders if he could have a word with you. I told him you were busy, but he wonders anyway." Her tone suggested that it was her strongly held opinion that if Mr. Diller had any sense of propriety whatsoever, he would have faded directly into the ground upon being told that Mrs. Conger was busy.

Rose suppressed a grin and did her best to impersonate the grande dame that Mrs. Goodrich obviously expected her to be. For a long time, when she had first come to live in the Conger house, Mrs. Goodrich had frightened her to death, and she had been painfully aware that she did not meet the standards that Mrs. Goodrich had set for the senior Mrs. Conger-in-residence. But she had eventually come to realize that, whatever she did, Mrs. Goodrich would see her as Mrs. Goodrich wanted to see her. In the last couple of years Rose had found a certain enjoyment in trying to play the role. So now, for the benefit of the old housekeeper, she stood up, drew herself as erect as she could, and tried to sound imperious.

"It's unusual that he should call without an appointment, isn't it?"

Mrs. Goodrich nodded a vigorous agreement.

"But I suppose it would be useless to try to send him away."

Again Mrs. Goodrich nodded vigorously.

"So I suppose you may show him in."

The door closed, and in a moment it reopened to allow George Diller to enter. Rose promptly relaxed and smiled at him. He was a little younger than she, and sported a full beard. He was one of the teachers at the White Oaks School, but since he seemed to have a special way with the children he taught, he also drove the van that picked them up and delivered them home every day. The school had tried other drivers, but things always seemed to go better when George Diller drove, as if the children, trusting him, tried to behave better for him.

"What was that all about?" he said, glancing back toward the door.

"You heard?" Rose replied, chuckling.

"You sounded just like my Aunt Agatha, down in Boston. She could order a servant to kill himself, and he wouldn't dare disobey. Fortunately for everyone, she never did."

"Mrs. Goodrich would have loved your Aunt Agatha. She's convinced that's the way a proper lady should talk, so I do my best for her. It's kind of fun, really."

"Well, it almost scared me off. But not quite."

"That's good. Would you like some coffee?"

"Not enough time. The kids won't wait long."

Rose glanced out the window and saw Sarah climbing into the front seat of the van. In the back, six or seven children stared out at her, and she could see that one or two of them were already getting restless.

"Then what can I do for you?" Rose asked.

"Nothing for me. It's about Sarah. It isn't anything serious, but the staff at the school would like you and Mr. Conger to come in for a talk."

"Oh?" Rose looked concerned, and George hurried on.

"Really, it's nothing. I think they're thinking of making some changes in Sarah's program, and they want to talk to you first."

Rose nodded. "Of course. Is there any time that's best for the school?" She moved to the desk and opened her calendar.

"Not really." George shrugged. "Afternoons are best, after the kids have gone home, but if you don't have time, we can always work around you."

Rose knew they could. White Oaks was a very expensive school, and had a policy of going out of their way both for their students and the families of their students. Consequently, they found that they very rarely had to go out of their way. Parents, realizing that the school would do what it could for them, tried to do what they could for the school. So Rose searched for a free afternoon, and picked up a pencil.

"How's Thursday? Of course, I'll have to check with my husband, but I imagine he can get away."

"Fine," George said. "About four?"

"I'll mark it right now—" Rose broke off as she heard a little cry from the front of the house. She glanced up, and for a moment she didn't see anything amiss. Then she saw it: The van was moving.

"George!" she yelled. "Quick! The van!"

Without asking any questions, George headed for the door. It stuck, and he grappled with it for a moment. Rose was still staring out the window. The van was moving slowly, but it was picking up speed on the slight incline that led to the garage. She judged that if it hit the garage, it would stop with little damage. But if it missed the garage . . .

Her eyes moved across the wide lawn, and the unobstructed path that led directly to the edge of the cliff.

"The door," George yelled. "It's stuck!"

"Push down," Rose snapped. "It jams at the top." She glanced out the window again, and the van seemed to be veering a little to the left. It would miss the garage.

She heard George grunt, and spun to see him still struggling with the door. Behind her she could hear the terrified screams of the children as they realized what was happening.

"Let me do it," she cried, pushing him aside and grasping the knob. She lunged at the door and gave a quick yank. It flew open, and George was through it and running for the front door, a few feet away. In the middle of the doorway, Mrs. Goodrich stood frozen, her hand covering her mouth as if to stifle a scream. George shoved her aside, and she would have fallen if Rose hadn't moved quickly to catch her.

"It's all right," Mrs. Goodrich snapped. "Don't worry about me. Help Mr. Diller."

But it was obvious that there was nothing she could do. She watched as George raced after the coasting van. From where she stood it appeared that even if he caught up with it, he wouldn't have any way of stopping it before it shot off the edge of the cliff.

The driver's door was flapping wildly as George caught up with the van. He hurled himself into the driver's seat, and his left hand groped for the emergency brake as his right hand pulled the wheel around. He felt the rear wheels lock, and the van pulled around to the left and began to skid. There was nothing more he could do. He held his breath and waited. Behind him, the children screamed wildly, except for Sarah, who sat placidly in the front passenger's seat, staring out of the window.

It stopped only inches from the edge. If the door hadn't been open, George thought—but then he realized that there were too many ifs. He sat behind the wheel and waited for his nerves to calm down. By the time he was ready to begin guiding the children out of the van, Rose was there. One by one, they got the children out of the van, and Rose led them up to the house. Mrs. Goodrich, having seen that the van didn't go over the edge, had already disappeared into the kitchen. By the time all the children were safely in the house, she had produced a pitcher of hot cocoa. Rose left the children in her charge and went back to the van. George had climbed into the driver's seat again, and was preparing to jockey it away from the precipice.

"Be careful," Rose warned him.

With Rose waving him directions, he eased the van inward from the edge and, when it was far enough back, turned it around. He called to Rose to join him, and eased the vehicle back up to the driveway. When he parked it, he carefully left it in gear and checked the hand brake twice.

"What happened?" Rose asked him as they reentered the house.

George shook his head. "I don't know. I must have forgotten to set the brake. But I was sure I had. It's almost a reflex with me." He thought a moment, then shook his head. "I can almost see myself setting it, but I must not have."

An hour later, with the children calm once more, George Diller herded them all back into the van. If Rose noticed that George made sure that Sarah was in the back seat this time, she didn't comment on it. She simply stood on the porch and watched the van make its way down the driveway. Then she returned to her office and tried to concentrate on her work. It wasn't easy.

George Diller drove even more carefully than usual on his way back to the school, and he kept one eye on the rear-view mirror. But it wasn't the road behind him that he was watching. It was the children. Particularly, he watched Sarah Conger.

She sat in the back seat, and as they drove along the Conger's Point Road she seemed to be looking for something. Then George remembered. Every morning the van passed Elizabeth Conger as she walked into town to school. And every morning Elizabeth waved to Sarah as the van passed.

But this morning they were too late. There was no one to wave to Sarah.

At the end of the day Mrs. Montgomery would note in her records that Sarah Conger had been much more difficult than usual. It was one more thing she would have to talk to Sarah's parents about.

## FIVE

ROSE GLANCED AT HER WATCH AS SHE left the house; she had just enough time to stop at Jack's office and still not be late for her appointment. As she walked to the garage, she glanced at the scars on the lawn, and shuddered once more at the memory of the van careening toward the cliff. She wondered if she should have kept Sarah home for the day, and felt a slight twinge of guilt at the relief she had felt when George Diller had insisted that it would be better for Sarah to continue the day as if nothing unusual had happened. She made a mental note to devote a little extra time to Sarah that evening.

A quarter of a mile toward town, Rose smiled to herself as she passed the old Barnes place. She had a feeling that today, as she drove home, she would be able to take down the FOR SALE sign that had been hanging on the fence for months. And it's a good thing, she thought. It's been on the market too long. Another couple of months and it would take on that awful deserted look and be impossible to sell at any price. But she had a feeling that she finally had the right customers for the house. Unconsciously, she pressed the accelerator, and as the car leaped forward some of the feeling of depression that had been hanging over her all morning dissipated.

She slipped the car into her space behind Port Arbello Realty Company, and dropped her purse on her desk as she walked through to the front door.

"You have an appointment in fifteen minutes," the receptionist reminded her. Rose smiled at the girl.

"Plenty of time. I'm just going to run across the square for a minute and say hello to Jack." She knew she could as easily have telephoned, but she liked to keep up the charade of devoted wife. In Port Arbello, solid marriages counted for a lot in the business community.

On her way across the square she glanced quickly at the old armory, standing forbiddingly on the corner just south of the courthouse. Another year, she thought, and I'll find a way to buy it. Then it would be a simple matter of a zoning variance, and she could go ahead with her plan to turn it into a shopping center—not one that would compete with the businesses already surrounding the square, nothing with a major department store. Rather, she envisioned a group of small shops—boutiques, really, though she hated the word—with a good restaurant and a bar. That way, she could increase the value of the property without taking any business from the rest of the merchants. In her mind's eye she saw the armory as she would remodel it: sandblasted, its century-old brick cleaned of the years of grime, with white trim, and a few changes in the facade to give it an inviting look instead of the grim air with which it had always looked down on the town around it.

She jaywalked across the street to the *Courier* office and went in.

"Hi, Sylvia." She smiled. "Is my husband in?"

Jack's secretary returned her smile. "He's in, but he's a bear today. What did you do to him this morning?"

"Just the usual," Rose said. "Tied him up and thrashed him. He squalls, but he loves it." Without knocking, Rose let herself into her husband's office, closing the door behind her, and crossed to his desk, leaned over, and kissed him warmly.

"Hello, darling," she said, her eye not missing the fact that the intercom was open. "I hear you're having a bad day." As Jack looked at her in puzzlement, she pointed to the intercom unit on his desk. He nodded and switched it off.

"You seem cheerful enough," he said sourly.

"I am, now. But we almost had a disaster this morning." She recounted what had happened with the van.

"George is sure he set the brake?" Jack said when she had finished.

Rose nodded. "But he must not have. If he did, then there's only one explanation for what happened. Sarah." Jack seemed to lose a little of his color.

"So the school wants to talk to us about her on Thursday afternoon?" He made a note on his calendar.

"Not about what happened this morning," Rose said quickly. "Although I should imagine that will come up too. My God, Jack, they all would have been killed. Not one of them would have had a chance."

"And you really think Sarah might have released the brake?"

"I don't know what to think," Rose said uncertainly. "I suppose I'm trying not to think at all until we talk to the school."

"I could take the rest of the day off," Jack offered. "We could play a round of golf."

Rose smiled, but shook her head. "If you want to, go ahead. But not me. I have an appointment that I'm almost late for, and I think it's going to be a good one. I'm going to try to sell the Barnes place. If I can pull that off, it will do a lot more for me than a game of golf." She stood up. "For some reason, work seems to relax me."

"I wish it did the same for me," Jack replied. He didn't get up, and Rose felt a surge of anger that he wouldn't play the game with her. "Send Sylvia in as you leave, will you?"

Rose started to make a reply, then changed her mind. Silently, she left the office, forcing her face into a cheerful expression for Sylvia Bannister's benefit.

"He is a bear," she said to Sylvia. "And he wants you in his den. Got to run." Without waiting for the secretary to speak, Rose left the building and hurried across the square. By the time she had reached her own office, she had put her personal life back into its compartment, and was ready to greet her clients.

"So that's about it," Rose said a couple of hours later. "As far as I can tell, these are the only three houses in Port Arbello that come anywhere close to what you're looking for. I could show you more, but I'd only be wasting your time. Why don't we start with these two, and save this one for last." She picked up the listing for the Barnes property, tucked it beneath the other two, and stood up.

"Can we all fit in your car, or shall we follow you?" Carl Stevens asked.

"Let's take mine. That way I can give you a running commentary on the town. If you want all the dirt, you'll have to talk to my husband. I've only been here twenty years, and the people don't really trust me yet."

Barbara Stevens grinned at her. "That's why I love towns like this. If you weren't born here, people leave you alone. And you can't paint if people won't leave you alone."

They left the office, and Rose followed through on her promise. It wasn't true that she didn't have the dirt; every time she sold a house, its owners gave her a complete history of the house in question and the immediate vicinity. Rose knew who had slept with whom, who had gone crazy, and who had done "odd things" in every part of Port Arbello for the past fifty years. But she never passed the information on to clients. Instead, she stuck to her business. Where other real-estate people pointed out the house where they'd found old Mr. Crockett hanging in the attic, Rose pointed out the fact that the school was only two blocks from the property she was showing. Consequently, she got the sales.

She ushered the Stevenses quickly through the first two houses on her list. They were noncommittal, and she didn't push the properties. Then she turned onto the Conger's Point Road.

"Any relation?" Carl Stevens asked as he read the sign.

"We are the last of the Congers," Rose said, doing her best not to sound pretentious, and succeeding. "Unless I manage to produce a son, there soon won't be any Congers at all on Conger's Point Road."

"I think it would be wonderful to live on a road that was named after you," Barbara said.

Rose nodded. "I have to say I sort of get a kick out of it. From what I can gather, this road used to be practically the family driveway. My husband's family used to own practically everything between the town and the Point. But that was a hundred years ago. It's been built up for years. We still live on the Point, but the road passes us now. Sort of symbolic: The road used to end at our doorstep, but now it passes us by."

"You're a philosopher," Carl said. "Which side of the Point is the property that we're going to?"

"This side, but barely. As a matter of fact, if I can sell it to you, we'll be neighbors. The Barnes place adjoins ours. But don't worry, the houses are a quarter of a mile apart, and there's a strip of woods, a field, and some water between them. The Barnes place is on the mainland; we're out at the end of the Point. Here we are," she finished. She braked the car and turned in to the long drive that led to the old house. She heard Barbara suck in her breath, and wondered how long an escrow they'd want.

"My Lord," Carl said. "How big is it?"

"Not as big as it looks," Rose said. "It's an odd house, but I think you'll like it. Besides, if you don't, you can always change it. The first time I saw it, it struck me that an architect should have it. No one else could make it livable."

"What's wrong with it?" Barbara asked.

"Nothing, really," Rose said. She was parking the car in front of the building now, and she pointed to what appeared to be a pair of long, enclosed galleries, one above the other, that ran the length of the house. "See those?"

"Don't tell me," Carl said. "Let me guess. You go in the front door, and there's an entry hall that goes straight through the house. On each side of the entry hall there's a staircase, and the two staircases meet above the front door. From there, a hall extends the length of the house in both directions."

Rose nodded. "That's it exactly. With another hall on the bottom floor. It gives the place the feeling of an immense railroad parlor car. Every room has one door onto the hall. There's an incredible view of the ocean, but only from the far side of the house. And I don't have any idea at all of what to do about it. That's one of the reasons I brought you out here. Even if you don't buy it, I can get some ideas on what to do with it in case somebody else does."

They went into the house and explored it room by room, first the lower floor, then the upper. Rose, following her instincts, did little more than identify the use to which the Barneses had put each room. Finally they were back in the entry hall.

"Well?" Rose said. Carl and Barbara Stevens looked at each other.

"It does have some problems," Carl mused.

"And they'd be expensive problems, wouldn't they?" Barbara added.

"Not expensive," Rose said. "Very expensive. Count on putting in half again what you pay for it, and that doesn't include the plumbing. Also, it's going to need rewiring within five years, and a new roof in two."

"Honest, aren't you," Carl said with a grin.

Rose shrugged. "If I don't tell you now, you'll tell me later. And I wouldn't want the next-door neighbors mad at me."

"And they want how much for it?" Rose could see the wheels clicking in Carl's mind.

"Fifty-two five. If the floor plan weren't so weird they could get at least twice that."

"Okay," Carl said.

"Okay?" Rose repeated. "What does 'okay' mean?"

Barbara laughed. "It means 'Okay, we'll buy it.' "

"At the asking price?" Rose said vacantly.

"At the asking price."

Rose shook her head. "You're both crazy. You asked me how much they wanted for it, not how much I thought you could get it for. Don't you want to make them a lower offer?"

"Not particularly," Carl said.

"I see," Rose said numbly. "What am I saying? I don't see at all. If you don't mind my saying this, you're taking all the fun out of it for me. I get paid to write offers and counteroffers, and make everybody think he got a good deal. I've never heard of selling a house for the asking price. In fact, I know darn well you could get it for less."

Barbara nodded. "But it would take time. We don't want to wait. We don't want an escrow, and we don't want to finance it. We'll write you a check for it today. Can we move in this weekend?"

Rose nodded. "I suppose so," she said slowly. "There's no mortgage on it, so I guess there isn't anything to it but transferring the title. That doesn't take any time at all."

Carl began laughing. "You look like we've just spoiled your entire day. Let's go back to your office and get this thing settled. Then we'll go home and pick up Jeff and bring him out here. He'll love the place. He loves the ocean, and he loves climbing. That bluff should make him very happy."

Again Rose nodded. "Something's wrong," she said. "Selling a house like this isn't supposed to be this easy. Why are you in such a hurry to move in?"

"We're in a hurry," Barbara said, "because we've been looking for a house for a year, we know exactly what we want, we have the money to buy it and the talent to fix it, and it's just what we're looking for. Also, Jeff is fourteen years old, and we want to get him started in school before it gets too far into the year. In another month all the cliques for this year will be formed, and Jeff will be out in the cold till next fall. So if we can't move in next weekend, we probably won't move in at all. Can you arrange it?''

"Sure," Rose said. "There isn't anything to arrange. Like I said, you've taken all the fun out of it for me."

"Well," Carl said, "we'll do our best to make it up to you."

On the way back to town, Rose decided she liked the Stevenses.

Martin Forager stood in front of Jack Conger's desk, his eyes blazing. He kept his hands stuffed deep in the pockets of his plaid hunting jacket.

"I'm telling you, Conger," he was saying, "it's a disgrace. It's been two days now, and nothing's been done." He turned to stare out the window. "Nothing," he repeated.

"I'm sure Ray's doing his best," Jack began. Forager whirled.

"His best ain't good enough. I don't know what happened to my daughter, but I want to know."

Jack looked up helplessly. Martin Forager was a big man. He had planted his fists on Jack's desk and was leaning over him, glowering.

"I don't see what I can do," Jack said quietly.

"You can use your paper," Forager snapped. "That's what you can do. You can use it to light a fire under Ray Norton. Let him know that if he doesn't do something, and do it fast, the people of this town are going to get rid of him."

"I hardly think—" Jack started to say.

"I hardly think," Forager mimicked. "It didn't happen to your daughter, so why would you hardly think anything?"

Jack fought hard to control his temper. He began again.

"Just exactly what do you think happened to Anne?" he asked.

"Someone—" Martin Forager hesitated. "Did something to her," he finished lamely.

"Did what?" Jack asked.

Forager began to look uncomfortable. "Well—I don't know, really. But the doctor said . . ."

"The doctor said nothing much happened to her," Jack said firmly. "He told me so himself, at your request. He examined her thoroughly, and apart from a few bruises, which she could have gotten in any one of a number of ways, she isn't hurt. She certainly wasn't molested." He continued quickly, seeing the blood drain from Martin Forager's face. "I know, you never said she was, but that's what you've been thinking." He dropped his hands into his lap and slumped back in his chair. "Hell, Marty, that's what we've all been thinking. But apparently nothing happened. And you know how kids are. She came home late. Maybe nothing at all happened, and she made the whole thing up." He held up a hand as he saw Forager's temper begin to build again. "Don't start up again, Martin. If the doctor's report showed anything, anything at all I could get a handle on, I'd be raising as big a stink as you. But it doesn't. Unless Anne starts talking about what happened to her, there's nothing any of us can do."

Forager glared at him for a moment. "You mean like Sarah talks about what happened to her?'' he snarled. He turned away, and was out of Jack's office before he could see the effect of his words. Jack remained in his chair, waiting for his heart to stop pounding. He was shaking.

When Sylvia Bannister came into the inner office a few minutes later, Jack hadn't moved. Sylvia started to put a file on the desk in front of him, but stopped when she saw his face.

"Jack?" she said. "Jack, are you all right?"

"I don't know, Syl," Jack said quietly. "Why don't you close the door and sit down." He looked up at her. "If you have time?"

"I always have time," Sylvia replied, closing the door. She sat down in the chair in front of the desk and lit a cigarette. The beginnings of a smile came over Jack's face.

"That's almost automatic, isn't it?" he said.

"What is?" she said, glancing around.

"The cigarette. Haven't you ever noticed that you never light a cigarette in here when you know it's business, but you always light one when you know it's just going to be us talking? It's as though you use the cigarette to change roles from secretary to friend."

"Does it bother you?" Sylvia asked anxiously, looking at the cigarette with an embarrassment that was not like her. Jack shook his head.

"Not at all. I kind of enjoy it. It reassures me that you can read me like a book."

Sylvia relaxed again. "Then I'll try not to remember it every time I do it. You shouldn't have mentioned it; now I'll be self-conscious about it."

"Not you." Jack grinned. "You're the least self-conscious person I've ever met."

"Well," Sylvia said shortly, beginning to feel that Jack was avoiding whatever it was he wanted to talk about. "Instead of talking about my many, varied, and questionable virtues, why don't we talk about you? What happened?"

Jack shrugged. "I'm not sure anything did, really. Martin Forager just said something to me that shook me. Something about Sarah."

Sylvia drew on her cigarette and let the smoke out slowly, choosing her words. "Exactly what did he say?" she said softly. Jack recounted the conversation he had just had. When he was finished, Sylvia reflected quietly before she spoke.

"I think that's what's called a shot in the dark, Jack. He didn't even know what he was saying," she continued, as Jack looked unconvinced. "Jack, nobody in this town, including you, your wife, or me, knows what happened to Sarah. *Nobody* knows. But you have to face it. Sarah doesn't talk any more, and she goes to White Oaks, and everybody in town knows what kind of school it is. So there's bound to be speculation, and some of it's bound to focus on you."

Jack nodded. "I know. Just one more thing to worry about."

"One more? What else is there?"

"Well, there's the situation between Rose and me."

Sylvia wasn't at all sure she wanted to hear any more, but she knew she would. If only I wasn't so damned—fond—of him, she thought. She had almost used the word "love," but had shied away from it. Yet she knew there wasn't any use in shying away from it. She did love Jack Conger, and she knew it. Not that it made any difference. She had come to grips with being in love with her boss a long time ago, and it helped to know that he loved her too, in a certain way. Not a sexual way. That he had always reserved for Rose, and Sylvia was just as happy that he did. She wasn't sure she could handle an affair, and she was very sure that she didn't want to try. She liked things the way they were. In the office, she and Jack were close. They moved from a business relationship to a personal one and back again many times each day, and each was in tune with the moods and feelings of the other. It was, she supposed, like a marriage in some ways, except that it lasted only eight hours a day. Each afternoon Jack went home to his family, and she went home to her cat. For eight hours a day she had a job she loved and a man she loved. It was usually enough. But sometimes, like right now, she wished he wouldn't tell her everything, that he would hold back a little of himself from her. On the other hand, she knew that for the past year he really hadn't had anybody else. Not since the day he had carried Sarah out of the woods.

"Are things getting worse?" she said.

"I'm not sure if 'worse' is the word. What's your definition of 'worse'? Rose is starting to hate me, but why shouldn't she? My drinking seems to be getting a little worse, but not so you could notice. And then there's Sarah. Sylvia," he said, and the desperation in his voice was almost tangible. "Why can't I remember what happened that day?"

"You were drunk," Sylvia said. "People black out sometimes." She put it bluntly, but her tone held no condemnation, only understanding.

"But I've never blacked out before," he said. "Never. It makes me wonder exactly what I did to her in the woods. What did I do that I won't let myself remember?"

Sylvia lit another cigarette, and when she spoke her voice was gentle. "Jack, what's the use of killing yourself over it? If you'd done what you think you did, the doctors would have known immediately. There would have been some kind of damage to"—she groped for a word, then decided that he might as well hear it out loud—"her vagina. You didn't rape her, Jack."

The word hit him like a physical blow. "I never thought—"

"Yes you did," Sylvia interrupted him. "That's exactly what you thought, and it's exactly what you've always thought. And if you want the truth, that's probably what's at the root of your worries. Maybe Rose thinks it has to do with money and liquor. I don't know what she thinks, and frankly, I don't care. It's what you think that counts. And you think you raped Sarah. Well, you didn't, and you can't keep torturing yourself by thinking you did. It's over, Jack, and you've got to forget it. Maybe if you can forget it, you can stop drinking."

Jack avoided her eyes, staring instead at the blotter on his desk. He saw the note on the calendar, the note reminding him to go to White Oaks on Thursday afternoon.

"It's hard to forget it," he said, "when I have to face Sarah every day."

Sylvia nodded. "Of course it is. That's why the doctors suggested that she be institutionalized for a while. It wasn't just for her, you know. It was for you, too. It's hard to forget something when you're faced with reminders every day. Particularly reminders like Sarah."

"I can't put her away," Jack said miserably. "Not after what I did to her."

Sylvia came around behind him and put her hands on his shoulders. She felt the knots in the muscles, and began working to relax them.

"You're too hard on yourself, Jack," she said softly. "Much too hard. Let it go." But she knew he wouldn't.

## SIX

NEITHER OF THEM SPOKE UNTIL ROSE turned the car into the gates of the White Oaks School. Before them, an expanse of well-tended lawn rolled gently up a rise dotted with maple trees. A gardener rode back and forth across the leaf-strewn grounds on a midget tractor, his progress marked by exposed strips of lawn. Here and there stood piles of leaves, some of them intact, others already scattered by the group of children moving from one pile to the next, systematically rescattering the leaves. The gardener seemed not to notice but drove patiently onward. Rose smiled at the scene, but it only depressed Jack.

"I love this place," Rose said. "It's so beautiful, no matter what season it is." When she heard no response from her husband, she continued. "I should think it would be good for the children, just being in a place like this."

"If they even know where they are," Jack said flatly. "You'd think the gardener would get upset with them, wouldn't you?"

"I suppose they hired him partly because he doesn't get upset," Rose replied. "I don't suppose it's an easy place to work. I admire the people who can do it."

"I certainly couldn't," Jack said. "I don't see how any of the people here can stand it. Look over there."

He pointed across the lawn to a spot where a small boy, not more than six or seven, sat under a tree. He had found a stick and was methodically tapping the trunk of the tree with it, with the regularity of a metronome. Rose stopped the car, and they watched him. He simply sat there, beating a steady rhythm on the tree trunk.

"The poor child," Rose whispered, after several silent minutes had passed. "What do you suppose he thinks about? What do you suppose makes him that way?"

"Who knows," Jack said uncomfortably. He watched the boy for a while, and finally his expression softened. "I'm sorry, Rose," he said. "I don't really hate this place. It's just that it makes me feel so—so helpless. I see all these children, and they all seem to be part of another world, a world I can't touch. And it tears me apart to think my own daughter is part of this world."

Rose reached across the front seat and squeezed his hand. She put the car in gear again, and they moved toward the main building. Behind them, the boy still sat beneath the tree, slowly tapping at its trunk.

Dr. Charles Belter stood up as they came into his office, and came out from behind his desk to greet them.

"Mr. Conger," he said warmly, his hand extended. "Mrs. Conger. I'm glad you could both be here. You'd be surprised how hard it sometimes is for us to get even one parent out here, let alone both. Of course, some of the parents have a difficult time being here, simply because of the nature of our work." He looked carefully from Rose to Jack, and noted the response to his comment that showed in Jack's face. And you, Mr. Conger, are one of those parents, he said to himself. Aloud he invited them to make themselves comfortable, and told them that Sarah's teacher would be joining them in a couple of minutes.

Charles Belter was in his late fifties, and had the look that psychiatrists are supposed to have. He sported an immense beard (no doubt the model for George Diller's, Rose thought) and a walrus moustache, and still had a full head of bushy hair that was fast going gray. Behind his horn-rimmed glasses his blue eyes twinkled with a good humor that had always made it easy for him to relate to the children with whom he worked. Indeed, he had done his best for years to try to emulate Santa Claus, a role he was able to totally realize only once a year. The rest of the time, he felt, the red suit and bells would be a little too eccentric even for him. Consequently he contented himself with wearing a red blazer, which he did his best not to button. He didn't fool anybody.

White Oaks School had been his dream since the first day he had seen it, back in the days when it had been a tuberculosis sanitarium. Like so many similar facilities, the tuberculosis sanitarium had run out of clients. It was Dr. Charles Belter's dream that someday he, too, would run out of clients. But the prospects of that happening were dim, and he looked forward to spending the rest of his life at White Oaks. Which, he reflected, was not a bad prospect.

There was a tap at the door; then Marie Montgomery let herself into the office. Prim and thirtyish, she had a conservative look that suggested a spinsterish schoolmarm of fifty years earlier. People who had not seen her work always had reservations about Marie Montgomery; people who had taken the time to observe her in action were totally convinced of her abilities. Put her in a classroom full of disturbed children and her reserve disappeared. She seemed never to notice the children's peculiarities, and would work tirelessly with each of her ten students, seeing progress where others saw no change, inventing techniques where none had existed before. It was almost as if, by refusing to recognize her pupils' limitations, she overcame them. And, indeed, her pupils always seemed to make more progress than anyone else's. But now, as she perched herself in the vacant chair between Dr. Belter and Rose Conger, she wore a look of concern that went beyond her normal air of reservation.

"Marie," Dr. Belter said, "we've been waiting for you."

She smiled briefly. "I'm sorry. I was delayed for a minute. Oh, nothing serious," she went on as Dr. Belter's brow rose questioningly. "Just a matter of discipline. Two of the children seemed to want to discipline each other. They'll be all right."

"It must be difficult," Jack said.

"Not at all." Mrs. Montgomery was crisp but kind. "Don't forget, most of the children here don't really know there's anything the matter with them. They simply have a different standard of normality. And when you look at the state of the world, who's really to say they're wrong? Sometimes I watch Jerry tapping that tree trunk out there, and it occurs to me that that isn't really such a bad way to spend time. I sometimes wish I had his powers of concentration. Do you know, he's been working on that same tree for five months now? I'll be glad when he's finished."

"What's he doing to it?" Jack asked.

Mrs. Montgomery shrugged. "If you can find out, you're doing better than I am. But I'll know someday. Someday he'll tell me all about it. When he's ready. In the meantime, I have other things to keep me busy."

"Like Sarah?" Rose said.

The younger woman nodded. "Like Sarah. I hope you haven't been too worried. I asked George to make it absolutely clear that there isn't any emergency. I hope he did."

Rose smiled. "He did. But then we had an emergency of our own. I suppose he told you about it."

Dr. Belter's face clouded. "Yes," he said. "He did. Needless to say, that wasn't one of the things we wanted to talk about, since it hadn't happened when we decided to have this meeting, but I think—"

"Are you suggesting that Sarah had something to do with it?" Jack said coldly. "Because if you are—"

"I'm not suggesting any such thing," Dr. Belter said. "I doubt that we'll ever find out exactly what happened with the van. George Diller was sure he set the brake. He might be mistaken. Sarah, of course, can't tell us anything about it at all. But from my own observations of her, and from what Marie here tells me, I'm not going to suggest that Sarah released the brake. At least not deliberately. For one thing, saying Sarah released the brake implies several things. First, that she knew what would happen if she did. In other words, that she knew that if she released the brake the van would start to move, and that if the van started to move it would at best ram into the garage, hurting several of the children, and at worst plunge into the sea, killing everybody in it, including herself. Frankly, we're not at all sure that in her current state of mind Sarah is capable of putting all that together. It's possible that she is, of course, but her performance here doesn't indicate it. Further, we don't think she's suicidal, and releasing that brake would certainly have to be considered a self-destructive gesture.''

''In other words,'' Rose said, ''you don't think Sarah released the brake?''

Dr. Belter smiled wryly. ''I wish it were that simple,'' he said. ''It's entirely possible that she released the brake without the least idea of what she was doing. She may easily have been doing nothing more than displaying a fleeting interest in an object, with no concept of the possible ramifications of her actions. This, I'm afraid, is very much within the scope of her current behavior.''

There was a long silence as Rose and Jack digested what the doctor was saying. Jack shifted uncomfortably while Rose played with a glove.

''What you're saying, Dr. Belter, if I read you right,'' Jack said tightly, ''is that my daughter is dangerous.''

Dr. Belter sighed and began again. ''No, that's not exactly what I'm saying.''

''Not exactly,'' Jack repeated, ''but close?''

Dr. Belter nodded slightly. ''I suppose you could say that if you wanted to. What Sarah is, right now, is irresponsible. From what we have been able to observe, she is often totally unaware of the effects her actions could have. In other words, she acts without thinking. That can be a dangerous thing for anybody. For her, with the emotional struggles she is going through, it can obviously be disastrous. The incident with the van, I'll admit, is an extreme example, but it is certainly illustrative of what could happen.''

''If she actually released the brake,'' Jack said darkly.

''If she actually released the brake,'' Dr. Belter repeated. ''And, of course, we have no way of proving it either way. Believe me, nothing would make me happier than to be able to show that it was carelessness on George Diller's part. It would be much more simply dealt with. But I can't.''

''You said there's more,'' Rose said softly. ''What else is there?''

''Marie?'' Dr. Belter said, turning toward the teacher. ''Why don't you run through it?''

Marie Montgomery picked a file up from the desk and opened it.

''It's all so minor,'' she said. ''Really just little things, but when they're added up, I think we have to pay attention to it. First, Sarah seems to be retreating further into herself. It isn't anything major. It's just that a couple of months ago she would almost always respond to her name the first time it was spoken. Now she never hears until it's repeated, or if she does she seems to ignore it.''

''Then there's the matter of her concentration. It seems to be getting shorter. As a matter of fact, I have some figures on that, but, again, they aren't anything major. What it boils down to is that she spends less time with any one thing than she used to. That in itself wouldn't bother me particularly—attention spans seem to expand and contract like rubber bands around here—but with Sarah it isn't as if she gets bored with what she's doing, exactly. It's more as though she finds herself more interesting than the real world. It's getting harder to keep her focused on the real world, and that bothers me. It's beginning to look like we're losing touch with her, instead of getting closer to her." Marie Montgomery saw the flash of pain in Jack's eyes and hurried on. "That's really the major reason for this meeting. To find out if the same things are happening at home."

Rose shook her head. "I don't think so," she said doubtfully, "but of course I can't really be sure. I find it awfully hard to look at her objectively. I'm afraid I try to see progress where there might not be any."

"There's progress," Jack said, but his voice indicated that his statement might be more wish than fact.

"Jack," Rose said, as gently as she could. "What progress has there been, really?" She turned back to Mrs. Montgomery. "I wish I could tell you whether or not there really has been any change in Sarah, but I can't."

"We're not expecting you to be able to tell us anything today," Dr. Belter put in. "As we've tried to make clear, nothing major has happened. This is simply to alert you to something that might be happening. We aren't sure, and we're asking for your help. It would be very helpful for us, and for Sarah, if you could simply be aware that something may be going on that we don't know about, and try to notice anything unusual or different in her behavior."

"Well," Jack said carefully, "there was that thing with the Ouija board the other night."

"Ouija board?" Dr. Belter said. "I haven't seen one of those things in years. Do they still make them?"

"Not this one," Rose said. "Elizabeth found it in a storeroom or something. And the Ouija board really had nothing to do with what happened."

She recounted the incident of a few nights earlier, and Sarah's reaction to the cat brushing up against her. As she talked, Dr. Belter took a few notes.

"It was really nothing," Rose finished.

"And they were playing with a Ouija board?" Dr. Belter asked again. "Hmm." He made a final note and looked up. "Does Sarah spend much time with her sister?"

"That's putting it mildly," Jack said. "The worst part of each day is when Elizabeth leaves for school and Sarah has to wait for the van to bring her out here. They're practically inseparable."

"And how does Elizabeth react to Sarah?" the doctor asked.

"Considering her age," Rose said, "it's amazing. You have to remember that Elizabeth is only thirteen herself. But the way she takes care of Sarah, you'd think she was five years older. She seems to understand Sarah, somehow. She plays with her by the hour, and reads to her, and it never bothers her when Sarah suddenly wrecks whatever they're playing, or grabs a book out of her hands. And the other night, when Sarah screamed, it was as if Elizabeth didn't hear it at all. It upset Jack and me much more than it did either of the girls."

"It's strange," Jack said, picking up the thread. "Elizabeth talks to Sarah, and she never seems to notice that Sarah doesn't talk back. It's as if Sarah doesn't have to talk—Elizabeth seems to communicate with her or something. Sometimes Elizabeth makes me feel inadequate. I've tried to talk to Sarah so many times I can't count them, but as soon as I pick her up she starts wriggling around, and in a couple of minutes she's out of my lap and off to find Elizabeth."

"Has she shown any signs of violence at home?" Dr. Belter said quietly.

"Sarah? I don't think so," Rose said. "Why?"

"Again, it's nothing we can really put our finger on," Dr. Belter said. "The screaming when the cat brushed up against her reminded me of it. One day last week one of the children came up behind Sarah and touched her shoulder. She screamed, which isn't abnormal for her, but she also whirled around and hit the other child. She hadn't done that before, and we still don't know if it was an accident or if she struck at the child on purpose. Has she ever swung at either of you? Or at Elizabeth?"

Jack and Rose shook their heads.

"Certainly not at either of us," Rose said. "And if she'd ever done anything like that to Elizabeth, I'm sure we'd have heard about it." She paused a moment, as if reaching to remember something, then went on. "I'm afraid we don't really spend as much time with Elizabeth as we should. But Sarah takes up so much of our time. Well, Elizabeth doesn't seem to resent it."

"You're very lucky," Dr. Belter said. "Many parents find that they have more trouble with their so-called normal child than with their disturbed one. It's only to be expected, really. All children need attention, and when one is disturbed, the other often feels he needs to compete for his parents' attention. It sounds as if Elizabeth is a very exceptional child." He smiled and stood up. "Thank you for coming today. We'll be going over Sarah's case in our staff meeting tomorrow, and we may make some minor changes in her medication. Other than that, for the moment it's just a matter of keeping our eyes open and trying to spot a trend."

"Then that's it?" Jack said, getting to his feet.

"That's it," Dr. Belter said. "For the moment. I don't want you to feel alarmed. You should, however, be aware that if Sarah's condition deteriorates too far, we won't be able to keep her here. White Oaks is a school, not an institution." Seeing the anxiety in both their faces, Dr. Belter hurried to reassure them. "It's only an eventuality," he said. "For the moment, we aren't having any more problems with Sarah than with any of the others. And some of them are a lot worse than she is. For the foreseeable future, I look forward to having Sarah here."

"Can we take her home with us," Rose asked, "or has she already gone in the van?"

"She's waiting in my room," Mrs. Montgomery said. "One of the aides is with her. I'm sure she'll be glad to see you."

But Sarah wasn't waiting in Marie Montgomery's room.

* * *

In the house on Conger's Point, Elizabeth poured the last of a glass of milk into the cat's dish, and watched as Cecil lapped it up. Then she picked up the animal and listened to him purr.

"Come on," she said to the cat. "Let's go outside."

Scratching Cecil's ears, Elizabeth carried him from the house.

As she crossed the field, Elizabeth pulled the rubber band out of her ponytail and shook her head. The blond hair cascaded over her shoulders. Her step quickened.

No one saw her disappear into the woods.

# SEVEN

THE ROOM WAS A SHAMBLES: DESKS AND chairs were overturned; the items that were normally arranged across the top of Marie Montgomery's desk had been swept from it and now lay scattered and broken across the floor to the left of the desk.

"Jesus," Jack breathed. Before anyone could say more, they heard the sounds from the cloakroom—scuffling noises, as though whatever struggle had taken place in the classroom was now continuing in the small room behind the blackboard. The sounds were muted but somehow desperate. There were no cries, none of the shouts that should accompany the sort of battle that must have taken place. Led by Mrs. Montgomery, the three of them raced through the room.

In the back corner of the cloakroom the aide struggled with Sarah. The battle had come to a stalemate.

When she spoke, Mrs. Montgomery's voice was very low and completely controlled, but it held a note of authority that Rose Conger was sure had cut through worse confusion than confronted her now.

"Philip," she said, "what's happened here?"

Immediately the struggle stopped. The aide, who couldn't have been more than twenty, straightened and stepped away from Sarah.

The child was a mess. Her shirt was torn in several places, and she was covered with some sort of yellow substance. As soon as the aide let her go, Sarah's hand moved to her mouth, and she began chewing. Rose stared at her, and it was a few seconds before she realized what her daughter was doing. The yellow substance was chalk, and Sarah was chewing on a piece of it. Philip watched her for a second before turning to the small group that hovered in the doorway. Rose started to move toward her daughter, but Marie Montgomery's hand held her back.

"It's all right," she said quietly. "A little chalk isn't going to hurt her."

"It's not a little," Philip said. "She's been at it ever since you left. She must have eaten almost a full box by now."

"And you tried to stop her?" Marie asked.

The young man nodded. He looked miserable. "I couldn't do it, though. I was afraid of hurting her."

"You probably scared her half to death," Marie said. "If you'd let her alone, she might have stopped of her own accord. A little chalk won't hurt her."

"But a whole box?" Jack said. He took a step toward Sarah. The child shrank back farther into the corner of the tiny room, and began to gnaw on another stick. Her teeth made a strange grinding sound as she crushed the chalk into powder. She swallowed some of it, but most of it cascaded, mixed with saliva, into her lap. Jack felt a queasy feeling developing in his stomach.

Rose broke free from Mrs. Montgomery's grip, and quickly moved past her husband to pick up her daughter. Sarah let herself be lifted, but refused to open her hand when Rose tried to remove the chalk she clutched. Rose seemed to be about to struggle with her when Mrs. Montgomery spoke again.

"Let her have it, Mrs. Conger. Really, it won't hurt her. If she's had too much, she might throw it up. Otherwise, it'll pass right through her. If it could hurt her, we wouldn't use it here. Our kids do that all the time." She looked accusingly at the aide, who seemed to wither.

"It just seemed like she was eating so much of it."

"So you scared her half to death, and wrecked the room?" the teacher inquired drily. "Don't you think the cure was a bit worse than the illness?"

"I guess I just . . ." Philip trailed off. "Didn't think," he finished lamely.

"I guess you didn't," Marie said, but the chill was gone from her voice, and she was smiling again. "Well, next time, keep in mind that chalk doesn't hurt children, and that desks cost money. And you can think about it while you clean up my room." She turned and led the Congers out of the room, walking with them to their car.

"Are you sure it won't hurt her?" Jack asked again as he turned the key in the ignition.

Mrs. Montgomery shook her head. "She might throw up, but that's all." She waved to them as they drove away, then turned back to the building. She'd changed her mind, and was about to help Philip clean up the mess.

Rose, holding a now passive Sarah on her lap, was still trying to get the scene out of her mind when the vomiting began. She wasn't sure it was going to happen at first; she felt a couple of involuntary flinches in her daughter, but then Sarah lay still again in her mother's arms. Then, without warning, it came.

The yellowish stream shot out of Sarah's mouth and ran down into her lap, where it overflowed. Rose could feel the heat of it as it soaked through her wool pants. She felt more than saw Jack glance over to see what had happened.

"Don't look," she said tightly. "Just keep your eyes on the road and get us home as quickly as you can. Mrs. Montgomery said this might happen." She was trying to reach into her purse for the package of Kleenex that was always there, when the second convulsion hit. As she felt more of the vomit flow over her legs, she realized the Kleenex would be futile. Instead, she used her free hand to roll the window down.

The cold air hit her face and cut through the sickening sweet-sour smell of the vomit, and Rose began to fight down her own nausea. Then Jack had opened his window, too, and she felt more fresh air. It wasn't until Sarah began to throw up again that Rose realized their mistake. There was a window open, and Sarah was struggling to reach it.

"Dear God, this can't be happening," Rose said to herself as the mixture of freezing air and vomit washed over her face. She was sure she was going to lose her own battle with nausea as she began to struggle to get Sarah's face out of the wind.

The girl was crying now, and Rose began to panic as she realized what could happen to Sarah if she began to choke on her own vomit.

"Jack," she said. "I think you'd better try to stop the car. Don't look. Just stop the car."

"There's a rest area just up ahead. Can you make it?"

"I'll have to," Rose said.

She felt the car surge forward, then swerve to the right and brake sharply. She had the door open before the car had quite stopped. She swung out of the car and set Sarah on the asphalt of the parking lot. She was just able to get off the lot and onto a patch of bare earth when the first retching began. Mortified, she stood with her forehead resting against the trunk of a tree, her own vomit mixing with Sarah's as it splashed against her legs. In a couple of minutes, it was over.

She turned back to the car, and her teary eyes told her that for her daughter it was not yet over.

Sarah sat miserably in the spot where Rose had left her, and the convulsions were beginning again. Frantically, Rose looked for her husband. For a second he seemed to have disappeared, but then she saw him coming from the men's room, a sodden paper towel in his hands. Ignoring her, he went directly to Sarah, knelt beside her, and began bathing her face with the dripping towel. Rose watched the scene in silence, then began making her way to the women's room.

For a long time she ran cold water, scooping it up and pouring it over her face, as if the water could wash away the experience that preceded it. Finally she returned to the car.

They saw Mrs. Goodrich standing on the porch when they turned into the driveway. The Congers glanced at each other, and their eyes held for a moment. There was a sudden warmth between them that neither of them had felt for a year. When Rose spoke, it was not to wonder why Mrs. Goodrich was on the porch.

"I'm sorry about all that," she said quietly.

"It's all right," Jack replied, his voice gentle. "It's nice to know that

I'm still good at something, even if it's only looking after my sick women-folk.''

Rose saw the pain and tenderness flash in his eyes. She looked away, her gaze coming to rest on Sarah, who had fallen asleep in her arms.

''Do you think I ought to call the doctor?'' She shifted Sarah's weight so that the child's head was cradled on her shoulder.

''If it'll make you feel better. But I suspect it's all over now. She's got all that crap out of her system. I think we can wait till she wakes up at least. Then we'll see.'' He stopped the car in front of the house, got out, and went around to open the door for his wife. Mrs. Goodrich had left the porch and was coming toward them, her ample figure moving as quickly as her age would allow. As Jack pulled open the passenger door, she stopped.

''Lord have mercy,'' she muttered, her eyes taking in the mess that covered the inside of the car, Sarah, and Rose. Involuntarily she took a couple of steps backward.

''It's all right, Mrs. Goodrich,'' Rose said, disengaging herself carefully from the car so as not to disturb Sarah, in her arms. ''We had a little trouble, but it's over with now.''

Mrs. Goodrich surveyed the mess stoically. If she wondered what had happened, it didn't show in her face. ''I'll have to take a hose to the inside of that car,'' she said, almost making it sound like a threat.

''I'll take care of it, Mrs. Goodrich,'' Jack began. ''We can't really ask you—''

''I've cleaned up worse than that in my time,'' the housekeeper snapped. ''Besides, you've got other things to do.'' There was an edge to her voice that captured Jack's attention. Rose had already disappeared with Sarah into the house.

''Other things? What other things?''

''It's Miss Elizabeth,'' the housekeeper said. ''I think she's been playing where she's not supposed to.'' Jack waited for her to continue, and eventually had to prompt her.

''Well,'' Mrs. Goodrich said. ''I saw her come out of the woods not too long ago. I don't know why, but I'm sure she was playing on the embankment. She denied it, of course.'' The last was said with the certainty of one convinced, by a lifetime of hard experience, that children will deny anything and everything, even when caught red-handed.

''Elizabeth's usually pretty honest,'' Jack said gently. He was reluctant to nettle the old woman; when he did, it usually showed up at dinner in the form of overcooked food. Mrs. Goodrich peered at him over her glasses and stood her ground.

''I'm well aware of that, young man,'' she said, and Jack prepared to give in. Ever since he had been a child, he had known that when Mrs. Goodrich called him ''young man'' she meant business.

''Nevertheless,'' she went on, ''I think you'd better speak to her. She knows she's not to go into those woods, let alone anywhere near the embankment. And I know she was in the woods. I saw her come out.''

''All right,'' Jack said. ''I'll talk to her as soon as I clean up. Where is she?''

"In the field," Mrs. Goodrich said dourly, indicating that as far as she was concerned, the field was almost on par with the woods and the embankment. She pointed off to the distance, and, following her gesture with his eyes, Jack saw his older daughter. She was squatting down, and seemed to be looking at something.

He started to move toward the house but, seeing the glare Mrs. Goodrich was giving him, turned toward the field instead.

"No time like the present," he heard the housekeeper mutter behind him.

Elizabeth didn't see him until he was less than twenty feet from her. She suddenly looked up, as if she had heard something, but Jack was sure he had been silent. When she saw him a smile lit her face, and Jack could feel its glow brighten his spirits. He stopped, and the two of them studied each other for a moment. With her hair flowing free, Elizabeth looked more than ever like the girl in the portrait.

"How's my favorite daughter?" he said, breaking the silence.

"Am I?" she said, the smile growing even brighter. "Well, if I am, you deserve this for telling me so."

She stooped, and when she stood up there was a single buttercup in her hand. She ran over to him and held the flower under his chin.

"Well?" he said. "Do I glow?"

"I'm not going to tell you." Elizabeth laughed. "Did you bring Sarah home with you?" He nodded, and when Elizabeth turned and began to walk toward the house, he stopped her.

"Hold on. Can't you spend a little time with your favorite father?"

Elizabeth turned back to him. "I just thought——" she began.

"Never mind," Jack said. "Sarah had a little trouble on the way home, and your mother's cleaning her up. It's nothing serious," he added hastily as a look of concern twisted Elizabeth's face. "Just something she ate. She had a bit of an accident on the way home."

"Yuck!" Elizabeth said. "Does the car stink?"

"Mrs. G's cleaning it up. She wants me to talk to you."

"I thought she would," Elizabeth said. "She thinks I was out on the embankment today."

"Were you?" Jack tried to sound unconcerned.

"No," she said. "I wasn't. I don't know why she thinks I was."

"She said she saw you coming out of the woods."

"I know," Elizabeth said. "And I don't know why she thinks that either. I wasn't in the woods."

"Were you near them?"

Elizabeth nodded. "I thought I saw Cecil, and I was following him. But I don't think it was Cecil. It looked like him, but then, just as he was about to go into the woods, he jumped. 'Cecil' turned out to be a rabbit."

"How could you mistake a rabbit for Cecil?" Jack asked. "Of all the un-rabbitish cats I know, Cecil is the most un-rabbitish of them all."

"Search me," Elizabeth said. "But he sure looked like Cecil till he jumped."

"Well, I'm glad he did," her father said. "If he hadn't, you might have followed him into the woods."

"I'd have noticed," Elizabeth said. She was silent for a moment; then: "Daddy, why aren't I allowed to go into the woods or to the embankment?"

"It's dangerous, that's why," Jack said, his tone indicating that he would like to leave it at that. But Elizabeth was not to be put off.

"But, Daddy, I'm thirteen years old now, and I can take care of myself. I don't see how the embankment can be any more dangerous than the quarry, and you let me go there any time I want to."

"I'd just as soon you stayed away from there, too," Jack said.

"But why?" Elizabeth pressed. When there was no answer she said, "It's because of Anne Forager, isn't it?"

"Anne Forager?" Jack said guardedly.

"All the kids are talking about it. They say something awful happened to her, and that it happened out here. Is that true?"

"I don't know," Jack said truthfully. "I don't really think anything happened to her, and if it did, I doubt very much if it happened out here. At any rate, that doesn't have anything to do with you. It's just that the embankment is very dangerous."

"Not any more than the quarry."

Jack shook his head. "If you slipped at the quarry, you'd at least have a chance. You'd fall into deep water, and you can swim. With the embankment, you wouldn't hit water. You'd hit rocks and surf. That's a whole different story."

"I suppose you're right," she said. Then she looked up at him, and there was a glint of mischief in her eyes. "But in five years I'll be eighteen. Then I'll go see just what's at this embankment, and you won't be able to stop me."

"That's five years," Jack said. "In five years you could change your mind."

"I won't," Elizabeth assured him. Then she slipped her hand into his, and together they walked back to the house.

Dinner was a quiet affair for the Congers that night, at least at the beginning. Out of respect for the delicate stomachs of Rose and Sarah, Mrs. Goodrich had put together a light omelette, which she had restrained herself from burning. Conversation was dilatory, much of it in the form of encouraging remarks directed toward Sarah by her parents. Sarah seemed not to hear; instead she concentrated on her plate, calmly shoving each forkful of egg into her mouth, chewing stoically, and swallowing. To Elizabeth, Sarah seemed to be as she always was.

Mrs. Goodrich cleared away the plates and brought in the dessert.

"Here we go again," Elizabeth said.

"Hmm?" Rose inquired, turning her attention from Sarah to the older girl. Elizabeth grinned at her.

"I said, 'Here we go again.' We had the same pudding at school today. Except this is better."

"Oh?" Rose said. But she was not really interested; her attention was back on Sarah. "How was school?"

"Not bad. We got our history tests back. I think Mr. Friedman must have made a mistake. He gave me a perfect score."

Now both Rose and Jack turned to Elizabeth, and she could see the pleased expression in their eyes. But before they could speak, a sound rent the air.

Elizabeth turned, then ducked just in time to avoid the bowl of pudding that was flying toward her from her sister's place. The glass bowl shattered on the wall behind Elizabeth, but the sound of its crashing was inaudible over the shrieks and wails emanating from Sarah.

Her face contorted in rage, Sarah snatched all the silverware within her reach, and in a moment it was scattered across the room. One of the heavy silver knives shattered a pane in the French door and clattered to rest on the veranda outside. Her voice building, Sarah continued to howl as her arms moved wildly over the table, searching out other things to throw.

Rose sat as if frozen and stared at Sarah. Sarah had been so calm, and now—She began to rise as she saw Sarah's fists clutch at the tablecloth. She tried to prepare herself for the destruction that was imminent if her daughter followed through on what she apparently intended to do.

And then, over the din of Sarah's howling, she heard Jack's voice shouting.

"For God's sake!" he yelled. "Will you get her out of here?"

Rose's eyes widened, but the impact of his words seemed to free her from her chair. Wordlessly she swept Sarah into her arms, somehow freeing the clutching fingers from the tablecloth, and carried her from the room. As she passed Jack she sensed more than saw him slump weakly in his chair.

The dining room was suddenly silent, and the two of them sat there, Jack avoiding words, Elizabeth with nothing to say. Then, visibly, Jack began to pull himself together.

"I'm sorry," he muttered, more to himself than to Elizabeth. "Every time she does something like that I get the most horrible feeling. I get the feeling that I made her nuts." He began sobbing, but silently.

"And I guess I did," he mumbled. Then he too left the room, and Elizabeth was suddenly alone.

She sat quite still for a time, as if she had neither heard what her father said nor noticed the chaos around her. When eventually she moved, it was to begin cleaning up the mess. She cleared off the table first, then began on the wall and floor. She moved slowly, carefully, as if her mind was far from what she was doing. When she finished, she surveyed the dining room.

"I was so sure that was Cecil," she said, for no apparent reason. "But I guess it couldn't have been." She was silent, then spoke once more to the empty room. "I wish he'd come home."

Then Elizabeth, too, left the dining room.

# EIGHT

**T**O AN OBSERVER THEY WOULD HAVE seemed no different from any other family at breakfast. Perhaps one child—the younger—was much quieter than the other, but such is the case in any family. Only a particularly careful observer would have noted a slight air of strain around them, as if they were avoiding something. As, indeed, they were.

Rose Conger was maintaining an almost grim good cheer, doing her best to prevent the silence that was normal for Sarah from becoming the norm for them all. But she knew no one was paying any attention to her. She could see Jack, his face mostly hidden, trying desperately to concentrate on his morning paper. And she knew that Elizabeth was devoting more energy to getting food into Sarah than she was to listening to her mother.

"And, of course," Rose chirped, "they have a son." She waited for a reaction, but there was none. She said, a little more loudly, "A fourteen-year-old son." She was gratified to note that she suddenly had her older daughter's attention.

"Who does?" Elizabeth said, putting down the knife she had been using to slice Sarah's sausages.

"You haven't been listening. The new neighbors. If you hadn't been so engrossed, you'd have heard me."

Elizabeth smiled sheepishly. "I'm sorry," she said, with a grin that let it be known that she was apologizing more for the sake of form than for anything else. "Don't tell me you actually sold the Barneses' old place." She made a face. "I hate that house. Who would want to live there?"

"It's a family," Rose said, smoothing the tablecloth unconsciously. "An architect and an artist. And their son. His name's Jeff."

"A boy," squealed Elizabeth. "A real live boy! What's he look like?"

"I'm sure he'll be terribly handsome," Rose replied. "Isn't the boy next door always supposed to be terribly handsome?"

Elizabeth blushed, and the sudden flushing disconcerted Rose. And then it hit her that she had somehow come to think of Elizabeth as being older than she was. She had to remind herself that Elizabeth was only thirteen, and that thirteen-year-old girls are very likely to blush when boys are mentioned.

"Actually, I don't know what he looks like. But we'll all know over the weekend. Carl and Barbara—they're the new neighbors," she added for the benefit of Jack, who had finally put his paper down. "Carl and Barbara Stevens will be coming down this morning, and I'm going to spend most of the day with them." Jack looked at her questioningly.

"Well," Rose went on, a little uncomfortably, "since the Barneses aren't around, somebody has to show them how the house works. Particularly a house like that." She saw a shadow of doubt cross Jack's face.

"All right," she said, putting down her napkin. "Also, I feel like being a busybody neighbor and seeing what I can find out about them. So far they seem to be a delight, and I think it would be nice to have neighbors who are also friends. It would be fun to have people we like close enough for dropping in, and I intend to promote it."

"Well," Jack said, the shadow of doubt now growing into a cloud. "I'm not so sure that's a good idea." Rose saw his eyes flick involuntarily toward Sarah. It was so fast that she was sure he wasn't aware that he had done it; she was equally sure she hadn't imagined it. She decided to face the issue directly. She began folding the napkin into smaller and smaller squares.

"I see no reason why we should behave like hermits," she said slowly. "If there is a reason, I'd like to know what it is."

The color drained from Jack's face, and he stared at his wife.

"I—I should think—" he began. Then he fell into an uncomfortable silence.

"I should think," Rose said definitely, "that we should keep in mind what century we are living in. Having a daughter in White Oaks School is not something we need to be ashamed of. If you think it is, then you have more of a problem than Sarah does." She paused as she saw Jack signaling with his eyes to where Elizabeth sat, listening to what her mother was saying. Making up her mind, Rose turned to Elizabeth.

"What do you think?" she asked.

"About what?" Elizabeth asked carefully, unsure of the direction things were taking.

"Well," Rose said, casting about in her mind for the proper words. "About Sarah, I suppose."

Elizabeth looked directly at her mother—almost accusingly, Rose thought. She seemed to be struggling with herself, and almost on the verge of tears. Then, she found her voice as her tears overflowed.

"I think," she said, fighting back a sob with a small, choking sound, "that we all should remember that Sarah isn't deaf. She doesn't talk, but she hears." She stared beseechingly at her mother for a few seconds, then turned back to her sister. "Come on, Sarah," she said. "Let's go get ready for school." She took Sarah's hand, and led her out of the dining room. Silently, Rose and Jack watched them go.

" 'From the mouths of babes . . .' " Jack said softly. Then he saw the tears running down his wife's face. He moved from his chair and knelt beside her. She buried her face in his shoulder, and her body shook with her sobs.

"What are we going to do, Jack?" she said into his ear. "She makes me feel ashamed sometimes. Absolutely ashamed. And she's only thirteen."

Jack patted her gently. "I know, darling," he said. "I know. I guess sometimes children have an easier time of things. They seem to be able to accept things the way they are. And we have to fight it."

"It?" Rose looked up. Their eyes met, and there was closeness between them, a closeness Rose hadn't felt since the early years of their marriage.

"Life," Jack said. "Wouldn't it be nice if we could stop fighting life?"

Rose nodded. "But we can't, can we?" Jack didn't answer, nor did Rose expect him to.

A few minutes later Rose looked in on her daughters. Elizabeth, already dressed, was brushing Sarah's thick dark hair. Sarah sat quietly in front of the mirror, but Rose couldn't tell whether she was watching Elizabeth. She might have been, but she might also have been somewhere else, living a life that had nothing to do with this room, her sister, or anything else related to the house on the Point.

"Do you need anything before I go?" Rose said.

Elizabeth looked up and smiled. "An extra quarter for snack period?" she asked brightly. Rose shook her head. Elizabeth straightened up. "There," she said. "What do you think?" Rose noted that the barrettes Elizabeth had fastened in her sister's short, shiny hair did not match, and the part was not quite straight. She decided not to comment on it.

"What does Sarah think?" she countered.

"Oh, she loves it," Elizabeth said. "It keeps her hair out of her eyes."

"That counts for a lot," Rose said, smiling. "Could you do the same for me?"

"Sure," Elizabeth said eagerly. "Now?"

Rose laughed. "Later. I don't have time now, and neither do you. But maybe tomorrow," she added, seeing the light fade in Elizabeth's eyes. "Kiss me good-bye?"

Elizabeth approached her mother and tipped her head up to be kissed. Rose squeezed her quickly, then moved to the vanity, where Sarah sat, still apparently staring at her new hairdo. Rose knelt and wrapped Sarah in her arms.

"Have a good day, sweetheart," she whispered. She kissed the little girl several times, then hugged her once more. "See you this afternoon," she said.

Downstairs again, Rose stopped in the kitchen to speak to Mrs. Goodrich. The housekeeper looked up at her inquiringly.

"Has Cecil turned up yet?" Rose asked.

Mrs. Goodrich shook her head.

"Do me a favor and look around for him today, will you?"

"Cats can take care of themselves. He'll be back when he's a mind to," the old woman said.

"I'm sure he will," Rose said drily. "But would you mind having a look anyway? The children miss him. He might have gotten locked in somewhere."

"If he did, someone locked him," Mrs. Goodrich stated. Then she relented. "Sure. You go on now—I'll find him."

Rose smiled her thanks and went to find her husband. Jack had already left the house.

In the kitchen, Mrs. Goodrich continued loading the dishes into the dishwasher. She was convinced that no machine could get dishes nearly clean enough for someone to eat from, but she used the machine anyway. She simply washed them to her own satisfaction before loading them into the machine and left out the soap. She supposed the machine was good enough for rinsing, particularly since she rinsed them herself, too. She closed the door and pressed the button to make the dishwasher start. All that racket, she thought. It's a wonder they don't all smash. Then, over the noise of the washer, she heard another sound, from the front of the house. She moved to the kitchen door, opened it slightly, and listened.

"No, Sarah," she heard Elizabeth saying. "You can't come with me. You have to wait here for the van."

Mrs. Goodrich heard Sarah wail, and moved through the door.

"Oh, Sarah," Elizabeth was saying, a little louder now. "I wish you could come with me, really I do, but you simply can't. It'll only be a few minutes." There was another wail from Sarah. "Sarah, let go. I'm going to be late if I don't leave now."

When Mrs. Goodrich appeared in the front hallway, Elizabeth was valiantly trying to free herself from Sarah's grasp. The smaller girl held on to Elizabeth's wrist with both hands, and Elizabeth was making no headway at all. Each time she pried one hand loose, the other would grasp her anew. She saw Mrs. Goodrich, and signaled to her to hurry.

"Help," she said, keeping her voice as light as she could. "Just hang on to her till I get out of sight, and she'll be all right."

Mrs. Goodrich seized Sarah and held her firmly while Elizabeth put on her coat. "You hurry along now," the woman said. "The sooner you're gone, the easier time I'll have. Not that I'm saying I don't like having you around," she added.

"I know," Elizabeth grinned. "I'll see you this afternoon."

Elizabeth went to the front door, opened it, turned to wave to Sarah, then closed the door behind her. She tried not to listen as she heard Sarah's voice rise in a howl of anguish. Instead, she concentrated on the trees that lined the driveway. By the time she reached the Point Road, she'd almost convinced herself that Sarah had stopped her howling.

Behind her the battle that was raging was a strange one. Sarah's outraged screams filled the house, and she struggled, twisting and squirming in Mrs. Goodrich's arms. Her face set, the old woman drew every measure of strength she possessed to hang on as tightly as she dared, and hold the child without hurting her. Mrs. Goodrich saw no point in trying to talk to Sarah. She was sure the child would never hear her above her own din, and it would only be wasting her strength to try. Grimly, she held on.

Then Sarah bit her. The housekeeper felt the teeth sink into her hand, into the fleshy part at the base of the thumb. She steeled herself against the pain and lifted Sarah off the floor. She carried the child to a window and turned so that Sarah could see out. Sarah stopped howling.

Mrs. Goodrich set her down then, and examined the thumb. The skin was broken, but not badly.

"It's been a long time since a child did that to me," Mrs. Goodrich noted out loud. Sarah, her attention diverted from the window and the empty driveway beyond, stared up into the housekeeper's face. Looking down into the huge, empty brown eyes, a surge of pity swept over the old woman. She slowly knelt down and put her arms around the child. "But I don't suppose you meant anything by it, did you? And you're not rabid, so there's no real harm done." She continued to hold the child, soothing her until she heard the van coming up the driveway. Then she hauled herself to her feet and, taking Sarah by the hand, led her back to the front door. Sarah stood docilely while Mrs. Goodrich bundled her into her coat, and made no objection when George Diller led her to the van. Mrs. Goodrich stood by the door and watched the van till it was out of sight. She didn't wave; she was too tired from the struggle, and she didn't really think Sarah would see it anyway. When the driveway was empty once again, she closed the door slowly and retreated to her kitchen, where she bathed the injured hand, winced as she applied iodine, and bandaged it. Then she remembered the cat.

She was sure it was a waste of time, but she had agreed to make a search for Cecil, and she would. She decided to get the long climb to the attic out of the way first and work down from there. Getting to the second floor was no problem; she was used to that. She carried the key to the attic door in her pocket, but instinctively tried the door as she reached for the key. The key dropped back into her pocket as the door opened, revealing the steep staircase. "Supposed to be locked," she muttered to herself, pausing a moment to rest before tackling the stairs that led to the attic. As she climbed, she tried to remember the last time anybody had been up here. A month ago, when they had brought down the old portrait. She went into the attic and closed the door behind her.

"Cecil?" she called. "Here, kitty, kitty, kitty . . ."

Elizabeth was halfway into town when she saw Kathy Burton walking ahead of her.

"Kathy?" she yelled. The girl ahead of her stopped and turned around. "Wait up," Elizabeth called. She ran until she caught up with her friend.

"What are you doing out here?" she said when she was abreast of Kathy.

"I was baby-sitting last night," Kathy said. "At the Nortons'."

Elizabeth rolled her eyes. "They're weird," she said.

"What do you mean?"

"He's so much older than she is . . ." Elizabeth trailed off, mulling the peculiarities of her elders. Then another thought occurred to her.

"Your mother lets you baby-sit there?"

"Sure," Kathy said curiously. "Why wouldn't she?"

"I mean after what happened to Anne Forager . . ."

"Oh, that," Kathy shrugged. "My mother says nothing happened to her at all. She says she's a liar."

Elizabeth nodded. "That's what my dad thinks, too. But I'm not sure he believes it."

"Why?"

"I don't know," Elizabeth said. "He's just acting strange." She looked around, and pointed to a bird that swooped from a nearby tree. "Look," she said, "a jay."

Kathy followed her gesture, but missed the bird. "You sure are lucky, living out here," she said. "That's why I like to sit for the Nortons. I can stay over and walk back in the morning."

"I wish there was a bus," Elizabeth said. "It gets boring after a while."

"I wouldn't get tired of it if I lived out here," Kathy said confidently. "It must be fun to be able to go exploring any time you want to."

Elizabeth nodded, but her attention was no longer on Kathy.

A rabbit had flashed across the road ahead of the girls, and as Elizabeth watched it a strange expression crossed her face. She stopped, and seemed to be grasping at an elusive thought.

"There's a place," she whispered.

"What?" Kathy asked.

"A secret place," Elizabeth went on. She turned to Kathy and stared intensely into her eyes. "Would you like to go there sometime?"

Kathy's eyes widened. "What kind of place?"

"If I told you it wouldn't be secret any more, would it? If I take you there, you have to promise never to tell anybody about it."

"Oh, I wouldn't," Kathy said, the excitement of sharing a secret bringing a quiver to her voice. "It would be just ours."

Elizabeth seemed on the verge of saying something more when she heard the sound of a vehicle approaching from behind them. She pulled Kathy off the road, and the two of them waited while the White Oaks van passed them. George Diller waved and tooted the horn as he passed. From the back of the van the girls could see Sarah, her face pressed against the rear window of the vehicle, until the bus took a curve in the road, moving out of sight. When the van was gone, Elizabeth stopped waving, and she and Kathy once again began walking.

"What's wrong with her?" Kathy asked.

"Who?"

"Sarah," Kathy said.

"Who said something's the matter with her?" Elizabeth said defensively. It upset her to be asked questions about her sister.

"My mother," Kathy said matter-of-factly. "She said Sarah's crazy."

Elizabeth stared at the ground for a while before she spoke again.

"I don't think you should talk that way about Sarah."

"Well, is she crazy?" Kathy pressed.

"No," Elizabeth said.

"Then why does she go to White Oaks? That's a place for crazy kids. They come from all over the country to go there."

"And they live there, don't they?" Elizabeth pointed out. "If Sarah was crazy, wouldn't she have to live there too?"

Kathy thought it over. "Well, if she's not crazy, why does she go there at all?"

Elizabeth shrugged her shoulders. "I don't know. Something happened to her about a year ago. She was in the woods, and she fell or something.

And now she can't talk. If she went to school in town, everybody would laugh at her. But she'll be all right, as soon as she starts talking again.''

The two girls walked in silence for a while, and it wasn't until they were into town that either of them spoke again.

''Does Sarah know about the secret place?'' Kathy said suddenly.

Elizabeth shook her head. ''And you won't either, if you don't stop asking questions about it. It's a place you have to be. You can't talk about it.''

''Will you show me?'' Kathy asked defiantly.

''If you stop talking about it,'' Elizabeth countered. ''It's a very special place, just for me. But I suppose I could take you there, since you're a friend of mine.''

''When?''

But Elizabeth didn't answer. Instead, she gave her friend a mysterious look, then disappeared into the school.

Mrs. Goodrich spent nearly an hour in the attic, only part of it looking for Cecil. A quick inspection convinced her that the cat was not there, and she was about to go back downstairs when something caught her eye. She wasn't sure what it was—something out of place, or something missing, or something there that shouldn't have been there. She paused and looked around. For a long time she couldn't put her finger on what it was. It was more a feeling than anything tangible. As if someone had been here and moved things around, then returned them to their original places. Except that there was still an air in the attic. An air of having been disturbed.

The old woman began looking around more carefully, realizing as she did that the attic was as much the storehouse of her memories as it was the repository of the Conger family's castoffs. All the things that Congers had used and forgotten about were scattered around the attic—things that they had forgotten about but that Mrs. Goodrich had not. Her hand caressed the cradle that had been used for so many Conger babies—Sarah most recently, but Elizabeth before her, and their father before them. She wondered how many generations of Conger babies had slept in that cradle. And then she noticed that the intricate hand carving contained not a particle of dust. That was what had struck her about the attic: no dust. Everything that should have been covered with dust was clean.

She spent the next hour in the attic, looking for the dirt that should have been there. But it was not there, nor was Cecil.

Early in the afternoon she decided that, wherever the cat was, he was not in the house.

He'll come back, she thought. When he's a mind to.

## NINE

"**A**RE YOU SORRY YET?"
Rose asked the question as she peered over the edge of her highball glass at Barbara Stevens. She had been right; she did like the Stevenses, and was looking forward to several years of happy neighborliness. Opposite her, sitting next to Carl, Barbara stared right back at her.

"Sorry?" she said. "Sorry we bought the house?"

"Well," Rose said, her eyes wandering through the ugly square living room, now filled with packed boxes and disarranged furniture, "I told you it was a mess. And it sure is."

Barbara laughed, and the sound seemed to make the room less ugly. "It isn't all that bad. There are lots of possibilities." Rose was sure she heard a touch of uncertainty in the words.

"Name one." It was a challenge.

"Carl has dozens," Barbara said, neatly avoiding the hook. "I'll take over after the remodeling is done."

"In other words," Carl put in, "never. Barbara is thoroughly convinced that 'remodeling' includes paint, paper, and, if she can persuade me, new furniture. Then, when it's all finished, she comes out of her studio, looks around, and says, 'My, we have done wonders with this place, haven't we?'"

"Now, it's not that bad at all," Barbara protested. "Besides, you know damned well that you think an architect should have full control of everything that goes into a building, from the day the ground is broken until the day the building is torn down." She turned her attention to Rose and winked. "He even has stipulations in his contracts to carry his instructions forth unto the fourth generation. The sins of the fathers may not be visited on the sons, but they're sure going to have to live with them."

"Enough," Carl said, standing up and brandishing a bottle that the three of them had half killed. "Any more, anybody, or shall we call it a day?"

Rose glanced at her watch, and it struck her that she had spent a lot more time here than she had intended. But it had been fun, and she'd found out a lot more about the old house than she had even known. The three of them had spent most of the day exploring it from top to bottom, and the Stevenses were now well acquainted with the Barneses' lighting system, which had allowed some rooms to be lit only from other rooms. Some rooms, which Rose explained had been the children's, were without any switches at all, and the three of them had speculated that the Barneses had actually and literally kept some of their children in the dark on occasion. The day had gone fast, and it was close to four. Rose stood up.

"There's one more thing I should show you," she said pensively, "and I'd like to do it this afternoon."

Carl's brows rose curiously. "Sounds important."

"It may be, and it may not be. You'll know better than I, since I haven't met Jeff yet."

"Jeff?" Barbara echoed, now totally mystified. "What does he have to do with it?"

"Nothing, I hope," Rose said. "That's why I'd like to tell you about it now, before he gets here. Come on."

She led Carl and Barbara out of the house on the ocean side. There was a path leading along the cliff to the south, and it was along this path that Rose took the Stevenses.

"There should be primroses," Carl remarked. Barbara smiled at him appreciatively, but Rose appeared not to have heard the remark. She strode forward, and they walked for about a hundred feet before she stopped.

"There," she said, pointing.

Carl and Barbara stared out to sea, their eyes sweeping the horizon. The ocean was clear of boats and ships, an expanse of gray-green water broken only by the horizon and Conger's Point jutting out to sea another hundred yards south of them.

"It's beautiful," Barbara said. "But I don't know what I'm looking for."

"The Point," Rose said. "From here you have a good view of the north face of it. The woods at the top are really a pretty shallow stand. On the other side of the woods is our field, and, of course, on the other side of the field is our house. If it weren't for the woods, you'd have a straight shot at the house."

"So?" Carl said, still clearly baffled as to what Rose was getting at.

"It's the embankment," Rose said. "I think you ought to know about it. It's very steep, and it can be treacherous, particularly when the wind blows from the north. The sea can get wild out there, and the spray turns the face of the embankment into glass. There have been some accidents . . ." Her voice trailed off; then, catching the worried look in Barbara's eyes, she went on. "Oh, not for a long time," she said. "Not in this century, as far as we know. We've always been very careful about it, and the children are not allowed to go anywhere near it. In the Conger family, for generations children haven't been allowed to play either in the woods or on the embankment. Not only is it dangerous, but it's practically invisible. You can't see the face of the embankment from any point on our property, and only from a couple of spots over here. From your house it's totally out of sight. All you can see is the forest."

"Why haven't you cut the forest down?" Barbara said thoughtfully. "It wouldn't be as pretty, but at least you'd be able to see if any of the kids are playing along the top."

Rose smiled tightly. "I suggested it once. Part of it, of course, is the esthetics. Also, there's the wind. The woods protect the house pretty well when the wind is from the north. Which it is, during the winter. And, of course, the privacy thing. The Congers always liked the idea that none of their neighbors could see them."

"It's nice to be able to afford that sort of luxury," Carl murmured.

Rose nodded. "Very nice. If you can afford it, which we barely can. A couple of more tax hikes and we won't be able to afford it at all." She realized she was saying more than she probably ought, then realized that she didn't really care; in fact, it was nice to be able to admit to someone, anyone, that the Congers weren't what they used to be. Still, she decided it was time to get back to the subject at hand.

"So that's what I wanted to show you," she said. "Of course, you can do what you want, but I'd advise you to tell Jeff not to go anywhere near the place."

"Which would send him there directly, the minute our backs were turned," Barbara said. "I think we'll just have to trust to his good sense." She noted the expression on Rose's face, and her smile faded. "Is there something else?" she asked.

Rose hesitated a minute, then spoke again. "Yes," she said, glancing once more at her watch. "I don't have time to go into it all, but there's a legend about the embankment. There may be a cave there, and it's really quite dangerous." Rose smiled uncertainly. "I've got to be getting home. Both the girls will be there, and I don't like to leave them for long with nobody but Mrs. Goodrich."

"Mrs. Goodrich?"

"The housekeeper. She's getting older—she must be nearly seventy—and terribly set in her ways, but she's been with the family since long before Jack was born."

They chatted a little more on the way back to the Stevenses' new house, but Rose didn't go in again. She felt a sudden urge to get home.

Minutes later, she was striding along the Point Road, skirting the west end of the strip of woods. She saw a squirrel playing in one of the trees, something she normally would have taken a few minutes to enjoy, but she didn't give it a second glance. She passed the woods, and was walking along the edge of the field. Suddenly she stopped. Coming out of the woods, about one hundred and fifty yards from Rose, was Elizabeth. A couple of seconds later, Sarah, too, emerged from the woods. Rose felt her stomach tighten as she watched her children cross the field toward home. She didn't call out to them; indeed, she didn't even move until she saw them disappear into the house. Then, when they were no longer visible, she continued on her way. But her pace was slow, and her mind was filled with thoughts. None of them made any sense. All of them were foreboding.

When she got home, she didn't call out a greeting. Instead, she went directly to the small study at the rear of the house, poured herself a drink, and sat in the wing chair. As she waited for her husband to come home, she studied the old portrait above the mantel. It did look like Elizabeth.

So much like Elizabeth.

She sipped the drink, stared at the picture and waited.

\* \* \*

She was still in the wing chair an hour later, when Jack came home. She heard his voice calling out as he opened the front door, heard the answer come from Elizabeth upstairs. Rose remained silent, and listened to his footsteps approach the study. She was watching the door when he came through. His eyes widened in surprise; then he grinned at her.

"Are we doing a role reversal? I'm the one who's supposed to sit brooding in the chair with a drink in my fist." His smile faded as he watched his wife's face. "Is something wrong?" he asked, and Rose was pleased to hear a concern that sounded genuine.

"Fix yourself a drink and sit down," she said. "And you might as well fix this one up. The ice has melted."

He took her glass, refilled it, and poured himself a neat Scotch. Setting Rose's drink on the table at her elbow, he seated himself opposite her.

"So what's up? Sarah?"

She shook her head. "I'm not sure, really." She recounted her day, skipping over most of it until she reached the end. She went over her final conversation with the Stevenses in detail, trying to remember exactly what she had told them. When she finished, he didn't seem particularly disturbed.

"Then what has you so upset?" he asked.

"On my way home, I saw the girls coming out of the woods. First Elizabeth, then Sarah."

"I see," Jack said quietly. "And you want me to talk to them?"

"Not both of them. Just Elizabeth. I don't care what you tell her, but convince her to stay away from there."

"Shall I tell her about the legend?"

"If you want."

"Well, Lord knows, if that won't do it nothing will. That legend has kept four generations of Congers away from that embankment."

"Four?" Rose said. "That many?"

"I think so," Jack said. He counted briefly on his fingers. "Nope. I'm the third. If it works, Elizabeth and Sarah will be the fourth. Well, no time like the present." He finished his drink and left the room.

Alone, Rose continued sipping from her glass and staring at the portrait. For some reason, Carl Stevens's words echoed in her mind. "The sins of the fathers . . ."

Then she remembered the rest of the quotation, and she shuddered: ". . . even unto the third and fourth generations."

Jack climbed the stairs slowly, wondering what he would tell his daughter. At the top he paused and squared his shoulders. The truth, he guessed. Or at least what the Congers had thought was some sort of truth, among themselves, for more years than he knew.

He found them in the playroom. A frown creased his brow as he saw what they were doing. Between them was the Ouija board, and Elizabeth seemed to be concentrating on it. Sarah was concentrating on Elizabeth. Jack cleared his throat, and when nothing happened he spoke.

"Elizabeth," he said, and regretted the sharp sound that filled the room. His daughters jumped a little, and Elizabeth opened her eyes.

"Daddy! Did you come up to play with us?"

"I came up to talk to you. Alone." His eyes shifted to Sarah on the last word, and Elizabeth picked up on the message. She stood up, then leaned over to whisper into her sister's ear. Sarah, to Jack's eye, did not respond, but Elizabeth seemed to be satisfied that Sarah would be all right by herself. She followed him as he led her out of the playroom and into her own room. When she was inside he closed the door, and Elizabeth knew that she had done something wrong. She sat on the edge of her bed and regarded her father respectfully.

"It's the woods, isn't it?" she said.

Her father looked at her sternly. "Yes," he said, "it is. Unless I'm badly mistaken, it was only yesterday that we had a talk about that. Now I understand you were in the woods today. With Sarah."

Elizabeth looked straight into his eyes, and he tried to find a clue in her own as to her mood. He wondered if she would be defiant, or angry, or stubborn. But he saw only curiosity.

"I know," she said. "I don't really know why I took Sarah to the woods today. We were in the field, playing, and then we were in the woods. I must have been thinking about something else, because I honestly don't remember going into the woods. The only thing I remember is suddenly realizing we were in the woods, and leading Sarah back out to the field."

Jack listened to his daughter silently, trying to decide if she was being truthful. He remembered his own youth, and all the times he had become so engrossed in something that he had lost track of his surroundings. He supposed it could have happened.

"Well," he said, "I expect you not to let it happen again. You're a big girl now, and you should be able to keep your mind on what you're doing. Or at least where you are, particularly when Sarah is with you."

"I take good care of her," Elizabeth said, and Jack thought he heard a defensive note in her voice.

"Of course you do," he said soothingly. "But please take good care of her only on this side of those woods." Now he definitely saw anger in Elizabeth's face. The beautiful features hardened slightly, and he realized he was going to have to amplify. While she posed the question, he tried to figure out where to begin his answer.

"I want to know why," she was saying. "I think it's getting absolutely silly. I'm old enough to go where I want to go, at least on our own property. When I was little, it was one thing. But I'm not little any more. You said so yourself," she finished.

"You're going to think we're all crazy," Jack said.

"Are we?" Elizabeth asked, but there was no twinkle in her eye.

"Who knows?" Jack replied, keeping his tone light. "Okay, I'll tell you the story. There's an old family legend."

"I know," Elizabeth said.

"You know?" Now Jack couldn't keep the surprise out of his voice. "How?"

Elizabeth widened her eyes and tried to look spooky. "The Ouija board," she intoned. "It knows all and it tells all." Then she burst into laughter at the expression on her father's face. It was a mixture of awe, surprise, and fright. "I'm kidding, Dad," she said. "I don't know what it's all about." She thought carefully, then went on. "In fact, I don't really know what I know and what I don't know, or where I found out. But I know there's some kind of story and it goes back a long way. What is it?"

Jack felt a strange sense of relief that she did not know the legend, and he began to tell it to her.

"It does go back a long way," he said. "Your mother and I were just figuring it out, and it's four generations, counting you and Sarah. It has to do with your great-great-grandmother. It all happened somewhere in the neighborhood of a hundred years ago, and she was already an old, old lady then. I don't know how many of the details I can remember, since I don't think anybody ever wrote the story down, but here's what is supposed to have happened:

"The old woman—I think her name was Bernice or Bertha, something like that—was in the habit of taking a nap every day after dinner, which was what we'd call lunch nowadays. Apparently every day she'd go upstairs and sleep for an hour, then come back down, and that was that. Except that one day she didn't come back down."

"You mean she died?" Elizabeth asked.

"No," Jack said. "She didn't die. When she didn't come down from her nap, they went upstairs, I imagine expecting to find her dead, but she wasn't. She was still asleep.

"To make a long story short, the legend has it that she slept for two days and two nights, solid. They tried to wake her up, and couldn't. They called a doctor, but he couldn't find anything wrong with her at all. I suppose she might have had some kind of stroke and gone into a coma, but at the time they didn't know much about such things. Anyway, she eventually woke up, and she didn't seem to have anything wrong with her.

"I suppose the family would have forgotten about it, except that a couple of days later one of the old lady's sons, who would have been my great-uncle, I think, walked into the house carrying a dead rabbit. Then he proceeded to jump off the cliff behind the house."

"You're kidding," Elizabeth breathed.

Jack shook his head. "If I am, then your grandfather kidded me when he told me the story."

"But why did he do it?" Elizabeth asked.

"No one ever found out." Jack shrugged. "Or if they did, they never told anybody. Anyway, when the old lady heard about it, she wasn't surprised. Apparently she said she'd been expecting it. And from then on until she died, she told everybody who was going to die, and when. She said she had gotten all the information in a dream she had while she'd been sleeping those two days."

"And she was never wrong?" Elizabeth asked doubtfully.

"Who knows? You know the way stories grow. She could have been wrong most of the time, but the only thing anybody would remember and pass along would be the times she was right. She probably predicted everybody's death every day, so sooner or later she hit the nail on the head. It's like astrologers. They say so much that some of the things have to be right.''

"Then what's the big deal?" Elizabeth said.

"Well, the last straw came just before she died. She claimed she'd had a vision.''

"A vision? You mean like angels or ghosts?''

"Not quite. A vision, but not of angels. She claimed that in the vision she had been taken to a cave in the embankment. Inside the cave, she was shown a shaft that led straight down. Her 'angel,' or whatever it was supposed to be, told her that the shaft was the gates of hell. According to the old lady, all sorts of awful things were supposed to happen if anybody ever went through the gates of hell. Or, I suppose, down the shaft. Anyway, she told the family that she had seen visions of horrible things in the future, and that the only way to keep them from happening was to see to it that no one went near that cave. She made everyone in the family swear never to go near the embankment where the cave is supposed to be. Then she died.''

Elizabeth stared at him silently for a minute before she spoke. He could hear incredulity in her voice.

"Is there really a cave there?''

"I don't have any idea.''

"You mean they believed her?" Elizabeth said. "You mean nobody ever even went to look for it?''

Jack licked his lips uncomfortably. "Someone did," he said slowly. "My grandfather.''

"Did he find it?" Elizabeth asked eagerly.

"No," Jack said. He hoped he could leave it at that, but Elizabeth wouldn't let him.

"Well, what happened?" she demanded.

"No one knows about that, either. He announced one day that he was going to find the cave, *if* there was a cave, and headed off by himself. When he didn't come back, a search party went to find him.''

"Did they?" Elizabeth asked. "Find him, I mean?''

"They found him. They found him at the bottom of the embankment. His foot was wedged between two rocks, and he had apparently drowned when the tide came in.''

An expression of horror came over Elizabeth's face. "What an awful way to die," she said softly.

"Yes," said Jack, "it is. The odd thing was that they couldn't figure out exactly what happened. His foot was caught, but not tightly. He should have been able to get it loose without any trouble.''

"Maybe he fell," Elizabeth suggested.

"Maybe, but they didn't find any bruises that would have indicated it. Well," he finished, "that's it. Whatever the truth of it, the whole family has always respected the old lady's dying wish. Except for my grandfather. If nothing else, it gives us a reason for staying away from a dangerous place. I hope you'll respect it as much as the rest of us have.''

Elizabeth was very quiet, and when she spoke her voice was low. "Daddy," she said. "Do you believe it?"

Jack considered the question, and could find no answer. He had lived with the legend for so long that it never entered his mind to question the truth of it. Now, looking at it in the cold light of his daughter's ice-blue stare, he shook his head.

"No," he said, "I don't suppose I do, really. On the other hand, I don't believe it's bad luck to walk under a ladder, but I still don't walk under ladders. So maybe, deep down inside, I do believe the legend."

Elizabeth seemed to digest this for a minute, and Jack was about to lean over to kiss her when she asked another question.

"What about the little girl?" she said.

"What little girl?" Jack asked blankly.

"I'm not sure," Elizabeth said. "It seems to me that I've heard somewhere that there was a little girl in the legend."

Jack reviewed the story in his mind, then shook his head.

"No," he said. "Not that I know of."

"Well," Elizabeth said, "there should be. Let's make one up." Now Jack could see the glint of mischief in her eyes.

"You do that," he said. "And tell me about it over dinner. See you downstairs in thirty minutes."

He kissed her, then left the room. As he descended the stairs, he heard her calling after him.

"I'll ask the Ouija board about it," she said.

He heard her laugh as she went back to the playroom.

## TEN

"WHAT EXACTLY DID YOU TELL HER?" Rose spoke in the dark, and her voice seemed to bounce off the walls and come back at her more loudly than she desired. Beside her, she felt Jack stir. She was sure he wasn't sleeping, but it was almost a minute before he answered her. In the silence, she began counting the ticking of the grandfather clock. She had reached forty when Jack finally spoke.

"The whole thing," he said. "The idea was to keep her away from the embankment, wasn't it?"

"I suppose so," Rose said unsurely. "How did she take it?"

She heard Jack chuckle in the darkness. "How would you take a story like that in this day and age? I'm not sure family legends and curses count for much any more."

"But a lot of it happened," Rose said.

"Some of it happened," Jack countered. "Granted that the old lady slept for a couple of days, that someone jumped off the cliff and someone else drowned. It still doesn't add up to much. And, of course, the old lady's vision at the end was probably nothing more than senility." He rolled over. "Still, it makes a good spooky story, and it's sure kept us all off the embankment for a lot of years."

"How did she take it?" Rose repeated. "Didn't she say anything?"

Jack smiled in the darkness. "She wanted to know about the little girl."

"Little girl?" Rose said. "What little girl? I never heard of a little girl before."

"Of course not. There isn't any. It just struck Elizabeth that there ought to have been a little girl involved in the legend. She said she thought she heard about one somewhere, but couldn't remember where. She said she'd consult the Ouija board."

Rose felt herself begin to shudder, but fought it off. "Ouija board," she said. "I'm not sure we should let her play with such a thing. Children are too suggestible."

She rolled over and nestled against her husband. She felt his body stiffen. Sighing, she moved away from him.

In her room, Elizabeth lay in her bed, listening to the murmur of her parent's voices. As the voices died away, the girl's eyes closed; then her breathing evened out and grew deeper. As the clock struck, her eyelids began to flicker. A sound struggled from her throat, then died away on her lips. She turned, and the covers fell to the floor. Her knees drew up, and she wrapped her arms around herself.

And then she rose from the bed.

She padded on her bare feet across the floor of her room and out into the hall. She moved, trancelike, to the attic door and stretched upward to take the key from the ledge above. Avoiding the loose third tread, Elizabeth glided up the steep stairs into the attic, unaware of the silent Sarah, who stood quietly watching the ascent.

After Elizabeth disappeared into the upper reaches of the house, Sarah returned to her bed, where she lay staring blankly at the ceiling.

Elizabeth stayed in the attic for an hour, but what she did there, and what she saw, didn't register on her memory.

Lying awake, Rose felt as if she were suffocating. She tried to ignore the feeling, but it persisted. Finally, in frustration, she left her bed and went to sit by the window. Moodily, she sat and smoked and peered out into the night. There was a full moon, and shadows played across the field. It was peaceful, she thought, and she considered going for a walk. The cliff would be beautiful, with the light dancing on the sea, and the surf, turned silvery by the moon, crashing below her. And then, as suddenly as the feeling of suffocation had come over her, it left her. She crushed the cigarette out and went back to bed. In a moment she was asleep.

Had she stayed by the window, she might not have returned to her bed, for she might have seen the shape moving across the field.

Elizabeth crossed the porch at the moment that Rose went back to bed. She moved slowly, carefully toward the field, as if feeling her way with her feet. Then, suddenly, she turned and began walking quickly toward the old barn that stood a few yards from the garage. She let herself in by the side door and moved to the tack room. She picked up a bag and a strange coil of rope and wood. She slung the coil over her head, grasped the neck of the bag, and left the barn. Then, her step no longer cautious, she moved across the field toward the wood. Soon she was enveloped in its black shadows.

The dress Elizabeth wore was old—much older than any of the clothes she kept for playing in the field. Its ruffled hem caught on branches as she drew nearer the woods, but the ancient material gave way with so little resistance that she felt no pull. Her blond hair, flowing over her shoulders in an old-fashioned way, caught the moonlight and, from a distance, seemed to form a halo around her head.

She moved surely and gracefully, her eyes staring directly ahead into the blackness before her. There was no path or trail, but she advanced as easily as though the way had been paved. Though the shadows were deep, and the underbrush thick, her feet found the places where no branches waited to trip her, or stones to bruise her foot, or vines to ensnare her.

And then Elizabeth emerged from the woods, and stood on the top of the embankment, staring out across the sea. It was gentle that night, and the surf murmured below, softly, invitingly.

Elizabeth began moving eastward along the edge of the embankment, slowly, as if waiting for some sort of signal to tell her she was at the right place. Then she stopped again, and stared once more out to sea. Finally she began moving down the steep face of the embankment, her small feet finding holds that would have been useless to a larger person. Occasionally her free hand moved out as if to steady herself, but most often it stopped short of touching anything. She moved steadily downward, disappearing now and then from the moonlight, then reemerging a few feet lower than before. Finally she disappeared into the shadow of a boulder, and crept into a hole that lay hidden in the blackness. Fifty feet farther down, the surf pounded against the Point.

Elizabeth crawled through the tunnel of the cave, pulling the long skirt up every few minutes, then creeping farther forward until the dress grew taut as she crawled across it. Then she would pause again, and pull the material from under her knees, spreading it once more before her. She felt her way forward, pushing the bag carefully, as if it would disappear if she pushed it too far. Then she stopped, crept as far over the bag as she could, and felt the floor of the cave in front of her. At the end of her reach she felt the lip of a shaft.

She moved a little closer to the edge and poked around in the depths of the bag. Her hand closed on a flashlight, and she drew it out. She tested it a couple of times, flashing the narrow beam on the walls that closed in around her. The tunnel widened into a room around the shaft, and the shaft itself appeared to be a well in the center of an oval room whose floor was littered with boulders.

Elizabeth removed the coiled object from around her neck, and, still clutching the flashlight, moved to the edge of the shaft. She pointed the light downward and stared into the depths. Far below, she wasn't sure how far, the light glinted on something that lay on the bottom of the shaft.

She laid the flashlight carefully in a cleft of stone, and jiggled it a little to be sure it was secure. Then she began uncoiling the object she had carried from the barn. It was a rope ladder that had once provided primitive access to the loft. For years it had lain in the tack room: the loft was no longer used, and the ladder had been deemed a danger to playing children. Elizabeth began wedging the ends of the rope into cracks in the boulders, chinking the rope tighter with bits of stone that lay scattered across the cavern floor. Finally she tested the ropes, pulling on them as hard as she could, bracing her legs against the boulders. The rope held.

She pushed the rest of the coil over the lip of the shaft. It clattered against the side of the shaft, then caught. She pulled it back to the surface and carefully untangled it. The second time, as she fed it carefully over the edge, it fell straight to the bottom. She felt a slight vibration as the bottom rung struck the floor below.

She picked up the bag and dropped it over the edge. She heard a soft *thunk* as it too hit the bottom. Then she worked the flashlight loose from its crevice, put it in a pocket of her dress, and began making her way down the ladder.

It was slow going, but Elizabeth didn't seem to notice the slime that rubbed off the walls of the shaft as she crept carefully from rung to rung, nor did the darkness frighten her. She felt the cool stone touch the sole of her foot as she found the bottom of the shaft. She reached into her pocket and pulled out the flashlight.

The yellowish beam flickered around the chamber at the bottom of the shaft. It was very much like the chamber above: smaller, and with a lower ceiling, but oval, and with a flat, rock-strewn floor. The shaft opened almost in the center of the small chamber.

Elizabeth played the light over the floor of the cavern, and the object which had glinted from above suddenly flashed once more. It was a gold bracelet, set with a small opal.

It was still on the wrist of its owner.

The skeleton lay directly below the opening of the shaft, sprawled in the position in which it had lain through the decades. Here and there small pieces of rotten cloth still clung to it, but they disintegrated into dust when Elizabeth touched them. The sack lay near it, where Elizabeth had dropped it, its impact having scattered some of the ribs across the floor. Elizabeth retrieved the bag and set it aside. Then she played the light over the skull. She picked up a rusted metal barrette that lay next to the skull and examined it carefully. She nodded to herself.

"I knew you were here," she whispered. "Everything will be all right now. You'll see."

She left the skeleton for a moment and found a new resting place for the flashlight. She left it on and trained it on the spot where the ancient bones gleamed palely in its light.

Elizabeth worked slowly, moving the bones carefully. She laid them out at one edge of the chamber, close to one of the walls. She found a small flat rock to cushion the skull, and when she was finished the remains lay on their back, the arms folded peacefully over the rib cage. Elizabeth smiled at the corpse, and there was a strange light in her eyes as she removed the bracelet from the fleshless wrist and slipped it onto her own.

She began moving some of the rocks around, wrestling a large one with a fairly flat surface into the center of the cavern. Then she moved four other, smaller rocks to form stools around the rough table. She placed the bag on the table and sat down on one of the stools.

From the bag she began removing a set of doll's clothing: a small blue dress, tiny stockings, and a pair of miniature patent-leather Mary Janes, together with a pair of white mittens and a small ruffled bonnet.

Then she opened the sack and Cecil lay on the rock slab, his body limp, his head at a strange angle from the broken neck that had killed him.

Elizabeth began dressing the dead cat in the doll's clothes, carefully working the dress over his head, front legs, and torso, forcing the forepaws through the sleeves, and meticulously buttoning the dress up along his spine.

Then she worked the tiny socks over his hindpaws, and forced the stockinged paws into the miniature shoes. She slipped the mittens onto the forepaws and, finally, put the bonnet on Cecil's head, tying the strings securely under his chin.

"Pretty baby," she murmured as she finished. "Aren't you my pretty baby?"

She set the grotesquely costumed animal on the rock opposite her and watched as it collapsed to the cavern floor. She tried to set it up twice more, but each time it fell. Finally she collected a number of small rocks and built a small pile of stones that would support the weight of the corpse. Eventually the dead Cecil sat propped across from her, its bonneted head lolling weirdly to one side. Elizabeth seemed not to notice the unnatural pose.

"And now we'll have a party," she said. "Would you like some tea?"

Her right hand picked up an imaginary teapot, and she skillfully poured from it into an equally invisible cup that she held steadily in her left hand. She set the imaginary cup in front of the dead cat.

"One lump or two?" she asked politely, offering her guest a bowl of sugar. Without waiting for an answer, she mimed placing two lumps of sugar in the cup that was not on the table.

"Well," she said, smiling brightly, "isn't this nice?"

Elizabeth waited, staring across at the tightly closed eyes of the cat.

"Are you sleeping?" she asked. She reached across the table and prodded the corpse with one finger. Then she left her seat and moved around to kneel beside Cecil. She carefully forced each eye open, peeling the lids far back until they did not snap shut again when she released them. She went back to her seat.

"There," she said. "Now we can have a nice conversation. Would you like a piece of cake?" Elizabeth picked up an imaginary cake plate and

offered it to the vacantly staring cat. When there was no response, she
pretended to scoop a slice of the cake onto a plate that was apparently
already waiting in front of Cecil.

"Now," she said, pausing to take a bite of the cake that wasn't there
and wash it down with a swallow of the imaginary tea. "What would you
like to talk about?"

She waited for a response again and glared at the limp, unresponsive
body that sat propped across from her. Empty eyes stared back at her.

"It's very rude not to talk when you're spoken to," she said softly.
"Nice children answer questions."

There was still no response from the corpse, and Elizabeth's face flushed
with anger.

"Answer me when I speak to you," she snapped. Still there was no
response.

She peered balefully at the cat, and her eyes flashed in the strange yellow
glow of the flashlight.

"Talk to me," she demanded, a hard edge of hatred coming into her
voice. "You talk to me, you disgusting child!"

Elizabeth's anger mounted as the dead thing across from her failed to
respond to her demands, and her voice rose and grew shrill.

"Don't you sit there like that, you bastard!" she yelled. "That's all you
ever do. I spend my life with you, and what do I get from you? Nothing.
*Nothing!* Well, now you'll talk to me, or I'll beat your ass bloody."

She suddenly leapt at the cat, grabbing the corpse and yanking it across
the table. She flipped it over, held it on her knee, and began spanking it. The
slapping of her hand against the cat's haunches echoed back at her, and she
put all her strength into the beating she was administering. Then she set the
cat back on the rock and smiled at it.

"There," she said. "Now that you've had what you deserve, we can get
back to our tea party."

She went on chattering mindlessly for a few moments, miming the
actions of refilling the cups and plates she imagined were before her. Then
she asked the cat another question and waited for a response. When there
was none, her anger flashed back, flooding over her like a red tide.

"Don't you do that to me, you fucking no-good monster!" she
screamed. "I hate it when you do that to me. Hate it, hate it, *hate it!*"

As her voice rose, she grabbed the cat and began swinging it over her
head, then brought it crashing down on the stone table. In her rage, she
didn't hear the crushing of the skull.

"You'll answer me," she raved. "God damn you, you'll talk to me or
I'll kill you!"

Suddenly she hurled the cat against the wall of the cave and grabbed the
bag once more. She reached deep into it, and when she withdrew her hand
she clutched a large butcher knife. Her anger cresting, she fell on the cat's
limp body and began slashing at it with the knife, her voice rising as she
cursed the unresponsive animal.

Suddenly she had the cat on the table again, and the knife flashed
through the air once more. Cecil's severed head rolled away from the torso

and fell to the floor. Elizabeth stared at it, not comprehending what had happened.

"Don't do that," she breathed. "Don't do that to me. I want you to talk to me. *Talk to me!*" she screamed once more, then stopped, her breath coming in gasps. She felt a pain throbbing through her head, and heard something that sounded like wind. Then the pain passed, and the sounds of the wind faded into a strange whimpering from above. She looked up into the darkness of the shaft.

Seeing nothing, she found the flashlight, and shined it upward. The beam illuminated Sarah's dark face, her huge brown eyes blinking in the glare of the light.

Elizabeth smiled up at her, and her face softened.

"Sarah," she almost whispered. "Did you see? Did you see that naughty baby? She isn't like you. She isn't like you at all. You're such a sweet girl, so sweet . . ." She turned back to look once more at the decapitated feline body, which lay, still clothed, on the rough rock. Then the light picked up the head, still encased in the old-fashioned bonnet, the eyes dully reflecting the glare from the flashlight.

"You should have talked to me," she hissed. "Really, you should have." She picked up the knife and placed it carefully on a ledge near the ceiling of the cavern.

Then she slipped the flashlight, still glowing, into her pocket and began to make her way back up the rope ladder. Sarah crept back from the edge as Elizabeth emerged from the pit.

"It's late," Elizabeth whispered. "But not too late." Then she slipped the bracelet that was still on her wrist off her own arm and onto Sarah's.

"This is for you," she said. "It's from Beth. She wants you to have it. She says it should belong to you."

Ignoring Sarah now, Elizabeth crept through the tunnel and emerged once more into the night. Quickly, she made her way back up the face of the embankment and disappeared into the woods.

Elizabeth lay once more in her bed, staring at the ceiling. She wished she could fall asleep again, but she couldn't. She had awakened from a dream which had fled as she opened her eyes, and now sleep would not come to her. She thought she heard a noise outside, and went to the window. There, making her way slowly across the field, she saw her sister. Elizabeth went downstairs and met Sarah at the front door.

She was covered with mud and slime, and her hands were badly scratched. She stared helplessly up at Elizabeth.

Silently Elizabeth took Sarah upstairs and into the bathroom. She cleaned her sister up and threw the filthy clothes into the laundry chute. Then she tucked Sarah into bed.

Elizabeth wondered where Sarah had been. But soon she slept. It was a peaceful sleep, and there were no more dreams.

# ELEVEN

MRS. GOODRICH OPENED THE TRAPDOOR at the bottom of the laundry chute and watched the clothes tumble to the floor at her feet. She picked up a particularly dirty pair of blue jeans with a ragged tear at the knee and looked at them critically.

"Just look at that," she said to the empty room. "I've never in my life seen anything so filthy. Looks like she's been crawling around in some kinda slime."

She fished out an equally dirt-encrusted shirt and examined it carefully. The filth had dried overnight, and it flecked off into the old woman's hand as she held the shirt to the light.

She sniffed at it, and her face wrinkled even more deeply as she recoiled from the smell of rotting seaweed. Her face tightened, and she turned toward the laundry-room door with an air of determination.

She found Rose and Jack Conger sitting silently in the dining room, and would have noticed the strain in the air if she hadn't had other things on her mind. She stumped into the room without her usual pause, and Jack looked up curiously. Mrs. Goodrich ignored him.

"Miz Rose," she complained, her Yankee twang taking on a hint of outrage. "Just look at these. I don't know how I'm supposed to get things like this clean." She held the shirt up for Rose's inspection, primarily because the filth showed up better against the white of the shirt than the blue of the denim. Mrs. Goodrich was a great believer in the best effects delivering the best result. She shook the shirt slightly, for good measure, and was gratified to see some of the dried mud flutter to the carpet. The vacuum would take care of that.

"What is it?" Rose asked curiously. "It looks like mud."

"Mud? You call that mud? I call it slime." She held the shirt nearer, and Rose was able to get a good whiff.

"It smells like dead fish," Rose commented, wondering what was expected of her. "Whose is it?"

"Miss Sarah's," Mrs. Goodrich stated. "I don't know what that child's been up to, but it should be stopped. She didn't get this dirt from playing in the yard, or even the field. I don't know how I can get it out." She did know, of course, but saw no point in admitting it. Over the years she had discovered that life was much easier if she feigned incompetence, and this seemed like a good time to exercise that knowledge.

"Well, do your best," Rose said, still not sure how she was supposed to deal with the situation. "I don't really see how we can find out where she picked up that dirt, under the circumstances."

Mrs. Goodrich, her feelings aired, stumped back out of the room, leaving the air filled with grumblings. Rose thought she heard a reference to things like this not happening in the old days, and wondered if it could have been true. Then she saw Jack staring at her, and suddenly felt uncomfortable. Briefly she wondered what had happened to the peace they had had so recently.

"Well, what was I supposed to say?" she said, feeling a little guilty but not sure why.

"Nothing," Jack said. "Don't worry about the dirt—Mrs. Goodrich can handle that with a good hard look. But where *did* Sarah pick it up?"

"I'm sure I don't know," Rose snapped. "Why don't you ask her?"

"That's cruel, Rose," Jack said quietly. "And not just to me. It's cruel to Sarah, too."

Rose took a deep breath, then exhaled slowly, willing the tension from her body. She chewed her lower lip for a moment, then tried to smile at her husband.

"I'm sorry," she said. "Of course you're right. But, God, Jack, what am I supposed to do about it? If she went somewhere by herself, there's absolutely no way in the world that we're going to find out where it was."

"It probably has something to do with the scratches," Jack said.

Rose nodded. "And she could have gotten those anywhere."

Then they looked at each other and they both remembered. Early this morning, Rose had looked in on Sarah. The child had thrown her blanket off in the night, and as Rose bent to cover her she saw that Sarah's hands were badly scratched, and one knee was scraped. But she had been clean. The wounds had been clean too. They'd assumed that something had happened during the night, that the wounds had been somehow self-inflicted. But now, with the filthy clothing, they had to reassess the whole thing. They each avoided the subject in a different way: Rose by stirring her coffee moodily, Jack by mopping up the last of his egg with a piece of danish.

"It did smell like the sea," Rose said at last.

"Around here everything smells like the sea," Jack countered.

"I suppose she could have decided to go down to the beach."

"In the middle of the night?" Jack said. "Besides, that trail's not slimy, and it's an easy trail. Even if it was pitch-black, all you have to do is keep one hand on the guardrail and walk. And the beach is sand."

"There are rocks," Rose offered, and it was true. There were rocks on the beach, but they weren't of the rough variety. They were, for the most part, beach pebbles worn smooth by years of tumbling in the light surf of the south side of the Point. The rough rocks, both of them knew, were on the north side, jutting out of the face of the embankment. Neither of them was willing to confront that possibility yet.

"What about the quarry?" Jack asked suddenly. "She could have walked over to the quarry for some reason. It's always muddy there, and God knows those old slag heaps are hard on the hands."

Rose stared speculatively into space and tried to believe in the idea of the quarry. It would be easy, except for the smell. Her nose wrinkled as she remembered the awful rotting kelp odor that had permeated the shirt. She decided to put it out of her mind.

"Well, I don't see that there's a thing we can do about it now," she said. "It's too late. Besides, we've got other things to worry about," she added pointedly.

Jack felt the familiar sick feeling begin to form in his stomach, the feeling he was not getting used to—and was experiencing more and more.

"Don't you think things are bad enough?" he asked, his voice carrying a quaver that he hoped Rose wouldn't hear. "Let's not make them any worse."

"How could it get any worse," Rose said bitterly. She kept her voice low, ready to break off the conversation if she heard the children coming downstairs. But she was not about to let it go. She remembered the previous night—his rejection, her long, thoughtful vigil at the window—and wondered how many more of them there would be, how many more of them she would be able to stand without blowing apart from the rage, the frustration, and the humiliation.

Last night she had taken herself in hand and squeezed her anger back, forcing herself to sleep through it. But this morning it was still there, waiting to be served up to Jack along with his coffee and orange juice. He had not been surprised.

"Don't you think it's time you got back into therapy?" she asked softly, trying another tack.

"I don't want to go into it," Jack said sourly.

"The subject or the therapy?"

"Take your pick," he said. "Is there a difference?"

"That depends," Rose said, deliberately keeping the poison out of her voice. "I know you don't get off on therapy—"

"I don't get off at all," Jack finished for her. "You're getting predictable."

"And you aren't?" Rose snapped, no longer bothering to hide the hostility she was feeling. "Listen to me," she hissed as he began turning away, as if his back might shield him from her words.

"It's no good, Jack, it's just no good. I'm a normal woman, with normal desires, and I deserve some kind of normal satisfaction. Although God knows why I should expect that in a home that's anything but normal. Maybe there's nothing we can do for Sarah, but I should think that you, at least, would want to do what you can before you get just like her."

"It's not that easy—" Jack began, but she didn't give him time to defend himself.

"What is easy? Is it easy to live with a man like you? Easy to live with a child like Sarah? Easy to keep on acting as if nothing is the matter? Business as usual? How long do you think I can keep it up? God knows, every woman that's ever married into this family has had her hands full just being the latest Mrs. Conger for this godforsaken village. But that's not enough, not any more. Not only do I have to be Mrs. Conger, but I have to be a loving mother to a traumatized child, a loving wife to an impotent husband, and push real estate on the side.''

"You don't have to do that," Jack put in, grabbing at the only available straw.

"Don't I?" Rose demanded. "Don't I? Well, let me tell you one more thing. Pushing real estate is the easy part. It's the only fun I get out of life any more, and besides, it gives us enough money to keep Sarah at White Oaks. So don't talk to me about what's easy. For Christ's sake, all I'm asking you to do is go and *talk* to somebody!''

*Talk to somebody. Talk to somebody.* The words echoed in his mind, bouncing back and forth off the inside of his skull. It sounded so easy.

Just go talk to somebody.

But about what? About what he'd done to Sarah? About why he'd done it? He wasn't even sure what he'd done, and if he wasn't sure what he'd done, how could he begin to be sure why he'd done it? And it wasn't as if he hadn't tried. He'd spent months with Dr. Belter. The psychiatrist had spent hours with him, hours with Sarah, hours with the two of them together, watching them interact, trying to discover from some clue in the way they related to each other what had happened. He'd beaten her—Jack knew that now. But he couldn't remember starting to beat her; he couldn't remember administering the blows. All he could remember was being in the woods, then carrying Sarah out of the woods. And her face. For some reason he could remember her face, the tiny, dark, great-eyed face, peering desperately up at him, the frightened eyes not understanding what was happening, pleading with him to help her.

If he could remember, he could deal with it. But it was as if it had all happened to somebody else and he had been a witness to it. A witness who didn't want to see.

They had even tried hypnosis. But that too had failed. Dr. Belter had warned him that some people simply cannot be hypnotized, and he had proved to be one of them. Deep inside he harbored the distinct feeling that he could have been hypnotized, but simply didn't want to be; that whatever was inside him was too fearsome to bring out, that he was protecting himself from a weakness too ugly to face. And it had formed a vicious circle, the guilt feeding on the doubt, the doubt growing as the guilt increased. Finally, when he could no longer face those awful silent hours with the doctor, sipping coffee and wishing desperately that he could bring himself to talk, if not about the incident with Sarah then at least about the impotence that had resulted, he had given up. He had come to terms with himself, and they were not easy terms. He would live with the guilt, and he would live with the impotence, and he would live with the questions about what had really happened. But he would not have to know. And he had come to believe that to know what had happened would be the worst thing of all.

He stared silently across the table at Rose, wondering if there was any way to convey all of this to her, trying to think of what he could possibly say, when he was rescued from having to say anything at all. Mrs. Goodrich's voice was pouring forth from the kitchen.

"Miss Sarah, you stop that, do you hear me?"

There was a crash, the sound of pots and pans falling to the floor, followed by the sound of Sarah's voice rising into the wordless wail that for a year had been her only means of communicating her pain to the world.

"Dear God," Rose breathed, letting her head sink into her hands. "How much more?" Then she pulled herself together and started toward the kitchen, wondering what it would be this time. She didn't see Elizabeth enter the dining room from the other door.

Elizabeth paused as her mother left the room and waited a moment, listening to the chaos from the kitchen. As it subsided, she relaxed and moved to the table. Still in his chair, Jack stared vacantly at the door leading through the butler's pantry to the kitchen, his face pale. Elizabeth reached out a hand to touch him.

"It's all right, Daddy," she said softly. "It's over now."

At the touch, Jack started. His mind registered the fact that he hadn't been aware of Elizabeth's presence, and he felt the fear sweep over him again. He tried to cover it with a smile.

"Hello, Princess," he said, fighting to control the shakiness in his voice. "I didn't hear you come in."

"I wonder what she was doing," Elizabeth said, standing close to her father. "I hope she didn't hurt herself."

"I'm sure she didn't," Jack said, though he was far from sure. "Have a seat, and I'll pour you some juice."

Elizabeth grinned at him crookedly. "How about if I sit on your lap?" she said.

"My lap? Aren't you getting a little big for that?"

"Sometimes I like to feel small again," Elizabeth replied. "Do you ever feel like that?"

"Everyone feels like that," Jack said, opening his arms. "Climb on up and be small for a while."

The girl sat on his knee, and Jack put an affectionate arm around her waist. And then the door opened once more, and Rose stood staring stonily at him.

"I beg your pardon," she said, her voice icy and her eyes accusing him. "I didn't mean to interrupt anything."

"You're not—" Elizabeth started to say, but she wasn't allowed to finish.

"Take your chair, Elizabeth," her mother snapped. Obediently Elizabeth left her father's lap and sat down in her chair. She reached for the orange juice and poured herself a glass.

Jack started to rebuke his wife, then changed his mind. "Is everything all right out there?" he said instead.

"Mrs. Goodrich has it under control, and Sarah seems to have settled down, but the kitchen's a mess. Mrs. Goodrich thinks she was trying to get at the knife case for some reason."

"The knife case?" Jack repeated. Elizabeth began buttering a piece of danish.

"Well, of course, she's not sure," Rose continued. "I can't imagine what she'd want to do with a knife."

"No," Jack said briefly, "I can't either." Then he searched his mind for another subject, something that would take all their minds off what had just happened. Suddenly he brightened and turned to Elizabeth.

"Did you ever find Cecil?" he said.

Elizabeth shook her head. "I don't know what happened to him. He must've run off somewhere. He'll be back. Cats are like that, I guess. I'd rather have a dog, anyway. They pay more attention to you."

"I asked Mrs. Goodrich to look for him the other day," Rose said, her foot moving to the button on the floor that would summon the housekeeper. "But I forgot all about it till this minute." Rose, too, was glad for the distraction from the unpleasantness that had clouded an otherwise beautiful morning. Outside the sun was shining brightly. The door to the butler's pantry opened, and Mrs. Goodrich's stocky frame appeared.

"Yes?"

"I'm sorry to bother you, Mrs. Goodrich, I know it hasn't been the best morning. But I was just wondering, did you ever find Cecil the other day?"

"I got better things to do than search for an independent cat," the housekeeper said shortly. Then she relented. "No, I didn't. And I searched this place from top to bottom." She seemed to think a moment, then spoke again. "Which reminds me. Somebody around here not satisfied with my work?"

"Not satisfied?" Rose said blankly. "What do you mean?"

"Well," Mrs. Goodrich said, shifting her weight from one leg to the other, "someone's been up in the attic, cleaning. If you'd wanted the attic cleaned, you might have told me. I'm getting along, but I can still keep this house."

Rose glanced at her husband and her daughter; they both shrugged their innocence. "I'm sure I don't know who cleaned it," Rose said, trying her best to suggest that it probably hadn't been cleaned at all. "And you didn't see any traces of Cecil?"

"Cats don't leave traces," Mrs. Goodrich said bluntly. She turned, then stepped aside. "'Scuse me," she said, and edged around the small form of Sarah, who had been standing, hidden behind the housekeeper's bulky form, through the whole conversation about the cat. Her eyes were filled with tears, and she was shaking.

Elizabeth moved quickly to her sister and put her arms around her, stilling Sarah's sobs with her embrace.

"It's all right, Sarah," she said softly. "If Cecil doesn't show up, we can get another cat. Or maybe even a dog," she added wistfully. Sarah's trembling increased, and she seemed about to scream. Then she relaxed under Elizabeth's loving smile.

Rose watched Elizabeth dry Sarah's eyes and lead her to the table, and wished once more that she had the compassion for Sarah that her older daughter clearly had. She banished the twinge of guilt she felt pass through her and poured more coffee, first for herself, then for Jack. It was in the way of calling a truce, at least for a while.

# TWELVE

PORT ARBELLO BASKED IN THE UNUSUAL
warmth of the fall afternoon, and the sun warmed not only the air
but also the atmosphere within the house at the end of the Point. By
noon, a feeling of peace had overtaken the house, a peace all the
Congers felt. The strain of the morning dissipated, and the undeclared truce
between Jack and Rose seemed to be blossoming into an armistice. Within
themselves, they wondered how long it would last, but each of them was
determined to enjoy it while it was there.

"I love Indian summer," Rose commented over lunch. "Let's do something this afternoon."

"Can't," Jack said apologetically. "I already promised Ray Norton a
round of golf."

Rose felt a caustic phrase concerning neglect of family rise to her throat.
She fought it down before it had the chance to ruin their lunch.

"I've got some work to do anyway," she said, and there was nothing in
her voice to suggest disappointment, hostility, or anything else that might
destroy the good mood she could feel in the room. Jack, who had been
expecting some sort of dart, looked up in surprise.

"I could cancel it," he offered, and Rose knew it was a genuine offer.

"No, you go ahead," she said, the intention being sufficient for the fact.
They finished lunch in the comfortable silence that often occurs between
people who love each other, but which had been absent from their lives for
so long. They greeted it with appreciation, and did nothing to disturb it.

Jack left for his golf game, and the children disappeared upstairs. Rose
wandered to her office in the small room at the front of the house and
shuffled some papers around. She found she couldn't concentrate. She left
the office and rambled down the hall to the study at the rear. She entered
the study, and something caught her eye. It was so fast, she wasn't sure it
had happened—one of those instants when one is sure one saw something,
but has no idea what. She glanced around the room, but nothing was amiss.
She closed the door behind her and sat down. It was a pleasant room, and
the sun streamed through the window. It flashed off an ancient brass spittoon
that had been converted to a standing ashtray, and it occurred to Rose that
that must have been what caught her eye as she entered. Then she glanced up
at the old portrait above the mantel.

It had to be an ancestor, she knew. The resemblance to Elizabeth was
too remarkable for the girl in the picture not to be a Conger. But which
one?

They had found the picture up in the attic more than a year ago. But then the trouble with Sarah—as Rose liked to phrase it—had started, and it had not been until a month ago that she had remembered the portrait and brought it downstairs. It was odd, she reflected, not for the first time, how the painting had been tucked away in a corner. The Congers, who had apparently been much given to ancestor worship, had a large rack in the attic upon which those ancestors not currently on display in the lower portion of the house could be neatly stored. At the moment, the group in storage included nearly everybody; only Jack's mother still enjoyed the light of day over the fireplace in the living room. Even with all the ancestors in residence, there had still been plenty of room in the rack for the picture of the young girl. But she hadn't been there. Instead, she had been hidden away in a corner.

The other odd thing was that the girl was not identified. The frames of all the other portraits bore neat brass plates giving the name, date of birth, and date of death of their subjects. Except this one. This one had once borne such a plate, as evidenced by the two tiny nail holes in the bottom rail of the frame, but it had been removed.

Rose stared at the portrait and wondered what had banished the little girl from the family gallery. Her imagination ran wild, and she entertained herself for some time creating scenarios to account for the girl's fall from grace.

And then it hit her. It had not been the sunlight on the spittoon that had caught her eye. It had been something in the portrait. She studied it carefully, trying to force her mind to make the connection again, to tell her what it was that she had recognized. Then it came to her.

It was the bracelet. The bracelet on the girl's wrist. She had seen it before, very recently. But where? It was a gold bracelet, and it seemed to be set with some sort of stone. It looked like opal, but in the old oil she couldn't be sure. It could have been something else.

She concentrated on remembering where she had seen the bracelet, why it was suddenly familiar. She drew a blank, and the longer she stared at the picture, the surer she became that it was not a real memory, but a simple déjà vu. The illusion of memory. She reached up to adjust the picture, which seemed to be tilted just slightly off center, and decided that she wasn't going to spend any more time worrying about a bracelet in a picture. She really did have work to do.

She returned to her study, determined to avoid looking out the window until she was well into the rhythm of her work. The day was just too pretty, and she knew that if she looked out too soon she would find an excuse to close her files and go out into the sun. But the sun could wait. She burrowed into the stack of papers on the desk.

She didn't really hear the door open an hour later, but was aware that she was no longer alone. She looked around and discovered that Sarah was with her, standing just inside the door, her huge brown eyes fixed on her mother. Rose put down her pen.

"Sarah," she said, and held out her arms. Slowly, almost warily, Sarah approached her. The little girl stopped when she was just beyond Rose's reach.

"She wants you to play with her," Elizabeth said from the door. Rose glanced up.

"I didn't see you," she said. "Come in."

"Not now," Elizabeth said. "I'm going outside for a while. Sarah wants you to play with her."

"What does she want me to play?"

"Whatever," Elizabeth said. "I'll see you later." She disappeared, and a moment later Rose heard the front door open and close. She turned her attention back to Sarah.

"What would you like to play?" she asked the silent child.

Sarah merely stood there; then, after a few seconds, she backed a few paces away from Rose and sat heavily on the floor. Rose frowned slightly, then left her chair and joined her daughter on the floor.

"Pease porridge hot," Rose tried, clapping her hands first on her thighs, then together, then silently outward. There was no response from Sarah, who simply sat on the floor, her face in repose, staring steadily at her mother. Rose decided to try it again, this time guiding her daughter's hands through the routine.

"Pease porridge cold," she said. "Now let's try it together."

She went through the routine again, and on the first "Pease" Sarah's hands clapped against her thighs. But as Rose resumed the chant, the child's hands continued to slap her thighs, never progressing to the other variations. Rose found herself playing with empty air. Determinedly, she continued the game. Sarah's hands clapped a steady rhythm against her thighs. Finally, when Rose stopped the game, Sarah's hands continued to move, clapping hollowly into the silence.

Rose watched the mindless clapping for a minute or two, then could stand it no more. She picked the child up and sat in a large chair, Sarah in her lap. The girl did not resist, but Rose had the distinct feeling that if she did not continue to support her daughter, the child would slip to the floor. She picked up a magazine from a table next to the chair, and began to leaf through it. Every now and then Sarah's hand would reach out to stop the pages from turning. The third time it happened, Rose realized that Sarah was stopping the pages wherever there was a picture of a cat.

"I know, darling," she whispered. "If Cecil doesn't come back in another day or two, we'll get you another cat."

And suddenly Sarah was gone. Before Rose could do anything, the girl had wriggled from her lap and dashed out of the room. Rose could hear her retreating footsteps pounding up the stairs, and started to follow. Then she stopped, realizing that there was little she could do, since she had no way of finding out from Sarah what had gone wrong. She stood in her office door for a minute, listening carefully, but heard no sounds from above. It wasn't until she was sure of the silence that she allowed herself to realize that she had not been expecting silence. She had been expecting pandemonium, an encore of this morning's tantrum. When it failed to materialize, she felt relief. She left the office door open and returned to her desk.

She had no idea how much later it was when she once more got the feeling that she was not alone. She glanced over her shoulder, and there, standing once more just inside the door, was Sarah. She seemed to start slightly when Rose glanced at her, and Rose turned quickly back to her work. But she was careful to listen for her daughter's slightest movement.

Sarah came into the room and began moving around, touching objects, picking things up to examine them, then putting them back where she had found them. Rose heard the small feet shuffling around the room, heard the tiny clicks as Sarah replaced the things she picked up. Then there was a silence, but Rose restrained herself from looking around to see what the girl was up to. Then she felt something touch her leg, and realized that Sarah had crept under the desk. Rose smiled to herself as she remembered how much fun she had had as a child pretending a desk was a cave. If her daughter was anything like she had been, she would be happy there the rest of the afternoon. Rose turned all her attention back to her work.

As the afternoon wore on, Rose was occasionally aware of movement under the desk, but it wasn't until she felt something being fastened around her ankle that she finally put her work aside. She sat very still, wondering what it was that Sarah was attaching to her. She waited, expecting something to touch her other leg, and she wasn't disappointed.

The girl was tying her feet together. Rose began planning the show she would put on for her daughter when Sarah had finished. She had tried the same trick as a child, tying her father's shoestrings together as he sat at his desk, and had been gratified when he stood up, stumbled violently, then crashed around the room for almost a full minute before collapsing to the floor in a hopeless tangle. At the time it had never occurred to her that her father had not actually been out of control of the situation, and, indeed, it wasn't until this very minute that she realized that he had put on the same carnival for her that she was about to stage for Sarah. Then she felt Sarah finish.

"Well," she said loudly. "That's that. I guess I'll stretch my legs." She could picture the child grinning and quivering with suppressed laughter beneath her.

Rose pushed away from the desk and moved her feet carefully to test the length of the string she was sure was hobbling her ankles. It seemed to be very long indeed, and she wondered how she was going to be able to fake the thing convincingly.

It wasn't until she was fully away from the desk that she realized that there was no string at all, that it was something entirely different that was around her ankles.

She reached down and felt something hard. When she looked, she felt her heart skip a beat, and had that feeling in her stomach that she often got when an elevator dropped away beneath her feet. It was the bracelet.

She pulled it from her ankle, forgetting about Sarah for the time being, and examined it carefully. Yes, it was the bracelet from the picture: gold set with a small opal. Tiny flecks of dirt clung to it, as if it had been lying outdoors for a long time. She stood up, intending to take it into the rear study for a careful comparison, and felt something else, something flopping against her other ankle.

She looked down once more, and didn't immediately recognize the other object. It was a pale, whitish color, but badly stained, and seemed to have a buckle of some kind on it. Then she realized what it was.

A collar.

A cat's plastic flea collar.

"Where in the world—" she muttered as she unfastened the collar from her ankle. She straightened up and examined the collar. It was dirty too, but it was not the same kind of dirt that was on the bracelet. The collar bore specks of a reddish-brown substance. It took a while for Rose to realize that the substance looked like dried blood. When she did realize what it was, she stepped to the office door.

"Mrs. Goodrich," she called. "Come here, please. Quickly."

When she turned back to the study she realized that Sarah was still under the desk, tightly crouched, her small face peering out of the darkness like a rabbit trapped in a hole. Rose stared back at the child, not having any idea what to say. When Mrs. Goodrich appeared at the door, Rose hadn't moved.

"I sure hope my pies don't get ruined," the old woman said, wiping her hands on her apron. Then, when Rose didn't turn around to face her, she stopped wiping her hands and spoke again.

"Is something wrong, Miz Rose?" she asked.

"I—I don't know," Rose said unsteadily. "Look at this."

She held out the flea collar, and Mrs. Goodrich reached to take it from her.

"Looks like a flea collar," the housekeeper said. "Same kind we put on Cecil." Her eyes caught sight of the stain. "Here, what's this?"

"I'm not sure," Rose said, hoping Mrs. Goodrich would offer an alternative.

"Why, it's blood," the woman said. "Well, if that don't beat all. Where'd this come from?"

"Sarah," Rose said vaguely. "Sarah put it on my ankle."

"Well, that's a peculiar thing to do," the old woman said. "Where do you suppose she got it from?"

"I'm not sure," Rose said. "I don't have any idea at all, really."

"Well, if she got it off that cat, I wish she'd tell us where the cat is." She sniffed the air. "I smell my pies." She bustled away, and Rose listened to her footsteps fade down the hall.

"Sarah?" Rose said. The child crept a little way out from under the desk. "Sarah, darling, it's all right," Rose said, not knowing if it was all right or not. "Come out from under there."

She reached down and gently pulled her daughter the rest of the way out, then picked her up and carried her upstairs. She set Sarah on the bed and covered her with a comforter. "Take a little nap," she said, and bent down to kiss her gently on the forehead. She was behaving with a calm that she did not feel.

She heard Jack's car coming up the drive as she went back down the stairs, and waited for him at the front door.

"Hi," he said, but the smile faded from his face when he saw how pale she was. "What's wrong?" he asked. "Has something happened?"

"I don't know," Rose said quietly. "Let's go into the study. I'll be with you in a minute."

She stepped into her office and picked up the bracelet and the collar. Then she followed Jack down the hall.

"Why don't you pour us both a drink," she said, closing the door behind her. Jack looked at her curiously.

"You sound upset," he said. "What's been going on around here?"

She told him what had happened and showed him the two objects. He examined the collar briefly, then turned his attention to the bracelet.

"This looks familiar," he said slowly. "I'd swear I've seen it before, but I can't remember where."

"The picture," Rose said.

"Picture?" Then he looked to where she was pointing, and his eyes found the bracelet on the little girl's wrist. "Good Lord," he breathed. "Are you sure it's the same one?"

"I haven't compared them yet, but yes, I'm sure," Rose said. "And the strangest thing is that earlier, before Sarah put it on my ankle, I was looking at the bracelet in the picture. I was almost sure I'd seen it somewhere before, other than in the picture."

"Has Sarah been wearing it?" Jack asked.

"I don't know. If she has, I hadn't noticed it consciously. But I suppose she must have been."

Jack moved to the picture and held the bracelet up next to its representation in the portrait. It was the same bracelet.

"It's the collar that worries me more," Rose said, taking a long swallow from her drink.

"The collar?"

"Well, where do you suppose she got that? And how do you suppose the blood got on it?"

"You mean Cecil?" There was clear disbelief in his voice.

"What else could it be?"

"Oh, now, come on, Rose. Sarah loves that cat."

"I know," Rose said miserably. "But put it all together. The cat's gone, Sarah was apparently trying to get at the knives just this morning, then she got upset at pictures of cats this afternoon. And now that." She pointed to the bloody collar.

"You think she's killed Cecil."

The words hit Rose, and she recoiled almost visibly. She realized that that was exactly what she thought; she had merely refused to put words to it. She nodded dumbly.

"I don't believe it," Jack said. "I just don't believe it."

"Then where did she get that collar? And the bracelet, too, for that matter."

"I don't know," Jack said. "But I don't believe she killed Cecil. She wouldn't do a thing like that."

"How do we know she wouldn't, Jack? How do we know what she would do or wouldn't do?" She was on the verge of tears, and Jack reached out to comfort her, but she turned away.

"What do you think we ought to do?" Jack said.

"Call the school, I suppose," Rose said. "Talk to Dr. Belter. He wanted to know if anything unusual happened. And God knows this is unusual."

"What are we going to tell him?" Jack said uneasily. "That Sarah found a couple of things and we think she killed the cat?"

"I don't know," Rose replied. "I'll just tell him exactly what happened and see what he thinks about it."

"When are you going to call him?" A note of belligerence had crept into his voice.

"Right now," Rose replied, moving to the phone. She dialed the telephone, and was connected to the doctor a couple of minutes later. He listened to her story, and when she finished he asked some questions.

"How is she now?" he wanted to know.

"Sarah? I guess she's all right. She doesn't seem to be upset, if that's what you mean. She's upstairs, sleeping."

Dr. Belter considered, then spoke again.

"Why don't you both come to the school on Monday? You and your husband? Then we can talk about it. Can it wait until then?"

"Well, I suppose so," Rose said, but she wasn't sure it could. Dr. Belter heard the uneasiness in her voice.

"I'll tell you what. If anything else happens, you call me, and I'll be right out there. Otherwise, I'll see you on Monday."

"All right," Rose agreed. "I suppose that'll be fine. Thank you, Doctor." She hung up the phone, and was about to tell Jack what had been arranged when she saw his eyes move from her own to a spot behind her and the blood drain from his face. She whirled around, not knowing what to expect.

It was Elizabeth, and she was a mess. The dress that had been so clean when she left the house was now filthy, covered with mud, and the muck was streaked over her face as well.

"My God," Rose said. "What happened?"

"I'm sorry," Elizabeth said, and it was the voice of a small girl. "I was out by the quarry. I slipped in the mud."

"What were you doing out there?" Jack demanded. "You could have killed yourself."

Elizabeth seemed on the verge of tears. "I said I was sorry," she repeated. "I'm all right. It's—it's only mud."

"That dress," Rose snapped. "You've ruined that dress. Get it off immediately and give it to Mrs. Goodrich. Maybe she can save it."

Elizabeth burst into tears and fled from the room. Rose watched her go,

and doubted that Mrs. Goodrich would be able to save the dress. It looked
to be as ruined as the afternoon. Rose, too, felt like crying.

"Oh, shit," she said miserably.

"It's only a dress," Jack said soothingly.

"No it's not," Rose said. "It's everything." She felt the hopelessness
sweep over her.

## THIRTEEN

"AND THAT'S WHERE WE ARE AS OF
now," Dr. Charles Belter concluded, closing the file in front of
him. He glanced around the room, noting that Marie Montgomery looked unhappy and Josephine Wells looked annoyed. The
three of them were waiting for Jack and Rose Conger, and Josephine Wells
had suggested that it would be a good idea to review the entire file before
their arrival. The mind of a bureaucrat, Dr. Belter had thought, but he had
complied. Now he looked at Josephine Wells. "Any questions?"

"It strikes me," Josie Wells said, and Dr. Belter noted to himself that
things invariably "struck" Josie Wells, "that there must be a lot more going
on here than we know about."

Dr. Belter tried to keep his face straight, and did his best to nod gravely.
"Go on," he said, knowing that she would anyway.

"It strikes me," Miss Wells said again, and this time Charles Belter had
to fight down an impulse to do exactly that, "that we should be looking
beyond Sarah as an individual, and trying, rather, to fathom the greater
socio-psychological factors involved within the structure of the prime unit."

"If you mean we should talk to her family," Dr. Belter remarked drily,
"that's exactly what we're about to do. If they ever get here." He glanced
at his watch and noted that it was still five minutes until the time the
Congers were due. He braced himself to tolerate further pontificating from
the social worker.

"What I'm trying to say," Miss Wells said, tapping her front teeth with
the end of the Pentel she always carried, apparently for no other purpose,
since she rarely took notes, "is that what we seem to have here is a clear
case of regression." Miss Wells, who felt that her Master of Social Welfare
degree qualified her as a psychologist, a sociologist, and a sage, leaned back
and looked pleased with herself.

"And?" Dr. Belter prompted.

"And therefore it strikes me that we should be trying to find out toward
what she is regressing."

Dr. Belter shot a glance to Mrs. Montgomery, but the teacher's face was a bland mask of innocence. Marie Montgomery had discovered long ago that with Josie Wells it was best to sit quietly and listen. Any response was all too likely to carry Miss Wells further into the mazes of gobbledygook that she mistook for erudition. Marie caught Dr. Belter's glance, and wondered how he was planning to deal with the social worker's impossible idea.

"I think you're absolutely right," Dr. Belter said gravely. "I suggest that you have copies made of the entire file immediately, and begin comparing common factors between the prenatal experience of Sarah and the postpartum depression futeriundus of her mother." The doctor was pleased to see Josie Wells's Pentel scribble a word. He wondered how many books she would search before she finally decided there was no such word as "futeriundus." Then it struck him that it was more likely she would simply attach a meaning to the word, and proceed to carry out his instructions. He sighed to himself and cursed the necessity of having a social worker in his midst. When he saw the Congers driving up to the building, his sigh became audible. He braced himself and put on a broad smile as they were ushered into his office, so that neither of them was aware that he was, while greeting them, examining them minutely.

He noted the obvious strain in Rose's face, the strain that had been growing there for a year. It didn't seem any worse than the last time he had seen her, but there were other signs now, signs that her composure was wearing thin. Her hair, usually perfectly set, was beginning to show the first signs of disarray. Not that it was messy—not by any means; it simply wasn't as perfect as usual. And there was a tiny spot on the jacket of her pants suit, a spot that most people would never notice but nevertheless a spot that Dr. Belter knew Rose Conger would not normally tolerate.

Jack, on the other hand, seemed totally unchanged. It should be showing, Dr. Belter thought. Unless he's some sort of monster. But Charles Belter did not believe people were monsters, so he looked more closely. He found what he was looking for in Jack's fingernails: He was beginning to chew on them. Not enough so they looked chewed, but just slightly uneven, as if he would chew one, then smooth it out with a file, leaving it shorter than the others.

"Sit down," Dr. Belter said warmly. "We've just been discussing Sarah. Since you didn't call again, I gather yesterday was quiet?"

"Well," Rose said, "I'm not sure what quiet is any more. If you mean nothing happened, nothing out of the ordinary, I suppose you could say nothing happened. But I'm afraid I have to say that I think she's getting worse."

"Rose!" Jack said. "I don't think that's fair."

"No," Rose said tiredly. "I know you don't think it's fair. And it may not be. I will grant you that I'm not a psychologist, and I will grant you that I have no training in the sort of disorders Sarah has. But I'm a mother, and I know how I feel. And I feel worn out, and I feel sick, and I feel my daughter isn't getting any better—"

"That's a lot different from getting worse," Jack interjected.

"All right, maybe I'm wrong. You tell us," she appealed to the doctor.

Then she recounted the events of Saturday, leaving out none of the details. Dr. Belter listened carefully, as did the teacher and the social worker. When Rose was finished, he leaned back in his chair, closed his eyes, and seemed to be considering something. No one in the room spoke, and it passed through Jack's mind that the doctor looked just like Santa Claus. Had he known of the thought, Dr. Belter would have been pleased.

Eventually he opened his eyes again, and turned to Marie Montgomery. "Any ideas?"

She shook her head. "Not at the moment. Frankly, it doesn't sound to me like Sarah's getting worse."

Jack's eyes lit up. "No?" he said eagerly.

"Well," Marie Montgomery said carefully, "it seems to me that the fact that she was able to concentrate on something as long as she did in order to get that collar onto your ankle indicates that she may be getting a little better. Granted, it was a macabre thing for her to do—at least, it seems so to us, but it may not have been macabre to her at all. It may have been something else entirely." She reviewed the incident with the magazine and Sarah's reaction to the pictures of cats. "She may have been trying to tell you something."

"Such as?" Rose asked.

The teacher shrugged. "That's the hard part. You have to remember that Sarah's mind isn't working the same way as yours and mine. There's really no way for us to know what she was trying to communicate. But whatever it was, it must have been important. She doesn't normally spend that much time doing anything, let alone anything that takes the dexterity of fastening one of those plastic collars. They're tricky."

Dr. Belter nodded his head in agreement, and seemed to come to a decision in his own mind. He spoke to his colleagues. "I think I'd better talk to the Congers alone, if you don't mind."

Josephine Wells started to protest, but Mrs. Montgomery was already on her feet. "Of course," she said, over the social worker's voice. "If you need us, page us." Before Josie could say anything, Marie Montgomery was pulling her out of the office. Dr. Belter waited until the door was closed before he spoke.

"You two are having a rough time of it, aren't you?" he said at last. Rose and Jack stared at him, each waiting for the other to speak. The silence lengthened, until Rose broke it.

"Yes," she said, barely audibly. "We are. And it isn't all Sarah."

Dr. Belter's head bobbed. "Not directly, anyway. Do you want to tell me what's going on at your house?"

Rose waited for Jack to speak, but when he didn't she began talking about their problems. As she talked she became aware of a strange detachment, as though she were talking about two other people, not herself and her husband. She recounted the fights and the cruelties they had inflicted on each other, and was surprised to discover that she was being fair; she was presenting Jack's side of things as well as her own. When she was finished, Dr. Belter turned to Jack.

"You want to add anything?"

"No," Jack said. He smiled at his wife. "I have to hand it to you—I couldn't have been that fair."

"Mrs. Conger," Dr. Belter said, "has it occurred to you that maybe you should be in therapy too?"

"What do you mean?" Rose said defensively.

Dr. Belter smiled easily. "Well, let's face it. Generally speaking, I consider emotional problems to be a communicable disease. If one person in a family is having problems, others usually are too, if for no other reason than that it is difficult to live with someone who is mentally ill. It is quite easy for someone with no particularly severe problems to develop some severe problems simply because of the extra pressure involved in living with a person as disturbed as Sarah."

"And you think I'm developing some severe problems?"

"Are you?" Dr. Belter tossed the question back to her.

Her initial impulse was to deny it, but Rose realized that she couldn't, not if she was honest. She remembered the moments of panic she was having, the tight feelings in her stomach, the sudden flashes of anger she felt, the way she had begun to overreact. An image came to her mind of Elizabeth fleeing from the study in tears, simply because Rose had yelled at her about getting her clothes dirty.

"You're suggesting that I could use some therapy too?" she asked noncommittally.

"I'm suggesting that both of you could use some therapy. You don't seem to be handling your problems very well, either of you, which is understandable, considering the circumstances. All I'm suggesting is that you both could use some help."

"Maybe we should throw in Elizabeth, too, and qualify for a family discount," Jack said. When the chuckle died away, Dr. Belter's face took on a serious cast.

"What about Elizabeth?" he said.

"She's incredible," Rose said. "Other than when I yelled at her on Saturday for getting her dress dirty, she's been an angel. She's patient with Sarah, takes care of herself. Sometimes I wonder what I'd do without her."

"She must be an amazing child," Dr. Belter mused. "Generally, a child her age, with a sibling like Sarah, would show at least intermittent hostility toward the sick brother or sister. It's because of the extra attention the sick one gets, of course, and it's perfectly natural."

"Well," Rose said, "we've had none of that sort of thing."

Jack grinned. "I guess Elizabeth is the only one of us who's immune to the family curse." He laughed, but his laughter faded when he noticed that the doctor had not joined him.

"Ah, yes," Dr. Belter said, leaning back once more and closing his eyes. "The Conger family curse."

"You've heard about it?" Jack said.

"Around Port Arbello, who hasn't? As a matter of fact, I probably know more about your family curse than you do."

"Oh?" Jack said guardedly. "How so?"

Dr. Belter smiled at him. "I make it a practice to find out everything I can about all my patients, and their families. So when I first met you people, I started snooping."

"And what did you find?" Rose asked.

"A certain Reverend Caspar Winecliff," Dr. Belter said, savoring the name.

"You mean the old Methodist minister?" Jack said, his brows arching. "We hardly know the man."

"Ah, but he knows you," the doctor intoned, enjoying the baffled looks on the Congers' faces. Then he dropped the air of mystery.

"Actually, Caspar Winecliff simply has a passion for local legend and folklore, particularly with reference to New England curses and that sort of thing. My personal opinion is that he enjoys the subject because he thinks it's wicked and flies in the face of his good Methodist background. If you ask me, he believes every word of every legend he's ever heard, though of course he denies it. And the Conger legend happens to be his favorite."

"You're kidding," Jack said. "I knew the legend wasn't any great secret, but I didn't know anybody was that interested in it."

"I didn't either, until I was down at the library one day asking some questions. I was hoping to find some old papers or something that would have the legend written up. They didn't, but the librarian put me onto Caspar Winecliff. How much do you know about your legend?"

Jack recounted as much of it as he knew, and when he was finished the doctor nodded his head.

"That's it, all right, except for the story about the little girl."

Jack and Rose glanced at each other, and Dr. Belter thought he saw alarm in their eyes.

"What little girl?" Jack said apprehensively. For some reason, an image of the portrait in the study came to his mind.

"It has to do with the relative who went off the cliff," the doctor began, looking inquiringly at Jack.

"I know about him," Jack said. "I'm not sure what his name was."

"It was John Conger, actually," Dr. Belter said seriously. "The same as yours."

Jack felt a chill in his spine. "What about him?"

"Well," Dr. Belter said, "the story is that the reason he jumped off the cliff was that he had just molested and killed a little girl. His daughter."

The blood drained from Jack's face, and he stared coldly at the doctor. "Just what are you trying to say?"

The doctor smiled reassuringly. "I'm not trying to say anything. I'm just telling you the story. And, of course, it could be entirely apocryphal. Caspar Winecliff tells me they never found a body, and, for that matter, there don't seem to be any records of John Conger's ever having had a daughter."

Rose saw the portrait in her mind's eye, with the nameplate removed from the bottom of the frame.

"Did Reverend Winecliff have any idea of how old the girl was, or what she looked like?" She was almost afraid to hear the answer.

Dr. Belter shook his head. "Nothing about what she looked like, but she was supposed to have been about ten or eleven years old."

"About the same age as Sarah?" Jack said, a distinct edge in his voice.

"Yes," Dr. Belter said, meeting his troubled gaze, "about the same age as Sarah."

"Dr. Belter," Rose said, "just what are you getting at? It sounds as though you believe in the whole silly legend."

Dr. Belter thought carefully before he answered, and when he spoke he chose his words precisely.

"Whether or not I believe in the legend isn't what's at issue here. What's at issue is whether or not your husband believes in it. Do you, Mr. Conger?"

Jack started to speak, but the doctor stopped him.

"Don't answer quickly, please. Think about it. And try to think about it on two levels. I'm sure your conscious mind doesn't believe that there could be any kind of curse on your family. In this day and age we tend to think of such things as silly. But there is also your subconscious mind. Often we find that the things our conscious minds refuse to take seriously our subconscious minds deal with in a very serious manner. Essentially, that is what dreams are all about, and, sometimes, neuroses and psychoses. One might say that mental illness results when our conscious minds and our unconscious minds try to do each other's jobs. So think about it before you answer my question."

Jack did, and found that he was amazed by the answer he came up with. He smiled sheepishly at the doctor.

"Okay," he said. "I guess I have to admit that I do believe in the legend, including the curse. I suppose with us Congers it's like religion. We were brought up with it, and while we know it's nonsense, it's still lurking there, just below the surface."

Dr. Belter nodded. "But you say you never heard of the little girl before?"

Jack shook his head. "No. I'm sure. I'd have remembered. Why?"

"Isn't it obvious? If the story of the little girl is true, there are some pretty strong parallels between what happened to her and her father, and what happened to you and Sarah. Except that with you and Sarah no molestation took place, and nobody died. But otherwise, it's the same thing."

"History repeating itself?" It was Rose's voice, and the two men turned to her. "I don't believe it."

"That's not exactly what I meant," Dr. Belter said. "Although the effect would be the same. Do either of you know anything about voodoo?"

"That it's a lot of hoodoo," Jack said, too quickly.

"Not quite," Dr. Belter replied. "It's based on the power of suggestion. Essentially, what it boils down to is this: If someone believes strongly enough that something will happen, it will, in all likelihood, happen. For instance, voodoo tradition has it that you can cause pain in a person by sticking pins in an effigy of that person. The catch is that the person has to *know* that pins are being stuck in the doll. Once he knows the pins are being placed, his own mind will create the pain. Do you see?"

Jack mulled it over. "In other words, you think I might be a victim of the legend, simply because I believe in it?"

"That's it," Dr. Belter said. "Simplified, but that's essentially it."

Rose smiled wryly. "Except that we didn't know anything about the relevant part of the legend. The little girl. You said yourself that there's no evidence she exists."

"But she does, Rose," Jack said quietly. "Don't you want to tell Dr. Belter what she looked like?"

Dr. Belter turned questioningly to Jack.

"We found a picture in the attic," Jack explained, and went on to tell the doctor about the portrait.

"But how can you be sure it's the same little girl? How can you even be sure it's a Conger child?"

"Because," Jack said, his voice a whisper now, "the girl in the picture looks exactly like Elizabeth."

"I see," Dr. Belter said after a long silence. "Mr. Conger, are you sure you never saw that picture before, or heard anything about it?"

"Not until a year ago," Jack said definitely. "Not that I can remember."

"Not that you can remember," the doctor repeated thoughtfully. "But we don't always remember everything we want to remember, do we? I think maybe it would be a good idea to try to find out exactly what you do remember."

Jack appeared to be about to object, but at the look on Rose's face, a look that told him he'd better agree, he sagged in defeat.

"Very well," he said. "When shall we begin?"

Dr. Belter examined his calendar. "How about two weeks from tomorrow, at one P.M.? Both of you."

Before Jack could protest Rose said, "We'll be there."

The session with Dr. Belter ended.

Neither of the Congers felt better about anything.

They were more frightened than ever.

## FOURTEEN

FIFTEEN MILES FROM WHITE OAKS SCHOOL, while Jack and Rose Conger sat chatting with Dr. Charles Belter, the final bell rang through the halls of Port Arbello Memorial School, and the children poured out of the classrooms. Elizabeth Conger picked Kathy Burton's face out of the crowd and hurried toward her.

An eager smile lit Kathy's face. "Is today the day?" she asked.

"What day?" Elizabeth's face was blank.

"Is this the day you're going to take me to the secret place?"

Elizabeth looked at her oddly, and Kathy's eyes widened as she felt a thrill of excitement run through her. Then she sagged with disappointment.

"I can't," Kathy said. "I'm supposed to go right out to the Nortons' to baby-sit."

"That's all right," Elizabeth said, her eyes suddenly seeming to bore into Kathy's. "The secret place is only a little farther out than their house, and it won't take very long."

"I don't know," Kathy said doubtfully, "I told Mrs. Norton I'd be there right after school."

The two girls left the school building and began walking toward the Conger's Point Road. As they left the town behind, Elizabeth began talking quietly about the secret place and the wonderful times she had there. As she talked, Kathy Burton began to wish she hadn't promised Mrs. Norton her baby-sitting services for the afternoon.

"Why don't we go tomorrow?" she asked.

Elizabeth shook her head. "No. It has to be today."

"Well, I don't see why it can't wait," Kathy sulked.

"It just can't, that's all," Elizabeth stated. "But if you don't want to go . . ." She let her voice trail off.

"But I do want to go," Kathy insisted. "It's just that I promised Mrs. Norton." She waited for a response from her friend, but when none came she looked at her watch.

"Maybe if we hurry," she said. "I could be a little late."

Elizabeth smiled at her and quickened her pace. "It'll be all right," she said. "You'll see. You'll love the secret place."

As they passed the Nortons' driveway, Kathy felt a twinge of guilt and wondered if Mrs. Norton was watching for her. When she didn't see anybody, or hear anyone calling her, she relaxed. When they were out of sight of the Nortons' house, she spoke.

"How much farther is it?"

"Not far. Just past the old Barnes place. Have you seen the people who bought it?"

"He's cute," Kathy said. "What's his name?"

"Jeff Stevens. He's fourteen. His mother's an artist."

"Does he know about the secret place?" Kathy asked.

Elizabeth shook her head. "I don't think I'll tell him," she said. "We'll keep it just for us."

They passed the old Barnes house, and looked curiously at it. They'd both heard that it was being remodeled, but from the outside it looked the same as ever.

"It sure is ugly," Kathy said.

"The Barneses were crazy," Elizabeth commented. "It's even weirder on the inside."

"You've been in it?" Kathy asked.

"Not for a long time," They were coming to the woods now, and Elizabeth took Kathy by the arm. "We go through here," she said. Kathy looked at the woods nervously.

"I don't know," she said. "I'm not supposed to go in there. They think that's where something happened to Anne Forager."

"Nothing happened to Anne Forager," Elizabeth scoffed. "You know what a liar she is."

Kathy mulled it over. It was true, Anne Forager *was* a little liar, and she did want to see the secret place, but still . . . She made up her mind.

"All right," she said. "But you lead. I don't know the way out here."

They left the road and plunged into the woods. Their route took them through the center of the woods, and every now and then they caught a glimpse of the sea through the trees on one side or the field on the other. There was no trail, but Elizabeth seemed to have no trouble making her way through the underbrush. Kathy stumbled now and then, and had to call to Elizabeth to wait. She was determined not to fall behind. Then Elizabeth made a left turn, and in a couple of minutes they stood on the embankment, high above the surf.

"Isn't it beautiful?" Elizabeth whispered.

"Is this the place?" Kathy asked, looking around. Somehow it was not what she had expected.

"No," Elizabeth answered. "It's over that way." She led Kathy along the embankment, and at a certain spot, a spot that looked to Kathy to be no different from any other spot, Elizabeth started down the face of the embankment. Behind her, Kathy stopped.

"It looks awfully dangerous," she said. Elizabeth turned and looked up at her, and Kathy thought she saw something in Elizabeth's eyes, something that made her uneasy. "I'm not sure I ought to," she said nervously. "I really should be at the Nortons' by now."

"Are you chicken?" Elizabeth said scornfully. "Look, it's easy." She leaped from one rock to another, and Kathy had to admit to herself that it did look easy. Besides, she wasn't chicken, and she wasn't going to let Elizabeth think she was. She began picking her way down the embankment, trying to follow the path Elizabeth had taken. It was not so easy.

Kathy told herself that she was having a harder time of it just because she hadn't done it before. Next time, she assured herself, she'd know the way and be able to go as fast as Elizabeth. She glanced up and saw Elizabeth disappearing behind an immense boulder. That must be it, she said to herself.

When she got to the boulder Elizabeth was waiting for her. Kathy crouched down in the deep shadow that cast the crevice between the boulder and the face of the embankment in almost total darkness.

"Is this it?" she whispered, and wondered why she was suddenly whispering.

"Almost," Elizabeth whispered back. "Look." She pointed to a spot deep within the blackness, and Kathy suddenly realized that it was not a darker shadow, but a small hole in the embankment.

"We aren't going in there, are we?" she whispered.

"Sure," Elizabeth whispered back. "Are you scared?"

"No," Kathy lied, and wondered how much face she would lose if she turned back now. "It's awfully dark, though, isn't it?"

"I have a light," Elizabeth said. She reached into the hole and pulled out the flashlight from its niche behind a rock just inside the mouth of the cave. She clicked it on and shined it into the opening.

"It's a tunnel," Kathy whispered. "Where does it go?"

"To the secret place," Elizabeth said. "Come on." She crept into the tunnel, and Kathy saw that there was enough room for Elizabeth to crawl along without hitting the roof of the cavern. Swallowing her fear, she followed Elizabeth.

In half a minute they were in the cavern surrounding the shaft. Elizabeth waited for Kathy to emerge from the tunnel, and heard Kathy say, "This is neat."

"We're not there yet," Elizabeth said. "The secret place is down there." She shined the light into the shaft, and heard Kathy suck in her breath.

"Where does it go?" she breathed.

"Down to the secret place. I have a ladder, see?" Elizabeth directed the beam of the flashlight to the rope ladder, which still hung in the shaft, securely anchored to the rocks on the cavern floor.

"I've never climbed one of those before," Kathy said, wondering if her lack of experience would get her off the hook.

"It's easy," Elizabeth said. "Look. I'll go first, and when I get to the bottom I'll hold the light for you. It isn't very far, and you won't fall. Besides, even if you do, you won't fall far enough to hurt yourself. I've done it lots of times, and there wasn't anybody to hold the light for me."

"How did you find this place?" Kathy asked, wanting to delay the moment when she knew she would have to conquer her fear.

"I don't know. I guess I've known about it for a long time. My friend told me."

"Your friend?"

"Never mind," Elizabeth said mysteriously. "Come on." Holding the light, she began climbing down the rope ladder, and in a few seconds she was on the floor of the pit. She shone the light up and saw Kathy's frightened face peering down at her.

"I can't see you," Kathy hissed.

"That's because I'm behind the light," Elizabeth hissed back. "Come down."

Kathy pondered the situation. She was afraid of the shaft, and of going down the ladder, but she didn't want Elizabeth to know how frightened she was. She glanced back toward the entrance to the tunnel, and the blackness there made up her mind for her. She wasn't about to try to make her way through the tunnel in the total darkness behind her. She eased herself over the lip of the shaft, and her feet found the ladder. The descent was much easier than she had thought it would be.

"I have some candles," Elizabeth whispered, keeping the flashlight trained on Kathy's face. In the glare, Kathy barely saw the flare of the match as Elizabeth struck it. Elizabeth put the match to two candles, then snapped the flashlight off. For a moment Kathy couldn't see anything in the gloom except the twin points of light, and Elizabeth's face looming in the glow.

"This is spooky," she said uncertainly. "I'm not sure we should be down here."

Her eyes began to adjust to the gloom, and she looked around the cavern. There didn't seem to be much to it—just a large, uneven room with some boulders strewn around. In the middle, some of the boulders had been arranged in a circle, like a table and chairs. Then Kathy saw something behind Elizabeth.

"What's that?" she asked. Elizabeth stepped aside, and Kathy's eyes slowly took in the skeleton that was neatly laid out along the wall.

Her scream was cut off by a sharp slap.

"You have to be quiet down here," Elizabeth said, in a whisper that seemed to Kathy to echo through the cavern more loudly than her scream. She wanted to scream again, but the sting of the slap kept her silent.

"We're going to have a party," Elizabeth whispered. "Just you and me and my baby."

"Baby?" Kathy repeated hollowly. "What baby?" She wasn't sure what Elizabeth was talking about, and her mind, clogged with confusion, couldn't seem to get a hold on anything. Then she knew that Elizabeth must be referring to a doll.

"Sit down," Elizabeth ordered her. "I'll bring the baby."

Slowly, Kathy sank onto one of the rocks that served as a stool and watched in fascination as Elizabeth produced a sack and placed it on the tablelike boulder.

"It's broken," Kathy said as Elizabeth pulled a bundle of doll's clothes from the bag. "There's no head."

"Yes there is," Elizabeth muttered. "Here." She pulled the bonnet out of the bag and set it on the table. It rolled over, and the cavern echoed with another scream as Kathy saw the distorted features of the cat's face, the eyes open but sunken in now, the stump of flesh at the severed neck beginning to putrefy.

Kathy fought to control herself. She thought she was going to throw up.

"I don't want to stay here," she said, her voice quavering with the beginnings of hysteria. "Let's go home."

"But we have to have a party," Elizabeth said, her voice carrying a silky sweetness that somehow frightened Kathy even more. "That's why we came here." She began propping the body of the cat up on one of the rocks, and Kathy watched in horror as Elizabeth tried to balance the head on the decapitated torso.

"Stop that!" she cried. "Don't do that!" She felt the sting of another slap, and this time she struck back. Her hand flashed out, but before it could make contact with Elizabeth, the other girl had leaped on her.

Kathy felt Elizabeth's weight coming down on her and tried to brace herself, but there was nothing to brace herself against. She rolled off the rock to the floor of the cavern, and felt Elizabeth's fingernails digging into her face. She screamed again.

"Don't do that down here," Elizabeth said, the silkiness gone from her voice and her breath coming in quick, shallow gasps. "Down here you have to be quiet. My friend doesn't like noise."

Beneath her, Kathy whimpered, and tried to regain control of herself. She had to, she knew, or the beating would continue. She forced her body to go limp.

"Let me up," she whispered desperately. "Please, Elizabeth, let me up." The beating ceased then, and Kathy felt the pressure ease as Elizabeth let go of her. She lay quietly, her eyes closed tightly, waiting for whatever would come.

"Sit there," she heard Elizabeth hiss. "Sit over there, and I'll pour us some tea."

Kathy opened her eyes slowly, and looked around. Elizabeth was sitting on the rock nearest the end of the dangling rope ladder, and Kathy felt her hopes fading. She had thought she might be able to climb out of the shaft before Elizabeth could stop her. Now, she could see, that would never happen. She got shakily to her feet, and sat carefully on the rock opposite Elizabeth. Between them, the macabre corpse of the cat sat propped on a third rock, its lips stretched back in a deathly grin. Kathy tried not to look at it.

"Now," Elizabeth said. "Isn't this nice?"

Kathy nodded dumbly.

"Answer me," Elizabeth snapped.

"Yes," Kathy whispered, afraid to raise her voice.

"What?" Elizabeth demanded, and Kathy was afraid for a moment that Elizabeth was going to hit her again.

"Yes," she said, louder this time.

"Yes what?" Elizabeth said relentlessly.

"Yes," Kathy said, wrenching every word out, "this is very nice." Elizabeth seemed to relax, and smiled at her.

"Tea?" Elizabeth asked.

Kathy stared at her.

"Answer me!" Elizabeth demanded. "Do you want some tea?"

"Y-yes," Kathy stammered. "Some tea . . ."

Elizabeth began to mime pouring tea and passing a cup to Kathy. Kathy hesitated for a split second, but quickly pretended to accept the invisible cup Elizabeth was holding out to her. There was an odd, wild look in Elizabeth's eyes, and Kathy felt panic beginning to grow in her. She wanted to bolt for the ladder, but knew there was no way she could get to it before Elizabeth got to her.

"I think we should go now," Kathy said slowly. "I really think we should. Mrs. Norton will be looking for me."

"Fuck Mrs. Norton," Elizabeth said quietly. Kathy's eyes widened at the word, and her fear grew.

"Please, Elizabeth," she said fearfully. "Can't we go now? I don't like it here."

"You don't like it?" Elizabeth said, glancing around at the dimly lit cavern. The flames flickered, and shadows danced evilly on the walls. "It's my secret place," Elizabeth went on. "And now it's yours, too. Only we know about this place."

Until I get home, Kathy thought. She fought to stay calm, and watched Elizabeth carefully.

Elizabeth was engrossed in the tea party, and was busy pouring for the wreckage that had been her pet, and pretending to pass cakes around. Her eyes fell once more on Kathy.

"Talk to me," she said.

"Talk to you?" Kathy repeated. "About what?"

"They don't talk to me, you know. None of them do. They only talk to Sarah, and she can't answer. So I come here, and my friends talk to me." She was staring into Kathy's eyes again, and there was a cold light in her own eyes. "All my friends talk to me here," she said again. Kathy licked her lips.

"I—I like your secret place," Kathy said carefully, hoping she was choosing the right words. "I'm glad you brought me here. But, please, I'm going to be awfully late for my job. If I get in trouble, I won't be able to come here with you again."

"You will," Elizabeth said with a smile, but the smile only made Kathy more uncomfortable. "You'll learn to love this place. You'll learn to love it as much as I do."

"Y-yes," Kathy said. "I suppose I will. But I have to go now. I really do," she pleaded.

Elizabeth seemed to consider it, then nodded.

"All right," she said at last. "Help me clear off the table."

She stood up and began to go through the motions of stacking up all the imaginary dishes. Kathy watched her in silence, but when Elizabeth glared at her she stood up and tried to convince Elizabeth that she was helping. She also tried to move near the shaft, but Elizabeth managed to keep herself between Kathy and the ladder.

"Blow out the lights," Elizabeth commanded. She stood at the bottom of the ladder, the flashlight in her hand.

"Turn on the flashlight," Kathy countered. Elizabeth snapped it on.

"Will you hold it while I climb up the ladder?"

Elizabeth nodded. Kathy moved toward the ladder.

"The candles," Elizabeth said softly. "I told you to blow them out."

Obediently Kathy turned back to the stone slab. She blew out one of the candles, then stooped over the other one. Just before she blew on its tiny flame, she stared over the flickering light and saw Elizabeth smiling at her. She blew out the candle.

As the flame died, Elizabeth snapped off the flashlight and darted up the rope ladder. Below her she could hear the first scream of terror burst from Kathy's throat.

"Eliiiiiiizabeth!" Kathy wailed. "Nooooooo! Oh, God, Elizabeth, don't leave me here!"

The screams built in intensity, and Elizabeth heard the other child stumbling around in the blackness of the pit, knowing that Kathy was trying to find the end of the rope ladder that should have dangled somewhere in the suffocating darkness. But she had already pulled the rope ladder out of the pit. Kathy's screams echoed around her, resounding off the walls of the upper chamber, pounding against her eardrums. She coiled the ladder, then moved once more to the top of the shaft. She threw the beam of light downward and watched as Kathy swarmed into it like a moth around a lightbulb.

Kathy's face tipped up, drained of blood and shining palely in the uncertain light of the electric torch. Her mouth was contorted into the shape of the screams that tore upward from some spot deep in her guts, and her arms were upraised, pleading.

"Noooooo!" she screamed. "Pleeeeeaaaase nooooo!"

Elizabeth held the flashlight steady and stared down at her friend.

"You have to be quiet in the secret place," she said softly. Then she snapped the light off and moved to the entrance of the tunnel by memory, surely, swiftly. She began crawling toward the surface.

By the time she emerged on the embankment, the roaring of the surf drowned out whatever remnants of the screams might have found their way through the tunnel, and Elizabeth was pleased that she no longer heard sounds from the secret place.

She began making her way deftly up the embankment and disappeared into the woods.

# FIFTEEN

MARILYN BURTON DIDN'T BEGIN WORRYing until eight o'clock that night. If she had been home earlier in the day she would have begun worrying then, but, having closed her shop at six as usual, she had decided to treat herself to a dinner out. She didn't mind eating alone; in fact, she rather enjoyed it. She talked to people all day in the store, and it was a relief to spend a few hours by herself, alone with her thoughts. She heard the phone ringing as she put her key in the door, just before eight, and a feeling came over her that something had gone wrong, that she was about to be alone with some thoughts she wouldn't enjoy.

"Marilyn?"

She recognized Norma Norton's voice immediately, and the feeling of unease intensified.

"Yes?" she said. "Something's happened, hasn't it?"

There was a short pause before Norma spoke again. "Well, I don't know," she said uncertainly. "That's why I'm calling you. I've been calling you all afternoon."

"Why didn't you call me at the store?"

"I did, but the line's out of order."

Marilyn frowned, then realized that she hadn't had any calls all afternoon. Nor had she had any reason to call out. The sound of her daughter's name brought her mind back to Norma Norton.

"I'm sorry," she said, "I was drifting. What about Kathy?"

"That's what I want to know," Norma said, her exasperation coming clearly over the line. "What about Kathy? She never showed up after school."

"She didn't?" Mrs. Burton said blankly. "That's strange."

"It's damned inconsiderate is what it is," Norma fumed. "I thought she might have gotten sick, but she could at least have called."

"Just a minute," Marilyn said. "I'll check here. I just got in." She set the phone down, but even as she walked toward Kathy's room she knew it would be empty. She was doing the same thing she had done when they'd called her to tell her that Bob was dead. Postponing the inevitable. Even knowing what she was doing, she still walked through the entire house before she returned to the telephone.

"She's not here," she said. She stood dumbly, waiting for the woman at the other end to pick up the conversation. There was a long, awkward silence as the memory of Anne Forager's strange story went through both their minds. Neither of them wanted to mention it.

"Maybe she went over to see a friend," Norma Norton said gently. "Maybe she forgot all about babysitting for me today."

"Yes," said Marilyn numbly. "I'll tell you what. Let me make a couple of calls, and I'll call you back when I find her. She certainly owes you an apology."

"Do you want me to call Ray?"

"Of course not," Marilyn replied, too quickly. "I'm sure everything is fine." But she knew it wasn't. She dropped the receiver back in its cradle and sat silently for a few minutes. Postponing the inevitable. Then she picked up the phone and dialed.

"Mrs. Conger?" she said. "This is Marilyn Burton."

"Hello," Rose said warmly. "Don't tell me you've finally decided to sell that store of yours?"

"No," Marilyn said. "That's not why I'm calling. I was just wondering if Kathy's out there."

"Kathy?" Rose said blankly. "No. Isn't she home?" She reproved herself for asking a dumb question. "I'm sorry," she said immediately. "Of course she isn't home, is she?"

"No," Marilyn said reluctantly. "I wish she were. Is Elizabeth there?"

"Yes, of course," Rose said. "Just a minute, I'll call her."

Jack looked at her curiously as she went to the door of the study. "Kathy Burton hasn't gotten home from school yet," she said. "Mrs. Burton is wondering if Elizabeth knows where she might have gone." She stepped into the hall and called Elizabeth's name, then waited until her daughter came down the stairs.

"It's Kathy's mother," she explained. "She's wondering if you know what Kathy was doing this afternoon."

Elizabeth walked to the phone, and picked it up.

"Mrs. Burton? This is Elizabeth."

"Hello, dear, how are you?" Marilyn Burton plunged ahead without waiting for an answer. "Did you see Kathy this afternoon?"

"Sure," Elizabeth said. "She walked most of the way home with me. She was baby-sitting for the Nortons today."

"And she walked with you all the way to the Nortons'?"

"Farther," Elizabeth said. "We were talking about something, and she walked with me all the way past the Stevenses' house."

"Stevenses?" Marilyn Burton said blankly. "Who are they?"

"Oh, they're the people who bought the Barnes place," Elizabeth said. "They just moved in."

"I see," Marilyn said. "And Kathy was going to go right back to the Nortons'?"

"That's what she said," Elizabeth replied. "I tried to talk her into coming here for a little while, but she said she didn't have time."

"I see," Marilyn Burton repeated, though she had barely heard what Elizabeth had told her. "Well, I'm sure she's perfectly all right."

"Didn't she get to the Nortons'?" Elizabeth asked.

"No," said Marilyn Burton. "She didn't. But don't worry. I'm sure she's somewhere." She dropped the receiver back in its cradle, then called Norma Norton back.

"Norma?" she said. "It's Marilyn. I think you'd better call Ray."

Rose saw the apprehension in her daughter's face as Elizabeth hung up the phone.

"What is it?" she asked. "Has something happened to Kathy?"

Elizabeth shrugged and shook her head slowly. "I don't know. She never got to the Nortons'."

"Where did she leave you?" Jack asked.

"At the edge of the woods," Elizabeth replied. "We were talking about the Stevenses, and Kathy was hoping if we walked by, maybe she'd get a glimpse of Jeff."

"And did you?" Rose asked archly.

Elizabeth shook her head. "I don't think anybody was home," she said. "At least, we didn't see anybody. So when we got to the woods Kathy said she had to be getting back to the Nortons'."

There was an uncomfortable silence, and Rose was sure that all three of them were thinking about Anne Forager. "Well," she said finally, breaking the silence. "You'd better get back upstairs before Sarah misses you."

"Yeah," Elizabeth said blankly. "I hope nothing's happened to Kathy." She searched her parents' faces, as if looking for reassurance that her friend was all right. Rose did her best to smile brightly.

"I'm sure it's nothing serious," she said, with a confidence she didn't feel. Then she decided to voice what they were all thinking. "After all, nothing happened to Anne Forager, did it?"

"No," Elizabeth agreed. "But she's a little liar anyway. Kathy isn't like that." She left the room, and Jack and Rose listened to her steps echoing up the stairs.

"We ought to get a carpet for that staircase," Jack said absently.

"That's a stupid thing to say," Rose snapped. She stopped, surprised at what she'd said. Jack stared at her.

"What did you expect me to say?" he said coldly. "Are we supposed to sit here speculating on what might have happened to Kathy Burton?" He saw the anger flare in his wife's eyes, and wished he'd kept his mouth shut. He picked up his glass and headed for the bar in the corner of the study.

"I wish you wouldn't do that," Rose said.

"Do you? Well, I'm sorry," Jack said irritably, and poured twice as much liquor into the glass as he had intended to. He was preparing for the battle he could see brewing when the phone rang again. This time it was Ray Norton.

"That you, Jack?" he said when Jack picked up the receiver.

"Hello, Ray," Jack replied. "Shall I guess what you're calling about?"

"I was wondering if it would be all right with you if I dropped over for a couple of minutes."

"Here?" Jack said. "Why here?"

"Well," Ray answered. "It seems like Elizabeth was the last person to see Kathy—"

"You're talking like she's dead," Jack interrupted.

"I didn't mean to." Ray Norton was apologetic but firm. "But she does seem to be missing, and I'd like to hear Elizabeth's story straight from her."

"What do you mean?" Jack said defensively.

Ray Norton heard the tone of his voice, and hurried to dispel Jack's thoughts.

"Stop jumping to conclusions," Ray said. "I just don't like getting information secondhand, even from a mother. In fact, especially from a mother. I'd rather get it directly from the source, and from what I know of Elizabeth, she's a pretty reliable source. Can I drop over for a few minutes?"

"Officially or unofficially?" Jack asked.

"Oh, come on, Jack," Ray replied. "If you're wondering if you need a lawyer—"

"No," Jack interrupted, "I was wondering if I should have a drink waiting for you. See you when you get here." He dropped the phone back on the hook, cutting off Ray Norton's relieved laughter, and turned to his wife.

"We're having company," he said.

"So I gathered," Rose said drily. "I take it he wants to talk to Elizabeth?"

"That's it." Jack nodded. "I guess Marilyn Burton's pretty upset, and gave him a garbled version of what Elizabeth told her."

"Well, she has a right to be," Rose said. "Upset, I mean." She looked at the drink in Jack's hand and was suddenly sorry she'd criticized him.

"If I apologize for snapping at you, would you mix me one of those?" She smiled.

Jack mixed the drink, and they sat in front of the fireplace, waiting for Ray Norton's arrival. "I wonder what really happened," Jack said finally.

Rose glanced up at her husband, and saw that he wasn't looking at her but at the portrait of the little girl. She, too, stared up at it for a moment.

"What do you mean?" she countered. "You mean to her? Who knows? Who even knows if there really was a girl such as Dr. Belter was talking about. And even if there was, there's no way of knowing if that's the girl."

"If there *was* a girl, that's the girl," Jack said positively.

Rose looked quietly at him, trying to fathom what was going on in his mind. "You sound so sure," she said at last.

Jack's lips pursed, and he frowned a little. "Yes," he said slowly. "I do, don't I. And you know what? I am sure. I can't tell you why, but I'm sure there was a girl and that that picture *is* the girl. And it terrifies me." Then they heard the sound of a car coming up the drive, and Jack stood up to go to the front door. While he was out of the room Rose examined the portrait once more, and thought about the legend.

What nonsense, she thought. What utter nonsense.

Ray Norton closed his notebook and smiled at Elizabeth. "I wish all witnesses were like you," he said. Once more he ran through Elizabeth's recounting of what had happened that afternoon.

"And you're sure you didn't hear my wife calling to you?" he said.

"I'm sorry," Elizabeth said. "But we didn't. In fact, we were both listening for her. Kathy said she'd have to go in if Mrs. Norton called her, even though we were early. I'm sorry we didn't hear her."

Ray Norton nodded noncommittally. Norma hadn't called to the girls as they passed the house, hadn't even seen them. Ray liked to throw a curve now and then, just to see if a witness would change his story. But Elizabeth hadn't. They'd been alone, and they hadn't seen anybody or anything unusual, but of course, as Elizabeth explained, they hadn't been looking for anybody, either. Except while they were passing the Nortons', they had been engrossed in talking about Jeff Stevens.

"And you didn't turn around and wave?" Ray said once more.

"I cut across the field," Elizabeth said. "So I couldn't have seen Kathy anyway. The woods would have been in the way."

"Okay." Ray sighed. He looked at Jack. "I'll have that drink now, if it's still around. I probably shouldn't, since I'll have to go into town, but I hate things like this." He caught Rose's frown and remembered that Elizabeth was still in the room. "Not that anything has happened," he added hastily. He took the drink that Jack was offering, gratefully. "Thanks."

"Can I ride into town with you?" Jack asked. "As a newspaperman, not as a friend. I'd like to be on top of this one, after what I took from Martin Forager. Besides, I still have all of this afternoon's work to catch up on."

"Fine with me," Ray said, draining the drink. "But I can't guarantee what time you'll get back."

"I'll find a way," Jack said. He went to find a coat, and while he was gone Ray looked up at the portrait.

"It looks just like you," he said to Elizabeth.

"I know," Elizabeth said. "But it isn't. It's somebody else. She's not at all like me."

Rose and Ray Norton stared after her as she left the room.

"Now what did that mean?" Ray said, puzzled.

"Don't ask me," Rose said. "She and Sarah found an old Ouija board up in the attic. Maybe she's been talking to ghosts."

"Right," Ray said with mock seriousness. "I'm sure that's what it is." Jack returned, his coat buttoned up to his chin.

"See you when I see you," he said, and kissed Rose perfunctorily. The two men left the house, and seconds later Rose heard Ray Norton's car grinding away down the driveway. Not knowing why, she fixed herself another drink.

Ray Norton pulled the car up in front of the Port Arbello *Courier,* but didn't turn off the engine.

"Looks like you got burglars," he commented, pointing to a shadow moving across the drawn curtain of Jack Conger's office. Jack smiled.

"Looks like Sylvia is trying to catch up on my work, is what it looks like."

Ray Norton shook his head ruefully. "Sure wish I could get a secretary like that. At the station they don't even want to do their own work, let alone mine."

"Yes," Jack said easily, "it is a problem, isn't it. On the other hand, Sylvia can do my work better than I can, and your girls can't do your work at all. Any idea how long you'll be?"

"None whatever. Call me when you're through, or I'll call you. If you wander over later, and ask me nicely, I'll fill you in on what's happening with Kathy Burton."

"What do you think's happening?" Jack asked.

The police chief looked grim. "If we're lucky, it'll be the same story as Anne Forager. But we won't be lucky."

"You sound awfully sure," Jack said.

"Call it a hunch. And knowing kids. Don't quote me, but I tend to agree with the people who say nothing happened to Anne. She's always been that kind of kid. Kathy Burton's different, though."

"Oh?"

"Norma and Marilyn Burton have been friends for years, ever since they were kids. So I know Kathy. She's a good kid. Responsible, not the kind that would have let Norma down the way she did today, unless something happened. Been that way ever since her father died." Norton shook his head sadly. "That was a tough break, for Kathy and her mother both. I really hand it to them."

"It was a hunting accident, wasn't it?"

"Yup. Just about three years ago. Really dumb one. He wasn't wearing the colors, and someone mistook him for a buck. I tell them the same thing every year: Wear the colors. There's always one or two who don't listen. But Burton's the only one who ever caught a shot for his trouble." The chief glanced at his watch. "Well, enough jawboning. Got work to do." He shifted the car into gear as Jack got out. "See you later."

Jack watched him pull away and head around the square to the police station. It was one of the things he liked about Port Arbello—being able to watch the whole town from his front door.

He had been right: Sylvia Bannister *was* in his office, and she *was* trying to do his work. She smiled at him as he came in.

"You just wrote one of the best editorials that's ever come out of this office," she told him.

"Oh? What's it about?"

"Read it yourself," she said, handing him a sheaf of papers. "Pure dynamite. You are fearless, courageous, and willing to put your reputation on the line. But modest and humble."

"Sounds great," Jack said. "But what am I being all this about?"

"Rose's plan for the armory."

"How'd you hear about that?" Jack asked, puzzled. "That's supposed to be a secret."

"Not in this town," Sylvia said. "Anyway, you're against the plan."

"I am?" Jack said blankly. "That'll be great for me at home."

"It won't hurt. You couldn't very well be for it—everyone would accuse you of corruption. This way, you get credit for being honest and courageous and Rose gets her plan talked about."

"Have you talked this over with Rose?" Jack said doubtfully.

"Of course," the secretary said. "Who do you think thought of the idea? Didn't she tell you about it?"

"She doesn't tell me about much," Jack said, and a sudden wave of despondency flowed over him. He saw Sylvia's face cloud over.

"I'm sorry," she said. "I thought maybe things were getting better."

Jack smiled, but it was a wry smile. "I thought they were. But you can never tell. One day things seem to be going well, and the next all hell breaks loose."

"And today all hell broke loose?"

Jack shrugged and slumped into a chair. He folded his hands over his stomach and stretched his legs. He was comfortable, and he hadn't been comfortable for a long time.

"Not really, but it might yet. The night isn't over."

Sylvia looked at him curiously, and he filled her in on the disappearance of Kathy Burton. When he was finished she seemed puzzled.

"Well, I'm sorry to hear about Kathy, of course, but I don't see how it could have any bearing on you and Rose."

"Rose has problems with reference to me and young girls," he said quietly. He saw the outrage flash into Sylvia's eyes, and it pleased him.

"But that's ridiculous," Sylvia declared. "For God's sake, she's been with you all day. What does she think, you spend all your time, even when you're with her, making trouble for children?"

Jack held his hands out helplessly. "I know. But it makes her nervous. And I suppose I can't blame her, all things considered."

"Well, I think it's awful," Sylvia said, and Jack could hear indignation boiling in her. "Is she going to hold one incident against you the rest of your life? I don't think you should stand for it. Really, I don't!"

"My God, Sylvia," Jack said. "You sound really angry."

"Well, I guess I am," the secretary flared. "I guess I just don't think it's right. We know you didn't really do anything to Sarah, and we know you weren't responsible for what happened. Not really. You were drunk . . ." She trailed off.

"But I am responsible," Jack said quietly. "I wasn't that drunk, and I guess I did beat her. So I do deserve some punishment." His voice grew quieter. "But it gets hard sometimes," he said softly. "You have no idea."

"Oh, I might have some idea," Sylvia said gently. She came to stand behind him, her hand resting gently on his shoulders. As she continued to talk, her fingers began massaging the tight muscles of his neck, and he relaxed under her touch. "I'm not inhuman, you know. I hurt. I carry some pain and guilt with me, too. And I do the same thing you do. Try to hold it in, and try to deal with it. Sometimes I wish I could do what you do and get drunk a few times." She smiled wanly. "But I don't. I'm not allowed."

"What stops you?" Jack said quietly.

"Me, I suppose. Me, and my puritan background, and my high ideals, and all the other stuff that got bred into me and keeps me from liking myself."

Jack reached up, and his hand closed over hers. He felt her stiffen, but she did not pull her hand away. Slowly he drew her around until she stood in front of him and he was looking up into her eyes. They were blue, a deep blue, and Jack had the feeling he had never seen them before. He stood up.

"I'm sorry," he whispered, and put his arms around her.

"Sorry?" she said. "For what?" She tried to keep her eyes on his, but she couldn't. After a moment she broke their gaze and leaned her forehead against his chest.

"I'm not sure," Jack said above her head. "For everything, I guess. For all the trouble you've had, and for all the things I haven't been able to give you." He tilted her head up and kissed her.

It was a soft kiss, a tender kiss, and it surprised Jack. He had not planned to kiss her, nor had he realized he wanted to. But as he kissed her it became very clear that he did want to kiss her and did not want to stop with a kiss. He felt a heat flood through him that he had not felt in a long time. And then he felt Sylvia pull away, and he was ashamed.

"I'm sorry," he repeated, and this time he was sure she knew what he meant. And then he had the distinct feeling that she was no longer in a serious mood, that, indeed, she was laughing at him. He looked at her, and there was a mischievous delight playing in her eyes and at the corners of her mouth.

"I thought you weren't supposed to be able to do that," she said, suppressing a giggle. Jack felt his face flush as he realized what she was saying.

"I haven't, for the last year," he said nervously. "I certainly didn't expect—" He began floundering. "What I mean is, I hadn't intended—"

"Don't apologize." Sylvia laughed. "Be happy. At least you know the problem isn't all yours. Apparently it's your wife you don't turn on to, not everybody."

Jack stared at her, and he felt a weight lifting off his whole being. Maybe, he thought, things aren't so bad after all.

"Now what do we do?" he said.

She shrugged and walked from the room. "Nothing," she tossed back over her shoulder. "Not for a while, anyway." He heard her close the front door of the office behind her, and realized she was right. He would need time to think. So, he hoped, would she.

# SIXTEEN

PORT ABRELLO SAT UP LATE THAT NIGHT. At ten o'clock, when she was usually in bed, Marilyn Burton found herself getting into her car and driving out the Conger's Point Road to spend however long it took with Norma Norton. The two women sat drinking coffee and talking quietly about anything except their children, each of them mentioning several times that the coffee would surely keep them awake all night. They carefully avoided mentioning that they expected to be awake all night anyway. Instead, they simply went ahead and drank the coffee.

Shortly after eleven, Martin Forager appeared at the police station, his breath reeking of whiskey and his manner truculent.

"Well," he demanded. "Now what have you got to say for yourself?"

Ray Norton glanced up at Forager, and his finger stopped dialing the telephone on his desk. He was in the last stages of organizing a search party, and Marty Forager's interruption was annoying. But he put his annoyance aside and spoke mildly.

"About what, Marty?"

Forager sat heavily in the chair opposite the police chief, a surly expression darkening his face. "She hasn't showed up yet, has she?"

"No," Norton agreed, "she hasn't. But I still don't see what you're getting at."

"I know what this town thinks," Forager challenged. "I hear the rumors too. They think my Annie lied. That nothing happened to her."

"By now Anne was home, wasn't she?" Norton replied quietly. He glanced at his watch. "Unless I'm wrong, Anne came in at eleven. It's nearly eleven thirty now."

Forager glared at him. "You wait," he said. "You just wait, and you'll see. She'll turn up, and she'll turn up with the same story."

"I don't care what story she has," Norton said. "I just hope she turns up."

"She will," Marty Forager repeated. "You just wait."

"I will, Marty," Ray Norton said as the man opposite him got to his feet. "Where you heading?"

"Saw Conger's lights on," Martin Forager said thickly. "I thought I'd go over there and see what he's up to."

Ray Norton put on his best policeman manner. "I think I'd go on home if I were you," he said, his voice turning it from a suggestion into an order. Forager swung slowly around to stare at the police chief.

"You telling me what to do?"

"Not really," Norton said affably. "But it's a busy night around here, and I think it's a busy night at the *Courier,* too. And it doesn't concern you, Marty. Go on home, and talk to Jack Conger in the morning if you still think you want to."

"You and he are pretty buddy-buddy, aren't you?" Forager said suspiciously. "And you both live out on the Point Road, where all the trouble seems to be, don't you?" He leered drunkenly at the policeman, who considered the advantages of putting him in the one cell Port Arbello possessed to sleep it off. He decided against it. Instead, he smiled agreeably.

"That's right, Marty. I though you knew. Ever since I got to be chief of police and Jack Conger took over as editor of the *Courier,* we've been entertaining ourselves by kidnapping little girls. The woods are full of the bodies, but nothing will ever be done about it, because everybody knows that Jack and I are buddies and covering up for each other. In fact, and don't spread this around, we're queer for each other, and the real reason we're out messing with little girls is so that no one will suspect that it's really each other we turn on to." He stood up. "Now, why don't you go out and spread that one around, even though I asked you not to? It's at least as plausible as the story your daughter told."

He immediately regretted his last statement, but then he realized that Forager was too drunk to put together everything he'd said.

"That's all right," Forager muttered under his breath. "You'll see. Somethin's going on in this town, and it started with my daughter. You'll see." He shambled out the door, and Ray Norton stepped out from behind his desk to see where Forager was headed. He watched until he was sure the drunken man wasn't headed toward the offices of the *Courier,* then went back to his desk. On an impulse, he picked up the phone and dialed quickly.

"Jack?" he said when he heard his friend's voice answer. "If I were you I'd lock my front door."

"What are you talking about?" Jack Conger said, and Ray Norton thought he heard a sharpness that didn't fit with the light tone in which he'd couched his suggestion.

"Sorry," he said. "I didn't mean to scare you. Marty Forager's wandering around tonight, and he's pretty drunk. He was just here, and he said he was going to see you next."

"Is he headed this way?" Jack asked.

"Nah. He looked like he was heading for the tavern, but after a couple of more belts, he just might forget what I told him. Or worse, he might remember."

"What'd you tell him?" Jack asked curiously.

Ray Norton recounted the ludicrous story he had made up for the benefit of the drunk, and was surprised when Jack Conger didn't seem to think it was funny.

"That's great," Jack said, annoyance twisting his voice.

"Well, I wouldn't worry about it," Norton said uneasily. "I imagine he'll forget all about it by morning."

"I hope so," Jack Conger replied. Then he changed the subject. "What about Kathy Burton?"

"Nothing." Ray Norton replied, shifting to his business tone. "She hasn't turned up, and no one's seen her. I don't know what to think. Marilyn Burton's out at my house now, and Norma's staying up with her. I have a feeling they'll be up a long time."

"Along with the rest of the town," Jack observed. He had swung his chair around, and was staring pensively out the window. There was a lot of traffic; cars cruising slowly around the square, and knots of people standing talking under the street lamps. He knew what they were talking about, and it made him uncomfortable. "This town talks too much," he said.

"Only when they have something to talk about," the police chief responded, "and that's not often enough. How much longer are you going to be over there?"

"I've about got it wrapped up. What about you?"

"Same here. I was just finishing the calls for the search party when Marty came in. The boys should all be here in another half-hour, and I want you, too."

"Why me? Not that I'm objecting."

Norton chuckled. "You'd better not. We're starting the search at your place, and I need you to help me lead it. Since we know the area best, and we're both more or less responsible citizens, I thought we'd split into two groups. I'll take my bunch to the quarry and you can comb the woods."

Jack felt a sudden chill, and beads of sweat formed on his forehead. He hadn't been in the woods for a year. He tried to keep his discomfort out of his voice when he spoke again.

"All right. I'll close up here and head over your way. See you when I get there."

He didn't bother to wait for the chief to say good-bye before dropping the phone back in its cradle. He cleared his desk off and locked it, then his office. He left the lights on in the main office of the paper, and made sure he locked the door behind him when he stepped out onto the sidewalk. What with the traffic, and the questions of the curious, it was a half-hour before he made it to the police station. That worked out to just about ten feet a minute.

Rose Conger had tried to work after her husband had left the house, but hadn't been able to concentrate. She had given it up, and turned her attention to a book, but again had found herself unable to concentrate. Finally she had given it up, and simply sat, listening to the old clock strike away the quarter-hours, the half-hours, the hours. The night was beginning to seem endless. Then she had decided to call Norma Norton, to see if she had heard anything about Kathy. Norma, a bit uncertainly, had invited her to come over and join the watch. Though their husbands were close, the women had never hit it off particularly well—partly, Rose suspected, because Norma Norton regarded her not as a human being but as *the* Mrs. Conger. She welcomed the opportunity to try to dispel the image.

"I'd love to," she said. "I've just been sitting here getting more nervous by the minute. Let me find out if Mrs. Goodrich is still up. If she's not planning to go to bed for a while, I'll have her keep an eye on the girls. I'll be there in ten minutes, or call you back."

She found Mrs. Goodrich watching television in her room off the kitchen, and the old woman assured her that she'd be up most of the night. "Seems like the older you get, the less sleep you need," she said grumpily. "Or maybe it's just arthritis. But you go ahead. Nothing's happened in this house for fifty years that I haven't been able to handle."

Rose thanked her and went upstairs to check on the girls. They were sleeping peacefully, and she kissed Sarah lightly on the forehead. She didn't want to disturb Elizabeth. Two minutes before the end of the allotted ten, she had parked her car in the road in front of the Nortons', and a minute later she was gratefully accepting a cup of coffee from Norma.

"I'm so sorry about what's happened," she told Marilyn Burton. "But I'm sure Kathy's all right. It'll be just like Anne Forager." The trouble was, none of them knew what had happened to Anne Forager. They sat together, an uneasy group, and tried to numb their fears with caffeine.

Elizabeth's eyes snapped open when she heard the click of her bedroom door closing. She didn't know why she had pretended to be asleep when her mother opened the door. Usually she would have spoken, if only to say good night. But she had kept her eyes closed, and maintained the slow, steady, rhythmic breath of sleep. And now, with the door closed again, and her eyes open, she still maintained that slow, steady rhythm. She lay quietly, listening to the night sounds, and heard the purring of her mother's car as it moved quickly down the driveway.

When the sound of the engine faded from her hearing, she rose and went to the window. She stared off across the field, and almost felt that she could see into the woods that stood darkly in the night. For a long time she remained at the window, and a strange feeling came over her, a feeling of oneness with the forest and the trees and a desire to be closer to the sea beyond the woods. She turned away from the window and, her eyelids fluttering strangely, began to dress.

A few moments later she left her room and moved to the top of the stairway. She paused there, seeming to listen to the silence, then began to descend, as silently as the night. She passed the grandfather clock without even noticing its loud ticking. At the bottom of the stairs she turned and began making her way toward the kitchen.

She didn't hear the droning of the television set in the little room next to the kitchen; if she had, she might have tapped at the door, then opened it to see Mrs. Goodrich dozing fitfully in her chair.

Elizabeth opened the refrigerator and stared blankly into its depths for a moment. Then her hand moved out and her fingers closed on a small package wrapped in white paper. She closed the refrigerator door and left the kitchen. In the little room next door Mrs. Goodrich's sleep was not disturbed by the soft clicking of the front door, or by the heavy chiming of the clock as it struck midnight.

Elizabeth moved across the field quickly and faded into the woods. Once she was there, hidden by the trees, her pace increased.

The lights of the searchers bobbed in the darkness around her, but if she was aware of them she gave no sign. Twice Elizabeth disappeared into the shadow of a tree only seconds before one of the searchers would have discovered her, and just before she emerged from the woods onto the embankment she passed within ten feet of her father. She neither noticed him nor made any sound that could have penetrated Jack's concentration. He was too intent on overcoming his fear of the forest to have heard. He forged on, stolid in his grim search for Kathy Burton.

Soon Elizabeth was once again on the embankment over the sea. She listened to the surf, and it seemed to her to be a sound she was used to, a sound she had lived with for much longer than she could remember. She began making her way down the embankment, until she disappeared into the black shadow behind the boulder.

The sounds of the surf, or something else, prevented her from hearing the snapping of twigs and the breaking of branches behind her as others fought a path through the woods above.

Kathy Burton wasn't at all sure she was hearing anything, she had been hearing so much in the past hours. First there had been the sound of her own screams, echoing back at her like some vile, dying creature, hammering into her ears. She had screamed until her voice gave out, then had lain on the floor of the pit for a long time, crying to herself, her body heaving with exhaustion and fear. Then the panic had passed, and she had begun listening to the muffled sound of the surf, which made a soft backdrop of noise, preventing silence from multiplying the terror of the unrelieved blackness. And then she had begun hearing the small sounds, the tiny scurrying sounds to which she had at first been able to attach no meanings. Her mind began producing images in the darkness, images of rats chasing each other around the cavern, circling just beyond her reach. As the images in her imagination grew stronger, she began to feel the rats, if rats they were, moving closer to her, sniffing the air toward her, and her fear grew. She retreated to the top of the rock that only a few hours earlier had served as the table for Elizabeth's manic party.

She had stayed there, huddled against the darkness, and had felt herself growing smaller. She imagined herself disappearing, and it was the least frightening of her imaginings, for if she disappeared she would at least be away. And she wanted to be away, desperately.

As the hours had worn on, her joints had become stiff from the inactivity, and from the dank chill that pervaded the cavern. Finally she had been forced to move, but she had not dared to leave the flat surface of the rock, afraid of what she might encounter in the darkness that surrounded her.

And now she heard a different noise, a scuffling noise from above. She felt a scream forming in her aching throat, but she held it back. The scuffling continued.

Kathy craned her neck, trying to find, somewhere in the darkness above, the shaft that led out of her prison. She thought she knew where it was, for there was the slightest draft, nothing more than a general disturbance of the air, and she was sure that the shaft lay directly above that tiny current of air that was the only real movement in the pit. Earlier she had stood up and tried to reach the low ceiling of the cave, but it was just out of reach, and the inability to even locate the limitations of her confinement had only served to increase her fear. She lay on her back now, her face tipped upward into the draft of air she was sure came from the shaft.

And then she was blinded. She felt her face contract as the light struck her eyes, dazzlingly brilliant. Like a doe trapped in the beam of an automobile's headlight, she was frozen to the stone slab.

Above her, Elizabeth held the flashlight and peered down into Kathy's terrified face. There was a wild look in Kathy's eyes that somehow comforted Elizabeth, and she smiled to herself. Then she heard Kathy speak.

"Who is it?" Kathy managed, her voice sounding strange to her ears. "Please, who is it?"

"Be quiet," Elizabeth hissed down at her. "You must be quiet here."

"Elizabeth?" Kathy asked uncertainly. Then, when she heard no answer, she repeated the word.

"Elizabeth," her voice rasped. "Please, Elizabeth, is that you?"

Above her Elizabeth continued to hold the flashlight steady with one hand, while the other hand pulled at the white paper that wrapped the bundle she had brought from the kitchen. When the paper was free, she spoke.

"Here," she said, her voice almost as harsh as Kathy's strained rasp. "Here's your dinner."

She flung something downward, and watched as the piece of raw and bloody meat slapped wetly into Kathy's face.

Kathy didn't see it coming, and when the slab of meat hit her she recoiled reflexively, and her voice found itself once more. A howling of fear mixed with revulsion at the unknown wet coldness that had hit her face roared out of her throat and filled the cavern with sound. The dull roar of the surf disappeared, and all the small noises were drowned in the sound of Kathy's terror. And then Elizabeth's voice, harsh and ugly, cut through the scream.

"God damn you!" Elizabeth shouted. "Shut your fucking mouth! Shut up!" she kept screaming, as Kathy's voice slowly died away. "*Shut up!*" And then the silence closed over the cave again, until the murmur of the surf found its way in once more.

"Eat it," Elizabeth commanded. "Eat your dinner."

Below her, Kathy's eyes began to adjust to the rent in the darkness. She looked down and saw the raw steak gleaming redly in the circle of light from the flashlight above. She stared at it and tried not to listen to Elizabeth's voice commanding her from above.

"Pick it up," Elizabeth was saying. "Pick it up, you little bitch, and eat it! Come on, pick it up and eat it. Pick it up. Pick it up. Pick it up."

The voice from above took on a hypnotic quality, and suddenly Kathy found herself holding the limp and bloody object in her hands. And then the order from above changed.

"Eat it," Elizabeth commanded. "Eat it. Eat it. *Eat it!*" Helplessly, Kathy moved the raw meat to her lips. The light clicked off.

Kathy sat for a long time, crouched on the slab of rock, the piece of meat clutched in her hands, listening to the scuffling sounds dying away above her. And then, finally, it was silent; still she sat in the blackness, like some wary animal, waiting for an unseen enemy to leap forth from the night.

She became aware of the fact that she was hungry. Slowly her mind began to focus once more on reality, and she wondered how long she had been trapped in the hole, how long it had been since she had eaten. She thought about the bloody object in her hand. Somewhere in her mind she found some little note, some scrap of information, that told her that some people ate raw meat. She felt her stomach jerk, and for a moment she thought she was going to throw up. Then the nausea passed, and once more she felt the pangs of hunger. She made up her mind.

Kathy forced the raw meat into her mouth and began chewing. She was glad now for the dark. She knew she wouldn't have been able to eat it if she had been able to see it.

The scuffling began again when she was halfway through the steak. She stopped gnawing at the meat and listened. It grew louder; then, when it sounded as though it was directly above her, it stopped.

Kathy started to say something, then thought better of it. Acting more on instinct than on reason, she suddenly leaped from the rock, something in her subconscious telling her that the danger from the pit was less than the danger from above. She huddled against the wall of the cavern and waited for the beam of light to come once more through the shaft, heralding a fear that would be bigger than the fear of the darkness and the silence. But there was no beam of light, no rasping, ugly voice obscenely commanding her from above. Instead, there was a sharp crash, as though some object—some hard object—had been dropped from above. There was another silence, and then the scuffling began again, fading slowly away until it melded fully into the background of the surf. Kathy stayed huddled against the wall.

When her legs told her that she would have to move, she began groping her way once more toward the center of the cavern. Her hands found the large slab of stone, and she began cautiously going over its surface, not wanting to find the object that had been dropped, but afraid not to find it.

And then her fingers brushed against something. She drew away as though the object were hot, then moved back. She began examining the object with her fingertips. It was hard, and round, and sort of flat. It seemed to be covered with some sort of cloth—and then she knew what it was. She picked up the canteen and shook it. It sloshed.

Carefully she unscrewed the top and sniffed at the contents. There was no odor.

Finally she worked up her courage and tasted it. It was water.

Thirstily, Kathy drank. The water was soothing to her painful throat.

As she awoke the next morning, Elizabeth's eyes widened in surprise at the pile of dirty clothes sitting in the center of her bedroom. She stared at it curiously, wondering where the clothes could have come from. She decided that Sarah must have left them there during the night, and gathered them up. Depositing them in the laundry chute, she went downstairs for breakfast.

A few minutes later Sarah woke up, and she too found a heap of filthy clothes on the floor of the room. She got out of bed and put them on. Then Sarah, too, went downstairs and silently took her place at the breakfast table. Her parents looked at her in horror. Elizabeth stood up, came around beside her, and took her hand.

"Come on, Sarah," she said gently. "You don't want to wear those to school."

Elizabeth led her sister back upstairs as Rose and Jack Conger looked at each other. Neither of them could think of anything to say. They were too frighened.

## SEVENTEEN

TIME CREPT SLOWLY THROUGH PORT Arbello that week. Marilyn Burton, still valiantly postponing the inevitable, opened her shop each day, and each day she smiled at her customers and assured them that, no, she was sure nothing too bad had happened to Kathy and she would turn up. Deep inside, though, she knew that Kathy would not turn up.

Ray Norton expanded the search parties, and the men of Port Arbello began a systematic search of the entire area, each day sweeping a wider arc around the town. Norton did not expect them to find anything, but it kept them busy, and kept them from listening too closely to Martin Forager's charges, repeated drunkenly in the tavern each evening, that the police weren't doing anything. Norton hoped he could keep the searchers working for at least ten days, at the end of which time he hoped to have something more solid to go on than a simple vanishing.

The women of Port Arbello found they were drinking much more coffee than usual, and burning much more gas than usual, as they all took to transporting their children to and from school. All except the people along Conger's Point Road, where Anne Forager had allegedly been attacked, and where Kathy Burton had apparently disappeared. The families on Conger's Point Road did not discuss what was happening, nor did they consult each other on the best way of handling the situation. It was as though, individually, they had each decided that nothing would happen if they did not admit that anything was wrong. So the children of Conger's Point Road continued to walk to and from school each day. If anyone noticed that there was an unusual amount of automobile traffic on the Point Road as each of the mothers found an errand or two to do in town during the hours the children would be walking, no one commented on it. Silently they preserved the appearance of normalcy, and the sight of the constant search parties reassured them.

Thursday morning Elizabeth found herself almost running from the house to the Conger's Point Road. She would have cut across the field, coming to the Road at the base of the woods, but she felt slightly embarrassed. When she got to the Road she glanced quickly to the right, then deliberately slowed her pace and tried to assume an air of nonchalance. For the third morning in a row, Jeff Stevens was waiting for her.

Tuesday morning she had assumed it was a coincidence. She hadn't questioned him about how he happened to leave his house just as she passed the woods. Instead, she had simply fallen in beside him, and surrendered her books when he had taken them from her.

Wednesday morning he had been waiting for her by the Stevenses' mailbox, and she wondered if he had been told to escort her to school. As if he had read her thoughts, he reached for her books and smiled.

"Tomorrow morning you can carry mine," he'd said. "I'm glad you live out here. It isn't any fun, walking by myself."

So on Thursday morning Elizabeth approached Jeff and held out her hands.

"My turn," she said, grinning at him. When he failed to respond, she spoke again. "You said I could carry your books today."

Jeff handed his books over silently and told himself not to forget to get them all back before they were in sight of the school. The teasing had been bad enough when he'd carried Elizabeth's; if she were seen carrying his, he'd never live it down.

He tried to think of something to say, but nothing came to his mind. Which was all right with him, since he seemed to find himself stammering a lot when he tried to talk to Elizabeth. He wondered if he was developing a crush on her, and decided he probably was.

"You're awfully quiet this morning," Elizabeth said, making Jeff blush a deep red.

"I was . . . uh . . . I was just thinking about Kathy Burton," Jeff managed to say, and the blush deepened. What was wrong with him? He'd known what he was going to say. Why couldn't he just say it?

"I wonder what happened to her," Elizabeth said, frowning a little. "Maybe Anne Forager wasn't lying after all."

"Except she's still around, and Kathy isn't." This time Jeff pronounced each word carefully and managed not to stammer.

"I hope they find her," Elizabeth said. "She's a good friend of mine. She baby-sits for the Nortons a lot, and we used to walk together."

Jeff suddenly found himself hoping maybe they wouldn't find Kathy Burton. He wasn't sure he wanted to walk with Elizabeth and someone else too. He decided being fourteen was lousy.

He forgot to retrieve his books from Elizabeth until they were inside the building. Thursday morning Jeff Stevens took a terrific ribbing at school.

By Thursday afternoon Port Arbello had begun to accept the reality of the situation. Marilyn Burton found that her cash receipts were dropping back to a normal level; fewer people were stopping by "just to have a little chat" and staying to buy an article or two out of guilt more than need.

Ray Norton was beginning to cite the cars that were habitually overparked on the square; he had decided on Thursday morning that an investigation of a missing child should not be used as an excuse for overlooking less serious matters.

Things were getting back to normal.

Mrs. Goodrich was once more in the laundry room, and when she saw the extra sets of filthy clothes she shook her head ruefully. She thought about separating them from the rest of the laundry and bringing them up again to Miz Rose, then remembered what had happened the last time she had taken such action. She decided it would be wasted effort. So she put the soiled clothing in a tub and added extra soap and bleach to them as they soaked. Two hours later, when they came out of the dryer, they were as clean as new. As clean as Mrs. Goodrich's demanding standards called for.

Outside the Port Arbello school, Elizabeth Conger stood uncertainly, searching the faces of the children as they emerged from the building. For a moment she thought she might have missed the one she was watching for. Then she suddenly smiled and waved. When there was no response from the object of her efforts, she called. "Jimmy," she yelled. A small boy looked up. "Over here," she called, waving once again.

Jimmy Tyler was small for his age, but not by so much that it was a strong disadvantage to him. It was only an inch, and his father had told him that by the time he reached his next birthday he would surely be as big as the other eight-year-olds. But when you are seven, eight seems like a long way off, so Jimmy made up for his slight disadvantage in size by being more agile than anybody else. Particularly in climbing. Jimmy Tyler would climb anything, and one of his favorite sports was climbing higher and faster than any of his friends. Then he could look down on them, and that made him feel good.

He looked up when he heard his name, and saw Elizabeth Conger waving at him. He waved back, then saw that she was waiting for him. He hurried his step.

"Want to walk home with me?" Elizabeth asked him. The Tylers lived even farther out the Point Road than the Congers, and this week, much to Jimmy's surprise and pleasure, Elizabeth had been waiting for him each afternoon, and walking home with him. He liked Elizabeth, even though she was a girl. He supposed that, since she was almost twice as old as he, that didn't count. Anyway, none of his friends had teased him about walking with a girl yet.

"Okay," he said brightly.

They walked silently for most of the way, and it wasn't until they were in front of the Stevenses' house that Jimmy spoke.

"This is where it happened, isn't it?" he said curiously.

"Where what happened?" Elizabeth asked.

"This is where Kathy Burton disappeared," Jimmy said, his young voice expressing no particular reaction to Kathy's disappearance.

"I don't know," Elizabeth said. "I guess it must be."

"Do you suppose they got her?" Jimmy asked, pointing to the ugly old house above the sea.

"No, I don't," Elizabeth said flatly. "Those people aren't like the Barneses were."

"Well," Jimmy said doubtfully. "I still don't like that house."

"I used to think it was haunted," Elizabeth said, teasing him, "when I was your age."

"I don't believe in ghosts," Jimmy said, wondering whether he did or not.

"You don't?" Elizabeth said, but there was a new sound in her voice, as if she was suddenly talking more to herself than to Jimmy. "I didn't used to, but now I'm not so sure."

"Why?" Jimmy said.

Elizabeth seemed to jump back into the here and now. "What?" she asked.

"I said, why?" Jimmy asked again. "Why do you believe in them now if you didn't used to?"

"Oh," Elizabeth said. "I don't know." She suddenly felt uncomfortable, and quickened her pace. Jimmy Tyler almost had to trot to keep up with her.

"Slow down," he said finally. "I can't keep up."

They were near the woods now, and Elizabeth paused, staring into the trees.

"If anything's haunted around here, it's in there," she said.

"In the woods?" Jimmy asked. "Why would anybody want to haunt a woods?"

"Because of something that happened there. Something bad, a long time ago."

"What happened?" Jimmy demanded.

"I don't know," Elizabeth said. "I almost know, but I don't know yet."

"Will you tell me when you find out?" Jimmy's voice rose a notch. "Please, Elizabeth? Will you?"

Elizabeth smiled down at the child beside her and reached down to take his hand.

"I'll tell you what," she said softly. "I'll try to find out what happened this afternoon. Can you come over to my house at four thirty?"

"I don't know," Jimmy said doubtfully. "Why don't you call me? My mother doesn't usually let me go outside that late. It's starting to get dark by then now, and she doesn't like me to be outside in the dark.''

"If you want to know what happened in the woods," Elizabeth said enticingly, "come over at four thirty. It won't be dark till after five. Besides, Sarah wants to play with you."

"How do you know?" Jimmy said truculently. "Sarah can't talk."

"I just know," Elizabeth said. "You be here by four thirty, and I'll tell you about why the woods are haunted."

"All right," Jimmy agreed finally. "But it better be good. I don't believe in ghosts." He started to walk away.

"By the mailbox," Elizabeth called after him. "Meet us by the mailbox." Jimmy Tyler nodded and waved, and Elizabeth watched him continue down the road. She wondered what she'd tell him that afternoon, and why she'd told him the woods were haunted at all. It occurred to her that it was a silly thing to say. Jimmy was right, of course. There was no such thing as ghosts. Well, she'd make up some kind of story, and at least Sarah would have someone besides herself to play with. That would be nice.

At four thirty Elizabeth and Sarah were waiting by the mailbox that stood across the road from the end of the Congers' long driveway. Elizabeth saw the small form of Jimmy Tyler trudging toward them and waved. He returned the wave.

"See?" Elizabeth said to Sarah. "Here he comes, just like I told you."

Sarah stared at Elizabeth, and there was nothing in the huge brown eyes that told Elizabeth that her younger sister had even heard her. But she knew she had. She smiled at Sarah, but Sarah still did not respond. She simply stood, patiently waiting, as Jimmy Tyler approached.

"I can't stay very long," Jimmy said when he caught up with the girls. "My mother told me I have to be in before it gets dark." He glanced at the sun, which was falling steadily toward the horizon behind them.

"Let's go out in the field," Elizabeth suggested. "Let's play tag."

"Does Sarah know how?" Jimmy said, neither knowing nor caring whether the subject of his question could hear or understand him. Elizabeth looked at him reproachfully.

"Of course she does," Elizabeth said. "And you'd better hope you're never It, because she can run a lot faster than you. She can even run faster than me."

"Who is going to be It?" Jimmy wanted to know.

"I will be," Elizabeth said. "I'll give you both till I count to five to get away. One—two—three—" Jimmy Tyler was already bounding across the field. Sarah simply stood there, looking at her sister. Elizabeth stopped counting and put her hands gently on Sarah's shoulders, bending her knees a little so she was on the same level as the smaller girl.

"We're going to play tag," she said softly. "And I'm It. You have to get away from me." Sarah seemed not to hear for a moment; then she bolted suddenly, as if the idea had at last penetrated her mind, taking off across the field in the direction that Jimmy Tyler had taken. "Four—*five!*" Elizabeth called out the last number and set off after the two other children.

She knew she could catch either of them whenever she wanted to, but she didn't try too hard. They seemed to be enjoying dodging away from her, and a couple of times she deliberately let her foot slip when she was only inches from one of them, and listened to Jimmy laugh as she tumbled to the ground. Then, when she sensed Jimmy's interest in the game lagging, she suddenly caught up with him. "You're It," she cried, dashing away from him. He stopped suddenly, as if stunned at the turn the game had taken. Then he grinned happily and set off after Sarah.

Sarah played the game with a determination not to be found in other children. When Jimmy ran toward her, she turned and fled from him at a dead run, her head bent forward, her small legs pumping beneath her steadily. It was quickly obvious that Jimmy didn't stand a chance of catching up with her. Elizabeth worked her way around and headed Sarah off. When she got close to her sister, she called to her, and the sound of her name caused Sarah to look up. She broke her stride and paused for a minute. Elizabeth dashed toward Jimmy as Sarah watched.

"I told you you'd never catch her," she crowed to the boy.

"But I bet I can catch you," Jimmy shouted back, and he shifted his concentration from Sarah to Elizabeth. Chasing Elizabeth was more fun, anyway; she dodged around, and didn't try to keep a straight course. He began trying to outguess her, and didn't notice that as Elizabeth darted to and fro she was working her way closer and closer to the woods. He didn't realize it until she suddenly collapsed in a heap and let him catch her.

"I give up," she laughed, trying to catch her breath. "I can't outrun you."

He fell on the grass beside her, then sat up.

"Look," he said. "We're almost into the woods."

"Yes," Elizabeth said. "I didn't think we were this close. Maybe we'd better go back."

"No," Jimmy said firmly. "I want to hear about the woods. Did you find anything out?"

"There isn't anything," Elizabeth said. "Nothing at all."

"I'll bet there is." Jimmy pouted. "You just don't want to tell me."

"Well," Elizabeth said slowly, gazing off into the trees, "there is a secret place. Only Sarah and I know about it."

Jimmy's eyes widened with interest. "A secret place?" he echoed. "What kind of secret place?"

Elizabeth shook her head. "I don't think you'd like it," she said. "It's kind of scary."

"I'm not afraid," Jimmy declard. "I'm not afraid of anything. Where is it?"

Elizabeth smiled at him. "It isn't really in the woods," she said. "It's on the other side."

A frown knit Jimmy's brow. "There isn't anything on the other side. Only the ocean."

"That's where the secret place is," Elizabeth insisted.

"I want to go," Jimmy demanded, his voice rising a little.

"Shhh," Elizabeth cautioned him. "Don't frighten Sarah."

"Does she frighten easily?" he wanted to know.

"Sometimes. Not always, but sometimes."

Sarah sat quietly with them, and it would have been impossible for an observer to tell whether she was following the conversation. She would look first at one, then at the other, but not always at the child who was speaking. She seemed to be hearing a conversation of her own, a conversation completely separate from the one Elizabeth and Jimmy were having. Jimmy looked at Sarah speculatively.

"Is she afraid of the secret place?" he asked.

"I don't think so," Elizabeth said uncertainly.

"Are you?" Jimmy asked, hearing the hesitation in her voice.

"I don't know," Elizabeth said after a long pause. "I think maybe I should be, but I'm not."

"I want to see it." It was no longer a request, but a demand. Jimmy Tyler set his face in an expression of stubbornness and looked steadily at Elizabeth. "I want to see it," he repeated.

"It's getting late," Elizabeth said carefully.

"I don't care," Jimmy said firmly. "I want to see the secret place, and I want to see it now."

"All right." Elizabeth gave in. "Come on."

They got to their feet, and Elizabeth led them into the woods. She did not move through the woods as swiftly today, or as sure-footedly. Instead, she moved carefully, and several times had to stop and look around, as if she was looking for markings on a trail. At last they came out of the woods and stood on the embankment.

"Where is it?" Jimmy asked. "Is this it?" There was disappointment in his voice. Elizabeth looked around and wasn't sure which way she should go. She felt uncomfortable today, and something inside her was telling her not to go any farther, to turn back before it was too late. But she didn't know what it would be too late for. All she knew was that she seemed to have lost her bearings somehow, and was unsure of which direction to take. She heard a strange buzzing sound in her ears, a buzzing that didn't drown out the sound of the surf, but seemed to make it hazy. She struggled with herself, and was almost on the verge of turning back into the woods when she heard Jimmy's voice.

"Look," he was saying. "Sarah knows the way. Let's follow her."

Elizabeth looked frantically around, and there was Sarah, picking her way slowly down the face of the embankment, moving back and forth from one toehold to the next. Jimmy followed behind her, his agile little body having no difficulty in keeping up. Elizabeth hung back for a moment, then reluctantly followed.

As she moved down the embankment, the confusion lifted from her, and she knew where she was going. Her step grew sure, and she began moving with the suppleness and agility that had always before taken her so swiftly to the large boulder that hid the entrance to the cavern tunnel.

And then they were there. The three of them huddled together in

the shadow of the immense rock, and Jimmy looked at Elizabeth quizzically.

"Is this it?" he said, his voice implying that it was less than he had
expected.

"This is the entrance," Elizabeth whispered. "Come on."

And suddenly she was gone. Jimmy stared at the spot where she had
crouched an instant before, and then he realized that there must be a tunnel.
Eagerly, he followed Elizabeth into the hole in the face of the embankment.

In the pit, Kathy Burton was not immediately aware of the scuffling sounds
from above. She lay on the floor of the cave, the water container clutched in
her hand. She had lost it once in the darkness, and had had to spend what
seemed like an eternity searching for it, ranging back and forth across the
cold damp floor of the cavern, not knowing whether she was searching all
the area or only circling over a small portion of it. At one point in her
gropings in the dark her hand had closed on a strange object, and it had been
a few moments before she realized that it was a bone, a part of the skeleton
that still lay neatly along one wall.

Another time her hand had brushed against the furry surface of the
corpse of the cat, and she had retched for a few moments before being able
to continue her search.

The smell in the cave was getting foul, for the flesh of the cat was
beginning to rot, and Kathy had had to relieve herself several times. Mixed
in was the sour smell of her retching.

She had found the water bottle at last, and had developed the habit of
clutching it whenever she was awake. When exhaustion overcame her and
she fell into a fitful sleep for a few moments, the bottle stayed beside her,
and it was the first thing she groped for when she woke up.

She had stopped hearing the sound of the surf long ago, she wasn't sure
when, and the only sounds that still registered on her mind were the scrap-
ings of what she thought had been rats. It had turned out that they weren't
rats, but tiny crabs, scuttling among the rocks, finding refuge and food
among the small pools of sea water that collected here and there from
seepage. She had not yet tried to eat one of them, but she was afraid she was
getting close to the point where she would have to. She was pondering the
wisdom of this when she suddenly became aware of the sounds from above.

She froze where she was and waited quietly. She wanted to cry out, but
was afraid to; she didn't know what was above her. And then the beam of
the flashlight hit her, for the first time in three days. By now her eyes were
so used to the total blackness that the light was physically painful. She heard
a voice above her, but could not make out the words.

"Look," Jimmy Tyler was saying, his voice kept low by sudden fear.
"There's somebody down there."

"Shh," Elizabeth said. "They'll hear you."

"I'm afraid," Jimmy said, his fear of the cave overcoming his fear of
being thought a coward.

"It's all right," Elizabeth soothed him. "They can't get up here."

And then Kathy Burton opened her eyes, and moved her head into the beam again, looking upward. She tried to speak, and found to her dismay that she couldn't. All that came out was a low gurgling sound.

"It's Kathy," Jimmy said. "We've found Kathy Burton."

"Yes," Elizabeth said slowly. "We have, haven't we." Jimmy Tyler did not notice the strange tone that had crept into her voice, the odd rasping sound.

"What's wrong with her?" he whispered. "Is she all right?" He raised his voice. "Kathy," he called. "It's me. It's Jimmy."

Below, Kathy Burton felt a surge of relief come over her. She was safe. Jimmy Tyler would bring help, and she would get out of here.

"Go get someone," she whispered hoarsely.

"I can't hear you."

She heard his voice echo down. "Help!" she croaked, a little louder.

Jimmy turned to Elizabeth. "We've got to get her out of here," he said. "I'd better go get someone."

"No," Elizabeth whispered. "Let's get her out now. There's a ladder here. Look." She showed him the ladder. "It won't hold me, but I'll bet it would hold you. You can climb down and find out if she's all right. If she is, she can climb back up with you."

Jimmy considered it for a moment. He had never climbed a rope ladder before, but, on the other hand, he was the best climber he knew. And he thought of how neat it would be if he got the credit for saving Kathy Burton after the whole town hadn't been able to find her.

"It's all right," he called down the shaft. "I'm coming down."

And suddenly, in the pit, Kathy realized with terrible clarity what was about to happen. She tried to call out to him, but her voice wouldn't carry through her fear. She watched in horror as the rope ladder appeared in the shaft. She tried to get up, to move to the ladder and grasp the end, but she was too weak. She watched in silence as Jimmy Tyler started climbing slowly down the ladder.

It happened when he was a little more than halfway down: Above him, Elizabeth gathered all her strength, and clutched at the rope ladder with both hands. And then she yanked.

If he'd been expecting it, Jimmy would have been all right. But he wasn't expecting it, and he felt first one hand and then the other come loose from the slippery ropes. He was falling. He tried to break the fall, but it was too late. He landed on his head beside Kathy Burton, and lay still.

The shock of it forced a scream from Kathy's ragged throat, and she found enough strength to make a single lunge at the rope ladder. Helplessly she watched it disappear up the shaft once again. And then she heard the ugly, rasping voice that she had come to associate with Elizabeth.

"Take care of him," Elizabeth said. "Take care of your little brother. He needs you."

The light clicked off, and Kathy listened as the scuffling sounds faded away once more. She began groping in the dark for Jimmy Tyler.

It was almost dusk as Elizabeth and Sarah made their way through the woods, and as they crossed the field night fell darkly over Port Arbello.

## EIGHTEEN

THE NEXT DAY THERE WAS NO SCHOOL IN Port Arbello. The school had opened as usual, but by nine o'clock it had become obvious that the teachers would be sitting in all but empty classrooms. The few children who showed up were dismissed. But they refused to go. All had explicit instructions from their parents not to leave the school. They would be picked up, even the ones who lived only a block or two away.

The panic had built all through the night, from the moment Jimmy Tyler's mother had called Ray Norton to advise him that her son had not come home that afternoon. Well, actually, he had come home, she admitted under questioning, but he had gone right out again to play. And then he had not come home.

No, she did not know where he had gone.

Yes, she supposed she should have found out, but she had assumed that he was going to stay near their house; after all, there weren't any children his own age to play with. In fact, the only children close enough to be convenient were the Conger children.

Ray Norton's forehead creased into a frown when Lenore Tyler mentioned the Conger children. That made three cases in the area, though he was still inclined to doubt Anne Forager's strange story. He wondered what time Marty Forager would show up to begin abusing him about his handling of things in general and the case of his daughter in particular.

When he finished talking to Lenore Tyler, Norton started to call Jack Conger, then thought better of it. He decided to wait awhile and see what developed. He turned his attention instead to another problem, a problem that he thought could be potentially worse than the one of the missing children. The children's disappearance was a fact. There was nothing he could do about it for the moment, except try to find out where they had gone.

The reaction of Port Arbello to the disappearances was something else again. This, Ray Norton thought, was predictable, and he didn't like what he saw coming.

Port Arbello was not used to dealing with crime. Port Arbellans, in fact, were part of that great mass of Americans who knows that crime exists but never feels it personally. They lived in an atmosphere of trust; they had no reason not to. For most of his career, Ray Norton's time had been taken up with citing speeders (most of them tourists) and keeping the peace at the tavern. There had been an occasional suicide in Port Arbello, but that was not unusual for New England, particularly during the winter. The crimes that plagued the country, the urban crimes that make urban people barricade their doors, were essentially unknown in Port Arbello. There had never been so much as a mugging, let alone a murder, at least not in the last hundred years. The town was so innocent, indeed, that it was only in the last few days that the people had begun installing new locks on their doors. Until now they had felt perfectly comfortable with the old locks, locks that could be opened with almost any key that came to hand.

But now they were frightened, and Ray Norton found it worrisome. Particularly with a man like Marty Forager doing his best to fan the fires. Ordinarily nobody paid much attention to Marty Forager, but now he had something to use as leverage, and Ray Norton was convinced that he would use it to his best advantage. Ray was very much aware that Martin Forager resented the position he held in Port Arbello. Not that he could blame him; who, after all, would want to be known as "poor Marty Forager"—a phrase always accompanied by a sorrowful shake of the head and words of pity for his wife and daughter.

He was pondering the situation, trying to figure out the best way to defuse it, when his main worry appeared in his office.

Marty Forager loomed over him, and Ray Norton could see immediately that he had already been drinking.

"I came to tell you," Forager said, his voice surly. "There's going to be a meeting tonight. A town meeting. Since you don't seem to be able to do anything about what's going on in this town, we're going to see if we can come up with some ideas of our own." He stared down at the chief of police as if waiting to be challenged. Ray Norton looked up at him.

"Am I invited?" he asked mildly. The question apparently took Forager by surprise, as he stepped back a pace.

"No way we can keep you from coming," he said reluctantly. "But you ain't running it," he added.

"I would assume that Billy Meyers will be running it," Ray said quietly. "He's still president of the council, isn't he?"

"This's a citizens' meeting," Forager sneered. "Not a council meeting. Nobody's gonna run it."

"I see," Norton said, standing up. He was pleased to note that Forager moved back another pace. "In that case, you can count on me showing up. I always wanted to see a meeting nobody was running. It ought to be fascinating."

Marty Forager glowered at him, and Ray thought he was going to say something more. Instead, Forager simply wheeled and stalked silently out of the police station. Norton watched him go and decided it was time to call Jack Conger.

"Jack," he said when the editor was on the phone. "I'm afraid we've got trouble."

"Not another child," Jack said. "I don't think the town could stand it."

"No," Norton replied. "It's not that. It's the town I'm worried about now. Martin Forager was just here again." Quickly he filled Jack in on what Forager had told him, and made sure that the editor understood Forager's manner as well as his words.

"In other words," Jack said after he'd heard Ray Norton out, "you see a lynch mob developing."

"I wouldn't say that," Ray said slowly.

"Not for publication, anyway," Jack gibed at him. "But that *is* what you're saying, isn't it?"

"Well, I don't think it's gone that far yet," the police chief began.

"—But that's the direction it's taking," Jack Conger finished for him. "Any ideas about who Forager wants to string up?"

"I think I'm at the top of the list," Ray replied, trying to put some banter into his voice. Then he became more serious once again. "Frankly, it's you I'm worried about."

"Me?" Jack said, his voice reflecting a disbelief he did not feel. "Why me?"

"Well, we might as well face the facts," Norton said. "All the things that have been happening have been happening near your place."

"That's not quite true," Jack corrected him. "Anne Forager says she was near our place, but no one knows for sure. Kathy Burton was last seen near our place, but it would be more exact to say she was in front of the Stevenses' house. After all, Elizabeth said they parted at the woods, and that's right at the property line. And as for Jimmy Tyler, we don't know anything about him at all. The Tylers live a good quarter of a mile farther out than we do. So why do you think they'll focus on me?"

"It's natural," the policeman said smoothly. "Everything's happening on Conger's Point Road. So who comes to mind when you think of Conger's Point Road? Conger, of course."

"I see," Jack said slowly. "What do you think I should do?"

"I think you should come to that meeting tonight, and I think you should come to it with me."

"After what you told Marty Forager about us?" Jack said, still managing to cling to a shred of humor, however black. Ray Norton chuckled.

"Well, if we have the name, as the man says, we might as well have the game. Seriously, though," he went on. "I think you'd better plan to be at that meeting tonight, if for no other reason than not to be conspicuous by your absence."

"Well," Jack said doubtfully, "I'm not sure I go along with your reasoning, but I'll be there, if not as a private citizen then as the editor of the *Courier*. If they all know they're going to be quoted, it might help to keep the lid on things."

"Maybe with some of them, but not with Marty Forager. I think he's beginning to think of this whole mess as a one-man crusade."

"Yes," Jack mused. "He is that sort of person, isn't he? Do you want to ride in to the meeting with me?"

"Fine," Ray agreed. "Pick me up a little before seven. I'll find out where it's going to be, and either get back to you or tell you when I see you." The conversation ended.

* * *

"Is there anything I ought to do?" Rose asked.

They were in the small study. Rose had listened in silence as Jack told her of the meeting he would have to attend, and the direction that Ray Norton was afraid it was going to take.

"Maybe I ought to go with you," Rose continued.

"No," Jack said. "I don't see any reason for that. I think you ought to stay here with the girls."

Rose looked at him, trying to fathom his mood. He seemed worried about something, but she wasn't sure what it was.

"Surely you don't think anything's going to happen to them, do you?" she asked.

Jack shrugged. "I don't see how. Not as long as you're here and they stay in the house," he said. "But I'd feel more comfortable if I knew what was going on."

"Jimmy Tyler," Rose said slowly. "That's odd."

"What's odd?"

"That he should disappear. I mean, suppose Anne Forager's story is true, and frankly I'm beginning to think it is. Well, then, at least it makes some kind of sense for Kathy Burton to have disappeared. But Jimmy Tyler?"

"I don't see what you're getting at," Jack said, although he was afraid he did.

"Well, let's face it," Rose said. "There haven't been any kidnap notes or ransom demands, have there? So what does that leave? A nut. Some crazy person who gets turned on to children. Little girls. Except that now Jimmy Tyler is missing, too, and he doesn't fit the pattern."

"If there is a pattern," Jack said reluctantly.

"Isn't there?" Rose was looking into his eyes. "Don't you see a pattern?"

"Yes," Jack said finally, "I suppose I do." He hoped that what was hanging between them, unsaid, would remain unsaid. "And it doesn't help matters that it's all happening out here, does it?"

"No," Rose said quietly. "It doesn't." She was about to say more when Elizabeth appeared at the door. Rose wondered how long she had been standing there.

"Mother?" Elizabeth said uncertainly.

"Come in, darling," Rose said, glad of the interruption.

"Is it true that Jimmy Tyler's gone too?"

Rose glanced at Jack, unsure of how to handle the question, and saw that she was on her own. She could see no point in denying it.

"Yes, he's been missing since yesterday afternoon."

"What time?" Elizabeth wanted to know.

"Why, I don't know," Rose responded, puzzled. "I don't think any-body knows, really. But no one's seen him since after school."

"I walked home with him yesterday," Elizabeth said slowly, as if trying to remember something.

"You did?" Rose said. "You didn't tell me that."

"I guess it didn't seem important," Elizabeth said, and Rose got the definite impression that her daughter was thinking about something else.

"Is something bothering you, dear?" she asked the girl.

"I—I don't know," Elizabeth said hesitantly. "It's just that I'm not sure—" She broke off, and Rose prompted her again.

"Sure of what, Elizabeth?"

Elizabeth shifted her weight from one foot to the other, uncomfortable. Finally she sat down and looked at her mother, a worried expression on her face.

"I don't know, really," Elizabeth said. "But I thought I saw Jimmy yesterday afternoon."

"You mean after you walked home with him?" Jack asked.

Elizabeth nodded. "But I'm not sure it was him," she said, as if it was somehow important that whoever she had seen might *not* be Jimmy Tyler.

"Where did you think you saw him?" Jack pressed.

"In the field," Elizabeth blurted. "Playing with Sarah."

"But you couldn't see them clearly?" Rose asked, knowing what was coming.

"They were too far away," Elizabeth said miserably. "They were almost to the woods."

"I see." Rose sighed. She avoided looking at Jack, afraid to see if he was feeling the same thing she was feeling. Instead, she spoke again to her daughter.

"They were by themselves?" she asked, and hoped that Elizabeth wouldn't hear the implied criticism. After all, Rose reflected, she *isn't* Sarah's nurse. She wished she could have retracted the question, but didn't see how she could.

"Yes," Elizabeth said apologetically. "I was in my room. I wouldn't have seen them at all if I hadn't looked out the window. I thought Sarah was in her room. I—I'm sorry."

"It's all right," Rose heard Jack say. "You aren't responsible for Sarah." Rose wished she'd said it. "Why don't you go upstairs, honey, so your mother and I can talk."

Elizabeth left the room. Rose had the impression that she left only because she had been told to, that she wanted to stay. But there was nothing more to be said. She looked at her husband, but he was avoiding her gaze. The silence stretched until Rose could bear it no more.

"I don't know what to think," she said at last. "I'm not sure I want to think at all."

"Maybe we'd better call Dr. Belter," Jack said.

"No," Rose said, too sharply. "I mean, call him about what?"

Now it was Jack's turn to sigh tiredly. "Don't you think it's time for us to face up to it?" he said.

"I don't know what you're talking about."

Jack smiled ruefully. "What do you suppose would happen to us if we both decided to bury our heads in the sand at the same time?"

"All right," Rose said after a short silence, her voice stronger. "You're right, of course. I suppose we're going to have to accept the possibility that Sarah is getting dangerous. Is that it?''

"That's it," Jack said. "Of course, it may easily not be true, but I don't think we can sit here and do nothing. Not considering what's been happening."

"Let's talk to her," Rose said desperately. "Let's at least try to talk to her before we do anything."

"What good'll it do?"

"I don't know," Rose said. "But we can at least try, can't we?" Her eyes were beseeching him, and finally Jack stood up.

"All right," he said. "Shall I go get her?"

"No!" Rose said immediately. "I'll get her. You wait here."

While she was gone, Jack mixed himself a drink. The hell with the meeting, he thought.

A few minutes later Rose was back, leading Sarah by the hand. She followed along docilely, almost as if she were unaware of what was happening. She wasn't resisting, but she didn't seem to be actively involved, either.

Rose sat the child down, then knelt beside her. Sarah sat quietly on the sofa, staring vacantly into the air in front of her face. After a minute or two her right hand went up and her thumb disappeared into her mouth.

"Sarah," Rose said quietly.

Sarah continued to sit, sucking her thumb, apparently not hearing her mother's voice.

"Sarah," Rose repeated, a little louder. "Do you hear me?"

Sarah's head turned, and she peered blankly at her mother. Rose made a distinct effort not to turn away.

"Sarah!" Jack said sharply. The child's head swung around, and her gaze fell on her father. Jack met her eyes for a moment, but he was not as strong as Rose. He broke the eye contact, and sipped his drink.

"Sarah," Rose said again. "Were you playing with Jimmy Tyler yesterday?"

No response.

"We need to know," Rose said. "Can't you at least nod your head? Were you playing with Jimmy Tyler yesterday? Jimmy Tyler!" she repeated, more loudly, as if her child were hard of hearing. Her frustration rose as her daughter continued to stare vacantly into her eyes. Her hand moved to her forehead and brushed back a nonexistent stray hair.

"Sarah," she began again. "We know you were playing with Jimmy Tyler in the field yesterday. It's all right. All we need to know is if you went into the woods. Did you go into the woods?"

No response.

"For God's sake, Sarah," Rose pleaded. "It's terribly important. Please, please, try to understand. He went home, didn't he? Jimmy Tyler went home?"

Sarah continued to stare at her mother. The silence hung heavy in the room. And then, very slowly, Sarah shook her head.

* * *

The meeting in town was chaotic, and Jack was sorry he had agreed to take Carl Stevens with him. Jack was embarrased for the town, and he knew he had not been good company. All he could see, first on the way to Ray Norton's house and then as they drove into Port Arbello, was a vision of Sarah staring darkly into the distance and slowly shaking her head. Over and over again Jack tried to tell himself that it was a good sign, that Sarah finally had responded to something. But over and over he would remember what she had responded to, the question Rose had asked, and despair would close in on him again. Jimmy Tyler had not gone home. Sarah knew that Jimmy Tyler had not gone home. The time was getting very near when all of them—he and his wife and Elizabeth and Mrs. Goodrich—were going to have to accept the fact that Sarah would no longer be with them. But not yet.

The faces of the people of Port Arbello loomed around him, and Jack found himself unable to meet some of the eyes that he imagined were staring at him accusingly. Marilyn Burton greeted him warmly, but he was sure he heard a false note in her voice. Lenore Tyler smiled and waved, and Jack wondered why she hadn't spoken. Had she guessed?

Although Marty Forager had claimed that there was to be no chairman at the meeting, he did his best to run it his way.

"There's something going on in this town," he shouted, "and it's going on out at Conger's Point."

Suddenly all the eyes in the packed auditorium were turned on Jack, and he realized he would have to say something.

He stood up and faced the town. Suddenly they were no longer his old friends; suddenly he was no longer Mr. Conger of Conger's Point Road. Suddenly Conger's Point was something to be afraid of, not respected. And he was the man who lived there.

"I don't know what's going on," he began, and a murmur ran through the crowd, a murmur that Jack was afraid could turn the crowd into a mob. He'd have to do better than that. He listened to his own words and wondered where they came from.

"My daughter saw Jimmy Tyler yesterday afternoon."

"How did she tell you that? Sign language?" a mocking voice shouted from the rear. Jack flinched and fought to contain his sudden rage.

"Elizabeth saw Jimmy Tyler," he heard himself say. "Down by the old quarry. She talked to him. She told him to go home. She told him it was a dangerous place to play, but he didn't pay any attention to her. She told me that when she came home, just before dark, he was still there. That's all."

Jack sat down, and felt the eyes of the town staring curiously at him. He wondered if they knew he was lying, and tried to convince himself that he had lied only because of the way the meeting was going, because of the feeling he had gotten of a mob on the verge of rampage. But he knew that that wasn't true either. He had lied to protect his daughter. His baby daughter.

Then they formed a posse. They called it a search party, but Jack knew it was a posse. Ray Norton tried to stop them, but there was nothing he could do. Perhaps if Marilyn Burton hadn't been there, or Lenore and Bill Tyler had stayed away, Norton could have controlled the situation. But the fact was that they were there, and their very presence, combined with the rantings of Martin Forager, aroused in them the desire to *do* something. Anything.

And so they went out to the old quarry. Ray Norton made sure that he was in the lead, and found a spot to park his car that effectively blocked the road. If there was anything there, Ray Norton wanted to make sure it stayed there. He didn't want any evidence obliterated by fifteen cars driving over the soft ground. Norton organized them as best he could, and the men of Port Arbello spread out to search the area. It was ironic that the only person to find anything was Martin Forager.

What he found was tire tracks. They were fresh, and they were of an odd sort. As the men gathered to examine them, Jack Conger smiled to himself. The tracks would strengthen his story.

They were preparing to leave the quarry when Ray Norton drew him aside.

"Well," Jack said when they were sitting alone in Norton's car, "at least you have something to work on."

"Yeah," Norton said, but he didn't look too hopeful. "I just wonder what those tracks will lead to. If you ask me, we'll never even find the car that left them. But that's not what I wanted to talk to you about."

Jack looked at the police chief questioningly. Norton looked uncomfortable, as if he weren't quite sure how to begin. He decided that the best way was the most direct way.

"Look, Jack," he said. "I know what I'm about to say sounds silly, but I have to say it anyway. Or, rather, ask. How much do you know about the old legend about your family?"

Jack tried to smile, but underneath the smile he felt chilled.

"I know there is one," he said carefully. "What's it got to do with all of this?"

"Nothing, probably," Norton said. "If I remember right, there was supposed to be a cave involved, wasn't there?"

Jack nodded. "Yup. The old lady claimed it was somewhere in the embankment. But of course she never claimed to have seen it, except in her so-called vision."

"Well, what about it?"

Jack looked at the policeman blankly. "What about it?"

"Does it exist?"

"The cave?" Jack said incredulously. "Are you serious? My God, Ray, the cave was never anything but the figment of an old lady's imagination. If someone told the same story today they'd say she was senile. And they'd be right."

"But didn't anyone ever look for it?" the police chief persisted.

"Sure," Jack said. "My grandfather did. And it cost him his life. That embankment is a dangerous place. It's steep and slippery and treacherous. Fortunately, we've had the legend to keep all the kids away from the place."

"And none of them ever went to find out if there was anything there?"

Norton said curiously. "You know, when I was a kid the one thing I always wanted to do was go look for that cave. But I couldn't."

"Why not?" Jack asked. "The embankment was there."

"Ah, but it was on the Congers' property. Don't forget, when I was a kid your family was almost royalty around here. We may have wandered all over everybody else's land, but not the Congers'."

Jack chuckled, remembering. It had almost been like that when he had been a boy. "Well, let me set your mind at rest," he said. "Of course I went to look for the cave. And I imagine my father did too. But I didn't find it, probably because it simply isn't there. If it was, I'd have found it."

"Okay," Norton said. "I was almost hoping you'd never looked, and that we could turn the damned thing up. I can't turn the whole town out searching for it, not when all I have to go on is an old tale of a senile woman's visions. We'd probably lose three men in the looking. So I guess it's back to the quarry. I hope you won't have any objections to my sending out a crew to drag it?"

"Of course not," Jack said. "Any time you want. But, God, I hope they don't find anything."

"So do I," Norton agreed. "So do I."

An hour later Jack Conger was home. He went upstairs to say good night to his daughters, and it seemed to Rose that he was staying much too long with Elizabeth. She was on the verge of going up to see what was keeping him when he came down. When he entered the study he looked tired but he was smiling.

"Well," he said, fixing himself a nightcap. "If nothing else, at least I've bought us some time."

## NINETEEN

NEITHER ROSE NOR JACK SLEPT THAT night, but they were quiet, each of them with their own thoughts, each of them wanting to postpone the time when they would have to make decisions.

They tried to avoid their thoughts as they lay in bed, side by side, separated by their fears. Jack kept repeating the story he had told to the town meeting, over and over, until even he began to believe it. Before the blackness of night began fading into a gray dawn, he had almost convinced himself that Sarah had not been playing in the field with Jimmy Tyler; that instead Elizabeth had seen Jimmy at the quarry and instructed him to go home. But with the dawn the truth came back at him, and reality reentered his life along with the sun.

As if by mutual consent, they began talking about it at breakfast. They had risen early, since neither of them had slept, and they sat in the silent house, sipping coffee and trying to figure out what they should do.

"I suppose we should call Dr. Belter," Rose said.

"No. Not yet." Jack knew she was right, but somehow calling Dr. Belter symbolized defeat for him, and he wasn't ready for that yet. "I mean, what could we tell him?" he went on, and he knew he was rationalizing as much for himself as for his wife. "Because Elizabeth saw Sarah and Jimmy playing together is no reason for us to jump to conclusions."

"No," Rose agreed. "It isn't. But it seems to me we have a duty that goes beyond our own family. If Sarah has anything to do with this, even if she only has something to do with Jimmy Tyler, I think we have to tell *somebody*. And Dr. Belter seems the logical person to tell. And, of course, there's Sarah to be considered."

"Sarah?"

Rose wore a pained expression, and Jack knew it was difficult for her to say the things she was saying. He wondered if it was as difficult for her to speak as it was for him to listen.

"What about her?" Rose said. "If she is doing something, and I'm not saying she is, she isn't responsible. She needs help. How can she get the help she needs if we aren't even willing to talk about what she's doing?" She stopped talking for a moment and stirred her coffee fitfully. "Maybe we ought to search the woods," she said. "If something did happen, it must have happened there. Unless they got as far as the embankment." She smiled, but there was no warmth in it. "At least we know there's no cave, so we don't have to look for that."

"I don't know whether there's a cave or not," Jack said quietly. Rose looked at him sharply.

"What do you mean? Didn't you tell Ray Norton last night that you'd spent most of your boyhood looking for it and it doesn't exist?"

"Yes," Jack said uncomfortably. "That's what I told him. But it wasn't any truer than anything else I told anybody last night."

Rose set her cup down and stared at him. "You mean you lied about the cave, too?" she said incredulously.

He nodded miserably, and it struck Rose that he looked very much like a small child caught with his hands in the cookie jar. For some reason it made her want to laugh, though she felt anything but mirthful.

"Why on earth did you lie about that?" she asked him when her laughter died. Her voice was mocking, and it made Jack flush.

"Because I didn't want them poking around the woods and the embankment, that's why," he said vehemently.

"But they'll poke around the woods anyway," Rose said, taking on the voice of a teacher with a recalcitrant pupil. "Besides, they've already searched the woods. They did that when they were looking for Kathy Burton."

Then a thought came to her, and she searched Jack's face carefully, looking for the answer to the question that had come into her mind. It was there, in his hangdog expression, in the defensive light that glimmered in his eye.

"You believe it, don't you?" she said. "You believe in the legend. Is there a cave there?"

"I don't know," Jack said softly. "I never looked."

"Why not?" Rose demanded. "Are you going to sit there and tell me that, with a wonderful legend like that, you never once, you and your friends, never once went looking for that cave?" Her eyes widened in astonishment as he shook his head. "Well, for heaven's sake. That legend actually worked." Now her laughter came in gales, partly at the idea of her husband putting enough faith in the legend never to investigate it, but mostly as a simple release. A release of the stress she had been carrying. It was not pleasant laughter, and it did not make the house ring. Instead it echoed dully through the room, and then came back to hang heavily between them.

"I think," Rose said finally, "that it's time we had a look at that embankment. If there is a cave there, I think we should know about it. I think the whole town should know about it."

"You look if you want," Jack said softly. "Frankly, I'd rather not know."

Jack Conger arrived in his office early that morning, before any of the staff had gotten in. When they arrived, at eight thirty, they found his office door closed and the red light above it lit. All of the staff except Sylvia Bannister respected the warning light.

Sylvia ignored it.

She walked into the inner office without knocking. Jack looked up but did not speak.

"Bad night?" Sylvia said sympathetically.

Jack put down his pencil and leaned back, rubbing his eyes. "It depends on what you call a bad night. If you call lying to the whole town, lying to the chief of police, asking your oldest daughter to lie too, getting no sleep, and then topping the whole thing off with making yourself look like a fool to your wife—if you call that a bad night, then I suppose I had a bad night. Otherwise it was fine."

Sylvia sat down. "Do you want to tell me about it?"

"No," Jack said irritably. "I don't. I want to be left alone, to try to get my head straightened out. If that's all right with you."

He was already staring again at the piece of paper on the desk in front of him, and chewing on the end of the pencil, so he couldn't see the look of hurt that came into Sylvia's face. She stood up and smoothed her skirt.

"Of course," she said coolly. "I'm sorry I bothered you." She left the room, and when Jack heard the door close he looked up again, looked helplessly at the door through which the woman had just passed. He wanted to call her back. He didn't.

He worked for an hour, writing and rewriting, and when he was finished he read what he had written. Then he crumpled the pages and threw them into the wastebasket.

It had been an editorial, and when he had finished writing it and reread it he realized that it could as easily have been written by Martin Forager as himself. He had attacked the police chief, even suggested that perhaps it was time Ray Norton was replaced. He had demanded some answers about what had really happened to Anne Forager. And he had suggested, but in terms that denied their own content, that it was time for the citizens of Port Arbello to form a lynch mob. He had not, of course, used that term. He had called instead for a "protective association," but it amounted to the same thing. In short, he had written a hypocritical, self-serving editorial, designed to undermine the police chief and at the same time entrench Jack Conger as a concerned citizen. Jack Conger realized that he was trying to throw Ray Norton off a trail that Ray Norton didn't even know he was on. A trail that could lead only to Sarah, who couldn't possibly be considered responsible for anything she might have done. He retrieved the editorial from the waste-basket and read it once more. He decided, objectively, that the editorial had served its purpose very well.

He burned it in the wastebasket and picked up the telephone. It was time to talk to Charles Belter.

Dr. Charles Belter listened carefully to everything Jack Conger told him. It took more than three hours for Jack to put it all together for the doctor, and several times he had to backtrack, going over a point several times, filling in background or amplifying. Dr. Belter listened patiently, interrupting as little as possible; he felt it was important to listen not only to what was being said but also to how it was being said, and in what order. The mind tended to attach priorities to things, Dr. Belter knew, and often much could be learned not from the points being made, but from the order of the points and their relative importance to the person making them. When Jack finished Dr. Belter leaned back, his hands folded comfortably over his ample stomach.

"So you don't know whether or not there really is, or was, a cave?" he said.

"Was?" Jack repeated. "What do you mean, was?"

"Only that there might have once been a cave, but that it got filled in, or collapsed. It isn't important. Just a mind that deals with details functioning in its usual picky way. Forget I said it. The important thing is that you don't know whether or not the cave is real."

"No, I don't. And I don't see how it matters."

Dr. Belter lit a cigarette and shook the match out before he spoke again. "I don't know," he said at length. "Does it matter?"

"What are you getting at?" Jack asked suspiciously.

Dr. Belter smiled at him. "Well, it just seems to me that you've attached a lot of importance to that cave. After all, you did go so far as to tell the chief of police that it definitely doesn't exist. That tells me a couple of things."

"Such as?" Now there was definite hostility in Jack's voice.

"First, that you think there is a cave. If you were really sure that there was no cave, and that the legend was only a legend, why would you want to try to talk Norton out of searching for it? After all, if you're sure it doesn't exist, then you don't have to worry about it being found, do you?"

"What's the second thing?" Jack asked, without conceding the first.

"Why, that's easy," Dr. Belter said with a grin, leaning forward over his desk. "You're not only sure there's a cave, but you're afraid of what might be found in it."

"That's the stupidest thing I've heard of in a long time," Jack said angrily.

"Is it?"

Jack knew he was reacting more out of fear than out of anger, and he wondered why. What was he afraid of? Then he decided he wasn't afraid *of*; he was afraid *for*. He was afraid for Sarah.

"It's Sarah I'm worried about," he said nervously.

"Are you?" the doctor asked, and Jack thought he heard a mocking tone in his voice. "Let's talk about that for a minute then. Exactly what are you worried about? Are you worried that Sarah has been terrorizing little children, then shoving them into a cave? That's what I would call one of the stupidest things *I've* ever heard of. For one thing, take a look at Sarah's size. She's not big, is she? In fact, she's small for her age, and a bit underdeveloped." He noticed the look of anger that was coloring Jack's face and held up a hand. "Oh, come on. I didn't say she was abnormally small or underdeveloped. Physically she's well within the normal range. But on the small side of the average, rather than the large side. Now tell me, do you really think a girl the size of Sarah could do much to a girl the size of Kathy Burton? Kathy Burton, from what I've found out, was big for her age, and somewhat athletic. So, considering that she's also a year older than Sarah, I don't see much chance that Sarah could have done anything to her. Anne Forager and Jimmy Tyler I don't know about. They're both younger than Sarah, and a bit smaller. But Kathy Burton wouldn't have taken any guff off of Sarah."

"I understand that children with . . . mental problems . . . sometimes show remarkable strength," Jack said.

"You've been watching too many movies. Oh, sure, it can happen, but it's rare, and it only happens for short periods of time, under what we call hysterical conditions. The same things happen with so-called normal people. The mother who lifts the car off her crushed child? Those things can happen. Under severe stress, the body simply shoots itself up with adrenalin, and you have a surge of strength. But it's rare, and it's for very brief periods of time. Seconds, not the time it would take to do what you're suggesting."

"I'm not suggesting a thing," Jack said coldly.

"Aren't you? I think you are. I listen carefully, you know. It's my profession. And here's what I heard you saying. Not directly, mind you, but by implication. And all because Elizabeth said she saw Sarah playing with someone who looked like Jimmy Tyler.

"You see Sarah dragging children into the woods, beating them, and then taking them and dumping them in a cave somewhere. Am I right?"

Jack shifted in his chair with discomfort. The doctor had stated his thoughts too closely. "Go on," he said, not at all sure he wanted to hear any more, but feeling that he must.

"Well, if you don't mind my saying so, that theory is ridiculous. Not only would Sarah be totally unable to sustain the kind of abnormal strength that would be necessary for such a feat, but even if she could, can you imagine the difficulties in hauling someone your own size down the face of that embankment? You've said yourself that it's tricky for an adult by himself. It sounds like it would be impossible for a child carrying another child of almost the same size."

Jack thought it over and felt an odd sense of relief. The doctor was right; it didn't make sense. He and Rose had been overreacting. And why not? The last days had not been easy for anyone in Port Arbello, and Rose and Jack Conger were no exception. He felt a grin come over his face, and it felt good.

"Well, that's done with, anyway," he said. "Have you got any other ideas?"

Dr. Belter leaned forward, and his expression took on a seriousness that made the grin fade from Jack's face.

"Yes, I have. Mr. Conger, have you ever suffered from blackouts? Recently?"

It took nearly a full minute for the implications of what the doctor had just said to sink into Jack's mind. When it finally did and he grasped what Dr. Belter was suggesting, he had to fight to control himself. Trembling, he got to his feet.

"Only once, Doctor," he said coldly. "And we both know what happened that time. Since then, never." He left the doctor's office without another word, and without waiting for Charles Belter to respond.

"How can you be sure?" the doctor said to the closed door and the empty room. "How can you be sure you never have blackouts?"

It was noon when Jack returned to the paper. He closed the door behind him, and a moment later the red light above his door flashed on. The staff of the *Courier* looked at one another curiously, but none of them was willing to speculate on what was going on. Instead, they all glanced at the clock and began drifting away to lunch. When the office was all but empty, Sylvia Bannister looked at the closed door. She hesitated a minute, then punched the button on the intercom on her desk.

"I'm going to lunch now," she said. She waited for an answer, and when none came began putting on her coat. She was ready to leave the office when the intercom suddenly came alive.

"Can you spare me a minute?" Jack's voice crackled through the wire.

Sylvia took off her coat and rehung it on the hook. Then she smoothed her skirt and entered the inner office.

She had been prepared to be cool to her employer, but the expression on his face changed her mind.

"You're not all right, are you," she said, making it more a statement than a question. Jack looked up at her, and she was sure she saw tears trying to make their way out of his eyes.

"I just got back from talking to Dr. Belter."

"I wondered where you went," Sylvia said, lowering herself into the chair opposite him. "Why did you go see him?"

"I'm not sure, really. I thought I was going to talk about Sarah. About what to do about her. But he didn't want to talk about Sarah."

"Oh?"

"He wanted to talk about me."

Sylvia smiled at him reassuringly. "Is that such a bad idea? We can all stand to talk about ourselves now and then. And you haven't been having it too easy lately, have you?"

"That wasn't what he wanted to talk about. He seems to think that I might be the one who's after the kids."

Sylvia stared at him in complete disbelief. "You? You must have misunderstood him."

"No. I didn't misunderstand him. He wanted to know if I've been having any blackouts lately."

"That is the most disgusting thing I've heard in a long time," Sylvia said, her voice reflecting the sickness she felt in her stomach. "That happened a year ago. Not last week, not last month. A year ago. Thirteen months, actually. Does he seriously think it would happen again now? Three times? Besides, we know where you were when the children disappeared."

"On the day Kathy Burton disappeared I was in his office, as a matter of fact," Jack said, smiling thinly.

"Then what's he trying to do?" Sylvia demanded.

"I don't know," Jack said. "But, God, it scares me. If that's what he think, what will the rest of the town think?"

"I haven't any idea, but I know what I think. I think it's insane, and I think Dr. Belter needs to have his own head examined."

She stood up. "And I think you and I should go have some lunch. At my place."

Jack looked at her with no comprehension.

"Jack," Sylvia said softly, "don't you think you've absorbed enough? Take some time off for yourself. Even if it's only a few hours with me. You need it. Really, you do. And so do I."

They drove in silence to Sylvia's house, and talked quietly while she fixed their lunch. They avoided the sensitive subjects, but it wasn't the studied avoidance that created a distance between Jack and Rose when they were consciously staying away from something. Instead, it was an easy avoidance, a mutual agreement to talk about things that made them comfortable, and they grew closer.

They didn't go back to the *Courier* that afternoon. They started to, but they changed their minds. Instead, they spent the afternoon in Sylvia Bannister's bed, and it was good. It was good for both of them. For the first time in a year, Jack Conger lay comfortably in a woman's arms. Sylvia Bannister was content. And, for the moment, so was he.

The two children in the cave clung together, as they had for almost thirty-six hours. Jimmy Tyler had been unconscious for the first hour he was in the cave, and for a long time Kathy had been sure he would die. But he hadn't died, and eventually he had awakened, terrified in the darkness. Kathy had tried to soothe him and explain to him what had happened. Her voice had been weak, and she had had several periods of incoherence, but the very sound of a human voice in the blackness had seemed to soothe Jimmy, and eventually he had calmed down. And then they had waited.

They stayed close together, never moving far enough apart so that they couldn't touch each other, and when they slept, they slept in each other's arms.

Jimmy was terrified by the strange scrabbling sounds, but when Kathy told him what they were he tried to catch one of the tiny crabs. Eventually he succeeded, and popped one into his mouth. It was bitter, and he promptly spat it out, retching. Kathy gave him a mouthful of the water to wash the taste away.

They talked now and then, Jimmy mostly, since Kathy's voice was weak and her throat hurt her badly now, but for the most part they simply sat silently, holding hands, wondering how long they had been trapped in the cavern and how long they would be kept there.

It was during one of the times that Jimmy was talking that Kathy suddenly squeezed his hand.

"Shhh!" she hissed. He felt her hand grasp his even more tightly, and stopped talking. Above him Jimmy heard an odd scuffling sound. As the scuffling grew louder, Kathy's hand continued to tighten on his, until it began to hurt. He sensed that the sounds from above were frightening Kathy, and the fear was contagious. He forgot the pain in his hand as he strained to hear what was happening overhead.

"Put your hand over your eyes," Kathy whispered to him. He didn't know why he should, but he followed her instructions. A moment later he saw a dim red glow through the flesh of his fingers. He opened his fingers slightly and saw a beam of light shining down from the shaft above. Squinting, he removed his hand from his eyes, then opened his eyes completely as they grew used to the light. Kathy still sat huddled next to him, one hand clutching his, the other clasped tightly over her eyes.

"It's all right," he whispered. "If you squint the light doesn't hurt your eyes."

Tentatively, Kathy took her hand from her face, and began letting her eyes adjust to the unaccustomed light. The light held steady, and there was silence from above. Curiously, the two children looked at each other. While they were searching each other's faces, they heard a plopping sound. Jimmy started to speak, but Kathy clapped a hand over his mouth. Both of them saw the small package, wrapped in white paper, that lay in the middle of the pool of light. Jimmy struggled free from Kathy's grip and scurried into the light to snatch it, like a rat snatching a piece of cheese from the middle of a floor, then darting back to its hole.

He unwrapped the package. "Look," he said. "Sandwiches."

Kathy looked at the food, and her hunger overcame her fear. She grabbed at one of the sandwiches and shoved it into her mouth. Jimmy was gobbling at the food with the hunger of a small child not used to going without.

The nausea hit both of them simultaneously, and suddenly both of them were lying on the floor of the cave, retching furiously. The sandwiches, the wonderful gift from above, were stuffed with sand. Sand, and seaweed.

From above they head the awful, maniacal laughter, and they knew that it was Elizabeth up there, holding the light steady, watching them puke. Instinctively Kathy and Jimmy squirmed away into the protective darkness, like subterranean animals creeping away from the sun. When they were completely out of the pool of light, the beam of whiteness suddenly disappeared, and they heard the sounds of Elizabeth creeping away toward the surface. Kathy and Jimmy cried quietly, clutching each other's hands.

## TWENTY

T HE FOLLOWING SUNDAY WAS ONE OF those leaden, gray days when fall seems to take a perverse pleasure in giving a preview of the winter to come. In Port Arbello the weather only accented the depression that hung over the town, and the tavern did a brisker business than usual. On an ordinary Sunday morning, only Marty Forager could be counted on to step over the threshhold, announcing that he was there for "services." He would then stay through the day, and shuffle out only after he had finished "vespers." But on the Sunday following Jimmy Tyler's disappearance, the churches of Port Arbello found their pews packed for the early service, and the tavern found its stools packed for Marty Forager's services.

The Congers did not go to chuch that Sunday morning, nor did they show up at the tavern. They wouldn't have gone to the tavern anyway, and they had omitted church by mutual consent, neither stating why they chose to stay home, neither wanting to hear the reasons voiced. It was as if they sensed something coming, and hoped they might be able to avoid it by staying in their house. They were observing their morning coffee ritual, silently, when the telephone rang.

"I'll get it," they heard Elizabeth call from upstairs. A moment later they heard her call down again. "It's for you, Mother. Mrs. Stevens."

"Barbara," Rose said, trying to sound more cheerful than she felt. She had, indeed, been growing as depressed as anybody else in Port Arbello, but was able to hide it by using her "professional" voice. "I was beginning to think you people had——" She'd been about to say "died" when she thought better of it. She didn't bother to try to find a better word. "That was a hell of a thing to say, wasn't it. Well, I guess that's what's on all our minds these days.''

"That's why I'm calling," Barbara Stevens replied. "I'm tired of the only topic of conversation in Port Arbello, and I should imagine you are too. And the weather's too lousy to work on the house, so Carl thought a game of bridge on a wet afternoon might be in order. Do you play?''

"I'd love to," Rose said. "What time and where?"

"Here, about one-ish. And bring the girls."

"Let me check with Jack. I'll call you right back."

She hung up the phone and returned to the dining room.

"That was Barbara Stevens. She and Carl want us to come to their place for a game of bridge this afternoon. With the girls," she added as Jack looked doubtful.

"I don't know. You know how Sarah can be in a strange place."

"Then we'll leave them home with Mrs. Goodrich," Rose said promptly. Jack saw that there was going to be a bridge game and decided to go along with it gracefully, even though he hated the game.

"Why don't we play here instead?" he suggested. "Unless there's some reason why the Stevenses want us at their place?"

"Fine," Rose said, smiling. "Barbara said one. Is that all right with you?"

Jack glanced at his watch automatically. "I can't see any reason why not," he said.

Rose grinned at him. "Except that you hate the game, right?" Without giving him time to answer, she continued. "Well, at least it will give us something new to think about. After this week, you might even find you enjoy it.''

The same thought had occurred to him, and he smiled at Rose, then watched her leave the room. He listened to her talking to Barbara Stevens, but didn't really hear what she was saying. He was, instead, trying to decide why it was that ever since the afternoon with Sylvia, which had been wonderful, he had been feeling better about his marriage. He supposed that it was simply that he was feeling better about himself. He found that he was actually looking forward to the bridge game. It was nice to be looking forward to something.

"One club."

"Pass."

"One spade."

"Pass."

"One no-trump."

The bid was passed out, and Barbara Stevens looked at her partner.

"Does your husband make you play one bids?" she asked.

"Only if he thinks he can set me," Rose replied. Barbara looked first at Jack, then at Carl.

"Well, boys, what about it? Do I have to play this one?"

Jack examined his hand carefully, then closed it and threw it in. "Not when fourth best is a four from a seven," he said. "You underbid. Score yourself forty, and we'll count ourselves lucky."

Carl Stevens dealt the next hand, and as he began sorting it he glanced up at the ceiling.

"Mighty quiet up there," he observed. "I didn't know three children could be that quiet. Knock on wood." He finished sorting his cards, and tried to keep his glee from showing.

"Two no-trump," he announced, and was pleased to hear a groan from the women.

Upstairs, the three children sat on the floor of the playroom, finishing a game of Monopoly that Sarah had won, primarily because both Jeff and Elizabeth taking turns playing on her behalf, had made good deals for her. For her part, Sarah was sitting quietly, staring at the Monopoly board and occasionally picking up one of the pieces to examine it carefully before putting it down on the exact spot from which she had picked it up.

"She's just lucky, that's all," Jeff commented as he shoved the last of his money over to Sarah. Sarah, as if sensing somehow that the game was over, suddenly swept the board clean. Elizabeth began picking up the scattered money and sorting it out again. She smiled at Jeff.

"She does this all the time," Elizabeth said. "Whenever I play a game with her, she always wins. Then she dumps it." Elizabeth did not add that the only active part Sarah ever took in any of the games was in the dumping. She was sure Jeff understood that without being told. "Have you ever seen a Ouija board?" she asked him.

"You mean one of those things that's supposed to tell your fortune?"

"They don't really tell your fortune. You're supposed to be able to talk to spirits with them."

"I don't believe in spirits," Jeff said. Then: "Do you have one?"

Elizabeth nodded. "I found it up in the attic. Sarah and I play with it all the time. Want to try it?"

"Sure," Jeff said. "Why not?"

Elizabeth finished packing the Monopoly set in its box, then pulled out the Ouija board. She set it on the floor between Jeff and herself, then called to Sarah, who drifted back from the window she had been looking vacantly out of. Silently Sarah sat down on the floor and rested her fingers on the indicator.

"What do we do?" Jeff asked.

"It's easy," Elizabeth said. "Just put your fingers on that thing, the same way as Sarah, and then ask a question. Pretty soon it starts moving."

"All by itself?" Jeff said skeptically.

"Sure. Come on. Let's try it."

She put her fingers on the indicator, and after a moment, and feeling a bit silly, Jeff did likewise.

"Is anybody there?" Elizabeth intoned. For nearly a minute, nothing happened. Jeff was about to give it up as stupid when he thought he felt a vibration under his fingers. Then the indicator moved. It slid across the board and stopped at the "B."

"Did you do that?" he said to Elizabeth.

She shook her head. "Shh. You shouldn't talk."

Jeff's lips tightened, and he felt the indicator try to move again. He pressed down, trying to immobilize it. He could feel it straining under his fingertips and glanced surreptitiously at Elizabeth to see if she was trying to move it. She looked relaxed. Under his fingertips, which were growing white from the pressure he was applying, the indicator started to move.

"You can't stop it," Elizabeth whispered. "I tried that too. I thought Sarah was moving it. But I couldn't make it stop."

Jeff watched, fascinated, as the indicator moved across the board to stop at the "E." He tried once more to hold it immobile, but it moved relentlessly onward, coming to rest at the "T."

"Bet," Jeff said. "What's that supposed to mean?"

"It hasn't stopped yet," Elizabeth said. "But I know where it's going." The indicator swung slowly over the other way now, and stopped at "H." A sensation came over Jeff, and he knew that the indicator wouldn't move again.

"Beth," he said. "That's your name. Short for Elizabeth."

"I know," Elizabeth said. "But it isn't me. It's a spirit, and the spirit's name is Beth. She must want to tell me something."

"Why not me?" Jeff said, grinning. "I'm here too, you know."

Elizabeth shook her head seriously. "No, it's me she wants to talk to. I've talked to her before."

"Sure you have," Jeff mocked. "I suppose she was your great-great-grandmother, or something like that?"

Now Elizabeth looked at him nervously, and seemed to be less sure of herself. "Why did you say that?" she asked uncertainly.

"What?" Jeff countered.

"What do you mean, my great-great-grandmother?"

Jeff seemed to be baffled. "I didn't mean anything. Isn't it always a great-great-grandmother that people talk to?"

"Have you heard anything about my great-great-grandmother?"

"Why should I have?" Jeff challenged.

"I don't know," Elizabeth said. "I just thought you might have heard about the legend."

"What legend? Don't tell me Beth *was* your great-great-grandmother. Because if you do, you're crazier than your sister."

"Don't talk that way about Sarah," Elizabeth snapped. "It's not nice." She turned to Sarah. "Don't listen to him, Sarah. He doesn't know anything."

Jeff looked embarrassed and tried to mumble an apology. Then he asked Elizabeth to tell him about the legend.

"There's supposed to be a cave on the Point somewhere," she began. "My great-great-grandmother, or maybe it's three greats, had a dream about it. It was an awful dream, and the cave is supposed to be an awful place. My father told me that my great-great-grandmother said it was the gates of hell. Anyway, she had a dream about it, and then terrible things started happening."

"What sort of terrible things?" Jeff asked eagerly. "Did people get killed?"

"I guess so," Elizabeth said. "I think Beth was one of them."

"Who was she?"

"I'm not certain," Elizabeth said. Her voice had softened to a whisper, and a strange blank look had come into her eyes. "She was only a little girl when she died. A little younger than Sarah. I keep asking her what happened to her, but she won't tell me. But it had something to do with the woods, and the cave. That's why we're not supposed to go there."

"Is that all?" Jeff seemed disappointed, as if he had been expecting much more than what Elizabeth had told him.

"Well, there was my great-great-uncle. He killed himself."

"How do you know?"

"I just know. He came home one day, and he was carrying something. I think it was a dead cat, or something like that. Maybe it was a rabbit. Anyway, you know that study in the back of the house?"

"The one with the picture of you in it?"

Elizabeth nodded. "But it isn't a picture of me. Anyway, they say my great-great-uncle took the cat or the rabbit or whatever it was into the study. Then he went out to the back of the house and jumped off the cliff."

Jeff's eyes widened. "Really? Into the ocean?"

"Of course into the ocean," Elizabeth said. "There isn't anything else down there, except for the rocks."

"Gosh," Jeff breathed. "Did anything else happen?"

"There was one other person, my great-grandfather. They don't really know what happened to him, but he went to look for the cave one day, and he never came back."

"Did they ever find him?"

"Yes. But he was dead. He got his foot caught in the rocks, and when the tide came in he drowned."

"I don't believe any of it," Jeff said, hoping there was more.

"I don't care if you believe it or not," Elizabeth said. "It happened."

"Who told you?"

"My father. And his father told him. Or his mother. Anyway, it's true."

"Have you ever seen the cave?" Jeff demanded.

"No," Elizabeth said uncertainly. "But nobody else has ever seen it either."

"Then how do you know it's real?"

"I just know."

"How?"

"I just do."

"Well, if you can't tell me how you know, then you don't know," Jeff said tauntingly.

"I *do* know," Elizabeth insisted. "Beth told me," she blurted out.

Jeff rolled his eyes. "Sure she did. Except that you don't even know who she is."

"I do too," Elizabeth said shakily. "She—she's the girl in the picture downstairs. The one who looks like me."

Jeff looked at her with scorn. "Sure she is," he sneered.

"She is," Elizabeth insisted. "She talks to me through the Ouija board, and she told me so."

Jeff lounged back, propping himself up on one elbow, and grinned at Elizabeth. Neither of them noticed that Sarah had moved out of the circle and was back at the window, staring out and shifting her weight nervously from one foot to the other.

"I'll tell you what," Jeff said. "If you can tell me where that cave is, then I'll believe the rest of it."

Elizabeth looked at him petulantly and tried to figure out how to convince him.

"Well," she said nervously. "There's a place . . ."

Sarah turned from the window and stared vacantly across the room at Elizabeth. Neither Elizabeth nor Jeff seemed aware that she was there.

"What kind of place?" Jeff said, disbelief filling his voice.

"A—a secret place," Elizabeth said.

Sarah began screaming. The first high-pitched wail tore out of her throat as she charged across the room. Her face contorted, she grabbed the Ouija board and flung it at the window. It shattered the glass, then clattered down onto the roof of the porch.

Jeff leaped to his feet and stared at Sarah, who was running wildly around the room, as if she was looking for something. Suddenly she bolted for the door, flung it open, and disappeared into the hall. Jeff, his face pale, looked helplessly at Elizabeth, but Elizabeth was unruffled. She went to the window, opened it, and picked the Ouija board from among the splinters of glass in which it lay, brushing her finger against one of the fragments accidentally as she did. Carefully she sucked at the wound after making sure it didn't have any glass in it. When she was finished she turned back to Jeff and smiled. "It's all right," she said. "It happens all the time. Don't worry, she'll be all right."

As Sarah's first scream resounded through the house, Barbara Stevens dropped her cards, and her hands flew to her mouth.

"My God," she said. "Something's happened to the children." She was halfway out of her chair before Rose could stop her.

"It's Sarah," Rose said. "It's all right. It happens every now and then, and I know it's awful, but please, just sit still."

Barbara sank uncertainly back into her chair, her face pale, and Carl Stevens sat as if rooted to his seat as the screams built in intensity. And then they heard the pounding of feet coming down the stairs.

The door of the living room flew open, and the room was immediately vibrating with the agonized screams of the hysterical child. Sarah looked around wildly, her eyes seeming to be searching for something but seeing nothing, and then she was across the room, charging toward the French doors, her arms outstretched.

She hit the doors full force, and her hands struck the wood frames of the panes rather than the glass itself. The doors buckled under the strain and flew open, banging back against the walls, shattering the panes. Sarah was already across the porch.

"Jack," Rose cried out. "Stop her! Hurry!"

Jack was already on his feet, and as the Stevenses looked on in horror, he bolted across the room and through the doors. They heard Sarah's screams begin to fade as she raced into the field, and watched in fascination as Jack chased her. In her hysteria Sarah moved unnaturally fast, and the three people in the living room saw that she was almost outrunning her father. She was heading toward the woods.

In the sudden silence of the house, Rose moved to the French doors to watch the pursuit. Upstairs, directly above her, Elizabeth and Jeff also watched the activity in the field, which, in the grayness of the day and the slight drizzle, seemed to be some manic form of tag. No one spoke, and time almost seemed to stop as Jack Conger tried to catch up with his fleeing daughter.

Jack felt the rain in his face as he leaped the five steps from the porch and dashed into the field. He could see Sarah ahead of him, her small legs pumping as she charged headlong for the forest. He had thought he would have no trouble catching her, but as she maintained the distance between them Dr. Belter's words came back to him and he realized that her body was working on adrenalin, not strength. He wondered how long she could hold her pace.

She began slowing perceptibly when she was a little more than halfway across the field. She ran straight as an arrow, as if she had a spot picked out and was heading for it. As he chased her Jack felt his feet slip on the wet grass, and twice he stumbled. Sarah did not, and each time Jack lost his footing she widened the gap again.

And then, finally, she began to falter, and Jack could feel that the race was almost over. He would catch up to her at the forest's edge, or slightly inside it.

Inside it. The thought chilled him for some reason, and then he felt an odd sensation. His system had now taken over for him, and he felt the tingling of adrenalin as it coursed suddenly through his body. He saw the woods loom up in front of him as he lunged after Sarah.

His arms closed around her legs, and he felt her fall more than he saw it. And then she was wriggling in his arms, trying to get free of him, and her screaming mounted. The two of them struggled there in the mud, and Sarah's thrashing became stronger, as if for some reason her fears had multiplied. He almost lost his grip on her, and then, as suddenly as it had begun, it ended.

Her screams stopped, and she lay in the mud, her small chest heaving with the exertion, her throat choking on tight little sobs. Jack picked her up gently and turned toward the house.

He started across the field, his mind a blank. Then it began to come back to him. This was like another day, a day a year ago when he had carried

Sarah across this field, and it had been raining, and she had been crying. That day her dress had been torn, and she had been bleeding. Reluctantly he looked down at the limp child in his arms.

Her face had gotten scratched in the struggle, and there was a thin line of blood on her left cheek. Her denim overalls were muddy, and the bib had been ripped open and flapped beneath her. Jack felt panic building in him.

He looked toward the house, and through his blurred eyes he saw them waiting for him, waiting for him to bring his child home, waiting for him to tell them what he had done. What had he done? He didn't know what he'd done. He was bringing his child home. But they were waiting for him. Why were they waiting for him?

He no longer felt the rain on his face, or the spongy softness of the wet field under his feet. It was as if he was walking through a tunnel, and he didn't know what lay at the other end, nor did he know what lay at the end he was coming from. He felt himself getting dizzy, and he forced his eyes from the group that waited for him at the French doors. He forced himself to look up.

He saw Elizabeth. She stood at a window on the second floor, and she was watching him. She was smiling at him. It was a gentle smile, and it comforted him.

Jack felt the panic begin to recede, and he concentrated on watching Elizabeth—on watching Elizabeth as she watched him, beckoned him onward, somehow comforting him as he carried Sarah through the rain.

Elizabeth disappeared from his view as he stepped onto the porch. The panic came upon him once more.

He carried Sarah into the living room and laid her gently on the sofa. Then he gave in to the panic and the hysteria and began to sob. He backed away from Sarah, as if he never should have carried her into the house at all, and watched, strangely detached, as Rose and the Stevenses gathered around her, clucking over her and fussing. No one saw him leave the room. They were busy with Sarah. He found his way up the stairs and into the bedroom he shared with Rose. He lay down on the bed and began to cry. He was remembering. He hated it.

Downstairs, the three adults in the living room stared helplessly at the sobbing child on the sofa. All they could do, they knew, was wait till it passed. But the sobs were heart-rending, and it almost sounded as though Sarah was trying to say something.

They strained their ears and tried to make words out of the strange sounds that were being wrenched out of Sarah, as if by some unseen force.

"Secret," she seemed to be saying. "Secret . . . secret . . ."

But they couldn't be sure.

## TWENTY-ONE

BARBARA STEVENS FELT TOTALLY HELP-less as as she watched Rose try to comfort Sarah. The child lay trembling on the couch, and her vacant eyes darted wildly around the room, as if searching for a way out. If there were any coherent thoughts going through her mind, it was impossible to interpret what they might be.

"It's all right, baby," Rose crooned over and over. "It's all going to be all right now. It's over, and Mother's here." She was trying to cradle the child's head in her arms, but Sarah kept jerking spasmodically. It was all Rose could do to keep her on the sofa.

The Stevenses' eyes met over the crouching Rose, and a look of pity passed between them. Then they heard a noise at the living-room door and saw Elizabeth and Jeff standing there. Carl started to wave them back upstairs, but Rose had seen them too.

"It's all right," she said. "She's quieting." She turned her attention to the two children, who were now inside the living room, standing quietly, though Jeff was fidgeting.

"What happened up there?" Rose said quietly. She glanced at both children, but her gaze settled on Elizabeth. "What set her off?"

"I don't know," Elizabeth said. "We were playing with the Ouija board, and then I started telling Jeff about the old family legend."

"Was Sarah listening?"

"I don't know," Elizabeth said again. "I wasn't really paying much attention to her. Jeff and I were arguing."

"Arguing?" Barbara Stevens asked. "What about?"

"She was telling me a story," Jeff said. "It was really crazy, and she got mad when I told her I didn't believe it."

"But it's true," Elizabeth insisted.

"About the cave?" Barbara asked. Her son looked at her in surprise.

"You mean you've heard about it too?"

"Yes, I have. But whether it's true or not, you shouldn't have argued with Elizabeth about it."

"But—" Jeff began, but his father cut him off.

"No buts," he said. "You know better than to argue about something you don't know anything about. Apologize to Elizabeth."

For a moment it looked as if Jeff was about to argue some more, but then he turned to Elizabeth. "I'm sorry I argued with you," he said, then couldn't resist adding, "but I still don't think there's a cave."

Elizabeth opened her mouth, but Rose spoke first.

"It doesn't matter right now whether there's a cave or not. What matters is what got Sarah so upset. What happened?"

Elizabeth picked up the story. "I was telling Jeff about the legend, and I got to the part about the cave. And we started arguing about whether or not it was real, and then all of a sudden Sarah started screaming. There's a broken window in the playroom."

"A broken window?"

"She threw the Ouija board through it," Jeff explained.

"What in the world were you doing with the Ouija board?" Carl Stevens wanted to know.

Jeff started to speak, but this time it was Elizabeth who got there first.

"We were just playing with it. It spelled out 'Beth.' "

"That's your name," Barbara Stevens said with a smile.

"Yes," Elizabeth said, shrugging. She flashed a quick glance at Jeff, and he caught her meaning immediately. *Don't let the grown-ups know too much about it. It's our secret.* He smiled at her.

"But what set Sarah off?" Rose said doggedly, casting about desperately for a rational reason for her daughter's outburst. Please, she begged, directing a prayer heavenward. Let me understand. Just once.

Jeff and Elizabeth looked at each other and shrugged. Rose was about to begin cross-examining them, but changed her mind when she saw her husband making his way slowly down the stairs. He didn't come into the living room, though. Instead, he started across the hall toward the back study. The back study and the bar, Rose thought.

"Well," she said, "I guess that more or less takes care of our bridge game, doesn't it. I don't think I could concentrate on the cards any more." She produced one of those bright and cheery smiles that tell the recipient it's time to leave. The Stevenses got the message.

Carl glanced at his watch nervously. "It's time for us to be getting home anyway," he said. "I'm sorry this had to happen. If there's anything we can do . . ." He trailed off helplessly, knowing there wasn't.

"We'll do it again," Barbara said quickly, coming to his rescue. "Soon. Call us, okay?"

Rose smiled at them, and Elizabeth escorted them to the door, holding the door open while they got into their coats. Outside the rain still fell quietly from the gray skies.

"Not too pleasant," Carl said.

"No," Elizabeth agreed. "But we get used to it." As they left, neither Carl nor Barbara was sure whether Elizabeth had been referring to the weather or to her sister's outburst.

Neither of them spoke until they had turned onto the Point Road.

"It must be hard," Barbara said finally.

"What?"

"Having a daughter like Sarah. I feel so sorry for them both."

Carl nodded his agreement. "I'm not sure I could cope with it at all, let alone as well as they do. Elizabeth is remarkable too," he added. "They're lucky to have her. In a way, I suppose, it balances things out."

"She's crazy," Jeff commented from the back seat. Carl reproved his son for talking that way. It never occurred to him that Jeff might be talking about Elizabeth, not Sarah. And it didn't occur to Jeff that his parents had misunderstood him.

Elizabeth watched the Stevenses drive away through the rain, then quietly closed the door and went back to the living room. She watched her mother try to comfort Sarah for a moment, then walked over and knelt beside her.

"I'll do it," she said. "I can calm her down."

Rose stood up in relief. She never knew what to do in these situations, and she always wound up feeling helpless and frustrated—feelings which she was sure were somehow transmitted to Sarah. Gratefully she let Elizabeth take over, and when she saw that Sarah was indeed getting through her seizure, or whatever it was, she started grimly for the study in the rear of the house. There, at least, she would be dealing with the familiar, and her husband, at least, would understand what she said. Until he got too drunk. An image of Martin Forager flashed into her mind, and then Forager's features suddenly faded and were replaced by Jack's. She shook off the image and went into the study without knocking. Jack was sitting in the wing chair, a stiff drink in his hands, his eyes fixed on the portrait of the young girl hanging above the cold fireplace.

"I could have Mrs. Goodrich build a fire," Rose volunteered cautiously.

"It wouldn't make any difference," Jack said dully. "I'd still be cold." His eyes didn't move from the portrait.

"Are you all right?" Rose asked.

"I suppose so. I'm sorry I fell apart like that. I had a bad time out there."

"I noticed," Rose said, a trace of acid edging her voice.

Jack held up a hand. "Don't start, Rose, not now. I'm still on the edge, and I don't want to talk about it yet."

"You're going to have to, sooner or later."

"I know. But let's make it later, shall we?"

Rose sat down in the other chair by the fireplace, then felt the chill of the room. She decided to ask for a fire anyway, and went to find Mrs. Goodrich. When she returned Jack hadn't moved, but his drink was fuller than it had been when she left. She knew he'd finished the first and refilled his glass, but he didn't seem to have changed his position at all. His eyes were still fixed glassily on the portrait, as if it held some sort of magnetic force over him. Rose, too, gazed at it, and tried to see whatever it was that Jack was seeing.

A few minutes later Mrs. Goodrich came in to build the fire. She said nothing, nor was she spoken to. When she left the room her employers still sat silently, gazing at the picture. Only now, a fire blazed cheerfully at their feet. Mrs. Goodrich, returning to her small room by the kitchen, felt vaguely worried. She picked up her *TV Guide* and settled herself into her chair.

\* \* \*

Elizabeth slipped out the front door and made her way through the drizzle to the barn. When she was inside she walked quickly to the old tack room and pulled the door shut behind her. She took off her raincoat and hung it on a peg. Then she began to unbutton her dress. When all the buttons were open, she slipped it off and folded it neatly. She set it on an empty shelf and covered it with an ancient horse blanket. Then she rummaged around in the pile of old hay in one corner of the tack room and pulled out a small bundle of wadded material. She shook it out. It was the old dress she had found in the attic, torn and stained now, but still in one piece. She put it on carefully, then began loosening her ponytail. When the blond hair was flowing freely over her shoulders, she glanced around the tack room, then opened the door once more. In a moment she was out of the barn and walking slowly across the field toward the wood. The rain began to fall harder now, and by the time she was twenty yards from the house her dress was sodden, her hair streaming. She didn't feel it. She moved slowly but deliberately through the storm.

She reached the edge of the woods, and didn't pause to enjoy the protection the trees gave her from the downpour. Her hair was plastered shroudlike over her shoulders now, its wet sleekness accenting the features of her face. Her pace quickened, and she moved through the woods with a sure-footedness that would have seemed impossible to an observer, had there been one.

Lightning was beginning to play across the horizon when she emerged from the woods, and a roll of thunder greeted her as she stepped out onto the crest of the embankment. It was dark, very dark, though the sun had not yet set. The storm seemed to blot it out almost completely, and the sea, barely visible through the rain, had the menacing look of an animal in the night. Elizabeth, slowed by neither the rain nor the darkness, began gliding down the face of the embankment. As the storm intensified she disappeared behind the boulder that guarded the entrance to the tunnel.

She found the flashlight in its niche next to the tunnel entrance, but didn't turn it on until she had reached the upper chamber. By now the stench from the dead cat, mixed with the sour smells from the children's vomiting, had fouled the air throughout the cavern, but Elizabeth didn't seem to notice it.

She crept to the top of the shaft, clicked the light on, and peered down. She could see nothing except the large flat table-rock, but she could hear soft moaning drifting upward. She knew Kathy and Jimmy were still down there, cowering somewhere in the darkness. She smiled to herself and began to lower the rope ladder into the pit.

She tested it briefly, then began to climb down, the still-lit flashlight casting eerie shadows as it glowed in the pocket of her peculiar, old-fashioned dress. She felt her foot hit the floor of the cave and stepped away from the ladder. She drew the flashlight from her pocket and shined it around the cavern.

Kathy Burton and Jimmy Tyler sat huddled together against the wall of the cavern opposite the place where the skeleton lay. Kathy's eyes were tightly shut against the sudden brightness of the light, but Jimmy Tyler held one hand out, shielding himself from the worst of the glare. He was squinting, trying to see past the source of the light. Kathy was whimpering softly to herself, and except for the hand clasped over her face was apparently unaware of what was going on. Jimmy didn't try to get up, but his eyes moved alertly in the light. Elizabeth shifted the beam to the old skeleton, and a sound crept from her lips as she saw that it was in disarray, the bones scattered a couple of feet in every direction.

Elizabeth reached into her pocket and brought out some candles she had found in the tack room and a small cigarette lighter she had taken from the house. She wedged the candles into cracks in the walls and lit them, placing the lighter carefully into a crevice just below the candles. Then she snapped the flashlight off, and it disappeared back into the large pocket of her dress. The flames of the candles flickered, then grew steady, and a warm light suddenly bathed the interior of the cavern.

Ignoring the two children huddled together, Elizabeth began tending to the old bones opposite them. Tenderly she moved each bone back into its proper position, and in a few minutes the skeleton was complete again, its arms folded once more over its empty rib cage. Only then did Elizabeth turn her attention back to Kathy Burton and Jimmy Tyler.

"It's time to have another party," she whispered. Kathy didn't seem to hear her, but Jimmy shrank closer to the girl next to him, his mind filling with fear. He knew this was Elizabeth, but she was not the Elizabeth he had known all his life. It was another Elizabeth, a terrifying Elizabeth.

She was covered with mud, and her hair, muddy now, as well as wet, clung to her face and shoulders. The torn dress, soaking wet and slimy with the muck of the cavern, clung to her body in lump folds, and there was an emptiness in her face that reminded Jimmy of his grandmother, when he had seen her at her funeral two months ago. She looks dead, Jimmy thought. Elizabeth looks dead. He tried to burrow in closer to Kathy Burton.

As he watched in horrified fascination, Elizabeth found the remains of the dead cat, its doll's clothes now covered with the cave slime, and propped it up carefully on one of the rocks that sat like stools around the table-rock. She discovered the head of the cat, now eyeless, but still wearing it's grotesque bonnet, and tried to balance it on top of the torso. When she couldn't make it stay, she grasped the head firmly and ground it into the torso like an orange onto a juicer. The rotting flesh of the torso gave way, and the end of the spine protruded upward into the foramen magnum. The head held, squatting deeply between the cat's shoulders.

"Come to the table," Elizabeth said softly, beckoning Jimmy Tyler to leave the security of the cavern wall and join the cat at the strange table. He shook his head.

"Come to the table," Elizabeth repeated, her voice becoming menacing. Jimmy Tyler pulled his knees up to his chest, and tightened his grip on Kathy Burton's hand.

Elizabeth moved toward him, and her hand drew back to strike him. Just before the blow was delivered, Jimmy scuttled away from Kathy and crouched, shivering, on one of the small rocks.

Elizabeth turned to Kathy.

"You too," she ordered. Kathy didn't move, but her eyes flickered open a little, and her mouth worked as if she was trying to speak.

"Now," Elizabeth demanded. This time the blow fell, and Jimmy Tyler cringed at the sound of the sharp slap against Kathy's face. Still Kathy didn't move. Instead, a small gurgling sound escaped her lips.

Elizabeth glared down at the inert child for a moment, then began dragging her toward the center of the cavern by her feet. Weakly Kathy Burton tried to kick loose, but Elizabeth's grasp was firm. In seconds Elizabeth was setting Kathy on the third stool. When she stepped away Kathy slumped back to the floor, and Elizabeth kicked her.

"Sit up when you're at the table," she snapped. Kathy seemed to become slightly conscious of what was going on, and managed to pull herself upright. "That's nice," Elizabeth said. She stepped back and looked over the strange tableau.

"Now," she said. "Kathy, you're the mother. And Jimmy's the father. And Cecil is your baby. Your crazy baby. Feed your baby, Mother."

Kathy sat quietly, barely able to keep herself upright.

"I said to feed your baby!" Elizabeth demanded. When Kathy still made no move toward the cat, Elizabeth raised her fist and brought it down hard on Kathy's back, driving her face first into the center of the table. "You do what I tell you," Elizabeth snarled through her teeth.

"If Mother can't feed the baby, you do it," Elizabeth said to Jimmy. He looked at her, puzzled, trying to figure out what he was supposed to do. He saw her fist closing again, and decided the best thing to do was to pretend. He quickly mimed putting a bottle in the baby's mouth.

"She's too old for a bottle," Elizabeth hissed. "She eats real food."

Jimmy quickly pretended to pick up a spoon and shovel some food toward the cat.

"Talk to her," Elizabeth commanded. "Talk to your baby."

Jimmy froze for a moment, then found his tongue.

"Nice baby," he said. "Here's some nice food for the nice baby."

"*Her name's Sarah!*" Elizabeth screamed. "Don't you even know your baby's name? What kind of a father are you?"

"Sarah," Jimmy repeated quickly. "Here's some food for nice little Sarah."

He continued pretending to shove food into the dead cat's mouth, and kept babbling at it, not knowing what he was saying but being careful to call the cat Sarah every few seconds.

"She doesn't answer, does she?" Elizabeth said softly. Jimmy shook his head.

"Do you know why she doesn't answer?" Elizabeth asked smoothly.

Jimmy shook his head again.

"*Because she's crazy!*" Elizabeth screamed. "But children are supposed to answer when they're spoken to, aren't they?"

Jimmy nodded dumbly.

"Then she's a bad child," Elizabeth said. "She's crazy and she's bad. Punish her." Jimmy didn't move. "*Punish her!*"

His eyes fixed on Elizabeth, and on the hand that was flexing rhythmically into a fist. Jimmy slowly picked up the dead cat. The head tumbled from the body and rolled into the shadows. Shuddering, he put the corpse over his knee and began spanking it.

Elizabeth smiled.

Kathy still huddled over the table, cradling her head in her arms, and she must have moved slightly, for Elizabeth's attention was suddenly drawn to her.

"Don't sleep at the table," she said menacingly. Jimmy, afraid that Kathy was about to receive another of Elizabeth's terrible blows, reached out to shake her.

"Don't touch her," Elizabeth commanded. "You don't like to touch Mother, do you? She wants you to touch her, but you don't like to. We know what you like, don't we?" She leered at the little boy, who stared at her in bewilderment.

"You like the baby, don't you? We know you like the baby better than you like Mother, don't we?" And suddenly her voice rose, and the cavern was filled to overflowing with the sound of her words.

*"Well, if that's what you want, that's what you can have!"*

Elizabeth leaped on Jimmy, and began pulling at his clothes. He struggled, but he was too weak from hunger and fear to fight very hard. Soon, before he had a chance to realize what was happening, Elizabeth had stripped his clothes from him and flung them in a corner. Naked, he huddled on the floor of the cavern.

Elizabeth picked up the torso of the dead cat.

"This is what you want, isn't it?" she hissed. "You want your baby, don't you?"

And she fell on Jimmy Tyler, forcing the rotting flesh of the dead cat against his crotch, mumbling incoherently that if he wanted it so badly, here it was. Jimmy Tyler's helpless sobbing mixed with Elizabeth's ramblings, filled the cave. He didn't understand what was happening to him.

Kathy Burton, the strange sounds penetrating her fogged mind, looked up and watched the vile scene that was transpiring in front of her. She couldn't grasp it at first, couldn't sort it all out into anything that made sense. Then her mind cleared a little more and she realized what was happening. She looked on in horror as Elizabeth continued in her efforts to force Jimmy Tyler to copulate with the corpse.

Kathy Burton screamed, and with the last of her reserves of strength she pulled herself to her feet and moved toward the spot where Elizabeth struggled with Jimmy Tyler.

"Don't," she croaked. "Please, Elizabeth, don't."

Elizabeth wheeled, and Kathy wished she hadn't tried to interfere. She began backing away, the light in Elizabeth's eyes driving her backward until she reached the wall of the cavern. Her terror grew as she saw Elizabeth pick up a rock from the floor of the cavern. She felt the strength suddenly ebbing from her body when Elizabeth raised the stone over her head, and she began collapsing to the cavern floor as Elizabeth brought the rock downward.

For Kathy Burton, the horror was over.

\* \* \*

An hour later Rose Conger found her older daughter emerging from the shower.

"I was just going to tell you that if you wanted a shower before dinner, you should get started. I see I'm too late."

Elizabeth nodded and smiled at her mother. Rose smiled back, and silently thanked God for sending her Elizabeth. Without Elizabeth, she didn't know how she would manage.

"Will you bring Sarah down with you?" she said.

"Sure," Elizabeth replied. "As soon as I get dressed."

In the cave, Jimmy Tyler lay where Elizabeth had left him, too weak and too confused even to try to find his clothes. He lay shivering, naked in the darkness.

## TWENTY-TWO

ROSE LAY STIFFLY IN BED LATER THAT night, listening to the rain pound on the roof, her thoughts as turbulent as the weather outside. She could hear nothing from Jack's inert form beside her, but she sensed that he wasn't asleep.

"There's something about that portrait, isn't there?" she said finally. Jack snapped on the lamp by his side of the bed and raised himself up on one elbow.

"Do you feel it too?" he asked.

"No," Rose said flatly. "I don't. But all evening long you sat and stared at it. What is it about it? It's as if you're trying to see something in it."

Jack lay back down again and stared at the ceiling.

"I'm not sure," he said. "It just seems like—like the portrait should look more like Sarah than like Elizabeth."

"Sarah? Why Sarah?"

"Nothing I can put my finger on. Just a feeling. I keep thinking about what Dr. Belter told us. About the little girl who was supposed to have been killed. I keep getting the feeling that the picture must be of that girl."

"What does that have to do with Sarah?" Rose's voice was sharper now, as if she was guarding herself against what was to come.

"I remembered today. I remembered it all. Rose, that day a year ago. I almost killed Sarah."

"But you didn't."

"No, I didn't," Jack said miserably. "I wanted something else."

"Something else?"

"I wanted to rape her," Jack said quietly. He waited for a response from Rose, and when there was none he went on. "I don't have the vaguest idea of what it was all about, but today, when I was bringing Sarah back in from the rain, I looked up and saw Elizabeth watching me. And then, suddenly, I remembered it all. I remembered being in the woods, and watching Sarah crawl under a bush. And suddenly I wanted her. Sexually. Don't ask me to explain why—I don't know. It was the most awful thing I've ever felt in my life. I felt like I was someone else, but I was still myself. It was like I was being made to do something, or want to do something, that I didn't want to do. And then an awful feeling came over me that . . . that Sarah was seducing me."

Rose sat up. "Seducing you?" she demanded. "Seducing you? My God, Jack, she was only ten years old!"

"I didn't say she *was* seducing me. I said I *felt* like she was. And so I started beating her. I really wanted to kill her. Oh, Jesus, Rose, it was awful." The pain of memory swept over him once more, and he began crying softly. Rose, failing to understand what had happened to him, her own feelings in turmoil, searched for something to say.

"What's all this got to do with the portrait downstairs?" she asked finally.

"I'm not sure," Jack muttered. "When I look at that portrait I get the strange feeling that what happened to Sarah a year ago, happened to that girl a long time ago."

"And that, I suppose, takes you off the hook, doesn't it?" Rose said icily. "Suddenly, instead of being the aggressor you're the victim? My God, Jack."

Jack cringed at her words, but Rose plunged on.

"And what about today? Were you a victim again today? Did some strange force come over you again today? Were you not yourself again today?"

"What are you talking about?"

"I saw it today, Jack. I saw it all. And I was ashamed that Carl and Barbara Stevens saw it too."

Jack sat up and stared at his wife. "I don't know what you're talking about," he said.

"I'm talking about you out there in the field with Sarah. I'm not sure which was worse, watching her charging across the field, screaming, or watching you rescue her. You were vicious, Jack. It wasn't like you were helping her. It looked like you were attacking her! It was like it was all happening all over again."

Jack sat up, his eyes blazing. "Are you out of your mind? Today was nothing like a year ago. Nothing at all. For one thing, I was stone sober today."

Rose frowned. "Maybe you don't have to be drunk," she said. "Maybe something more serious is wrong with you."

Something snapped inside Jack, and he grabbed Rose by the shoulders and pinned her down to the bed.

"We'll see who I can rape," he snarled, and as Rose lay back limply, as if he weren't worth fighting against, his rage grew. He grabbed at her nightdress and tore it from her body. Still she lay there, taunting him with her passiveness. He hurled himself on her and tried desperately to mount her.

And he couldn't.

Now she began squirming under him, and for a moment he wasn't sure whether she was trying to free herself or help him.

"You can't do it, can you?" her mocking voice came from beneath him, slightly muffled by his chest. "Only little girls? Well, I'm not a little girl, Jack. I'm a woman, a real woman. Now get off me." She pushed up against him, and once more he tried to thrust himself inside her. Again he failed.

Then the struggle began in earnest, and Rose suddenly became frightened by what might happen to her. She redoubled her efforts, and finally succeeded in freeing herself. She scrambled from the bed and turned to face him. His eyes blazing, his anger still growing, he stared at her, and Rose was frightened. She felt she knew what Sarah must have experienced in the woods that day so long ago. She reached out to pick up an ashtray from the table by the bed.

"Don't come near me," she screamed. "I swear, Jack, if you so much as lay a finger on me, I'll—"

"You'll what?" Jack thundered. "You'll kill me? Do you really think I care?" He was standing now, and the bed separated them. Both of them were shouting, neither hearing the other. And then, when they both paused for a breath, they heard it. Someone was tapping at their door. They stared at each other, stricken. The children.

But it was Mrs. Goodrich's voice out in the hall. "Are you all right?" she was saying. "Land sakes, you're waking up the whole house."

There was a silence; then Rose spoke. "It's all right, Mrs. Goodrich," she called softly. "I'm sorry we disturbed you. We were just—just talking about something."

"Some people like to sleep at night," Mrs. Goodrich said. They heard her retreating back toward the staircase, her footsteps heavy as she plodded down.

"I suppose the children heard it all, too," Rose complained.

"Don't try to blame it on me," Jack said. "You might try listening to me once in a while, instead of accusing me."

"You're never responsible, are you?" Rose said, making an effort to keep her voice down. "You'll never take the responsibility for anything, will you?"

"Yes," Jack said. "I will. But not for everything, Rose. Not for everything." He began dressing.

"Where are you going?" Rose demanded.

"You don't need to know," Jack said. Then he smiled cruelly. "I'll take the responsibility for where I'm going. And I'll take the responsibility for what I'm going to do."

He left her standing next to the bed in her torn nightgown, and she hadn't moved when she heard his car roar off down the driveway two minutes later. Only when the noise of the car had faded did she sink back down to the bed. Shakily she reached for a cigarette and lit it. The smoke, sucked deeply into her lungs, seemed to calm her.

She finished her cigarette and lay down on the bed, turning off the light. She lay still for a long time, keeping her breathing even and forcing her tense muscles to relax. She tried to sort out her thoughts, and when that failed decided to drift with them and see where they led.

Thirty minutes later, she was still trying to relax her muscles, and her mind was as chaotic as it had been when she lay down. She decided to get something to eat.

She padded into the kitchen and turned the light on. She listened for a minute and heard the rhythmic snoring of Mrs. Goodrich in the next room. She crept to the refrigerator and opened it.

She thought she heard the click of a door opening as she poked among the leftovers neatly packaged on the shelves of the refrigerator, but it wasn't until she felt a draft on her legs that she turned around. The back door stood open.

A stab of fear ran through her, and she instinctively moved toward the drawer where the knives were kept. Then she saw who had opened the back door.

Sarah, her flannel nightgown soaking wet and covered with mud, her dark hair glistening with the rain, stood by the knife drawer, as if trying to decide whether to open it or not.

"Sarah?" Rose breathed, her heart pounding and a terrible fear rising in her. "Sarah," she said again.

She approached the child and knelt down. She reached out to touch Sarah, very gently, for fear that her daughter was sleepwalking and not wanting to wake her if she was. But at the touch Sarah turned around and stared at her mother. She blinked a couple of times, and Rose was sure she was awake.

"Sarah," she said quietly. "What is it? What were you doing outside?"

Sarah peered blankly at her mother, and Rose didn't know whether she had been heard or not. Then a large tear formed in one of Sarah's eyes and slowly ran down her face, streaking the mud in its path. It collected on her chin, then, when it was too heavy to hang on any longer, fell to the floor. Rose gathered the girl into her arms. Sarah did not resist.

"Come on," Rose said. "I'll take you upstairs and put you to bed."

She picked the little girl up and closed both the back door of the house and the refrigerator door. Snapping off the kitchen light and crooning to the child who shivered in her arms, she made her way upstairs to the bathroom. She set Sarah down and began running a tub of hot water. Then she went to get towels.

When she returned, Sarah still sat where Rose had left her, unmoving, as though she were thinking about something. But her eyes, the huge, beautiful brown eyes, still seemed vacant, staring at the tub of water. Rose undressed her and placed her in the tub.

When she finished bathing Sarah, Rose put her to bed. She tucked the child in carefully, then sat with her till she was sure Sarah was asleep. Finally she left Sarah's room, leaving the light on, and went downstairs. She knew she would not sleep if she went back to bed; knew she would not sleep until her husband came home. She wished he were home now, or at least had told her where he was going. She sat in the study and waited. Above her the little girl who looked so much like Elizabeth smiled down at her. The picture comforted Rose, and made her waiting easier.

Jack drove fast through the storm, the pounding of his heart echoed by the beating of the windshield wipers as they fought vainly to keep the glass clear in front of his eyes. He didn't need to see, really; he was so familiar with the Point Road that he felt he could have driven it blindfolded, navigating by the bumps and chuckholes.

He drove automatically, his mind racing, his thoughts chaotic. Then he saw the lights of Port Arbello glowing dimly ahead in the rain, and he knew where he was going.

He pulled the car into Sylvia Bannister's driveway, and left it there for anybody who wished to see. The house was dark, but he didn't consider going elsewhere. Instead, he walked up to the front door and knocked loudly. When there was no response, he knocked again, louder. Finally he saw a light flash on and heard feet coming toward the door.

"Who is it?" Sylvia's sleepy voice called.

"It's me. Jack."

He listened as she unfastened the chain and threw the bolt. Then the door opened, and she squinted out at him.

"Excuse me," she said, and flipped the switch for the porch light. "I didn't mean to leave you in the dark."

"It's all right," Jack said, grinning crookedly. Seeing her made him feel better. "I seem to be in the dark a lot these days anyway."

She pulled the door open and let him step inside before she closed it again, and fixed the chain and deadbolt. "I suppose it's silly," she said. "But they make me feel safer." Then she looked at him closely, and concern came into her face. "Are you all right?" she said. "Let me get you a drink. You look like you need one."

"I do," Jack said. "I suppose I shouldn't but I could really use one."

"She's got you convinced, hasn't she?" Sylvia said as she led him to the kitchen.

"Convinced?"

"That you're an alcoholic," Sylvia said, pouring them each a drink.

"I suppose I am." Jack accepted the glass she handed him.

"No," Sylvia said definitely. "You're not. Martin Forager is an alcoholic. You're not. At least not yet. But I suppose if you wanted to you could become one. Do you?"

"I'm not sure sometimes. But yes, sometimes I do want to become one. Sometimes I'd like to stay drunk all the time. I would, except I suffer from terrible hangovers. They don't show, but God, do they hurt."

"Well, I suppose as long as you're suffering you're safe. At least, that's what my mother taught me. Do you want to sit here, or shall I build a fire?"

"This'll be fine," Jack said, settling into one of the chairs at the kitchen table. "It makes it different from home. Mrs. Goodrich does not tolerate any Conger sitting in the kitchen. I think she thinks it's beneath our dignity. Not that we have any dignity left, after tonight.'' He told Sylvia what had happened at home.

"It must have been awful,'' she said when he had finished.

He swirled his drink and smiled wryly. "Well, it wasn't pleasant. So I took off, and here I am.''

"I meant the remembering. It must have been terrible.''

Jack nodded. "It was. In a way, I wish I hadn't remembered. Not knowing what I'd done was bad enough. I think knowing what I was trying to do is even worse.''

"Nonsense,'' Sylvia said. "You seem to be forgetting something. You didn't rape her, and you didn't kill her.''

"But I wanted to,'' Jack said miserably.

"Wanting to do something and doing it are two entirely different things. If I had to feel badly about all the things I've wanted to do, I'd be a mess. And this town wouldn't be in very good shape, either. I can think of at least three people right off the bat that I've wanted to kill. I mean really kill. Complete with fantasies of doing it, and getting away with it. So stop feeling bad.'' She glanced at his drink, then held her own glass up. "And fix us both another. I'm not your secretary now, you know. I'm a woman, and I want to be waited on.''

"You can kick me out if you want to go back to sleep,'' Jack said. "But I hope you don't.''

"Kick you out? Not much chance of that. You might fire me in the morning, when you're my boss again. Besides, I happen to like you.''

"Do you, Sylvia?'' Jack said seriously. "Do you really? I guess I haven't been feeling particularly likable lately.''

"And it hasn't occurred to you that that might have something to do with the way Rose has been treating you? It's hard to feel good about yourself when someone you love is making you feel bad about yourself.''

"I'm not sure I love her,'' Jack said slowly.

Sylvia glanced at him, and the corners of her mouth flickered upward. "I suppose I could read a lot into that, if I wanted to, but I won't. You love her, Jack, even if you don't believe you do. You're used to her, and a lot of love is nothing more than habit.''

"I thought love had something to do with passion,'' Jack said, trying to keep his voice light.

"Passion? I'm not sure passion has anything to do with it at all. Look at me, for instance. I've loved you for a long time.'' She smiled at his expression of surprise. "You didn't know? Well, why should you? It wasn't the kind of love that demands attention. It was the kind of love that's comforting. I knew it was there, and it helped me. If you didn't know it was there, or nobody knew it was there, it didn't matter. It was my love, and I liked it. And it had nothing to do with passion.''

"And what about the other afternoon?''

"That was passion,'' Sylvia said softly. "And I liked it. But it scares me.''

"Scares you?''

"Yes. I keep wondering—after the passion dies, will I still have my love? Or will that fade too? I don't want it to, Jack. I want to be able to go on loving you."

Their eyes met, and Jack reached out to touch her hand.

"And I want you to go on loving me, Sylvia. I want you to very much."

Together they walked to Sylvia's bedroom and closed the door. Their drinks sat forgotten on the kitchen table, and the ice in the glasses slowly melted.

Rose heard the car grinding up the driveway and glanced at the clock. He'd been gone almost three hours. She wondered if he'd notice the light under the study door when he came in, or whether he was too drunk. She heard the front door open, and her husband's footsteps in the hall. They stopped, then started again, and she heard him coming toward the study. He'd seen the light.

She waited till the study door opened before she spoke.

"I hope no children disappear tonight," she said coldly. "I won't be able to vouch for your whereabouts." She looked at him icily, but he didn't flinch. She realized he was sober.

"If it becomes necessary, Sylvia Bannister can tell anyone who's interested where I've been tonight. And what I've been doing."

"I see," Rose said quietly, absorbing what he was telling her. "I suppose I should have known. She's been in love with you for years. I didn't know it was mutual."

"I didn't either, until recently," Jack said. "Are we going to have a fight about it?"

"Do you want one?" Rose countered.

Jack smiled and sat down. "No, I don't. I've had enough of fighting, Rose, with you, with everything. If you really want to know, I didn't want to come home tonight. Sylvia sent me."

"Sent you?" Rose asked, her brows arching. "Was she afraid the neighbors would talk?"

"No. She was worried about you. She likes you, you know."

"And I like her. But not so much that I'll let her take my place."

Jack chuckled. "It wasn't very long ago that you were thinking about leaving me."

"A woman has pride. If I left you it wouldn't be so that you could marry Sylvia Bannister. You'd be so broke that you wouldn't be able to marry anyone."

"I see," Jack said, standing up. "Somehow this conversation seems to have gotten out of hand. I have no intention of asking you for a divorce, at least not right now. So I think I'll go to bed."

"Not yet," Rose said. She realized that it sounded like a command, and that Jack wouldn't respond to a command. Not tonight. She softened her voice. "Please," she said. "Something happened tonight, and I don't know what it means or what we should do about it."

Jack sank back into the chair he had been occupying. "You mean after I left?"

Rose nodded. "I couldn't sleep, and after a while I decided to get something to eat. I went down to the kitchen, and while I was there Sarah came in."

"So?"

"I'm sorry. She came in from outside. She was dripping wet and covered with mud. Needless to say, I haven't the slightest idea where she'd been, or why."

"What did you do?"

"What could I do? I took her upstairs, bathed her, and put her to bed. I waited till she fell asleep, then came down here. I've been here ever since, trying to figure out what she could have been doing."

"Did she do anything in the kitchen?"

"If you mean, did she make one of her scenes, no. But I had the strangest feeling. I was burrowing around in the fridge when she came in, and I didn't hear her. I didn't realize there was anyone there till I felt the draft from the open door. When I realized there was someone in the room, my first thought was to grab a knife. And that's when I saw Sarah. She was standing by the knife drawer, and it seemed like she was trying to make up her mind about something."

"About what?"

"I don't know," Rose said uncomfortably. Then: "Oh, yes, I do know. It seemed to me that she was trying to choose one of the knives. I'm probably wrong, but that's the way it seemed."

Jack considered it, turning everything over in his mind, but he could come up with no answers.

"Is she still in her room?" he asked.

"Yes. I'd have heard her if she'd come down."

"Well, I don't see what we can do tonight. Let's go to bed, and look in on her. Then I'll call Dr. Belter in the morning. I doubt if it's anything serious, though. She was probably sleepwalking."

"No," Rose said definitely. "She wasn't sleepwalking, I'm sure she was awake, and I'm sure she knew what she was doing. And I'm very much afraid of what it might have been."

She was thinking of Kathy Burton and Jimmy Tyler, and Jack knew it. But he saw no reason to try to talk to her about it. It would be better to let Dr. Belter handle it in the morning.

"Come on," he said gently, "let's go to bed."

As he led her upstairs, he realized that Sylvia was right. He did love his wife. He loved her very much. He hoped it wasn't too late for them.

## TWENTY-THREE

THE NEXT DAY, COLUMBUS DAY, DAWNED bright and cold, with a north wind rattling the house at the end of Conger's Point. By nine o'clock the brightness was gone, and the gray skies blended into an almost invisible horizon with the leaden sea. There was a heavy swell running, and the surf pounded at the Point with a winter strength.

"I know it's a holiday," Rose heard Jack saying into the telephone as she came down the stairs. "But I think it's pretty important. She seems to have been sleepwalking."

Fifteen miles away, in his cramped apartment at White Oaks, Charles Belter was stifling a yawn. He came awake at the word and his brows knit into a frown. Sleepwalking? It didn't fit the pattern. "Just what do you mean by sleepwalking?" he inquired. He yawned again, covering the mouthpiece of the telephone, and reached for his coffee. He was glad Jack Conger was at least aware it was a holiday, even if he didn't intend to respect the fact.

"Well," Jack was saying, "I'm not really sure she was sleepwalking. It just seems to be the most logical explanation. She was wandering around in the rain last night."

Belter set his coffee down and straightened up. "In the rain?" he said. "You mean outside?"

"That's right."

"What time was this?"

"I'd say about eleven thirty. Maybe midnight."

"How long was she outside?"

"I don't have any idea. We didn't know she'd gone anywhere. My wife came down to get something to eat, and while she was in the kitchen Sarah came in. Soaking wet and muddy."

"I see," Dr. Belter said. "Did she seem to be all right otherwise?"

"I—I don't really know," Jack faltered. "I wasn't home."

When there was no reply, Jack felt he ought to explain a little more. "I had to go out for a while," he said.

"What time did you get back?" Dr. Belter inquired, hearing something in Jack's voice that made him want to pry a little.

"I'm not sure," Jack hedged. "Late. I guess around three."

"I see," Dr. Belter said again. "May I assume you want to talk to me today?"

"If it wouldn't be too inconvenient for you. We think we're going to have to make up our minds about what to do with Sarah, and we'd like to talk it over with you. And after last night it suddenly seems urgent."

It seems urgent to you, anyway, Dr. Belter thought. Aloud he said, "Suppose you and your wife come out here about one?"

"Shall we bring Sarah with us?"

Dr. Belter thought about it. "I don't think so," he said. "There really isn't any need for it, and most of the staff is off today, so there isn't anyone around to look after her while we talk."

"All right," Jack said. "We'll see you at one, then." He hung up the phone and smiled at Rose. She did not return his smile.

"One o'clock," he said. "But he doesn't want us to bring Sarah."

Rose looked doubtful. "I don't know," she said. "I hate to leave her alone."

"She won't be alone. Elizabeth will be here, and Mrs. Goodrich."

"It just seems to me, with everything that's been happening, it's not a good idea to leave the children alone."

"I don't call being left with Mrs. Goodrich being left alone. When I was a boy she used to watch me like a hawk when my folks were away. I think she had visions of the Lindberghs in her mind."

"That was a long time ago," Rose commented. "She's getting a bit old to be watching children."

"Not that old," Jack said.

"Oh, I don't know," Rose said. "I suppose I wouldn't worry, but with Sarah . . ." Her voice trailed off, and she poured some coffee into her cup. Jack pushed his toward her, but she ignored it.

"It'll be all right," Jack insisted, and reached for the coffeepot.

"What will?" Elizabeth asked. Jack looked up and smiled at his daughter. He looked for Sarah behind her, but she wasn't there.

"Where's your sister?" he asked.

"Still asleep," Elizabeth replied. "She didn't want to wake up this morning, so I left her in bed. If you want, I'll go up and get her." She paused, then repeated her question. "What'll be all right?"

"We have to go see Dr. Belter this afternoon," Jack said. "Your mother's a little worried about leaving you and Sarah alone while we're gone."

"Won't Mrs. Goodrich be here?"

"Of course she will."

"Then why should you worry?" Elizabeth asked her mother. "I'm old enough to stay by myself, and I can take care of Sarah."

"I'm sure you can," Rose said reassuringly. "Ordinarily I wouldn't worry at all, but with the things that have been happening lately, I just want to be extra careful. That's all."

Elizabeth smiled at her mother. "Well, stop worrying. Nothing's going to happen."

It began drizzling at noon, and Rose wished she didn't have to go out. She looked longingly at the fireplace in the study and thought about how nice it would be to simply curl up on the sofa and spend the afternoon reading. But she couldn't. There were things that had to be done, and decisions that had to be made. But not right now. She sank down into the wing chair and stared moodily into the fire. She felt melancholy coming over her, and tried to force it away. She glanced up at the portrait, and found that her first thought was that it actually was a picture of Elizabeth. She reminded herself that it was not, and wondered once more who the girl in the portrait was. Could she really be the little girl that Dr. Belter had heard about? No, she told herself. The whole thing is silly. She stood up and straightened the picture. In the flickering light of the fire the child's expression seemed to change a little; something in the eyes. She looked again and decided that her own eyes were playing tricks on her. Whatever she'd thought she had seen was gone.

"Well," Jack said from the door, "we might as well get going."

"Already?" Rose said. "We have plenty of time." She wanted to put it off, and she knew it. She had a feeling about today, a feeling that today was going to be some kind of turning point. She wanted to put the interview with the doctor off as long as possible.

"I know," Jack said gently. "I'm not looking forward to it either. But it's something that has to be done."

"Yes," Rose sighed. "I suppose so. All right. Let me put on my coat. Are the girls downstairs?"

"I think they're in the playroom."

"Call them down, will you? I want to kiss them good-bye."

Jack looked at her curiously. "Rose, we're only going to talk today. You're acting like it's the end of the world or something."

She smiled tightly. "I suppose I am. But call them down anyway, will you?"

She began putting on her coat and heard Jack's voice calling from the foot of the stairs. When she got to the front door the children were waiting for her.

She kissed Elizabeth perfunctorily, then knelt by Sarah and put her arms around the child. She nuzzled Sarah's cheek, and felt the little girl withdraw slightly.

"You be good now," she whispered. "Mommy and Daddy have to go out for a while." She stood up again and smiled at Elizabeth. "We should be back by four thirty or five," she said. "Please stay in the house."

"Who wants to go out in that?" Elizabeth said.

"I know," Rose agreed. "It's awful, isn't it?"

"I wish it would snow," Elizabeth said. "At least it's pretty. This is depressing."

Rose smiled at her daughter's use of the word. She was definitely growing up, if she was starting to find the weather "depressing."

She left the house with her husband and got into the car. She turned to wave to the children as they drove away, then began preparing herself for the interview with Dr. Belter.

Elizabeth watched the car until it reached the Point Road, then closed the door. She was about to go upstairs when the phone rang.

"I'll get it," she called to Mrs. Goodrich. "Hello?" she said into the receiver.

"Who's this?" a voice asked.

"It's Elizabeth. Who's this?"

"Jeff Stevens. What are you doing?"

"Nothing. My parents had to go some place, and I'm taking care of Sarah."

"Oh." Jeff sounded disappointed. "I thought we might go look for the cave," he said.

"The cave? I thought you didn't believe there was a cave."

"I don't. And if we can't find it you'll have to admit I'm right, won't you?"

"I don't know," Elizabeth said noncommittally. "I don't see how our not finding it would prove it isn't there. That doesn't make sense. All it would prove is that we didn't find it."

"If it's there, we can find it. You want to try?"

Elizabeth thought about it. "Why don't you come over here?" she said. "Will your parents let you?"

"They're out playing golf," Jeff said.

"In the rain?"

"It doesn't bother them. They always play until it snows. Sometimes they even play in the snow."

"Weird," Elizabeth commented.

"Yeah," Jeff said. "I'll see you in a little while."

Elizabeth hung up the phone and went to find Mrs. Goodrich, to tell her Jeff Stevens was coming over. In the kitchen she could hear the sound of the old housekeeper's television droning from the next room. Elizabeth tapped lightly on the door. When there was no response, she tried the door, and finding it unlocked opened it and looked into the room. Mrs. Goodrich was sitting in her chair, facing the television. She was sound asleep. Elizabeth smiled to herself and closed the door again.

Twenty minutes later Jeff Stevens arrived, and Elizabeth led him to the back study. Sarah followed silently along behind, her wide brown eyes seeming to take in everything and see nothing.

"This is where my great-great-uncle left the rabbit," Elizabeth said, pointing to the wing chair.

"And that's the little girl who was supposed to have been killed?" Jeff asked, pointing to the portrait above the fireplace.

"That's Beth," Elizabeth said, nodding her head.

"She looks just like you," Jeff said.

"I know. But she isn't me. I don't like her."

Jeff grinned at her. "You sound like you know her."

"I do," Elizabeth said. "I've talked to her."

"That's dumb," Jeff said. "You can't talk to dead people."

"Yes you can," Elizabeth insisted. "With the Ouija board."

"It didn't say anything the other day," Jeff said sarcastically. "All it did was spell out a name. And I'll bet you did that."

"It was her," Elizabeth said defiantly.

"Well, if it's all true, let's go find the cave. If there is one, I'll bet that's where your friend Beth is."

"I don't know," Elizabeth said. "The cave is supposed to be on the embankment, and I'm not supposed to go there."

"I'm not either," Jeff said. "But I'm not going to let that stop me. Are you chicken?"

"No, but I just don't think we should."

"You're afraid we won't find it and you'll have to admit you're wrong."

"All right, then," Elizabeth said suddenly. "Let's go." She turned to leave the room, and Jeff smiled. It had worked.

Elizabeth found her coat and put it on. "We'll have to take Sarah with us," she said. "I can't leave her here by herself."

"What about the housekeeper? Can't she watch her?"

"She's asleep. Besides, she wouldn't know what to do if Sarah gets upset."

Jeff decided it was better to take Sarah with them than not to go at all.

"All right," he agreed. "Let's go."

Elizabeth put Sarah into her coat and buttoned it up. Then the three children left the house.

The rain seemed to have let up slightly as they crossed the field, and when they were in the woods the trees protected them from it almost completely. As they entered the woods, Jeff looked around.

"Which way?" he asked.

"There's a path," Elizabeth said. "You can hardly see it, but it's there. Come on." Her voice seemed suddenly different to Jeff, and he thought her eyes looked odd.

Silently and quickly she led the way through the woods, and Jeff was amazed at her sure-footedness. Elizabeth seemed to know exactly where she was going, and where to put each foot in the tangle of roots and rocks that carpeted the path. Nor did she look back to see if the others were keeping up. Twice Jeff had to call to her to wait, and he stopped two more times to help Sarah, who was picking her way with great difficulty. And then they emerged from the woods and stood on the embankment. The rain had begun coming down harder now, and the wind whipped it into their faces. Below them the sea looked angry. Jeff felt himself shiver a little, and wondered if he should have talked them into this. The embankment looked as dangerous as his parents had told him it was.

"Where do you suppose it is?" he said, hoping that Elizabeth would suggest that they give it up.

"I'm not sure," Elizabeth said. "Let's try this way." She led them along the embankment, and Jeff was about to suggest that it was too dangerous when Elizabeth suddenly started making her way down the face, following a path that Jeff couldn't see at all. He watched her move surely from rock to rock and decided that if she could do it, so could he.

But he found it more difficult than he had imagined. The rocks were slippery, and he couldn't seem to find the same toeholds that had served Elizabeth so well. He made his way slowly, trying to keep one eye on Elizabeth to try to see where she was putting her feet. Now and then he glanced back to see how Sarah was faring, but she seemed to be able to keep up with him, and in a couple of minutes he stopped worrying about her. The rain was making the rocks more slippery every minute, and he was afraid he was about to lose sight of Elizabeth as she made her way nimbly downward. He called to her, but she didn't hear him over the roar of the wind and the surf. And then she disappeared behind a large boulder.

He crept cautiously along, picking his way from one rock to another, and concentrated on keeping the large boulder behind which Elizabeth had disappeared in sight. Behind him Sarah was matching his slow pace.

"Here."

Jeff jumped at the sound of the word, and peered into the shadow of the huge stone. There was Elizabeth, crouching low to protect herself from the rain and wind.

"What?" he said.

"It's here," Elizabeth told him. "I found the cave."

Jeff frowned and searched the darkness. "There's nothing there," he said.

"Yes, there is," Elizabeth insisted. "Come down here."

He climbed down till he was beside her. "Where?"

"Right there," Elizabeth said, pointing. Then he saw it. There, in the rock's deep shadow, almost invisible in the darkness, was a hole in the embankment. He moved closer and peered in. He was aware of Sarah behind him, pulling at him and making small, sobbing noises. He shook her off, and when she reached out for him again Elizabeth took her hands and stared into her eyes. A moment later, Sarah was calm.

"What do you suppose is inside?" Jeff asked.

"I don't know," Elizabeth replied. "Shall we look?"

Jeff looked doubtfully at the hole. It seemed just large enough to crawl into, and he wasn't sure it led anywhere. Still, he didn't want to look like a coward.

"I'll go first," he said, trying to sound much more confident than he felt.

He made his way into the tunnel, and found that there was enough room to crawl comfortably. He eased forward, feeling his way in the darkness.

Behind him Elizabeth took the flashlight from its hiding place, but she didn't turn it on. She followed along behind Jeff. Sarah followed Elizabeth.

Jeff wasn't sure how far they had gone in the tunnel, but in the blackness it seemed like a long way. He was beginning to get frightened, and was on the verge of telling Elizabeth that he thought they had gone far enough when he felt a change around him. Though he could see nothing in the blackness, it felt as though there was more space around him than there had been. He reached out and realized that he was right. He could no longer feel the close walls of the tunnel. He wondered how large the cavern they were now in was, and crept cautiously onward. His hand felt the lip of the shaft, and he stopped. He felt around in the darkness, trying to determine how deep the drop was. He felt Elizabeth bump into him. He drew himself up and crouched in a squatting position next to the shaft.

"There's something here," he said. "It drops off. I can't tell how deep it is, or how wide."

And then he felt the push from behind him, and he grabbed wildly in the dark. But there was nothing for him to grab on to, and he felt himself falling through the darkness. He hit the bottom before he could scream, and the blackness deepened. Jeff Stevens lay still on the floor of the pit.

In the upper cavern, Elizabeth turned on the flashlight and moved to the edge of the shaft. She shined the light downward. It illuminated Jeff's inert form sprawled by the large flattish rock that she had used as a table for her tea parties. She could see nothing else in the pool of light, and after a moment she set the flashlight down and began uncoiling the rope ladder. Behind her, Sarah emerged from the tunnel and sat cross-legged, trembling, watching her sister. Elizabeth lowered the ladder into the shaft, and a moment later, the flashlight glowing dimly in her coat pocket, she disappeared down into the blackness below. Sarah crept forward and peered into the depths.

The candles still stood wedged into the cracks where she had left them, and the cigarette lighter still lay in its crevice beneath one of the candles. When she had lit the candles, Elizabeth turned off the flashlight and looked around.

Kathy Burton lay where she had fallen, her forehead badly discolored from the blow of the rock. Her eyes were open, and her face was beginning to bloat. Elizabeth poked at her curiously, and when there was no movement Elizabeth tried to close the eyes. They wouldn't close.

Jimmy Tyler lay naked, huddled against the wall of the cave. His eyes, too, were open, but they held the expression of a small and terrified creature. He was whimpering and shivering. When Elizabeth approached him he seemed not to see her, and there was no reaction when she touched him. He was clutching the torso of the dead cat to his chest, as if it were a teddy bear. The smell of death filled every corner of the cavern, and Elizabeth breathed deeply of it. She smiled at the skeleton that lay against the wall.

"It's good, isn't it?" she whispered. "Look, they're all here now. Mommy and Daddy and their baby. And your father, Beth. I brought your father to visit you today. Do you want to talk to your father?"

She dragged Jeff Stevens's unconscious body over to the skeleton and laid it out next to the fleshless bones. She moved the arms of the skeleton so that Jeff lay in its cold embrace.

Slowly Elizabeth began setting up another tea party, the last tea party. She dragged the body of Kathy Burton from the spot where it lay and wrenched it into a sitting position on one of the small stones that surrounded the table. It pitched forward and lay face down on the larger slab of rock. Then Elizabeth began working the torso of the cat loose from Jimmy Tyler's grasp. He fought with her mindlessly, unaware of what was going on but not wanting to be disturbed in whatever place his mind had taken him to. He fought passively, his small arms trying to hold on to the body of the cat, but he did not try to kick out at Elizabeth. He fought silently, against a force that no longer made any sense to him. The cat slipped loose from his grip, and his arms closed on the empty space.

She propped the cat up once more, but was not able to make the head balance on the rotting shoulders. She watched it roll off, and let it lie where it came to rest, a no-longer-recognizable object in a soiled blue bonnet.

Then she began moving Jimmy Tyler. He didn't resist; he didn't realize that anything was happening to him. With nothing left to hold on to, he seemed to give up, and Elizabeth was able to prop him up, his vacant eyes staring blankly off through the flickering candlelight.

Elizabeth began talking, but her speech was incoherent. Her voice kept changing pitch, and it was as if she were two people, first one and then the other.

As she talked she began to grow angry. She demanded that the objects of her anger respond to her, and when they didn't her rage only increased.

"Answer me," she cried, and the voice was not her own. "I want to know why you did it! Why did you leave me here? It's dark here, and it's cold. It frightens me. Why do you want to frighten me? Why can't I come out of here and be with everyone else?"

There was a silence, as she waited for an answer. But there was no answer.

"You're all alike," she hissed. "All of you. None of you have ever changed. You love *her*." She kicked at the body of the cat, and it fell at the base of the cavern wall. "You always pay more attention to her. Why can't you pay attention to me, too?"

And then she seemed to change again, and she stared down at the unconscious Jeff. "You're where you want to be now, aren't you? I wouldn't help you that day, would I? So you put me down here, by myself. But I knew you'd come back. And you'll stay with me this time. This time you'll stay. You and *all of them*."

Elizabeth snatched the knife from the ledge where it had long lain hidden and whirled to face the children. *"You'll all stay with me now!"* she screamed.

She fell upon the body of Kathy Burton, hacking at it with the knife, chopping wildly, tearing at the flesh of the corpse. When it lay dismembered, she turned to Jimmy Tyler.

He screamed as the knife plunged into his stomach, then fell gurgling to the floor of the cavern as she drew it out again and stabbed at his throat. He wriggled beneath her, his body responding reflexively as the knife cut at him. Elizabeth lay on top of him, the knife flashing in the yellow light of the candles as she continued to slash at him. In her fury she did not hear the low moans that came from Jeff Stevens as he slowly regained consciousness.

He was trying to remember what had happened. He'd been in the dark, and somebody had pushed him. He'd been falling. In the cave. He was in the cave. But it wasn't dark any more. Instead, there was a yellowish glow, as if candles were burning. And sounds. Strange, gurgling noises. He opened his eyes and tried to move his head.

He saw Elizabeth. His stomach heaved as he realized what she was doing. She was stabbing at something, but there was so much blood he couldn't see what it was. He heaved himself to his hands and knees and looked again. It was a little boy. Elizabeth was stabbing a little boy.

"No!" he cried out. He tried to get to his feet, but he was too dizzy. He saw Elizabeth turn, and heard her speak.

"You!" she cried. "You made me do this, Daddy. You did it to me, and now I'll do it to you. You'll stay here with me, Daddy. You won't leave me alone again."

He knew then that she was insane, and he tried to protect himself, but there was nothing he could do. His mind, still numb from his fall, seemed incapable of deciding which muscles to move, and his arms and legs wouldn't respond properly. Through hazy eyes he saw the knife flash out at him, but he felt nothing. He only saw the blood gush from his arm. Again he tried to move away, or raise his arm in defense, but he felt paralyzed. Terror welled up in him, and the knife was flashing at him. Again and again. Soon he saw nothing. He wondered why he felt no pain. It should hurt, he thought; dying should hurt. But it did not hurt, and Jeff Stevens drifted slowly into death. As the fog began to close over his mind, Jeff began to pray.

Elizabeth continued to slash at him long after he died, and when she was done his body was no longer recognizable. It lay in pieces, scattered across the floor of the cavern, mixed with the dismembered corpses of Jimmy Tyler and Kathy Burton. And then her rage was spent, and Elizabeth sat in the midst of the gore and stared curiously around her.

"Why did you do that?" she said softly. "I don't understand why you had to do it. They didn't do anything to you. They were your friends. And besides, it all happened so long ago. So very long ago." She crawled across the floor of the cavern, and knelt over the skeleton.

"You shouldn't have done it, Beth," she said, her voice a little stronger. "You should have left them alone. They weren't who you thought they were. He wasn't your father. Your father died a long time ago. And the others. They weren't my parents, and that cat wasn't Sarah. It was only a cat, Beth. A poor, helpless cat. Why did you make me do it? I don't hate them, Beth. I don't. It's you who hate them. It's you who hate all of them. Why can't you leave them alone? They didn't do anything to you. None of them did. *None of them.*" And she was angry again, but now she was angry at Beth, poor Beth, who had died so long ago.

Elizabeth grabbed one of the arm bones and raised it over her head.

*"Die!"* she screamed. *"Why won't you die and leave us alone?"* She brought the bone down, crushing the skull. "Die," she whispered once more. "Please die, and leave me alone."

And then it was over. Elizabeth stood up and walked to the rope ladder. She didn't blow out the candles; they would die of their own accord. Nor did she pull the ladder up from the shaft. There was no need to now; she would not be coming back, nor would anyone use the ladder to escape. Elizabeth crept through the tunnel and emerged from the hole in the embankment. She began climbing upward, away from the cave.

In the darkness, Sarah stared down into the flickering yellow light below. Then, slowly, she began making her way down the ladder.

Sarah worked slowly in the pit, trying to fit the pieces back together.

When she was finished, she found the canteen of water she had dropped down the shaft so long ago. She put the mouth of the bottle to the lips of each of the dead children, and tried to make them drink.

Then she sat down, and looked around her.

She sat for a long time, waiting.

## TWENTY-FOUR

I T WAS FOUR THIRTY WHEN DR. CHARLES Belter wound up the meeting with Jack and Rose Conger. He was not convinced that anything had been accomplished, nor was he convinced that anything needed to be accomplished. He had spent the better part of the afternoon not in attempting to second-guess the direction that Sarah's illness might be taking, but in reassuring her worried parents. That was half the battle, he had discovered, in dealing with a case like Sarah's. The parents read too many books, and of the wrong sort. They were convinced that their children were turning into some sort of monsters, and no matter what happened, they projected the worst. His job, he had found, was not so much to treat the child as to calm the parents.

And he had succeeded. As they drove home through the rain they felt better about everything. Dr. Belter had told them not to worry. They had faith in the doctor; they wouldn't worry. The rain came down harder, and they could feel the temperature dropping.

"Early winter this year," Jack commented as he turned off the Conger's Point Road. "This could turn into snow any time."

"I always like the first snow out here," Rose said. "Sometimes I think the house was designed for winter. The snow seems to soften it somehow." She looked through the rain to the old house, looming up ahead, and felt a strange sense of foreboding. It's the weather, she thought. Rain always makes the place so gloomy.

The phone started ringing as they opened the front door.

"Got it," Jack called, and picked up the receiver with one hand as he unbuttoned his dripping coat with the other. "Hello?"

"Jack? Barbara Stevens. We just got home from playing golf—"

"In this weather?" Jack said, disbelieving.

Barbara chuckled. "Some of us will play in anything. But I'll tell you something, just between us. That old shack that serves as a clubhouse needs a new roof."

"It needs a new everything, but there aren't enough members to do it. Besides, I doubt that anybody but you would be out there on a day like today."

"It was pretty wet," Barbara admitted. "Anyway, I was just wondering if Jeff is over there. He was supposed to be home all afternoon, but he isn't here. And since he doesn't really know anyone yet except you, I thought he might be playing with your kids."

"We just got in ourselves," Jack said. "Hang on, and I'll find out if he's here." He set the receiver on the table and turned to Rose, who was watching him curiously.

"Barbara Stevens," he said. "She's wondering if Jeff is here."

Rose felt a sinking sensation in her stomach. She was remembering a similar telephone call, a call that had come from Kathy Burton's mother only days ago. How many days? She couldn't remember. Her feeling of foreboding increased.

"What's wrong?" Jack asked his wife, seeing her face lose its color.

"Nothing," Rose said. "I was just thinking—" She broke off. "Nothing," she said again. "I'll call Elizabeth."

She stepped to the foot of the stairs and called upward, her voice echoing through the house. In a moment they heard a door open and close, and footsteps approaching the head of the stairs. Then Rose saw her daughter.

"Hi," Elizabeth said. "I didn't hear you come in. I was reading."

"Didn't you hear the phone ring?" Rose asked curiously.

"Yes, but when it stopped after the second ring I figured Mrs. Goodrich had gotten it. Is it for me?"

"No," Rose said. "It's Mrs. Stevens. Is Jeff here?"

"Jeff?" Elizabeth asked. "He left hours ago."

The feeling of foreboding flooded over Rose.

"Then he was here?"

Elizabeth nodded. "Oh, yes. He came over right after you left. He said he wanted to hunt for the cave."

"The cave?" Rose frowned.

"You know. The legend. He said it doesn't exist, and he wanted to go look for it. He wanted me to go with him, but I wouldn't. I told him it was too dangerous. Besides, it was raining."

Jack, who had been listening to the conversation between Rose and Elizabeth, picked the telephone up again.

"Barbara?" he said. "Apparently he was here, but that was early this afternoon. Elizabeth doesn't know where he was going, but apparently he said something about wanting to hunt for the cave."

"The cave?" Barbara asked. "You mean the one on the embankment on the Point?"

"I guess so," Jack replied. "If there really is one. It's mostly just an old family legend. No one's ever found it."

"The embankment's dangerous, isn't it?" Barbara said, worry sharpening her voice.

Jack decided to be truthful. "Yes, it is. That's one of the reasons we've kept the legend going. It's been a useful tool for keeping children away from a dangerous place."

"I know. Rose told me about it when we moved in. We told Jeff to stay away from there."

"Then I'm sure he did," Jack said reassuringly. "He probably just decided to go for a hike and lost track of time."

"I don't know," Barbara said, the anxiety in her voice rising. "He doesn't know the area, and he's usually pretty responsible about things."

"But he's a teenager," Jack reminded her. "They can be counted on not to be counted on."

"I suppose so," Barbara said doubtfully. "Well, I won't start worrying for another hour. If he isn't home by six, I don't know what we'll do."

"I'm sorry I couldn't help you more. If he turns up here, we'll call you." They said good-bye, and Jack hung up the phone. He turned to Rose, and the worry he had not allowed to show in his voice was etched on his face.

"It's like the others, isn't it?" he said.

Rose nodded mutely. It was too much like the others. And then she remembered Sarah. Sarah had not been standing behind her sister at the head of the stairs. She glanced upward and saw Elizabeth still standing where she had been, waiting to be told what Mrs. Stevens had said.

"Where's Sarah?" Rose said, finding her voice.

"Sarah?" Elizabeth repeated the name. "In her room, I guess. Or the playroom." She fell silent and appeared to be listening. "Just a second," she said. "I'll look."

They heard her footsteps in the hall as she made her way first to Sarah's room, then to the playroom. When they heard her approaching the head of the stairs again, and did not hear the soft murmur of her voice speaking to her sister, they knew that she had not found Sarah. Elizabeth reappeared at the head of the stairs and started down.

"She's not up here," she was saying. "She's probably with Mrs. Good-rich."

As they began searching downstairs, Rose knew they would not find Sarah. Instead of joining in the search, she went into her little office and sank into the chair at her desk. For some reason she found some security there, some security she was suddenly sure she was going to need.

"Well," Jack said, trying to keep his voice steady. "She isn't down here, either. Mrs. Goodrich thought she was upstairs."

"She's got to be here," Rose said desperately. "Look upstairs again. She might be in our room, or the guest room. And the attic. Look in the attic."

She did not volunteer to join in the search, for she was sure it was useless. Sarah was not in the house. Rose sat in her desk chair and listened as Elizabeth and Jack made their way systematically through the house. There was a silence as they searched the third-floor attic; then she heard them on the second floor, and finally coming down the stairs. They came into the small office, and Jack shook his head. "Nothing," he said. "She's not here."

"I didn't think she would be," Rose said. "Not when she wasn't in her room." They looked at one another, unsure of what to do next.

"The barn," Elizabeth said suddenly. "Maybe she went out to the barn." Without waiting for an answer from her parents, she left the room, and they heard the front door open. And then they heard Elizabeth scream.

It was not the same sort of scream they were used to from Sarah, the frustrated scream of a child who finds herself unable to communicate by any other means. Elizabeth's was a scream of horror. It froze Jack and Rose momentarily; then they were on their feet, racing for the front door. They found Elizabeth on the front porch, staring wildly out at the field. They followed the direction of her eyes, and Rose felt a scream emerging from her own lips. She was able to suppress it only by clamping her hand over her mouth.

From the woods, a small form had emerged, and was now making its way across the field toward the house. It was Sarah, and even from here they could see that she was soaking wet and covered with mud. And there was something else. Something that streaked her face and arms, and stained her clothing with a redness that they knew was not mud.

It was blood. Sarah was covered with blood.

"Jesus God," Jack muttered, his mind almost unable to accept what his eyes were seeing. And then he remembered that Elizabeth, too, was watching the strange apparition that was coming slowly across the field. He took his daughter's arm and pulled her into the house.

Elizabeth seemed dazed, and she did not resist as Jack led her upstairs and into her room.

"Stay here," he said. "Don't come downstairs until I come up to get you." He looked at her closely, and saw that her face was pale and she was shaking. "Are you all right?"

She nodded, and her mouth moved. "What's wrong with her, Daddy?" she said in a small voice. "Is she hurt?"

"I don't know," Jack said. "But it will be all right. Just stay here, and it will be all right." Elizabeth, suddenly seeming much younger, peered up into his face, and he gathered her into his arms. She began sobbing quietly.

"It's going to be all right, honey," Jack whispered. "I'll take care of her." He rocked her gently, and she calmed down. He laid her on the bed. "Try not to think about it," he said. "I have to go down and help her now, but I'll be back in a little while. Try not to think about it," he repeated, and knew that there was no way she would be able to blot what she had seen out of her mind.

Rose was still standing on the front porch, her hand still clamped over her mouth, and tears were streaming down her cheeks. Sarah was still in the field, getting closer to the house, moving slowly, the object she carried dragging in the mud behind her. It was getting colder, and there was snow mixed with the rain now.

Small sounds started to come out of Rose as she tried to come to terms with what she was seeing. The object in Sarah's hand was clearly visible now, and as the realization of what it was came to Jack he had to fight down the rising nausea in his stomach.

It was a child's arm, and it had been severed at the shoulder. It seemed to be badly lacerated, and the blood was slowly oozing from it, dripping from the ragged stump that bumped through the mud behind Sarah.

Sarah seemed unaware of the rain and snow, or of the cold. She moved forward steadily, her vacant eyes fixed on her parents as they stood on the porch waiting for her. Jack wanted to go to her, to pick her up and carry her home, but he was unable to. Helplessly he stood next to his wife as their daughter came toward them.

And then she was home. She stood at the bottom of the steps to the porch and stared blankly up at them. Then she lifted the severed arm and held it out, presenting it to them as if it were a gift.

The hysteria she had been holding back swept over Rose. Her mouth opened jerkily, and the scream that had been struggling in her throat burst forth to resound across the field. The trees in the woods almost seemed to tremble with the screams that tore out of the tormented woman's being. Her eyes began playing tricks on her, and all she could see was the arm, the bloody arm, suspended against a background that was fast going black. It seemed to grow before her eyes, and then all she could see was the stump, the ragged flesh surrounding the bone. Her screams rose to a hysterical pitch.

Elizabeth's first scream had awakened Mrs. Goodrich, and she had sat peering dazedly at her television set, unsure whether or not it had been the source of the sound that had awakened her. When she began hearing Rose's screams she realized that it had not been the television. She got to her feet and headed stiffly for the front of the house.

The anguished cries grew as she approached the front door, but it wasn't until she was on the porch that she realized the cause. Her eyes widened at the sight of the bloodied, mud-covered child. She fought down the nausea and glanced at Rose, quickly realizing that it was the mother, not the daughter, who needed immediate attention.

"Take care of Miz Rose," she commanded Jack. She moved forward and, swallowing hard, disengaged Sarah's fingers from the wrist of the dismembered arm. Taking Sarah by one hand and holding the grisly arm in the other, she led Sarah into the house. She took her quickly to the kitchen, and stood her in front of the sink. Then she wrapped the arm in a towel and set it aside. She began working on Sarah, stripping her clothes from her and wiping her off. Then she wrapped the child in an old blanket from her own room and went to the phone. She dialed the number for the police station and asked for Ray Norton.

"Ray," she said. "This is Mrs. Goodrich out at the Congers'. You'd better get out here fast. Something bad's happened. And bring a doctor with you. That one from White Oaks, if you can get hold of him. He knows us."

The police chief started to ask some questions, but the old housekeeper cut him off.

"When you get here," she said. "I've got other things to do." She hung up the telephone and returned to Sarah. The child sat meekly waiting, and offered no resistance as Mrs. Goodrich led her upstairs to the bathroom.

Mrs. Goodrich's command had brought Jack to his senses. He grabbed Rose and shook her.

"It's all right," he said. "Mrs. Goodrich is taking care of her." When Rose continued screaming, he shook her harder and yelled at her. *"It's all right!"* he shouted, and her screams suddenly stopped. She stared at him, her mouth working, her eyes wide.

"Come on," he said. He led her into the house and forced her to come with him to the back study. He poured two large tumblers of brandy and handed one of them to Rose. "Drink this," he commanded. "You need it."

Wordlessly she accepted the glass and drained half of it. Then, shakily, she sank to the sofa.

"What shall we do?" she breathed. "Oh, God, Jack, what shall we do?"

"Call Dr. Belter," Jack said quietly. "I'll call Dr. Belter. And Ray Norton." But neither of them made a move toward the telephone. They simply sat there, staring at each other, trying to assimilate what they had seen. They were still there, sitting in the study, when Ray Norton arrived.

He had been getting ready to go home when the call came. He had known immediately that something was wrong. Very wrong. In all the years he had known her, he had never known Mrs. Goodrich to use the telephone. So he called the White Oaks School and told Dr. Belter to meet him at the Congers'. Then he had gotten into his car and raced out the Conger's Point Road, using the siren for the first time since he had had it installed.

The front door stood open, and he didn't bother to ring the bell. He went in and closed the door behind him. He could hear water running somewhere upstairs, but there were no other sounds. He started for the stairs, then changed his mind and went down the hall to the back study. He opened the door and saw Jack and Rose Conger sitting quietly by the fireplace, their faces pale. Neither of them moved when he came into the room.

"Mrs. Goodrich called me," he said softly. "She said something happened out here."

"Yes," Jack said dully. "Only we don't know what." He fell silent, and Ray Norton moved closer.

"Are you all right?" he said. "What happened?"

"You'd better call Dr. Belter at the White Oaks School," Jack said. "I was going to do it myself, but . . ." His voice trailed off again.

"It's done," Norton said. "Mrs. Goodrich told me to call him. He's on his way." He paused, unsure whether he should wait for the doctor before pressing Jack and Rose for information. Whatever it was, it seemed to be over now. He got a feeling of shock from the house, but not of emergency. It was as if something terrible had passed over them, leaving them stunned. He decided to wait for the doctor. He noted the empty glasses in the hands of both the Congers, and, though he supposed that he shouldn't, he refilled them.

"You look like you need this," he said gently. He sat down, and together they waited for Dr. Belter. The sound of running water upstairs suddenly stopped, and the house was silent. Then Rose began to cry, very softly.

*  *  *

It was almost thirty minutes before they heard the doorbell ring, and Ray
Norton stood up to answer it. Then they heard the heavy clumping of Mrs.
Goodrich's feet coming down the stairs, and the murmur of voices. A
moment later the housekeeper opened the study door and let the psychiatrist
in. Without waiting to be asked, Mrs. Goodrich came into the room and
closed the door behind her.

"I put her to bed," she said. "She's asleep. And I looked in on Miss
Elizabeth. She's scared, but she's all right."

Dr. Belter looked curiously at Jack and Rose Conger.

"What happened?" he said, and when there was no answer, he turned
to the housekeeper. "What happened?" he asked again.

"Well," Mrs. Goodrich said shortly. "It isn't pretty, and I don't know
for sure what it's all about. I was in my room, watching television, and all of
a sudden I heard the most awful commotion. It was Miz Rose, and she was
screaming. 'Course, I didn't know who was screaming till I got to the front
porch, and after I got there I didn't pay much attention. It was Miss Sarah.
She was standing there, in the rain, all covered with mud and blood. And she
had something in her hand."

"What?" the doctor asked when the old woman fell silent. Mrs. Goodrich shot a glance toward Rose. "What was she carrying?" the doctor
pressed.

"It—it was an arm," Mrs. Goodrich said. "It's in the kitchen. I left it
there when I took Miss Sarah up to the bathroom."

"Oh, Jesus," Ray Norton breathed. He looked helplessly at the doctor,
wondering what to do. Dr. Belter realized he would have to take charge for
the moment.

"You'd better come with me," he told the police chief. "I don't see
what good it will do right now, but we'd better have a look at it."

The two men went to the kitchen and unwrapped the bloodstained
towel. Ray Norton felt his stomach rebelling at the grisly sight.

"A child," Dr. Belter said. "It's the right arm of a child."

Norton nodded dumbly. "How old?"

Dr. Belter shrugged. "Hard to say, but it looks like a small child. No
more than eight or nine."

"The same age as Jimmy Tyler," Ray Norton said softly. "And the
blood hasn't coagulated yet."

"It couldn't have happened very long ago," the doctor said. "It must
have been this afternoon."

They rewrapped the arm and returned to the study. Ray Norton looked
at the Congers uncomfortably.

"I know this is going to be hard," he said, as gently as he could, "but
I'm going to have to ask you some questions."

"I know," Jack said dully. "Can Dr. Belter take Rose upstairs? I think
she ought to lie down. I saw everything she saw."

"Of course," Norton replied, signaling the doctor to take Rose from
the room. He waited till they were gone, then sat down opposite Jack.

"What happened, Jack? Take your time. I know it must have been awful, but I have to know what happened."

"I don't know. We got home from White Oaks, and Sarah wasn't in the house. We searched, and then Elizabeth said she might be in the barn. She was going out to look, and when she got to the porch she screamed. Rose and I went out to see what was wrong, and . . . we saw her." He winced a little, seeing the gruesome scene once more. "She was covered with blood, and she was dragging that—that thing. God, Ray, it was awful."

"She was coming out of the woods?"

"Yes."

"Well. I know this isn't going to be pleasant for you, but I'm going to have to put together a search party. If Sarah found that thing in the woods, we've got to find the rest of the—" He broke off, not wanting to say what was in his mind.

"My God," Jack whispered suddenly, "I forgot."

Norton jerked his head up.

"It's Jeff Stevens," Jack continued softly, staring helplessly at the policeman. "He's missing too."

Norton stared back at Jack in disbelief. "Jeff Stevens?" He repeated the name as if he'd never heard it before. "The kid in the old Barnes house?"

Jack nodded dumbly.

"Shit," Norton muttered under his breath. Then: "Are you sure?"

"It's all the same," Jack said hopelessly. "He was in this area, he didn't show up at home. Just like the others."

Norton stood up. "I'll call his parents. I wonder if his father will want to be part of the search party."

"I suppose," Jack said. "We have to find out what's happening, don't we?" He paused a moment, then went on. "I'll come along too, Ray. The least I can do is help look."

Norton shook his head. "Not you," he said. "You've been through enough."

He went to the telephone and began making a series of calls. By the time he was finished, Carl and Barbara Stevens were on their way over and a search party had been organized. He looked out the window toward the woods. It had begun snowing, and it seemed to be falling harder each minute.

As he watched, the woods slowly disappeared into the snowstorm.

They searched the woods, first in the fading light of dusk, then using lights, but they found nothing. If there was a trail, the snow covered it, and as the night wore on the storm grew. After four hours they gave it up. The search party returned to the house on Conger's Point, but soon they began drifting back to town. There was nothing to be accomplished on the Point. In town, where there were no Congers to overhear, the people of Port Arbello could talk.

In the house on Conger's Point, only Ray Norton and Dr. Belter remained. They sat in the study with Jack Conger, and the three of them talked. There was no talk of whether something should be done with Sarah; only of what should be done. Jack Conger was tired. He was tired and he felt terribly alone. He sat with the doctor and the police chief only because it was his daughter they were discussing, his family. But he was beyond caring what they decided to do. He would do whatever had to be done. He poured himself another drink and seated himself by the fire. He envied Rose, who lay sedated and asleep upstairs.

Dr. Belter was just finishing a long explanation of the details of Sarah's illness. When he was done, Ray Norton lit his pipe, something he rarely did, and leaned back.

"Well, I just don't know what to do," he said at last. "I'm going to have to tell people something, you know."

Dr. Belter smiled tightly. "Tell them what you want. If you ask me, which I suppose you're about to do, I don't have any answers. I wish that search party had found something. But they didn't, and we can't change that."

Norton nodded his agreement. "Let me ask you a question. Is it possible, *at all possible,* for Sarah to have killed the children?"

"I don't know," Dr. Belter said hesitantly. He didn't like to deal in possibilities. He had seen so much that he was inclined to think that practically anything was possible. He saw that his answer was going to be unacceptable to the chief of police, so he weighed his words carefully.

"Let me put it this way. I have to say that, yes, it is possible for Sarah to have killed all three of the missing children. I say that not because I think she did, but because at the moment we don't have any alternatives to choose from. If I were you I'd keep searching. If this snow lasts through the winter, I'd continue looking in the spring. Somewhere out there is the rest of that body, and maybe two more bodies besides. And I certainly don't think that you can charge Sarah with anything on the basis of one arm. I admit, it's ugly. I admit, at the moment we don't have much else to think. But you should also be aware that if you try to claim that Sarah is responsible for the dismembering of one child and the disappearance of two others, nothing is going to happen. Any psychiatrist you find will tell you the same thing I will. Sarah is not responsible for what she does. She is almost hopelessly schizophrenic. I say almost because with her kind of disorder there is always a chance that she'll come out of it. But even if she does, there's no guarantee that she'll be able to tell you what happened. She probably won't remember. Frankly, if I were you I'd keep the case open."

"And what about Sarah?" Ray Norton said uneasily. "What if she is responsible?"

"I don't think there's too much question about Sarah's future. I'm sure that after the last couple of days the Congers will agree that it's time she was institutionalized. It'll be the best thing for her, and the best for them. They can't go on living as they have been." He looked to Jack, and Jack nodded his agreement.

"When?" Jack said.

Dr. Belter thought it over. "Tonight, I think. I don't see any reason why your wife should have to go through it. It isn't easy to see your child leave your house for the last time. And it will be better for Sarah, too. I can take her to White Oaks for tonight, and we can talk tomorrow about the best place for her.''

Jack nodded mutely. He wondered why he didn't feel anything, but he didn't.

"I'm sorry," Ray Norton said. They had moved into the hall, and Ray was standing uncomfortably by the front door, wanting to get away. "If there's anything I can do . . ." His voice trailed off as Jack shook his head.

"Thanks, Ray," he said. "I don't know. I guess I'm feeling numb."

Jack started up the stairs to pack a suitcase for Sarah, and Ray Norton put his hand on the front door.

"Wait a moment, please," Dr. Belter said softly to the police chief.

Norton's hand dropped from the doorknob, but he didn't meet the psychiatrist's eyes. For the last hour he had heard a lot of things he hadn't wanted to hear, and he was embarrassed. He was acutely aware that there was such a thing as knowing too much about your friends, and he had a distinct feeling he was about to hear even more. He was right. Dr. Belter led him back to the study and quickly filled him in on every detail of the Conger cases, both Sarah's and Jack's.

When the doctor was finished Ray Norton stared at him, unable to conceal the animosity he was feeling toward the man.

"Just exactly why are you telling me all this?" he asked. "It seems to me that what you're doing is unethical at best and probably illegal at worst."

Dr. Belter stared at the fire in front of him. He was very much aware that what Norton was saying was true. What he was doing was both unethical and illegal, but he had thought it over carefully before deciding to go ahead. And now it was too late—he had already begun.

"You're right, of course," he said uncomfortably. "And believe me, if I thought there was any other way of going at this thing I wouldn't be doing what I'm doing right now."

"I don't see what you hope to accomplish," Norton said.

"You mean you don't want to see." Belter's reproach was mild. "What I'm suggesting," he said, his voice hardening, "since you want me to spell it out, is that I think there's a distinct possibility that Jack Conger might be involved in all this mess."

"I don't see how," Norton observed. "You yourself admit that he was in your office when at least one and possibly two of the disappearances took place."

"That's not quite true. We don't actually know when the disappearances took place. All we know, really, is when and where the children were last seen. And, as it happens, they were all seen on or near the Conger property. As for when they actually met with . . . whatever it is they met with, we don't know, do we?"

Norton reluctantly agreed. "Just what are you proposing? That I charge Jack Conger with killing three children? Granted, I suppose we could use your files to establish a record of previous assault, but where does that get us? Without any bodies, and with you yourself acting as a witness for an alibi, there isn't a chance in the world of making it stick."

"And, of course," the doctor added, "you don't think he had anything to do with it."

"No," Norton said flatly. "I don't."

Dr. Belter leaned back in his chair and folded his hands across his stomach. "Then what do you propose to do?"

"Nothing," Norton said. "Come spring, I'll have those woods searched again, and I'll have a good search made for that cave. Other than that, I propose to see what happens next. If any more children disappear, I'll reassess the situation. But if you want my opinion, I think it's over with."

"You really think Sarah did it all?" the psychiatrist asked in disbelief.

Norton nodded. "I'm no shrink, but for my money she did it. And I'll stick to that opinion till I have something more solid to go on. The word is already all over town that Sarah Conger went berserk—those aren't my words, but they're the ones that will be used—and she's going to be put away. And in a town like Port Arbello a story like that counts for a lot. The town will calm down, and when the word gets out that Sarah's been taken wherever you take her it'll calm down even more. I don't propose to stir it all up again, and I don't propose to have the whole town talking about something that happened to Jack Conger a year ago. I assume I can count on you not to tell anyone else what you've told me?"

"That goes without saying," Belter said stiffly. "But do me a favor, will you? Talk to Jack Conger. Don't grill him, just talk to him. You don't even have to do it officially."

"Why?" Norton demanded.

Belter smiled thinly. "Just to prod him. You might be absolutely right— he may have nothing to do with all this. But then again, he might. In any case, my professional opinion is that he's pretty near the end of his rope emotionally. If you let him know that you're aware of that, it might make him nervous. Nervous enough to make himself get some help before something happens that he is mixed up in."

"I'll think about it," Norton said noncommittally. "If there's nothing else, I have a lot of work to do." He stood up, and the two men shook hands formally and coldly. When the police chief had left the house Dr. Belter thought for a while about the two folders in his office and the look on the policeman's face as he'd left. Norton, he knew, would not be coming for the files. And he wouldn't press the matter himself. Tomorrow he would seal Jack Conger's folder and put it away in the dead files, the special cabinet he kept for the records of patients he didn't think he'd be seeing again.

Suddenly weary, he turned and went upstairs to help Jack, who was just finishing with the packing. He looked as though he'd been crying.

"I'll give her a shot," Dr. Belter said, "and she won't even wake up. You can be at school tomorrow morning if you like. It might make things easier. For you and your wife, if not for her. Frankly, I doubt she'll even be aware of what's happening. I'm sorry, but I imagine all this will make things worse for her." Then he smiled, seeing the expression on Jack's face. "Don't forget," he went on, "we don't really know what goes on in the mind of a child like Sarah. Often I suspect that a child's schizophrenia is much harder on the family than it is on the child. A person's mind generally takes him where he wants to go. Sarah will be all right. Maybe not by your standards, or by mine, but she's living where she wants to live. All we can do, really, is wish her well.''

"But what's going to happen to her?" Jack asked dazedly. He picked up his child and began carrying her downstairs. He knew it would be the last time.

Dr. Belter waited until they had reached the front door before he answered Jack's question.

"It's hard to say," he murmured at last. "With Sarah, only time will tell what's going to happen. All I can advise you to do is go on with your life. There's literally nothing you can do for Sarah." At the look of pain in Jack's eyes, he relented. "I didn't say forget about her. By all means go on loving her. But it's time to stop living your lives around her. You and your wife and Elizabeth are still a family, you know."

Jack wondered how much of a family they would ever be again.

"If I can be any help to you, please let me know," Belter went on. "It isn't the end of the world, you know. It's just been a very bad year. For you, and everyone else in Port Arbello. But it's over now." He held out his arms to receive the sleeping child.

Jack looked once more into the face of his daughter, and kissed her gently.

"I love you," he whispered. "I always have. I'm so sorry, my baby. So very sorry."

Then he placed his child in the doctor's arms, and Sarah Conger was taken away from the house on Conger's Point. As he watched the car taking his daughter from her home, Jack Conger wondered if it would, indeed, be all over now. He hoped so.

He stood alone in the driving snow and watched the taillights disappear. He raised one hand in a final salute.

"Sarah," he whispered. And then again: "Sarah . . ."

## TWENTY-FIVE

A WEEK PASSED, THEN TWO. PORT AR-bello began to return to normal, though it was a slightly different normal. Most of the children returned to walking to school, but some of them kept on riding. "What happened once could happen again," some of the parents were saying.

Three days after Sarah walked out of the woods, Carl and Barbara Stevens put their house on the market. Rose Conger was surprised when she got the listing for it, and turned it down. She explained that she was taking some time off to recuperate, but that was only part of the truth. The rest of it was that she couldn't face seeing Barbara Stevens again.

Marilyn Burton continued to operate her dress shop, and people noticed that she was beginning to talk to herself. For a while many of the women in Port Arbello made an effort to drop in on her as often as possible, but it didn't seem to do any good. After a while they stopped dropping in, and if Marilyn Burton's habit became worse, no one knew about it.

Martin Forager did his best to keep the talk alive, but as the days dragged on and nothing else happened, people began to tell him to let it be; they'd just as soon forget. He couldn't, of course, and few nights passed without Marty Forager suddenly standing up in the tavern and drunkenly demanding that someone find out what really did happen to his daughter. After a while people stopped paying attention.

Jimmy Tyler's parents acted as if nothing had happened. They kept his room just as it had been on the day he disappeared, and always set a place for him at the table. Mrs. Tyler told everyone that she expected Jimmy home any day now, and that the waiting was hard. But she also insisted that she was holding up well under it and it would all be over soon, when Jimmy came home. The people of Port Arbello clucked sympathetically, but shook their heads when Mrs. Tyler wasn't around. They saw another Port Arbello legend in the making.

For Jack and Rose Conger, the weeks after Sarah left their home were difficult. Rose stayed in the house almost all the time; after the second week she telephoned the Port Arbello Realty Company to tell them she would not be back. They were not surprised; rather, they were relieved. They had been trying to figure out the most diplomatic way of telling her that her services would no longer be necessary, that Conger was no longer a name to be proud of in Port Arbello.

Jack Conger couldn't stay at home. He had a paper to run, and he had to try to act as if nothing were wrong. It was impossible, of course, and he imagined that people were looking at him strangely even when they weren't. He found that he was spending most of his time barricaded in his office, talking to no one but Sylvia Bannister.

Sylvia had come into his office on his first day back at the Port Arbello *Courier* and had closed the door firmly behind her.

"Are you going to be all right?" she had asked him without preamble.

"That depends on what you call all right," he had said. "I intend to go on living, and go on working, if that's what you mean."

"I suppose that's what I meant," Sylvia had said. Then she had left his office as abruptly as she had entered it.

The Congers told Elizabeth that her sister had finally had to be put in an institution, and she had accepted it without further explanation. She had not asked any questions about the day Sarah had come out of the woods, and while they thought it was a little odd, they accepted it gratefully. Neither Jack nor Rose wished to discuss that day, and they counted themselves lucky that Elizabeth, too, seemed to want to forget it.

*  *  *

In early November, about a month after Sarah was sent to the Ocean Crest Institute, Jack and Rose Conger were sitting in the small study at the back of the house. Jack was reading; Rose was trying to read. Without knocking, Elizabeth came into the room and sat down on the sofa beside her mother. When Rose looked up to see what she wanted, Elizabeth was staring at the portrait of the young girl that hung above the mantel. Rose glanced up at the picture.

"Sometimes it's hard to remember that she isn't you," Rose mused. Elizabeth looked at her mother sharply.

"Well, she isn't," Elizabeth said petulantly. "I don't think she looks anything like me at all."

Jack set his book aside and smiled at his daughter. "You wouldn't have said that two years ago, or three. Of course, you're older than she was when that picture was painted, but when you were that age you looked exactly like her."

"I'm not like her," Elizabeth said flatly.

"Well, no one said you are, dear," Rose said. "All your father or anyone else ever said was that you looked like her."

"I don't want to look like her," Elizabeth said, her face growing slightly red with anger. "She's an awful person, and I don't want anything to do with her. I wish you'd take the picture down."

"Take it down?" Rose said, puzzled. "Why on earth should we take it down?" She examined it once more, trying to see what her daughter could dislike in it. She could see nothing.

"Because I want you to," Elizabeth said. "I think it should go back in the attic, where you found it."

"I don't see any reason to put it away," Jack said. "I should think you'd be proud of it. Not every girl has a portrait like that of herself."

"It isn't me," Elizabeth insisted, her anger swelling. Her parents glanced at each other nervously.

"Well," Jack said, hesitating, "if it means that much to you—"

"It does," Elizabeth declared. "I never want to see that picture again. I hate it." She paused and glared at the picture, at the little girl who looked so much like Elizabeth smiling down at her. "I hate you!" Elizabeth suddenly shouted at the picture. Then she ran from the study, and a moment later her parents heard her pounding up the stairs to her room. They looked at each other again, and there was worry in their eyes.

"What do you suppose brought that on?" Jack said.

Rose thought about it a moment, and when she spoke it was in a manner of thinking out loud.

"She seems to be changing lately. Have you noticed it? She isn't like she used to be. She's starting to get a little sloppy. Just little things. And she's started arguing with me. It used to be that if I asked her to do something she either did it immediately or it was already done. Lately she's started arguing with me, or simply not doing what I ask her to do. And she flat out refused to do something for Mrs. Goodrich the other day. You should have heard Mrs. Goodrich!"

Jack chuckled. "I have heard Mrs. Goodrich. Thirty years ago I flatly refused to do something she told me to do. I heard her then, and it was the first and last time I ever refused to do anything she asked me to do.''

"I suspect it'll be the last time for Elizabeth, too.'' Rose smiled. Then her smile faded, and her voice grew serious again.

"But, really, Jack, haven't you noticed it too? Or is it just my imagination?'' Rose bit at her lower lip anxiously. "I'm afraid my imagination works overtime these days.''

Jack thought it over and realized that Rose was right. Elizabeth had been changing, but it wasn't anything serious, as far as he could see. Elizabeth, in his opinion, was simply beginning to act like any other thirteen-year-old girl.

"I wouldn't worry about it if I were you. After all, she's been through just as much as we have, and her life's changed just as much as ours. We can't expect her to be the same as she always was. You're not and I'm not—why should she be?''

"I don't know, really,'' Rose said thoughtfully. "I'm not sure I'm even worried. In a way, it's kind of a relief. She was so perfect, she sometimes made me feel incompetent. I could never handle Sarah the way she could.''

Jack seemed to stiffen, and Rose realized that it was the first time either of them had mentioned Sarah in a month. They hadn't been to visit her yet; it was almost as if they were trying to pretend that she hadn't existed. But she had.

The next day they drove to Ocean Crest, forty miles south of Port Arbello. It was close enough to make visiting Sarah easy, but far enough away so that Port Arbello would be able to feel safe. Sarah would be there for a very long time.

It was a difficult visit. The child sat in front of them, her enormous brown eyes fixed on a spot somewhere in space, somewhere Rose and Jack could not go.

She did not resist when each of them embraced her, nor did she respond.

"She's always like that,'' the nurse explained. "So far she hasn't responded to anything. She eats, but the food has to be put in her mouth.'' When Rose seemed to be on the verge of tears, the nurse hastened to explain.

"It isn't anything to worry about,'' she said. "Sarah's had a bad trauma, and she's reacting to it. She's temporarily withdrawn, just as normal people do. Except that she was already so withdrawn that now she's practically shut down. But she'll come out of it. I'm sure she will.''

They made the drive home in silence. When they were in the house Rose said, "Fix me a drink, will you? I feel like I need one. I'm going up to say hello to Elizabeth.''

"Kiss her once for me,'' Jack said. He headed for the study as Rose disappeared upstairs.

A couple of minutes later, when Rose went into the study, she found her husband standing in the middle of the room, staring at the empty place on the wall above the fireplace.

"It's gone,'' he said. "She put it back in the attic.''

Rose stared at the blank space herself, then went to the study door. "Elizabeth!" she called.

"What?" The muffled shout came through indistinctly from upstairs. Rose's eyes narrowed, and she went to the foot of the stairs.

"Come down here," she said sharply.

"In a minute," she heard from upstairs.

"Now!" Rose commanded. She stalked back to the study. A very long minute later Elizabeth walked into the room.

"You used to knock before you entered a room," Rose pointed out to her.

"Oh, Mother," Elizabeth protested.

"Don't whine," Jack said sharply. "It doesn't sound attractive. Did you take that picture down?"

"What picture?" Elizabeth said evasively.

"You know perfectly well what picture," Rose snapped. "The one above the fireplace."

"Oh, that," Elizabeth said offhandedly. "I told you I hated it."

"Where did you put it?"

"Back in the attic," Elizabeth said. "That's where it belongs." Then she marched out of the study.

"Well," Jack said, "I guess that's that."

"I don't know," Rose said. "We certainly don't have to leave the picture there. It seems to me that if we want to hang *our* picture in *our* study in *our* house, *our* daughter is no one to tell us we can't."

"But if it means so much to her—" Jack began.

But Rose cut him off. "It's not that. It's just that she's starting to act like an only child."

"In a way," Jack said softly, "she is, isn't she?"

The picture of the unknown child stayed in the attic.

BOOK TWO

# THE PRESENT

# TWENTY-SIX

RAY NORTON DROVE SLOWLY ALONG THE Conger's Point Road, partly because he was keeping only one eye on the road and partly because he was getting older, and driving more slowly was a part of getting older. He would be retiring next year, and he was ready. Port Arbello was changing, and Ray Norton was changing, and he no longer felt that he was the best chief of police the town could have. He'd kept this feeling a secret, but he knew it was an open secret. As the years had worn on he had turned more and more of the work of his department over to his deputy chief. Port Arbello had ten policemen now, and even they weren't enough.

Not like the old days, Norton thought as he stopped the slowly cruising car entirely. Everything's changing.

He was parked by the Congers' field, and he was watching the work that was going on in the woods on the far side of the field. An apartment complex was being built there, and though Ray Norton didn't approve of it, even he had to admit that, for what they were doing, they were doing a good job. The complex would fit well on the Point, long and low, snug to the ground against the north winds of winter.

As he watched the building progress it occurred to him that what he really resented was not the building itself, but the fact that the building would spell an end to what had become, for him, an annual tradition.

Each spring for the past fifteen years Ray Norton had spent several of his days off searching the woods for some trace of the three children who had disappeared that autumn the snow had come early. The first spring he had been joined by a search party, and they had combed the woods for days, then moved on to the embankment, searching for some trace of the missing children or the entrance to the cave that was supposed to be hidden there. They had found nothing. Whatever might have been there had vanished with the snow. They had continued the search for the cave until one of the searchers lost his footing among the rocks and nearly lost his life when he tumbled to the stony beach below. After that people stopped showing up for the search. From then on Ray Norton had searched alone.

He had never found anything, but the search had become a habit with him, and each spring he would return to the woods, make a careful search, and then move on to the embankment. And each spring he would find nothing. Well, the search was over now. The woods were being torn up, and the foundations of the apartment buildings were being anchored to the embankment.

Ray Norton left his car and began trudging toward the woods. You never know, he was thinking. They might turn up something I missed.

From the old house at the end of Conger's Point, Elizabeth Conger watched the white-haired police chief making his way slowly across the field. Each spring she had watched him, and each spring she had asked him what he hoped to find.

"Don't know," he would say. "But I can't just let it go. Something's out there, if something's anywhere. And I'll find it, if it's there."

She had often wondered exactly what it was he hoped to find, and what he would do if and when he found it. It would have to be this year, or it wouldn't be at all.

She glanced at a clock and saw that she still had three hours before it would be time to leave for Ocean Crest.

Sylvia Bannister was driving north, and it had not been her intention to make any stops until she reached Maine. But when she saw the sign for Port Arbello she turned off. As she drove toward the town she wondered why.

She had left Port Arbello a year after Sarah's commitment, and had not been back in the fourteen years since. Now, as she drove into town, she decided that it was time to take one more look at her past.

She intended only to drive around the square, but she found herself stopping at the offices of the Port Arbello *Courier*. Before she went in she glanced across at the grim old Armory, still unchanged from the old days. So, she thought, Rose never followed through on her project to convert it to a shopping arcade. Just as well. She pushed open the door to the *Courier* and knew at once that Jack Conger was no longer there.

Everything was changed, and most of the old staff was gone. But she spotted one familiar face, a face that looked at her curiously.

"Miss Bannister?" the person said, and Sylvia realized that the young man had been a copy boy when she left. Now he was an editor. Things *did* change.

"I was looking for Mr. Conger," she said doubtfully. "But I get the feeling he isn't here any more."

The young man stared at her. "You mean you didn't hear?" he asked. "He died. Nine or ten years ago."

"I see," Sylvia said. "What about Mrs. Conger? Does she still live out on the Point?"

The young editor shook his head. "Only Elizabeth. Mrs. Conger died the same time that Mr. Conger did."

He didn't explain, and Sylvia left the office. She almost decided to leave Port Arbello and continue northward, but she changed her mind. She wasn't sure why, but she wanted to see Elizabeth Conger. She turned her car around and headed out the Conger's Point Road.

The house hadn't changed, and Sylvia parked her car in front of the porch. She glanced out at the woods as she mounted the steps, and a chill ran through her body as she wondered what had really happened out there. She noticed the construction as she rang the bell.

A tall and strikingly beautiful young woman answered the door and looked at her curiously. From the blond hair Sylvia Bannister knew at once who it was.

"Elizabeth?" she said.

The young woman nodded. "May I help you?" She thought she knew the woman from somewhere, but she wasn't sure. And so many strangers knocked on her door, asking her questions about the past. Questions she couldn't answer.

"I'm not sure if you'll remember me," Sylvia said. "I'm Sylvia Bannister."

"Of course," Elizabeth said, opening the door wide. "My father's secretary. Please, come in."

Sylvia glanced around the house as Elizabeth led her through to the back study. Nothing, it appeared, had changed.

"I don't know why," Elizabeth was saying, "but we all seem to wind up living in here. I hardly ever use the living room any more, and Mother's old office is completely closed off."

"I heard about your parents," Sylvia said gently. "I just wanted to stop by and tell you how sorry I am."

"Don't be," Elizabeth said. "It may sound harsh, but I'm sure they're happier now."

"Do you mind if I ask you what happened?" Sylvia asked.

"Not at all. It's been almost ten years since they died, and I don't mind talking about it any more. And maybe you could answer some questions for me. If you don't mind."

"Not at all," Sylvia said. "I'll tell you whatever I can."

The two women sat down, and Elizabeth told Sylvia what had happened to Jack and Rose Conger.

"It happened about five years after they had to send Sarah to Ocean Crest," she said. "Just after my eighteenth birthday, to be exact. Of course, we'll never know exactly what happened, but Dad took Mother out sailing one day. And they didn't come back. Everyone assumed there had been some kind of an accident, but a week after it happened the manager of the marina, I can't remember his name, found all the life preservers from the *Sea Otter* stuffed into one of the lockers. Since Dad was always careful about things like that, they decided that it wasn't an accident after all. Apparently Dad just took Mother out, and sank the boat with both of them on it." She paused a minute and seemed to think. "I've started to put it all together, I guess. At the time, of course, it didn't make any sense to me at all. But over the years I've started to find out more and more about what must have been happening to him. I think I can understand it now. I think it just got to be too much for Dad. Apparently the town never stopped talking about what happened that fall, and somehow they got the idea that Dad was involved in it. Anyway, you know how Port Arbello is. They have long memories, and stories get worse every time they're told. Toward the end Mother wouldn't leave the house at all, except if Dad took her on a trip out of town, and Dad . . . well, I guess he just got tired of having people staring at him all the time."

"Why didn't they just leave town?" Sylvia asked.

"Why don't I?" Elizabeth asked. "I guess for us Congers this place is home. It isn't easy giving up everything that's familiar to you. Dad could never do it, and I can't either. Besides, there's Sarah to think about too, you know."

"Sarah?" Sylvia's eyes flickered with interest. "How is she?"

"Much better," Elizabeth said. "As a matter of fact, she's coming home today, for the first time."

"Will she be able to stay?"

"Not this time. But eventually, we hope. Not that Ocean Crest is a bad place to be. Actually, she's very happy there."

"Yes," Sylvia said, "I imagine she is."

"But we still, or I should say she still, has to remember what happened that day she came out of the woods with that—that thing in her hands. It's the only thing she still can't remember. She remembers what happened between her and Dad—" Elizabeth suddenly stopped talking, and stared at Sylvia in embarrassment.

"It's all right," Sylvia said. "As a matter of fact, I can probably tell you more about that incident than Sarah can, even if she remembers it."

"Could you?" Elizabeth asked. "I don't know why, but I've always felt that it was the major cause of what happened to Dad and Mom."

"It undoubtedly was." Sylvia sighed. "Jack talked a lot about it to me. We were very close, you know."

Elizabeth nodded. "There's been some gossip. I was never very sure how much truth there was to it, but I knew Mom and Dad weren't getting along. Especially after Sarah got sick.''

"That was the root of the trouble," Sylvia said. "Jack was never the same after that terrible day in the woods." She fell silent for a minute, then continued.

"We had an affair," she said stiffly, her face coloring. "It didn't last long, only a year. I finally broke it off. I don't know why, really. I suppose partly because I felt sorry for Rose and partly because I was afraid of what would happen when it came to an end. Often, it seems, it's easier to handle endings if you bring them on yourself. So I ended the affair, and left Port Arbello. And do you know," she went on, "when I left I had the feeling that for Jack, life had ended. I suppose that sounds conceited, but I don't mean it to be. It didn't have anything to do with me. He just seemed tired out. Really, when I think about it I'm surprised he held on as long as he did."

Elizabeth nodded. "I think he did it for me. I don't think it was any coincidence that he killed himself right after my eighteenth birthday. He waited until I was old enough, and then he just sort of—went away . . .''

"It must have been terrible for you," Sylvia said.

"It was, at first. And it still isn't easy. I've had to sell off some of the land just to support myself and Sarah. I decided to get rid of the woods. It seemed like they'd been in the family long enough. I guess I hoped that if I got rid of them, and that awful embankment, it would get rid of the legend and the gossip as well."

"I'm sure it will," Sylvia said. Then she glanced at her watch. "Gracious. If I'm going to get to where I'm going, I've got to get started. Thank you for telling me what happened to Jack. Have I been any help to you at all?''

"Of course," Elizabeth said. "I'm glad to know my father had some happiness in his life." Then she too glanced at the time. "I'm sorry this has to be such a short visit," she went on. "Come back and see me again?''

Sylvia assured her that she would, but both women knew that they wouldn't meet again. Elizabeth waved to Sylvia as she drove down the drive, then glanced once more at her watch. She still had an hour before it would be time to leave for Ocean Crest. She went to look in on Mrs. Goodrich.

Though the old housekeeper had never admitted to her true age, Elizabeth was sure she was well into her eighties. She still lived in the little room next to the kitchen, and did her best to keep up the pretense that she was looking after Miss Elizabeth instead of the other way around—brewing fresh coffee for her each morning, and managing to put together something that passed for lunch, though Elizabeth had grown accustomed to waiting for the old woman to fall into her afternoon nap and then going to the kitchen to fix something to tide herself over until dinner.

Elizabeth was worried about Mrs. Goodrich; it wouldn't be much longer until the old woman would need full-time care, and Elizabeth didn't see how she was going to afford it. Unless what the doctors had told her was true, and Sarah really would be allowed to come home. She tapped lightly at Mrs. Goodrich's door.

"Is that you, Miz Rose?" the ancient voice quavered. Elizabeth shook her head a little, in sorrow. More and more lately the old woman had been mistaking Elizabeth for her mother, and Elizabeth supposed that it was a sign of increasing senility.

"It's me," she said gently. "Miss Elizabeth." She opened the door, and the old woman stared at her blankly. Then her mind seemed to clear, and she smiled tentatively.

"Oh, yes," she said uncertainly, "where's your mother?"

"She'll be in later," Elizabeth promised, knowing that later Mrs. Goodrich would have forgotten that she had asked for Rose. The first time this had happened, Elizabeth had tried to explain to the old woman that Rose was dead, and a look of horror had come over Mrs. Goodrich's face.

"Oh, dear," she had clucked. "What'll become of poor Mister Jack now?" Elizabeth had stared at her for a moment before she realized that the old housekeeper must have forgotten what had happened. These days she simply ignored it. She closed the door.

Elizabeth glanced around the kitchen now, and thought she ought to do the dishes and save Mrs. Goodrich the effort. Her arthritic hands could no longer hold on to wet dishes, and she had a hard time seeing what she was doing. But Elizabeth found she didn't mind having the role of servant thrust upon her. Mrs. Goodrich had served her family well for a long time. The least they could do for her was take care of her in her old age.

And besides, Elizabeth didn't really have much else to do. Without being aware of it, she was becoming more and more like her mother, sticking close to her home, going into Port Arbello only when there was shopping to do or errands to be run. It did not occur to her that, at the age of twenty-eight, she was beginning to behave like a spinster twice her age. Nor did it occur to her that her lifestyle seemed odd to many people.

Elizabeth Conger was, in actuality, fairly content with her lot in life. She had her home, which she loved, and she had her cat, an ancient Persian she'd named Cecil, after the one that had disappeared. Her father had brought the kitten home to her soon after Sarah had gone to Ocean Crest. The cat was decrepit now, and needed a great deal of care. Elizabeth had considered having Cecil put to sleep, but hadn't been able to find it in her heart to do it.

She glanced around the kitchen again and wondered where to start. Then, just as she had made up her mind to do it, she changed her mind and decided to go for a walk instead.

She looked in on Mrs. Goodrich once more and found the old woman sound asleep. As she was putting on her coat at the front door, she felt Cecil rubbing against her ankle.

"You want to come along too?" she asked the cat. "I know you, though. You'll be perfectly happy walking for about ten feet, then you'll want to be carried."

The cat looked up at her and mewed.

"Oh, all right, come on," Elizabeth said, opening the front door. The cat bounded out into the bright spring sunlight.

Elizabeth, seeing Ray Norton's car still parked on the Point Road by the field, decided to go over to the woods and watch the construction. She had avoided the woods for years, until she had had to walk the property with the real-estate agent she had listed it with. Even then she had not felt comfortable about the woods or the embankment. But now, with the construction work going on and the area bustling with activity, it had lost its threat, and she found she enjoyed going there.

She found Ray Norton sitting with his back to a tree, patiently watching the work.

"May I join you?" She smiled.

The old policeman looked up in surprise. "Well, look who's here," he said. "Since when are young Congers allowed to play out here?" His eyes were twinkling, and Elizabeth laughed softly.

"Not that young any more," she said. "And besides, it's all different since they took over." She made a gesture that encompassed all the men and machinery around them.

"Hmph," Norton snorted. "If you ask me, it was better the way it was."

"I don't know," Elizabeth mused. "I know I shouldn't say it, but I'm kind of glad it's all happening. For the first time in my life I feel comfortable out here." She stared out to sea for a moment, then spoke again.

"Mr. Norton, do you suppose there ever really was anything out here?"

"For instance?" Norton countered.

"Oh, the cave, I suppose. I know you've been searching for it for years, and you've never found it, but you think it's here somewhere, don't you?"

"I don't know," the old man said. "For a long time I didn't believe it was here, then I did believe it. Now I don't know what I think. I guess when you get to be my age that's normal. At least I hope it is, because it's the way I am."

"Will you be coming back?" Elizabeth asked him. "I mean, when all this building is done and there are people living here. Will you still come out each spring to look around?"

Norton shook his head. "I doubt it. For one thing, I'll be retired by this time next year. And for another, this place just won't be the same. If I don't find what I'm looking for this year, I won't find it."

Elizabeth stood up and patted the old man on the back.

"You'll find it," she reassured him. "Whatever it is, if it's here you'll find it." She glanced at her watch. "I've got to get going," she said. Norton looked at her curiously.

"Sarah's coming home today," she explained. "Just for a visit, to see how it goes. But it'll be the first time in fifteen years." She paused, then winked at Norton. "And I didn't even clean up the kitchen," she added. "I thought it would be homier that way." She turned and started back through the woods, picking her way carefully through the brambles. Twice she caught her foot. She'd be glad when it was all cleared away.

The old policeman watched her until she had disappeared into the trees, then turned his attention back to the workmen.

So she's coming home, he thought. Well, that's nice.

If he was going to find anything after all these years, he was going to find it today. He made himself comfortable and kept on watching. It was all right; he didn't have anything better to do. When he thought about it Ray Norton realized that he hadn't had anything better to do for fifteen years.

Three hours later, as Ray Norton looked on, one of the pile drivers setting the foundations for the apartment complex broke through the roof of the upper cavern. The light of day shined dimly down on the gates of hell.

## TWENTY-SEVEN

OCEAN CREST INSTITUTE, WHICH HAD dropped the word "Mental" from its name several years ago, sprawled over twenty-five acres of woods and lawns on a bluff above the Atlantic. It looked as much like a resort hotel as its management could make it, and it was able to keep its costs within reason only through the grace of an enormous endowment that had accumulated over the years from the bequests of wealthy families grateful for the care and discretion that Ocean Crest had shown their members whose eccentricities had gone beyond the harmless. No bars marred the view from the windows of Ocean Crest; instead, bulletproof glass had been installed in the units that housed those patients deemed to be dangerous. Sarah Conger had lived in one of those units for four years, never knowing that she could not have left by one of the windows. She had never tried. Residents of Ocean Crest rarely tried to leave; if they ever wandered off, it was usually through confusion, not a desire to escape.

After the first four years Sarah Conger had been moved out of the security unit and into a small house that she shared with three other adolescent girls and a housemother. An outsider, not knowing that all the girls were victims of mental disorders, would have thought them only unusually quiet. There were rarely any outbursts of any kind from the girls. Rather, they lived as close to a normal life as Ocean Crest could make for them. The director, Dr. Lawrence Felding, was totally committed to the idea that the mentally ill need "asylum," not treatment. If you want someone to be normal, Dr. Felding maintained, you have to treat him as though he is. People, he had discovered, tend to live up to nonverbal expectations much more readily than to stated orders.

On the other hand, Dr. Felding saw to it that very little at Ocean Crest was left to chance. What he had done was develop a level of planned spontaneity that seemed to work for his patients. Often residents of Ocean Crest were surprised to discover that a friend known for months, or even years, whom they had always assumed to be another resident, was a psychiatrist. The doctors of Ocean Crest happily conducted therapy over card games, picnics, and "chance" meetings in lounges.

It was only when residents were being considered for discharge that formal meetings were held with doctors. And after fifteen years at Ocean Crest, Sarah Conger was starting to have formal meetings with her doctors.

"How does it feel to be going home?" Larry Felding was asking her.

Sarah lit a cigarette nervously and shook the match out before answering. "It doesn't feel like going home at all," she said. "I've spent more than half my life here. This is home."

Larry Felding laughed easily. "Careful. If you say that in the wrong place, people will say you're getting institutionalized."

Sarah grinned at him, and Larry Felding remembered all the years when Sarah Conger had never grinned, had simply sat mutely staring out at the sea, her face expressionless. Her silence had been complete for three years, and it had been another five before she had begun to speak in complete sentences. When she had been at Ocean Crest for ten years she finally smiled, and it was then that Felding had begun to be hopeful that she would eventually recover. For the last year or so it had been rare that Sarah Conger was not grinning. Her good humor faded now only when someone tried to talk to her about the events that had occurred just before she had come to Ocean Crest. Then her grin would fade, and she would become uncomfortable. She could not remember what had happened. Larry Felding was sorry that he was going to have to kill that grin now, but he didn't see any way out of it.

"While you're at home, Sarah," he said, "I want you to try to remember."

"Remember?" Sarah said, the grin predictably fading. "Remember what?" Felding looked at her over the top of his half glasses, and Sarah squirmed. "All right," she said. "I know what you're talking about and I won't pretend I don't. And I know I have to remember all of it." Then her smile sneaked back onto her face. "Of course," she said slyly, "if I don't remember, I can't be discharged, can I?"

"No," Felding replied, examining his fingernails. "But I could always kick you out for malingering, couldn't I?"

"Not you," Sarah said complacently. "You couldn't kick a squirrel out of here." Then she turned serious again. "I think I'm afraid to remember, Larry. I really think that's what it is."

"Bully for you," Felding commented. "After fifteen years you've finally discovered that we don't face what we're afraid to face. Shall I put that on your chart?" Then he leaned forward and the banter left his voice. "Of course you're afraid, Sarah. When you do remember, it's not going to be pleasant. In fact, I'm afraid it's going to be very unpleasant. But you won't remember all of it at once. It'll come back to you in bits and pieces, like the day in the woods with your father. You won't have to face it all at once. But you have to face it. Otherwise we won't ever be able to call you 'well,' whatever that means. So while you're at home I want you to try to remember what happened."

"All right," Sarah said reluctantly. "I'll try. But I'm not going to promise anything. Is there anything special I should do? Anything that might help to jog my memory?"

Felding shrugged. "Who knows? You might try wandering around in the woods or the field."

"The woods are being torn down," Sarah said. "Elizabeth had to sell them off to keep this place going, remember?" Her infectious grin was back, and Larry Felding decided not to disturb it again. He sighed in mock embarrassment.

"I know," he said. "But I have to pay for my Rolls-Royces some way." He stared out the window at the battered Chevy that was technically his, but which everyone at Ocean Crest used as a sort of public transportation system. He saw another car pulling into the slot next to his.

"Speaking of Elizabeth, here she is. Are you ready?"

"I'll go get my bag," Sarah said, standing up. "I suppose you'll want to have your usual private chat with the family."

"You've been here too long," Felding said sourly. "You're catching on to how this place works." Sarah winked at him, and he smiled back at her. "Tell Elizabeth to come in, will you?"

"Okay. How long shall I take to get my bag? The usual ten minutes?"

"Get out of here!" Felding cried, and Sarah fled, giggling to herself. She met Elizabeth in the hall.

"Hi," she said. "Larry wants to talk to you, but I think I just upset him. Go in and calm him down." Still laughing, she left the building and started across the lawn to the house she had been living in for the last five years.

Elizabeth tapped lightly on the open door and stuck her head inside. Felding's eyes were twinkling when he looked at her.

"Come in," he said, waving. "I just kicked your sister out."

"She said she'd upset you. What happened?" Elizabeth wasn't sure whether she should be concerned. When Felding laughed, she relaxed.

"Sometimes I almost wish for the old days when she didn't say anything at all. She takes a very strange pleasure in needling me. Was she like that when she was a child?"

"From the day she was born. She was sassy, but she was happy. It made it all the harder when she got sick. She was so different all of a sudden." She was silent for a moment, remembering. Then she shook off the memory and met Dr. Felding's eyes. "Sarah said you wanted to talk to me?"

"Yes. I always like to have a little chat with a resident's family before they go home for the first time. To prepare them for anything that might happen."

"And something might happen with Sarah?" Elizabeth asked anxiously.

"I don't know." Dr. Felding was frank. "It all depends, really, on Sarah."

"Sarah? I don't understand."

"I've asked her to do something while she's home," Felding explained. "I've told her that I want her to use the time to try to remember what happened that day she walked out of the woods."

"I see," Elizabeth said noncommittally. "Is there anything you'd like me to do?"

"Only if you want to."

"If it'll help Sarah, I'll do anything," Elizabeth said earnestly. "You know that."

"Well, you don't need to sound so serious. I don't have anything terrible in mind. Tell me, is the house much different from when Sarah left?"

Elizabeth shook her head. "That house hasn't changed much in generations, let alone years." Then her expression clouded over a little. "Except for Sarah's room," she said, half apologetically. "Mother painted it and got rid of all of Sarah's things."

Felding's face fell a little. "What do you mean when you say 'got rid of'?" he asked.

"If it's important," Elizabeth reassured him, "they're all still there. In our family 'get rid of' means put in the attic. I'm sure all of Sarah's things are up there. Is it important?"

"It's hard to say. It could be. What I'd like you to do is go through all of Sarah's old things with her. Make an adventure out of it."

"It would be." Elizabeth smiled. "I haven't been up in that attic in years. In fact, I'm not sure I've been up there since Sarah came here." She thought for a moment. "Once, maybe, but that's all."

"Then it should be fun," Felding said. "Who knows what you'll find up there. And something might jog Sarah's memory."

"I feel sorry for her, in a way. That was a terrible day. I don't remember too much about it myself. Just seeing Sarah across the field, all covered with—" She fell silent, as if forcing the memory from her mind. "Well," she said shortly, "anyway, I feel sorry for her. I suppose she does have to remember it all, but it seems a shame, after all these years, digging it up again."

"I know," Felding said gently. "But it has to be done."

He heard feet in the hall outside and glanced at the clock. Exactly ten minutes. Sarah was back.

"It looks just the same," Sarah said as Elizabeth turned into the long driveway that led to the house. "Only smaller. I remembered it as being much bigger than it is."

"They say that always happens with a house you only remember as a child. The house doesn't get smaller, but you get bigger. The result is the same. You don't feel bigger, so things must have gotten smaller."

She parked the car in the garage, and they began walking to the house. Without realizing it, Elizabeth had adopted her father's old custom of using only the front door, and she headed in that direction now.

"Just like Father," Sarah commented. When Elizabeth looked at her curiously, Sarah went on. "Don't you remember? He would never use any door except the front door. It was practically a ceremony."

"I'd forgotten, I guess," Elizabeth confessed. "You really remember that?"

"Oh, I remember practically everything now, even during that year before I went to Ocean Crest. Except for the last few weeks. There are some fuzzy patches, and I can't seem to get through the fog. And I'm not sure I want to. I suppose Larry told you."

"Do you call all the doctors at Ocean Crest by their first names? Or is Dr. Felding special?"

Sarah laughed. "He's not special, except in the way all the people at Ocean Crest are special. We call all of them by their first names. Don't forget, I didn't even know Larry was a doctor during the first years. I just thought he was another nut."

An expression of consternation crossed Elizabeth's face. "How can you talk that way?" she said.

"What way?"

"Referring to yourself and everyone else at Ocean Crest as a nut?"

"Sorry," Sarah said. "I forgot. I usually don't say that in front of outsiders. It seems to bother them, like it bothered you. But it doesn't bother us," she said serenely. "We think 'nut' is a much better word than 'paranoid schizophrenic' or 'manic depressive.' It sounds so much more human."

"I'll never get used to that place," Elizabeth said. "But it seems to work, so I guess it's all right."

"Why don't you check in?" Sarah suggested lightly. "Who knows? If you try real hard, maybe you can be crazy too. But it's not easy," she added, her voice taking on a more serious tone. "It takes a lot of energy to be the way I was for so long. Maybe I was just too tired to talk."

"Like Mrs. Goodrich," Elizabeth said, feeling a sudden desire to change the subject. It was a lot easier for Sarah to talk about her illness than it was for her.

"How is she?" Sarah asked.

"As well as can be expected, considering her age," Elizabeth replied. "She might not know who you are, and she might say some strange things. I just wanted to warn you."

"I'm used to people saying strange things," Sarah said, her grin lighting her face. "Lead me to her."

Elizabeth unlocked the door, and they stepped into the entry hall.

"Just the same," Sarah said. "Just like I remember it." She moved from room to room, taking in everything. "You haven't changed anything, have you. Don't you get bored with it?"

"Bored with it?" Elizabeth repeated. "Why should I?"

"I don't know. I should think you'd want a change now and then, that's all."

For some reason Elizabeth suddenly felt slightly uncomfortable. "I suppose I'm my father's daughter," she said, a little stiffly. "He never wanted things to change either."

"I hope you're not completely your father's daughter," Sarah remarked. "If you are, I don't think I want to go to the woods with you."

Elizabeth felt her stomach knot, and looked at her sister with horror. "How can you say such a thing, Sarah?"

Sarah's grin faded, and she looked into Elizabeth's eyes. "I think we'd better have a little talk, Elizabeth," she said. "I can wait to see Mrs. Goodrich. Where's a good place?"

"The back study," Elizabeth said. "I use it more than any other room in the house." She led the way, feeling uneasy about what Sarah might have to say to her. She decided to fix herself a drink.

"Fix me one, too?" Sarah asked her, and when Elizabeth looked at her strangely, Sarah went on, "We drink at Ocean Crest, too."

She sat down and waited until Elizabeth handed her a glass and took a chair opposite her.

"Look, Elizabeth," she said. "I know you thought I said a horrible thing when I made that crack. But you have to understand some things about me. I know what happened out in the woods, and I know it was a horrible thing that Dad did to me. But it's over. I mean, it's really over. I've been through it all—the pain, the anger, the resentment, everything. And yes, I joke about it now. For a long time that incident with Father was the end of my life. But it isn't any more. It's over with, and in the past. It's like it happened to someone else, and if I joke about it I guess it's just one of the tools I use to deal with it. My kidding about it can't hurt Dad; he's dead. And there isn't any reason that it should hurt you, either."

"It just seems so—so—" Elizabeth groped for the right word, and couldn't find it.

"Macabre?" Sarah suggested. "I suppose it is, but believe me, it's better for me to joke about it than sit in silence and brood on it. So let me be myself, all right?" She smiled, and Elizabeth returned the smile uncertainly.

Elizabeth and Sarah returned to the little study after dinner, where they sat sipping brandy and enjoying the fire.

"Do I really look like Mother?" Sarah asked suddenly. Mrs. Goodrich had insisted on calling Sarah "Miz Rose" even after Elizabeth had explained that it was not Rose but Sarah, home for a visit. Mrs. Goodrich had remained unconvinced.

"Quite a bit, really," Elizabeth said. Then an idea occurred to her. "You know, all of Mom and Dad's old photo albums are up in the attic. Why don't we go up there and find some pictures of Mother when she was your age? Maybe the resemblance is greater than I can see. And we can dig out all the toys we had when we were kids."

"I detect the fine hand of Larry Felding at work," Sarah chuckled. "But I'll give you credit. You did that very well. And I suppose I can't put it off forever. Let's go up. Maybe something will jog my memory."

The two women went up to the door that blocked the stairs to the attic and found it locked.

"I hope we don't have to break it down," Elizabeth said. "I haven't been up here in years, and I don't have any idea where the key is."

Sarah suddenly reached up and ran her fingers along the ledge above the door. A moment later she had put the key in the lock and the door was open.

"How did you know about that?" Elizabeth said curiously. "I certainly didn't know there was a key up there."

"I don't know," Sarah said with a shrug. "I suppose I must have seen someone put it up there years ago, or something. Who cares? Let's see what's up there." She reached for the light switch and started up the stairs.

"Well, for heaven's sake," she said when they were in the attic. "Will you look at that."

"At what?" Elizabeth said. It just looked like an attic to her, and she didn't see anything odd about it.

"That corner," Sarah said, pointing. "It's so clean. Attics are supposed to be dusty."

It was true. In one corner, where an old picture was propped facing the wall, there was no dust anywhere, not even on the floor.

"That is odd, isn't it?" Elizabeth said. "I can't imagine this old place is so tight. There must not be any vents in that spot."

"You don't suppose Mrs. Goodrich comes up here to clean, do you?" Sarah said.

Elizabeth shook her head. "She hasn't been upstairs in years. Anyway, why would she clean just one corner? Well," she went on, shrugging the mystery away, "Let's get to it, shall we?"

They started going through the attic, and found a box marked "Sarah."

"Here it is," Elizabeth said triumphantly. "Prepare to face your past." Sarah touched the box reluctantly, as if it might be hot. Then she seemed to get a grip on herself.

"No time like the present," she muttered, and opened the box. Inside was a jumble of clothing, children's books, and toys. She lifted each item out, and they all seemed familiar to her. She recognized some of the clothes as having been favorites, and held others up in disgust.

"Ugh," she said. "Remember this?" It was a brown scarf, and Sarah was holding it by two fingers. "I used to hate wearing this, it was so itchy. Why do you suppose Mother didn't just throw it away?"

"It wasn't Mother," Elizabeth said. "It was Dad who insisted on keeping everything. I think the whole history of the Congers is probably up here somewhere."

Sarah snorted. "With the history we have, you'd think they'd have wanted to bury it, not store it," she said. "Isn't there supposed to be some sort of curse on us or something?"

Elizabeth looked at her sister curiously. "I didn't know you knew about that," she said slowly.

"Oh, sure," Sarah said. "Didn't you know? It's all written up in my records, first at White Oaks, then at Ocean Crest. What nonsense. Secret caves and everything."

"Ray Norton's still looking," Elizabeth said.

"Ray Norton?" Sarah said, without any particular interest. "Who's he?"

"The chief of police. Every year he comes out here, searching around in the woods and the embankment."

"Well," Sarah said, "I wish he'd find something. Then maybe I could remember those last few weeks and get on with it." She reached into the bottom of the box. "What's this?"

She held up a doll, one arm of which was broken off at the shoulder. It was an odd doll, old-fashioned, and dressed in a blue dress with ruffles down the front and around the hem. On its head, framing the faded porcelain face, was a tiny bonnet.

"I don't remember this," Sarah said. "Where do you suppose it came from?"

Elizabeth examined it carefully, and an odd feeling came over her. Then she realized that it was the right arm that was missing. Fifteen years ago it had been a child's right arm that Sarah had dragged across the field from the woods.

"I don't know," Elizabeth said, quickly putting the doll down. "I've never seen it before either."

She heard the doorbell sound two floors below, and felt a strange sense of relief at being called out of the attic. She didn't know why, but the doll had affected her more than she thought it should have.

"Who could that be?" she said. Then, when Sarah started to rise, she spoke again. "I'll get it," she said. "Why don't you see if you can find the doll's other arm? It looks terrible without it."

Elizabeth left the attic and hurried down the stairs. She paused before she opened the door. "Who is it?" she called.

"Ray Norton," a voice came back to her.

Elizabeth opened the door and let the police chief in. As soon as she saw his face she knew something was wrong. The blood had drained out of it, and there was a strange look in his eyes.

"What is it?" she said. "Has something happened?"

"Is Sarah with you?" Norton asked.

"She's upstairs," Elizabeth replied. "We've been poking around the attic. What's happened?"

"I'm afraid I have some bad news for you," Norton said. "Can we go into the study?"

"Of course," Elizabeth said. "Shall I call Sarah?"

"No," Norton said. "I'd like to talk to you alone."

"All right," Elizabeth said. "Go ahead. I just want to run up and tell Sarah I'll be a while. Will it take long?"

"No." The old policeman shook his head and started down the hall.

A minute later Elizabeth joined him in the study and closed the door behind her.

"You've found something, haven't you?" she said. "In the woods."

"We found something," Norton agreed. "But it wasn't in the woods. The construction workers broke through the roof of the cave today."

"The cave?" Elizabeth said blankly. "You mean the cave in the legend? But I thought—we all thought it didn't exist."

"I know," Norton said gently. "But it turns out it does exist."

"Was—was there anything in it?"

Norton nodded mutely; then, after a pause during which he seemed to be trying to decide how much to tell her, he spoke.

"I know Sarah was supposed to be here for a couple of days, but you'd better take her back to the hospital in the morning," he said.

"Tomorrow morning?" Elizabeth said. "Why? What did you find?"

"A mess," Norton said. "There were four skeletons in the cave, and the remains of a dead cat as well. We've already identified three of the skeletons. All three of the kids that disappeared fifteen years ago. And Jimmy Tyler's skeleton was missing a right arm."

"You said four skeletons," Elizabeth said softly. "Who is the fourth?"

"We don't know," Norton said. "It appears to be much older than the other three. All we know so far is that it was another child, probably a girl."

"I see," Elizabeth said.

"Anyway," Norton said uncomfortably, "for now we're keeping it quiet. But by tomorrow afternoon the word will be out, and this place will be crawling with people. Reporters, photographers, thrill-seekers. The whole works. And I don't think you'd want Sarah subjected to all that."

"No," Elizabeth said shortly. She paused and her eyes met those of the police chief.

"Mr. Norton," she said. "What's going to happen?"

"I don't know," Norton replied. "I'll know better tomorrow, when I've had a chance to talk to the coroner and the district attorney." He stood up nervously, wanting to leave. "You'll excuse me if I don't stay," he said. "I really shouldn't have come at all, but I knew Sarah was here, and I just wanted to . . ." He trailed off, unsure of what else to say.

"I know," Elizabeth said. "And I appreciate it. Thanks for coming out."

She accompanied him to the front door and watched until she saw the taillights of his car fade away down the driveway. Then she snapped the porch light off and slowly climbed the stairs up to the attic.

As she climbed, she tried to think what she was going to tell Sarah.

## TWENTY-EIGHT

SARAH SLEPT RESTLESSLY THAT NIGHT, and woke several times. It didn't seem fair that she would have to go back to Ocean Crest in the morning, but she supposed that Elizabeth was right and she shouldn't stay in the house with only Mrs. Goodrich. Not that she thought anything would happen, but still, she wasn't used to being on her own, and Ocean Crest had agreed to let her come only because Elizabeth would be with her all the time. And now Elizabeth had to go out of town for the day. She punched at her pillow and tried to go back to sleep.

When she first heard the noises from over her head, Sarah was sure she was imagining them. When they persisted, she began listening. Someone, she was sure, was moving around in the attic. She got out of bed and slipped into her robe, then went to Elizabeth's room. The bed was rumpled but empty. Sarah went to the attic stairs and listened. Movement. Silence, then more movement. She started to go up to see what was going on, then changed her mind. Instead she returned to her room, but left the door slightly ajar. She sat on the edge of her bed and lit a cigarette. The cigarette was almost finished when she heard the sound of footsteps coming down. She went to her bedroom door and peeked out. Elizabeth was coming out of the attic. Sarah watched her close the attic door and return the key to its place on the ledge above it. Then Elizabeth returned to her own room and closed the door. The house was silent, and Sarah returned to her bed.

When she came down the next morning, Elizabeth was waiting for her in the dining room. There was a pot of coffee and a plate of blueberry muffins. Elizabeth smiled.

"This is nice, isn't it?" she said. "I hardly ever use the dining room any more. I seem to rattle around in it by myself. But this takes me back. Coffee?"

Sarah nodded and sat down. She stirred at her coffee. "What were you up to last night?" she asked suddenly.

Elizabeth looked at her in surprise. "Last night? Nothing. I just went to bed. Why?"

Sarah decided not to confront her sister with what she had seen the night before. Apparently Elizabeth didn't want to admit to having been in the attic.

"I don't know," Sarah said, shrugging her shoulders a little. "I just thought I heard something in the attic. I thought maybe it was you." She watched her sister carefully, looking for something that would tell her Elizabeth was holding back information. But Elizabeth looked genuinely puzzled.

"In the attic? I didn't hear anything. But then, I sleep like a log. What time was it?"

"I don't know. Late. One or two, I suppose. I couldn't sleep, so I was smoking a cigarette. I could have sworn I heard someone moving around up there." She grinned at Elizabeth. "I thought maybe it was you, still looking for the missing arm."

"Well, it wasn't me," Elizabeth said. "Unless I've started sleepwalking. Did you take a look?"

"No. I decided not to. Attics in the middle of the night aren't my cup of tea." She buttered a muffin and ate it. "I wish I didn't have to go back this morning," she said.

A cloud seemed to cross Elizabeth's face. "I'm sorry too," she said abruptly. "But it just can't be helped. There's some legal thing that's come up, and I have to attend to it today. Apparently they can't continue with the construction till it's taken care of."

Elizabeth had decided to come as close to the truth as possible without telling Sarah of the discovery of the cave the previous day. "I suppose we ought to get started pretty soon," she said.

They finished breakfast in silence.

Dr. Lawrence Felding watched the two women park the car next to his and slipped the file on his desk into the top drawer. He put on an expression of surprise as Sarah and Elizabeth entered his office.

"What are you doing here?" he said. "Have I lost a day?"

Disappointment was apparent in Sarah's dark eyes, but she tried to keep her voice light.

"I got kicked out," she said. "Actually, something came up and Elizabeth has to be out of town for the day. So here I am."

Felding put on his best puzzled expression. "Why don't you go get rid of your suitcase, and I'll have a chat with your sister," he said.

"The usual ten minutes?" Sarah asked.

"Give me twenty, so I can get all the details." Felding grinned. The grin disappeared as Sarah left his office.

"Sit down," he said to Elizabeth. "I had a call this morning from the police chief in Port Arbello. Horton?"

"Norton," Elizabeth corrected him. "Ray Norton. He came out to see me last night. I guess you weren't surprised when we drove up, then."

"No," Felding said. "I'm afraid I have some bad news for you."

"Bad news?" Elizabeth repeated.

"Norton discussed the whole mess with the district attorney up there. He wants to prosecute."

"Prosecute?" Elizabeth enunciated the word as if she'd never heard it before.

"The D.A. seems to think he can build a case against Sarah. It seems they've been storing that arm all these years, and it fits one of the bodies they found."

"Jimmy Tyler's," Elizabeth said softly. "I was afraid of that. When Mr. Norton told me about it last night I assumed that must be whose arm she brought out of the woods that day. But it never occurred to me that they'd still have it." She looked up, her eyes appealing to Felding for some reassurance. "But I still don't see—I mean, everybody knows that Sarah was—was—" She faltered, not wanting to say the word.

"Insane?" Felding finished for her. "Of course they do. And, of course, that will be the plea if they try her, and there isn't a chance in the world that she won't be found innocent on grounds of insanity. But they say they have to go through the motions, in order to close the case."

"But what good will it do?" Elizabeth flared. "It won't bring those children back to life, and it won't help Sarah. My God, it'll be awful for her!"

"I know," Larry Felding said uncomfortably. "But I don't see any way to avoid it. If she hadn't made so much progress over the years there wouldn't be any trial. She'd be judged unfit to stand. But, unfortunately, she isn't. Right now she's of pretty sound mind."

"Except she still can't remember what happened that day," Elizabeth pointed out. "How can they try her for something she can't even remember?"

"Well, there isn't much we can do about it. What we have to do now is tell her."

"Tell her?" Elizabeth breathed. It hadn't occurred to her that Sarah would have to be told, but of course she would. Elizabeth tried to get used to the idea. "When?" she asked.

"I think now," Felding said. "It's going to be all over the papers by this afternoon, and she's going to know then anyway. I thought it might help if you were here when I told her." He smiled and added, "You know, it might just jolt her into remembering what happened. It might turn out that she didn't have anything to do with it."

Elizabeth chewed her lip. "That's true, isn't it? God, wouldn't that be wonderful?"

A few minutes later Sarah came back to Dr. Felding's office.

"I'm glad you waited," she said to Elizabeth. "I was afraid you might leave without saying good-bye." Then she noticed the strained looks on both Elizabeth's and Dr. Felding's faces, and she sank into a chair.

"Something's wrong, isn't it?" she said, her eyes flashing from one to the other. "You didn't have to go out of town today, did you, Elizabeth?" Sarah looked at her sister accusingly. "Well, what is it?" she cried. "Please, tell me what's happened."

Larry Felding told her what had happened. What had been found in the cave, and what was going to happen in the days to come. As she listened, the blood drained from Sarah's face.

She couldn't believe what she was hearing.

The cave was real.

Four bodies. One of them with an arm missing.

A dead cat.

A knife.

The blood. The blood and the mud.

She began remembering, and she felt her mind beginning to go numb.

Images flashed before her: Stumbling across the field in the middle of the night. Following someone. Who was she following?

Creeping through the woods, trying to keep up with the fleeting shadow ahead of her.

Rocks. Slippery rocks. Her ankle was twisting. She couldn't catch up. She tried, but then the shadow disappeared.

Darkness, and a closed-in place. And then a beam of light shining in the darkness. And rope, there was rope. What was the rope for?

And sounds. Children's voices. Cursing, yelling.

A shaft. She seemed to be looking into a shaft, and there was light. Light was flickering off something. But what?

A knife. She saw a knife flashing in the yellow light.

And then a face looked up at her. A face. Whose face?

She remembered.

Pain flashed through Sarah's head, and she raised her hands to her temples. She looked wildly around the room. The face was there, there in the room with her. Her sister.

"Elizabeth——" she cried. "Elizabeth . . ." And then another name came to her, a name she had heard in the darkness. "Elizabeth," she cried again, her voice rising in a shriek. Then *"Eliza . . . beth. Beth! Beth!"*

And then something snapped in Sarah's mind, and her hands fell limply to her lap. The color slowly returned to her face, but there was no expression. Her eyes—the eyes that had become so expressive, dancing merrily in the impish face—had gone vacant.

"Sarah?"

Elizabeth said the word softly, tentatively. She reached out to her sister, but there was no response. Sarah sat quietly, and the vacant eyes peered almost sightlessly from the expressionless face. "Sarah?" Elizabeth said again.

Dr. Felding roused himself. It had happened so fast. He should have been ready with a hypodermic needle and a sedative. But it shouldn't have happened so fast. It should have been gradual, should have come back to her slowly, in pieces. But it had all crashed in on her, and she hadn't been ready for it. She hadn't been able to handle it. Sarah Conger's mind had closed down again. He wasn't sure why, but he knew that for Sarah it was over. The past had locked her in its grip again. He looked helplessly at Elizabeth.

"I'm sorry," he said. "My God, I'm sorry."

"What happened?" Elizabeth faltered. "What's happened to her? She's all right, isn't she?" There was a note of desperation in her voice, and Felding pressed a button under his desk that would signal a nurse to come in with a sedative.

"She's all right," he said soothingly. "She remembered, that's all. It all came back to her."

"But," Elizabeth stammered, "but look at her . . . she's—she looks like she used to . . ." Elizabeth began softly crying as she realized what had happened. Her sister was gone again, and this time she might never be back.

It wasn't until late that afternoon that they let Elizabeth go home, and even then Dr. Felding insisted on driving her. They were followed by someone else from Ocean Crest, who would bring the doctor back.

"I don't think we could have stopped it," Felding was saying. "It was too fast. She just caved in. I don't know what to tell you."

Elizabeth felt numb. She kept hearing Sarah's voice calling her name. "Elizabeth . . . Elizabeth . . ." And then that other name. Beth. Beth. Something stirred deep inside of her.

"She loved you very much," she heard Felding saying now. "That's why she was calling you at the end. She wanted you to help her." He reached over and patted Elizabeth's hand, and wasn't surprised when she withdrew it. They were in the Conger driveway now.

"Do you want me to come in with you?" Felding asked gently.

Elizabeth shook her head. "No," she said, "but thank you. I'll be all right. Really I will."

Reluctantly Felding let her get out of the car alone, and watched her until she disappeared into the house. Then he parked the car, and got into his own as it pulled up behind Elizabeth's. He glanced at the house once more, then drove away. One day, he thought, the past will let go and Sarah will be free.

Elizabeth sat in front of the fireplace, staring at the blank space above the mantel. The name kept running through her mind.

Beth.

Beth.

Sarah hadn't been calling for help. She had been accusing. But whom had she been accusing? Elizabeth struggled with her mind, feeling there was something she should remember. Had there been somebody in the attic last night? Had Sarah really heard something? She decided to go up and look around.

In the attic she found herself drawn to one of the far corners, a corner she hadn't been in for years. The corner where the old portrait lay.

Elizabeth picked up the portrait and leaned it against one of the rafters of the sloping roof. She looked at it and couldn't remember why it was that she had wanted it taken out of the study. The child was so pretty, all dressed in blue, with ruffles down the front and around the hem. And a little bonnet perched on the head, only partly covering the blond hair that cascaded over her shoulders. Elizabeth decided to take it back downstairs and rehang it in the study. Then she glanced at the spot where it had lain, and she saw the doll—the doll with the missing arm. It was propped up on what looked like an old book, and the book seemed to be familiar. She decided to take all three things down to the study.

She carefully hung the portrait over the mantel, adjusted it to be sure it was straight, then stood back to admire it. It was right, she knew. It belonged there.

She propped the doll on one of the chairs, the strange old-fashioned doll. Then she noticed that the doll was dressed the same way as the girl in the picture. It must have been her doll, Elizabeth thought. Beth's doll.

Elizabeth seated herself in the wing-back chair. Beth's doll, she repeated to herself. Why had she thought that? Was that the name of the girl in the portrait, the girl who looked so much like herself?

She picked up the old book and opened it. Somewhere, on the edges of her memory, she thought she had seen it before. A long time ago.

It was a diary, handwritten on lined, yellowed paper, and the writing was that of a child. The words were carefully formed in a clear, old-fashioned hand that bore the odd look of a young person practicing penmanship. Much of it was faded and illegible, but Elizabeth could make out pieces of it.

*He keeps looking at me.*

*He was watching me today. He watches me when I play in the field.*

*My father tried to hurt me today.*

*I wish he'd go away. I wish my father would go away. Mother wants him to go away too.*

*He tried to hurt me again today. Why does Daddy want to hurt me?*

There was more, but Elizabeth couldn't make it out. She turned the pages of the old diary slowly, then closed it. She reopened it at the front and reread the inscription on the first page. It was written in a strong hand, a masculine hand, and it had not faded. The initials under it were the same as her father's: *J.C.* The diary must have been given to the little girl by her father.

She set the diary aside and stared up at the portrait. It was your diary, she thought. It was yours, wasn't it?

Cecil, her ancient cat, came into the room then, and nuzzled against her leg. She took him into her lap. She stroked the old cat for a long time and continued to stare up at the portrait.

Late in the evening, Elizabeth stood up. She glanced at the broken doll one more time; then, carrying Cecil, she walked to the kitchen. She opened the knife drawer and took out the largest of the knives. Without bothering to shut the drawer again, she went back to the study and stared mutely at the portrait.

"All right," she said at last. "All right."

Cradling the cat against her bosom with one hand and holding the knife with the other, Elizabeth Conger walked slowly out of the house.

She started across the field, toward the forest and the embankment beyond. As she walked through the night, the odd inscription in the diary ran through her mind over and over:

*Suffer the Children,* it had read, *to Come Unto Me.*

Elizabeth Conger was answering the summons.

# PUNISH
# THE  SINNERS

For Linda and Jane
The Grey Ladies
with the Red Roses

# PROLOGUE

H E REACHED UP AND GRASPED THE DOOR-knob carefully, half-hoping it would be locked. When it wasn't, his eyes widened in anticipation, and he began pushing the door open very slowly. When you are four years old, and you are going to do something that you are not sure you should do, you try to do it either very slowly or very quickly. The little boy was doing it very slowly.

He pushed the door to his parents' bedroom open just far enough for his small body to slip in, then closed it again behind him. He looked around, though he already knew the room was empty. On the other hand, when you are four, very few rooms are truly empty.

He tiptoed across the room to his mother's closet, and again half-hoped the door would be locked. When he found that it wasn't, he made up his mind to go ahead and do it. He pulled the door open and stepped into the closet. There they were: his mother's shoes.

He had seen a picture in a book once—a little boy, all dressed up in his mother's clothes—his tiny feet lost in the immense high-heeled shoes, his body swathed in the folds of a red dress, and his face just barely visible peering out from under the brim of a large sunbonnet. His mother had thought the little boy in the picture was adorable.

So now he stepped into a pair of his mother's shoes, and tried to balance his weight on those tiny little heels. It was difficult, but he managed it. Then, while he was trying to figure out how he was going to get to the hatbox perched almost out of sight on the shelf far above his head, he heard the sound.

It was the click of a doorknob, and even before he heard the next sound, he knew that someone had come into the room. He turned quickly; the closet door was almost closed. Maybe, if he held very still, and stayed very quiet, whoever was in the bedroom wouldn't notice the closet door at all . . .

He crouched down on the floor of the closet. More sounds. Footsteps, and two voices. It was his parents, and they were both in the bedroom. He heard the bedroom door close.

"I just don't like doing it now," he heard his mother say. "It seems so—so dirty, I guess."

"You mean you don't like doing it in the light." His father, angry. "The trouble with you, Ruth, is that you're prissy. You need a touch of the whore in you."

The little boy wondered what "the whore" was.

There was a scuffling noise, and then his mother's voice: "What about the children?"

"What about them?" his father rumbled. "Elaine's at school, and the kid's outside somewhere doing God knows what."

The little boy sank farther back into the depths of the closet. Suddenly it was very important that he not be discovered. He wasn't sure why, but he knew it was important.

He listened to more scuffling sounds, and heard some words that he couldn't quite make out. He began to wonder what was happening on the other side of the closet door, but he was afraid to peek out and see.

When his mother began to moan, the little boy conquered his fear. He crept to the crack where the door stood slightly ajar, and pressed his eye close. He could see the foot of the bed, but that was all. His mother moaned louder; he decided to risk pushing the closet door open a little more. And then he saw them.

They were on the bed, and they didn't have any clothes on. His father lay on top of his mother. She was crying or moaning and struggling with his father. But she had her arms around his neck, and between the moans she was saying, "Yes . . . Yes . . . Oh, God, yes!"

As he watched the strange scene on the bed, the little boy became frightened. He thought maybe he ought to help his mother, but he was scared of his father. His father had hit him before; he didn't want to be hit again. And he wasn't really sure that his mother wanted any help. Still, her cries were getting louder, and now she really did seem to be struggling. But her arms were still around his father, and she was kissing him.

The little boy's eye was caught by another movement in the room, and he realized that the bedroom door was opening again. He held his breath, then let it out again when he saw Elaine standing in the doorway. She would know what to do, he thought. She was sixteen years old, and almost all grown up. If his mother needed any help, Elaine would be able to provide it. He watched as Elaine moved toward the bed, waiting for her to say something, do something. But she didn't. She just stood there by the bed—watching.

Just as the little boy was about to call out to his sister, he saw her suddenly raise her hands above her head.

He saw the meat cleaver from the kitchen clutched in her hands.

And he saw the cleaver flash down, and heard the sound as the hard metal slashed through his father's skull.

He heard his mother cry out, and he watched in confusion as she tried to struggle free of his father's weight. He wondered why Elaine didn't help his mother, now that she had stopped his father from doing whatever he was doing.

He realized that Elaine wasn't going to help his mother. He watched, horrified, as his sister raised the cleaver again, and brought it down into his mother's face. He thought he heard his mother scream, but it was too quick for him to be sure. Frozen, he watched as his sister raised the cleaver—again and again—bringing it flashing through the air. Long after they had both stopped moving, the knife continued to flash until all he could see was silver and red.

Terrified, the little boy huddled in the closet, wondering if his sister was going to find him and start hitting him, too. But she was standing still now, looking at what she had done. And then she started moving again. She dropped the bloody cleaver on the bed, and knelt down on the floor, as if looking for something he couldn't see.

She stood up again, and pulled a chair to the center of the room, directly below the light fixture in the ceiling. She climbed up onto the chair and began tying something to the light fixture. It was an electrical cord, the kind his parents used when they needed something longer than the cords that came on the electric things. He wondered why she was tying it to the light fixture. Everybody knew that electric cords have to be plugged in for them to work.

He saw his sister tie the other end of the cord around her neck, and he realized what she was going to do. He'd seen this before. She was going to hang herself. He'd seen pictures of it. But if she hung herself, who would take care of him? He had to stop her. The little boy finally found his voice.

He screamed and as the wail escaped his throat, the girl on the chair spun around and lost her footing. As the chair fell away from her, the closet door swung open, and their eyes met. And then her neck snapped. It was over.

The little boy watched helplessly as his sister swung slowly back and forth. Finally he moved toward her, and reached out to touch her. She felt strange. She didn't feel like his sister anymore. He wondered what to do.

Much later—he didn't know how much later—he heard a scream. He didn't respond to it. He was huddled in the corner of the closet, his knees drawn up under his chin, his arms wrapped around his legs. He thought he heard some other noises too, and even later, he was aware that the closet door was being pulled open. It wasn't until a pair of arms reached down and picked him up that he started crying. When he started, he cried for a long time.

They kept him in a hospital for the first day after the discovery of the gruesome scene in the bedroom. The nuns took care of him, and asked him a lot of questions, but he couldn't answer any of them. He wanted his mother and his father. They didn't come to see him.

On the second day they took him to the convent. He didn't know what a convent was, only that it was a big building, and there were lots of nuns there who fussed over him a lot. And there were other children there, children who lived there. The little boy wondered if he, too, was going to live there.

As he went to sleep the second night, he wondered if his parents would come to see him. And Elaine. He wondered what had happened to Elaine. As he drifted off to sleep, he thought he saw her. She was looking at him, and there was something wrong with her. Her neck looked funny—stretched out and tilted at an odd angle.

When the little boy screamed, a nun hurried into the room and put her arms around him. The nun held him until he went back to sleep.

On the third day they took him to church and the little boy realized that his parents weren't going to come and get him. He realized that they were in the boxes at the front of the church, and that after the boxes were taken away, he wouldn't see them again.

He asked if it would be all right if he looked at his parents before they were taken away, but he was told that he couldn't. He wondered why.

During the funeral service the little boy kept looking curiously around the church, and shortly before the service ended, he tugged at the black folds of the habit the woman next to him was wearing. He knew she was a nun, and that she would take care of him. He tugged again at her habit and she leaned down to put her ear close to his lips.

"Where's Elaine?" he asked. "Isn't she going to be here?"

The nun stared at the little boy for a moment, then shook her head.

"She can't be here," the nun said finally. "You mustn't think about her anymore, or talk about her."

"Why not?" the little boy asked.

"Never mind," the nun admonished him. "Your sister was an evil child, and she has sinned. You mustn't think about her."

The funeral mass ended, and his parents were taken from the church. He watched them go, and wondered what had happened to them.

And what had happened to his sister.

And why he was by himself.

But, of course, he wasn't by himself. He was in the convent, but no one would tell him why. He heard someone—one of the sisters—say: "He'll get over it. He'll forget. It will be better that way."

The little boy did not forget. Not while he was small, and not while he grew up. Always, he was aware that something had happened. Something had happened to his parents, and to his sister. And his sister had caused it to happen.

His sister was evil.

She had sinned.

He knew that God forgave sinners.

But who punishes them?

By the time he was ten, he had stopped asking. Nobody had ever told him the answer.

# BOOK ONE

# THE SAINTS
# OF NEILSVILLE

# ONE

PETER BALSAM TRUDGED TO THE TOP OF Cathedral Hill and stared up at the forbidding stone facade of the Church of St. Francis Xavier. The desert heat seemed to intensify, and Balsam could feel sweat pouring from his armpits, and forming rivulets as it coursed down his back. He sank down on the steps in front of the church, and stared at the vista below him.

The town was called Neilsville, and it lay shimmering in the heat of the Eastern Washington desert like some dying thing writhing in agony with each tortured breath, unable to end its misery.

There was an aura about Neilsville, an aura that Peter Balsam had felt the minute he had arrived but had not yet been able to define.

A word had flashed into his mind the moment he had gotten off the train two hours earlier. He had put it immediately out of his mind. It had kept coming back.

*Evil.*

It covered the town like the stink of death, and Peter Balsam's first impulse had been to run—to put himself and all his possesions on the next train east, and get away from Neilsville as fast as he could.

But the next train would not be until tomorrow, and so, reluctantly, he had gone to the apartment that had been rented for him. He had not unpacked his suitcases, not put his name on the mailbox, not tried to order a phone, not done any of the other things that one normally does to settle into a new home.

Instead, he had tried to tell himself that the pervading sense of foreboding, of something desperately wrong in the town, was only in his imagination, and had set out to explore the place.

After two hours he had climbed Cathedral Hill, and now he was about to present himself to the man who had brought him to Neilsville.

He slipped into the gloom of the church, dipped his fingers into the holy water, made the sign of the cross as he genuflected, and slid into a pew. Peter Balsam began to pray.

He prayed the prayers the nuns had carefully taught him in the convent, the prayers that had always before brought him peace.

Today there was no peace. It was as if fingers were reaching out to him, grasping at him, trying to pull him into some strange morass that he could feel but not see.

Balsam concentrated on his prayers, repeating the familiar phrases over and over again, until the rhythms of the rosary overcame the fear within him.

*"Holy Mary, Mother of God, pray for us sinners . . ."*

In the study of the rectory next to the church, Monsignor Peter Vernon paced slowly back and forth. He had watched Balsam's slow progress up Cathedral Hill, and had expected to hear the faint tinkling that would announce his visitor. Now he realized that Balsam must have stopped to catch his breath after the long climb.

The priest went back to the window, and stared out once more, taking in the familiar dry vista of Neilsville, then focusing on the five girls who were playing on the tennis courts below him—four of them together, one alone. As he continued to stare down at them, each of them, in turn, glanced up at him as if they had felt his disapproving glare. One of them waved impudently, and the priest quickly stepped back from the window, embarrassed at having been discovered watching them, and angry at his own embarrassment.

He resented the girls, resented the way they acted so respectful in his presence, then sneered at him from a distance. When he had been a child, such impudence had not been tolerated. The nuns had demanded respect all the time, and the boys in the convent had given it, unquestioningly. But times had changed, and these girls didn't live at St. Francis Xavier's, didn't have the constant supervision he himself had had at their age. This year, he told himself, things would be different. This year, with the help of Peter

Balsam, he would take a stronger stand. This year, he would teach them respect, and humility. It was for this purpose that he had summoned Peter Balsam to Neilsville.

It had not been an easy thing to do. From its inception, the parish school had employed only nuns on the teaching staff, and they had resisted when Monsignor had told them he was bringing in a layman to teach psychology. Psychology, they had told him, had no place at St. Francis Xavier's. It should be left to the public school. And as for a man—and not even a priest at that—teaching at St. Francis Xavier's, it was simply unheard of. Monsignor Vernon had explained to them: he had been unable to find anyone else who could teach both psychology and Latin. Then, when they still resisted, he had invoked his authority as their religious superior. They, like most others, had wilted under the brooding stare of the Monsignor. The priest had invited Peter Balsam to come to Neilsville.

Knowing Balsam's background, Monsignor Vernon had felt it unlikely that his old friend would refuse. Balsam hadn't.

Peter Balsam emerged from the church, recoiling from the hot blast that assaulted him as he stepped into the fierce sunglare. He told himself once again that the fear the town instilled in him was only in his mind. It was just that it was all so different from what he had grown up with, so dry and parched-looking.

He told himself that he should stay, should give Neilsville a chance. He had lived with fear too long, and this time he should overcome it. As he walked to the rectory next to the church, he told himself that the discomfort he was feeling came only from his own imagination. But he didn't believe it, for as he climbed the steps to the porch of the rectory, he again felt something pulling at him, something from outside himself. Something in Neilsville.

He glanced around for the doorbell as he crossed the porch. He was about to knock on the door when he saw a neatly lettered card taped to the inside of the glass panel in its center. "Please come in," the card read. Balsam obediently tried the doorknob, and entered the foyer of the rectory. To his right stood a small table, and on the table rested a silver bell. Balsam picked up the bell, and shook it gently, sending a clear, tinkling sound through the house. A silent moment passed before he heard the click of a doorlatch somewhere down the hall and saw a figure emerge from a room. Then Pete Vernon was striding toward him, tall, purposeful, one hand stretched out in greeting.

"Peter Balsam," he heard the priest's voice boom. "How long has it been?" A moment later, even before he had a chance to say hello, Balsam found himself being propelled down the hall and into the room from which the priest had appeared a few seconds earlier.

"Pete—" Balsam began tentatively, as Vernon closed the door of what was apparently his study. Suddenly Balsam realized that he was even more nervous than he had thought. Something in his old friend had changed. He seemed taller, and more confident, and there was a brooding quality in his eyes, a darkness that Balsam found unnerving. "It's been a long time," he finished lamely. "Thirteen or fourteen years, I guess."

"Sit down, sit down," Vernon said. He indicated two large easy chairs that flanked a stone fireplace, and settled into one of them before Balsam had reached the other. As he sank slowly into his chair, Balsam became acutely aware that Pete Vernon was examining him closely.

"I'm afraid I'm a bit rumpled," he said, grinning uncomfortably. "It's quite a hill you have here."

"You get used to it," Vernon said. "At least I have. Welcome to Neilsville."

The Monsignor saw Balsam's grin fade, and his own brows furrowed slightly. "Is anything wrong? The apartment not satisfactory?"

Balsam shook his head. "The apartment's fine. I'm not sure what it is. It's hard to explain, but ever since I got off the train, I've had this strange feeling. I can't really put my finger on it. I keep telling myself it's only my imagination, but I keep getting the feeling that something's—" He broke off, trying to find the right word. He hesitated over using the word "evil," though that was the word that kept coming to mind. "—that something's not right here."

He felt a sudden chill coming from the priest, and realized he'd said the wrong thing. Neilsville had been the Monsignor's home for nearly fifteen years, and the first thing Balsam had done was insult the place. He tried to recover from the blunder.

"But I'm sure I'll get used to it," he said quickly, and only then realized that he had committed himself to stay. The priest seemed to relax again, and smiled at him.

"And your wife?" he asked smoothly. "Linda, isn't it? When will she be joining you?"

"I'm afraid she won't be joining me at all," Balsam said carefully. "I'm afraid we're separated. Sometimes things just don't work out."

"I see," Vernon said in a tone of voice that told Balsam he didn't see at all. "Well, that's most unfortunate."

Balsam decided to try to make light of it. There was no point in trying to explain what had gone wrong and no sympathy in the priest's steely gaze. "That depends on how you look at it," he said, forcing a smile. "From our point of view—Linda's and mine, that is—it was the marriage that was unfortunate, not the separation."

Balsam's smile faded as he watched Vernon stiffen. He had made another mistake: Pete Vernon was a priest, and a failed marriage was nothing to make light of.

"I shouldn't have said that," he said quickly. "Of course the whole thing has been very painful, and I'm afraid it will take time." A lot of time, he thought to himself, but the priest seemed mollified.

"Of course," Vernon said, his voice suddenly taking on a fatherly quality Balsam had never heard before. "If there's anything I can do . . ." He trailed off and then he suddenly shifted his chair. When he spoke again, it was with annoyance.

"I wish you'd told me all this before," he said. "Such things make a much bigger difference in towns like Neilsville than they do in bigger cities. It isn't going to make things easier for either of us."

My God, Balsam thought, is he going to fire me before I even get a chance? Aloud he said, "I don't really see why my marital status is anyone's business but my own."

Vernon smiled tolerantly at him. "I'm afraid you have a lot to learn about Neilsville. Here, such matters are everybody's business. Well, I don't really see that there's anything to be done about the situation. I mean, here you are, and Linda isn't here, and that's that, isn't it?"

Balsam hoped his sigh of relief wasn't audible.

"Pete," he began, but broke off when the priest held up his hand.

"Since we're talking about the less pleasant aspects of Neilsville, there are one or two more things I should tell you right now. First, while we're old friends, and it's perfectly natural for you to call me Pete, in this parish we tend to be a bit on the formal side. Everybody, and I mean *every*body, calls me Monsignor. It may seem stiff to you, but there are reasons for it. So I'd suggest that you try to get into the habit of using my title yourself." He smiled wryly at the look of stupefaction on Balsam's face. "I wish it weren't necessary," he said, "but I'm afraid it is. If people overheard you calling me Pete instead of Monsignor, they'd take it as a sign of disrespect."

"I see," Balsam said slowly, hoping he'd matched the tone that Vernon had achieved earlier with the same phrase. "Doesn't that sort of thing tend to isolate you from everyone?"

Vernon shrugged helplessly. "What can I do? That's the way things have always been done here, and that's the way the people here like it. We have a duty to our flock, don't we?" Before Balsam could reply, the priest stood up. "Suppose I take you on a little tour?" he suggested. "We might as well get you used to the lay of the land." He smiled warmly, but Peter Balsam suddenly wondered just how much of that warmth was real.

Monsignor Vernon led Peter Balsam from the rectory across the tennis courts to the school building. The four girls who had been playing doubles stopped their game and stared at the two men. Peter Balsam grinned at them self-consciously, while the priest studiously ignored them.

The fifth girl, absorbed in trying to serve balls against the wall of a handball court, didn't seem to notice them at all.

"They really gave me the once-over," Balsam commented when the two men were inside the school building.

"It was me they were staring at," Monsignor Vernon said stiffly. "They do it on purpose. They think it embarrasses me."

"Does it?" Balsam asked mildly, and was surprised when the priest grasped his arm and turned to face him.

"No," he said, his dark eyes boring into Peter's. "It doesn't bother me at all. Will it bother you?"

"Why should it?" Balsam asked in confusion, wondering why the priest was reacting so strongly.

The Monsignor dropped his arm as quickly as he'd grasped it. "No reason," he said shortly. "No reason at all."

But as they began their tour of the school, Peter Balsam was sure that there *was* a reason. He told himself it was nothing more than a function of their common background. Growing up in the convent, neither of them had ever learned how to deal with teen-age girls. And now, in their mid-thirties, it was probably too late for either of them to learn. So, in their own ways, each of them coped with his discomfort—Balsam by grinning foolishly, and Vernon by ignoring them completely. As they began their tour of St. Francis Xavier High School, Peter Balsam put the entire incident out of his mind.

On the tennis court the four girls gave up their game and gathered together. Judy Nelson, a few months older than the other three, was snickering.

"We really bugged him that time," she said. "He always tries to pretend we don't exist."

"Only during the summer." Penny Anderson shuddered. "During the year you can't get away from him." If any of the girls heard her, they didn't respond. They were still watching the two figures as they disappeared into the school building.

"Did you see what happened when I waved to him?" Karen Morton asked. "I thought he was going to freak. I hate the way he stares at me."

"Everyone stares at you," Judy replied, trying to keep the envy out of her voice. "And the way you flash your body around, who can blame them?" Judy was pleased to see her friend blush.

"She can't help it," Janet Connally defended Karen. "We can't all afford to get new clothes every week."

Karen Morton flushed again, unsure whether her overdeveloped figure or her poverty was the most shameful, and wishing someone would change the subject. To her relief, the fourth girl in the group did.

"That must have been the new teacher with Monsignor," Penny Anderson said. "My mother picked him up at the train this afternoon and took him to his apartment. She says he's weird."

"Then he'll fit in here just fine," Judy commented. "If you ask me, this whole town's weird." She shuddered a little, but the other three girls ignored it: Judy had hated Neilsville as long as they could remember.

"Are you going to take his course?" Penny asked Judy.

"I wouldn't miss it," Judy said, a conspiratorial look coming over her face. "Let's all take it."

"I don't know if my mother will let me," Penny said doubtfully. "She doesn't think they ought to be teaching psychology."

"Nobody does, except Monsignor," Janet put in. "And I keep wondering why he wants it so badly. I mean, it seems like the last thing he'd want us to know anything about."

"Maybe he had to put it in," Karen suggested. "Maybe the Bishop insisted."

"Oh, who cares?" Judy Nelson said impatiently. "The point is, if we can all get into that class, and they don't split us up like they usually do, we can get away with anything. I mean, a new teacher, who isn't even a nun? It'll be too much. After the first week he won't know what hit him."

"It would be fun," Penny agreed. "But I'll have to work on Mother."

"And speaking of mothers," Judy cut in with a grimace, "I have to meet mine down at Osgood's to buy a new dress. You want to come along?" The question was addressed to the group, but only Karen Morton responded:

"I'll come. We'll find you something sexy to wear to the party Saturday."

"As if she'd let me buy something sexy," Judy groaned. "She thinks I'm twelve years old." The two of them wandered off, leaving Penny and Janet alone on the court. After a moment, Judy spotted the fifth girl still silently serving balls to herself on the handball court. She nudged Karen, then turned and called to her friends, loudly enough for the other girl to hear, "You coming, or are you just going to stand there and watch the elephant play?"

Janet Connally's eyes widened in surprise at her friend's meanness, but she said nothing. She just tugged at Penny's arm, and began walking away. At the other end of the court Judy Nelson was giggling at her own wit.

The object of Judy's wit, Marilyn Crane, wanted to shrink up and die. She'd heard the crack, as she knew she was intended to, and she tried to hold back her tears.

It wasn't her fault she was clumsy, she told herself. It was just the way things were—the way things had always been. All her life, ever since she was small, she'd been too big, and too homely. All her life her mother had read her the story of the ugly duckling, and tried to convince her that someday she'd grow up to be a swan. But Marilyn knew it wasn't true.

She tried to swat another ball neatly against the concrete wall, but missed. She glanced quickly around, relieved to see that she hadn't been observed.

She scooped up her balls and stuffed them into a can. She would have done it much earlier, but the foursome had arrived, and Marilyn hadn't wanted them to think she was leaving just because they were there. Staying had been even worse, since what little skill she had developed over the summer had immediately escaped her with the arrival of an audience. With the stoicism she had developed over her fifteen years of life, she had stuck it out. Now, finally, she was able to make her escape.

She decided to go into the church. It would be cool in there, but more important, in the church she knew she could find solace from her confusion. It was only there, sitting in the chilly gloom, that Marilyn felt she belonged, that no one was laughing at her, or making cruel remarks just loudly enough for her to overhear.

In church, Marilyn would be close to the Blessed Virgin, and the Blessed Virgin always brought her peace.

Indeed, when she sat in the church, staring up at the statue of the Madonna, it was almost as if the Virgin were alive and reaching out to her. Marilyn wanted to reach back, to touch that presence who brought her peace.

But each day, for Marilyn Crane, there was less and less peace. One day, she knew, there would be none at all. And on that day, she would finally touch the Sorrowful Mother, and her own sorrow would be transferred to the Mother of God.

Marilyn slipped into the church, and silently began praying for forgiveness of all her sins.

# TWO

AS THEY MOVED FROM ROOM TO ROOM, exploring St. Francis Xavier's High School, Peter Balsam began to feel increasingly uncomfortable. Most of the parochial schools he had seen had begun to take on the same casual flavor as the public schools, emphasizing secular subjects rather than religious training. But here in Neilsville, the classrooms were stark, decorated only with a small statue of the Blessed Virgin, placed in identical niches in each of the rooms. As the tour progressed, Monsignor Vernon became aware of Balsam's discomfort.

"I told you we were formal around here," he said with a tight smile. "I suppose you think we are a bit backward."

Once again, Peter tried to make light of his feelings. "I was just wondering how St. Francis Xavier himself would feel about all this," he said. "As I recall, the old boy was pretty famous for his lack of formality. In fact, he tended to be pretty merry about most everything, didn't he?"

Monsignor Vernon paused a moment, his hand resting on the doorknob of the only room they hadn't yet inspected. He looked at Balsam for almost a full minute, and when he spoke it was obvious that he was choosing his words carefully.

"Let me put it this way," he said. "Despite the fact that St. Francis Xavier was a Jesuit, this is obviously not a Jesuit school. The fact of the matter is that Neilsville, and the people of this parish, myself included, tend to feel much more at home with the Dominicans than with the Jesuits. Do I make myself clear?"

Balsam tried to keep his smile genuine, and his voice easy. "Perfectly," he said. "Although I have to admit that I tend to associate the Dominicans with the Inquisition. I'll do my best to get over it."

Monsignor Vernon stared at him once more, then a smile began playing around his lips. "I hope you will," he said, his voice taking on a warm heartiness. He unlocked the door of the last classroom, then stood aside to let Peter enter. "This room is going to be yours."

Balsam looked around the room with more curiosity than he had felt in any of the others. It seemed the same: square, overlooking the schoolyard, a blackboard on one wall, desks perfectly lined up in five rows of six desks each, with his own desk squatting forbiddingly in one corner, so placed that none of the students could ever be obstructed from his view. At the back of the room, as in all the other rooms, there was a niche for the ever-present statue of the Virgin Mary. But in this room the niche contained a different statue. Balsam stared at it for a moment, then turned to Monsignor Vernon. He was surprised to see that the beginnings of a smile had grown into a full-fledged grin.

"I don't get it," Balsam said finally, moving closer to the statue and examining it carefully. "Who is he?"

"That," Monsignor Vernon replied in the jovial voice Peter Balsam remembered from their college days together, "is St. Peter Martyr."

When Balsam still looked blank, Vernon continued, "That's the Dominican you're going to have to get used to. While St. Francis Xavier may have been famous for his merriment, St. Peter Martyr was equally famous for his vigilance in the matter of heresy."

"Heresy?" Balsam repeated, still not seeing the point.

The grin faded from Monsignor Vernon's face. "My idea of a joke," he explained. "I thought, since you're going to be teaching pyschology, and some of the modern psychological theories seem pretty heretical to the Church, that it might be amusing to put St. Peter Martyr in here. To keep an eye on you."

Balsam shook his head sadly, then looked closely at the man who had once been his friend, trying to determine if the priest really had thought it would be amusing to put the statue in his room, or whether he was trying to say something to Balsam, to warn him about something. It was impossible to tell.

"Well," the Monsignor said finally, breaking what was fast turning into an embarrassing silence, "suppose we go back to the rectory for a few minutes? There're a few things we should talk about, and I have some excellent sherry. If it isn't too early?"

"Fine," Balsam agreed distractedly, not really hearing the question.

They returned to the rectory in silence, Balsam wondering how his friend could have changed so much in so few years. He had remembered Pete Vernon as someone who tended to take life as it came, and make the most of it. Now he seemed to have turned completely around, and taken on an odd stiffness, almost an awkwardness, he'd never had in their school days. Well, Balsam told himself as they reentered the study, I shouldn't have expected him to be the same. We all change, and he has a lot of responsibilities. Balsam decided he was simply going to have to change his perspective with respect to Pete Vernon. Then he smiled to himself slightly as he realized that the change in Pete would certainly make it easier for him to remember to call him "Monsignor."

The priest handed him a glass of sherry, then picked up a folder from the desk that sat in one corner of the room, bringing it with him when he returned to the chair opposite Balsam. The two men sipped their sherry in silence for a moment, then the priest spoke.

"I have something here that intrigues me," he said, tapping the folder. Balsam looked at him inquiringly.

"The synopsis of your thesis," Vernon continued. "I keep going over and over it and I get the distinct impression that whoever wrote the summary left a lot out."

Suddenly Balsam relaxed: he was on familiar territory.

"I can well imagine," he said. "You have no idea how much trouble that thesis caused. For a while there, I thought I was going to be tossed out of St. Alban's."

Vernon fingered the folder. "I can well imagine." He read the title of the thesis aloud: " 'Suicide As Sin: An Investigation of the Validity of the Doctrine.' It almost sounds as if you were challenging the Doctrine. Were you?" He looked pointedly at Peter.

Balsam shrugged his shoulders. "That depends on what you mean by 'challenge.' All I set out to do was take a look at the Doctrine of the Church in light of what psychologists now know about the phenomenon of suicide."

"And that's not challenging the Doctrine?" the priest asked.

"Not in my mind," Balsam said. "But I'm afraid at St. Alban's they didn't see much difference between my investigation and an actual challenge."

"I don't suppose they did," the Monsignor commented. "In fact, neither do I."

"Well, I suppose the best way to explain it is in terms of a trial. What I was doing, I thought, was conducting a preliminary hearing to see if there was enough evidence for a trial."

"And was there?"

Balsam shrugged. "Who knows? I found a few conflicts between the Doctrine of the Church and the science of psychology. As to the resolution of the conflicts, I'll leave that to better minds than mine."

Monsignor Vernon suddenly leaned back in his chair and seemed to relax. For the first time, Balsam realized that the subject of his thesis had disturbed the priest. He decided that a little explanation was in order.

"It's just always seemed to me that the Doctrine of the Church with reference to suicide is a bit inhuman," he began.

Monsignor Vernon smiled thinly. "The Doctrines of the Church are concerned with God," he said. "That which may seem inhuman isn't necessarily un-Godly."

Balsam's brows arched. Spoken like a true Inquisitor, he thought. Aloud he said: "It just seems to me that anybody who is deranged enough to want to kill himself can't be called rational, and certainly deserves the same considerations the Church gives to what we like to call 'morons and savages.' "

"Your analogy doesn't work," Vernon replied stiffly. "Morons and savages are not responsible for themselves, not because they are morons and savages *per se*, but simply because they have no capacity for understanding the Doctrines."

Balsam decided not to press his point. "Well, as I said, it's going to have to be left to better minds than mine to decide whether or not the Doctrine should be changed. I took no stand whatsoever in the thesis, which is probably why it passed."

"And you came to no conclusions of your own?" the Monsignor pressed.

Balsam shook his head. "As far as I'm concerned, all I did was raise more questions. I don't think I'm qualified enough in either psychology or theology to come up with any answers."

Monsignor Vernon nodded his head slowly, as if digesting what Balsam had just said. When he spoke again, it took a moment for Balsam to see the continuity.

"I should tell you that there has been a lot of concern expressed in the parish about the course you're going to teach," he said. "I'm afraid there's a strong feeling that psychology has no place in a religious school. Frankly, I had some doubts about whether or not I'd chosen the right man for the job."

"And?" Balsam prompted him.

Monsignor Vernon smiled grimly. "Let's just say I feel a bit better about it now. A few minutes ago I was about to give you a strong warning against teaching our students anything that is contrary to the Doctrines."

Which warning you have just given me, Balsam said to himself. "And you don't think you have to now?" he asked, trying to keep his voice level.

"I think you'll do just fine," Vernon said, standing up. "But I think I was wise to put St. Peter Martyr in your room," he added. Balsam wondered if he saw a light in Vernon's eye. He decided he didn't.

"Maybe I'd better study up on St. Peter Martyr," he said. "Since we're going to be roommates."

Vernon clapped him on the shoulder and Balsam felt himself being steered toward the door. "Maybe you should," the priest agreed. "He was a fascinating man. Believe me when I tell you that he never had any trouble at all in determining what was, and what was not, in conflict with the Doctrines of the Church. If you ever have any doubts about what to teach your class, consult St. Peter Martyr. Or me, for that matter. The sin of pride aside, I have almost as fine a sense of right at St. Peter did."

"I'll keep it in mind," Balsam said dryly, and wondered if the priest had heard him. They were near the front door now, and Monsignor Vernon seemed lost in thought.

"You know," he said, as he opened the front door, "I was just thinking. I have a study group—pretty informal, for Neilsville—that you might be interested in joining. Particularly if you want to find out more about Peter Martyr. He's our favorite saint. Or have you drifted completely away from such things?" He looked with a sudden intensity into Peter Balsam's eyes. Balsam met the priest's gaze for a moment, then broke away from it.

"Not completely," he said uncertainly. "But I think it'll have to wait. I've got a lot of preparing to do for my classes."

"More than you know," Vernon said in a tone that made Balsam look inquiringly at him. Seeing the confused look on Balsam's face, the priest continued. "We decided it should be the junior class that got first crack at the psychology course," he said. "And in the junior class we have four girls who will undoubtedly all want to take your course."

"The four who were playing tennis?" Peter asked, acting on intuition.

"Those are the ones," the priest said darkly.

"Should I be worried about them?" Balsam asked.

"That's up to you," Vernon replied. "But a word of warning. They've been almost inseparable since they were tiny, and most of the sisters have found the only way to handle them is to split them up. Otherwise they band together, and your class becomes nothing more than a gossip and note-passing session. A drawer in my office contains nothing but the notes that have been confiscated from them over the last nine or ten years. Someday I'm going to read them all, just to see what they always think is so important that it can't wait until after class."

Balsam felt a twinge of concern run through him. Teen-age girls had always made him uncomfortable, and the prospect of confronting a close-knit band of them terrified him. But he wouldn't let his fear show.

"Thanks for warning me," he said, "but my instincts tell me it should be interesting to have all four of them in a psychology class."

"And you always follow your instincts?" Monsignor Vernon asked.

Balsam looked at him steadily. "No," he said quietly. "Not always."

"Good," the priest said. "Then you should fit in well here." And before Balsam could reply, the priest had quietly closed the rectory door.

For a long time, Peter Balsam stared at the closed door of the stone house. What did he mean by that?

But there were no answers in the stone façade of the rectory. Slowly, Peter Balsam started down the slope that would take him back into the heart of Neilsville. As he walked, he didn't see the town at all. All he saw was an image in his mind. An image of the statue in his classroom; the statue of St. Peter Martyr. It was a warning, he was sure. But of what?

From his window in the rectory, Monsignor Vernon watched Peter Balsam make his way down the hill. It would be all right, he decided. He hadn't been sure, but now that he had talked to Balsam, he knew. Now that Peter Balsam was in Neilsville, everything was going to be all right again.

As he made his way down Main Street, the sense of foreboding that had come over Peter Balsam on his arrival in Neilsville rose again, and he wondered what had happened to his resolve. He had intended to tell Pete— "Monsignor," he corrected himself—that he wasn't going to stay. But he had not done it. Instead, he had let himself be led. Ever since they had been boys together, it had been like that. Almost as if Pete Vernon held some kind of power over Peter Balsam.

As if the slightly older Vernon knew something that Balsam did not.

Once, indeed, Pete Vernon had said something that had stuck in Peter Balsam's mind: "Our lives are entwined," he had said. "They always have been, and they always will be." Balsam had dismissed it at the time, told himself that the older boy was only trying to get his goat. But now, nearly twenty years later, here they were, together in Neilsville . . .

He became acutely aware of people staring at him as he walked along the sidewalk, and he resisted the impulse to return their stares. He concentrated, instead, on looking the town over.

Perhaps without the heat and dryness of the desert, Neilsville could have been pretty. Its frame buildings, which would have been attractive set among the maples of the Midwest, looked only stark here in the arid country between the Cascades and the Rockies. They seemed to be waiting for something, some force of nature that would weld them together into a community. But it hadn't happened. Each store, each house, stood huddled into itself, and as Peter Balsam walked among them he wondered if it was only he who felt the odd sense of rejection that seemed to personify the town. Surreptitiously, he began to examine the people of Neilsville.

There was a sameness to them that he had seen nowhere else. They all seemed to be of a type, slightly older than their years—not a healthy kind of age, a wise kind of age, but rather a tiredness. A fear? The same wariness that he had perceived in the buildings was in the people—as if they were waiting for something to happen, and whatever it was, it was not going to be pleasant.

He caught several of them staring at him. They didn't turn away in embarrassment when he confronted them. Instead, they met his eyes, and their lips tightened. Only then would they turn and whisper to their companions. Balsam wondered what they were saying to each other, but he could not hear.

He stopped at the corner of First and Main to wait for Neilsville's lone traffic light to change, and realized that he was standing in front of the office of the telephone company. He went in. Behind the counter, an elderly woman sat pensively at an empty desk. She looked up at him.

"I suppose you'll be wanting to order a phone?" she asked.

Surprised, Peter nodded. "How did you know?"

"Around here," the woman drawled, "everybody knows everything." She pulled a form out of the top drawer of her desk. "It's Balsam, isn't it?" she asked. Peter nodded. Without asking him any more questions, the woman began filling in the spaces on the order form. Finally she pushed it toward him for a signature. As he checked over the information she had gleaned from God-knew-where, she suddenly spoke.

"You used to be a priest, didn't you?"

He looked up, startled.

"Not actually," he said. "I started studying for the priesthood, but didn't finish."

"One of those," the woman muttered. Then, as Peter signed the order for the telephone, she spoke again.

"I understand Margo Henderson got off the train with you."

Peter decided to ignore the disapproving note in her voice.

"Yes, she did. Very pleasant woman." More than pleasant, he remembered. Beautiful. And at the same time he remembered Margo Henderson with pleasure, he remembered the woman Pete Vernon had sent to meet him at the station with annoyance. Anderson, her name had been. Leona Anderson.

"Divorced," the woman behind the counter said, jarring Peter back into reality. He realized she was still talking about Margo.

"Well," Peter said, smiling, "there are worse things to be."

"Are there?" the woman said, not returning his smile. "We're mostly Catholic in Neilsville, you know."

"But not entirely," Peter said. "I understand there's a public school as well as St. Francis Xavier's. And I think I noticed a few other churches, too."

The woman behind the counter looked him up and down, and Peter felt her gaze taking in his curly brown hair. Apparently she didn't approve of that, either. "There's room enough in Neilsville for everyone. If they behave themselves." Her tone said she didn't think Peter would.

"That's strange," he said. "Someone else said the same thing to me earlier today. A woman named Leona Anderson."

"Leona's a very wise woman."

"I'm sure she is," Peter agreed dryly. She had also struck him as a very unpleasant woman, who had made her distaste for him plain, from the look in her eye as she introduced herself to the moment she delivered him to his apartment. "When will the phone be put in?"

"Four days," the woman said without consulting a calendar. "That's how long it takes to process the order."

Since there seemed to be no room for argument, Peter thanked the woman for her services and left the office. She watched him go. When he was out of sight she picked up the telephone on her desk and quickly dialed a number.

"Leona? That man Balsam you told me about. He was just here, ordering a phone. I think you're right, and you'd better talk to Monsignor. I don't know what it is, but there's something wrong about that young man. If you ask me, trouble just came to Neilsville."

## THREE

FOUR DAYS LATER PETER BALSAM WAS BE-ginning to feel a little easier about Neilsville. He had created a space for himself: his books were neatly arranged on the bricks and boards that nearly covered one wall, and he had spent more than he had intended on the plants that now hung from hooks in the ceiling and brackets on the walls. And, of course, there was the telephone. He stared at the green instrument on his desk, and wondered why the installation of the phone that morning had made him feel "connected." It wasn't as if he had anyone to call, nor was there much likelihood that anyone would call him. And then, surprisingly, the telephone rang. He stared at it uncomprehendingly for a moment, then picked it up and spoke a tentative hello, ready for whoever had called to discover he had dialed a wrong number and hang up.

"Peter Balsam?" A woman's voice, vaguely familiar, somewhat shy.

"Yes," Peter answered, wondering if he should recognize the voice.

"It's Margo Henderson," the woman continued. "From the train?" Balsam felt a surge of pleasure run through his body.

"Hello," he said again, this time with warmth.

"That's better," Margo said. "For a minute I thought you didn't remember who I was."

"I didn't," Balsam admitted. "Actually, I thought it was going to be a wrong number. I just had the phone put in this morning. It usually takes a few days before anybody can get the number."

"Not in Neilsville." Margo laughed. "You're the most interesting thing to happen in years." She paused for a second, and Peter was about to respond when she plunged ahead. "I was wondering if maybe you'd like to take me out for dinner tonight," she said.

Peter was momentarily nonplussed, then recovered himself.

"I'd love to," he said. "But I have a problem. No car."

"That's no problem. I happen to have a very serviceable Chevy. If you're not too proud to allow yourself to be picked up by a woman, I'll see you about seven-thirty."

"Well, fine," Peter said, not really sure if it was fine or not, but willing to give it a chance. "Do you know where I live?"

"Let me see if I can figure it out," Margo replied. "If you don't have a car, you must be within walking distance of St. Francis Xavier's. So you must live in that new apartment building on Third Street, just off Main."

"A regular Sherlock Holmes," Peter said.

Margo chuckled. "Not really. See you at seven-thirty."

Balsam was about to say something else when he realized he was holding a dead phone in his hand. He stared at it, wondering why she had hung up so abruptly, then decided she had probably been calling from work, and someone had been waiting for her. With a shrug, he turned his attention to other things.

An hour later, Peter Balsam found himself walking slowly up the hill to St. Francis Xavier Church. As he walked, he noticed that Neilsville, though still bleak, no longer seemed as threatening as he had originally thought. Familiarity, he thought: he was getting used to the town. He was no longer seeing only the strangeness of the structures in Neilsville. Now he was noticing their uniqueness as well. Some of the houses, he was beginning to realize, were rather interesting in their own way. Yards were, for the most part, neat and well tended, as if the people of Neilsville, knowing that the surrounding landscape was always going to be barren, had decided to create some green oases within the desert. But it wasn't until his third day in Neilsville, when he had decided to venture away from Main, that Peter had discovered this softer side of Neilsville. Now he walked purposefully along, enjoying the shade of the tree-lined streets and enjoying, too, the privacy the side streets afforded him. On Main Street, he had been too aware of the constant stares of the people of Neilsville as they tried to size up this stranger in their midst. But on Elm, if people watched him from their windows, Peter Balsam was blissfully unaware of it.

He reached the top of the hill and made his way into the cool, dark church. Just inside the entrance he dipped his fingers in the font and genuflected, then moved down the aisle, genuflected once more, and sank into a pew. For a few moments Balsam simply sat, absorbing the serenity of the church, letting his eyes adjust from the glare of the summer afternoon to the soft light filtering through the stained glass of the clerestory windows.

Slowly he became aware that he was not alone. A few pews ahead of him, near the alcove dedicated to the Blessed Virgin, a girl sat motionless, her head bowed. He recognized her as the girl who had played alone on the handball court.

Her lips moved silently in prayer, and her fingers worked at the beads clutched in her hands. Balsam watched her for a few minutes, then began to feel as if his stares were intruding on her privacy. Self-consciously, he forced himself to concentrate on his own meditations, and ignore the lonely presence of the girl.

Thirty minutes later they met at the door of the church. He hadn't seen her rising from her pew at the same time as he had risen from his own, and he had almost forgotten her presence. But as the two of them emerged from the shadows of the church into the white-hot afternoon, and the somnolence that he always felt in church left him, Balsam smiled at the girl. She looked at him uncertainly, and seemed about to hurry away, so he spoke.

"Hello," he said.

Marilyn Crane looked at the man mutely, and tried to find her tongue.

"You seem to come here as often as I do," Balsam continued. "It makes a nice break from the heat of the day, doesn't it?"

Her eyes widened, and Balsam wondered if it was possible that the girl hadn't noticed him yesterday and the day before, as the two of them silently sat in the church. Apparently she hadn't.

"I'm Peter Balsam," he said, offering her his hand.

Marilyn Crane stared blankly at the proffered hand. Then, as if coming out of a daze, she grasped it and introduced herself.

"I'm Marilyn Crane," she said. "You're the new teacher, aren't you?"

Balsam nodded. "Are you going to be one of my students?"

She smiled shyly and bobbed her head, almost as if she was apologizing for her presence. "Latin Three," she said. Then she added, as an afterthought: "And the psychology course, I hope."

"You hope?" Peter repeated. "All you have to do is sign up for it."

"I don't know if I can," Marilyn said softly. "I asked my parents if I could take it, but they said they'd have to talk it over."

"Well, you can tell them for me that I promise not to put any crazy ideas in your head," Balsam said, grinning.

Suddenly the girl seemed to relax, and the two of them began slowly walking back down the hill toward town.

"How did you know that was what my parents were worried about?" Marilyn asked suddenly, when they were halfway down the hill.

Balsam tapped his head. "I'm a psychologist," he said darkly. "I have ways of knowing things."

Marilyn looked at him sharply, then, as she realized he was kidding her, she laughed, a hesitant, hollow sound. Listening to it, Balsam was sure he knew the reason it sounded strange: this child rarely laughed.

"You spend a lot of time in church, don't you?" he said mildly.

Marilyn nodded. "I like it there. It's so cool, and quiet, and I can be by myself but not feel lonely, if you know what I mean."

"I know exactly what you mean," Balsam replied. "I feel the same way."

Marilyn looked at him wonderingly, and for the first time in her life felt that there might actually be someone else in the world who understood how she felt.

"I usually pray to the Sorrowful Mother," she said. "For some reason, she always seems to make me feel better."

Balsam didn't respond right away, and Marilyn glanced quickly at him to see if her words had put him off. But no, he merely seemed to be thinking about something, so she continued walking beside him in silence. It was a nice silence, she thought. Not like the silences that so often fell over groups of her acquaintances as she approached.

Had Peter Balsam been aware of the silence he probably would have broken it. But he was thinking about what the girl had said, or, more accurately, of the way she had referred to the Blessed Virgin. The Sorrowful Mother, she had said. It had been a long time since Balsam had heard that appellation applied to the Holy Mother. He wondered briefly how she had happened to use it, but quickly decided not to question her about it. Not yet, at least. The child seemed nervous, like a rabbit on the alert, ready to shy away at the least provocation. And Balsam felt that it was important that she not shy away. Important for him, and important for her.

"Well," he said finally as they approached the corner of Third Street, "this is where I get off." He pointed down the street. "I live down there," he continued. "In the new apartment building."

A look of comprehension came over Marilyn's face, and she bobbed her head. Peter suddenly realized that she had been afraid he was rejecting her. He smiled at her, saying, "Come over and see me if you want to. I'm always home, or most always, and my name's on the mailbox."

"Oh," Marilyn gasped. "I—I couldn't do that—" she stammered.

Balsam looked blank. "You couldn't?" he asked. "Why on earth not?"

Now Marilyn appeared totally flustered. "I—I don't know," she floundered. And suddenly Peter understood. There had never before been a teacher in Marilyn's life who didn't wear a habit or live in a convent. What he had just suggested was so totally beyond her experience as to be almost incomprehensible.

"Well," he said briefly. "Don't worry about it. And don't forget to give my message to your parents. I think the psychology class is going to be very interesting, and I'd like to have you in it."

As Marilyn looked dumbfounded, Peter smiled at her once more, and started down Third Street. After he had gone a few yards, he turned and waved, and suddenly Marilyn waved back. Peter Balsam continued down the street toward his apartment.

For a few seconds longer, Marilyn watched the retreating figure of the new teacher, then continued home. Suddenly the world did not seem so bleak to her. She liked the new teacher, and she would talk to her parents again about taking his psychology course. Then she suddenly stopped, and there on the sidewalk of Main Street, Marilyn Crane crossed herself, and silently repeated a prayer of thanks to the Sorrowful Mother for bringing Mr. Balsam to Neilsville. Then she opened her eyes and continued walking. Across the street, Judy Nelson watched her from the drugstore window, and smiled.

The bell rang at precisely seven-thirty. Peter Balsam opened the door to find Margo Henderson smiling at him with a brightness that was almost too cheerful. He held the door for her to come in, and closed it firmly behind her. As the door clicked shut, the smile faded slightly, and she laughed nervously.

"I feel like a wicked woman," she said, shrugging off the light jacket she had thrown over her shoulders and glancing quickly around the apartment. "Do you happen to have a spare drink around here?"

"Scotch or bourbon?" Peter said, wondering if he should offer her wine instead, and wishing he'd thought of a clever retort.

"Scotch, with about ten splashes of water." She gave the room a more careful inspection while Peter mixed two identically weak highballs. "I like this," she declared as she took one of the glasses from him. "Books and plants—the two things I can't live without." She tasted the drink. "And you make perfect drinks, too. Maybe we should get married."

Peter choked on the mouthful of scotch-and-water he had been about to swallow, then realized she had been kidding. As his face reddened, Margo laughed again.

"I'm sorry," she said. "I didn't mean to kill you off." She patted him on the back until his coughing subsided. He sank to the couch and looked at her. And then, when he saw the twinkle in her eye, he suddenly began laughing.

"I am *so* glad to see you," he declared. "You haven't any idea." Then he looked at her quizzically. "What did you mean, you feel like a wicked woman?"

"This is the first time in my life I've ever asked a man for a date. Now, maybe you have women calling you all the time, but for me this is a new and daring experience. In fact, I'd give odds such a thing has never been done in Neilsville before."

"Well, I'm glad you called," Peter said. "If I sounded a little strained earlier, it was just out of surprise that the phone rang at all. I'd been staring at it, feeling very plugged into the world, when I realized nobody in town was likely to call. And then it rang, and here you are. Where are we going for dinner?"

"I'm not sure," Margo said, suddenly pensive. "I'd thought about Clyde's, where the food is good and the music isn't too offensive, but then it occurred to me that it might be the better part of valor to go out of town."

"Out of town?" Peter repeated blankly.

Margo nodded. "Maybe I'm being paranoid, but considering you're brand new in town, and teaching at St. Francis Xavier, and I'm divorced, and . . . well, all things considered, I think we might do better to go somewhere where neither one of us will be recognized. If you aren't starving, I thought we might drive over to Moses Lake. It's forty minutes away, but I know a good Italian place there."

Balsam started to protest, but then he remembered the frown on Leona Anderson's face when he had accompanied Margo off the train, and the remarks Monsignor Vernon had made about the "formality" of Neilsville. "Formality," he thought, was the wrong word. He was getting the distinct impression that Neilsville was downright narrow-minded.

"Fine," he agreed, finishing his drink. Then he smiled at Margo mischievously. "Do you want to meet me around the corner, or shall we risk walking out to your car together?"

"Not to worry," Margo said sheepishly. "I parked in the alley."

The restaurant hunched shabbily in the middle of an asphalt parking lot, lit garishly by a sign advertising the name of the place—Raffaello's—and, in much larger letters, Olympia Beer. But inside it had been decorated in checkered red-and-white tablecloths that somehow managed not to be cute. And the food had been delicious. Peter leaned back in his chair, picked up the cup of cappuccino in front of him, and looked at Margo. He decided she was really quite beautiful.

"Feel better?" she asked him, winking over the rim of her glass as she drained the last of her wine.

"What makes you think I wasn't feeling good to start with?" Peter countered.

She shrugged slightly. "I don't know," she mused. "There was just a look about you. Like something was panicking you. I supposed at first it was me, but I've changed my mind. I think it was Neilsville."

Balsam nodded guiltily. "You hit it right on the head," he admitted. "I have to confess that I've been getting pretty nervous about the whole thing. At least until yesterday. Yesterday I finally decided to take a chance and walk on a street other than Main. Behind the scenes, Neilsville doesn't seem quite so bleak as it does on Main Street."

"I guess most towns are like that," Margo agreed. "You don't really get a feel for them from the downtown area. You have to see where the people live. And even then, it's not easy. People in small towns aren't as friendly as they're supposed to be. Unless you're a native, of course. If you're not, forget it. You're a newcomer for at least twenty years."

"I thought that only happened in New England," Peter laughed.

Margo shook her head. "Small towns are small towns, wherever you go," she said. Then she changed the subject. "How did you find your friend the Monsignor?" she asked, and Peter thought he detected a trace of acid in her voice.

"Not the same as I remembered him," he admitted. "But I don't suppose I was the same as he remembered me, either."

"Mmmm," Margo mumbled, avoiding his gaze.

"You don't like him, do you?" Peter said suddenly.

"I don't know." Margo was pensive. "I suppose Monsignor is something of a reflection of the town. And I'm not going to try to tell you that the town hasn't been hard on me. At least the Catholic part of it." She looked across the table at Peter, wanting to say something more, but not wanting to risk offending him. But he seemed different from the rest of the Catholics she knew, and she decided to take a chance. "There's something evil about them," she said hesitantly. "Or maybe that's the wrong word. But ever since I was divorced, and pretty much excommunicated from the Catholic community, I've noticed something. I can't put my finger on it, but I'm sure it's there. They stare at you. They talk about you. They make you feel like a freak. And your friend Monsignor Vernon is the worst of them. Every time I see him, I feel his eyes on me, boring into me, as if he's examining me, and finding me lacking. And the rest of them aren't much different." She suddenly felt embarrassed, as if she'd said too much, and tried to put on a cheerful face. "I'm doing all right, though," she added quickly.

Balsam shook his head in wonder. "I don't know," he said slowly. "It all seems so strange to me, almost medieval."

"It is," Margo said bitterly. Then she brightened. "Let's talk about something more cheerful. Have you seen your classroom yet?"

Balsam grinned crookedly at her. "I thought we were going to talk about something more cheerful," he said.

"Well, there must be something cheerful to talk about," Margo laughed. "Neilsville isn't all that bad." She paused thoughtfully, then brightened. "Let's not talk about Neilsville at all. Why don't you tell me about you?"

Peter hesitated a split second, then decided there was no reason not to tell her about his childhood.

At least the part of it he could remember, the part after he was taken to the convent.

He began telling Margo about growing up with the Sisters, then deciding to enter the priesthood.

"And that, I suppose, was the first of the mistakes," he said.

"Mistakes?"

"Sometimes it seems like my life was a series of mistakes. I only entered the priesthood because it seemed the natural thing to do. But I soon found out it wasn't for me, so I left the seminary and went to St. Alban's." He grinned. "Remind me to model my robes for you sometime."

"You still have them?"

"In the bedroom closet. I guess nobody ever throws things like that away. Anyhow, I took a degree in psychology, and then went to California on a counseling job. But it didn't work out any better than the priesthood. So I decided to go back to St. Alban's, and get a master's degree. And I got married." A frown creased Margo's face. "Didn't I tell you that?" He hurried on. "I thought I had. Not that it matters. I'm separated."

"Does Monsignor Vernon know?"

"I told him. He didn't seem too pleased."

"I'll bet," Margo agreed. "What happened? To your marriage, I mean?"

"I'm not sure. Looking back on it, I don't think Linda and I ever should have gotten married in the first place. I suppose we needed each other at the time—we were both pretty lonely people. Anyway, she found someone else not to be lonely with."

There was a note of bitterness in his voice, and Margo decided not to press the matter. "What brought you to Neilsville?"

"Monsignor Vernon. I got a letter from him, asking me if I could teach both Latin and psychology. When I wrote back and told him I could, he offered me the job here. So here I am."

"And you don't like it." It was a statement, not a question.

Peter moved uncomfortably in his chair. "I don't know. I get what they call bad vibes from the town. It's as if there's something going on here, something under the surface, that's always about to erupt, but never does."

Margo stared at him. "That's it, exactly," she said. "That's exactly how I feel. But I thought I was the only one."

"Well, now there's two of us." Peter smiled. He reached for the check and stood up.

An hour later, when they pulled up in front of his apartment house, he took her hand, squeezed it, and opened the car door.

"Next time," he said, "it's going to be your turn. I want to know as much about you as you know about me." Then he got out of the car, closed the door firmly, and turned to go into the building. Margo waited for him to turn and wave. When he didn't, she felt slightly disappointed.

As she drove home, Margo decided she liked Peter Balsam. She liked him very much. Next time, she would tell him about herself. And she was sure there would be a next time, even if she had to call him again. But she didn't think she would. Next time, she was sure, Peter would call her.

Later, as she was preparing to go to bed, Margo suddenly remembered that there was something Peter hadn't told her. On an impulse, she reached out to pick up the phone, but it rang before she touched it. It was Peter.

"I hope I didn't wake you up," he said.

"No. As a matter of fact, I'm glad you called."

"I'm not really sure why I called."

"Maybe because I wanted to talk to you."

"You mean, you made me call you?"

"Maybe I did," Margo said mysteriously.

Peter chuckled. "I don't believe in that kind of thing."

"Don't you? Maybe you should." Then: "Peter?"

"Yes?"

"I was wondering about something. When you were a child—how did you get to the convent in the first place?"

There was a silence, and then Peter's voice, sounding slightly hollow, came over the line. "I don't know, really. The sisters never really tell you where you came from."

Twenty minutes later, as Margo was trying to fall asleep, she was still thinking about what he had said, and wondering where, thirty-some years ago, Peter Balsam had come from.

## FOUR

IF THE FIRST DAY OF SCHOOL AT ST. FRANCIS Xavier High School did not engender the same enthusiasm as the last, it was not only because the first day marked the beginning of another nine months of regimentation. It was, as far as the students were concerned, much worse than that; it meant another nine months of being reminded of their constant failure to live up to the standards set by Monsignor Vernon and the Sisters, another nine months of constant invasions of their privacy as the Sisters swooped down on them, demanding to know exactly what it was they were whispering about, or inspected their lockers, or suddenly seized their notebooks to determine exactly what was being written in them, or subjected them to any of the other minor or major indignities that plagued their lives. And, of course, the first day was the worst, for they had only just gotten used to the freedom of summer when it was torn from their grasp.

And, of course, there was Monsignor Vernon, ever-present, ever-watchful, constantly ready to criticize, seldom ready to praise. He had been there this morning, waiting on the steps of the school, watching them return for yet another year. There he would remain for the next nine months, if not on the steps, then in the corridors, his black-garbed figure looming over them, his piercing black eyes boring into them, discovering in them—each of them—minute flaws to be condemned.

As they walked together down the stairs to the first floor of the school and made their way slowly toward Room 16, neither Judy Nelson nor Karen Morton was in the best of moods. They stopped in front of Judy's locker, and she began working the dial. As usual on the first day of school, it took her three tries before the metal door suddenly clicked open. Judy pulled the door wide open and tossed her history book inside. She stared at it bitterly.

"Do you suppose Sister Kathleen meant it when she said we'd go through that whole thing in the first semester?" she asked of no one in particular. The three inches of history sat depressingly thick on the floor of the locker.

"Who reads it?" Karen said, tossing back her long blond hair. "All you have to do is glance at the headings, and study the quizzes at the end of the chapters. Everybody knows Sister Kathleen hasn't made up a test of her own in forty years."

"She gives me a pain," Judy groused. "Did you believe her this morning? She thinks we spent the whole summer 'being carnal,' as she puts it. Is that the same as screwing?"

Karen giggled, but her face turned red, and Judy wondered if she'd touched a nerve. She decided to press the point, and see what happened.

"I mean, the way she was talking, she must think we don't do anything except talk about sex, or dream about sex, or *have* sex, for that matter. Well, if you ask me, that says a lot about where her head's at." By now, Judy was pleased to note, Karen was showing definite signs of nervousness. Now, she thought, was the time to pounce. "Of course," she mused, trying to sound as if she didn't have anyone in particular in mind, *"some* of us do have a few sins to worry about, don't we?"

"I wouldn't know," Karen said sarcastically. "But personally, if I have any talking to do on that subject, I'll do it in the confessional. Not to Sister Kathleen, and certainly not to you." Then, before Judy could reply, Karen caught sight of Marilyn Crane coming down the hall, and said, "You know, maybe it wouldn't be so bad being like Marilyn. At least the Sisters never seem to worry about *her* 'losing her soul in sin.' "

Judy slammed the locker shut, and glanced down the hall to the spot where Marilyn stood trying to work the combination to her locker. "If I were her," she said acidly, "I'd really be in trouble." She smiled wickedly at Karen. "After all," Judy purred, "isn't suicide supposed to be the worst sin of all?"

"Judy—" Karen breathed, her eyes widening at her friend's cruelty. "That's an awful thing to say. I mean, I don't like her any better than you do, but still—" Before she could finish what she was saying, a sharp scream interrupted her. She whirled to see Marilyn Crane staring into her locker, one hand clapped over her mouth to stifle the scream. If she hadn't turned so quickly, perhaps Karen would have seen the tiny smile that was playing around the corner of Judy Nelson's mouth. It was not a pleasant smile.

Twenty feet away, Marilyn Crane stared, horrified, into the depths of her locker. There, where earlier had been only a neat pile of books, lay a frog.

Or at least what had once been a frog. The creature was spread out on a dissecting board, its legs pinned as if it had been crucified, the contents of its belly laid artfully around the corpse. Penned in neat letters across the bottom of the dissecting board was a message. "Jesus Loves You—But No One Else Does."

Marilyn felt a wave of nausea rise in her stomach, and pressed her hand harder over her mouth. Who could have done it? And why? It was crazy. It was sick. *She* was sick. Then she got hold of herself.

No, she told herself. Don't get sick. That's what they want. Don't give them the satisfaction. She heard a noise behind her, and turned to see three of the Sisters hurrying toward her. Her first impulse was to wait for them, and show them what was in her locker. But there would be a fuss. They would question her. Eventually, they would find out who had put the frog in her locker—and she would only get blamed for being a tattletale. Thinking quickly, she scooped up the dissecting board and shoved it into the large carry-all that served her both as purse and book-bag, praying the frog wouldn't make too much of a mess before she could get downstairs to the girls' room and get rid of it. She slammed the locker shut and turned to face the three nuns who were now gathered behind her.

"What happened?" The voice was cold, accusing. Marilyn looked up at the cowled face of the nun who had spoken, and recognized Sister Elizabeth. Helplessly, she turned to the others. Sister Marie's countenance seemed gentlest, so it was to her that Marilyn directed her answer.

"Nothing," she said slowly. "I—" She cast around for a likely-sounding excuse for her short scream. "I pinched myself on the hinge of the locker," she finished, holding up an undamaged finger as proof that the accident had been more frightening than harmful.

Sister Elizabeth looked at her skeptically, and opened her mouth to challenge the girl. But before she could speak, the third nun, the same Sister Kathleen who only moments ago had been the subject of conversation for Judy and Karen, reached out and patted Marilyn gently.

"Some day, Marilyn," she said softly, "you're going to have to learn to be less clumsy."

Ordinarily such a statement would have hurt, but this time Marilyn was grateful. For once, her reputation for awkwardness had served her. She smiled sweetly at the nun, and in her mind begged forgiveness for the lie. Down the hall, she noticed that Karen Morton and Judy Nelson were losing interest in her plight.

"That's Marilyn," Karen commented. "She'll probably slam her locker on her nose before the week's over." The two girls laughed, and started on down the hall toward Room 16.

At the end of the corridor a door shut softly as Monsignor Vernon turned back into his office.

Inside Room 16, Peter Balsam was nervously awaiting the arrival of the psychology class. So far, the day had gone remarkably well. After all, Latin was Latin, and most of his students had taken it before. They knew what to expect. But the psychology class was different. All morning he had felt a certain electricity coming from some of the Latin students; he assumed these were the ones who had registered for the new course as well, and they were trying to size him up, trying, from the way he handled the Latin classes, to figure out what the psychology course would be like.

And, of course, there had been Sister Elizabeth, the rather stern-looking nun who had stormed into Room 16 between first and second periods to inform him that in her opinion his course was a mistake, and that, even before it had begun, it was already disrupting the school. She was having discipline problems, she declared, and he was to blame. The students were so busy talking about him, and his new course, that they paid no attention to her. Balsam, realizing that humor would be useless with Sister Elizabeth, solemnly promised her that he would see to it that his course created no more disturbances. Sister Elizabeth, carrying an air of skepticism with her, had marched wordlessly out of his room.

Then, between the second and third periods, Sister Marie had stopped in. In contrast to Sister Elizabeth, Sister Marie had been all smiles. When he had promptly called her Sister, she had held up a hand in protest, and asked him to please, at least when they were alone, just call her Marie. And, she had confided in an excited whisper, despite what the others might say, she herself thought it was about time they started teaching something useful at St. Francis Xavier's. Then her face had taken on a slightly wistful look and, as if suddenly realizing she might be on the verge of complaining, she had beaten a hasty retreat.

Finally, just a few moments ago, it had been Sister Kathleen. She had marched into the room, checked to be sure it was empty, then closed the door firmly behind her.

"It's my duty to speak to you about an unpleasant subject," she had announced. Without waiting for any response from Peter Balsam, she had plunged ahead.

"I'm sure you are aware that it isn't easy for us to maintain a suitable moral climate for the children here," she said, looking him in the eyes. Then her gaze shifted, and Balsam had the distinct feeling that she was suddenly losing her nerve. He thought he knew what was coming, and he wasn't disappointed.

"The modern world is not all I might wish it to be," Sister Kathleen continued. "I'm afraid the moral laxness that seems to have invaded the rest of the world has succeeded in penetrating St. Francis Xavier School, if you know what I mean." She looked at him darkly, and Balsam looked right back at her, trying not to reveal that he had, indeed, caught her meaning. She decided he was obtuse, and she would have to be more specific.

"What I'm trying to say," she went on uncomfortably, "is that I hope you have no plans to discuss anything—well, *carnal* is the word, I suppose— in your psychology course." She spat the word psychology out, as if it were extremely distasteful.

"It's a psychology course, Sister," Peter had reassured her softly. Then he couldn't resist his impulse. "Not a course in sex education." He almost chuckled out loud as the nun turned scarlet and fled from the room.

A moment later he had heard the sharp scream from the hallway, but by the time he had reached his door the three nuns who had paid him visits that morning had the situation well in hand. Also, he was sure, all but Marie would resent his intruding into the matter. So he had retreated back into Room 16, to await his students. And one by one, they were drifting in. He recognized some of them and noted that as they came into the room they headed directly for the seats they had occupied in earlier classes in Room 16. One of these, Janet Connally, had started for the third-row seat she had occupied earlier, then, as if remembering something, moved up to the front rank, and carefully set her books on one of the adjoining seats, her sweater on the other. When Peter Balsam caught her eye, she smiled at him, then self-consciously glanced around the room, nodding in recognition to her friends.

A moment later a pretty, dark-haired girl came into the room, glanced quickly around, then went directly to the seat on which Janet Connally's sweater was resting, picked up the sweater, and sat down. She handed the sweater to Janet, and whispered something in her ear. The two girls giggled, and Balsam wondered what had been said. Sister Elizabeth, he realized, would have found out immediately, probably with an intimidating look. Balsam had neither the assurance nor the technique to make such a ploy work, so he simply pretended not to hear the giggles.

A few minutes later Karen Morton and Judy Nelson breezed into the room, waved at Janet Connally and the dark-haired girl (who Balsam decided must be Penny Anderson) and took two of the remaining seats in the front row. The fifth seat, next to Karen Morton, was stacked with Karen's books. Balsam wondered whom it was being saved for. Just before the bell rang signifying the beginning of the class period, he found out.

Jim Mulvey, his hair a bit too long, and his clothes looking slightly rumpled, slouched into the room, shoved Karen Morton's books to the floor, and sank into the last seat of the front rank. While Mulvey fixed Balsam with a slightly sullen look, Karen glared at her boyfriend and retrieved her books from the floor. When Jim turned to her, she was all smiles.

Peter Balsam picked up the roster and noted that there was one more name on the list than there were students in the room. Though he was already familiar with almost half the class, he began calling the roll. Before he'd even begun, he knew who was missing. Marilyn Crane. He glanced at the list once more. Yes, her name was on it. He looked out at the twenty-nine faces in front of him. Marilyn's was not among them. He began calling the roll, half concentrating on matching names to faces, half wondering what had happened to Marilyn.

When he was halfway through the list, the door to Room 16 creaked open, and Marilyn Crane crept into the room and slid into the single vacant seat in the back row. At the sound of the door opening, every head in the room had turned. And then, starting from the point where Judy Nelson and Karen Morton sat together, the whispering and giggling began, rippling through the room, swirling toward Marilyn. Balsam stopped calling the roll, and stared out at the teen-agers, waiting for them to notice the sudden quiet.

When the silence finally came, he fixed his gaze on Karen Morton and Judy Nelson. Judy regarded him steadily, with an almost challenging look in her eyes. But Balsam was pleased to see that Karen Morton had the good grace to blush and quickly find something fascinating in her notebook. He resumed calling the roll, taking care to give Marilyn Crane a reassuring wink when he got to her name. In another minute, he was done. He set the list down on his desk, and looked once more at the class.

"Well," he said, "I suppose we might as well get to it. This class isn't going to be like any of the others, so those of you who think you have me all figured out from Latin classes can forget it." That should throw them off, he thought, and was pleased to see the looks of consternation he'd produced. There was a rustling in the room, as thirty teen-agers suddenly realized they were going to have to reassess things. The four girls in the front row glanced nervously at each other.

"As some of you know," Balsam continued, looking at them placidly, "I generally seat my classes alphabetically." An almost inaudible groan went through the room, and several of the students began gathering their belongings in preparation for the seating shift. "However," Balsam continued, "this class is different. In this class you can sit where you want, and you needn't feel you have to use the same seats every day. It may make it a little harder for me to learn your names, but don't worry about it. So, if any of you want to change seats now, feel free."

About half the class began trading seats. Nobody in the front moved, nor did Marilyn Crane: the front row had already decided where to sit, and Marilyn Crane had no reason to move—no one had invited her to sit by them. Balsam noticed, however, that the boy who eventually did sit next to Marilyn—Jeff Bremmer, if his memory served him correctly—smiled and spoke to her. While they resettled themselves, Balsam wondered how many, if any, of his students had figured out that he had just gotten them to tell him something about themselves without saying a word. He knew they would continue to tell him about themselves as they rearranged themselves through the term. It would be particularly interesting to watch the front row, the four girls Monsignor Vernon had mentioned to him, and the boy, Jim Mulvey, who was apparently Karen Morton's boyfriend.

When they were finally settled in their new seats, Balsam began telling them what he hoped to accomplish in the psychology course. He would not, he told them, be spending too much time on the field of abnormal psychology, though he would delve briefly into some of the more exotic forms of madness. That earned him an appreciative laugh.

But what he was most interested in, he told them, were the possibilities the course offered for them all to get to know themselves, and each other, better. In this class, he announced, he intended to stay as far away as possible from the formalized teaching methods that were the norm at St. Francis Xavier's. Instead, he hoped the students would learn from each other as much as from him. At the same time they were teaching each other, he told them, they would be teaching themselves. If they all worked together, it should prove an interesting and valuable year.

Balsam glanced at the clock, and saw that he had only fifteen minutes left. Behind him, where it had been for forty-five minutes now, a map of the Holy Roman Empire covered much of the blackboard. Balsam now directed the attention of the class to the map.

"Behind the map," he told them, "there is a picture. I'm going to raise the map for just a second, then pull it down again. Then we'll talk about what you saw."

Quickly, before the students could begin buzzing among themselves, Balsam raised and lowered the map, exposing for not more than a second a large black-and-white print, done with a pen in great detail.

"Well?" he said, turning back to the class. "How about it? What did you see?"

In the front row, Judy Nelson's hand slowly rose.

"Judy?" Balsam said, then, as she started to stand up, he waved her down. "Not in this class," he said, smiling. "Let's save the calisthenics for Latin, shall we?"

Judy's eyes widened in surprise; this had certainly never happened at St. Francis Xavier's before. Not only she, but the entire class seemed to relax. She sank back into her seat.

"Well?" Balsam prompted her.

Judy started to speak, then giggled self-consciously, "I'm sorry," she said. "It's just not easy to answer questions sitting down. None of us has ever done it before."

Again the class laughed, and Balsam was pleased. So far, everything was going exactly as he planned it.

"That's all right," he said easily. "You'll get used to it. Now, if you haven't forgotten completely, what did you see in the picture?"

"Well," Judy said slowly. "I think it was a skull. At least that's what it looked like to me."

Balsam nodded. "Anybody else see a skull? Raise your hands." All the hands in the room went up, except one. Marilyn Crane sat, her hands folded on the desk in front of her, her face betraying the shame of having missed out on something.

"We seem to have a dissenter," Balsam said, trying to let Marilyn know with a smile that it was all right with him if she hadn't seen a skull. "What did you see, Marilyn?"

The girl looked as if she was about to cry. She didn't want to be the only person who hadn't seen what everyone else had seen. But she'd seen something different, and she wasn't going to pretend she hadn't.

"I—I suppose it sounds silly, but all I could see was a woman looking at herself in a mirror."

Another ripple of laughter passed over the class, but it was derisive, not happy. Before it had died away, Balsam had reached behind him and let the map roll upward into its case, exposing the picture. And then, as they studied it, the class stopped laughing, for Marilyn had been right. A second look revealed that the picture was, indeed, a highly detailed drawing of a woman peering into a mirror. It was captioned "Vanity." Balsam let them absorb the lesson in silence for a moment.

"You see?" he said at last. "Nobody was wrong, and nobody was right." The class looked at him, baffled, and Balsam realized he had presented something totally new to them—a situation in which there was no wrong and no right.

"What you've just seen," he told them, "is what we call an experiment in stimulus response. As you may have noted, not everyone reacts to a given stimulus with the same response. How one responds to a given stimulus depends on one's psychological make-up." And then, realizing that only Marilyn Crane had responded differently from the rest, he decided to add something for her benefit. "The fact that only Marilyn didn't see the skull is interesting, isn't it? You must be an awfully morbid group." He winked at them, so they would know he was only kidding. But he'd made his point; no one turned to stare at Marilyn. Instead, they stared at each other.

Balsam glanced at the clock; there were still five minutes left.

"You know," he said, directing his attention to the class once again, "you all surprise me. For fifty minutes now, I've had something carefully concealed on the desk. And not one of you has asked me what it is." The students looked at each other uncomfortably. "I hope that will change by the end of the term," Balsam continued dryly. "A little curiosity may have killed the cat, but it never hurt a student. So gather round."

He pulled a cloth away, and the students clustered around his desk to see what it was that they should have asked about. It was a wooden box, with a glass top, known as a Skinner box. Under the glass was a white rat. As the students looked on, Peter Balsam flipped a switch on the side of the box, and the rat began pounding at a small lever inside the box. Each time it hit the lever, a small pellet of food fell into the box. The rat promptly gobbled it up.

"Conditioned response," Balsam told them. "The rat has learned that the food will only come out when the light is on and he presses the lever. So every time the light goes on, he presses the lever." He switched the light off; the rat sat still.

Around him, the students were talking among themselves, and speculating on the possibilities of the experiment. In the middle of their discussion, the bell rang. Immediately, the discussion ended, and the students began moving back to their seats to gather up their books and notebooks.

"And that," Balsam said loudly enough to attract their attention, "is another example of conditioned response. See you tomorrow."

They stared at him for a moment, then burst into spontaneous laughter. As Balsam watched them drift out of the room, he decided it was going to work. The psychology class was a success.

He pulled open the bottom drawer of his desk, and took out the brown bag that contained his lunch. Then, as he began slowly munching on a sandwich, a vague discomfort came over him. At first he couldn't pinpoint the cause of his anxiety, but as he continued eating his lunch it all came clear to him.

It was the picture, and the way the class had reacted to it. Why, out of thirty students, had all but one of them seen the image of death? Why had only Marilyn Crane, of all the students, seen a woman and a mirror? The ratio was wrong—the class should have been fairly evenly split in their initial perception of the picture.

But they weren't.

# FIVE

INEZ NELSON HEARD THE TELEPHONE RING, and glanced toward her husband. His eyes remained fixed on the TV. It rang again, and Inez glanced at the ceiling, as if expecting to be able to see Judy running toward the upstairs extension. When it rang for the third time, Inez sighed, got up from her chair, and walked into the kitchen, half-expecting it to stop ringing before she could pick it up. It didn't.

"Mrs. Nelson?" Inez immediately recognized the voice as Karen Morton's. "Is Judy there?"

"Just a minute," Inez said. She laid the receiver on the kitchen counter and went to the foot of the stairs.

"Judy!" she called. "For you! Karen Morton!"

"In a minute," Judy's muffled voice called back. Inez walked slowly back to the kitchen and picked up the receiver. "She'll be here in a minute," she said. She stood by the phone, idly waiting to hear her daughter's voice before she hung up.

"Karen?" Judy's voice came on the line. "I was just going to call you." Her voice dropped slightly, and her tone became confidential, "I saw him today. I mean he *spoke* to me."

"Who?" Karen asked without much interest.

"Lyle," Judy said, as if Karen should have known. "Lyle Crandall. Isn't he gorgeous?"

"If you like that type," Karen said. She was not about to admit that she agreed that Lyle Crandall was, indeed, gorgeous.

"I think he's neat," Judy went on. "He looks just like Nick Nolte, only better. Is he coming to your party?"

"I suppose so," Karen said, sounding bored. "I mean, I guess he'll show up with Jim Mulvey, and you better believe Jim's coming."

"But he's not coming with any of the girls?" Judy asked.

"It's not going to be that kind of party," Karen said. Then, after a slight pause, she added, "At least not at first. But you never know what might happen, do you?"

Judy felt a wave of anticipation run over her, and wondered if the party was really going to turn out the way Karen had implied. "What about your mother?" she said. "Isn't she going to be there?"

A slight snicker came over the wire. "She has to work Saturday night," Karen replied. "At first she told me I couldn't have a party if she couldn't be here, so I told her I was only going to have some girls in. She thinks we're going to make fudge or something."

"What if she finds out boys are going to be there?" Judy wanted to know.

"She doesn't get off till midnight," Karen said confidently. "By then we'll have gotten everybody out of the house." Then, in a near whisper: "Did you tell your mother you were coming over early?"

"Of course," Judy said. "You don't think I'm going to wait till everyone's there and then change my dress, do you?"

Karen giggled. "That might be interesting," she said.

"Maybe for you," Judy said archly. "I'm a little more modest."

"In that dress?" Karen said. "I didn't think you bought it because you thought it was modest. I thought you bought it because you thought it was sexy."

"It is, isn't it?" Judy breathed. "Do you think Lyle will notice?"

"How can he miss?" Karen said sarcastically. "With that neckline, and the way it fits, everyone will notice you." Then she paused a moment. "What if your mother finds out which dress you bought?"

"She won't," Judy said confidently. "Besides, even if she does, I can talk her into letting me keep it." Then, remembering that her mother sometimes stood at the foot of the stairs listening to her when she was on the phone, Judy glanced down the stairwell. No one was there, but she decided enough had been said about the new dress.

"What do you think of Mr. Balsam?" she asked, changing the subject.

"I guess he's okay," Karen replied, not wanting to commit herself to an opinion until she found out how her friends felt about the new teacher. "At least he's different from the Sisters. But he'll probably change. In a week his class won't be any different from the others."

"I don't know," Judy said, suddenly thoughtful. "Janet says he's completely different in Latin than he is in psychology. She says it's like having two different teachers."

"Really?" Karen was suddenly curious. "What do you mean?"

"I'm not sure," Judy said. "I guess he teaches Latin the same way the nuns do, making you stand up to recite, and all that. Janet says she thinks it's because he doesn't really know Latin very well, and he's trying to cover up."

Karen giggled. "Maybe he's just crazy, and he's trying to cover that up by teaching psychology. You know what they say about psychologists—most of them need one."

Now both girls laughed, but in the middle of the laughter Judy thought she heard a click, as if someone had picked up the other phone in the kitchen.

"Well, I have to go now," she said, cutting into the laughter. She hoped Karen would pick up her signal. "So I'll come over an hour earlier on Saturday, and help you get ready, all right?"

There was a short silence while Karen tried to fathom why Judy was breaking off their conversation so suddenly. And then, with the antennae that teen-agers share, she knew what was happening. "That'll be great," she said. "If I can get Penny and Janet to come early too, it'll almost be like having two parties. See you tomorrow." She hung up the phone, congratu-

lating herself on how quickly she had caught on and helped Judy fool whoever was eavesdropping on them.

Judy Nelson replaced the phone on its cradle, then stuck her tongue out at
the instrument, as if it had been responsible for her mother's violation of
what Judy regarded as a personal and confidential conversation.

But the click she had heard had not been her mother picking up the
downstairs phone; rather, it had been Inez finally replacing the receiver.
Now she was back in the living room, and she was fuming. She glanced at
her husband, and saw that he was still intent on the baseball game. Well,
there wasn't any use in trying to talk to him anyway. He would simply
rebuke her for listening in on something that was none of her business, then
tell her that, since tapping telephones is illegal, she couldn't use anything she
had heard against Judy. That, she thought, is what I get for marrying a
lawyer. Purposefully, Inez moved to the stairway. George Nelson glanced
up.

"Going upstairs?" he said.

"I have to talk to Judy," Inez said, certain that if she told her husband
what she was going to talk about, he would stop her. "It won't take a
minute."

"Tell her if she wants, I'll beat her at backgammon in about a half
hour," George said. Then his eyes locked once more on the TV screen. Inez
stared at him for a moment, then shook her head grimly. There would be no
cozy games between father and daughter *this* evening, not if she had anything
to do with it. She marched up the stairs, entered Judy's room without
knocking, and closed the door behind her.

From the bed, Judy looked at her mother, and was about to complain
about her having come in without knocking, when she realized something
was wrong. Her mother was angry. And then she knew. The phone. The
click hadn't been her mother picking up the phone. It had been her mother
hanging up. She had heard the wrong part of the conversation.

"I see you know why I'm here," Inez began. Judy weighed the chances
of bluffing it out. Just how much had she said about the dress? She tried
desperately to remember. Too much.

"Do I?" Judy countered.

"I think you do," Inez could feel her temper rising. "I heard you
talking to Karen just now."

Judy stared defiantly at her mother.

"You bought that dress, didn't you?" Inez demanded, her voice accusing.

"Which one?" Judy stalled.

"Don't talk to me that way, young lady," Inez snapped. "You know
very well which one. The one I distinctly told you you couldn't have. You
bought it, and stashed it away at Karen Morton's, didn't you?"

"Well, what if I did?" Judy blurted out. "That dress you wanted me to
buy made me look twelve years old. And the other one looked nice."

"Nice enough to help you get into trouble with Lyle Crandall? Well, it isn't going to work. Tomorrow afternoon you're going to get that dress and return it to the store.''

"Oh, all right," Judy said, giving in on the theory that simply returning the dress was a comparatively mild punishment.

"And you can forget about going to that party," Inez added.

"Mother—" Judy began, but Inez cut her off.

"Don't!" she said, holding up her hand. "If I were you, I'd think more about my sins than how I could get around my mother!"

Judy stared at her in bafflement. "Sins?" she said blankly. "What are you talking about?"

Inez's eyes narrowed. "Do you want me to count them out for you? You can start with the lie. You lied about the dress."

"I didn't," Judy said defensively. "You never asked me which one I'd bought." It was a technicality, she knew, but she hoped it would work. It didn't.

"You would have lied about it, if I had asked you," Inez snapped. "There's a commandment about honoring your father and your mother, you know."

Suddenly it was too much for Judy. She leaped up from the bed, and stood staring at her mother. And then she burst into tears.

"Don't say that," she screamed. "Wanting to grow up doesn't have anything to do with you. It's something I want to do for me, not to spite you! Can't you understand that?" Then, as she saw that her words had had no effect on her mother, Judy fled to the bathroom and locked herself in. She felt the anger well in her, and wished it would resolve itself into more tears. But, instead, it turned into more anger, and she suddenly felt trapped. Trapped like that rat in Mr. Balsam's box. Well, she'd show her mother. She'd find a way to get even, and her mother would be sorry.

Outside the bathroom, Inez Nelson stared at the closed door. She listened for a moment, hoping to hear a sound that would tell her what was happening inside. But there was no sound, and she knew that Judy was sulking again, something that seemed to be happening more and more lately. Well, this time she wouldn't give in, and she would see to it that Judy didn't find a way to get her father on her side. But she hadn't reckoned with her daughter's determination.

The thought had crossed Peter Balsam's mind that it might not be a bad idea to give Margo Henderson a call, and invite her out for a drink. Then the call had come from the rectory, and he had found his plans for the evening abruptly changed.

Monsignor Vernon—he was still having trouble with that; he had almost called the priest "Pete"—had asked him to come up to the rectory for a "chat." Something in his voice told Peter it was a summons, not an invitation; it was a command. So he had trudged up the hill and arrived at the rectory at precisely nine o'clock. Monsignor Vernon had met him in the foyer, as before, and led him down the hall to what apparently was his private den; at least, if others used it, Peter Balsam hadn't seen them yet.

The Monsignor had closed the door behind them, and offered Balsam a glass of sherry. This, Balsam realized, was a ritual, and he wondered if he was expected to decline the offer. Well, if he was, it was too bad. The least the priest could do if he was going to ruin Balsam's evening was give him a drink. Peter accepted the sherry and took one of the comfortable chairs by the fireplace without waiting for an invitation.

"Well," Monsignor Vernon said amiably, sinking into the other chair and holding his glass up to the light. "This is nice." Balsam was unsure if he was referring to the sherry, or things in general. He grunted noncommittally.

"How did it go?" the Monsignor asked him suddenly. "The first day of school, I mean?"

Balsam shrugged. "As well as can be expected, I suppose." Then he grinned. "I mean, I'm still alive, and nobody even shot a spitball at me."

Monsignor Vernon smiled icily. "They wouldn't," he said shortly. "We leave that sort of thing to the public schools."

Balsam nodded somberly, a sudden image of Sister Elizabeth flashing into his mind. With her around, he imagined, discipline problems were kept to a minimum at St. Francis Xavier's.

"I suppose I should get to the point," the priest said, shifting in his chair. So I was right, Balsam thought. This was a command performance. He waited quietly for the Monsignor to begin.

"I had a chat with Sister Elizabeth this afternoon," the priest began. "She seemed a little upset about you. She thinks you have what she called a 'cavalier attitude.' "

Balsam smiled at the term, but when he saw that the priest was not smiling, his expression quickly sobered.

"And you agree with her?" he asked carefully.

"I'm not certain," the priest said pensively. "That's why I wanted to talk to you this evening. I've been thinking about the talk we had the other day, about your thesis. It occurred to me that I'm still not sure where you stand."

"Where I stand?" Balsam repeated, trying to fathom the Monsignor's meaning.

"I suppose this will sound strange to you," Vernon said, trying to smile, with very little success. "But I must know exactly where you stand with reference to the teachings of the Church."

"Well, I haven't left it," Balsam said.

"No, you haven't, have you?" Monsignor said speculatively. "But then, there are various ways of leaving the Church, aren't there? And it seems to me that your thesis was certainly a step, however tentative, in that direction."

He paused then, as if waiting for a response from Balsam. When none was forthcoming he continued. "Well," he said abruptly, "there's no point in beating around the bush. We're here to determine whether you do, or whether you do not, accept the Doctrines of the Church. Since you seem to be particularly well versed in at least one of them, we might as well begin with that one."

Balsam's first instinct was to simply stand up, walk from the room, proceed down the hill, pack his things, and catch the first train out of Neilsville. Then he thought about it, and decided that there was no point in evasion. If the issue was so important to the priest, he would face it.

"Fine," he said at last. "Where do you want to begin?"

"I thought I just made that clear," the Monsignor said. "Do you accept the Church's Doctrine that suicide is a mortal and irredeemable sin?"

"I thought I told you the other day that I don't think I'm qualified to make any judgments at all about that."

"Are you qualified to have faith?" the priest countered.

"I don't think it's a question of faith," Balsam replied quietly.

"Then let me put it in purely intellectual terms," Monsignor Vernon said. Unexpectedly, he stood and took Balsam's glass. "More?" he asked. Surprised, Balsam nodded. The priest refilled the glasses, handed one to Peter, and regained his chair.

"There are reasons why we have the Doctrines, you know," he said, and Peter could tell from his tone that he was about to receive a lecture. He nodded anyway, on the off chance that it might cut the lecture short. It didn't.

"The Doctrine against suicide exists for many reasons," the priest said. "Most important, of course, suicide is in obvious conflict with natural law, since it involves the destruction of natural order." Balsam was tempted to bring up the phenomenon of lemmings hurling themselves periodically into the sea. He decided against it. The Monsignor would merely say there could be no comparison between human self-destruction and subhuman self-destruction. During this sequence of thoughts Balsam had lost track of the priest's line of reasoning. He seemed to have shifted from the subject of natural order to the subject of absolution.

"You realize," Vernon was saying, "that one of the greatest problems a suicide presents to the Church is the problem of absolution . . ."

Not to mention the problems the suicide is causing for himself, Balsam thought. He went on listening.

". . . The very act of suicide, if it is successful, precludes the possibility of confession and absolution for the sin. There can't be any question but that the suicide has separated himself from the Mother Church, and, therefore, from God."

"*Extra ecclesium nulla salus,*" Balsam muttered.

"Pardon me?" the priest said.

"Outside the Church there is no salvation," Balsam translated for him.

"I know the Latin," Monsignor Vernon said dryly. "I simply didn't hear the words clearly." Then he paused, and stared hard at Balsam. "Do you have 'problems' with that Doctrine as well?"

Balsam shrugged. "I hadn't thought about it," he said wearily. He leaned forward in his chair, and decided to try to explain his thinking to the priest.

"Look," he said, "I don't know what's been going on here in Neilsville, but everywhere else, at least everywhere I've been, a lot of people are raising questions. And these aren't people who have left the Church, or are contemplating leaving it. They're simply some thoughtful people who would like to see the Church bring itself a little closer to the twentieth century.''

"And that includes challenging the Doctrines?" Vernon asked darkly.

"Not necessarily," Balsam said. Was there no getting through to this man? Pete Vernon had always seemed so reasonable in school. What had happened? He made one more try. "It's not really a matter of challenging the Doctrines," he said. "It's simply a matter of bringing the Church more in touch with the needs of people.''

"The Church is concerned with the needs of God," Monsignor Vernon said stiffly, his voice taking on a coldness that almost frightened Peter.

"There are those of us who don't think the needs of God and the needs of man are any different. And we would like to see the Doctrines reflect that." After he spoke he realized that he had taken a stand. The Monsignor was glaring his disapproval.

"The Doctrines are infallible," Monsignor Vernon declared. "They do not need modification. Or do you also challenge the Doctrine of Infallibility?''

Balsam found himself suddenly angry. The man sounded like a medieval Inquisitor. "The Doctrine of Infallibility itself is only about one hundred years old," he pointed out, trying to contain himself. "And, unless my memory is way off, I don't think there was any kind of unanimity when that particular Doctrine was adopted.''

Suddenly the priest was on his feet, glaring down at Balsam with an intensity that frightened him.

"Peter Balsam," the priest hissed, his eyes glinting, "it is exactly the sort of thinking I have heard from you tonight that is destroying the Church. We will not tolerate it at St. Francis Xavier's. I do not know, and do not particularly care, what your private thoughts may be—obviously you are very close to falling from grace—but I will not stand for your contaminating the children of this parish with your ideas. It has been my duty and privilege to protect my flock from ideas such as those you've expressed, and I will not fail in my duty now. Do I make myself clear?''

Now Balsam stood up, and gazed at the priest levelly. "You do," he said tightly. "And I have to tell you that what I'm hearing sounds as if it came straight out of the thirteenth century.''

Suddenly the priest relaxed a little, and moved away from Balsam. When he turned to face Peter again, there was a slight smile on his lips that could have been genuine. Peter doubted it was.

"If you've studied your history, you know that there were a lot more saints in that century than in this. Maybe we should consider that fact before we talk with such self-satisfaction about our 'modern times.' ''

"We know a bit more about human beings now," Balsam said.

"Perhaps," Monsignor replied. "But they certainly knew something we've forgotten—how to deal with heresy and sin." He paused, and when he continued it was more to himself than to Peter. "Or at least some of us have. Not all of us.''

\* \* \*

Ten minutes later, as he walked back down the hill, Balsam was still trying to figure out what had happened to his old friend, Pete Vernon. Though a definite physical resemblance remained, Monsignor Vernon had nothing else in common with the Pete Vernon with whom Peter Balsam had grown up.

As he was leaving, the Monsignor had urged him once more to attend a meeting of the study group he led. Perhaps he should, Balsam decided. Perhaps it was the study group that had affected Monsignor Vernon so strongly, and made his religion so rigid. What was it the priest had said they called the group? The Society of St. Peter Martyr. The same saint whose statue stood in the alcove of Room 16, keeping tabs on him. Peter Balsam decided to attend the next meeting of the Society. If he was still in Neilsville.

After Balsam left the rectory, and he had carefully locked the front door for the night, Monsignor Vernon returned to the den, carefully locked that door as well, and lit the fire that was already laid in the fireplace. Then, unaware of the uncomfortably high temperature that was turning the small room into an oven, he began to pray. He prayed for a long time, and by the time he was finished, the flames had died. All that remained in the fireplace was a bed of coals, glowing hotly in the darkness. A bed of coals, he thought, that glowed for the heretics and sinners. Smiling contentedly, Monsignor Vernon took himself to bed. He would sleep peacefully tonight. Tomorrow he would begin his work.

## SIX

THE NEXT DAY, A SUBTLE SHIFT HAD taken place in the seating pattern of the psychology class. Though the same five people still ranged across the front row, Judy Nelson was not sitting next to Karen Morton. Today she had moved herself to the end of the row, and Penny and Janet had each moved in a seat. Balsam had wondered, when he first noticed this, if something had happened between Karen and Judy, or whether the four girls were in the habit of changing places, and sharing each other. That, he knew, was unlikely—in many ways adolescents tended to be much more rigid than adults.

Today, Balsam hadn't bothered to cover the Skinner box. As he talked to the class, he occasionally glanced down at the rat, which sat calmly gazing back up at him, almost as if it knew it was going to be called upon to perform, and was awaiting its cue.

Balsam was talking to the class about frustration, and he had tried to put a capital "F" on the word when he had first used it.

"Frustration," he had said, "might be defined as the feeling one gets when one has to sit and listen to a psychology lecture when one would rather be doing almost anything else."

The class had chuckled nervously, as if they were a little embarrassed at being caught out. But at least they were all paying attention; all that is, except Judy Nelson, who seemed lost in her own world. From what Balsam could observe of the sullen expression on her face, it was not a pleasant world.

He was right. Judy was still sulking about the scene she had had with her mother the night before. She had spent most of an hour locked in the bathroom, waiting for the slight tap at the door, and her mother's plaintive tone asking her if she was all right—the signal that she had won, that her mother had given in. But it didn't come. Finally, Judy had given up the bathroom in favor of a frontal assault. She had gone downstairs to play backgammon with her father. But he had only looked at her coldly and announced that he had changed his mind—there would be no backgammon that night. Judy, bursting into tears, had fled back to the bathroom. There she had waited. And waited. Evenutally she had heard her parents come upstairs, and heard them call her a cheerful good-night. Then she had heard their door close as they retired for the night. Judy had considered throwing another tantrum, but had discarded the idea. Instead, she had taken her anger to bed with her, where she had no trouble at all in transferring it to Karen Morton.

The "if onlies" had begun: If only Karen hadn't called her. If only Karen hadn't begun talking about the party. If only Karen hadn't mentioned the dress. Ignoring the fact that she, too, had talked about the party, bragged about the dress, Judy had quickly decided that the whole thing was Karen's fault. So, today, she had snubbed Karen in the morning, then carefully seated herself two seats away when they had arrived at Room 16. Now, as Mr. Balsam droned on, she glanced across at Karen, and mentally criticized everything about her, from her bleached hair and plucked brows to the too-tight dress that was stretched across her too-large bust. It was all Karen's fault, Judy told herself again. And then she saw all the students standing up and moving to the front of the room, and realized she hadn't heard a word Mr. Balsam had said. Coming out of her reverie, Judy got up and joined the group clustered around the strange box with the rat in it.

"Now," Peter Balsam was saying, "watch carefully. As you can see, I've arranged a maze in the box. A simple one. Two correct choices, and it's easy to get through. For you and me, anyway. But it looks different to the rat, since he can't see the whole thing, and wouldn't know what to think of it, even if he could see it. Now, watch what happens."

He dropped a pellet of food at one end of the maze, and placed the rat at the other. Then he replaced the glass top on the box. The rat sniffed a couple of times, caught the scent of food, and began snuffling around. It started through the maze, came to a dead end, snuffled some more, retraced its steps, and got back on the right track. Then it missed the second turn, and came up against another dead end. Unfazed, it backtracked again. This time its efforts were rewarded.

"Let's try it again, and see what happens," Balsam said. He opened the box, lifted the rat out, and put in another food pellet. The rat made it to the food with only one wrong turn. The third time he repeated the experiment, the rat went directly to the food. It had learned the route.

"Okay," Balsam said. "I'm sure everyone understands what's been happening. I've encouraged the rat to learn by rewarding him with food. So far, so good. Now let's try something else. He picked up a small piece of wood from the desktop, and held it up for the class to see.

"Let's add a new element," he said. "Let's put this into the maze right here." He carefully added the new barrier to the maze.

"But if you put it there," Janet Connally pointed out, "he won't be able to get through at all."

Balsam smiled at her. "Exactly," he said. "Now let's see how the rat reacts." He put the rat back in the box, and quickly replaced the glass top. The rat hurried through the maze until it suddenly bumped into the new barrier. It sniffed at the barrier a couple of times, and tried to prod its way past. The barrier held. Then the rat began moving more rapidly, poking in every corner, frantically searching for a way past the barrier. When it found none, it leaped against the barrier a couple of times, then strained upward and clawed at the glass. Finally, it sat very still, trembling, immobile.

"What happened?" a voice asked softly.

"I frustrated it," Balsam said. "And when it couldn't find any outlet for its frustration, it threw in the towel."

"You mean it just stopped trying?" Balsam recognized the voice now. It was Marilyn Crane. He glanced up at her, and saw an expression of compassion on her face.

"That's right," he said. "It stopped trying. It will probably try again in a few minutes, since it can still smell the food. But it will stop again, and unless I take the barrier away it will just give up completely."

"But I still don't understand what happened." Penny Anderson looked worried.

Balsam smiled at her. "I led it to expect something," he said. "I taught it that if it went through the maze in a certain way it could expect a reward at the end. And then, just as it had gotten used to the game, I changed the rules. All of a sudden it doesn't know what to expect, and finds that it isn't even in control of the situation. So it's frustrated. Unless I relieve the frustration, it will get neurotic. In fact, if I tried, I could drive that rat completely crazy. All I'd have to do is keep changing the rules on it, let it learn the new rules, then change them again. Mainly, it's a matter of being inconsistent. As long as the rat knows what to expect, he's all right. It doesn't bother him that he can't get food when the light is out. He just waits for the light to come back on. I set the rule long ago, and never varied it. With the maze, I did something different. I was inconsistent."

"I think I see," Janet said carefully. "It's like with my parents. As long as they do what I expect them to do, I feel safe. But every now and then they do something unexpected, and it upsets me."

"That's it," Balsam said. "It's all a matter of consistency. Lack of consistency leads to frustration, and from there on it's a downhill slide."

Just then the bell rang, and the class, without thinking, began moving to their desks. One or two laughed self-consciously.

"Conditioned response," Balsam heard Janet Connally whisper to Penny Anderson. Then the two girls were gone, disappearing into the hall with the rest of the class. When he turned back to the rat, Judy Nelson was staring blankly down into the box. Balsam watched her in silence for a moment, wondering if she was aware that the room had emptied. She seemed to be lost somewhere in the depths of the maze, as she had been lost somewhere in another world during his lecture. When he finally spoke, she looked up in surprise.

"Has he moved yet?" Balsam asked her.

"No," she said uncertainly. "He just sits there. It's too bad, isn't it?"

"What is?" Balsam inquired.

"I'm not sure. I mean, it just seems like it's too bad the rat doesn't have more control over his surroundings. It's like he wants to do something, but just can't do it."

"Exactly," Balsam said, moving closer to her and looking down at the rat. The rat, still trembling, stared balefully back at him, almost as if it were reproaching him.

"That's one of the things that make rats nice for experimentation," he explained. "Because they don't have much control over their environment, it's much easier to get dependable results. Or magnified results."

Judy peered at him now, a puzzled expression on her face.

Balsam began again. "If the rat were human it wouldn't be nearly so easy to reduce it to a point of total frustration. For instance, if the rat were a person, it would have first gone over the entire maze, making sure it hadn't taken any wrong turns. Then it would have investigated the barrier, trying to figure a way to get through. And then, if that failed, it would have started figuring a way to break the glass, so it could go over."

Judy nodded her head. "And if that didn't work?" she asked quietly.

"Who knows?" Balsam shrugged. "If I were that rat, I suppose I'd be busy tearing that cage apart, or I'd kill myself trying." His attention had wandered back to the rat again, but as he finished what he was saying he glanced once more at Judy. There was an odd look on her face.

"Is something wrong?" he asked her.

Judy shook her head negatively. "No," she said shortly. "I—I'm fine, really." She glanced at the clock. "I'm going to be late if I don't hurry." She moved to her chair, and quickly began gathering her belongings. As she was about to leave the room, Balsam stopped her.

"Are you sure you're all right?" he said.

She nodded quickly, and started for the door.

"If something's wrong, I wish you'd tell me what it is," Balsam tried again. "Or maybe you should talk to Monsignor."

At the mention of the priest, Judy suddenly turned back, and stared at Balsam.

"Monsignor?" she said blankly. "You must be kidding!" And then she was gone.

Balsam stared after her, her words echoing in his ears. *You must be kidding!''* And the look on her face, a mixture of resentment, bafflement, and, it seemed, contempt. And why not? Balsam reflected. Why had he suggested she talk to the Monsignor? Certainly the priest was the last person Balsam would go to if he had a problem; why should the students feel any differently? Perhaps he should have suggested one of the nuns. But which one? Sister Elizabeth? Hardly. What about Sister Kathleen? All Judy would have gotten was a lecture, a warning about her sins. And, if she had been sinning, a lecture wasn't what she needed.

Then he came, in his mind, to Sister Marie. Of course. Quickly, Balsam stepped into the hall and looked up and down. But Judy was gone. He went back into his room, fed the rat, and pulled his lunch bag from his desk. He took one bite and put his sandwich down. Maybe he could convince Sister Marie to talk to Judy and find out what was wrong. Because something *was* wrong. He was sure of it.

He found the nun in the library, deeply engrossed in a copy of *Christian Century,* which she quickly closed when she realized someone was approaching. Then, when she saw who it was, she smiled and waved. As Balsam drew nearer she laughed, and reopened the magazine. Inside was another magazine. Balsam saw that the nun had been engrossed in the theater column of *The New Yorker*.

"Catching up on your religion?" he grinned, sitting down across from her.

"It's terrible, isn't it? I always feel so guilty about it, but I do love the theater, there's no sense denying it."

Peter glanced once more at the magazine that was so neatly concealed inside the *Christian Century*. "Unlikely reading material for St. Francis Xavier's," he commented.

Sister Marie nodded emphatically. "If you promise not to tell anyone— and I mean *any*one—I'll let you in on a secret."

"Who would I tell?" Balsam said.

"Well, this is my own guilty secret. I've never told anyone until now. But I think it'll be safe with you." Her eyes were twinkling merrily, and Balsam decided he'd been right. If anyone should talk to Judy Nelson, it was Sister Marie. Her voice dropped conspiratorially.

"The library gets *The New Yorker* every year as an anonymous gift," she said.

"From you?" Balsam said.

"Oh, no, I couldn't," Sister Marie said, horrified at the suggestion. Then she went on, "My sister, however, could, and does. Every year, when Monsignor gets the notice of renewal, he talks about canceling it. But he's afraid to, because he thinks it would get back to whoever donates it, and they might cut off any other donations they're making to the Church."

"And would she?" Balsam asked.

"Heavens, no," Sister Marie said, laughing happily. "That's the best part of it. My sister happens to be a Baptist. She sends in the subscription each year as a favor to me. She doesn't give a nickel to the Church. In fact, she says I'm the only Catholic she can put up with at all! Isn't it wonderful?"

The two of them laughed for a moment, then Peter grew serious. He decided he liked Sister Marie very much.

"I wonder if you could do me a favor," he said slowly.

"Of course," Sister Marie responded. "Unless it's something wicked. Then I'd have to confess afterward, but I'd probably do it anyway."

"You're impossible," Peter said, smiling at her.

"I try." Then, as his smile faded, she grew serious. "What is it?" she asked.

"I'm not sure, really. But I thought you might be able to find out. It's one of my students, Judy Nelson." The nun nodded shortly, acknowledging that she knew Judy.

"Something's bothering her," Balsam continued, "and I can't get her to tell me what it is." Briefly, he told Sister Marie what had transpired after his class and that he had suggested that Judy talk to Monsignor.

"She wasn't too receptive to that idea," he finished.

"No, I don't imagine she was," Sister Marie said briefly, and Peter Balsam thought he detected a bitterness in her voice. He thought she was about to say something about the priest, then appeared to change her mind. She smiled at him reassuringly.

"I'll see what I can do," she said. "Mind you, I'm not guaranteeing anything. Sometimes I think our habits get between us and the children. I think we scare them. But I'll find her this afternoon, and see if I can find out what the trouble is. All right?"

Suddenly Balsam felt better. He smiled at the nun, and stood up.

"I'm sorry to dump this on you," he began, but Sister Marie held up a hand.

"Don't be sorry," she said. "Try to do what you think is right, and try not to worry too much about the consequences. If things go too far wrong, God will take care of them."

Balsam started to reply, then changed his mind. He smiled at her once more, then turned to go. Behind him, he heard her voice.

"Mr. Balsam?" He turned around. The twinkle was back in her eye. "There's something else you should know. One thing you can count on with Judy—if she can find a reason to be dramatic, she'll *be* dramatic. Whatever it is, I'm sure it's not serious."

Balsam nodded, then made his way back to Room 16. He finished his sandwich, sharing it with the rat, and prepared for his next class. Latin III. By the time the class convened, he was totally immersed in conjugating irregular verbs in the past perfect.

He had forgotten about Judy Nelson.

At a quarter to four that afternoon, Marilyn Crane hurried down the hall toward the lockers. She was late and she still had to stop at church before she went home. As she began spinning the dial on the lock, hoping it would open on the first try, she was vaguely aware of someone leaning heavily against the wall a few feet away. She didn't look up; not enough time. She turned to the last digit, and grasped the handle of the locker. It wouldn't move. Quickly, she twirled the dial again, until she felt a slight click. She tried the handle once more, and this time it moved. Marilyn pulled the locker door, and started to put her books inside. Then she gasped, and her hand flew to her mouth.

Inside was a crucifix, suspended upside down from one of the coathooks at the top of the locker. The face of Christ had been smashed. She looked frantically for a note, some explanation, but there was none. She stared vacantly at the dangling, obscenely defaced crucifix, then slammed the locker shut and closed her eyes tightly, but the image stayed before her. Then, as she began silently praying, she felt the eyes on her. She opened her own, and looked around, recognizing the person of whom she had been vaguely aware a moment earlier. It was Judy Nelson, and she was leaning against the wall, staring at Marilyn. Marilyn looked quickly away.

Judy Nelson! Would Judy have done something like this? She knew Judy didn't like her. None of that group did. Marilyn remembered the frog yesterday. Was Judy in the biology class? She could feel the other girl's eyes still on her.

No, Marilyn told herself, don't think that. Judy wouldn't do something like that. It has to be someone else; someone I don't even know. She wanted to believe it, believe that only a stranger could be so heartless. She forced herself to turn and look at Judy Nelson.

It was then Marilyn realized that something was wrong. Judy hadn't moved, nor had her expression changed. It came to Marilyn that Judy wasn't looking at her, but beyond her, at something off in the distance. She wondered if she ought to speak to Judy. Probably not. But she couldn't just walk away, could she?

Why not? Hadn't Judy said mean things to her?

So had everyone else. And Judy seemed to need help.

Marilyn closed her eyes again, and silently begged the Sorrowful Mother to give her strength. And she thought she felt strength flowing into her. She moved down the hall until she was next to Judy.

"Judy?" she asked. "Are you all right? Is something the matter?"

Judy Nelson seemed to come out of her reverie. She looked coldly at Marilyn, as if she hadn't noticed her before.

"I'm fine," she said; her tone told Marilyn she wasn't. ·

"Can I help?" Marilyn offered, determined not to be put off by Judy's coldness.

Judy stared at her again, and Marilyn thought she was going to walk away without saying anything. But then she seemed to change her mind. Her face went slack, and suddenly looked very tired.

"Nobody can help me," she said. Then she turned, and silently walked away, down the hall. For a moment, Marilyn was tempted to follow her, and try to find out what was wrong. She watched until Judy disappeared around the corner. Then, shrugging, Marilyn walked down the hall the other way, and left the school building to go into the church. As she sat in the pew, silently praying to the Blessed Virgin, she imagined she heard music in the background. It was a singsong sound, like Gregorian chants, and Marilyn wondered where it was coming from. When it stopped, she realized that it hadn't been coming from anywhere. It must, she was sure, have been coming from inside her head. She left the church, and walked down the hill toward home.

Inez Nelson heard the front door open and then close, and wiped her hands on her apron. "Judy?" she called. "Is that you?" She started toward the front of the house, glancing at the clock to determine how late Judy was. But before she had gotten halfway down the hall she heard her husband's voice.

"It's me," George Nelson called out. He stepped into the hall, almost bumping into his wife. "Judy not home yet?"

"No, she isn't," Inez said, suddenly worried. Why would she have been calling Judy, if Judy were already home? Didn't he *think*?

"Maybe she went over to Janet's or Penny's," George suggested.

"She should have called if she did," Inez pointed out, when, as if on cue, the phone began to ring. George looked triumphant.

"See?" he said, and picked up the receiver. "Nelson residence."

"Mr. Nelson?"

"Yes," George said, a little uncertainly. He didn't recognize the voice.

"This is Mrs. Williams, at the emergency room of the hospital."

"The hospital?" George repeated blankly.

"Neilsville Hospital," Mrs. Williams repeated. "I'm afraid I have to ask you to come down here. Your daughter's here." Then, when George failed to respond, she continued, "You *are* the father of Judy Nelson?"

"Yes," George said weakly, the color draining from his face. "What's happened? What's wrong?"

He listened, trembling, then quietly dropped the receiver back on the hook and turned to his wife.

"What is it?" she said. "What's happened?"

"I'm not sure," George said slowly. "She says—" he faltered, then blurted out, "Judy tried to kill herself."

## SEVEN

J UDY  NELSON  LAY  PROPPED  UP  IN  BED, glaring at the nurse who was adjusting the bandages on her wrists. In one corner of the room her bloodstained clothes lay in a pile: she had refused to allow them to be taken away, and rather than provoke a scene the nurses had decided the clothes could wait.

"Your parents will be here any minute now," one of the nurses said gently, patting Judy on the hand. "How are we feeling?"

"I don't want to see them," Judy muttered, pulling her hand away.

"Of course you do," the nurse smiled. "We all want to see our parents, don't we?"

Judy glared at the nurse. "*I* don't," she snapped. "Why don't you leave me alone?"

The nurse didn't answer her, merely moved to another chair, a little way from the bed. She ignored Judy's sullen stare and occupied herself with several unnecessary readings of Judy's chart.

In the reception area of the emergency room, Mrs. Williams was trying to explain the situation to Inez and George Nelson. George seemed to be listening carefully, but Inez was tapping her foot nervously, as if waiting for all the "nonsense" to be over with, so she could see her daughter.

"We don't really know what happened," Mrs. Williams was saying. "Or perhaps I should say we don't know *why*. Judy won't talk to anybody about it, and until she does, well . . ." Her voice trailed off, and she shrugged eloquently.

"Could you tell me exactly what you *do* know?" Inez asked sharply.

Mrs. Willams sighed. These things were so difficult. Thank God they practically never happened. Brusquely she began telling the story to the Nelsons.

"Apparently Judy didn't leave the school this afternoon. Instead, she went to the girls' locker room, off their gymnasium, and waited until she thought everyone had gone home. Then she found a razor blade, and cut her wrists." When she saw the color draining from Inez's face she hastened to explain. "It isn't as bad as it sounds," she rushed on. "As a matter of fact, it's next to impossible to do enough damage to yourself with razor blades to die, except under certain circumstances. Mostly, it just hurts a bit, and causes a lot of mess. Anyway, Judy must have gotten scared as soon as she cut herself, because she called the police right away. Of course the police called us, but by the time our ambulance got there, it was all pretty much over with."

"Over with?" George asked. "What do you mean, over with?"

"One of the janitors at the school found her," Mrs. Williams said. "Fortunately, he wasn't the kind to get upset at the sight of blood, and he had her wrists bandaged before anybody else could get there. It wasn't the best bandaging job I ever saw, but it wasn't the worst, either. Doctor put in a few stitches and rebandaged the wrists, and Judy should be fine in a day or so." Mrs. Williams tried to smile brightly, as if the whole incident were no worse than a scraped knee.

"I want to see her," Inez said suddenly.

"Yes," Mrs. Williams began. "I . . . I'm sure you do. But I'm afraid you'll have to talk to the doctor first." Now she was showing definite signs of discomfort.

"The doctor?" George said. "Which doctor?"

"Dr. Shields," Mrs. Williams said nervously.

"Shields?" George Nelson repeated. "He's a psychiatrist, isn't he?"

"Yes—" She started to explain. Inez cut her off.

"A psychiatrist? Just to bandage Judy's wrists? I don't understand."
Mrs. Williams was sure she did understand; she just didn't want to face it.

"I'm sure you do," she said. Suddenly, since the issue was met, she felt on firmer ground. "With wounds like Judy's, calling in a psychiatrist is standard procedure."

"Wounds like Judy's?" Inez said vaguely.

"I think she means self-inflicted wounds," George said quietly. Inez's face remained blank. Shock, George realized; she must have gone into shock and blocked out the details of what happened. He signaled Mrs. Williams aside.

"Is Dr. Shields around?" he whispered. "I'd like to talk to him, and I think he should probably have a look at my wife, too."

Suddenly understanding his meaning, Mrs. Williams stole a glance in Inez's direction. She was gone. Quickly she looked up and down the hall. Inez was striding purposefully toward Judy's room.

"Mrs. Nelson," she called, but it was too late.

Inez Nelson pushed open the door to the hospital room, and stepped in. She didn't see Judy at first but she heard her.

"Get her out of here," Judy screamed. "I told you I didn't want her in here!"

Inez whirled, and saw her daughter propped up in bed. She could barely recognize her. Judy's face was contorted with anger, and she was tearing at the bandages at her wrists. Inez started to move toward the bed. Before she could get there Judy had pulled the bandages off, and ripped at the stitches. Blood spurted from her wrists. She began screaming at her mother again.

"I hate you," she shouted. "Get out of here! *Leave me alone!*"

Inez tried to put her arms around her daughter, but Judy wriggled away, leaving Inez's blouse bloodied. She stared down at herself, and the horror of it washed over her. Inez, too, began screaming, and a moment later, after she'd pressed the emergency bell, the nurse began trying to separate mother and daughter. It took her only a second to realize that of the two, the mother was far worse off than the daughter. Inez was hysterical; Judy, screaming and struggling against her mother, seemed to know exactly what she was doing. Just as the nurse herself was beginning to panic, help arrived in the form of Mrs. Williams and George Nelson, followed by a press of orderlies and nurses, who crowded into the room, creating further confusion. Three burly orderlies were attempting to pull a shrieking Inez Nelson away from the bed when Dr. Shields arrived, sized up the situation in an instant, and began issuing orders. Within minutes, sedatives were administered to both Judy and Inez Nelson.

"I'm sorry, Doctor," Mrs. Williams said when the room had been cleared, "I tried to keep her away but I couldn't."

"It's all right," Dr. Shields said calmly. "I don't see that there's much damage done."

"Keep her out of the room?" George Nelson repeated, "Keep her out? Why did you want to keep Inez—my wife—out of the room?" He looked from Mrs. Williams to the doctor, then back again.

"It was my fault, really," Dr. Shields said. "Judy said she didn't want to see her mother right now, and I should have been here when you arrived to explain it to you. I'm sorry. The whole thing was really my fault."

But George Nelson hadn't heard the last. "Didn't want to see her mother? Why? I don't understand."

Dr. Shields looked at him sympathetically, seeing the man's confusion and helplessness. "Could you wait a couple of minutes?" he asked George. When George nodded mutely, Dr. Shields patted him on the back. "Fine," he said. "Mrs. Williams will get you a cup of coffee, and by the time it's cool enough to drink, I'll be back. Then I'll try to tell you what's happening, and what's going to happen next." When a look of fear came over George's face, the doctor felt compelled to add: "It isn't as bad as it looks." Then he smiled reassuringly, and disappeared down the hall. George Nelson sank into a chair, prepared to wait. He wondered why he suddenly felt that this was just the beginning. He was sure that it *was* as bad as it looked—and probably much worse.

Peter Balsam heard about Judy Nelson from a very agitated Sister Marie, who called him as soon as she heard about it from Sister Elizabeth—who had gotten all the details from the janitor. Sister Marie seemed to think the whole thing was her fault—she had been unable to find Judy during the afternoon. And now this had happened. Sister Marie felt terribly guilty. Balsam assured her that no matter what had happened, there was no reason for the nun to blame herself. He did not add, since he could see no reason to increase her worries, that he, too, felt responsible for Judy. Perhaps if he had tried a little harder to talk to her, if he had spent a little more time with her . . .

On an impulse, Balsam decided to go to the hospital.

Mrs. Williams looked up at the man who hovered uncertainly over her desk, and put on her best professional smile.

"Yes?" she said. The young man in front of her looked very uncomfortable. "Do you need to see a doctor?" she added solicitously.

"Me?" Balsam said in surprise. "Oh, no . . . no, I'm fine. I was just wondering if I'm in the right place."

"That depends on the problem," Mrs. Williams smiled. "What can I do for you?"

"I wanted to find out about Judy Nelson," Balsam said. He was vaguely aware that the two men who sat huddled together a few feet away had stopped talking and were staring at him. "Is she still here?"

Mrs. Williams nodded. "Oh, yes," she said. "I'm afraid she isn't allowed any visitors yet." She paused, then continued, "Are you a friend of the family?" Dumb question, she admonished herself. If he knew the family, he'd be talking to Mr. Nelson, not to me. In front of her, the young man was shaking his head.

"Not exactly," he was saying. "I'm one of her teachers. My name is Peter Balsam. Why don't you just tell Judy I was here—"

He started to turn away, then stopped. The two men who had been seated were now standing.

"Mr. Balsam?" one of them was saying now. "The psychology teacher?"

Balsam nodded.

"I'm George Nelson," the man said, offering his hand. "Judy's father. This is Dr. Shields."

Balsam took the proffered hand, and smiled an acknowledgment to the doctor.

"Hello," he said. "How is she? Is she all right?"

"She's going to be fine." The doctor answered for George Nelson. "We were just talking about the whole situation. Why don't you join us?" He indicated the chairs, but Balsam waited until the other two were seated before he sank into the third chair.

"What happened?" Balsam asked. The two men looked uncomfortably at each other.

"That's just what we were trying to figure out," Dr. Shields said. "I'm afraid we don't really know."

"I heard the janitor found her in the gym," Balsam said softly. "With her wrists—cut." He had almost said "slashed," but the word seemed too graphic.

"It was in the locker room," Dr. Shields corrected him, "and fortunately it isn't serious. Now we're trying to figure out why."

"Why?" Balsam repeated the word bluntly.

"Why she cut herself," George Nelson said miserably. "She just never seemed like the kind of girl who would do something like that."

The word "dramatic" popped into Peter Balsam's mind. Sister Marie had used it, at lunch time. She had said Judy tended to be dramatic. He wondered if he should mention it to the two men. They seemed to be waiting for him to speak.

"Has she talked about it?" Balsam asked.

The doctor shook his head. "No. All she's said is that she doesn't want to see her mother. Frankly, I don't think the situation is all that serious. In my experience, which I admit is very limited, someone who really wants to commit suicide doesn't call the police immediately after the attempt."

"She called the police?" Balsam asked.

George Nelson nodded. "That's right. And the cuts aren't deep. But we still think there must be a reason for it. I mean, a sixteen-year-old girl doesn't just *do* something like that, does she?" He looked from the doctor to Balsam, then back to the doctor.

"Did you see her today?" the doctor asked Balsam, ignoring Nelson's question.

"Yes, of course," Peter said. "She's in my psychology course."

"Did anything seem to be bothering her?" the doctor pressed.

"I'm not sure," Balsam began uncertainly. He didn't want to raise any false alarms. "I mean, I think something was on her mind, but I haven't the slightest idea what it was. She stayed for a minute or two after class, but when I tried to draw her out, she wouldn't talk about it. So I suggested she talk to Monsignor."

"Monsignor?" the doctor asked.

"Monsignor Vernon," George Nelson filled in. "The priest who runs the school. Did she talk to him?"

"I don't know. Frankly, I'd pretty much forgotten about it until Sister Marie called me."

Dr. Shields looked at Balsam questioningly, and Peter felt compelled to continue.

"After I suggested Judy talk to Monsignor, I got to thinking maybe she'd be better off talking to a woman. I tried to catch up to her, and suggest that she talk to Sister Marie, instead. But she was gone, so I found Sister Marie, and asked her to try to talk to Judy."

"And did she?" the doctor prompted him.

"I wish she had," Balsam said unhappily. "But she didn't. She said she looked for Judy after school, but couldn't find her."

"She must not have looked very hard," George Nelson said bitterly. "Judy was there all afternoon."

"What happens now?" Peter asked, deciding not to pursue the question of whether or not Sister Marie had made a proper search for the girl.

The doctor shrugged helplessly. "I'm keeping her here for observation," he said. "Standard procedure. But whether she'll start talking about what happened is anyone's guess. With kids, sometimes it's hard to get through."

Suddenly there seemed very little left to say, and Peter Balsam began to feel uncomfortable—there must be things the doctor would want to talk about with the patient's father. He stood up uncertainly, grateful when the two men also rose from their chairs. The doctor extended his hand.

"I'm glad to have met you," he said with a smile. "I hope we see each other again."

"But in happier circumstances," Peter replied, accepting the doctor's hand. He turned to George Nelson.

"I can't tell you how sorry I am about this," he said softly.

Nelson tried to smile at him, but found it difficult. "Thanks for coming," he said. "I'll tell Judy you were here. Or someone will."

A few minutes later Peter Balsam was walking slowly back through the streets of Neilsville. As he approached his apartment, he had a feeling of something left undone, as if there were someone he should talk to. He glanced up toward Cathedral Hill, and saw the short spire of St. Francis Xavier Church. Monsignor. He should talk to Monsignor. Peter Balsam didn't stop at his apartment. Instead, he increased his pace, and hurried up the hill.

He let himself into the rectory, and rang the silver bell. He waited. When there was no response, he rang the bell again. Still no response. He was about to leave when he noticed a thin band of light gleaming from beneath the door to the den. Balsam made his way down the hall. He stood quietly for a moment, listening.

At first there was silence, but a second later he heard the sounds of praying. An odd sort of praying: not the steady rhythms of the rosary, but short, staccato bursts of religious ejaculations. He listened for a moment, and had started to move away from the door when he heard another sound, a sound he hadn't heard since his childhood days in the convent. He stared at the door, wondering if he was really hearing what he seemed to be hearing. It was then that he noticed that the door was slightly ajar. Before he quite realized what he was doing, he had pushed the door partway open.

In the center of the room, kneeling on the floor, Monsignor Vernon was praying. He was staring heavenward, but from where Balsam stood, it almost seemed as though the priest was praying to the chandelier that glowed dimly above.

He was stripped to the waist, and sweating profusely, whether from the heat of the fire that flickered on the hearth, or from religious fervor, Balsam was unsure. In one hand the priest held a rosary; in the other was clutched the flagellum. With each ejaculation, Monsignor Vernon was beating his naked back with the whip. It was not the soft, symbolic flagellation the nuns Balsam had grown up with indulged in. Monsignor Vernon was punishing himself, and the welts on his shoulders showed vividly against the pale white of his skin. Embarrassed, Peter Balsam quickly pulled the door closed and backed away, wishing he hadn't seen the strange ceremony within.

Then the praying stopped, and a strange silence fell over the rectory. Balsam picked up the small silver bell and rang it once more. He thought he heard a movement in the den, but he wasn't sure. He turned away, about to leave the rectory, when he heard Monsignor Vernon's voice.

"Hello?" The voice sounded muffled, and uncertain.

"It's me," Balsam called. "Peter. I can come back . . ."

"No," the voice came again. "I'll be right with you. Just give me a moment."

Balsam wondered how the priest would look, if his fervor and exertions would show in his face. But when Vernon appeared a moment later, he seemed relaxed, as if he had been doing nothing more strenuous than reading a book. Looking at him, Peter wondered if he could possibly have imagined the strange scene of a few minutes earlier.

"Peter," Monsignor Vernon greeted him with a joviality that Balsam had not heard since their college days. "Come in, come in. I was just praying, and didn't hear the bell."

In the den, the lights had been turned up, and the fire, with another log thrown on it, was dancing brightly.

"A little warm for that, isn't it?" Balsam asked. The priest grinned self-consciously.

"I guess so," he said. "But every now and then I want a fire, and it doesn't seem to matter how hot it is outside." Then the brief flash of joviality faded, and Monsignor Vernon's face took on a serious expression. "I suppose you want to talk about Judy Nelson?" he asked in a tone that told Balsam that despite what he might wish, the priest did not want to discuss the matter.

"I just came from the hospital," Balsam said tentatively.

The priest's brow arched. "Did you?"

"No one knows what happened. Judy won't talk about it."

"I don't imagine she would," Monsignor said in a disapproving tone. "But I imagine she'll talk to me about it."

"Oh?" Balsam inquired. The priest nodded, almost imperceptibly, but did not explain.

"I was wondering," Balsam said carefully. "Did you happen to talk to her today?"

"I did," the priest said, "but the conversation is confidential. I heard her confession this afternoon." Then he looked sharply at the teacher. "What made you think I might have talked to her?"

"Because I suggested it," Balsam said nervously. "I mean, I didn't suggest she confess, but I told her I thought she ought to talk to you. Or to someone."

"I see," the priest said. He folded his hands carefully. "Was there a reason? For your suggesting she talk to me?"

"I—I thought she needed someone to talk to, and since she didn't seem to want to talk to me, I suggested you."

The priest considered this for a moment, then asked what had caused Peter's concern.

"It was her manner, more than anything," Balsam began, trying to recreate the scene in his mind. "She stayed after my class." He recounted as best he could the conversation he had had with Judy. When he was finished, the priest seemed to think it over, then asked a question.

"Was there anything you said, anything at all, that might have caused this?"

Balsam thought. He didn't think there was. And then he remembered. It seemed so insignificant. He hadn't meant anything by it. But now, considering what had happened, he decided he'd better tell the Monsignor about it.

"There was one thing," he said carefully, trying not to attach any great importance to his words, and succeeding only in making them sound even more important. "We were talking about an experiment I conducted during the class today. It had to do with frustration, and I was demonstrating a point with a rat and a maze. Judy seemed a bit distracted during the lecture, but when I started the experiment she perked right up. Then, while we were talking, she asked me what I'd do, if I were the rat. And I told her, I think, that I'd probably do what I could to relieve my frustration, even if it killed me. Or die trying. Something like that. I can't remember my exact words."

The priest was staring at him coldly. "Let me get this straight," he said. "Am I to understand that, while talking to a student you knew was having a problem, you talked about dying as a solution to the problem?"

Balsam felt a knot form in his stomach, and his mind reeled. No, he told himself, that's not what I did. Or, at least, that's not what I intended.

"It wasn't exactly like that," he said aloud, but the priest cut him off.

"Then exactly how was it? Exactly what did you say?"

Balsam thought hard, and the words suddenly came back to him, as if they were written in front of his eyes. "I said: 'If I were that rat, I'd be busy tearing that cage apart, or I'd kill myself trying.'" Suddenly the words sounded ominous.

"Kill yourself," the priest said. Then he repeated it. "Kill yourself. Well, I suppose that tells us what put the notion into Judy's head, doesn't it?'' The priest shook his head sadly. "Well," he said, "what's done is done, isn't it? And when it comes right down to it, the final responsibility rests with Judy herself, of course." He smiled at Balsam, but Balsam felt no warmth from the smile. "You shouldn't feel guilty about it," the priest continued. "She may have already had the idea. Still, it was an unfortunate phrase to have used. If I were you, I'd be a lot more careful in the future. Children can be so—suggestible." He stood up, and Peter was grateful for the signal that the conversation was over. He, too, rose from his chair.

"You know," the Monsignor said as he walked Balsam to the rectory door, "you ought to think about a couple of things." Balsam looked at him questioningly. "You might be wise to try to find a little more faith within yourself. Faith in the Church." When Peter looked puzzled, the priest continued, "The Devil works in strange ways, just as does the Lord. Granted, talking about how a rat might react, given a chance and some brains, certainly doesn't seem particularly significant. Talking about suicide is a different matter."

"I wasn't talking about suicide," Balsam snapped, his anger rising. "I was only using a figure of speech."

"So said many a heretic," Monsignor Vernon said softly.

"Heretic? What are you talking about?" Balsam cried. He gazed at his old friend, but nothing in the priest's eyes revealed what was going on in his mind. "I'm sorry, but I can't see how any of this could possibly be construed as heresy—or anything even resembling heresy."

"Don't you?" the priest said. "Pray, Peter. Pray for guidance. You might try praying to St. Peter Martyr. I find he can be very helpful." And then the door of the rectory closed, leaving a furious Peter Balsam standing helplessly on the front porch. Fuming, he began the walk back to his apartment.

Peter Balsam closed the book slowly, and put it back on the shelf. He had not taken Monsignor Vernon's advice; had not prayed for guidance to St. Peter Martyr. Instead, he had looked the saint up, to see just who it was that Monsignor seemed to think could be so helpful. What he found was one of the old Italian Inquisitors. St. Peter Martyr, it seemed, had been one of the zealots who had dedicated a short thirteenth-century life to the eradication of sin and heresy from the Christian World. And, from what little Balsam had been able to find out, St. Peter Martyr had been personally responsible for the imprisonment, torture, and death of hundreds of heretics. In the end, though, he had lost: he had been assassinated by two heretics, thus earning for himself the title, Martyr.

Balsam sat for awhile, staring off into space and wondering what it was about St. Peter Martyr that appealed to Monsignor Vernon. What was it that had made the priest into a fanatic?

Then Balsam paused. Maybe the priest wasn't a fanatic. Maybe he, Balsam, was being oversensitive. He didn't know. Suddenly, he wasn't at all sure there was any way of finding out.

# EIGHT

THERE WAS A TENSION IN THE AIR OF ST. Francis Xavier High School the next morning, the sort of tension that can only be brought about by a particular kind of shock. It was almost as if Judy Nelson were not coming back; as if she had been kidnaped, or murdered, or died in an accident. Perhaps, had Judy been a student at the public high school, the tension would not have been quite so great. There would have been a certain relief that she hadn't died, mixed with the horror at what she had done. But at St. Francis Xavier's the attempt was as shocking as the completion of the act would have been.

The Sisters sensed it immediately, and dealt with it in the only way they knew how—they ignored it. Judy's absence was noted in the records of attendance, but was not commented about, at least not in the classrooms. Of all the Sisters, Elizabeth had the fewest problems in the classroom. Her students, accustomed to her strict discipline, contained their urge to talk; more conscious than ever of Sister Elizabeth's sharp tongue and equally sharp ear, they saved their whispers for the breaks between classes, doing their best to vent their pent-up feelings in the five short minutes they had to move from one classroom to another.

Karen Morton was feeling the tension more strongly than anyone else that morning. She and Judy had most of their classes together, and while Karen had often resented the slightly edged comments Judy had been in the habit of making about both her appearance and her boyfriend, Karen missed her friend. And she was also finding that she had become the object of the other student's curiosity, as though her closeness with Judy made her privy to the answer to the question that was on everyone's tongue that morning: Why? Why had Judy done it? And what was going to happen to her now?

Karen felt everyone watching her as she moved through the halls. She lowered her eyes and wished once more that she had dressed differently this morning. Suddenly her sweater felt too tight, and she was uncomfortably aware of the way her skirt hugged her hips. Somewhere, in the back of her mind, something was telling her that she should be in mourning. And then she realized that was ridiculous—Judy was in the hospital, not the mortuary. She turned the corner into the hall where all four of the girls had managed to be assigned lockers, and was relieved to see that Penny Anderson and Janet Connally were waiting for her. She tried to smile at them, but couldn't.

"Karen?" Janet said as her friend approached. "Are you all right?"

Karen nodded mutely, and wondered for a minute if she really was all right. "People just keep staring at me," she said. "I feel like Marilyn Crane."

"They stare at you for different reasons, though," Penny Anderson put in. Then she couldn't contain herself any longer. "Why do you think she did it?" she said. "I mean, if anybody was going to try to kill herself, you wouldn't think it would be Judy." She shuddered a little. "It's too weird."

"I don't know," Karen said. "But everybody looks at me like it's my fault. And Sister Elizabeth! She *glared* at me this morning! I wanted to crawl under my desk."

"That's just Sister Elizabeth," Janet Connally said comfortingly. "She glares at everybody. You should have heard Sister Kathleen this morning. She spent the whole hour talking about sin. She wouldn't mention Judy's name at all. But she sure got her message across. The way she was talking, Judy might as well have——" She broke off, as she realized what she had been on the verge of saying. "I mean," she went on lamely, "Sister Kathleen kept talking about how the intent is as sinful as the act, and all that stuff. But I don't see how it can be."

Karen Morton shrugged. "I don't understand half of what they tell us. Sometimes I think they're trying to scare us."

"Well, they certainly succeeded with Judy," Penny Anderson said. "My mother says they probably won't let her come back to school." It was a thought that hadn't occurred to either of the two other girls, and they stared at Penny in dismay.

"Not let her come back?" Janet said softly. "Why?"

"Mother says what Judy did was even worse than getting pregnant," Penny said. "And you know what happened to Sandy Taylor last year."

The three girls looked at each other. Sandy Taylor had simply not been at school one day. They had all been told that Sandy had "gotten sick," but it hadn't taken much effort to figure out the truth, especially when Sandy's boyfriend had left school a couple of days later. It seemed to them that there was, indeed, a strong possibility that Judy Nelson might not be allowed to return to school.

It was then that Marilyn Crane appeared at the end of the hall. Janet Connally started to wave to her, but felt a nudge from Penny. Immediately, her hand fell back to her side. Behind Marilyn, the figure of Monsignor Vernon loomed, authoritarian and scowling.

Marilyn, unaware who was behind her, approached the group excitedly. She had something to say that they would want to hear; she was bursting with the story of seeing Judy the previous afternoon, just before she had—— Marilyn couldn't say the words, even to herself. *Before she did what she did.* She quickened her pace, but then, abruptly, the three girls turned away. The look of eagerness fell away from Marilyn's face, and she stopped. She tried to pretend she hadn't been about to approach them at all, that she had some other urgent business in this part of the school. She spun around, and nearly collided with Monsignor Vernon.

"Oh," she said in surprise. "I'm sorry. I——I didn't know you were there." She looked helplessly at the scowling priest, bracing herself for the scolding she was sure was about to fall upon her. But it didn't come. The Monsignor seemed not to notice her. He merely stepped around her, and continued down the hall. A few feet away, the girls who had been clustered together scattered like leaves before a breeze. She had been so hopeful. Now, again, she was alone. Holding back her tears, Marilyn decided she would skip lunch that day, and spend the time in church, consoling herself under the comforting presence of the Sorrowful Mother.

A few minutes later, Marilyn Crane slipped into the one empty seat in the back row of Room 16. She could see that there was also an empty seat in the front row: the seat Judy Nelson had occupied the day before. No one had sat in it today, and she didn't think it was likely that anyone would sit in it tomorrow, either.

Peter Balsam surveyed the class. The same thing was on their minds that had been on the minds of his last class, and the one before that. But the psychology students didn't stop buzzing among themselves when they came into the room, as the other classes had. And he had himself to thank—if "thank" was the word—for he had certainly done his best to let them know that they were not expected to behave here the same way they were expected to behave elsewhere at St. Francis Xavier. They had believed him. They were talking about Judy Nelson, and they weren't making much of an attempt to keep him from knowing about it. He decided, on an impulse, to face the issue squarely.

"Well," he said, "I guess there isn't much question what we're going to be talking about today, is there?"

His words silenced them. They stared at him, consternation clouding their faces, a wariness passing over them, as though they weren't sure what to expect.

"I know it's on all your minds," he said calmly, "and I don't suppose you've had a chance to talk about it in any of your other classes. Since what happened to Judy Nelson is definitely of a psychological nature, let's talk about it, get it all out in the open, and then maybe tomorrow we can get back down to business."

When the class continued to stare at him mutely, Balsam was taken aback. He had expected a flood of questions. Instead he was getting nothing. Finally, almost tentatively, one hand rose. It was Janet Connally.

"Yes, Janet?"

"Did—did Monsignor tell you to talk to us about Judy?" Her voice quavered, and Balsam was aware that she was almost frightened of her own question. He shook his head, and smiled at them.

"This is between you and me. In fact, I have an idea that Monsignor might prefer me not to mention the subject at all. But this class is for you, not for Monsignor. So why don't we get on with it?"

The ice broke. Immediately, five hands went up, and Balsam was hard-pressed to decide whom to call upon first. He chose Karen Morton, telling himself that her hand had been just a shade faster than any of the others. But he knew he had really called on her first because she was one of Judy's friends. "Karen?"

"I—I don't really know what I want to ask," she began uncertainly. "I mean, there's so many questions, I don't know where to start."

"Start anywhere," Balsam said gently.

"Well, can you tell us what happened?" Karen asked. "I—well, we've just heard so many rumors that we don't really know how bad it is."

"It isn't bad at all," Balsam said. "The cuts aren't deep, and Judy is only in the hospital now so the doctors can keep an eye on her."

"You mean they're afraid she might do it again?" It was Penny Anderson, and she hadn't bothered to raise her hand. She had simply blurted the question out. That pleased Balsam.

"No, I don't think anyone's afraid she'll do it again. It's simply that whenever anyone attempts to take his own life, he's kept under observation for a few days. In fact, I think it's a state law. Basically, it's not so much out of fear that the victim will try it again, as out of a desire to let the person calm down, and try to find out what led him to do it in the first place."

"Why did she do it?" This time it was Janet Connally.

"Well, Judy might know," Balsam said. He wondered if they would rise to the bait. Jim Mulvey did, and Balsam was surprised. Maybe he'd underestimated Mulvey.

"Might?" Jim said. "What do you mean? I should think if anybody knows why she did it, Judy would."

"That's what you'd think, isn't it? But what Judy did, what anyone who tries to kill himself does, isn't particularly rational. Usually it's an impulsive act, and after it's over the person wonders why he tried it in the first place. Unfortunately, all too often, it's too late. Judy was lucky. She's going to be fine."

"But what makes someone do something like that?" Balsam heard the question, but wasn't sure who had asked it.

"Any number of things," he said. "Haven't you ever gone to bed at night and thought how nice it would be if you just didn't wake up in the morning?" All of them squirmed uncomfortably. "Well, sometimes people decide not to take a chance. They decide to see to it that they won't wake up. But more often than not, what they're really trying to do is cry out for help. They don't want to die. Not really. They just want someone to help them. So they do something to attract attention to themselves."

"But it's a sin," Marilyn Crane's voice said softly from the back of the room. Everyone turned and stared at Marilyn. She did not notice. She was concentrating on Peter Balsam.

There it was: *It's a sin.* How was he to answer it?

And then he thought he saw an answer. "I'm not so sure," he said carefully. "What I mean to say," he continued into the shocked silence, "is that I'm not sure that a suicide *attempt* should be considered a sin. I mean, if the act isn't completed, then where's the sin?"

"Sins thought and considered are no different than sins committed, are they?" Again, Marilyn Crane.

"Well, that's certainly what we've all been taught," Balsam began. And then he stopped.

It took a moment before the class realized what had happened. Monsignor Vernon was coming slowly toward Mr. Balsam, a scowl creasing his forehead, his black eyes flashing. A hush fell over them. Something was about to happen. When it came, though, it seemed anticlimactic.

The priest reached the front of the room and turned to face the class. He made the sign of the cross and blessed them. Then he dismissed them. Monsignor Vernon watched in silence as the room slowly emptied. Then he turned to Peter Balsam.

"We will go to the rectory," he said.

Inez Nelson hurried into the main entrance of Neilsville Hospital, and glanced quickly at the clock. She was right on time, noon sharp.

Inez followed the green arrows to the psychiatric area, no more than three rooms, that served the mental-health purposes of Neilsville. She glanced nervously around, hoping not to see any familiar faces. There would be enough talk as it was, without her being seen going into this section of the hospital.

No one seemed to be around at all, so Inez seated herself in the small waiting area. A minute later she heard a door open, and looked up. Margo Henderson was standing in the doorway, smiling at her.

"Inez," Margo said genially, "I'm so glad to see you." At the look of consternation on Inez's face, Margo continued hurriedly, "Of course, I wish it could have been under happier circumstances, but Dr. Shields tells me that Judy's going to be just fine." She paused a moment, hoping there would be some response. "Well," she said, "Dr. Shields will be with you in just a minute. Why don't you sit down?" Margo indicated the chair Inez had risen from, then seated herself at the desk. So, Inez wasn't going to speak to her. Margo tried not to be bitter about it. Of course Inez was under a strain, but still . . . And then Margo remembered that Inez Nelson was Leona Anderson's best friend. And it had been Leona who had been the prime force in squeezing Margo out of St. Francis Xavier parish. Leona and Monsignor Vernon. Well, damn them both, Margo told herself. She picked up a pen, and began moving some papers around on the desk. She could feel Inez's eyes on her.

"It was an accident," Inez said suddenly in the silence. "I want you to know it was an accident." Margo looked quickly up at Inez, and saw the desperation in the other woman's eyes. Who was Inez trying to convince, Margo or herself? "Of course," she said shortly, and returned to her work. A moment later a buzzer sounded on her desk.

"Dr. Shields is ready for you now," she said, in an even, professional tone. "Right through there." She indicated the door she had recently emerged from, and watched Inez until her former friend had disappeared from view. Then Margo shook her head sadly, and went back to work.

Inez Nelson felt no better when she left Dr. Shields's office than she had when she entered. She still wanted to see her daughter; she was not to be allowed to do so. Instead, she had been forced to listen to a lot of psychological doubletalk. She was Judy's mother, and she was sure she knew better than any of them what Judy needed. And yet, she was frightened and feeling very unsure of herself. Maybe the doctor was right. As she hurried out of the hospital, Dr. Shields's words rang in her ears.

"Judy's being manipulative," he had said. And he had been right. But Inez was sure there was more to it than that. There had to be something else. Dr. Shields, himself, must have thought so. If not, why would he have said what he did?

*"Always look for the reason. Somewhere, there will be one. It may not make sense, but it will be there."*

What was he talking about? What did that mean? Inez Nelson felt more baffled, and more frightened, than ever.

## NINE

PETER BALSAM SAT GLUMLY IN THE DEN of the rectory, and wished Monsignor Vernon would open the window. He glanced around, and became aware that the den, which he had thought comfortable so short a time ago—only days ago—now seemed oppressive and crowded. He glanced at his watch, wondering how long this meeting was going to last; he had already been here for most of an hour, and the priest had yet to say a word. Instead, the Monsignor had alternately prayed, then glowered at Balsam. Once, Balsam had risen as if to leave. Monsignor Vernon had curtly told him to sit down. Balsam had sat, reluctantly at first, then angrily, and finally with curiosity.

Then, with a suddenness that startled him, the priest spoke.

"You're a stubborn man, Peter," he said. "But so am I. Except that I prefer to think of myself as tenacious. Tenacious in my beliefs, tenacious in my determination to do what is right, and tenacious in my determination to see that those around me do what is right."

"I was doing what I thought was right," Balsam said softly.

"Right?" The priest almost shouted, *"Right?* Don't deny what you were telling your class; I heard it. Every blasphemous word of it!"

"Don't be ridiculous," Balsam snapped. Immediately he regretted his choice of words. The priest was turning scarlet. "I'm sorry," he went on, trying desperately to remove his anger from his voice. "I didn't mean that quite the way it came out."

"But you did mean it, didn't you?" Monsignor Vernon said icily.

"I don't know." Balsam felt weary. "Let me try to put it this way. I was brought here to teach psychology, not the catechism. And today my students needed to understand what happened to Judy Nelson, and why it happened, and they needed reassurance. They did not need to be told that what Judy Nelson did was a mortal sin, and that her soul is forfeit, and a whole lot of medieval nonsense!''

The priest was on his feet now, towering over Balsam. ''Let us say,'' he snapped, ''that is what *you* thought they needed. *I* say they needed something quite different, and I am in a much better position than you to define the needs of the students in this school.'' Peter felt himself sink deeper into the chair as the priest raged on. ''The last thing in the world my students need is a lot of confusing, self-contradictory, pseudo-scientific claptrap. Perhaps, if these students were going on to college, they might need a small dose of what you call 'psychology.' But for the most part they aren't going anywhere. What they need are the tools to make their lives easier right here, in Neilsville. That is what the Church is for. To give people faith, and through faith, salvation.'' He paused and Peter could see the priest's effort to calm himself. ''The world is a complex enough place without confusing our children and undermining their beliefs. In fact, it is exactly such talk as I've heard from you that is responsible for the decay of our society. You leave people nothing to cling to, nothing to console themselves with. And I will not tolerate it. Do you understand me?''

''I think I understand you perfectly,'' Balsam replied coldly. ''And I think it might be best for both of us if I resigned my position here immediately. As it is, there is no way I can teach my class effectively.''

Something almost like fear flashed over Monsignor Vernon's face, but was gone in an instant.

''That's a foolish stance,'' the priest replied, ''and I think you know it.'' The rage he had been displaying only a moment earlier vanished, to be replaced by a countenance that seemed almost genial. He took his chair opposite Peter's once more, and leaned forward, his elbows on his knees, his head resting on his clasped hands. ''Peter, why can't you understand that you are not dealing with an enormous high school in an urban area? Why can't you understand that the needs of our students are not the same as the needs of students in, say, Philadelphia? We are not dealing with sophisticated people here. It isn't just because of me, and what I'm sure you think is my narrow-minded outlook. It's much deeper than that. It has much more to do with the people who live here than it does with me. In fact,'' he went on, a conspiratorial smile taking form, ''I don't know if you're aware of it, but there was a great deal of pressure put on the Bishop not to add your course to the curriculum at all. All I'm asking you to do, really, is exercise a certain amount of caution. Surely there's enough material so that you can do a little judicious picking and choosing, isn't there?''

''You mean censor my material?'' Balsam asked warily, feeling his resolution weakening and resenting it.

Monsignor Vernon sighed. ''Yes, if that's the way you want to put it.''

''So much for freedom of thought,'' said Balsam.

''I didn't tell you to stop thinking,'' Monsignor said. ''All I've done is suggest you put some limitations on what you say to your students.''

''Isn't it the same thing? How can my students think, if they're given nothing to think about?''

"Is it really so important? Frankly, what our students need is a lot more faith, not a lot more to think about."

"Ignorance is bliss?" Balsam remarked.

"In some cases, yes," the priest replied, his voice taking on a softness Peter hadn't heard before. "I know it sounds strange to you, but it's quite true. Living here for twelve years has opened my eyes to a lot. There was a time when I would have agreed with you—I wanted to know the truth about everything. But as I've grown older, I've discovered that the truth, or what we try to tell ourselves is the truth, is a very difficult thing to live with. And I've discovered that Truth—God's Truth, as taught by the Church—is a much better thing. It gives me peace, and it gives peace to my flock. If it all strikes you as a restriction on your freedom, let me remind you that God puts many restrictions on all our freedoms."

Listening to him, Balsam thought it all sounded quite reasonable, put in those terms. But the bottom line still read "repression." Repression of thought, of ideas.

"Well," he said, standing up again, "I still have the feeling I'm not the right man for the job here. I'm sorry, but you'd better start looking for a replacement. If there's one thing I've always valued, it's freedom. Not only my own freedom, but the freedom of those around me. People have to be exposed to all kinds of ideas, and have the freedom to choose among them."

"That's nonsense," Monsignor snapped. "And, frankly, you surprise me. You were raised to be a good Catholic, and I would have thought your faith would be stronger." His eyes were flashing again, and Peter once more wanted to draw away from the force of the priest's faith. But there was no place to go. "It is faith and belief in the word of the Lord that brings salvation, not any kind of self-serving 'science' that does nothing but provide excuses for the worst kinds of immoral behavior," Vernon was saying now, "and as for your resigning your post here, if I were you I'd think twice about that, and then twice more." He paused, a weariness coming into his voice. "It wasn't easy for me to bring you here, Peter, and one more failure on your record is not going to help you. You have a history of not finishing things, and I'm beginning to understand why. You hide from reality. You refuse to face things as they really are, and prefer to find what you call evidence to back up your own weaknesses. If I were you, Peter, I'd think about it, and pray about it, before I made up my mind to leave Neilsville. God had a purpose when He sent you here. You have no right to turn your back on that purpose, and on the Lord, until you have completed whatever task He sent you here to perform. And I think I know what that task is."

"Direct line?" Peter said, but Vernon went on, ignoring the sarcasm, his voice building as he spoke.

"I think He sent you here to help me. This is not an easy time to live in, and the Faith of the Church is under attack from every direction. I think He sent you here to me, not to turn and run again, but to be shown the powers of the Faith, and be restored to the Church." Balsam stared at the priest. "Yes," the Monsignor intoned, as if he were no longer aware of the other man's presence, "that is it. He sent you to me to help me carry on the work of St. Peter Martyr. To help me bring the heretics back to the fold. To punish the sinners." And suddenly he looked directly at Peter Balsam, his eyes glowing. "Pray Peter," he said urgently. "Pray for guidance, and stay here with me. Together we will finish what was begun so long ago."

Monsignor Vernon fell to his knees, and began to pray. For a moment Peter Balsam wondered if he was expected to join in the prayers. But the priest seemed to have fallen into a reverie, and Balsam suspected he was no longer aware of his surroundings. He looked at Vernon with concern, and pity. He would pray, and try to find some guidance. And he would think.

Peter Balsam walked slowly down the hall, and left the rectory. A minute later, he stepped into the cool freshness of the church.

He sat quietly in the gloom for a while, trying to gather his thoughts together, and make some sense out of the confusion. What had the Monsignor been talking about when he asked Balsam to stay and help him finish what had been begun "so long ago"? And all the talk of "bringing the heretics back to the flock" and "punishing the sinners." It reeked of the Inquisition. Had Peter Vernon, somewhere on the way to becoming a monsignor, also become a fanatic? It certainly seemed so. Still, some of what the priest had said had made sense. Balsam had run away from things, and did like to find what the priest had called "excuses" for his failures. Except, Balsam noted to himself with wry amusement, he preferred to call them "rationalizations."

A figure suddenly brushed past Balsam. Marilyn Crane. He glanced quickly in the direction from which she had come. Yes, she had been praying to the Blessed Virgin. Balsam hoped the girl had found more comfort in the saint than he had been able to give her in class. He glanced around the church, wondering if others had sought sanctuary from the sun and their problems. But the church was empty now. Peter Balsam began wandering through the side aisles, looking at the statues of the various saints.

It wasn't until he had paced almost to the altar that he noticed it. Then, quickly, he crossed the nave and examined the statues in the opposite alcoves. It was the same. Except for the obligatory statues of the Blessed Virgin and St. Francis Xavier, for whom the church was named, all the other saints, at least the ones he was familiar with, were Dominicans of the thirteenth and fourteenth centuries. There was St. Dominic himself, and St. Peter Martyr, and a statue of the Blessed James the Venetian. And the Portuguese St. Sanchia, who had originally welcomed the Dominicans into Portugal. There were others, some of whom Peter Balsam vaguely recalled. There was one who was totally unfamiliar. Saint Acerinus. Balsam searched his memory and couldn't remember the saint at all. That was no surprise: there were so many saints, and he had never been particularly interested in keeping track of them. In fact, he was rather pleased with himself for recognizing as many as he did. What disturbed him was that they were all Dominicans, all of the period of the Inquisition. And it had been the Dominicans who had been primarily charged with carrying out the Inquisition. Hadn't it crossed his mind, just minutes ago, that Monsignor's ramblings had "reeked of the Inquisition"? Balsam stared around at the statues of the saints. Suddenly he had an urge to get out of the church, to get away from the sanctified visages that seemed to be glowering down at him, accusing him.

He hurried out of the church, and back to his classroom. A few moments later, at exactly one o'clock, the bell rang. The afternoon was about to begin. Peter Balsam was sure it was going to be a long afternoon.

When the doorbell rang Peter Balsam glanced up from the book he had been reading, but didn't leave his chair. He looked at the clock: it couldn't be Margo—she was just getting off work. The doorbell rang again.

"Peter?" Margo's voice came through the door, a bit muffled, but definitely Margo's. "Are you in there?"

Now he jumped out of the chair and threw the door open.

"You're early," he said. Then he reached out to take the bag that seemed about to spill from her arms. "Let me take that."

He peered into the bag. "Good Lord, are we expected to drink all this?"

"That depends," Margo grinned. "It depends on how serious your problem is, and how long it's going to take to solve it. If there's any left over, I'll think up a problem of my own for another night." She winked at him, making the wink seductive. "Besides, it might be a long night."

She had closed the door, and was taking off her jacket. Peter watched her, watched the sensousness of her movements, and enjoyed the manner in which she managed to be sexy without being lewd. He felt desire growing in him. As Margo hung her jacket in the closet, Peter's eyes never left her.

"I took off early," he heard her saying. "Whatever's wrong, you made it sound so serious when you called that I decided Dr. Shields's reports could wait." She looked around as if she expected to see his problem lurking in a corner somewhere. Then she surveyed Peter carefully.

"Well, the apartment's in one piece, and so are you, so it can't be nearly as awful as you made it sound on the phone. Maybe I should reclaim those bottles immediately."

Suddenly, now that she was in the room with him, the problems didn't seem nearly so heavy. In fact, the entire afternoon was already fading into a haze, like a half-remembered nightmare. But it wasn't, it was real. He had a decision to make, and he wanted Margo's input before he made it.

"I'm thinking about quitting," he announced. He moved into the kitchen and opened the wine she'd brought while Margo digested this bit of information. When he came back into the living room and handed her a glass, she looked at him speculatively.

"Aw, heck," she said cheerfully. "And you just got here, too." Then she turned serious. "I don't understand, Peter. What happened today?"

He told her about his talk with the Monsignor, and about the class session that had preceded it, and when he was finished she looked at him blankly.

"I don't see what the problem is," she said.

"Oh, come on, Margo. You're bright. Can't you see? The man's crazy. He's a fanatic."

Margo considered his statement. When she spoke, she seemed to be making a very conscious choice of words.

"Peter," she began, "I don't know if Monsignor Vernon is crazy, or a fanatic, or what. But I do know that while what he said to you this afternoon may have *sounded* fanatic, or crazy, or whatever, it isn't. Not here. Now, whether the town get its ideas from Monsignor Vernon, or he gets his ideas from the town, I can't say. The kind of thinking that goes on around here actually gets scary sometimes. Do you know, there were several times after my divorce when I actually thought I should leave town? Really, it's true! All the people I thought were my friends—Inez Nelson for example. I saw her today, at the hospital. She'd hardly even speak to me, even when I was working. She thinks I'm a sinner. Can you imagine that? In this day and age? A sinner But that's the way things are around here." Then she flashed him a smile. "Maybe you can help change things."

Peter shook his head sadly. "Not me. Either I fit in, or I run away. That's the kind of person I am."

"You can change." Margo shrugged. "If I can change, you can change. And let me tell you, I've had to change a lot in order to survive the last couple of years. Every time I hear Leona Anderson make a crack loud enough for me to hear, I just turn around and wink at her. I used to cry, though." She stared into her drink, and swirled the liquid around. Then she looked up at Peter. "Winking is better," she said softly. "It doesn't hurt so much when you wink. For me, it was either wink or run. Learn to wink, Peter."

"I don't know," Peter said. "I'm just not sure what to do. I don't like what Monsignor's doing, and I don't like what his kind of religion is going to do to the kids. But what can I do? There's a little matter of obedience, you know. It's not like I have a union to complain to. All I have is the Church, and I'm sure you know they don't take kindly to underlings griping about their superiors."

"But what if you're right?" Margo asked. "What if Monsignor is crazy, or a fanatic? Shouldn't something be done about it?"

"Sure, but how do you prove that someone who professes total faith in the Church has too much faith? It's self-contradictory."

Margo thought about it, and wasn't sure she grasped his idea. So she changed the subject. They made small talk, the kind of talk people make when they're consciously avoiding something, and ate dinner. It wasn't until they'd finished washing the dishes and opened the second bottle of wine, that the subject of the Church came up again.

"Have you ever looked at all the saints in the church?" he said suddenly. Margo looked at him questioningly, then shrugged.

"I wouldn't know one saint from another," she said. "Why? Is something wrong with them, too?"

Peter chose to ignore the hint that he was reaching a bit far to find fault with St. Francis Xavier. Instead, he tried to explain his misgivings.

"They're all right out of the thirteenth and fourteenth centuries," he said. "Dominicans. Which is odd right there, when you consider that the church was named for St. Francis Xavier, who happens to have been one of the original Jesuits."

Margo frowned, as if she was trying to remember something. "You know," she said finally, "it seems to me that I remember a time, about five years ago, when I noticed one day that we had different saints in the church. As though the ones I was used to had suddenly been replaced. But I didn't pay much attention to it. At the time I told myself I just hadn't really noticed them before. But maybe he changed them."

"Changed them? Who?"

"Monsignor Vernon. Five years ago, when he became Monsignor. Maybe he changed them. Didn't you tell me he's big on the Dominicans? Which ones are they? The ones there now?"

"Mostly Italians," Balsam said. "St. Dominic, and Monsignor's special favorite, St. Peter Martyr, who also graces my classroom, and a few others. Then there's St. Sanchia, who wasn't Italian, but helped the Dominicans establish themselves in Portugal. And one I've never heard of, someone named St. Acerinus. I haven't any idea who he was, but he probably fits right in with the rest of them."

"You don't sound like you approve of them," Margo grinned. "Aren't all the saints supposed to be wonderful, lovable people?"

Balsam chuckled. "That depends. For instance, take St. Peter Martyr. I looked him up the other day. If you check him out in *The Lives of the Saints,* he seems to be a wonderful fellow. Teacher, priest; spent a lot of time convincing heretics that they should come back to the fold. Spent hours and hours, arguing with them, showing them the error of their ways."

"What's wrong with that?" Margo asked.

"Nothing. Except it turns out that Peter Martyr's idea of arguing with someone often involved torture, imprisonment, or burning at the stake."

"Good God," Margo breathed. "That's horrible."

Balsam nodded. "They were all like that. Most of the saints in St. Francis Xavier Church were part of the Inquisition. I haven't read much about it, but what I have read chills my spine."

"The Inquisition," Margo said with a shudder. "And 'heretics.' What a word! It sounds archaic."

"It didn't when Monsignor used it today," Peter said. "You know," he went on, "I get the strangest feeling when I talk to Monsignor. He doesn't seem the least bit worried about the Inquisition. In fact, I get the feeling he wishes it had never come to an end."

"Maybe it hasn't come to an end for him," Margo mused. Then she brightened. "That saint you've never heard of. Can't you look him up?"

"I already tried," Balsam said, smiling. "Apparently I'm not the only one who never heard of him."

"What do you mean?"

"See those books over there?" He pointed to four thick volumes on his desk. Margo glanced at them, and nodded. "Those are *The Lives of the Saints.* The nuns used to give them to us for Christmas. And as far as I can tell, they've never heard of St. Acerinus, either."

"You're kidding," Margo said.

"Look for yourself. The complete index is in the fourth volume."

Margo picked up the book, and flipped through the pages. When she couldn't find the saint she was looking for, and was convinced that St. Acerinus, indeed, was not listed in the index, her eye ran up and down a couple of columns. Then she paused, startled. "Hey!" she exclaimed.

"Oh, God," Peter groaned. "You found it."

"You're a saint!" Margo cried. "Here's your name, right here. Saint Peter Balsam. What does it say about you?"

"Never mind," Peter said. "He's an early one. Third century." But she hadn't heard him. She was busy picking up one of the other volumes, searching for the entry headed "Peter Balsam." He fell silent and watched her read the page devoted to the saint whose namesake he was. When she finished, she closed the book and grinned at him.

"Well," she said mischievously, "that settles it."

"Settles what?"

"Your problem. You aren't going anywhere, Peter Balsam. You're going to stay right here in Neilsville." Her voice suddenly turned serious. "Saint Peter Balsam didn't knuckle under, and he didn't run away. He stuck to his guns, and stood up for what was right."

Balsam smiled wryly. "And look what happened to him."

"Well, of course he died, but that was a long time ago."

"Was it?" Peter said. "When I talk to Monsignor, nothing seems long ago."

But he knew she was right. He would stay in Neilsville, as long as he could. He had a feeling his students needed him. And of course there was Margo. She needed him too. Or did he need her? He decided not to worry about it. Instead, he opened another bottle of wine.

"Here's to Saint Peter Balsam," he said, and raised his glass.

Margo did not go home that night.

# TEN

THE REST OF THE WEEK PASSED SLOWLY IN Neilsville, almost as if the town were waiting for a signal, something to tell it that a crisis had passed. The signal did not come. Judy Nelson was very much on their minds.

By Saturday her closest friends, Penny Anderson, Karen Morton, and Janet Connally, had all been to visit Judy, first separately, and then together. They had seen that she was not dying; indeed, she seemed to them to be in fine shape—she questioned them about classes, wanted to know what work she'd missed, and made them promise to fill her in on all the details of the party on Saturday that she would not be able to attend.

The subject all her friends wanted to talk about was carefully avoided. No one wanted to be the first to bring it up, and Judy herself didn't mention it. But the bandages on her wrists kept it at the front of all their minds.

Since that first day, Peter Balsam had resolved to make no further mention of Judy Nelson's attempt on her own life. For the moment, he told himself, it was better to let it drop. He was sure he had gotten his point across in the few minutes before the Monsignor had suddenly appeared. Balsam had kept a careful eye on the class, particularly on Judy's friends, with the intention of talking privately with any who seemed overly disturbed by the incident. But they all seemed to be doing fine. Every evening he was seeing Margo, and that helped. Monsignor Vernon had apparently forgotten the stormy session earlier in the week, for he treated Balsam the same way he had from the beginning, with a formal cordiality that induced a certain respect but no warmth.

Harriet Morton, Karen's mother, had considered canceling her daughter's party, but after consulting with Leona Anderson had decided to let it continue as scheduled. After all, it was only going to be the girls, and they probably needed the diversion. Canceling the party, she and Leona had decided, would only draw attention to a situation best ignored. Now she glanced impatiently at her watch.

"Karen?" she called up the stairs. She reached in her purse and fished for her keys, keeping one eye on the stairs as she waited for her daughter to come down. She heard Karen moving around on the floor above, and called again. "Karen! I have to go now. Will you come down here?"

"Coming," Karen called, and a moment later appeared on the stairs.

"Now, is everything all set for the party?" Harriet asked anxiously. Karen shrugged.

"Not yet. Penny's coming over early to help me. Can I use your punchbowl?"

Harriet sighed. "You'd better wash it first."

Karen looked as though having to wash the bowl might well dissuade her from using it. "Then *don't* wash it," Harriet said. "You can all get dust poisoning, if there is such a thing." The two of them laughed, and Harriet realized with a rush how much she loved her daughter. She gave Karen a quick squeeze and a kiss, and hurried out the door. "Have a good time," she called over her shoulder, "and I'll see you all later."

"By then it'll all be over," Karen said, waving. It had better be, she thought with a twinge of guilt. No telling what might happen if her mother came home and found the boys there. She closed the door after her mother, and went back upstairs, where she continued working on the dress that Judy Nelson had intended to wear that night. Just a few alterations, and it would fit Karen perfectly.

An hour later, as she bit off the last thread, Karen heard the doorbell.

"It's unlocked," she called down the stairs, and a moment later heard Penny Anderson's voice.

"Hi! Are you upstairs?"

"Come on up. I just finished my dress for tonight, and you can tell me if it fits right."

A minute after that Penny appeared in the doorway, and gasped at the sight of the black dress Karen was proudly holding up.

"Where did you get it?" Penny breathed. "It's beautiful. But it must have cost a fortune!"

"It's Judy's, really," Karen told her. "She wasn't supposed to buy it, but we snuck it over here so her mother wouldn't find out. She was going to return it to the store on Monday, so I just—" She hesitated, then blurted out the truth. "Well, I took it in at the hips a little, since now she won't be wearing it at all. Do you think the store will notice?" She offered the dress to Penny for inspection.

Penny looked at the new seams critically. "If they don't look at it too closely," she decided. "The new seams are perfect. Of course, you can still see where the old ones were. But why should they even look? Put it on."

Karen slipped into the dress and modeled it for Penny.

"It's great," said Penny. "Really sexy. I wish I had a figure like yours."

"Be glad you don't," Karen said. "Nothing fits me right, and I always look like some . . ." She trailed the sentence off, unwilling to use the word "tramp."

"Not in that dress, you don't," Penny assured her. "And you know what? I'll bet if you take off that makeup, and just let your hair fall, you'll look really great."

Together, the two girls began experimenting with Karen's hair and face. Half an hour later they surveyed the results in the mirror, and Penny giggled. "You know what? You look just like Judy always wanted to look. If she could just see you in that dress she'd die!" Then she realized what she'd said, and the two girls stared at each other.

"Why do you suppose she did it?" Karen asked. "Have you asked her?"

Penny shook her head. "I don't think I want to know. It's creepy, if you ask me. And it must have hurt like crazy."

"I don't know," Karen mused. "I guess if you're feeling so bad you want to die, you don't care."

Penny shuddered a little. "I don't think I could do it. I couldn't stand the pain." Then she smiled. "But I could sure stand to get the treatment Judy's getting. All she does is lie there in bed, and get waited on hand and foot, while she watches television all day."

"Yeah," Karen said slowly. "But suppose she'd died? What do you suppose that would be like?"

"Don't you ever think about it?" Penny asked her. "I think about it all the time. I like to picture my own funeral sometimes."

The thought had never occurred to Karen. Now she saw a picture in her mind's eye. "That could be kind of neat," she said. "I think I'd want a very small funeral. Just you and Janet and Judy, and my mother. And Jim, of course. It would be horrible for him, and he'd probably throw himself on my coffin." The prospect pleased her—a devastated Jim Mulvey, his own life forever destroyed by the untimely death of the girl he had hoped to marry, prostrated on the casket, crying openly over his loss.

"My funeral would be much more dignified," Penny said. "Of course, everyone would be there, and there'd be masses of flowers. And my parents would be in the front row. I don't think they'd cry. Instead, they'd be helping everyone else get through it. You know how my mother is; she'd be trying to take the attitude that life goes on, but of course inside she'd be a wreck. And it would kill Daddy, though he wouldn't let anyone know it. They'd probably be dead themselves within a year. After all, what would they have left to live for?" Then, as the dramatic image of her parents wasting away with unexpressed grief faded, Penny snickered. "Can you imagine Marilyn Crane's funeral?" she giggled. "Three faded roses, and everyone there to make sure she was dead."

"Who'd even care if she was dead?" Karen said flippantly. She began taking off the black dress. "We'd better get started, or we'll never be ready by the time everyone shows up." She hung the dress up carefully, and pulled on a pair of jeans. "Come on," she said. "You can help me wash the punchbowl."

An hour and a half later, the party was in full swing, except that so far, none of the boys had arrived. Then, as Karen and Penny were joking about having spiked the punch (they hadn't) the front door opened, and Janet Connally arrived. With her was Jeff Bremmer.

"Jeff was helping me out with a science project this afternoon, so I invited him along," Janet explained. Jeff looked around the room, and saw that he was the only male in sight.

"I don't know," he said uncertainly. "Maybe I shouldn't have come."

"Don't be silly," Penny said. "Everyone else is coming. Someone had to be first. Just don't tell anyone you were here. Karen's mother thinks this is a hen party."

Now Jeff was really unnerved. "I think I'd better go," he said. But a moment later a car pulled up in front of the house, and Jim Mulvey and Lyle Crandall appeared at the door. Suddenly, Jeff felt better about the party.

"Hey," Jim Mulvey said, whistling at Karen. "Now that's what I call a dress."

"You like it? It's the one Judy was supposed to wear tonight."

"Looks better on you," Jim assured her. Then he winked. "I got some beer here. Can I put it in the ice box?" When Karen looked uncertain, he reached out and squeezed her around the waist. "Come on," he said. "It's only a little beer. Us guys get thirsty." He pulled out a can of Olympia and held it up in Lyle Crandall's direction. "Want one, Crandall?"

"Sure," Lyle said. "And give me one for Jeff." Jim Mulvey tossed him another can and Lyle opened both of them. "Try this on for size, Jeff," he said, handing him the can.

Jeff considered the possibility of giving it back. Then he changed his mind. He held the can up to his lips, and the bitter fluid choked him. He flushed a deep red as the other two boys laughed at him.

"So what's been coming down?" Jim Mulvey asked of nobody in particular as he popped the tab on his own beer.

"We were talking about Judy Nelson," a voice said from somewhere in the background. "And killing yourself in general."

There was a wave of laughter through the room. Judy Nelson had become something to joke about.

"The guy next door killed himself years ago," Lyle Crandall put in.

"You're kidding," Jim said. "Who was that?"

"I can't remember their names anymore, and his wife moved away right after it happened."

"What'd he do?"

Lyle laughed and began to tell the story but Janet Connally cut him off.

"Ugh," she said with a shudder. "That's horrible. Let's talk about something else."

"I think it's interesting," Jim Mulvey grinned. "If you were going to kill yourself, how would you do it?"

Suddenly they were all talking about the best way to commit suicide. Pills, it was decided, were best, and after that gassing oneself. The more painful ways were discarded, as either too scary or too messy. And then, when they had exhausted that subject, they turned to speculating upon who in their classes were the most likely candidates for a suicide. No one mentioned any of the people at the party. If anybody noticed, nobody commented on it. When they were done, they agreed that if anybody at St. Francis Xavier's was actually going to kill himself, it should be Marilyn Crane. As Jim Mulvey put it, "She should do herself a favor." Everyone laughed, and someone suggested that Marilyn could even invent a new method—she could bore herself to death. Everyone laughed at that, too, except Jeff. He felt sorry for Marilyn, and decided that coming to the party had been a mistake. He argued with himself about leaving, but in the end he went to the refrigerator and helped himself to another beer. By the time it was half drunk, he felt much better about everything.

Just before nine o'clock, the telephone rang. Karen motioned for quiet before she picked up the receiver, then, after she had spoken into the phone, waved to everybody. "It's all right," she cried. "It's Judy." As the party resumed, Karen chatted with Judy Nelson. When she finally hung up, she waved again, until she had everyone's attention.

"Judy has a wonderful idea," she said. Then she began explaining what Judy's wonderful idea was.

At exactly nine o'clock the telephone rang at the Crane home. Geraldine Crane picked it up, and was pleasantly surprised when a voice asked for Marilyn.

"For me?" Marilyn said curiously, coming into the room. "Who is it?"

"Don't know." Geraldine shrugged. She handed the phone to Marilyn, and sat back down in the chair she had vacated when the phone rang. She picked up the book she had been reading, but didn't open it. Instead, she listened to Marilyn's side of the conversation.

"I don't think so," Marilyn was saying. "It's getting awfully late, and I think I'd better stay home." There was a silence, then: "No, really—I'm not feeling well. Thanks anyway." Then she hung up the phone and started out of the room.

"Who was that, dear?" her mother said.

"No one."

"Don't be silly. It was someone. Who was it?"

"Karen Morton," Marilyn said. She made another attempt to get out of the room, but again her mother stopped her.

"Well, what did she want?"

"Nothing."

"Marilyn, she must have wanted something. It sounded like she wanted you to go somewhere. Where?"

"Over to her house."

"Really?" Geraldine was elated. Marilyn was rarely invited to go anywhere, and almost never by people her own age, except that nice Jeff Bremmer. "What for?"

"She said it was a party. A come-as-you-are party. They want me to come."

"Why that sounds wonderful," Geraldine said enthusiastically. She remembered going to that kind of party herself, years ago, and it had been lots of fun. People had shown up in the most ridiculous outfits.

"Well, I'm not going," Marilyn said quietly.

Geraldine decided to take the bull by the horns. It was time Marilyn started mixing with the other children, she thought. "Of course you're going," she said. "Why on earth shouldn't you?"

"It's late," Marilyn said. "It's nine o'clock, and I want to go to early Mass tomorrow."

"You can go to a later one, and sleep in," Geraldine replied.

"But Mother, look at me. I'm a mess."

"That's what makes come-as-you-are parties fun," Geraldine said, more sharply than she had meant. "Now put on your coat and I'll take you right over to Karen's."

Marilyn surveyed herself in the mirror. She had been about to go to bed with a book, and she was wearing a flannel nightgown and an old pink bathrobe that she had insisted not be given to the Goodwill. Her hair was in curlers, and her face was covered with cream.

"I don't want to go," she insisted. But Geraldine was adamant. She brushed Marilyn's objections aside and packed her into the car.

Five minutes later, with a coat covering her bathrobe, and slippers on her feet, Marilyn Crane was deposited in front of the Morton house. Without giving her daughter time to voice any more objections, Geraldine Crane drove away. She was sure that finally her ugly-duckling daughter was going to be accepted by the flock. Marilyn, sure that the flock was playing a trick on her, moved slowly up the walk to the door. The house seemed dark, suspiciously quiet. She reached out, and tentatively rang the bell.

* * *

At ten-thirty Saturday night, Harriet Morton glanced around the diner where she and one other waitress had spent the evening with very little to do. Only two tables were occupied, and they were both in the other girl's station. And something was nagging at her. She had a feeling that she should be at home. She glanced at the clock, then heard the voice of the other waitress behind her. "Why don't you call it a night?" Millie was saying. "You've been jumpy as a cat all night, and it's not as if I can't handle it by myself." It was a tempting offer, but Harriet thought about the tips she might miss. Millie read her mind. "Tell you what I'll do. I'll punch you out when I leave, and we'll split any tips that come into your station between now and closing. Which, if we're lucky, should come to about twelve and a half cents each. Go home, will you? I can tell you're worried about something."

"It's probably silly," Harriet replied. "It's just that Karen's having a party tonight, and it's the first time I've ever let her have one when I wasn't there."

"Afraid it's turned into an orgy?" Millie grinned. "Go on, take off. I'll handle the mob." She looked sourly at the two lone diners who were poking unenthusiastically at the mess of potatoes and gravy that was billed as "real home cooking."

Five minutes later Harriet was in her car, and ten minutes after that she was pulling into the driveway. From the outside, the party seemed to be over—the house was dark. And then, as she closed the car door, she heard the music. Soft music, not the loud rock she had expected. She tried the door. Unlocked. As she snapped on the lights, she heard the sounds of scuffling in the living room. And there they were.

Harriet surveyed the guilty-looking teen-agers who were scattered around the living room trying to look as though they hadn't been caught— except that their clothes were mussed and the girls' makeup had somehow transferred itself to the boys' faces. Well, it was bound to happen someday, Harriet told herself. They *are* growing up. She steeled herself to give them the lecture she knew her husband would have given them, had he been alive. Of all the kids, it was her own daughter who was staring at her with the most resentment. The others looked properly ashamed; Karen, however, looked mad. It didn't occur to Harriet that Karen's anger was not so much directed at Harriet for the lecture she was giving, as at the fact that Karen was afraid of what the other kids might say when it was over. Karen could see her stock slipping. Her mother, she had always said, let her do what she wanted. Now the truth was coming out. Harriet Morton was just as strict as all the rest of the mothers of Neilsville.

Karen whispered into Jim Mulvey's ear. "We'll sneak out when this is all over with," she said softly. "Then maybe we can finish what we started." Jim felt a sudden tightness in his groin. Was it really finally going to happen? All of a sudden he was a little bit afraid.

Peter Balsam steered Margo's car into her driveway, and came to a stop. He turned and smiled at her.

"Are you coming in for a nightcap?" Margo asked.

Balsam shook his head. He wanted to accept, wanted to take her in his arms, but something held him back. "Not tonight," he said, avoiding the hurt look in her eyes. "I've got some reading to do." Then: "You're sure you don't mind if I take the car?"

Margo smiled. "Not if you bring it back in the morning. And I figure the best way to guarantee my seeing you in the morning is to loan you the car. Somehow, you just don't strike me as a car thief." She kissed him quickly, then got out of the car. "See you in the morning. Shall I fix some breakfast?"

"That'd be great," Peter said. "And Margo? Thanks for riding along with me."

She grinned. "I was just looking out for my car. Next time you decide you have to drive to Seattle, you can do it alone. Trip's too long for me." She waved at him and disappeared into her house. A moment later she heard him put the car in gear and back out of the driveway. Five minutes later, Margo Henderson was in bed.

Balsam made his way slowly through the back streets of Neilsville. He didn't want to be seen driving Margo's car. He suspected there was already a certain amount of gossip and he didn't want to fuel that particular fire. He was only five blocks from home, and beginning to relax after the trip, when he saw the figure sitting forlornly on the curb. As he drew abreast of the odd apparition, a face peered up at him, and he recognized Marilyn Crane. His foot hit the brakes, bringing the car to a fast enough stop to send the books piled neatly on the back seat tumbling to the floor. Peter Balsam backed the car up, and rolled down the window.

"Marilyn?" he called. "Marilyn, is that you?"

She had been about to walk away, hoping to disappear into the shadows, when she recognized his voice. Uncertainly, she turned, and Peter could see that she had been crying. She peered at the car, as if unsure whether to come closer or run away. Peter opened the door and got out. He started around the car.

"Marilyn? It's me, Mr. Balsam. What's wrong? What are you doing wandering around in a bathrobe?"

"I—I'm all right," she said, but it was obvious she wasn't. And then she remembered the day they had walked from the church into town together, and how Mr. Balsam seemed to understand her. Suddenly her tears started flowing again. "No, I'm not all right. I'm terrible, if you really want to know. Can I get in your car?"

"Of course you can." Instinctively, he reached out and took her arm to guide her into the car. By the time he shut the door firmly behind her, she was sobbing uncontrollably. He hurried around to the driver's side. Then, instead of driving away, he pulled the car closer to the curb, and turned off the engine. He reached out to touch the unhappy child, and she clutched at his hand.

"What is it, Marilyn?" he said softly. "Can't you tell me?"

"It—it was awful," she said. "They were all so mean." She looked at him beseechingly. "Why are they all so mean?"

"I don't know," Peter said gently. "Why don't you start at the beginning?"

Marilyn nodded vigorously, and did her best to control the sudden fit of crying that had overtaken her, as she told Peter Balsam what had happened to her that evening.

"It was awful, Mr. Balsam," she said, reliving the experience. "I stood there, and rang the bell, and I knew it was some kind of horrible joke, and I waited, but no one answered the door. And then, when I was about to leave, Mother drove away, so I didn't have any choice. So I rang the bell again, and then I could hear them inside. They were all giggling, and I knew they were giggling at me. And finally Karen opened the door, and asked me to come in. I wanted to run away right then, but I hoped that maybe—well, maybe it wasn't a joke at all, and that Karen had dressed up so that *everyone* would look as bad as I did, and she'd be the only one there that looked nice. So I went in. And they were all waiting for me. All of them—Penny and Janet, and Lyle and Jeff—all of them. And there I was. And they were laughing at me. I tried to tell Mother—I knew it was going to happen!" She began crying again, and Peter let her cry, knowing that nothing he could say could take away her humiliation. He let her cry it out. Then, when her sobbing eased off, he squeezed her hand.

"Would you like me to take you home?" he said softly. Marilyn seemed terrified.

"No," she said. "Not yet. I can't go home yet. Mother'd be furious with me. She'd tell me I was being too sensitive, and that I should have laughed right along with everyone else, then stayed and had a good time."

"Maybe you should have," Peter suggested gently.

"But I couldn't have. Don't you see? They didn't invite me because they wanted me. They only invited me so they could laugh. Once the joke was over, they didn't want me to stay. Oh, God, I wanted to die! It was so awful!"

"I'll tell you what," Balsam said. "Why don't we go somewhere, and I'll buy you a Coke?"

Marilyn looked at him hopefully, then her face sagged in disappointment. "Like this? I can't go anywhere looking like this."

Balsam couldn't help grinning at her now, but he was careful not to laugh.

"You managed to get here looking like that, didn't you?"

"That was different. I just had to get away from Karen's."

"How long ago was that?"

She shrugged listlessly. "I don't know. A half-hour. Maybe an hour."

"Do you mean to tell me you've been wandering around like that for an hour?" She nodded. "And you don't want to go home yet?" She shook her head. "All right, then, we'll go to a drive-in, and you can stay in the car while I buy a couple of Cokes. How's that sound?"

She looked at him gratefully. "Could we?" she implored him. "I just don't want Mother to find out what happened. She wouldn't understand at all, and she'd just get mad at me, and tell me I did everything wrong."

"It's all right," Balsam assured her. He started the car, and a few minutes later he pulled it into the back corner of the parking lot at the A & W. He went inside, and felt curious eyes on him as he bought two Cokes. When he returned to the car, Marilyn had calmed down considerably.

"You don't know what it was like," she said, sipping on her Coke.

"How do you know?" Peter said. "You're not the only one who's ever been caught in something like that." Then he proceeded to make up a story about his own past, in which he was made to look as ridiculous as Marilyn had been made to look tonight. He told himself that it didn't matter that the story wasn't true. What mattered was that Marilyn realize that she wasn't the only person who had ever been humiliated in public. She listened to him in silence. When he finished, there was just the tiniest trace of a smile at the corners of her mouth.

"That story wasn't true, was it?" she said.

"No," Balsam admitted. "But it could have been, and the stories that are true are still too painful to talk about." He thought about his wife, Linda, and the other man. The man he had found her with. That, he thought, was humiliation. But he couldn't tell Marilyn about it.

"What'll I do now?" she suddenly asked him. "I mean, how can I face them at school on Monday?"

"Don't worry about it," Balsam said. "Just act as if nothing happened, and I'll bet nobody will mention it at all. And listen carefully in my class on Monday. I think I'll have a special lecture—a little talk about people who feel good by making other people feel bad. With no names mentioned, of course. And don't be surprised if I act like you don't exist. I wouldn't want anyone to think you and I had planned anything in advance."

It worked. Marilyn smiled at him now, and the tears were gone.

"Thanks for finding me tonight," she said softly. "I guess you're the only person in the world I really needed to talk to tonight." She handed him her empty paper cup, and Peter Balsam got out of the car to throw it away, along with his own. Then he drove her home, in a comfortable silence.

"Marilyn?" her mother called from the living room as she closed the front door behind her. "How was the party?"

"Fine, Mother," Marilyn responded. She saw no reason to let her good feelings be dissipated by a lecture from her mother.

"Who brought you home?"

Before she could think of anything else to say, Marilyn blurted out the truth.

"Mr. Balsam?" Geraldine Crane repeated. "How on earth did that happen?"

"He—he was just driving by, and saw me walking," Marilyn said, stretching the truth only a little. "He offered me a ride, and since I felt silly walking dressed like this, I accepted."

Geraldine Crane considered this for a moment. She wasn't sure she approved. After all, the man was practically a stranger. "Well, I wish you wouldn't do things like that," she said. "If he ever offers you a ride again, turn him down."

"Oh, Mother," Marilyn said. "For heaven's sake, he's one of my teachers."

"But we don't really know him, do we?" Geraldine asked darkly. "Better to be safe than sorry."

But Marilyn had already slipped up the stairs. She didn't hear what her mother had said.

Leona Anderson wondered if she should call Geraldine Crane that night, or the next morning, or at all. It had been quite shocking. It was a good thing her bridge game had run late, and that she happened to drive by the A & W just when she had, or she wouldn't have seen it at all. There they were, just as brazen as trash, that Mr. Balsam and Marilyn Crane. And her in her bathrobe, no less! And in Margo Henderson's car. It really was too much.

And then, on reflection, Leona Anderson decided not to call anyone that night. She would wait until morning, and then tell Inez Nelson at church. Between the two of them, she and Inez would be able to decide what should be done. Leona had no doubt that something should be done.

Peter Balsam glanced at the clock as he entered the apartment. Nearly midnight. He was weary from the long drive, but he'd gone all the way to Seattle just for these books and they beckoned to him now. He picked up the most formidable of them, Henry Lea's *The Inquisition of the Middle Ages*.

He opened the book to the index, and began running his fingers down the columns. Then he began leafing through the book, reading a paragraph here, a page there, consulting the index once again.

Peter Balsam did not sleep at all that night. By dawn he knew much more about the saints that adorned St. Francis Xavier church than he had at midnight. What he had discovered wouldn't have let him have much sleep even if he had gone to bed. As the sun rose above Neilsville, and the intense heat of the last days of summer baked the town, Peter Balsam continued his reading. And every now and then, as if it were winter, he shivered.

# ELEVEN

KAREN MORTON WAS WALKING UP CATHEdral Hill, alone. Usually, on Sunday mornings, she waited at the foot of the hill, at the corner of First and Main, for Penny Anderson, Janet Connally, and Judy Nelson. But this morning Judy would not be coming. This morning Karen had no desire to see Penny or Janet. Or anyone at all. She wished she were home, closed comfortably into the security of her bedroom.

It had not been an easy morning for Karen, and it was not showing any promise of getting better.

She had thought of staying in bed, pleading illness, but quickly decided that wouldn't work. She had sensed, even before she saw her mother, that no excuse would be accepted today. She was going to have to get up, have to face her mother's anger, have to go to church. She was going to have to confess her sins. That was what was frightening her, for Karen knew she had a lot to confess. And so, even earlier than usual, Karen had gotten up, dressed, and gone downstairs. There just hadn't seemed any point in prolonging it.

Her mother had been in the kitchen. She hadn't spoken to her when Karen came down for breakfast. She simply stared at her, then turned back to the stove where she was frying eggs. Finally, her back still to Karen, she had asked the question Karen hadn't wanted to hear.

"What time did you come in last night?" she said quietly.

"I'm not sure," Karen hedged.

"Well, I am," Harriet snapped. "It was after two o'clock. Where were you all that time?"

"Jim and I went to—to the A & W," Karen said. She knew immediately she had made a mistake.

"Did you?" It was an accusation, not a question. "Did you, indeed? It must have been interesting, sitting there in the dark. The A & W closes at midnight."

Karen sank into a chair next to the kitchen table, and waited in silence for the onslaught of her mother's wrath. But it didn't come. Instead, Harriet Morton silently continued fixing their breakfast, silently set the plates on the table, and silently sat down. For Karen, the silence was much worse than any lecture.

"I'm sorry," she had whispered finally. Again, her mother stared at her. Then, at last, Harriet Morton began to speak.

"I don't know what to say," she began, and Karen had a sinking feeling in her stomach. Those were the words her mother always used when she was about to invoke Karen's father. She waited.

"If your father were alive," Harriet had gone on, "I could leave this whole matter up to him. But he isn't alive, and I have to deal with it. I suppose, when it comes down to it, that I shouldn't blame you. I know it can't be easier for you, not having your father around, than it is for me. But I'd hoped you were old enough to be trusted by now. Apparently I was wrong. Apparently all the things your father and I tried to teach you went in one ear and out the other. Well, there isn't anything I can do about it now. But there are a few things I can do about the future. First, there won't be any more parties. Since I won't be able to supervise them, you won't have them."

"For how long?" Karen asked softly. She had been expecting this.

"How long?" Harriet had said, looking at her blankly. "Why, until you're eighteen, of course. As long as you're my responsibility."

Karen had gasped. "But Mother—"

"And of course you won't be seeing Jim Mulvey any more," Harriet went on. She looked deeply into Karen's eyes, and added, "Unless, of course, you have to get married. I've been praying all night that that won't happen. But if it does, it's a cross we'll both have to bear."

Karen stared at her mother in dismay, and then burst into tears and fled the table. Her mother found her lying on her bed, crying.

"It's time for church, Karen," she said softly.

"I'm not going," Karen sobbed into her pillow.

"Of course you are," Harriet said. "Isn't it more important for you to go this morning than ever before? You need the church this morning, Karen. Now get off that bed, change your clothes, and go."

She was nearing the top of Cathedral Hill. Other worshipers were streaming toward the church of St. Francis Xavier. Karen did not join in their Sunday-morning chatter, and there was an air about her that kept people from calling a greeting to her. Karen Morton had something on her mind.

She made her way up the steps, and through the foyer. Then she dipped her fingers in the font, genuflected, and started down the aisle to the pew she and her mother usually occupied. Behind her, someone whispered a quick greeting. Karen didn't reply. She sank to her knees, and began the prayers she repeated every Sunday morning. Then she sat on the pew, and tried to pay attention to the Mass.

An hour later, when the Mass was over, Karen stood up reluctantly. Now was going to be the worst time. Now she was going to have to go to the confessional. She knew it was supposed to make her feel better; she knew that her sins would be forgiven. Until this morning, going to confession *had* always made her feel better. But this morning was a special morning. This morning she had a difficult confession to make. Karen steeled herself, almost lost her resolve, then slipped quickly into one of the confessionals that stood to the left of the doors. She clutched her beads, made the sign of the cross—"In the name of the Father, and of the Son, and of the Holy Ghost. Amen."—and knelt.

"Bless me, Father, for I have sinned," Karen began. "It has been a week since my last confession." Then she paused, wondering where to start. "I am guilty of the sin of lust," she said softly. She heard the slightest intake of breath from beyond the grille, and was immediately fearful.

"What are your sins, my child?"

Karen knew the voice. She had heard it in the halls of the school for too many years not to recognize it, even when it was pitched to the low level of the confessional. It was Monsignor Vernon.

"I—I—" Karen wanted to run from the tiny confessional, run out of the church and down the hill. She tried to get hold of herself. From the other side of the grille the Monsignor's voice inveighed her to begin.

"But it isn't easy . . ." Karen faltered.

"Nothing in this world is easy, my child," the priest said softly. "But we must confess our sins. What have you done?"

She told him. She began telling him all that had transpired during the week, and during the week preceding. She confessed to being deceitful, and told him first about helping Judy Nelson with the dress. Then she began telling him about the party the night before, and about being deceitful toward her mother. She told him about the trick she had pulled on Marilyn Crane, and the hurt she had caused Marilyn. And then she told him about the last hours of the night, when she and Jim Mulvey had sat in his car, hidden in the darkness.

"I—I let him touch me, Father," she whispered. She felt the heat between her legs once again, just as she had felt it last night, and a wave of guilt swept over her.

"You let him touch you?" Monsignor asked. "Let him touch you where?"

"I—I'm not—" Karen stammered. Then she blurted it out. "I let him touch me all over."

There was a long silence from the other side of the grille. Then the Monsignor spoke again.

"Exactly what do you mean when you say you let him touch you all over?"

In the darkness of the confessional, Karen Morton flushed a deep scarlet, and wished for a moment that she could die.

"Bless me, Father, for I have sinned," she mumbled again.

"I cannot forgive sins that have not been confessed," the inexorable voice came out of the darkness. Karen squirmed in embarrassment.

"He—I let him touch me on my chest. And between my legs," she said miserably.

"And did you touch him?" the priest continued relentlessly.

"Yes." The word was almost inaudible, and Karen wondered if she had been heard. But she couldn't bring herself to repeat it. Then the voice began talking to her.

"Lust is a most grievous sin, my child. Your soul is in grave danger, and you must be on your guard against the evil that is within you."

"I am trying, Father," Karen said miserably.

"The Devil walks among us," she heard the priest saying. "He is constantly with us, leading us out of the paths of righteousness. Guard yourself against him, my child, and be wary. He will appear as a friend, but he will lead you astray." Then the voice fell silent, and Karen wondered about the words. What was the priest trying to tell her? Was he saying that Jim Mulvey was the Devil? It didn't make sense. Then he spoke again.

"Is there anything else?" he said.

Karen searched her mind. It was almost over. Soon, she would be absolved of her sins, and free to go. She tried to remember if she had left anything out of the confession, but the strain of it had left her confused.

"No, Father," she said finally.

"Your sins are many, child, and your penance must be heavy."

Karen felt her heart sink. Many times she had seen people come out of the confessional and walk down the aisle toward the altar. There they would kneel, and spend the rest of the day. Often, she had wondered what prayers they were saying. Now she was sure she was about to find out.

"You will leave the confessional on your knees, and approach the Holy Virgin. For your sins, say one hundred Rosaries, and between each Rosary, recite the Apostles' Creed. Do you understand your penance?"

"Yes, Father." Karen wanted to cry. Leave the confessional on her knees? She didn't remember anyone ever having done that before. People would stare at her. They would know that she must have done something terribly wicked. She wished she could die. Then she realized the priest was saying the words of absolution. Quickly, she repeated the Act of Contrition. "Oh my God," she began, the words coming automatically through her confusion, "I am heartily sorry for having offended Thee, and I detest all my sins because I dread the loss of heaven and the pains of hell; but most of all because they offend Thee, my God, who are all-good and deserving of all my love. I firmly resolve, with the help of Thy grace, to sin no more and to avoid near occasions of sin." As she finished, she heard the words of absolution.

"I absolve you from your sins, in the name of the Father, and of the Son, and of the Holy Ghost. Amen. Go in peace, my child." The shutter closed over the grille, and Karen Morton was alone in the confessional. She sat for a long time, wishing she had the courage, or the cowardice, to ignore the penance, to leave the confessional and walk out of the church into the sunlight. But Karen Morton was in fear of her Lord, so she grasped her beads firmly, pushed the door of the confessional open, and, still on her knees, crept out into the church. She stared at the image of the Holy Virgin and kept her eyes firmly fixed on that peaceful face as she made her pitiful way down the aisle. By the time she reached the statue, and began telling her beads, the pain in her knees was almost as great as the agony in her mind. Her lips moving silently, she began the Apostles' Creed.

Peter Balsam stared out into the morning sunlight and wondered what he should do next. His first impulse was to call Margo Henderson, and he had already reached for the phone when he realized what he must do instead. He must go to church. He must pray. He must make his decision for himself. He knew that, in the light of what he had read last night, it was not going to be easy to pray this morning, not going to be easy to sit below the glowering countenances of the Saints of the Inquisition—the Saints of Neilsville—and come to a decision that made sense. But this morning, not much made sense to Peter Balsam. His long night's reading had shaken him to the core. Now, he had to find out if his faith had withstood the shaking or if it had crumbled.

He left his apartment, carefully locked the door behind him, and began the climb up Cathedral Hill.

He entered the church just as Karen Morton came out of the confessional and looked on in horror as she slowly made her way down the aisle to the alcove dedicated to the Blessed Virgin. For a split second he had wanted to go to her. When he saw the rest of the parishioners ignoring her, he changed his mind. He was still staring at her when he heard the voice behind him.

"I'd hoped you'd be here earlier," Monsignor Vernon's voice said softly into his ear. Peter Balsam jumped back, startled, then turned to stare at the priest.

"What on earth is going on here?" he demanded.

Monsignor Vernon looked at him impassively, almost as if he hadn't heard the question.

"Why did Karen Morton just go down the aisle on her knees?"

The priest smiled calmly, a look of peace in his eyes.

"That's between her and her Lord, isn't it?"

"Is it supposed to be some kind of penance?" Balsam demanded.

"It doesn't concern you," the priest countered. He turned, as if to move away, then turned back. "Will I see you at the next Mass?" he asked Balsam.

Balsam glanced again at Karen Morton, who was now engrossed in prayer, before he answered. Then he turned to the priest, and shook his head.

"I don't know," he said. "But I need to talk to you."

"To me?" Monsignor Vernon asked. "Very well. Shall we go to the rectory?"

"If you don't mind, I'd rather we went somewhere else. How about my classroom?"

The Monsignor shrugged indifferently and led Peter Balsam out of the church. A few minutes later he put his key in the door to Room 16, and stood aside to let Balsam enter first. Then he followed the teacher in, and pulled the door closed behind him.

"Is something wrong?" The question was not so much an inquiry as a prod. Balsam decided not to allow himself to be prodded. Instead, he approached the statue of St. Peter Martyr, and stood silently staring at it for several minutes. Then he turned quickly and spoke.

"He was a prize bastard, wasn't he?" Balsam had intended the words to be shocking. He succeeded. The priest immediately made the sign of the cross. Then his eyes flashed angrily at Balsam.

"I beg your pardon?"

"I've been reading up on him," Balsam said calmly. "On him, and on all the other saints you've got scattered around here. Almost all of them come straight out of the Inquisition, which I've also been reading up on."

The priest sat down on the edge of Peter Balsam's desk, arms folded in an attitude of exaggerated patience.

"I have a lot of Dominican saints here, yes," he said pensively. "And I suppose you're right—a lot of them do date from the period of the Inquisition. But I don't get your point."

Balsam felt his resolve beginning to crumble. "It's just this," he said, suddenly uncertain. "I got curious about the saints in the church and I decided to do some research. And then, the more I read, the more I realized that the kind of intolerance all these saints represented wasn't much different from the sort of thing we were talking about the other day. The day we were discussing what I can, and what I cannot, teach in my class."

The priest smiled dryly. "You think the Inquisition's being revived, right here in Neilsville?"

"In a word, yes, that's exactly what I think."

"Before I even argue the point with you," Monsignor Vernon said wearily, "may I inquire what the purpose of this meeting is?"

"Certainly," Balsam retorted. "This is to tell you that I've changed my mind. I don't think I can stay in Neilsville. In fact, after the reading I did last night, I'm not even sure I can stay in the Church."

Suddenly the priest looked stricken.

"You're not serious," he exclaimed. "You aren't really considering leaving the Church?"

Now that he'd said it, Balsam was suddenly no longer sure he meant it. He glanced nervously at the Monsignor, then back to the image of St. Peter Martyr.

"I don't know," he said uncertainly. "It's just that I can't stomach the sort of thing people like him stood for. And it seems to me that the Church hasn't really progressed very far since his day."

"Of course it hasn't," the priest intoned. "Why should it? Faith is absolute, and the Truth of the Lord is absolute. There is room within the Faith for differences of opinion."

As Balsam stared, the Monsignor's voice softened and he returned to himself. He smiled. "Peter, I know we've had differences of opinion. They are not at an end. We have always had our differences." He paused, as if weighing the prudence of what he was about to reveal, then continued with a sigh, "I hadn't intended to tell you this, but I selected you for the job here because of those differences." He left the edge of the desk, and began pacing the room, speaking as he moved. "I've been following your career very closely, Peter, much more closely than you ever knew. And I've worried about you. Of all of us, you've seemed to me to have had the most trouble, not only within the Church, but within yourself. I suppose some of it has to do with your childhood—"

"Forget that," Balsam snapped. "It has nothing to do with all this."

"Doesn't it?" the priest said quizzically. Then he smiled again. "Well, maybe it doesn't. At any rate, it's all academic. If you wish, I'll take the matter of your resignation under consideration. I will do it reluctantly, but I will do it. In the meantime, I wish you'd do me a favor. I wish you'd examine your own conscience, and I wish you'd make a greater effort to understand what the Dominican saints were all about. Their methods may seem a bit harsh today, but don't forget that some of the tales of that period have been grossly exaggerated. Primarily, they helped people to keep the Faith. And that, I think, is at the root of your problems right now. I think you're having a crisis of faith." He put his hand on Peter's shoulder. "It happens to us all," he said gently. "It's happened to me, since I've been here. But I've come through it. Of course I had the Society of St. Peter Martyr to help me. The Society could help you, too."

Balsam looked at the priest curiously. "Exactly what is the Society of St. Peter Martyr?" he asked.

The priest smiled enigmatically. "Come and see," he said. "We meet tomorrow night.'' When Peter seemed hesitant, he added: ''What harm can it do? It might even help. If nothing else, at least you'll understand us better. Then, if you still want to leave, I'm sure we'll be able to arrange it.''

Balsam sighed heavily. He had a feeling that something was wrong—that the talk had not gone as he had intended it to. He shrugged off the feeling and smiled at the Monsignor.

''Okay,'' he said. ''Tomorrow night?''

''Seven-thirty, at the rectory.''

The two men left the classroom, and walked together out of the school. ''Will I see you at Mass this evening?'' the priest asked.

''I don't know,'' Balsam answered honestly. ''But I suppose so. If I miss it, I can always confess.'' He regretted the facetious remark as soon as he'd made it, but the Monsignor was not listening.

''Then if not before, I'll see you tomorrow night.'' He turned and disappeared into the rectory.

Peter Balsam started down the hill. Then, as if remembering something, he went back to the church. There, still on her knees in front of the Holy Virgin, was Karen Morton, her fingers playing over the beads, her lips reciting the Rosary. As Balsam left the church and started again down the hill, he wondered how long she would be there.

If he had known Karen Morton would be in the church, praying on her knees, for the next eight hours, he might have changed his mind once more, and left Neilsville that afternoon. But it was already too late; things had already gone too far, and Balsam was already too enmeshed in it. The punishment was beginning.

# THE SOCIETY OF
# ST. PETER MARTYR

## TWELVE

INEZ NELSON HURRIED UP THE STEPS, AND through the main doors of St. Francis Xavier School. She was late, and she knew that Monsignor didn't like to be kept waiting.

She turned into the reception room and glanced nervously at the door that led to Monsignor's private office, wondering if she should tap at the closed door. Just as she decided against it she heard the click of the latch and looked up, relieved to see the priest smiling at her.

"Come in, come in," he said expansively. "It's a good thing you're late—Mondays are always my busy day. The work seems to pile up over the weekend, even though there isn't any school. Or maybe I just don't work hard enough on Fridays." He closed the door behind Inez, and offered her a chair. Then he moved behind his desk and sat down. His smile had disappeared.

"I suppose you've been to the hospital?" he asked.

Inez nodded. "I spent nearly an hour with that Dr. Shields——"

"The psychiatrist?" Monsignor interrupted her.

"Yes." Inez paused, choking back a sob. "Oh, Monsignor, I'm so confused and it's been worrying me all weekend. He says Judy is doing fine. But she won't talk about why she did it. All she'll tell him is that she's fine now, and that it won't happen again."

"And what does she say to you?"

Inez squirmed uncomfortably. "Well, that's just it, Monsignor. That's why I felt I had to talk to you. About so many things. But primarily about Judy. You see, she won't see me."

Monsignor Vernon's eyes opened in surprise. "Won't see you? What do you mean, she won't see you?"

"Just that," Inez said unhappily. "She absolutely refuses to see me." She was fighting tears. "And it's only me," she went on, her voice beginning to quaver. "She sees everyone else. Her father. Her friends. But she won't see me. And everyone says she's fine."

"Do they?" The priest's tone suggested to Inez that he didn't believe Judy could possibly be fine. "If she won't see you, I wonder how fine she could be?"

"That's exactly what I thought, too," Inez said. Suddenly she felt much better. "But I don't know what to do. If only I could talk to her, I know I could find out what's the matter."

The priest shrugged. "Frankly, I don't see what the problem is. Judy is only sixteen, and you *are* her mother. If you want to see her, I don't see how anyone can stop you."

Inez nodded vigorously. "That's exactly what I've been saying. But no one agrees with me. Oh, not that I can't see her if I demand to. Everyone says I can do that. But they all think it would be unwise. Dr. Shields, and George—my husband—both seem to think I should just wait. They say eventually she'll see me, and I suppose they're right. But in the meantime nobody seems to be taking my feelings into consideration. I feel like—well, I feel like such a failure." She looked guiltily at the priest. "Do you know what I've been doing? I've been going to the hospital every day at visiting hours, and visiting total strangers. Well, not total strangers, of course, but people I wouldn't normally go see in the hospital. Then I tell them that I was there visiting Judy, and I just decided to drop in." Now the tears came, and Inez stared miserably at the priest. "I just don't know how long I can stand it, Father," she said. "If it ever gets out that all this time Judy has been refusing to see me—well, you don't know what an awful feeling it is."

Monsignor Vernon offered her a Kleenex, and a smile. "It's difficult, I know," he said softly. "Sometimes I think everything is topsy-turvy these days, and we're expected to give in to our children all the time."

"I know," Inez said, sniffling into the tissue and trying to regain control of herself. "But I was beginning to think I was the only one who thought so."

"You aren't," the Monsignor replied, "although sometimes I think there are very few of us left who refuse to be manipulated by our children."

Inez looked sharply at the priest. *Manipulated.* The same word Dr. Shields had used. "That's it exactly," she said. "I feel like I'm being manipulated by Judy. As if she's trying to punish me."

"And that's undoubtedly exactly what's going on," Monsignor Vernon said emphatically. "You have no idea what it can be like here." He turned his chair, gazing out the window as he talked. "I have to have my guard up all the time. They're smart, you know. Brighter than we were, when we were young. But it isn't a good kind of brightness. It's a clever kind of brightness. They're always testing me, pushing me, to see how far they can go before I crack down on them. It must be even worse in the public schools. They have so few controls anymore. Thank God the Church recognizes the function of discipline in the raising of children! But it gets harder each year. Every year, they strain me more. Every year, more of them try to corner me. Well, I don't intend to tolerate it! This year, the children will find out who runs this school, and they'll find out it isn't them!" He suddenly spun the chair around again, and seemed almost surprised to see Inez Nelson sitting opposite his desk. He had almost forgotten she was in the office, and that it was to her that he was talking. Now she sat very still, unnerved by the intensity with which he had spoken. He broke the moment with a quick smile. "I'm sorry," he said, chuckling a little. "Sometimes I get quite carried away. Well, what were we talking about?"

"Judy—" Inez said distractedly. "We were talking about Judy. Which brings me to the other thing I wanted to discuss with you. Dr. Shields tells me that she'll be fine by the end of the week, and that she can come back to school a week from today. Next Monday."

"I see," Monsignor Vernon said carefully, licking his lips nervously. Inez Nelson noticed the gesture immediately.

"That's right, isn't it?" she said quickly. "I mean, there isn't going to be any problem, is there?"

"Actually, I don't know," Monsignor Vernon said hesitantly. "I mean, we've never before been faced with something like this, and I haven't quite been able to find out what to do about it yet."

"Do about it?" Inez asked blankly. "What's there to do? I don't understand."

"Well," the priest said slowly, "it isn't really the same as if she'd simply been sick, is it? What she did comes very close to sacrilege. Judy will have to confess and be absolved before she can return to school."

"Before?" Inez asked. "Why before?"

"Because of the nature of her sin. You must be aware that suicide is one of the most grievous sins that a Catholic can commit. Only God can forgive it, not the Church."

Inez was suddenly alarmed. Was Judy to be excommunicated?

"But she didn't—" she began. "I mean, she didn't actually do anything, did she?" she asked desperately. "I mean, yes, I suppose she tried, but Dr. Shields says he doesn't think she really meant to kill herself, and in any case, she isn't dead, is she?"

Monsignor gave the distraught woman his most tolerant look. "I'm afraid that isn't the point. The point is that she did, indeed, intend the sin.

That she didn't succeed was only a matter of luck, not intent. And I'm sure you're aware that a sin intended is every bit as offensive to God as a sin committed."

Inez Nelson stared at him helplessly. "But what's going to happen to her?"

"I'm afraid I can't answer that. There are grave philosophical and theological questions involved. I simply haven't the answers yet. But I intend to put the entire case before my study group tonight, and I'm sure that among the six of us we'll be able to find the answer. The Lord, through St. Peter Martyr, will guide me."

He rose from behind his desk, and led Inez out of the office. As she was leaving, he called to her, and she turned back, her face pale and her eyes beseeching him. He raised his hand in the sign of the cross. "May the Lord bless you and keep you, may the Lord make his face to shine upon you, and give you peace."

But as she walked out of the school, and slowly made her way to the parking lot, Inez Nelson knew there was going to be no peace for her. For her, or her daughter, or anyone else in Neilsville. As she got into the car, a cloud passed over the sun. Summer had come to an abrupt end in Neilsville.

The final bell had rung, and the students had poured out of the classroom into the halls. All but Marilyn Crane. She sat alone in the room, except for Sister Elizabeth, who was straightening up her desk.

It had not been an easy day for Marilyn; if she had had her way she would not have come to school at all. But her mother had insisted, and Marilyn had dragged herself up the hill. It had seemed steeper today than ever before, and when she had finally reached the school she had had to force herself to go in. All through the day she had heard the snickers, and the whispers, as the story of her humiliation on Saturday night spread through the halls. Everybody had heard. Suddenly it wasn't just her own classmates who snubbed her and turned away at her approach. Now the younger children, the children who had always been at least a little respectful, were pointing at her and giggling together.

She tried to ignore it all, tried to do as Mr. Balsam had suggested, and pretend that nothing had happened. She had spent the entire day waiting for the final bell, and now it had rung. But she still didn't leave her desk. Instead, she stared miserably down at the paper that lay accusingly in front of her. It was a test and it was marked B-minus.

The grade itself wasn't really bad. What hurt most was the note penciled next to the grade. There, in Sister Elizabeth's flowing script, was the real condemnation: "This is very disappointing. I know you can do better."

Marilyn wanted to cry. What did they want from her? She tried, she knew she tried. But, once more, she had failed.

As she stared at the grade, and the note beside it, anger churned in her. She fought it back. After all, who was there to be angry at, besides herself? She was the one who had gotten the grade. She was the one who hadn't lived up to Sister Elizabeth's expectations. Her anger turned to frustration.

What *did* they want, anyway? And even if she knew, why should she live up to their expectations? Why should she?

Why should she do anything at all?

And then, realizing the magnitude of the thought that had just gone through her mind, she quickly begged forgiveness. She decided to go to church. Things were always better in the church. The Blessed Virgin didn't demand anything of her.

Marilyn gathered her things, and left the room. As she did, Sister Elizabeth glanced up, looked at her curiously, and decided something was wrong with Marilyn Crane. She made a mental note to discuss Marilyn with Monsignor Vernon. Monsignor would know what to do. Sister Elizabeth went back to her work and put Marilyn out of her mind.

Peter Balsam arrived at the rectory punctually at seven-thirty. He let himself in, picked up the small silver bell, and rang it. When there was no response, he walked down the hall and tapped lightly at the study door. It was opened immediately by a man he didn't recognize, but who seemed to know who he was.

"Peter Balsam," the man said, opening the door just wide enough for Peter to slip through. He held his fingers to his lips. "Monsignor is saying the blessing."

The study was dimly lit, and as Peter looked around he realized that of the six men gathered in the small room, the only one he recognized was Monsignor Vernon. All the others were strangers, but he had the distinct feeling that he was no stranger to them. They stared at him and he felt as if he were being measured—and found wanting. As he pondered the possible significance of this, Monsignor Vernon finished the blessing, and smiled at him.

"Peter," he said expansively, "let me introduce you to the Society." He took Peter by the elbow and introduced him to the members of the Society of St. Peter Martyr one by one. All were priests, and all were from parishes outside of Neilsville. But as the Monsignor introduced them Balsam realized that, though they were all considerably older than Vernon, they shared certain traits with him. There was a tightness to their faces, particularly to Father Bryant, whose expression seemed frozen in disapproval. Father Martinelli, the eldest of them all, peered out from deep-set eyes that were almost invisible under bushy brows. He grunted a greeting to Balsam, but there was a note of displeasure in it, as if he felt this introduction should not be taking place. Father Prine, gnarled with rheumatism, extended his hand, but pulled it painfully back before Peter could shake it. The other two, whose names Peter didn't catch, greeted him formally, but offered no particular welcomes.

When the introductions were completed, Monsignor Vernon invited Balsam to sit down. The chair near the fireplace, the one he had occupied every time he had been in the study, had been left vacant. He wondered briefly whether this was by design or coincidence, deciding that either way he was grateful for the familiar touch.

"I've heard a lot about you," he said to the group in general. They stared. Just as the silence was becoming uncomfortable, Father Prine spoke.

"And we've heard a lot about you." There was something in the voice that told Peter that not all they heard had been good.

"All bad, I suppose," he grinned. The humor was lost on the old priest, who turned dourly to Monsignor Vernon.

"You'll have to forgive us," the Monsignor said to Peter. "We are a closed group, and we observe strict rules about speaking. While you are among us, you will observe them, too. But you are not to consider yourself a member of the Society of St. Peter Martyr. Not yet, at any rate. Whether or not we decide to initiate you into our order will depend on many things."

Peter was about to challenge the priest's use of the word "order," but he remembered the sanction against questions. He felt his temper rising, and had to fight down an impulse to leave. He restrained himself. He had come to the rectory for a reason. Here, he might find out just exactly how it was that Monsignor Vernon had changed from the rather casual student Balsam remembered from the seminary into the rigid dogmatist he had become. And if Balsam was to make any kind of adjustment to St. Francis Xavier's, he needed to understand his superior. He fought down his impulse to leave and sat quietly in the chair by the fireplace.

And the questioning began.

The questions seemed simple enough, at first, and Peter soon began to feel like a child being put through the Catechism.

He was asked to repeat the Apostles' Creed.

He was examined about his knowledge of the Immaculate Conception.

But as the questioning continued, each of the priests taking his turn, Balsam realized that they wanted more of him than a simple statement of his knowledge of the beliefs of the Church. They were trying to determine if there were flaws in his faith; if there were areas in which he was not in agreement with the Doctrines.

"Do you accept the Church as the true vessel of the Word of God?"

"Do you accept the Infallibility of the Pope?"

"Did you leave the priesthood because of doubts as to the Faith, or only as to your vocation?"

The questions rang in his ears, and he began to find himself agreeing with everything they asked, telling them what he knew they wanted to hear, not because he wanted to please them, but because, as they droned on, the questions lost their meaning. He began to feel that they were not asking him for his own responses, which would have been too complicated and ambiguous to fit into the narrow structure of their questions. Instead, they were inundating him with their own beliefs, and taking reassurance as he reflected those beliefs back to them.

An hour went by. Peter began to realize that he was no longer hearing the questions, that they no longer made sense to him. He held up a hand.

"Wouldn't it be easier if I just talked?" he asked. "I know what you're driving at, but at this rate we'll be here all night."

Father Martinelli glared at him. "You know nothing," the old priest quavered. "Answer the questions, please. If we wish your comments we will ask for them."

The questioning continued.

And then it was over. As if an unseen signal had been passed among the priests, the questioning suddenly stopped. Peter searched the faces, one by one, trying to read in their expressions their reactions to his answers. The faces were impassive.

Then he heard Monsignor Vernon speaking.

"It's time we took up the discussion for tonight," he said softly. "Which is, of course, the problem of Judy Nelson."

Balsam was baffled. Judy Nelson? Why was she to be discussed here? What possible concern was she to this group? The answer came soon enough. For the next ten minutes, as Peter listened in silence, the priests discussed what penance should be placed on Judy when she returned to school. The question of whether or not she should be allowed to return at all was disposed of very quickly; since she had not put herself beyond redemption, she was to be brought back into the fold. But the question of penance was not so easily resolved. Finally, as the discussion seemed to be getting nowhere, Peter interrupted.

"Don't you think it might be a good idea to talk to Judy before you decide on anything?" he suggested. Father Martinelli gazed at him with a detached curiosity.

"Not relevant," the ancient voice crackled. "Of what possible interest could anything she might say be to us?"

Peter was astounded. "It seems to me that it might be wise to find out why she did it, before you began handing down penances," he said.

"Nonsense," Father Bryant snapped. "Her motivations are of no concern to us. She has sinned, and in the eyes of the Church, it is the sin that matters, not the motivations of the sinner."

The five other priests nodded solemn agreement.

Balsam started to get to his feet. "Then you really have no need for me, do you? I'm a psychologist, not a priest, and certainly not a judge."

"Sit down," Monsignor Vernon said. Peter sat. "You are here for a reason. We have found, over the years, that a strictly structured examination of our own faiths has often served to reinforce that faith. That is what we have provided you with. But you are also here to discuss a specific problem that we don't feel qualified to handle."

Six pairs of eyes bored into Peter's. No one spoke until Peter broke the silence.

"What problem?" he asked.

Father Prine took over now.

"We are concerned for the safety of our children," he said, his voice muted but steady. "We can see no reason why young Judy shouldn't be allowed to return to school, yet we feel that somehow the other children must be protected from whatever——" He groped for the word, then found one he seemed reluctant to use. "——whatever evil is lurking in Judy."

Balsam wanted to tell the old priest that he was certain there was no "evil" lurking in Judy, that she was simply the victim of some psychological problems. He knew it was useless. It was not what they wanted to hear. He addressed himself instead to the thrust of the question.

"I'm not sure what could be done," he said slowly, "I mean, short of isolating Judy—and that would simply focus attention on the whole situation. It seems to me that the best thing to do is try to act as if nothing had happened, and hope things settle down of their own accord."

The priests appeared to be pondering the wisdom of this course. Finally Monsignor Vernon broke the silence.

"I wonder," he began. "I heard about something, or read about it. Relaxation therapy, I think it was called."

Peter Balsam's attention was suddenly riveted on the priest. Where had he ever heard of relaxation therapy? But the Monsignor didn't notice the sudden tension in the teacher, and continued talking, softly, reasonably.

"I was just wondering if it could be of any possible use in this situation. The students have been pretty keyed up lately. Do you think there's any way we could use this relaxation therapy to calm them down? Before Judy comes back next week, I mean?"

Balsam's mind was suddenly racing. There was danger here, but he couldn't define it. All he could put his finger on was the incongruity of the priest's suggestion. Of all people, Vernon was the last one Peter would have expected to suggest the use of what was, at best, an experimental process. His instincts told him to move carefully.

"I don't know," he said honestly enough. "I'm afraid I don't know much about the process, and from what I've read, I don't think it would accomplish much."

"But you don't know?" Father Bryant pressed.

"No," Peter said reluctantly. "I don't."

"In fact," Monsignor Vernon said, "it might indeed help them, mightn't it?"

Peter felt suddenly trapped. "I suppose it might," he admitted.

"Well, then," the priest said affably. "Why don't we leave it at this? You sleep on it, and do whatever you think best." He stood up, and Peter realized he was being dismissed. "I want to thank you for coming tonight. I think it's been good for all of us."

It wasn't until the door closed quietly behind him that Peter was sure his part in the meeting was over. Confused, he stood in the hallway for a moment, then, as he began to walk slowly toward the front door of the rectory, he heard the chanting begin. It was soft at first, then grew louder. Gregorian chanting, but somehow slightly wrong. As he left the rectory, Peter Balsam attributed the peculiar sound of the chanting to the fact that the participants were old, and their voices had weakened with age.

But as he walked slowly down Cathedral Hill, the sound of the chanting stayed with him, ringing in his head, imbedding itself in his mind.

He tried to figure out just what the Society of St. Peter Martyr was all about. He was sure it wasn't the simple "study group" Monsignor had claimed it to be. No, it was something else. He racked his memory. "Order." They had called it an order. Surely, in this day and age, they weren't attempting to begin a new order, one tied to the memory of a thirteenth-century inquisitor? That was absurd.

And there was something else that bothered him, something he thought about long after he got home that night. As he was drifting off to sleep, it came to him. The Society of St. Peter Martyr had not acted like any "study group" he knew of. No, the Society of St. Peter Martyr had acted like a tribunal.

Peter Balsam found it very disturbing. When he slept his dreams were filled with the sound of chanting, and the strange, intolerant visages of the members of the Society of St. Peter Martyr.

# THIRTEEN

A S HIS CLASS BEGAN DRIFTING INTO Room 16, Peter Balsam realized that he had been anticipating this hour all morning. His mind had been on his Latin classes even less than usual. The Latin students had sensed his distraction, and had taken advantage of it, spending the previous three hours mistranslating their lessons, winking at each other every time he failed to catch their deliberate errors, and passing the word, one class to the next, that today was a good day in Mr. Balsam's class—anything went! By fourth period, the psychology students were looking forward even more than usual to their offbeat class, and they came into Room 16 carrying an air of anticipation. It was almost as if they knew that Balsam had been lax with the other classes because he had something special planned for them.

Now, as the classroom slowly filled, Balsam had a sudden feeling of trepidation, his first such feeling since the decision had come to him. What he was about to do was an experiment, and an experiment he was unfamiliar with. He had gotten up early this morning, filled with a sense of purpose, and reviewed what little material he could find on the subject of relaxation technique, quickly realizing it was little more than a very light form of hypnosis, a period of induced relaxation, using both music and the human voice to put the subjects—a word Balsam hated—into a state resembling light sleep. Almost light sleep, but not quite. The music would be important and he had made his selection carefully from his limited collection of records and tapes. Feeling inspired, he had chosen religious music, a recording of Gregorian chants made by a small order of nuns in France. If the chanting of the Society of St. Peter Martyr the previous evening had put the suggestion into his head, he was unconscious of it. He busied himself setting up the record player as the last of his students hurried into the room.

The last to come in were Karen Morton and Marilyn Crane. Though they entered the room together, it was obvious to Balsam that it was only a matter of coincidence. Marilyn seemed almost unaware that anyone else was in the room. And Karen completely ignored Marilyn as she walked slowly toward the front row of desks. This morning she didn't seat herself immediately; instead, she piled her books on top of the desk, and approached Balsam, a little smile playing around the corners of her mouth. Balsam had a distinct feeling that she was about to play some kind of a game with him, and decided to end it before it got started.

"Take your seat, please, Karen," he said shortly, not seeing the hurt look that came over her at his rebuff. "We're already late getting started, and there's a lot I want to accomplish today." Then he turned his attention back to the class, and particularly to Marilyn Crane, who had moved lifelessly to her usual place at the back of the room.

As he finished setting up the sound system, Balsam began explaining what relaxation technique was all about, without telling them what he hoped to accomplish with it. He was afraid that if they knew he was planning more for them than a simple experiment, their guard would be up, and they wouldn't be responsive to the technique. A hand went up in the front row, Janet Connally's.

"Janet?"

"I'm not sure I understand," Janet said slowly. Then she grinned mischievously. "I mean, it sounds like I might fall asleep."

Balsam returned her grin. "You might," he agreed. "But don't worry about it. Today marks a momentous event at St. Francis Xavier's. Sleeping in class is permitted. In fact, a lot of you might wind up snoring through this whole thing, so let's get rid of the desks. Let's push them all over against the walls, and make enough room so everybody can lie down on the floor. If we're going to relax, we might as well go all the way."

The class exchanged looks, startled, then quickly began moving the furniture. When the job was half-complete, the door suddenly opened, and Monsignor Vernon appeared, his eyes quickly taking in the activity in the room. The activity stopped. It was almost as if someone had suddenly thrown a switch, and the motion had frozen. But instead of asking what was going on, the priest simply stared at Balsam, smiled briefly, and disappeared again.

When the door was safely shut, the clearing of the furniture continued.

There was a lot of giggling and whispering as the class settled itself on the floor, and Balsam didn't try to stop it. He wanted them to be relaxed, and if giggling and whispering would help, that was fine with him.

"All right," he said when they seemed as settled as they were going to be, "let's begin. I'm going to put on some music, and I want you to let yourselves float with it. As I said earlier, don't worry about falling asleep. There's no better relaxation than sleep, and that's what this is all about."

He set the needle on the record, and the music began. At the first notes, another wave of giggling went over the class, but it soon subsided. Slowly, one by one, each of the students succumbed to the persistent rhythm and monotony of the chanting. Balsam walked among them and saw that their eyes were closed. One or two of them were displaying that odd flutter of the eyelids that comes with light sleep. He began talking to them, telling them to become aware of their breathing, to imagine with each breath that they were sinking into the floor. Deeper and deeper into the floor. Breathe evenly. Listen to the music. Sink into the floor. Deeper. Deeper . . .

He went back to the front of the room and was about to continue when once more the door opened, and Monsignor Vernon came silently into the room. This time he was not alone. Behind him, the Society of St. Peter Martyr filed into Room 16. Almost before Balsam was aware of what was happening, the six priests ranged along the back wall, silent observers of whatever was about to happen.

Balsam looked quickly at the class; none of them had noticed the intrusion of the elderly clerics and their young leader. Their breathing remained even and deep, their eyes closed. Balsam began turning the volume of the music down, until it was an almost imperceptible background. And then, trying to keep his voice on an even tone that wouldn't interrupt the state of near-trance that had come over the class, he began to speak.

"Relaxation," he began, "is a technique designed to relieve internal pressures through the release of physical pressures. Basically, it helps us the way sleep does. But in simple relaxation, we try to put our bodies in a state almost resembling sleep while we let our conscious minds roam about, sorting out our anxieties and dissipating them harmlessly. What we are doing today is a little like lying in a hammock on a sunny afternoon, daydreaming. Daydreams, which we may think are just idle fantasies, are really much more. They're a means of bolstering our own identities, or reinforcing ourselves against the everyday pressures of life." He glanced quickly over the class, noting that so far nothing had disturbed any of the students. Jim Mulvey was snoring gently. Vaguely amused, Balsam wondered if any of the students were hearing him. He glanced at the back wall, where the Society stood impassively listening. Then he continued his lecture.

"Though we may sometimes feel that daydreaming is a waste of time, psychologists have known for years that it's a very important means of releasing pressures. It's a sort of safety valve. The human mind, of course, has developed many safety valves. One you're all familiar with is dreaming. Dreaming is really the unconscious mind clearing up the debris it has been otherwise unable to cope with. Daydreaming is similar, except that it occurs on the conscious level."

The class was still quiet, but the Society had shifted its attention. Their interest had moved to the class. They seemed particularly intent on two of the girls: Karen Morton and Marilyn Crane.

Feeling strangely uneasy, Balsam stepped up the pace of his talk.

"Occasionally," he went on, "the safety valves the mind builds for itself fail to operate. When this happens, we begin to see all kinds of things happen, as the mind attempts to cope with its problems. Things like nervous tics develop, or a person becomes unable to concentrate. Or irrational behavior can begin to occur. Some people, when their safety valves fail to relieve internal pressure, begin scratching themselves, almost uncontrollably.

Balsam heard a faint rustling sound in the room and tried to pinpoint where it had come from. Karen Morton seemed to be fumbling in her purse. Then she settled down again. The members of the Society of St. Peter Martyr still stood impassively against the back wall. If they were listening to him as intently as Balsam suspected, they showed no outward signs of it. He tried to pick up his train of thought.

"Sometimes," he continued, keeping his voice low, "all of our safety valves malfunction, and when this happens the results can be very serious indeed. The end result, of course, can be self-destructiveness."

With a shock Balsam realized what he had just said, and stopped abruptly. His eyes went to the dour faces of the Society. Now, instead of the almost blank expressions they had been wearing, they were staring at him with an intensity that almost frightened him. He was getting too close to the sort of thing the Society would brand as heresy, and Peter Balsam ranged around in his mind for a way out. He found it almost too easily.

"The Church," he continued smoothly, "has recognized this for centuries, long before the social sciences began to study the mechanisms of the human mind. From its very inception, the Church has realized the importance of releasing the pressures, and problems that can impair the functioning of the mind. To provide a mechanism for the release of pressure, the Church instituted the ritual of the confessional." He glanced quickly at the six priests and was relieved to see that they had resumed their impassivity. Then, as Balsam continued his lecture on the function of the confessional in the psychological health of those who used it properly, Monsignor Vernon smiled encouragingly at him, and led the five elderly priests out of Room 16. When they were gone, Balsam felt a sudden surge of relief. He continued his lecture, only now he felt free to concentrate on what he felt was the area of primary importance. He talked to them about Judy Nelson, and this time he was sure that his lecture would not be interrupted.

He told them that what had happened to Judy was simply a matter of too much pressure having been allowed to build up, with no release. When it had become too much for her to bear, she had behaved irrationally—she had become self-destructive. He tried to tell them that Judy was more to be pitied than blamed, and then, as he continued talking softly, he urged them to do their best to be kind to her when she returned to school, to try to understand and not to dwell on the details of what she had done.

He glanced at the clock, and saw that only ten minutes of the hour remained. He turned to the sound system, and quickly changed the record. The soft chanting was replaced by the discordant sounds of acid rock. Gradually, he began turning the volume up, until the room was filled with the vibrant sounds of the music. Soon a stirring was noticeable in the room, as the class began to come out of their almost stuporous state and become aware of their surroundings.

All of them, that is, except one.

Marilyn Crane, a strange look on her face, her eyes wide open and her mouth hanging slack, had risen to her knees. Her hands were clasped before her, and as the class stared, she began to pray.

* * *

Karen Morton noticed the blood on her hands while she was opening her locker. It was just a slight stickiness at first, and she would have ignored it except that when she removed her fingers from the lock, the brilliant redness of fresh blood remained. That was when she looked at the palms of her hands.

The odd part was that it didn't hurt, and she didn't know how she had done it. There, in the center of each palm, the skin was broken, and the flesh had a strange pulpy look as if she had been gouging at it. She glanced around to see if anybody had noticed her, but no one was near. She pulled a Kleenex out of her purse, and hastily wiped the stains off her locker. Then she hurried toward the stairs, wanting to get downstairs to the restroom before anybody saw that she was bleeding and asked for an explanation.

Safe inside the restroom, Karen examined the wounds closely. She felt something hard in one of them, and washed her hands carefully. When the blood was gone, she held up the injured hand and found something stuck in the wound. She worked it carefully loose, and rinsed it off. It was the broken point of a pencil. She washed both hands once more, dried them, and searched her purse. There, at the bottom, was a pencil, covered with blood, its point broken off. Sometime during the hour, she realized, she had fished the pencil out of her purse, and begun gouging herself with it. But she had no memory of any of it; none whatsoever.

She burrowed further into her purse and found a couple of battered Band-Aids she had been carrying around with her for months. She stripped the wrappers off and began applying them to her injured hands. It was while she was applying the Band-Aids that the pain began. It was very slight, at first, but quickly searing sensations began to shoot up her arms. By the time she had finished with the makeshift bandaging, Karen had made up her mind. She was going home for the rest of the day. She told no one where she was going, or why. She simply left the restroom, walked up the stairs, and out of the building. For the rest of the afternoon she worried about what had happened to her. As the afternoon wore on, Karen Morton became increasingly frightened.

"Marilyn?" Peter Balsam asked when he saw that there was no one left in Room 16 but himself and the girl. She gave no sign that she had heard. "Marilyn?"

Slowly her head swung around, and she stared at him in silence for a long time. Then her lips began to move, but no words formed.

"I saw her," she whispered finally, with a great deal of effort. "I saw her."

"Saw her?" Balsam repeated, baffled. "Saw who?"

And suddenly Marilyn was smiling, her face taking on a look of radiance that almost transformed her homeliness into beauty.

"The Virgin," she whispered. "I saw the Blessed Virgin. She came to me!"

"It's all right," Balsam said soothingly. He tried to keep his voice steady, but he felt his stomach lurch. Something had gone wrong; Marilyn had not come out of the semi-trance along with the rest of the class, and there was no one to turn to for help. Telling himself to stay calm, he decided to try to talk her back into reality.

"What did you see?" he asked quietly.

"She was beautiful," Marilyn said dreamily. "Only she wasn't smiling at me. It was as if she was in pain. And then, while I was watching her, she showed me her hands. They were bleeding. It—it was as if she had been—as if she had been—" She trailed off, unable to say the word.

"Crucified?" Peter Balsam asked softly. Marilyn nodded mutely.

"What does it mean?" she asked him, and for the first time Balsam was sure she was aware of his presence. "She was trying to tell me something, I know she was, but I couldn't figure out what it was. What was she trying to tell me?"

Balsam took Marilyn's hand and held it gently. "It's all right," he said soothingly. "It's all over now. You fell asleep and dreamed. That's all."

"No," Marilyn objected, pulling her hand out of his. "I know I wasn't asleep. I heard everything you were saying. You were talking about safety valves, and releases, and what happens when the safety valves don't work. And that's when she came to me. But I still heard you. You went on talking, and the priests of the Sanhedrin were here, listening to you, and watching the Sorrowful Mother, and then they went away. And then you talked about Judy Nelson, and the Virgin went away too. I know I wasn't asleep, Mr. Balsam. I *know* it." Marilyn stood up and began putting the room in order, and Balsam realized that whatever had happened, it was over now. But what had happened? Marilyn, at least, had been aware of the six priests' presence. He decided to probe a little further.

"You saw the priests?" he asked her. Marilyn nodded emphatically.

"The priests of the Sanhedrin. The Jews who condemned our Lord. They were here, six of them, and they were watching the Sorrowful Mother. But she wasn't paying any attention to them. She wanted to talk to me. But I don't know why."

Balsam wondered if he should tell Marilyn that the priests she had seen were very real. No, it would probably only upset the girl more. Instead, he decided to try to convince her that it was nothing but a dream.

"There was no one here, Marilyn," he assured her. "What happened was simply a mixture of a dream and reality. It isn't uncommon. With part of your mind you're aware of what's going on around you, but part of your mind is drifting. And things start to get mixed up. The real world gets mixed into your dream, and your dream seems all the more real."

"But it wasn't a dream," Marilyn insisted. "I know it wasn't a dream. I saw the Blessed Virgin, and her hands were bleeding!" Then, seeing the disbelief in Peter Balsam's face, she ran from the room, as if leaving his skepticism would confirm the reality of what she had seen.

Alone in Room 16, a deeply disturbed Peter Balsam sat thinking. A few minutes later he reluctantly concluded that he must discuss the incident with Monsignor Vernon.

*   *   *

Balsam wasn't surprised when he found the Society of St. Peter Martyr gathered in Monsignor Vernon's office. It was as if they had expected him, and when he entered the office they rose as one to greet him. As usual, the Monsignor acted the spokesman.

"Well, Peter," he said, smiling almost warmly. "We are pleased with the way you handled your class today."

Balsam smiled wryly. It was odd indeed that he was finally receiving praise for the one class that had gone totally wrong.

"I'm afraid I handled it very badly," he said. Monsignor Vernon looked at him questioningly, and Balsam related as well as he could what had happened to Marilyn Crane. The priests listened in silence. When Balsam finished they looked to Monsignor Vernon. The priest frowned as he thought over the implications of the odd incident.

"It would appear that Marilyn thinks she's had a religious experience," he said carefully.

Balsam nodded. "I tried to explain to her that it was much more likely that she simply fell asleep, but she wouldn't listen. And the more I think about it, the more worried I get."

"Worried?"

"I've been thinking about Marilyn and her entire personality structure," Balsam began. But before he could finish his thoughts, the Monsignor interrupted him.

"Marilyn's always been one of our best students, and one of our most religious ones, too."

"I'm sure she has," Balsam said dryly. "But I wonder how much of it is real."

"Real?" Vernon repeated. "I'm not sure what you mean."

"Marilyn doesn't seem to be a very well-balanced child. She has practically no friends, and the other kids shun her. It's almost as if they take a malicious pleasure in making her feel bad." He told them what had happened at the party the previous Saturday night. They listened, again in silence. "If you want my opinion," Balsam finished, "Marilyn uses her studies and her religion as an escape. Since she isn't particularly well accepted by her peers, she chooses to get her acceptance from her teachers and the Church."

"Is that so bad?" Father Bryant asked. "There are worse ways to compensate."

Balsam shrugged. "There are all kinds of ways to compensate, and I'm certainly not about to suggest that Marilyn has picked unhealthy ones. But any compensation, carried to an extreme, is unhealthy."

"I see," Monsignor Vernon said slowly. "You believe Marilyn's faith is questionable. You believe that what she thinks she saw this afternoon stemmed from—what?—hysteria?"

"I think it's possible," Balsam said, glad that the priest seemed to understand it so well. But then the Monsignor's expression changed, and the cold light that Balsam had come to recognize shone in his eyes—the cold light of his religious fanaticism.

"I disagree," he said flatly. "I've seen this sort of thing before. She's clever, you know. A very bright child. This is nothing more than an attempt to manipulate us. All of us. You, me, her friends, the sisters, everyone. Mark my words, an investigation of this matter will prove me right. You may call it hysteria if you wish. To me it is nothing more than a very clever kind of manipulation. It is out of wariness born of experience that the Church has set up machinery to investigate just such phenomena as Marilyn Crane claims to have experienced." And then, as quickly as the light of fanaticism had come into the Monsignor's eyes, it was gone. Suddenly he was smiling genially at a horrified Peter Balsam.

"It really isn't anything to worry about," he said now, the hardness in his voice gone. "Things like this happen all the time. I imagine that Marilyn will forget all about it by the end of the day. And if she doesn't, I'll have a talk with her." Then he paused for a moment, as if a thought had occurred to him. "And we mustn't forget," he said softly, "there's always the chance that the Blessed Virgin did visit Marilyn."

## FOURTEEN

PETER BALSAM HEARD HIS FRONT DOOR open, and called from the kitchen. "I'm in here, throwing together something that I hope won't poison us. Come in and fix us some drinks, will you?"

"I'm already here," Margo Henderson replied from the doorway. She surveyed the suit he was still wearing with distaste. "One of these days we're going to Seattle again, just to get you a new suit. Why don't you change? Just looking at you makes me feel uncomfortable."

"Can't," Peter said, grinning at her. Now that she was there, he was beginning to feel a little better. But not much; the grin faded. "I have to go to a meeting tonight, and it isn't the kind of meeting where you show up in jeans and a tee-shirt."

"As if you owned such things in the first place," Margo commented as she pried a tray of ice loose from the freezer. "What's the big meeting?"

"You won't approve," Peter said. He wrestled with a can opener, then helplessly handed the mangled soup can, together with the opener, to Margo. "It's the Society of St. Peter Martyr."

Margo glanced at him briefly as she took the can and completed the job Peter had botched. "I thought you were all through with them," she said levelly.

"I didn't say that," Peter hedged.

"No?" Margo's eyebrows arched. "Strange. That's the distinct impression I got last night."

Peter looked at her sharply. "Last night? I didn't talk to you last night."

"Of course you did," Margo said. "All right, so it was early this morning, if you want to get technical. But I call anything before dawn 'last night.'" Then, seeing the look on Peter's face, she frowned. "You really don't remember, do you?"

"There's nothing to remember," Peter declared. "I came home from the meeting, went to bed around eleven, and slept all night. I thought about calling you, but decided not to; it was too late."

Margo finished with the can, then mixed drinks for both of them before she spoke again. As she handed Peter his scotch-and-water, she looked at him carefully, trying to decide if he was playing some kind of a joke on her. She decided he wasn't.

"Well then," she said, biting her lower lip speculatively, "you've taken up some rather odd habits. Do you always make phone calls in your sleep? Because you *did* call me last night."

Peter searched his memory, but could find no recollection of any such thing the previous night. He felt a slight knot of fear in his stomach, but fought it down. "What did I say?" he asked, trying to keep his voice light. "Was I interesting?"

"No," Margo said shortly, "you weren't. All you said was that you'd gone to the meeting of that silly society of Monsignor's and that you weren't going back."

"Did I call it 'that silly society,' or are you editorializing?"

The smile crept back to Margo's face. "All right, so I didn't quote you exactly. If you want to know, I don't recall your exact words. I mean, it was late, and I was asleep and, well, you know how groggy people can get in the middle of the night. Anyway, I got the definite impression that you were not impressed with Monsignor and his funny friends."

"Funny friends?" Peter repeated. "I don't suppose those were my exact words either, were they?"

"No," Margo said again, beginning to feel exasperated, "they weren't. But if you ask me, any friends of Monsignor's have to be funny."

"I wish they were," Peter replied in a tone Margo found suddenly disturbing. "But I'm not sure there's anything funny about them at all." Briefly, he told her about the meeting of the Society the previous night, and the events of the afternoon. Margo listened to him carefully, and when he was finished she shook her head.

"But why do you want to go back again tonight?" she asked. "It seems to me you'd want to stay out of the whole thing."

"I don't know," Peter mused, as if trying to explain his feelings to himself as well as to her. "I can't figure out what they're up to. But I know they're up to something. Last night, just before I left their meeting, Monsignor Vernon told me I had been invited for a reason—to have my faith reinforced. And he was right. When I woke up this morning, I felt much better than I did last night."

"Better about what?" Margo asked.

Peter shrugged. "The Church. Until this morning I was almost ready to throw the towel in on the whole thing. But this morning I felt different. I felt I'd missed something, that there was something, somewhere, that would make everything clear to me. And I think that something may just be in the Society. Anyway, I decided I have to give it a chance." He smiled at Margo, hoping to erase the look of concern that had come over her face. "I don't see what harm it can do, and it might answer a lot of my questions."

Margo looked doubtful. When she spoke, skepticism edged her voice. "A miraculous transformation, Peter? Something happened to you last night, because you've certainly changed your tune."

"A man can change his mind," Peter said, trying to keep his voice light.

"Or have it changed for him," Margo pointed out. Silently, she decided to be waiting for Peter when he returned home that night.

He was let into the study, as the previous night, by one of the old priests—Father Martinelli, if he remembered correctly—and once again found Monsignor Vernon deep in prayer. But the room looked different to Peter Balsam, and he soon realized why. Tonight no lights were on. The curtains had been drawn tightly shut. The only illumination was provided by a fire glowing in the fireplace and tall red candles placed around the room. Seven chairs had been carefully arranged in a semicircle around the fireplace—the two large comfortable chairs and five others. Monsignor Vernon was kneeling at one of the chairs, using it as a makeshift prie-dieu. The other chair, opposite the one Monsignor Vernon knelt at, was waiting for Peter Balsam. He took the chair silently, steeling himself for another inquisition.

But tonight it was different. There was no discussion before the ritual got under way. Instead, as soon as Monsignor Vernon finished the silent prayers, the chanting began. The Monsignor led it, and with each phrase one of the other old priests joined in, the sound swelling until all the ancient clerics were chanting out the cadences.

At first Peter Balsam wondered if he was expected to join the chanting, but as he listened he realized that he couldn't participate: the phrases were unfamiliar. As he tried to follow the words, he discovered that it was not the thinness of the voices that made the chanting unintelligible; it was the language, a tongue sufficiently like Latin to sound familiar, but different enough—twisted enough, Peter thought with a shiver—to remain beyond his grasp.

As the cadences mounted, surrounding him, invading him, Peter Balsam felt his mind begin to wander. The fire flickering on the hearth almost seemed to recede into the distance, and the dancing shadows of the shimmering candles cast strange images on the walls. He began to feel as if he was being transported back in time to another age, an age where faith alone could transport a man into raptures.

Images began flitting through his head. His eyes, almost closed, drifted from one face to another, but instead of the five elderly priests and the youthful Monsignor, Peter Balsam saw the faces of ancient saints come suddenly to life. They were smiling on him and beckoning to him. A feeling of camaraderie came over him, and Peter Balsam happily gave himself over to the companionship of the small group.

Some time later, he became vaguely aware that the chanting had stopped, and that the Society was now involved in responsive prayers. He was dimly aware of Monsignor Vernon's voice, resonating softly through the room, and the thin, reedy voices of the five elderly priests as they made the responses. He tried to concentrate on the words, but, like the chanting, they were in a not-quite-Latin that he was unable to translate. Yet, like the chanting, the prayers held an insistent rhythm, a rhythm that grew, bearing a spiritual message that was very clear: Peter Balsam, the steady intonations seemed to whisper, you are in the presence of God. Be humbled, Peter. And be comforted.

And he was. As the rhythms overcame him once more, Peter Balsam uttered a silent prayer of thanksgiving to be part of this wondrous ceremony.

Time almost stopped for him then, and his thoughts ceased to flow as he gave himself up to the religious experience that was unfolding around him. As he sank deeper and deeper into a state of trance, his senses sharpened. He felt the searing heat from each individual candle; the tongues of fire on the hearth seemed to be licking at his feet. He heard the voice of the Devil calling out to him in his head, and tried to close out the beckoning whispers. He began to feel the heat of hell glowing around him, and as his discomfort grew he became frightened. And then, as he felt himself being drawn downward, he felt the hands of angels upon him. He was suddenly cooler, and his mind's eye saw the fires receding into the distance. As the angelic hands caressed him, he felt a calm come over him, and he began silently repeating the Acts of Faith and Contrition. Slowly, his ecstasy grew.

The fire still burned in the fireplace, as high as it had when the evening had begun. The candles were shorter, but how much shorter he couldn't discern. Around him, the six priests were gathered, sitting calmly, almost expectantly, in their chairs, watching him. Peter Balsam had no idea what time it was, nor how long he had been closeted in the study with the six priests. He discovered, to his own fascination, that he was not thinking about the ceremony at all; instead, he was almost entirely possessed by a feeling of fulfillment, as if he had, somehow, received answers to questions that he could not now even formulate. And he was tired, with the weariness of a man who had just run several miles. Somewhere in the back of his mind a memory stirred, then disappeared.

He wondered if he was expected to speak. He looked from one face to another, and for the first time tonight saw each of the priests distinctly. In the warm glow of the candlelight the gnarled old faces took on a kind of beauty, and Peter Balsam realized that there was a gentleness in these men that he had not seen before. They were smiling at him, and he returned their smiles.

"Welcome," Father Martinelli said softly.

"Welcome?" Peter repeated, just as softly. Suddenly, it was a word of many and marvelous meanings.

"We are glad to have you among us," Father Prine murmured.

Monsignor Vernon nodded agreement. "Once again we are seven. Now we can continue our work."

Balsam frowned slightly. "Work?" he asked. "What work?"

Monsignor Vernon shook his head. "No questions," he said quietly. "Not now."

The meeting of the Society of St. Peter Martyr was over. Peter Balsam had become a part of the Society.

He walked back to his apartment slowly, savoring the night air, and the first feelings of true peace that he had felt in a long time, certainly since he had come to Neilsville. He breathed deeply of the warm, dry air, and looked to the sky in search of the stars he felt should have been there. The sky was black, except for a pale, almost ghostly glow where the full moon far above the clouds shone weakly through the mists. By the time Peter Balsam reached his home, the rain had begun to fall.

Light glared in the living room, hurting his eyes. Squinting, he stepped inside, then drew back. Margo was lying on the couch, sound asleep, an open book sprawled across her breast. While he was wondering whether to wake her, her eyes popped open, and she jumped off the couch.

"What are you—" she began. Then she glanced wildly around and sank back down on the sofa.

"What am I doing here?" Peter asked, grinning at her. "I live here, remember?"

She looked up at him sheepishly. "I'm sorry," she said. "I was going to be here waiting for you, all bright-eyed and bushy-tailed, and dying to hear all about what happened at that meeting. So what do I do? I fall asleep. What time is it?"

Peter suddenly realized he didn't have the vaguest idea what time it was. When he looked at his watch, he wasn't sure he believed it.

"That can't be right," he muttered, holding the watch up to his ear.

Margo looked at him quizzically. "What can't?" she said. "What time is it?"

Peter sank down on the couch beside her. "My watch says three o'clock," he breathed. "But it can't be. I was only gone an hour or so."

Margo looked at him speculatively. "You've been gone seven hours, Peter," she said calmly. "What happened?"

"I don't know," Peter said blankly. He tried to explain to Margo what had transpired at the rectory that evening, but in the telling none of it made sense. It all sounded like a dream, like disconnected fragments out of some religious fantasy. Margo listened to the story quietly.

"Why don't you go get out of those clothes?" she said when he'd finished. "They look like they've been slept in. I'll put on some coffee and we'll try again." She grinned at him mischievously. "So far, it all sounds exactly like what I thought it would be. A bunch of silliness." But inside, she was more concerned than she had shown.

As she put the kettle on, Margo wondered if she was making a mistake. Perhaps Peter wasn't what he seemed to be. Perhaps he wasn't the nice, simple, rather straightforward person she had become so fond of. She spooned instant coffee into two mugs and tried to clear the last remnants of sleep from her mind while the water came to a boil.

A few minutes later, as she started into the living room with the two steaming mugs, Peter appeared in the doorway, his face pale.

"Margo—" he began.

She set the cups down quickly, and hurried to him. "Peter, what is it?"

"I don't know," Peter gasped. "When I took off my shirt, I—" He broke off again and unconsciously touched the belt of his robe.

"What *is* it?" Margo said, more urgently. He clutched his robe tighter around his torso, and stared at her, wild-eyed. Peter was frightened. Very frightened. She moved closer to him.

"Let me see, Peter," she said gently. His hands fell to his sides, and he let her untie the cord around his waist. Then she opened the robe, and let it fall to the floor.

On Peter's back, from his shoulders to his waist, were angry red welts. Though the skin was not broken, the marks had swollen and stood out in painful relief from the pale whiteness of his back.

"My God," Margo breathed. "What happened?"

Peter shook his head mutely. "I don't know," he said. And then the full horror of it struck him. He began shaking. And with the shaking came the tears.

"I don't know, Margo," he sobbed. "And that's the worst of it. I don't know where they came from!"

"They did something to you," Margo kept insisting. "While you were in that trance, or whatever it was, they did something to you."

Balsam shook his head in despair. "They couldn't have," he repeated yet again. "I would have remembered it. I wasn't unconscious. I was in some kind of odd state, I know, but I was conscious of my surroundings."

"But you thought you were gone only an hour or two, and it was seven hours. *Seven hours,* Peter! If you really remember everything that happened, how could you have lost five or six hours?"

"I don't know," Peter said helplessly. "I suppose something happens to your time sense when you go into a trance. But I know I wasn't unconscious. I know it."

As the dawn came, they gave it up. They were both too tired to retrace the same ground. Peter went to the window, and watched the sun rise slowly over Neilsville. The clouds had gone, but there was a heaviness in the air that said they would be back soon. Peter turned back to Margo.

"You'd better go," he said. "It's awfully late."

She nodded dully. "I know." Her voice was lifeless. She looked at his tired eyes and she wanted to put her arms around him, to feel his arms around her. "Oh, Peter," she said, the words choking her a little. "What are we going to do?"

He tried to smile at her, but the attempt failed. "I don't know," he said. Then a touch of irony crept into his voice. "I don't seem to know much of anything, do I?"

Now she did go to him and put her arms around him. "Yes, you do," she said softly. "There's an explanation for all this. And we'll find it. Really we will."

Peter wanted to believe her; he told himself that he did. But inside, he wasn't sure. Inside, he was terribly frightened, and terribly alone.

He sent Margo on her way, then sat for an hour, trying to fight off the sleep he was suddenly afraid of. At seven o'clock he called the school and told them that he had become ill in the night, and would not be in today. Then he went to bed and spent the day sleeping—and dreaming. In the dreams, there were many explanations of the strange marks on his back. But when he woke up every now and then, none of them made sense. Or maybe they did.

## FIFTEEN

"**Y**OU LOOK LIKE HELL."

Dr. Shields stared at Margo and motioned her into a chair.

"I feel like hell," she admitted. "I was up all night."

The psychiatrist put the report he had been reading into the top drawer of the desk, and leaned back in his chair.

"Peter Balsam?" he asked.

Margo nodded mutely, then, reluctantly, began telling him about the discussion with Peter that had kept her up all night. At first the psychiatrist listened in silence. Then, as she continued her story, he began interrupting her with questions. When she was finished, he sat with his hands folded in front of him, lost in thought.

"Do you want some advice, or did you just want to talk it out?" he asked finally.

Margo shrugged helplessly. "I don't really know. If you have any advice, I suppose I might as well hear it."

The doctor nodded noncommittally, then looked sharply at Margo. "Just how much does Peter Balsam mean to you?"

"I don't know," Margo said dully. "A lot, I thought. But after last night, I'm not so sure. The whole thing sounds so weird, I'm not sure I want to be involved at all."

"Well, it's not that bad," Dr. Shields said gently. "After all, you aren't involved with his problems. Yet."

"Yet?" she repeated.

"Yet. I mean, so far, everything that's happened to Balsam has only happened to him. Any time you get too uncomfortable with it, all you have to do is stop seeing him."

"But I'm not sure I want to do that. I want to know what's happening, before I make the decision. Does that make any sense?"

Dr. Shields nodded. "So how can I help? What's bothering you most?"

She looked at him levelly. "The marks on his back. The welts. Dr. Shields, you have no idea what they look like. They're awful!"

He leaned forward now, and stared at her intently. "Tell me about them."

She closed her eyes, and as an image of the strange markings on Peter's back came to her, she did her best to describe them. As she talked, a chill passed through her. When she was done, she looked at the doctor.

"Well?"

"You're sure the skin wasn't broken? Not even abraded?"

"I'm positive. And they didn't hurt him, either."

"That figures. It sounds to me like their origin is hysterical."

"Hysterical?"

"It's not an uncommon phenomenon. Although in this case it seems to me to be a rather bizarre manifestation. Essentially, it's the same thing as psychosomatic illnesses. The wish becomes the reality."

"It doesn't make sense," Margo said. "Are you telling me Peter has a subconscious desire to be beaten?"

The psychiatrist shrugged eloquently, but when he saw the expression his gesture brought to Margo's face, he tried to reassure her.

"It doesn't necessarily indicate that at all," he said. "The subconscious works in all kinds of strange ways. And don't forget the circumstances of the manifestation. If what you say is true—and I don't have any reason to doubt it—it sounds to me like Balsam's got himself mixed up with a pretty crazy bunch of priests. Do you think they practice flagellation?"

"As far as I know, priests don't do much of that anymore," Margo said, trying not to sound as defensive as she felt. "Besides, even when they did do it, it was ritual. They never used the kind of force that would leave marks like Peter has."

Dr. Shield's brows arched in skepticism. "Under normal circumstances, of course, they don't. But what about other circumstances? From what you've said, that society sounds like an odd group. And your Peter Balsam could fit in very well with them. Isn't it true that he once studied for the priesthood?"

"That was years ago," Margo said vehemently. "And he gave it up."

"Right," Dr. Shields pounced. "Gave it up to go into psychology. And you know what people say about us. No one's as crazy as a psychologist."

"Including you?" Margo asked.

"Did I ever say I was sane?" Dr. Shields replied, the first traces of a grin playing around the corners of his mouth. "I'll tell you what," he said. "Let's forget about it all for the time being. Well, not really forget about it, but I don't really think any of us, including your friend Balsam, knows enough about what's going on to make any reasonable judgments. So let's just keep our eyes open, and see what happens next. And tell Balsam that if he'd like to talk to me, I'm willing." Then he had an idea. "You know," he mused, "it would sure help if we knew what really went on in those meetings of the—what do they call it?"

"The Society of St. Peter Martyr," Margo said dully.

"Lovely name," the psychiatrist said sarcastically. He gave her a reassuring smile. "Go home and get some sleep. And Margo," he added as she opened the door to the outer office. She turned. "Be careful," he said seriously. "You don't really know very much about Balsam, do you? He might be very different from what you think he is. Granted, he seems like a nice guy. But he could be crazy, couldn't he?" Margo stared at him wordlessly, then closed the door behind her. Dr. Shields sank back into the chair behind his desk, and stared thoughtfully at the closed door. He liked Margo, and didn't want to see her hurt. He hoped he was wrong. But inside, he didn't feel he was. And if Peter Balsam was, indeed, as sick as Dr. Shields suspected, it could only mean trouble.

Then he remembered Judy Nelson, still a patient in the hospital. And who had come to the hospital right after she had been admitted? Peter Balsam.

For the rest of the afternoon, Dr. Shields tried to convince himself that Balsam's visit had been nothing more than the concern of a teacher for one of his students, that there was no connection between Peter Balsam and Judy Nelson's attempt on her own life. But when he went home that afternoon, he was still unconvinced. There *was* a connection. He was sure of it.

Geraldine Crane heard the front door slam, but went right on with her ironing. A moment later she glanced up to see her daughter come into the kitchen.

"You're early," she commented. Marilyn set her books down on the table and opened the refrigerator. "Don't spoil your appetite," she heard her mother say.

She poked around the refrigerator, then decided that a carrot would do for a snack. She moved to the sink and began peeling the carrot into the disposal.

"All the vitamins are in the peelings," Geraldine said. "If you peel it, there isn't any use in eating it."

Marilyn silently continued peeling the carrot, and wished her mother would leave her alone. Her wish was not granted.

"I was cleaning your room today," Geraldine said tonelessly. Marilyn wondered if she was going to be criticized for not keeping it clean enough, or if it would be something else. It turned out to be something else.

"I found your history test," Geraldine said in an accusing voice. "You might have shown it to me."

"I didn't want to," Marilyn said.

"I can see why." Her mother's voice stabbed at Marilyn. "Since when do you get B-minuses?"

Marilyn threw the carrot into the sink. Suddenly she didn't want it.

"It's only one test, and not an important one," she said defensively.

"One test?" Geraldine asked. "It may be only one test to you, but to me it says you aren't trying hard enough." She put down the iron, and turned to face her daughter. "I don't know what to do with you, Marilyn. It seems like no matter what I want for you, it never works out."

Marilyn was on the verge of tears. "It's only one test, Mother," she pleaded. "And it isn't that bad a grade. Greta got worse grades than that all the time."

Geraldine nodded. "Your sister didn't go to college," she said. "Greta got married."

"Well, maybe I will too," Marilyn blurted, regretting the words as soon as they'd been said. She had just opened a whole new can of worms, and she knew it.

"You have to date before you get married," Geraldine pointed out acidly. "And so far I don't see you doing much in that department, either."

"All right," Marilyn exclaimed. "I'm sorry, Mother! I'm sorry I'm not like Greta, I'm sorry I'm not popular, I'm sorry I'm a disappointment to you. I'm sorry, I'm sorry, I'm sorry."

Geraldine Crane sank down into one of the chairs by the kitchen table, and pulled Marilyn down into another. Suddenly she wished she hadn't spoken so sharply to her daughter, and now she tried to make up for it.

"There's nothing for you to be sorry about," she said gently. "I'm really very proud of you. I just want you to be happy." She paused a minute. "And you spend too much time in church," she went on. "You're too young to be spending all your time in church. Time enough for that when you're older."

"But I like it in church," Marilyn said through the lump that was suddenly blocking her throat. She didn't want to cry; she hoped she wasn't going to. "Maybe I should go into a convent."

"Don't be silly," her mother said. "That's no kind of life for you. All you need to do is make some friends, and try to get out of yourself a bit. No wonder you're not happy. If I spent as much time by myself as you do, I'd be miserable, too."

Marilyn could no longer hold the sobs back, but neither could she let herself go in front of her mother. She felt too alone. Before her mother could stop her, she had fled from the kitchen. Geraldine Crane sat silently at the kitchen table and listened to her daughter pound up the stairs. Then, though there was no one to see it, she shrugged helplessly and went back to her ironing. Bringing up Greta was so easy, she thought. Why is it so difficult with Marilyn?

She picked up another of her husband's shirts, and began pressing the sleeves, her mind on her daughter. The iron went back and forth over the same spot. It wasn't until she saw the brown of the scorch mark that Geraldine realized she was drifting, and put her mind resolutely back on the task at hand. It didn't occur to her that the same kind of preoccupation that had just caused her to ruin the shirt might also have caused her daughter to get a B-minus on the history test.

She heard Marilyn coming down the stairs a few minutes later, and wondered if she ought to call her into the kitchen and try to talk to her. But before she could make up her mind, Marilyn appeared at the door.

"I'm going to the hospital," Marilyn said in a voice that left no room for argument.

"The hospital?" Geraldine asked. "Whatever for?"

"I'm going to visit Judy Nelson," Marilyn said in a voice that was almost defiant. "If you want me to have friends, I guess visiting Judy is a good enough way to start."

"But I thought you didn't like Judy," her mother said curiously. "I thought you didn't like that whole group."

"Judy wasn't at the party," Marilyn said sullenly. Then, unexpectedly, she came over to her mother, and kissed her on the cheek. "I'm sorry," she said. "I know I'm not what you always wanted for a daughter, but I'll try to do better. I shouldn't let myself get so upset."

Before Geraldine could make any response at all, Marilyn was gone. Geraldine looked out the window, and saw her daughter get on her bike and pedal off. She frowned a little, with a vague feeling that something important had just happened and she had missed it. Then she put it out of her mind and went back to her ironing.

Marilyn saw them before they saw her. She stood inside the door and looked out on the half-dead garden behind the hospital. Penny Anderson and Judy Nelson were chatting together while Karen Morton flirted with one of the orderlies. Marilyn's first impulse was to leave, and either forget about the whole thing or come back another time. She fought the impulse down and stood inside the building, watching the group of girls and the orderly.

Then, after a couple of moments, Judy and Penny joined Karen. Marilyn could see their lips moving but couldn't hear their voices. She wondered what they were talking about.

"Don't look now," Penny was saying, "but I could swear that Marilyn Crane is standing just inside that door." The other girls started to turn, but Penny spoke again. "I said don't look now. What do you suppose she's doing here?"

"If she's watching us, she probably came to visit me," Judy said acidly.

"After Saturday night?" Penny asked. "I wouldn't think she'd want to see any of us, after what we did to her." She began giggling to herself, remembering the expression on Marilyn's face as she had realized why they had invited her to the party.

"She doesn't know I had anything to do with it," Judy said. "I was right here in the hospital, remember?"

"I wonder what she wants?" Karen said. Then, feeling the pressure of the orderly's leg against her own, she suddenly stood up. Things were going too far.

"Let's get out of here," Karen said nervously. "Marilyn isn't going to come over as long as we're here, and I don't want to talk to her anyway. Her pimples might rub off." She was pleased when the other girls laughed.

"Okay," Judy grinned. "You two get out of here, and I'll call you as soon as she leaves."

"That should be good for a laugh," Penny said. Then she and Karen wandered off, trying not to look at the door where Marilyn still hovered.

\* \* \*

Marilyn watched them go, and reached out tentatively to push the door open. Then something told her to forget it, to leave the hospital without talking to Judy. Too late. Judy was waving at her.

"Hi," Judy called. "What brings you out here?" Her voice sounded friendly, and Marilyn felt encouraged. Maybe this hadn't been such a bad idea after all.

"I—I thought you might want some company," she said hesitantly. She offered Judy the stack of fan magazines she had picked up in the drugstore on her way to the hospital. "I brought these for you."

Judy glanced idly at the covers. "Thanks," she said laconically. She stared at Marilyn, waiting for the other girl to speak.

"When are you going home?" Marilyn eventually asked.

"Who knows? As far as I'm concerned, I could go home today. But they won't let me out of here until I tell them why I did it—and I don't want to tell them."

The orderly looked sharply at Judy, and seemed about to say something. Judy didn't give him time.

"Why don't you leave us alone?" she said to him. "I mean, how can we talk with you sitting listening to every word?"

"I'm not supposed to leave you alone," the orderly replied. "You know that."

"Oh, that's stupid," Judy snapped. "Can't you just go over there and sit by yourself? That way you can still see me, but at least I can talk to Marilyn."

"Well . . ." the orderly began, on the edge of agreeing to Judy's request. Judy pushed him a little harder.

"Then go on," she urged. "Just for a few minutes." She took on an appealing little-girl look, and before the orderly could decide if it was sincere, he had taken the bait.

"Okay," he said, standing up. "But only for a few minutes. Then you have to go back to your room."

Judy pouted a little, but the pout disappeared as soon as the young man's back was turned. She grinned conspiratorially at Marilyn. "I have him wrapped around my little finger," she whispered. But Marilyn wasn't listening. She was thinking about something.

"What was it like?" she asked.

"What was what like?"

"What you did," Marilyn said. "You know—" Her voice trailed off, and she was afraid she'd said the wrong thing. A dreamy expression had come over Judy's face.

"It was weird," she said. "You know what? I really don't know why I did it. I was mad at my mother, but certainly not that mad."

"You didn't seem mad when I saw you in the hall that day," Marilyn mused. "You seemed more—sad."

Judy looked at her curiously. "You? I don't remember seeing you."

"Don't you remember?" Marilyn asked her. "It must have been just before you went to the gym and—and did it."

Judy shook her head slowly. "I don't remember anything like that at all," she said. "All I remember about that day is talking to Mr. Balsam. Then it all gets kind of fuzzy. But I remember being in the locker room, and I remember cutting myself. It didn't hurt at all. I just cut myself, and the blood started coming out. And I felt so peaceful. It was—well, it was almost like I feel sitting in church sometimes, listening to Monsignor celebrate Mass. A strange feeling comes over me, and I feel like I'm not in my body anymore. That's how it felt when I cut myself. Like I was watching it happen to someone else. And then I suddenly realized what I'd done. I mean, I suddenly realized it was me it was happening to. And I got scared. That's when I called the police. And then Mr. Jenkins found me." Judy paused, eyeing the other girl. "The rest was horrible."

"Horrible? What do you mean?" It seemed to Marilyn that the cutting would have been the hard part.

"They all wanted to know what happened. Why did I do it? How do I know why I did it? It just seemed like a good idea at the time. Now they're all afraid I'm going to try it again."

"Are you?" Marilyn asked, her voice serious. Judy shook her head emphatically.

"Not a chance. I suppose if I'd really wanted to kill myself, then I might try again. But I don't think I wanted to die. I think I just wanted to see what it felt like. But it's all over now." She grinned suddenly. "I've got too much to do. Who has time to die?"

Then the orderly was back, and Judy was standing up.

"Nap time," she said, with a hint of a sneer in her voice. "They treat you like a baby around here."

"If you act like a baby, you get treated like one," the orderly pointed out. Judy stuck her tongue out at him, but he ignored it. The two of them started walking toward the building. Suddenly Judy turned back.

"Thanks for coming," she said. Then, just before she disappeared into the hospital, she spoke again. "Killing yourself is really kind of neat. You should try it sometime." And then Judy Nelson began to laugh—a laugh that lingered in Marilyn's ears long after Judy disappeared into the shadows of the building.

Marilyn Crane sat alone for a long time, staring at nothing and trying to figure out the meaning of everything Judy had said. Then, she didn't know how much later, she finally left the bench and went back to her bike.

Before she mounted the bike and rode away from the hospital, Marilyn reached into the carryall. Her hand closed on a small object. She took it from the carryall and stared at it.

A small packet of razor blades.

Marilyn had no memory of having purchased them.

No memory of putting them in the carryall.

Yet there they were. She stared at them mutely, part of her mind wondering where they had come from, part of her mind accepting the fact of them. Carefully, she replaced them in her bag.

From a window on the second floor of the hospital, Judy Nelson watched Marilyn. There was a small smile on Judy's face as Marilyn pedaled away toward town. Judy watched until Marilyn disappeared, then got back into bed. She picked up the telephone, dialed, and waited while it rang.

"Penny? Marilyn just left."

"What did she want?"

"Who knows? Who even cares? But I'll tell you one thing. Something's going to happen to that girl!"

## SIXTEEN

THE BISHOP GLANCED ONCE MORE AT THE calendar on his desk, and noted the neatly inked appointment for five o'clock. "Golf," it read, "Joe Flynn." He had been looking forward to it all week until an hour ago, when his secretary had come in and calmly penciled in another appointment above the golf date: "Peter Balsam." His raised eyebrows had only produced a shrug and the explanation, "Fellow says it's urgent." So now he was going to be late for his golf date, and while he knew Joe Flynn would forgive him, he wasn't certain he would forgive this Peter Balsam for delaying him. Golf, after all, was important. The Bishop glared up at the clock on the wall, hoping the man would be late, even if only by a minute. During that minute he would have a legitimate excuse for slipping out the door behind his desk. He was counting the last fifteen seconds when the buzzer on his intercom sounded.

Muttering to himself, he pressed the switch. "Yes?" he barked as loudly and testily as he could, hoping to intimidate the unwanted visitor.

In the secretary's office, Father Duncan winked up at a nervous Peter Balsam and held a finger to his lips. Then he spoke into the intercom.

"Mr. Balsam is here to see you, Your Eminence. Shall I bring him in?"

"What're the chances of his going away if I say no?" the Bishop's voice growled from the box. Balsam felt himself turning red and wanted to flee. Father Duncan just grinned at him.

"None whatever," the priest said severely. "And I already called Joe Flynn and explained, so you can stop worrying about being late."

"Oh, very well then, show him in. But I wish you'd explain things to me the way you do to Joe Flynn. After all, you're *my* secretary."

Father Duncan stood up and beckoned Peter Balsam to follow him. "He always plays golf on Wednesday, so don't be surprised if he's a bit grumpy. And try to keep the meeting short. The later he is, the grumpier he gets. But his bark is much worse than his bite." Then, before Peter could reply, he pushed the door open and stood aside so that Peter could precede him into the Bishop's office.

Bishop O'Malley did not get up when Balsam entered his office, which surprised Balsam just a little. He heard the secretary make the introductions as he crossed the room to kneel in front of the Bishop. But he didn't make it.

"Must we?" the Bishop said, anticipating Peter. "Why don't you just sit down so we can get this over with as fast as possible, all right?"

An abashed Peter Balsam sank into the visitor's chair on the near side of the desk, and the Bishop smiled to himself. Threw him off with that one, he thought; score one for me. While Balsam recovered from the assault, the Bishop tried to decide which demeanor would prove most effective in getting this young man out of his office. He settled on a stern-superior image, and frowned across the desk.

"Father Duncan tells me you arranged this meeting yourself," he said severely, though the secretary had told him nothing of the sort. "Ordinarily, you would need the intervention of Monsignor Vernon in order to get this far." He watched Balsam squirm, and added another point to his side.

"I'm sorry, Your Eminence," Balsam said. "But I'm afraid I couldn't go through Monsignor—"

"Couldn't, or wouldn't?" the Bishop broke in. "There's a difference, you know."

"I do know," Balsam said, more sharply than he meant to. "I'm a psychologist." The Bishop mentally erased the two points he had scored for himself, and chalked up one for Balsam. Then he decided to give up keeping score—it just wasn't going to be his day. He smiled at Balsam.

"Sorry," he said. "Father Duncan didn't tell me that." Balsam took the statement as the sign of truce it was. He relaxed again.

"I couldn't go through Monsignor Vernon, sir, because I would have had to tell him what I wanted to talk to you about."

Bishop O'Malley picked up a pencil from the desktop and leaned back in his chair. He tapped his front teeth with the pencil for a moment, surveying the man across from him. "I gather you want to talk to me about Monsignor?" he inquired mildly.

Balsam nodded. "I don't know who else to talk to, or I wouldn't have bothered you. And I'm not sure it's really Monsignor Vernon I want to talk about. It's his society."

"His society?" the Bishop repeated. "I'm not following you." He glanced surreptitiously at the clock. Yes, he was going to be late.

"The Society of St. Peter Martyr," Balsam said, wondering if he was going to have to explain the whole thing to the Bishop.

"Oh, that bunch," the Bishop said nonchalantly. Suddenly he felt much better: this could be disposed of in a couple of minutes, and he could be on his way to the country club.

"Then you know about them?" Balsam asked eagerly.

"Well, they aren't any secret, are they? Seven old priests who get together every now and then to talk about 'the good old days.' " He looked at Balsam curiously. "You really came all the way over here to talk about the Society of St. Peter Martyr? I think you wasted your time." He stood up, ready to end the meeting. But Peter Balsam didn't move.

"I think there's more to it than that," he said softly. The Bishop stared at him for a moment, then sank back into the chair behind the desk. He was going to be late after all.

"More to it? What makes you think so?"

"Have you ever been to one of their meetings?" Balsam countered.

When the Bishop shook his head, Balsam began to describe the two meetings of the Society he had attended. The Bishop heard him out in silence, but throughout the entire recital the pencil drummed on the edge of the desk.

"Is that all?" he said when Balsam eventually fell silent.

"More or less," Balsam said equivocally. He'd left out the last part of the story, unable to bring himself to tell the Bishop about the strange marks on his back.

"It sounds like more," the Bishop commented dryly. "It sounds like you don't really remember too much about the meetings, and you're reading a lot into the Society that simply isn't there. Frankly, it doesn't seem to me to be in the least remarkable that seven old priests with not much to do have decided to entertain themselves by forming a discussion group."

"You keep saying seven," Balsam put in. "There are only six."

The Bishop smiled easily. "There used to be seven. Until Father George Carver died last year. Now it looks like they're trying to recruit you to round the number out again. Are you thinking of joining them?"

"According to them, I already have," Peter said hesitantly. The Bishop noted the hesitation in his voice, and picked up on it.

"Is there something you haven't told me?"

Balsam shifted uncomfortably in his chair, wondering whether he should tell the Bishop about the marks on his back. He decided against it.

"I really came here more to ask some questions than to tell you about the Society. I'd hoped you knew more about it than I do."

"I see. On the assumption that the Bishop is the source of all knowledge in the diocese. Well, I'm afraid that's a myth. If I tried to keep up with everything all my priests are doing, I'd never have time for the important things."

Like golf? Balsam wanted to ask, but didn't.

"Like golf," the Bishop grinned, reading his mind. "As for the Society of St. Peter Martyr, I'm afraid I know very little about it. As far as I knew it was simply seven old priests—"

"Monsignor Vernon isn't exactly old," Balsam broke in.

The Bishop peered at him over his glasses; this Balsam was showing a lot more spunk than he liked. On the other hand, he was finding it refreshing, in an odd way.

"Not in years, perhaps, but his thinking is a bit old-fashioned. As for the rest of them, well, their years match their thinking, for the most part."

"What do you mean?" Balsam asked. He thought he knew, but wanted the Bishop to spell it out for him.

"How can I put it?" the Bishop mused aloud. Then he put the pencil down and leaned forward in his chair.

"The Church is in a constant state of paradox," he began. "On the one hand we tell our flock, and each other, that we hold the keys to the absolute truth. But on the other hand we realize that there is no absolute truth. Truth changes along with the times. The trick to being comfortable within the Church is to balance tradition with change, and try to change tradition to keep up with the times. Unfortunately, all too many of us find it easier to cling to the traditions than move with the changes. All too many of us fail to see that keeping up with the times isn't destroying the Faith. And that, as I see it, is the basis of the Society of St. Peter Martyr. They're old-fashioned in their thinking, and they don't get much support from the Church, at least not in my diocese. They want to *Believe*. They need to lean on each other for support.

"They're terribly dogmatic, of course, and quite frankly I don't spend much time with them. I don't mean as the Society of St. Peter Martyr; I don't spend any time with the Society at all—I mean as individuals. I'm afraid I just can't be quite as—what's the word? religious?—as they'd like me to be. And, though I know I shouldn't say it, Monsignor Vernon's the worst of them."

The Bishop smiled wryly, then went on. "Young man, every time I talk to Vernon I thank my lucky stars I'm getting older. By the time that man gets to be my age, he's going to be absolutely impossible. In fact, I have to keep reminding myself that he's your age, not mine. He seems old already."

"I know." Balsam felt himself warming to the Bishop. "I went to school with him. He was just Pete Vernon then, and you wouldn't have recognized him."

"Wouldn't I? Don't forget, I've been watching him in Neilsville for twelve years now. I remember the young man who came out here from Philadelphia. He's a lot different now. Neilsville, I suppose. Towns like that do things to people. Too small. Inbred. I suppose it's inevitable that the clergy gets caught up in it too. I've often wondered if I'd have stayed with the Church if they'd sent me to a place like Neilsville." Then he brightened a bit. "Who knows? Maybe if I'd wound up in Neilsville, I'd have started a Society of St. Peter Martyr myself. Just between us, being stuck in Neilsville is certainly my idea of martyrdom."

"I know what you mean," Balsam replied. Then he picked up on something else. "Did Monsignor start the Society of St. Peter Martyr?"

"You mean you didn't know?"

Balsam shook his head. "I know he's their leader, but I'd assumed the Society had been going on for years."

"Not at all. Vernon started it about five years ago, at about the time he became Monsignor. I suppose it was his way of proving to himself that he'd 'made it.' "

"Seems a strange thing," Balsam commented.

"Petty conceit, I'd call it," the Bishop snapped.

"Conceit?"

Now the Bishop regarded him quizzically. "You mean you haven't figured it out?"

"You've lost me again," Balsam admitted.

"The names, man, the names," the Bishop cried. "Monsignor Vernon named the Society after himself!"

Balsam stared at the Bishop blankly. "Named it after himself?"

"You mean you didn't know?" The Bishop chuckled. "St. Peter Martyr's name was Piero da Verona. Now if you were to translate that into English, what would you come up with?"

"Peter Vernon," Balsam said slowly. "Or something close enough to that so it wouldn't make any difference. Is that what you mean?"

The Bishop nodded. "It makes you wonder, doesn't it?" Then: "What an unpleasant person he must have been."

"Who?"

"Piero da Verona. St. Peter Martyr."

Balsam's brows arched in surprise. "I beg your pardon?"

"You've read the story, haven't you? About how one of the so-called heretics was finally pushed too far by Verona's persecutions, and killed him one night?"

" 'So-called' heretics?" Balsam wanted to smile. He didn't.

The Bishop looked at him sharply, wondering if the young man was pulling his leg. "Oh, come on. I think we all have to admit that during the Inquisition the Dominicans were denouncing everyone who disagreed with them as heretics. But calling them heretics doesn't make them heretics, does it?"

"No," Balsam agreed, "it doesn't." Then he changed the subject. "What happened to the man who killed Verona?"

"Ah," said Bishop O'Malley, standing once more. "Now there's a wonderful case of the mysterious ways of the Lord. The murderer is a saint too!"

Balsam's eyes widened in astonishment. "Once more?"

"Possibly." Bishop O'Malley laughed. "I don't know what the truth of the matter is, and I don't suppose anybody else does either, but the story is that the man who killed Verona—his name escapes me if I ever knew it—repented, joined an order himself, and was eventually canonized. Not as fast as Verona, of course, who I think holds the record for quick canonization, but he eventually made it."

"As Saint who?"

"I haven't the slightest idea. There's so many saints I can't keep up with them." He glanced at the clock, and was surprised to see how late it was. "If you'll excuse me," he said to Balsam, "I'm going to be very late for my game."

Balsam leaped to his feet. "I'm sorry for having taken so much of your time," he apologized. The Bishop clapped him on the back, deciding he quite liked this young man.

"None of that," he said. "Any time. But next time, please go through proper channels. If you have to, lie to Vernon about it. Better that than having him find out you circumvented him entirely. Let him get wind of that, and you'll really find out what the Inquisition was like." Then a thought struck him. "You know, young man, maybe that's what they're up to. Maybe the Society of St. Peter Martyr is actually trying to resurrect the Inquisition. If they are, Neilsville would certainly be the place to start. It's always struck me as the kind of town that would love to have an Inquisition. Or a witch-burning. Tell you what, why don't you join up with the Society, and see if you can find out what they're up to? Who knows? It might prove to be interesting.''

Bishop O'Malley opened the door to his office and walked with Peter Balsam from the rectory to the car that Balsam had borrowed from Margo Henderson. He waved to Balsam as the younger man drove away, and decided that he did, indeed, like the boy very much. Feeling quite good, Bishop O'Malley got in his own car and set out for his golf game.

Had he known about the marks on Balsam's back, he would not have felt nearly so good. He would have known that something was happening in Neilsville.

Instead, he went happily to his golf game, where Joe Flynn beat him by three strokes. Which wasn't too bad; Joe Flynn usually beat him by five.

Peter Balsam entered his apartment and tossed the car keys to Margo Henderson.

"Not a scratch on it," he said. "You ready for the dinner I promised?''

Margo nodded, relieved to see that he seemed to be in a good mood. "Shall I fix you a drink first?" she asked.

"Sure. Then I'll tell you all about the Bishop. Right now I'm going to change my clothes.''

He walked quickly into the bedroom and stripped to his shorts. As he'd done this morning, he glanced in the mirror to check the welts on his back. This morning they had been as angry and red as ever.

Now they were gone.

He looked again, and tentatively touched the skin of his back.

No trace. Not a scar. Not a mark. His back was as clear as it had ever been.

When Peter Balsam returned to the living room a few seconds later and took the drink Margo offered, his mood had changed. The merriment was gone, and in its place was a certain thoughtfulness.

By the time dinner was over Peter Balsam had made up his mind.

He would join the Society of St. Peter Martyr.

Margo wasn't sure it was wise, but Peter insisted. Reluctantly, and only because the Bishop had suggested his joining the Society, Margo agreed. Despite her falling-out with the Church, she instinctively trusted the Bishop. And she was beginning to suspect she loved Peter Balsam.

But she didn't like it. She didn't like it at all.

## SEVENTEEN

PETER BALSAM FOUND THE NOTE IN HIS box on Thursday morning:

*The Rectory*
*Friday Night*
*8:00 p.m.*

There was no signature, not even any initials, and it was written—lettered almost—in a flowing script that appeared to have been produced by a quill. And yet, despite the lack of details in the note, Balsam was sure he knew what it was: the summons to his final initiation into the Society of St. Peter Martyr. He stared at it silently for a moment, then slipped it between the pages of the book he had been carrying. When he turned, he saw the smiling face of Sister Marie watching him quizzically.

"Is something wrong?" the nun asked.

"Wrong?" Peter repeated, somewhat startled. "No, nothing's wrong." He started to move away, but the nun stopped him.

"Are you sure? You look pale. Almost as if you'd just seen a ghost."

Peter hesitated for a moment, then suddenly pulled the note from the book he was carrying. He handed it to the nun. "What do you make of this?"

Sister Marie took the note from Balsam's outstretched hand and examined it carefully. She turned it over, glanced at the back of it, then returned it to Balsam.

"Odd," she said.

"Do you recognize the handwriting?"

Sister Marie looked puzzled, as if she wanted to say something but wasn't sure it was proper. Balsam pressed her. "You do recognize it, don't you?"

"I'm not sure," Sister Marie said slowly. "It was like a *déjà vu*. When you handed me the note, I had the strangest feeling that the same thing had happened before. But then, before I could remember, it was gone."

Balsam felt a pang of disappointment. He had hoped the nun would be able to tell him whose hand had written the message. Then she brightened, and asked to see the note again. This time she examined it even more carefully, and held it up to the light. When she finally gave it back to him she looked even more bewildered.

"I don't know," she said, hesitating in a way that made Balsam suspect she did. "I can tell you where the paper came from," she said. "That's easy: Monsignor Vernon. But you knew that, didn't you?"

"It seemed likely," Peter grinned.

"It's the hand that bothers me," Sister Marie said. "I know it isn't Monsignor's; I also know I've seen it somewhere before. But there's something amiss. Something on the edge of my mind that isn't quite right. It's as if I've seen it before, but it was different, if you know what I mean."

It's like Neilsville, Balsam thought to himself. You've seen it all before, but here it isn't quite right. Here, there's always something more than what can be seen. Aloud he said, "Try to remember, will you?" At his voice, the nun's expression changed from bewilderment to concern.

"Is it important?" she asked, not seeing how a simple summons to the rectory could be of that much concern to anyone.

"I wish I knew," Peter said. "It might be, and it might not be. I wish I knew who wrote this note."

"Well, don't worry about it too much," the nun smiled. "It'll probably come to me in the middle of the night, and if it does I'll write it down before I forget it."

"In the margin of *The New Yorker?*" Balsam asked mischievously.

"That, or something even worse," Sister Marie tossed at him. Then, before he could draw her out, she was gone.

Several times during Thursday and Friday, Peter Balsam spoke briefly with the Monsignor, and each time he wondered if he should mention the odd note. But the Monsignor never mentioned it, nor did there ever seem an opportune moment for Peter to bring it up. He wasn't sure, but he had the feeling that Monsignor Vernon was deliberately preventing him from asking any questions.

Late Friday afternoon, Balsam went looking for Sister Marie. When he found her, he had the distinct feeling that she wasn't particularly glad to see him. Her usual cheerful smile was nowhere in evidence, and the twinkle in her eye had faded.

"Sister Marie?" he said, as if he wasn't quite sure it was her. She seemed to jump a little, as if she hadn't seen him, though he was standing right in front of her.

"Mr. Balsam," she said, and Peter noted the use of his last name. Her eyes didn't meet his.

"You've been hiding from me today," he said, forcing a lightness into his voice that her manner did nothing to encourage.

"No, I don't think so," the nun said softly. Her eyes flitted from one part of the room to another, as if seeking escape.

"I was wondering if you'd remembered where you saw that handwriting before," Peter said as casually as he could.

"Handwriting?" the nun repeated too quickly. "What handwriting?"

"On the note," Balsam said, beginning to feel just a bit exasperated. The nun continued to look blank. "The note I found in my box yesterday morning? Surely you haven't forgotten?"

"Oh, that," Sister Marie said, laughing nervously. "I'm afraid it slipped my mind completely!" Again she glanced around the room, and Peter had the distinct impression she was about to dart off somewhere. He was right.

"I'm afraid you'll have to excuse me," she exclaimed. "I promised Sister Elizabeth I'd help her with some things this afternoon." Then, as if she were too aware that the excuse was lame, she added quickly: "Some tests. I promised to help her grade some tests." And then she was gone.

Though they'd made no plans to have dinner together Friday evening, Peter wasn't surprised when Margo Henderson appeared at his apartment shortly after he got there himself, nor was he surprised that she was carrying a couple of steaks that nearly matched the two he'd picked up himself on his way home. What did surprise him was that as soon as she was inside his apartment he gathered her into his arms and kissed her. She returned the kiss warmly, then pulled away from him.

"Now that was something new," she said. "I could get used to being greeted like that."

"Good," Peter replied. "Since we have two extra steaks, why don't you plan on being greeted that way again tomorrow night? And tomorrow night we can spend the evening together."

"They canceled the dance?" Margo asked. Peter snapped his fingers impatiently.

"Damn. I'd forgotten all about it." St. Francis Xavier's was holding its first dance of the school term that weekend. He grinned at her. "What do you think they'd say if you showed up with me to help me chaperone?"

"Me at St. Francis Xavier's? Monsignor'd have to exorcise the place after I left. But I'd love to have dinner." She paused, frowning prettily. "Although I have to admit I'm beginning to feel like a corporate wife—I have dinner with you, then sit by myself while you run around to meetings and social events." The glint in her eye told Peter that she was teasing, but he decided to take it seriously. He took her hands in his.

"It isn't fair, I know. And you don't have to do it, Margo. In fact, I wish you wouldn't."

The smile faded from her face and she grew serious. "Of course I don't have to do it, Peter, and you're very sweet to worry about it. But I'd rather have dinner with you and spend the rest of the evening worrying about you than spend the entire evening with anyone else. I thought you knew that."

"Maybe I was fishing," Peter said, the beginning of a grin playing around the corners of his mouth. Margo's face remained serious.

"Or maybe you were trying to tell me you care about me, in your own way. Well, all right. I know you care about me, and you know I care about you. That gives me the right to spend an evening worrying about you now and then. I will worry about you tonight—unless I can talk you into changing your mind."

Balsam smiled gently. "Why don't you wait for me and do your worrying here? Then, no matter how late I get back, we can find out what's really going on with the Society of St. Peter Martyr. Tonight I'm going to record the whole thing." He held up a small cassette recorder. Margo stared at it in silence. Suddenly she wasn't sure she wanted to know about the Society. In fact, she was almost sure she *didn't* want to know what went on at their meetings. But at the same time, she *had* to know. She made up her mind to be waiting when Peter came home that night. Silently, Margo began fixing dinner. There just didn't seem to be much to talk about.

The Society of St. Peter Martyr was waiting. All six of them were in the foyer, standing formally in a semicircle—expectant. He closed the front door behind him and stood looking at them. There was a long silence as the six priests surveyed him, and then Monsignor Vernon spoke.

"Peter Balsam," he said sonorously, "we have met, and it is our decision that you shall be initiated into the Society tonight."

"I see," said Balsam softly. He decided to risk a question. "Even though I'm not a priest?"

The Monsignor smiled faintly. "We have never had a . . . layman in the Society before, but we are prepared to make an exception for you. Our reasons," he declared, anticipating Peter's question, "will eventually become clear to you."

Peter remained silent. But he wondered why the Monsignor had hesitated over the word "layman." What other word had come into his mind?

The six priests turned suddenly, and began filing down the hall toward the study. Balsam quickly reached into the inside pocket of his jacket and activated the recorder before falling in behind them.

As before, the study was lit only by candles and the uneven glow of the fire. Once again the chairs were arranged in a semicircle in front of the fire, with the two easy chairs opposite each other, reserved for Monsignor and Balsam. In a few moments the seven men were seated.

The catechism began again, each of the priests in turn questioning Balsam's knowledge of the Faith. He answered the questions easily, giving the correct responses, careful to keep his voice level, to give no hint of his true feelings whenever he was mouthing a doctrine he questioned. As the inquisition went on—and he had the distinct feeling that it was, indeed, an inquisition—he wondered to what purpose it all was. The questions were the same ones he had answered before, and his answers were the same. No, he realized with a start, the answers were *not* the same. The first time he had sat in this room to be questioned by the six priests, it had taken him a while to realize what they wanted to hear. Tonight, he had known from the beginning. And his tone had been different that first night. He had made no effort to conceal his doubts about certain aspects of his faith. Tonight, Peter Balsam was acting the part of the true believer. And as he played his role, letting himself be led through the Doctrine and listening calmly to his own responses, he began to wonder if the role wasn't taking over the actor, to wonder how much of his earnestness was feigned and how much was real.

It was over, finally, though Peter Balsam didn't realize it at first. He looked from one stern face to another, wondering from which of them the next question would come. Eventually he realized there would be no more questions. The six clerics were looking at him with satisfaction; he had apparently passed their test. He wondered what would come next.

Suddenly they were standing, looming over him. "Peter Balsam," they asked in one voice, "what do you want of us?"

The question echoed in his mind. *What do you want of us?* His brain searched for the answer. He knew there *was* an answer; one single answer that they were looking for, and that if he was unable to give it, there would be no second chance. He was still trying to decide what to say when he heard his own voice answering.

"Solace in my Faith."

"And what do you offer us?"

"My body and my mind, for use in your holy work."

They reached out to him then, taking each of his hands, and drawing him to his feet. They offered him wine.

He had passed.

He was one of them.

He had told them what they wanted to hear, and he was glad.

The Society of St. Peter Martyr, once more seven strong, began to pray.

The same chanting he had heard before began once again, but this time Peter Balsam was aware that he was somehow able to take part in it. He mouthed the strange words easily, his lips and tongue forming one syllable after another as if he had been saying the unfamiliar Latin-like words all his life. As he chanted in unison with the others, part of his mind tried to reason out the source of his ability to match the priests word for word. He told himself that it was simply because he had heard the service once before, and it had remained imprinted on his memory. But another voice inside him told him there was more to it than that; that one hearing of the service was not enough for him to have it flow so easily from his lips.

He put the disturbing thoughts from his mind, and concentrated instead on trying to follow the service. It sounded, at first, much like the praises of the Lord that had been sung in the convent he grew up in. But, again, there was something different. The praises were there, but there were overtones of other things. Things in the odd not-quite-Latin that he could almost get a grasp on, but then would lose. Eventually he stopped trying to understand the words and began to feel them instead. They were words of exhortation. The Society was praising the Lord, yes, but it was also exhorting Him. To what purpose? Faster now, and faster, until individual words escaped him and there was only the rhythm.

The rhythm, insistent, inexorable, caught him up in its mysticism, transporting him into the same state of religious ecstasy he had experienced once before in this room. He began to lose consciousness of his physical surroundings, and was only aware of the presence of the light, and the warmth, and the spirituality of his companions. They were moving now, the circle closing in on him, surrounding him, and as the service grew more intense Balsam had the feeling of being at one with them, of joining them in an experience that was both frightening and exhilarating, as if, for the first time, the core of his soul was being touched by God.

And then the voice began.

It sounded far away at first, but it grew steadily louder until its throbbing tones echoed through the room. The glow of the candles and the heat and flicker of the fire held him but the chanting had stopped. Only the throbbing sound of a single voice filled his ears now. And then that, too, stopped. In the sudden silence, Peter Balsam reached out to touch the priest who was closest to him. In the odd light the priest seemed to glow white as an angel, and Balsam was sure he would find the support he was seeking. He tried to speak, but his mouth refused to open. From somewhere he heard another voice:

"He is with us. Saint Peter Martyr is with us."

And then the deep tones of the oddly disembodied voice once more filled the room, using the strange language that Peter could not quite understand. He was able to follow the meaning now and then, but only in snatches.

"You must find him for me . . .

"You must punish . . .

"They are everywhere . . .

"Celebrate . . .

"Punish . . .

"Sin . . .

"Sin . . .

"Celebrate . . . Punish . . . Sin . . ."

And then the voice was gone, and the chanting began again. And once more the strange trance came over Balsam, and he lost track of time, and of place, and of what was real and what was not. All was religion, and religion was all. And the chanting went on . . . and the celebration went on . . . and sometime during the long night, Peter Balsam felt himself slipping away, drifting in a fantasy that he had neither the will nor the desire to define.

Three hours before dawn, it ended. As before, Peter Balsam had no idea of what had happened. Only impressions, and a feeling of both exhilaration and exhaustion.

And, of course, a tape. As he left the rectory he felt the miniature recorder, still in the pocket of his jacket, still running. He switched it off, though he knew it must have stopped recording hours earlier. But the first two hours of the meeting were on the tape. At least it would be a beginning. But a beginning of what? He hurried his step, and by the time he got home he was almost running.

Margo was waiting for him, a strange expression on her face.

They listened to the tape together.

Margo sat at one end of the sofa, Peter at the other, and Peter was intensely aware of the distance between them. They only listened to snatches of the first part of the tape; the part that had recorded the catechism. Ten minutes after it began, Margo commented softly that whatever else was on the tape, Peter had certainly started out sounding like a good Catholic. He glanced at her, wondering what the remark meant, but her eyes were turned away from him. He reached down and advanced the tape through the rest of the first hour to the point where the chanting began.

When the first strange sounds of the almost religious music came out of the tiny speaker, Margo spoke again.

"There was a silence," she said suddenly. "What was happening during the silence?"

"You mean when they were accepting me into the Society?"

Margo nodded.

Peter thought back to the moment, then remembered.

"Wine," he said. "Monsignor Vernon passed a chalice of wine around." Margo's brow furrowed, and she fell silent.

They listened to the tape, watching the cassette player almost as if it were producing a visual image as well as emitting the peculiar sounds.

"It sounds almost like Latin," Margo said.

"I know. But it isn't. Not quite. It's close, but just different enough to make it mostly unintelligible. I can pick up a word here and there, but most of it sounds like another language."

"Like Spanish, sort of," Margo said.

"Spanish?" Peter said. He listened more closely, and suddenly the rhythms made more sense. And then it came to him. It wasn't Spanish at all. It was some kind of strange Italian.

"That's it," he said softly.

"What?" Margo asked, looking at him for the first time.

"That's it!" Peter exclaimed. "It's not Spanish, Margo, and it isn't quite Latin. It's some kind of Italian! And it makes sense, too. Not the words. I can't understand them, but I know what we're listening to! They're using a language that's between Latin and Italian."

Margo looked confused, and he tried to explain.

"The Romance languages all stem from Latin. French. Spanish. Italian. But languages change slowly. So what would early Italian sound like? It would be somewhere between Latin and modern Italian, wouldn't it? And St. Peter Martyr was an Italian from the thirteenth century! The Society is using the language of St. Peter Martyr! That must be it. Of course we can't understand all of it, any more than we can understand all of Chaucer's English."

"But where would they have learned it?" Margo asked.

"Who knows?" Peter said. Suddenly he felt much better about everything; the chanting had lost a lot of the mystery it had held in the flickering light of the rectory.

"How much of this do you remember?" Margo asked him suddenly.

"Not much," Peter said. "It all sounds vaguely familiar to me, but not nearly as familiar as it should. I mean, only a few hours ago I was taking part in that chanting."

Margo stared at him. "I thought you said you couldn't understand the words."

"I couldn't. And I still can't. But at the time I was able to keep up with it, without even trying. It was like the words just flowed out of me . . ."

His voice trailed off as he realized that now, in his apartment, the rhythms that had seemed so simple in the rectory seemed incredibly complicated.

And then he heard the voice.

It boomed sonorously out of the recorder, resonant and compelling. He recognized it immediately, and wondered why he hadn't known it during the service. It was Monsignor Vernon.

"What's he saying?" Margo asked. She, too, had recognized the priest's voice.

"I'm not sure," Peter said slowly, trying to conceal the sudden fear that was clutching at his stomach. "I . . . When I was there, I thought I was hearing the voice of St. Peter Martyr. It never occurred to me that it was Monsignor. And I can't understand most of what he's saying. It has to do with sin, and punishment, and celebrating. I don't know. I should be able to understand the Latin—I teach it. But it isn't quite Latin anyway. It's more like Italian and my Italian doesn't exist."

And then the booming voice stopped, and the chanting began again, accompanied now by a different sound. Slowly the chanting faded away, and the new sounds grew in volume. They began as a series of small whining noises, but as the tape ground on, the whines turned into moaning, mixed with heavy breathing and other sounds that seemed familiar to Peter but that he couldn't quite identify. Occasionally a cry of ecstasy penetrated the steady moaning.

Peter knew what he was hearing, but didn't want to admit it to himself. He listened to the tape, trying to shut it out, but at the same time fascinated. And he began to remember some of the images he had experienced in the rectory.

The angels, seeming to glow whitely in the flickering candlelight.

The closeness among the seven of them that he had thought was a spiritual closeness.

The caresses that he had thought stemmed from a religious experience.

Naked men, priests stripped of their vestments, stripped of everything, their bodies intertwined not spiritually but carnally, caressing each other not religiously but sexually.

He was listening to the sounds of an orgy, an orgy he knew he and six priests had participated in only hours earlier.

And then he heard his own voice crying out in that tight ecstasy that only comes with a sexual climax. His stomach knotted and he knew he was going to be sick. As he lunged toward the bathroom his right hand flew out, knocking the tiny recorder from the coffee table. But it didn't stop: the sickening sounds continued as he fled the room.

He stayed in the bathroom for a long time, waiting for the nausea to subside, not wanting to go back into the living room, not wanting to face Margo. Then, as he was beginning to hope that she might have left, he heard her rapping at the door.

"Peter?" she said, her voice quiet and gentle. "Peter, are you all right?"

All right? he thought. All right? How could I be all right? My God, what have I done? He sank to the floor of the bathroom, laying his cheek on the cool tile. He heard the click of the door opening, and realized that Margo had come in. Then he felt her touch him on the cheek.

"It's all right," she said softly. "Peter, it's all right."

He stared up at her, wanting to believe her, but sure that nothing would ever be all right again.

Darkness closed around him.

# EIGHTEEN

MARGO'S FIRST IMPULSE WAS TO CALL the hospital. Before she got to the phone, she had changed her mind. What could she tell them? They wouldn't believe her. Even if she played the tape for them, she was sure they wouldn't believe her. And besides, Peter had only passed out. She told herself that it wasn't anything serious: he had simply been overcome by exhaustion and the emotional shock of discovering what he had participated in.

She went back to the bathroom, and started moving Peter Balsam's unconscious body toward the bedroom. She would put him to bed, and then she would lie down on the couch and wait for him to wake up. Under the circumstances there just didn't seem to be anything else to do.

He didn't stir at all as she pulled and shoved him into his bed, but he looked so uncomfortable that she decided to undress him.

The first thing she noticed were the marks. The same marks that had been there a few days earlier. They were back, and they were identical to the earlier ones, standing red and angry all over his torso. She pulled his trousers off, then his underwear. The last garment seemed damp, and at first she thought he had simply been sweating profusely. But there was more. From Peter Balsam's body an odor emanated. The sweet muskiness of semen.

Margo Henderson buried her face in the soiled undergarment and cried. As the tears came, she realized that she had still been hoping. She had been clinging to a hope that the evidence of the tape had been false, that what she had heard was something entirely different from what she now knew was the truth. She had stumbled into a mess. And yet, even as she lay on the bed next to Peter, sobbing softly into the pillow, she realized she was not going to walk away; she would not—could not—leave him.

It wasn't Peter's fault, she told herself, forcing back the sobs. He didn't know what he was doing. He didn't know what they were doing to him. You watched his face as he listened, and he was shocked. So don't blame him; help him.

Margo rose from the bed, then pulled the covers up over Peter's naked body. She looked down at him, and realized how vulnerable he must be right now. When he woke, she must be close to him. He mustn't feel that she had abandoned him.

She went out to the living room, and stretched out on the sofa. The first glow of dawn was beginning to light the sky outside as Margo fell into a fitful doze interrupted by dreams that took all the peace from her sleep . . .

She was outside the rectory, and she knew what was going on inside. But she couldn't stop it. She could only crouch in the darkness outside, listening to the sounds, hearing first the chanting, and then the moaning, knowing that Peter was inside, that he was in the middle of that group of six strange priests, and that they were seducing him. Their hands were touching him, and their lips kissing him in a way that only her hands should have touched him, only her lips should have kissed him.

Then she was suddenly inside the rectory, inside that oddly lit room, watching the naked priests, their wrinkled bodies glistening sweatily in the candlelight as they stripped Peter's clothes from him, their fingers greedily playing over his smooth skin, their tongues clucking away in that strange language. And then they were holding him down and Monsignor Vernon, grown suddenly to a towering height, stood over Peter, his monstrous organ thrusting toward Peter's gaping mouth. The priest began advancing toward Peter, and Margo looked on in horror. She wanted to scream, but couldn't make any sound escape her lips. She tried to lunge forward, tried to rescue Peter from the grasp of the old men, but she couldn't make her feet move. They seemed to be mired in heavy mud. All she could do was look on in mutely fascinated horror as Monsignor Vernon, suddenly enveloped in a halo, forced his penis into Peter Balsam's mouth. And finally, as the immense glans disappeared between his lips, she screamed.

Margo woke up to the sound of her own scream, and felt her body shaking uncontrollably. She could feel a clammy sweat covering her like a wet sheet. And then she felt a hand touch her, and her eyes snapped open. Peter Balsam was bending over her. She stared silently at him for a second or two, suddenly unsure whether she was awake. And then she realized she was awake, and he was real, and she threw her arms around him.

"Oh, God, Peter," she cried into his ear. "I saw it all. I was there, right there in the room, and those priests—those six awful priests—they were naked and they were—they were doing the most disgusting things to you. And then the Monsignor—Monsignor Vernon—he—he—" She broke off, unable to continue.

"It's all right," Peter said softly, holding her closer. "It was only a dream. You had a bad dream."

She lay still in his arms for a moment, and her panic passed. And then she remembered. He should have been in bed. She had put him to bed, then lay down to doze, only a few minutes ago. What was he doing up? How could he be up already? She wriggled free of his arms and sat up. The sun was pouring brightly in the front window.

"What time is it?" she asked.

"Almost eleven," Peter said. "I woke up half an hour ago and decided to let you sleep. I guess I shouldn't have."

The dream came back to her, and she looked at him, tried to separate him from the Peter Balsam in her dream. But she couldn't quite do it, and she had to tell him why.

"Peter," she said softly, "there's something I didn't tell you last night. Part of my dream just now wasn't a dream. It was a memory. Last night I— well, I got so nervous waiting for you here that I decided to go for a walk. And I found myself walking up the hill. To the rectory."

"Is that why you looked so strange when I came in last night?"

She nodded miserably. "I already knew what had been going on at the rectory, long before I heard the tape. I must have been outside the window of Monsignor's study for hours, listening." She looked at him beseechingly. "You have no idea what it was like. I didn't want to listen, but I couldn't make myself go away. I stayed until it was almost over. I only got back here about forty-five minutes before you did."

"Why did you stay?" Peter asked gravely. "I don't think I would have."

"I had to. I had to see you, to see if you knew what was going on up there. And you didn't. I could tell from your face." Her voice rose. "Oh, Peter, they're doing such horrible things to you."

She flung her arms around his neck and clung to him. Only this time, Peter picked her up and carried her into the bedroom, kicking the door closed behind him.

"What are you going to do?"

It was an hour later, and they lay in bed, her head resting on his stomach.

"I'm not sure," Peter said. "I have to stop it. I can't let them keep doing what they're doing."

"But what can you do?"

"I don't know. I suppose I could take the tape to the Bishop, but frankly, I don't think he'd do anything. The only thing he could do is talk to Monsignor and the rest of them, and of course they'd deny they were doing anything wrong."

"But those sounds . . ."

"Religious ecstasy," Peter said, trying to make light of the whole mess. "The sounds we were making thirty minutes ago weren't much different."

Margo blushed, remembering, then spoke again.

"But you have to do something."

"I know," Peter said. "And I'm going to have to do it alone. No one's going to believe what's on that tape."

"I can back you up," Margo said softly.

Peter shook his head violently. "I'm going to have to do it on my own. I'll talk to the Bishop again, but I don't think anything will come of it. And believe me, I won't be going to any more meetings of the Society of St. Peter Martyr."

"What about the dance tonight?"

"I'll go, of course. That's going to come under the heading of acting as if nothing had happened. And all of a sudden I think it's important that I be there. Important for me, and important for the kids."

Then he remembered Sister Marie, and her strange evasiveness yesterday morning.

"And there's someone I have to talk to," he said softly, thinking: Someone who knows more about all this than she's told me.

He decided not to tell Margo about Sister Marie.

The gymnasium of St. Francis Xavier High School had that look of slightly seedy festivity produced by high-school students valiantly trying to convert a gymnasium into a ballroom. The crepe-paper streamers, already beginning to go limp as the dance was beginning, hung unevenly from the light fixtures and the basketball hoops, serving more to accentuate the unsuitability of the room than to lend their intended air of gaiety.

Marilyn Crane sat unhappily in one corner of the gym, the corner farthest from the door, and wondered for the tenth time why she had come. For the tenth time she answered herself; she was here to make her mother happy, and because her sister Greta had always come to the dances in the gym. The fact that Greta always had a date had not struck her mother as particularly relevant. So Marilyn sat in her corner, half hoping to be left alone and unnoticed, half hoping someone—anyone—would come over to talk to her. No one did.

The room began to fill up, and Marilyn watched the sisters in their black habits cruising among the students like so many dignified black swans in a flock of brightly colored, raucously quacking ducks. Marilyn wondered how they did it; wondered if that mystic self-confidence was issued to the sisters along with their habits. Marilyn particularly liked to watch Sister Marie, her wimple framing her pretty face in a way that seemed to accentuate her beauty rather than lend her an air of remoteness.

Sister Marie, unaware of Marilyn's scrutiny, was standing by the main entrance, greeting each of the students as he came in, and doing her best to keep her right toe from tapping to the music too obviously. Years of practice in front of a mirror had taught her the precise amount of movement she could make under the heavy folds of her habit without causing the telltale swaying of the material that had constantly given her away during her novitiate. But she still tended to get carried away, particularly since the advent of the rock era. Rock music always set her foot to tapping far in excess of the tolerance of her habit. She saw Janet Connally coming in, and smiled easily.

"All by yourself tonight?" she grinned.

"I get to meet more boys if I come alone," Janet said. "Besides, Judy couldn't come, Karen's here with Jim, and Penny is working the refreshment table with Jeff Bremmer."

"How is Judy?" Sister Marie asked, genuine concern in her voice.

"All right, I guess," Janet said slowly. "She came home yesterday, and she's supposed to be back in school on Monday."

"That'll be nice," Sister Marie said emphatically. "I've missed her."

"Sister Marie," Janet began. She wanted to ask the nun if she knew what was going to happen to Judy, but suddenly, without really knowing why, changed her mind.

"Yes?" the nun prompted her.

"Nothing," Janet said. Suddenly she felt nervous, and wanted to be elsewhere. "I think I'd better say hello to Penny." She moved off quickly, and her place was taken by Monsignor Vernon, who had been standing a few feet behind her.

"Monsignor," Sister Marie greeted him gravely, her cheerful smile disappearing.

"Sister Marie," the priest acknowledged her greeting, looking dolefully around the room. "Well." The word was uttered in a tone that conveyed deep disapproval.

"I think it looks nice," Sister Marie said tentatively.

"I wonder if it's the sort of thing we should be encouraging."

Sister Marie knew what was coming, knew how the Monsignor felt about frivolous activities—sinful activities. She knew about St. Peter Martyr, and about the Monsignor's fascination with the saint. Often, in the lonely privacy of her cell, she had wondered where that fascination had come from, and where it would lead the priest. And sometimes it frightened her. As it had frightened her when she finally remembered where she had seen that odd handwriting on the note Peter Balsam had shown her a few days ago.

Now, sensing that the Monsignor was about to launch into one of his tirades, she glanced quickly around for a diversion.

"I think I see Penny Anderson waving to me," she said, moving away from the priest. "I'd better see if she needs any help." Before Monsignor Vernon could make a reply, the nun was gone, gliding through the crowd, smiling and nodding to the students as they danced around her. The priest watched her go, his eyes noting the contrast between her dark habit and the brightly colored dresses of his charges. He felt his anger surging up, silently wished he could turn the clock back, turn time back to an easier day, when girls dressed modestly and a priest was respected.

Monsignor Vernon's expression grew even more severe as he watched the teen-agers merrily greeting Sister Marie as she made her way through the room. Not one of them had spoken to him. He turned, and walked back into the foyer of the gym, glad to be away from the glittering lights and festooning crepe.

Peter Balsam glanced at his watch as he hurried up the steps of the gymnasium: he was already ten minutes late, and he had intended to be at least that much early. He burst through the door into the foyer, and almost collided with the Monsignor. He felt his heart pound at the sight of the priest, and hoped his voice wouldn't give his feelings away. He wanted to back away, then turn and flee, but he forced himself to stand his ground and smile a greeting.

"Monsignor," he said. "Nice evening, isn't it?"

The priest seemed pleased to see him, and Peter began to relax. Maybe he was going to be able to pull it off after all.

"Sorry about last night," Vernon was saying. "I'm afraid time just slips away from us sometimes. I hadn't intended for the service to go nearly that late."

"Well, it was Friday night," Peter said, forcing his voice to remain neutral. "I'm afraid I slept in a bit this morning, though." He waited for the priest to respond, then became aware that the Monsignor was no longer looking at him, but seemed to be concentrating on something behind Peter. Peter turned, and saw Karen Morton and Jim Mulvey coming in the door. He smiled a greeting to his students, but they hurried by, studiously ignoring him. It wasn't until they had disappeared into the gym that he realized it hadn't been he they were avoiding; it had been Monsignor. The priest was glaring after them.

"Karen seems like a nice girl," Peter said, trying to keep his voice easy.

"Do you think so?" the priest said icily. "Then you aren't as perceptive as I thought you were. Excuse me, I'd better have a word with Sister Elizabeth."

Puzzled, Peter made his way to the door of the gym, and let his eyes wander over the crowd. Eventually he saw the Monsignor bending down to whisper into Sister Elizabeth's ear, and pointing toward a spot where Jim Mulvey and Karen Morton were dancing. A moment later, Sister Elizabeth was striding toward the couple, a ruler in her hand.

He watched curiously, wondering what the ruler was for. Then, as he looked on, Sister Elizabeth put the ruler between Karen and Jim. She looked at them severely when the ruler wouldn't quite fit, and pushed them slightly apart. When they were a foot apart, and the ruler could be passed between them without touching either of them, Sister Elizabeth was satisfied. She glared at each of them once more, then moved on to another couple.

Balsam almost laughed at the performance. The fact that Sister Elizabeth had not been kidding with her measurements made him stop. He looked around and saw that all the nuns were carrying rulers, and that they were all circulating through the room, meticulously making certain that the boys and girls were maintaining a foot of open space between them. All, that is, except Sister Marie, who was standing at the refreshment table chatting with Penny Anderson and Jeff Bremmer. Peter Balsam decided to have a cup of punch.

The nun saw Peter approaching, and had an impulse to hurry away. But then she changed her mind, and made herself smile at him.

"Some punch, Peter?"

Balsam's brows rose. "No more Mr. Balsam?" he said. The look of hurt in her eyes, and a sudden flicker of what he thought was fear, made him wish he hadn't said it. "I'm sorry," he said quickly. "I didn't mean it to sound sarcastic. I'm just glad to see you smiling at me again." He decided to change the subject. "Where's your ruler?" He gestured toward the nuns who were still steadily circulating through the room, measuring the gaps between the students.

"Oh, I have one," Sister Marie said, her sense of mischief getting the best of her. "But I use it differently." Deftly, she slipped the ruler from the sleeve of her habit, and stirred the punch with it. Then she looked at Balsam, and her manner changed slightly. "Could I talk to you for a minute?"

He followed her to a quiet corner.

"What is it?" he said gently. He thought the flicker of fear he had seen earlier was back, and growing.

"It's probably nothing," Sister Marie said nervously. "But I have to tell you about it. I'm sorry about the way I acted yesterday, when you asked me about the handwriting in that note. I told you I'd forgotten all about it. I lied. I didn't forget; I remembered. But for some reason, when I remembered, the strangest fear flowed over me. I almost felt like—well, never mind," she broke off.

She saw no point in telling Peter Balsam that she had felt like killing herself. Besides, it had only been an impulse, and it had passed almost immediately. But it *had* frightened her. Frightened her badly.

"You remembered the handwriting?" Balsam said, his heart suddenly pounding.

"Yes," Sister Marie said, nodding. "But I don't know what it means. It's very strange."

"What is it?" Balsam said impatiently. He had to know.

"It was years ago," Sister Marie said. "I was in Monsignor Vernon's office, and he suddenly offered to show me something. A relic. A relic of his favorite saint, Peter Martyr."

"A relic?" Balsam said curiously. "What sort of relic?"

"It was a letter. Just a page. But he told me it was written by St. Peter Martyr. And it was in the same handwriting as the handwriting on the note you showed me Wednesday morning."

"What did it say?"

"The letter? I haven't the slightest idea. It was in a language I couldn't understand. Almost like Latin, but sort of like Italian, too. I suppose if I'd had time, I could have figured it out."

"You speak Italian?" Peter couldn't believe his luck.

"And French, and Spanish. I majored in languages in college. So of course I joined the order, and where did they send me? Neilsville, Washington!"

Balsam hardly heard her. "You really think you could have understood that language?" he asked eagerly.

The nun looked at him, wondering why he was so curious about the relic. "I don't see why not," she said thoughtfully. "My Latin and Italian are both excellent, and since Italian grows directly out of Latin, I shouldn't have any problems with it."

"What if you *heard* the language?" Peter said.

"Heard it?" Sister Marie laughed. "Well, that's hardly likely, is it? I mean, who would speak it anymore?"

"But could you understand it?" Peter said urgently. The laughter faded from Sister Marie's voice.

"I suppose so," she said carefully. "I can't say. But I can try. I mean, if you aren't just being hypothetical."

"I'm not," Peter said. "Believe me, I'm not."

For the first time in several days, Peter thought he had a chance of getting to the bottom of the Society of St. Peter Martyr.

*   *   *

Jim Mulvey pulled Karen Morton to him, and squeezed her. A shiver of pleasure ran through her body, but she tried to pull away from him. "They'll see us, Jim," she whispered in his ear, gesturing toward the nuns. Sister Elizabeth, the one Karen feared most, had her back to the couple for the moment, but Karen was sure that it wouldn't be more than a few seconds until the sour-faced sister saw them pressed together and moved swiftly to break up the embrace.

"Let them see us," Jim whispered back, his voice heavy. "They just wish it was them instead of you." He pulled her to him again, pressing the swelling of his erection against her. "Put your hand down there," he whispered.

She wanted to, but she knew she shouldn't. She resisted the urge to touch him. Instead, she pulled away again.

"Not here," she hissed. "Everyone can see." She glanced around, and sure enough, there was Sister Elizabeth bearing down on them.

"Twelve inches," Sister Elizabeth said bitterly. "You know the rule." She brandished the ruler.

"I know it, but I can't quite manage it," Jim said innocently. "Will you settle for eight?"

Sister Elizabeth saw Karen blush a deep red, and wondered if she'd missed something. She glared at Jim, sure that he had gotten the best of her, but uncertain how he'd managed it. She scurried away, leaving Jim grinning triumphantly at Karen.

"That was a terrible thing to say to her," Karen said.

"Was it?" Jim leered. Then he winked at her. "Hey, I have an idea. You know that little room where they keep all the gym stuff?"

Karen nodded, remembering the equipment room, no more than a closet, really. "What about it?"

"Let's go in there," Jim said. "It's dark, and private. And no sisters with rulers."

Karen considered the idea. It'll only be for a couple of minutes, she told herself. What can happen in a couple of minutes?

Jim began dancing her toward the equipment room.

Marilyn Crane felt she was being watched. She told herself that she was only imagining it, that no one was paying any attention to her at all. That thought was even worse. Suddenly her corner became unbearable, and she looked around for refuge. Jeff Bremmer. Of all of them, Jeff was usually the kindest to her. She began working her way across the floor toward the refreshment table, dodging the dancing couples. She stepped aside to let Jim and Karen pass; they ignored her.

She rushed on toward the refreshment table, not speaking to anyone until she reached Jeff. He smiled half-heartedly at her.

"Hot in here," she said tentatively, dipping herself a cup of punch.

"Too many people," Penny Anderson said pointedly, staring into her eyes. Marilyn decided to ignore the crack, and turned back to Jeff.

"Can I help you with anything?"

Jeff glanced away from her guiltily, remembering that he'd been at the party when they'd all made her look like a fool. He looked to Penny Anderson for help.

"We can manage fine," Penny said. Then she relented. "If you want to get some more ice, it's out in the foyer." Marilyn's face broke into a smile, and she started toward the main doors. Behind her, she heard Penny's voice.

"She's really pathetic, isn't she?"

The words hit her like a physical blow. Marilyn hurried toward the door. Only now she knew she wouldn't be back, with or without the ice. She had to get out of the gym, get away from everybody, get to the church.

She had to get to the church. She had to.

The Sorrowful Mother. She had to talk to the Sorrowful Mother. The Virgin had come to her once; maybe she would again.

But then, just as she was about to pass through the doors, her way was blocked. She looked up into the piercing eyes of Monsignor Vernon. He returned her gaze, and seemed about to say something when Sister Elizabeth rushed up. Ignoring Marilyn, the nun spoke to the priest over her head.

"Monsignor," she said, her voice carrying a heavy burden of outrage. "It's happened. I knew it would if we let this kind of thing go on, and now it has."

"What's happened?" the Monsignor replied, his brow suddenly furrowed.

"Jim Mulvey and Karen Morton. I just saw them go into the equipment room together."

Suddenly, as Marilyn looked on, the Monsignor's face changed from its normally severe mask into a glowering visage of indignation. Thrusting Marilyn to one side, he began striding toward the closed door of the equipment room, scattering the dancers as he went.

Monsignor Vernon grasped the handle of the door of the equipment room, and yanked the door open. The small room was close and dark. The priest groped for the light cord, yanked it, illuminating two startled figures. There, under the naked bulb were Jim Mulvey and Karen Morton, their arms around each other, their bodies pressed close in a passionate kiss. The priest seized them, one with each hand, and thrust them out of the tiny room into the crowded gymnasium. He reached up and found the light cord again. The door began to swing slowly closed, and as he pulled the light switch he was suddenly plunged into darkness. He moved quickly toward the door but his foot caught on something. He tripped.

Monsignor Vernon fell to his knees, and as he caught himself he glimpsed the narrow band of light that came through the slightly open door. Deep inside him, a memory came to life.

Monsignor Vernon froze, staring through the crack in the door. High up in the rafters, the gym's lights glared balefully down on him. He felt himself growing dizzy. And then he saw the girl. She moved into his line of sight, and she seemed to be turning, turning slowly toward him. She had something in her hand, the girl. Something that glinted silver in the light. A knife. It looked like a knife.

Monsignor Vernon lunged to his feet and burst through the door.

Janet Connally, her silver net scarf held high as she danced, paused in mid-step as the priest, his eyes wild, threw the door open.

"Stop it!" he bellowed. Janet froze. The Monsignor stared around him. They were everywhere, the girls, all around him, they all looked alike. They all looked like her, like his sister. "Sinners!" he cried. "All of you are sinners!"

The students stared now, and began edging toward the door. Monsignor was angrier than they had ever seen him before.

"No more!" shouted the priest. "Do you think I don't know you? Do you think I don't recognize you? Do you think I will show you mercy? You do not deserve mercy! Beware for your souls, for you have sinned. Punishment will fall upon you."

And then, across the room, Monsignor Vernon saw Peter Balsam staring at him. The priest raised his hand, and pointed to the teacher.

"Heretic! Punishment will fall upon you," he bellowed. "Punishment at the hands of the Lord!"

And then, as quickly as it had come, the rage was over, the memory gone. Nervously, the Monsignor glanced around. A silence had fallen over the room, and when he spoke again, this time in a whisper, everybody in the room heard him.

"The dance is over," he said.

Five minutes later the room was empty, except for two people. Standing at opposite ends of the gym, as if waiting for the battle to begin, Monsignor Vernon and Peter Balsam stared at each other. And now, thought Peter, it's all going to happen.

He was frightened.

# BOOK THREE

# AUTO-DA-FÉ

## NINETEEN

THE CAFETERIA BUZZED WITH THE NOISE of high-school students at lunch, but Marilyn Crane didn't hear it. She sat alone, surrounded by empty seats, and concentrated on her sandwich. A few feet away from her, at the other end of the same table, Jeff Bremmer also sat alone. Every few seconds he glanced at Marilyn, and tried to figure out what he should say to her.

He knew she'd overheard Penny Anderson's remark on Saturday night. He had intended to follow her out to apologize for Penny. But then Monsignor had found Karen and Jim in the equipment closet, and blown his cool. Jeff shook his head, remembering the priest's outburst.

He glanced at Marilyn again, and decided to use the dance as an opening. "Boy, that was really something, wasn't it?" he said.

Marilyn looked at him, and wondered if he was talking to her. Then she realized there wasn't anybody else at the table; he *must* be talking to her.

"What was?" she asked warily, searching for a trap.

"The dance," Jeff said. "I knew Monsignor was a puritan, but I never expected anything like that."

"Well, they shouldn't have gone into the equipment closet," Marilyn said stiffly, allying herself with the priest.

Jeff tried another tack. "But calling Mr. Balsam a heretic? What was that all about?"

Marilyn shrugged. She didn't see how she could defend the priest against Mr. Balsam; he'd been too nice to her. But she wasn't going to agree with Jeff, either. "I don't know," she said carefully. Then she relented. "It was pretty weird, wasn't it?"

"Weird isn't the word," Jeff said. "It was really gross. I mean, just because Mr. Balsam isn't a priest doesn't make him a heretic. Jesus, who uses words like 'heretic' anymore anyway? If you ask me, Mr. Balsam's the best thing to hit this dump in years!"

"He probably won't stay," Marilyn commented.

"Why would he? Would you?" Without waiting for an answer, Jeff went right on talking. "But I'm glad he's here now. I like his class; he really makes me think about things."

"I know," Marilyn said. "But sometimes I'm more confused after his class than I was before. I mean, I used to think I understood things pretty well. But since I've been in his class, I just don't know anymore. Those rats are weird. It seems like he can make them do anything."

"It's just conditioning," Jeff said smugly. Then he frowned. "I wonder if you can condition people the same way you condition rats?"

Marilyn shrugged. "Why don't you ask Mr. Balsam?" There was something else on her mind. "That isn't really why his class makes me nervous," she said. "It just seems like the more I find out about psychology, the worse I feel about myself." Then, realizing what she'd admitted, Marilyn flushed. But suddenly Jeff was smiling at her.

"I wouldn't worry about it if I were you," he grinned. "I mean, you obviously aren't as bad off as some people around here." He nodded toward the door. Marilyn followed his glance. Judy Nelson was coming into the cafeteria.

The room fell silent. They had all been waiting for this moment; they had all known that Judy was back at school today, that she had spent the morning in Monsignor's office. No one knew what had gone on in there; but no one imagined it had been pleasant. Now here she was, sailing into the cafeteria as if nothing had happened. From the table next to Marilyn and Jeff, Janet Connally called out.

"Over here, Judy."

While Marilyn and Jeff looked on, Judy slid into a chair and was surrounded by her friends. The questions began.

Judy was enjoying it. They were hanging on her every word, and every couple of minutes someone she hardly knew stopped to welcome her back to St. Francis Xavier's. They all wanted to know what had happened to her; first in the hospital, then when she got home, and, most important, what had gone on this morning in Monsignor's office.

Judy answered the questions calmly, her voice soft and ethereal. As they listened to her, her friends began to feel that they were talking to a new Judy Nelson, a Judy who had passed through the valley of death and been transformed. It was exactly the impression Judy intended to give.

As Marilyn watched the scene being played at the next table, she began to wonder what had happened to Judy, if the attempt on her own life had really changed her, or if she was putting on an act. Chiding herself for the unkind thought, she turned back to Jeff. He wasn't there.

She glanced quickly back to the table where Judy was still regaling her friends, and saw that Jeff had joined Judy's group, and was hanging on her words along with everyone else. And then, as she watched, Mr. Balsam came into the cafeteria. She looked up hopefully; he always stopped to greet her. But today he walked right past her, intent on something else. Marilyn watched miserably as even Mr. Balsam joined the group around Judy Nelson. A couple of minutes later the teacher rose, and Marilyn's hopes surged again. Now he would pause at her table. But he didn't. Before Marilyn could summon the courage to call out to him, he was gone. Sadly, she turned her attention back to Judy Nelson's table.

Karen Morton had grown restive. She was tired of listening to Judy. Besides, didn't anyone want to hear what had happened to her at the dance? It wasn't fair. Ordinarily, the encounter with the Monsignor would be the major topic for the day, but Judy had eclipsed her. She stared glumly down at her hands. Then inspiration struck.

"Trying to kill yourself isn't such a big deal," she said, breaking into Judy's monologue. She was pleased when Judy fell silent and stared at her.

"Have you tried it?" Judy said knowingly. Karen smiled and held up her hands.

"How do you think I got these?" she said, displaying her palms. The scabs were nearly healed, but still clearly visible.

"Those?" Penny Anderson laughed. "I thought you said you didn't know how you got those!"

"I just didn't want to admit it," Karen said. She felt herself losing control of the conversation.

Judy Nelson confirmed the feeling. "If they weren't even bad enough to put you in the hospital, I don't think they count," she said acidly. "Besides, why should you want to kill yourself?"

"I'm not sure," Karen began, but Penny cut her off.

"I'll give you a reason," she said. "I've decided I'm going to take Jim Mulvey away from you."

Karen's mouth dropped open. All of a sudden it had all gone wrong. All she'd wanted was a little attention. Now they were all laughing at her, and Penny was saying she was going to take Jim away. That wasn't what she'd intended at all. She glared at Penny.

"You have about as much chance of doing that as Marilyn Crane!" she snapped. Then she stood up and walked quickly out of the cafeteria.

The remark hit Marilyn like a slap in the face, and her hand suddenly let go of the sandwich she was eating. She stared down into her lap, and her eyes filled with tears as she surveyed the purple stain that was spreading from the lump of jelly lying on her pale yellow skirt. Now she would have to spend the rest of the day pretending everyone wasn't staring at her dirty skirt. She stuffed the rest of her lunch back into its bag and hurried out of the room.

She started for her locker but suddenly changed her mind. Instead, she made her way to the church, and slipped into the pew in front of the Blessed Virgin. She reached into her purse to pull out her rosary beads. Before she found them her hand closed on something else.

It was the package of razor blades.

Her fingers closed on them and they felt good to her. Then, suddenly frightened, she dropped the blades and found the rosary. She began praying.

When she left the church thirty minutes later, Marilyn had almost succeeded in forgetting about the stain on her skirt. She hurried toward her locker and spun the dial quickly, intent on tossing the remains of her lunch into the metal box, and picking up her books for the afternoon. She pulled open the locker door.

Marilyn Crane screamed, but the scream was cut off as she gagged. A wave of nausea broke over her. Her Bible lay open on the bottom of her locker; on top of it was a white rat, its fur stained by the blood and gore that was oozing from it. Its throat had been slit, and it was disemboweled. The nausea passed, and the tears began. Marilyn Crane sank to the concrete floor, sobbing hysterically. Moments later Sister Marie appeared and gathered Marilyn into her arms. Then she led her slowly away toward the nurse's office.

Peter Balsam sat in his classroom after school, three books spread out in front of him. He was reading snatches from one page, then changing to another book, reading a paragraph here and a paragraph there, then picking up the third book. Slowly he was piecing it all together. And in its own weird way it was starting to make a strange kind of sense. He heard a noise at the door and glanced up. Karen Morton was standing uneasily in the doorframe.

"Can I come in?" she asked tentatively.

"I'm kind of busy," Balsam said, hoping she'd go away. She stood her ground.

"It'll only take a minute." Karen advanced into the room. Peter Balsam pushed the books to one side, and glanced at his watch. Maybe he could hold her to the minute.

"What is it?"

"I'm not sure," Karen said uncertainly. Then, seeing the impatience on Balsam's face, she hurried on. "It's Judy, I guess. She seems——" She hunted for the right word. "——different, I guess."

Is that all? Balsam thought to himself. "Well, of course she does," he said easily. "But I don't think she is, really. Oh, she may think she is, but don't forget: right now she's the center of attention around here. It'll all calm down in a couple of days, and things will be back to normal."

Karen started to say something, but Peter cut her off. "Look, I'm kind of busy right now. Can this wait till tomorrow?" He picked up one of the books, and had already started to read another paragraph. He had finally found the saint he was looking for, and he promptly put Karen Morton out of his mind.

The girl looked at him for a moment. She needed to talk, but he didn't want to listen. She felt her anger growing, and started out of the room. And then, just as she was at the door, she spun around.

"Maybe I should try to kill myself, like Judy!" she cried. "Then maybe you'd pay some attention to me."

The words jarred Peter loose from the book in front of him, but Karen was already gone. He could hear her feet pounding the floor as she ran down the hall. He started to get up to follow her, but another figure appeared in the door of Room 16.

Monsignor Vernon.

The two men faced each other coldly.

"You handled that rather badly," the priest commented.

"You aren't in any position to criticize," Balsam said icily, remembering the incident Saturday night.

The Monsignor ignored the remark. "What happened?" he said, and Peter knew the question was being put as the principal of the school. He explained briefly.

"I should have given her more time, I suppose," he finished. "But I'm afraid I was too involved in my reading."

"Oh?" the priest said, advancing toward the desk. "What is it that's so fascinating?"

Peter quickly gathered the books together and shoved them into the bottom drawer of his desk.

"It's not that interesting, really," he said as he closed the drawer firmly. "Just some old psychology texts."

The priest seemed to accept his explanation.

"There's going to be a meeting of the Society tonight," he said. "At the rectory, the usual time."

"I won't be there," Peter said.

The priest stared at him.

"Yes," he said. "You will be there. We need you."

And then he was gone. Peter stared after him. There had been something in the priest's voice, not a note of command, but something else. It was a note of knowledge, as if he didn't feel that he needed to order Peter to attend that night; it was as if the priest had some sort of secret knowledge, a knowledge that told him that something would compel Peter's attendance at the Society of St. Peter Martyr.

Balsam pulled the books out of his desk drawer, and left the school.

Two hours later, when he had finished his reading, it all made sense to him. Crazy sense, a sense he had difficulty accepting, but sense nevertheless. The Monsignor was right: he would attend the meeting of the Society of St.

Peter Martyr that evening. But only long enough to confront them with what they were doing, and why.

And then he would leave. If they wanted to go on without him, let them. Peter didn't think they would.

If the conclusions he had come to were correct, they needed him. But they would never have him.

## TWENTY

KAREN MORTON HURRIED DOWN THE front steps of the school, her eyes straight ahead, as if by looking to either side she might tip a delicate balance and give way to the tears that were welling inside her. She wouldn't cry. She would go straight home and spend the rest of the afternoon by herself. If nobody wanted to talk to her, that was fine with her; she certainly wouldn't make them.

It was Judy's fault, she told herself. Judy was supposed to be her friend. Some friend! When Karen had tried to talk about what she had done to herself, about gouging her hands, Judy had laughed at her. Well, maybe not out loud, but inside she had been laughing. And everybody was paying Judy all kinds of attention, even Mr. Balsam. Mr. Balsam should have listened to *her*. Judy's problems were all over with. Couldn't he see that? But what about Karen? Who would talk to her?

Ahead of her, Karen saw Marilyn Crane hurrying down the hill. For the first time, Karen knew how Marilyn must feel. She wanted to call out to her, wanted Marilyn to wait for her. But why should Marilyn wait? Wasn't Karen part of the group that had been making Marilyn's life miserable for years? Maybe she should apologize to Marilyn. No, that wouldn't work either. There was too much to apologize for. Besides, she didn't want to talk to Marilyn. She wanted to talk to a man. She wanted to talk to her father. He would have understood. He would have put his arms around her, and held her, and told her that it was all going to be all right. But he was dead, and there wasn't anybody else . . .

She heard a car pull up beside her, and recognized the sound of the motor immediately. Jim Mulvey. She kept walking; kept staring straight ahead.

She heard the sound of his horn, then his voice. "Karen? Hey, Karen?"

She stopped, and turned slowly. He was grinning and waving to her.

"Hop in," he called. She shook her head and started to turn away.

"Hey," Jim said, getting out of the car. "What's wrong? It's me, Jim."

He caught up with her and took her arm. She wanted to shake his hand off, but didn't.

When she turned to face him, Jim realized that something really was wrong with Karen. It looked as though she was about to start crying. The bantering quality left his voice, and it softened.

"Get in the car, Karen," he said. "I'll take you home." Karen let herself be led to the car, and for the first time since she'd known him, Jim Mulvey opened the door for her. She sat staring ahead as he circled the car and slid behind the wheel. They drove in silence.

"Do you want to talk about it?" Jim finally said. Karen shook her head. A minute later he slowed the car and pulled over to the curb. He turned to face her.

"I heard about what Penny Anderson said at lunch today," he said. "If that's what's got you upset, forget it."

"That's not it," Karen said dully. "Why don't you just take me home?"

But there was something in her voice that told Jim that she didn't really want to be taken home. He put the car in gear, but instead of driving Karen home, he headed out of town.

"Where are we going?" Karen asked, not really caring.

"Out by the lake."

"I want to go home."

"No, you don't," Jim said definitely. "You want to talk, so we're going to go sit by the lake and talk."

"I hate it out there," Karen complained. "It smells bad, and there's nothing there but scrub juniper."

"It's better than nothing," Jim said.

They finished the ten-minute ride in silence. Jim drove through the picnic area, and parked at the end of the dirt road that led to a primitive boat ramp. The lake was deserted. The silence lengthened, and Jim wondered what he should say. Then he decided not to say anything. Instead, he put his arm around Karen, and pulled her toward him.

She tried to resist when he kissed her, but his arms tightened around her, and his mouth found hers. And then, as the kiss deepened, Karen felt her body responding almost in spite of herself. She needed to be held, she needed to be caressed, she needed to be loved. Her arms went around him.

"Love me, Jim," she whispered. "Please love me." She heard him groan as her hand went to his lap and her fingers touched his erection. She pressed closer to him and helped him as he began undressing her.

"Jesus," Jim breathed half an hour later. "I never had it like that before. Let me know the next time you need to talk to someone." He leered at her, and winked, and Karen felt something break inside her.

He used me, she thought. He doesn't love me. He just wanted to fuck me. Fuck me. Fuck me.

She repeated the words to herself, over and over again, trying to make them take on that meaninglessness that comes when a word is used too often. It didn't work.

She had needed to be loved, and she had only gotten laid. She tried to convince herself that there wasn't any difference, but she knew there was. And now all the things they had been saying about her were true.

"Take me home," she said quietly.

Jim Mulvey started the car, turned it around, and began driving back to Neilsville.

Twenty minutes later he stopped in front of the Morton house. He let the engine idle, but didn't get out of the car.

"Aren't you going to open the door for me?" Karen asked.

"You can do it yourself," Jim said. He wasn't sure why, but he was suddenly angry with Karen. All they'd done was get it on, for Christ's sake. It should have made her feel better. And she'd sure acted like she liked it when it was happening. But now, nothing. Well, if she couldn't talk to him, she could damned well open the door herself. He glared at her.

Karen opened the car door, scrambled out, and slammed it behind her. Then, without looking back, she hurried toward the house. Not that it would have made any difference if she had looked back; as soon as the door had slammed, she'd heard the tires scream as Jim raced away.

Karen went inside, fixed herself a TV dinner, and tried to concentrate on the television. It didn't help. She needed to talk to someone, but there wasn't anybody to talk to. She glanced at the clock—her mother wouldn't be home for a couple of hours yet. But Karen had to talk to her, had to talk to her now. She picked up the phone and called her mother at work.

"Hi, Mom," she said, trying to keep her voice light.

"What is it?" Harriet Morton asked. All her tables were full; she really didn't have time to talk. "Are you all right?"

"I'm okay. I was just wondering if you could come home early tonight."

"If we're going to eat, I have to work," Harriet snapped. She dropped the phone back on the hook, picked up the coffee pot, and got back to work.

Karen stared at the dead phone, and felt like crying again. Even her mother wouldn't talk to her. She held back the tears and decided not to think about it. She wouldn't think about anything. She'd just watch television till her mother came home, then she'd let it all out. Only a couple more hours. She glanced at the clock.

Almost ten.

Only one more hour.

And then the phone rang. Karen picked it up eagerly; maybe her mother had changed her mind and was coming home.

"Hello?" she said. "Mother?"

But it wasn't Harriet Morton's voice at all. It was someone else, another voice, a voice Karen thought she recognized.

"You have sinned," the voice said. "You are evil. You must repent. Repent!"

And then it was over. The phone went dead in Karen's hand. She dropped it to the floor this time, not even bothering to put it back in its cradle.

So it was already out.

The talking was already starting.

And her mother still wasn't home.

She stared at the clock. Only five after ten.

The desolation swept over Karen Morton, but she still wouldn't let herself cry.

Maybe she should have let herself cry.

Maybe if she had let herself cry, she wouldn't have done what she did next.

Maybe she wouldn't have gone upstairs to the bathroom, locked the door, filled the tub with warm water, and begun cutting herself.

Maybe Karen Morton should have cried instead. But she didn't.

They sat like six birds of prey, the black of their clerical garb accentuating the paleness of their faces. They stared balefully at Peter Balsam, but he maintained his calm, returning them stare for stare, matching the coldness in their eyes with his own icy demeanor.

Inside, Peter Balsam was quavering.

He could tell they didn't believe him; he was sure they thought he had gone crazy.

The silence went on; Peter Balsam was determined not to be the one to break it. He wondered what was going through their minds. Had they simply decided to put what he had told them out of their minds entirely? Or were they thinking about his words, mulling them over, examining them?

"Just what is it you think you're going to tell the Bishop?" Monsignor Vernon finally said.

For the first time, Peter Balsam squirmed. Why had he told them he was going to go to the Bishop? Why hadn't he simply told them he was through with the Society of St. Peter Martyr, and let it go at that?

But they had insisted on knowing why he was leaving, and he had told them.

The had listened in silence as he told them about the chanting; they knew about that. It came to him then that the same things happened to all of them that had happened to him during those weird services: they knew something was happening, but they didn't know what. He tried to tell them. He wanted to tell them that they were all perverts, to detail for them exactly what they were doing during their rituals. But he found he couldn't. They were, after all, still priests. Priests, to be respected. The traditions he had grown up with took over, and he found himself unable to describe for them what went on between them. He merely told them that he had found the whole thing unspeakable.

"But you'll be able to tell it to the Bishop?" Monsignor had said mildly at the end of Balsam's recital.

"I won't have to," Peter said quietly. "I have a recording of everything that went on at the last meeting."

"A recording?" Father Prine said blankly. "What do you mean, a recording?"

Peter patiently explained it again.

"I wanted to know what goes on at the services," he said. "I couldn't remember myself; all I could remember was going into some kind of a trance, and it being much later than I thought it should be when I came out of it."

"Not unusual during times of devotion," the Monsignor said.

"It had nothing to do with devotion," Peter replied, his anger rising. "I don't know what it had to do with, but I wanted to find out what was going on. So I brought a recorder to the meeting, and recorded the whole thing. When I played the tape back, I was sick. Literally sick. If I played the tape for you, you'd all be sick."

"You're exaggerating, of course," Monsignor Vernon began, but Peter cut him off.

"I'm not exaggerating," he snapped. "The whole thing was absolutely depraved."

"I think we've heard enough," Monsignor Vernon said, standing up. "All you can tell us is that you heard a language that you think—you *think*, mind you; you don't *know*—might be some kind of mixture of Latin and Italian. And that we were all indulging in something you call depraved. Something you won't describe to us."

"I don't see that it's necessary," Balsam said. "I'm sure that when the Bishop hears the tape, he'll be convinced."

"Convinced?" It was the Monsignor again. He was pacing the room now. "Convinced of what?"

"Well, for one thing, I think he'll be convinced to put an end to your Society."

The Monsignor chuckled. "Convinced by the words of a heretic?" Peter noted that the fanatical light was beginning to come into Vernon's eyes. He told himself to be careful.

"Heretic again," he said softly. "Well, at least I know where that's coming from now."

"You finally figured it out?" The priest's voice was as soft as Peter's own.

Peter nodded gravely. "That, and a couple of other things." He stood up. When he spoke again he tried to keep his voice level. "Monsignor, I don't intend to spend any more time here discussing something that I don't think you're mentally competent to discuss. I know you think I'm a heretic—whatever that word means to you. But *I* think the Bishop is much more likely to come to the conclusion that you're sick. After all, when he hears your voice claiming to be St. Peter Martyr, and calling down the wrath of God on the sinners and heretics, what else can he conclude?"

If he had expected an outburst of protest, Peter Balsam was disappointed. A sudden silence fell over the small study, as the priests exchanged glances. But the atmosphere in the room had changed. No longer was it filled with hostility toward Peter Balsam. Suddenly there was something else. A sense of anticipation, as if something long awaited was about to occur.

Monsignor Vernon had stopped his pacing, and was staring at Balsam. The other five priests all looked uncertainly toward the Monsignor.

"Can it be true?" Balsam heard one of them whisper. But before he could answer the voice of Monsignor Vernon roared over him.

*"What did you say?"*

"I asked what else the Bishop can conclude," Peter said, trying to ignore the rage in the priest's voice.

"About St. Peter Martyr," the Monsignor thundered.

"During the last service you claimed to be St. Peter Martyr, and exhorted God to hand down punishment on what you called the sinners and heretics."

"It's happened," Father Martinelli breathed.

Peter whirled and stared at the old man. An expression of awe had come over the priest's face, and he was gazing at the Monsignor with adoration.

"What's happened?" Peter asked in a low voice, though he was sure he knew the answer.

"He's come to us at last," Father Prine said softly. "After all this time, St. Peter Martyr is finally among us."

Peter Balsam sank back into a chair. It couldn't be happening. And yet it was. They had heard him, but what he had told them hadn't shaken their faith in their young leader. Instead it had deepened it. Peter Balsam remembered the words of the Bishop. *"They want to Believe. They need to lean on each other for support."* Now, when they should finally have realized that the person they were all leaning on was unbalanced, they only drew closer.

Balsam's eyes moved to the Monsignor. An expression of rapture had come over him, and he was staring upward, his hands clasped in prayer, his lips moving silently. Suddenly he looked at Balsam, and the teacher saw the fierce light in the priest's eyes.

"And still you don't believe?" he said softly.

"No," Peter said. "I don't believe any of it."

"But you *must* believe," Monsignor Vernon said. "I tried to tell you so long ago, when we were in school together. But the time wasn't right. But you must have known. It's in the names."

"The names," Peter said tiredly. "You always come back to the names, don't you?" He peered quizzically at the Monsignor; he wasn't sure the priest was listening. But the others were. Balsam looked from one old face to another, and saw the same puzzlement in each of them.

"Hasn't he told you?" he asked them. They stared at him, waiting for him to continue. When he did, Balsam chose his words carefully.

"St. Peter Martyr was a man by the name of Piero da Verona. Peter Vernon, if you want to believe it. And he was killed by another man, a man named Piero da Balsama. Get it?"

"Peter Balsam," Father Martinelli whispered. "It's happening all over again! You are St. Acerinus."

"No!" Peter snapped. "I'm not St. Acerinus, I'm not Piero da Balsama. Any more than Monsignor Vernon is St. Peter Martyr. It's coincidence. Nothing more!"

And then it happened. Monsignor Vernon's voice was quiet, but it carried throughout the small room.

"I *am* St. Peter Martyr," he said.

It's a nightmare, Peter Balsam thought to himself. It isn't happening. None of it can be happening.

But it was. Around him, the five priests knelt, staring up at Monsignor Vernon. For them, in that moment, Monsignor Peter Vernon became St. Peter Martyr. Peter Balsam stood up, and his eyes met the Monsignor's over the heads of the kneeling clerics.

"I won't do it," he said softly. "I won't carry it any further. I won't be your heretic, and I won't kill you. If you really need a St. Acerinus, you'll have to find him somewhere else."

But the priest didn't seem to hear him. He stood quietly. His face was calm but the fanatic light gleamed in his eyes.

Peter Balsam walked from the study, and from the rectory. It would have to end now, he told himself. They needed him to sustain the fantasy. But he had withdrawn, and now it would have to end. And then, as he started down the hill, he heard it.

The chanting had begun again.

It had not ended.

Somewhere in Neilsville, a clock was striking the hour. It was ten, and the Society of St. Peter Martyr was holding a service, and Karen Morton was preparing to die.


Karen lay in the tub of warm water, and wondered why it didn't hurt. Judy Nelson was right; there was no pain at all. Only a kind of numbness.

Karen watched the blood flow from her wrists, watched it form strange patterns in the water, then move swiftly around her to turn the entire tub a bright pink.

As the pink slowly deepened into red, Karen wondered if she was doing the right thing. But it was too late. Too many things had gone wrong, and there was no one to talk to. If only there had been someone to talk to, someone to listen to her. But there hadn't been, and as the redness in the tub grew steadily deeper, Karen realized she didn't really care. Not any more.

She began to pray, but she kept her eyes open. She wanted to see the color of her death, as if perhaps by watching her life stain the water she could figure out why it had all gone wrong.

She never saw the color of death. Long after her eyes drifted closed, the water continued to darken. When she died, it wasn't from the bleeding.

It was from drowning.

At quarter of eleven, Karen's head disappeared beneath the surface of the crimson water.


At eleven-fifteen Harriet Morton unlocked the front door. "Karen?" she called. When there was no answer, she called a little louder: "Karen!?" Still no answer. Yet the house did not seem empty: she was sure Karen had not gone out.

Harriet went upstairs, but didn't call out to Karen again. When she saw the bathroom door, she felt a sudden surge of relief. Karen was in the tub. Of course. That was why she hadn't heard Harriet's first call.

Harriet tapped at the door. "Karen?" she called. "Are you in there?"

There was no response, so Harriet tried the door. It was locked. And then the fear hit her.

She pounded on the door, and called out her daughter's name. The silence buffeted against her.

Harriet picked up the telephone in the upstairs hall. The police. She would call the police. But something was wrong with the telephone. There was no dial tone. Only a strange buzzing sound.

Harriet Morton began to scream. She hurled herself against the bathroom door, and it burst inward. The sight of the bathtub, filled with red liquid, choked off her screaming.

At the end of the tub, barely breaking the surface, a foot was visible. The toenails were painted green. Harriet knew that only her daughter had ever painted her toenails green.

The neighbors called the police as soon as Harriet Morton began crying out into the night; the police called an ambulance. A moment later the night was shattered by the screaming of sirens.

By midnight a doctor had sedated Harriet Morton, and Karen had been taken away. But still the crowd lingered in front of the Morton house, talking quietly among themselves, trying to tell each other what had happened, trying to find a reason for the tragedy that had struck their town. Jim Mulvey was there. He wondered if it had been his fault.

## TWENTY-ONE

PETER BALSAM SAT WAITING OUTSIDE MONsignor Vernon's office the next morning. He was waiting to resign. There didn't seem to be anything else to do; he had discussed it with Margo late into the night before, then again this morning. They had gone over it all, piece by piece, trying to make some sense out of it. First Judy Nelson. Then the Society of St. Peter Martyr. Now Karen Morton. And Karen was dead.

There had to be a connection. Somehow all the strangeness in Neilsville was coalescing; Judy and Karen were its victims. And Peter was sure that the Society of St. Peter Martyr was involved.

But so was Peter Balsam. Margo had tried to talk him out of it, but all night long his certainty had grown. He had been Judy Nelson's teacher, and she had tried to kill herself. He had joined the Society of St. Peter Martyr, and Karen Morton had killed herself. Another of his students. It was as if whatever force was loose in Neilsville had been intensified first by the arrival of Peter Balsam, and then by his involvement in the Society. And so he would leave. He had already left the Society (for all the good it had done) and now he would leave St. Francis Xavier's and Neilsville.

And he would talk to the Bishop.

But first he would resign, and then he would go to Sister Marie for an exact translation of what was on the tape. He heard the heavy tread of the Monsignor, and stood up.

Monsignor Vernon stepped into the reception room and nodded curtly to Balsam. "I expected you to be here this morning," he said. "How long will it take?"

"What?" Balsam said, his guard dropping a little.

"Why, whatever it is you want to talk about this morning. It's Karen Morton, I assume."

"Her, among other things," Balsam said carefully. He felt suddenly off balance, as if he had had an advantage, and lost it.

They moved into the Monsignor's office, and the priest took his seat behind the desk, motioning to Peter to take the visitor's chair.

"No, thanks," Peter said. "This won't take long, and I'd rather stand." He cast around in his mind for the right words, and decided there were none. "I'm leaving," he said.

The priest's brows rose a fraction of an inch, but he said nothing. He simply sat in his chair, staring at the teacher, waiting for him to continue.

"I suppose you want to know why," Balsam said when the silence became unbearable.

"I think I have the right to know, yes," Monsignor Vernon said calmly. "I imagine it has something to do with Karen Morton."

"Among other things."

"Tell me about them."

Peter Balsam, without thinking about it, sank into the chair opposite the priest. "It isn't only Karen, although what happened to her was the final straw. I feel responsible for her death."

"You're not," the priest said, almost too definitely.

"Well, it's neither here nor there now, is it? But I do feel responsible. She wanted to talk to me yesterday, and I brushed her off. I shouldn't have done that. I should have known how important it was to her. I'm a psychologist, after all. But I didn't see. And I'm obviously not much of a teacher, either, am I? I mean, just look what's happening to my students." The feeble attempt at black humor failed even for himself.

"I've told you before, and I'm telling you again," the priest snapped impatiently, "you aren't responsible for Judy and Karen. You aren't a priest."

"But it isn't just them," Peter said softly. "There's more."

The priest's head came up and his eyes bored into Peter's. Peter hesitated, but forced himself to say what he'd come to say.

"I'm going to talk to the Bishop about you," he said, unable to meet the Monsignor's eyes. "I'm going to see him as soon as I'm released from my position here, to tell him about the Society of St. Peter Martyr. What you and those priests are doing is grounds for excommunication."

"Indeed?" the priest said incredulously. "Our prayers may be fervent, but they are still only prayers."

Something snapped inside Peter; he leaped to his feet and stood towering over the priest.

"Prayers!" he thundered. "You call that prayer? You have no idea what you're talking about. Fornication! That's what you're up to! You and all of them."

*"How dare you!"* the Monsignor roared. He was on his feet, his rage almost a palpable force in the room. "Have you any idea what you're saying?" If it was meant to intimidate Balsam, it failed. The teacher stood his ground, and glared right back at the priest.

"Cocksucker," he snarled. The priest recoiled.

"What did you say?" There was a look of horror on his face.

"The truth," Balsam said softly. "I called you a cocksucker and it's the truth. That's what you do, all of you. You get yourselves stoned some way, and you start in. And the saddest part of it is that you don't even know it."

The priest sagged into his chair and stared at Peter. "So that's what you meant last night?" he asked softly. "When you said we were depraved?" Peter nodded, and the priest shook his head gently. "Then it's even worse than I thought. I thought you were telling us we were perverted in a religious sense. But it's worse than that, isn't it? It isn't enough for you, is it? Now you have to accuse us of—of—" He broke off, unable to say the words. He stared balefully at Balsam. "Piero da Balsama," he said softly, "you killed me once, and now you try to disgrace me. But you will not do it. This time I shall triumph."

Now it was Balsam's turn to sag into a chair.

The man was insane. There wasn't any other word for it. But how should he deal with it? He tried to remember the books. The books had had the answers, but what were they? *Buy into the insanity.* That was it.

He remembered the technique. It was sometimes used in dealing with paranoia; Balsam was sure the priest was paranoid.

"What makes you think so?" he said now. "If I beat you last time, what makes you think I won't beat you again? Why should this time be any different?"

The priest's eyes flashed around the room as if he were looking for a hidden weapon.

"I know," he said softly. "I just know."

"Did God tell you?" Balsam sneered the word "God," trying to make it sound tainted.

"You don't believe me, do you?" Monsignor Vernon said. "But why should you? I'd almost forgotten—you're a heretic, aren't you?"

"If you say so," Balsam said evenly.

The priest continued to glare at him, but then something happened. It was as if a switch had been thrown, and the light suddenly faded from the Monsignor's eyes. He shook himself slightly, as if waking up from a sleep.

"What were we talking about?" he said, totally puzzled. Balsam thought fast; the paranoid state could have passed, or this could be simply another manifestation of it. He'd have to be careful.

"My resignation," he said. The priest still appeared to be puzzled, but then his face cleared.

"Ah," he said, clearing his throat. "Of course." He smiled genially, and leaned toward Peter. "Well, of course I can't stop you, but I'm afraid I'm going to have to ask you to wait a while. Oh, not long," he said quickly as Peter started to protest. "Just a few weeks. You see, I spoke to the Bishop this morning."

"The Bishop?" Peter said blankly.

The priest nodded. "He called me early, about Karen Morton. He's very concerned about the situation here, as am I. He seems to think there's something going on here, that whatever happened, first to Judy Nelson, and then, last night, to Karen Morton, are somehow connected." The priest's tone suggested that he didn't agree with the Bishop's assessment. "At any rate, he thinks it would be a good idea if we made the fullest possible use of your background in psychology. For some reason, he seems to think that of everyone here, you're the best qualified to deal with whatever's happening. Not, of course," he added, almost as an afterthought, "that anything *is* happening here. However, under the circumstances, we're going to have to ask you to stay a while longer."

Balsam thought it over. The Bishop, of course, was right. His resolution began to waver.

"And there's something else," the priest said somberly. "Were you aware that Karen Morton left a note?"

"A note?" No, Peter certainly wasn't aware of it.

"Yes," the priest lied. "A very disturbing note. She said something about us—you and me—to the effect that she thought, and I think I can quote it, 'something is going on between them.' Nonsense, of course, but if you left right now—well, I'm sure you can see my point. There would be talk, wouldn't there?"

Peter Balsam felt defeat wash over him. Yes, he agreed to himself, it certainly would cause talk. Particularly since it was true. But that "something" had gone on only in the meeting of the Society of St. Peter Martyr. How could Karen have known about that? Or did she? Maybe she had simply hit a nerve by accident. Not that it mattered. Either way, he was caught. Karen Morton was dead, and Peter Balsam was trapped. He looked up at his superior, and knew he was expected to say something.

"All right," he agreed. "I'll stay. But I'm still going to talk to the Bishop about the Society."

"I assumed you were," the Monsignor said coldly. "You'll be wasting your time." He stood up. "Is there anything else?"

"No," Peter said, his voice as cold as the priest's. And then something occurred to him. "Yes, there is," he added, eyeing Vernon carefully. "I was wondering where I might find Sister Marie. There's something I need to talk to her about."

An odd look passed over the priest's face, and Peter felt a surge of triumph. He had shaken the man. But then the Monsignor's face cleared.

"I'm afraid she's not here," he said smoothly. "She'll be away for a while."

"Away?" Peter asked warily. "What do you mean, 'away'?"

"Periodically, Sister Marie goes into retreat." He smiled thinly. "I'm afraid her vocation isn't always as strong as it might be, and we've found, both of us, that it helps her to get away from here now and then. She'll be back."

"But she didn't tell me she was going away," Peter protested, his hopes suddenly fading.

"Of course she didn't," the priest said easily. "Why would she?"

The interview was over.

"You should celebrate the Mass yourself," Father Martinelli said. He was sitting in the study of the rectory with Monsignor Vernon, though only he was sitting. The Monsignor was pacing.

"It's a sacrilege," he muttered.

"I don't see how," Father Martinelli said emphatically. "Whatever people may think privately, we know tonight's Mass is not for Karen Morton."

"That isn't the point," Monsignor Vernon replied. "Of course we know the Mass isn't for Karen Morton. How could it be?—she wasn't in a state of grace when she died. The point is that the people intend to *make* it a Mass for Karen. And the only way we can prevent that is to cancel the Mass entirely."

"And what will that accomplish?" the old man asked, tiredly. "We'll only face the same thing at the next Mass. There is no way we can stop our parishioners from praying for Karen Morton, and I'm not even sure we should try."

"But it's wrong," Monsignor Vernon insisted. "There's no other way of looking at it. When that girl killed herself she committed a sin beyond redemption. She has no rights within the Church whatsoever."

Father Martinelli sighed, and his ancient mind tried to sort out the problem. Technically, the Monsignor was right, and yet there was more to the problem. In the church, the parishioners were gathering, expecting to hear Mass, needing to hear Mass. Shouldn't their needs be met? He peered out the window of the rectory, and saw the people still streaming up the hill.

It had begun an hour ago. Ordinarily the turnout for a mid-week Mass was next to zero, even in a parish as devout as St. Francis Xavier. But today was different, and there could be only one reason. The people were coming because of Karen Morton. It had been this way all day. As the word of the girl's suicide spread through Neilsville, the people had begun drifting in and out of the church, praying briefly, and leaving only after silently lighting a candle.

And then, half an hour ago, they had begun arriving for the evening Mass. They kept arriving, until the church was as full as it ever was on Easter Sunday. Two things can fill the church, Father Martinelli reflected— the hope of eternal life, and the fear of unexpected, and inexplicable, death.

He had watched them stream into the church, and been pleased; Father Martinelli didn't really care about why people came to church. He only cared that they came. But with Monsignor Vernon it was different.

For the Monsignor, it wasn't enough that they were there; they had to be there for the right reasons. And to pray for Karen Morton wasn't, in Monsignor Vernon's strict religion, a suitable reason. And so they were discussing the possibility of canceling the Mass entirely.

"I'll have no part of it," the Monsignor said in a tone that told Father Martinelli the discussion was over. But then he relented. "If you want to conduct it yourself, I won't stop you. However, the consequences are your responsibility." Abruptly, the Monsignor left the room.

As he made his way to the church and began the vesting processes, Father Martinelli wondered what consequences the Monsignor could be talking about.

Peter Balsam dipped his fingers in the font, made the sign of the cross, and slipped into one of the back pews. In front of him, he saw Leona Anderson turn and glare. He pretended not to notice, and picked up his prayer book.

He glanced around the church, recognizing some of the people, just as the organ music surged out of the loft, and the service began.

The first disturbance came when the congregation saw that Monsignor Vernon was not conducting the Mass. They buzzed and whispered among themselves as the stooped figure of Father Martinelli moved unsurely up the aisle. Peter quickly searched for the face of the Monsignor, and was not surprised when he didn't find it.

The Mass began, but it was soon apparent that something was happening. Tonight, the responses, which normally brought only a few garbled murmurs from the congregation, came full-throated from the entire body of the church. Father Martinelli appeared to be unaware of anything unusual, and his quavering voice droned steadily on with the Mass. But Peter tried to locate a focal point for the phenomenon. He found it almost immediately.

Tonight, all of Karen Morton's friends, instead of sitting with their families, were knotted together near the center of the church. All of them— Judy Nelson, Janet Connally, Penny Anderson, and several others. Apart from them, sitting by herself, was Marilyn Crane.

Marilyn had come alone to the evening service, as she always did, and had taken her usual place near the statue of the Blessed Virgin. She had been engrossed in her prayers, begging the Sorrowful Mother to forgive her for the cruel thoughts she had had about Karen Morton in the past, and asking the Queen of Angels to intercede on behalf of Karen, when she had become aware that the church was filling up around her. Yet no one sat next to her. Suddenly she felt conspicuous, and found it difficult to concentrate on her devotions.

Then it began.

It was soft at first, a barely discernible murmur against the full tones of the organ, but then it began to grow, and, as the last chords of the organ died away, the church was filled with a different kind of music, the music of the human voice.

It was the girls.

They were clustered together, and clasping each other's hands, though otherwise it didn't seem that they were aware of each other's presence. Except for Judy Nelson, all of them were wailing, tears streaming down their faces, their heads tilted upward toward the church ceiling, as if they were searching for something in the heights.

Father Martinelli tried to ignore them and raised his voice to continue the mass over the growing wail.

But the sound continued to grow, and suddenly the girls were on their feet, swaying together, and crying out in a voice that seemed filled as much with exaltation as grief.

Father Martinelli faltered in the service, then stopped altogether. He glanced around for help, but there was none. Instead, he saw only troubled faces looking to him for leadership. Immediately he went into the benediction, and the organist picked up his cue.

As the girls' keening rose, filling the church, the organ blared out, mixing with the high-pitched lamentations and creating a chaos of sound that made the final words of the benediction inaudible.

It didn't matter. Already the congregation was beginning to move nervously toward the doors, embarrassed to be in the presence of such clearly expressed grief, unnerved by the adolescents' display of emotion.

To Peter Balsam, it was obvious that the girls were caught up in a hysterical response to their friend's death. He rose and moved toward them.

But, as quickly as it had begun, it was over. It was as if the girls had come out of a trance, and the moment they became aware of each other again, they looked at each other, giggled nervously, and hurried out of the church. Behind them, more slowly, Judy Nelson walked up the center aisle. As she passed the spot where Peter Balsam stood, she suddenly turned to him, and smiled. He supposed it was intended as a friendly smile, but it made him cold. He felt a shiver in his back, and quickly looked away. By the time he got hold of himself, and turned back to face her, she was gone.

Only one figure remained in the church. Marilyn Crane sat huddled in her pew, and seemed unaware of what had been going on.

As, indeed, she was. She had been concentrating on the Sorrowful Mother, and when the strange wailing had begun she was sure it was inside her own head. There was no other explanation for it; such sounds as these were never heard in any church Marilyn Crane had ever attended. And then, when they ended, she realized she was alone in the church. She decided that the Blessed Virgin wanted something from her, and was sending her a sign. She approached the statue, and lit a candle.

She waited for the message.

For a long time nothing happened. Then the urge swept through her. She wanted to put her hand in the flame. She fought the urge, but it grew inside her: this was the message from the Sorrowful Mother; this was the sign.

Marilyn Crane reached out and put the palm of her hand over the flame of the votive light. She lowered her hand until she could see the flame touching her skin. There was no pain. The Virgin was protecting her from pain. It was just as Judy Nelson had told her. It was beautiful.

Marilyn held her hand steady, and didn't remove it from the fire until she smelled the sickly-sweet odor of charring flesh. When she did pull her hand from the flame, she stood still for a few moments, staring awe-struck at the wound. Yes, she told herself, Judy was right. There is no such thing as pain.

As she pondered the new truth, Marilyn Crane crossed herself, thanked the Blessed Virgin for the message, and slowly walked from the church.

Peter Balsam had almost reached the sanctuary doors when something caught his eye, and he paused. Then he realized he was staring at one of the saints.

St. Acerinus.

St. Acerinus, the canonized Piero da Balsama.

The saint seemed to be staring down at him accusingly, as if Peter had started something, but not finished it. Peter Balsam told himself that he was being ridiculous, that he was imagining things. He tore himself away from the saint's sightless gaze, and started from the church. But he had a feeling of being watched.

When he turned around, Monsignor Vernon was standing in the chancel, observing him, a look of strange serenity on his face.

## TWENTY-TWO

EARLIER THEY HAD ALL GONE TO church; now they were gathered on Main Street, the parents at the drugstore, their children across the street. There was something new in Neilsville—a discotheque—and the St. Francis Xavier crowd had flocked there tonight.

Leona Anderson stabbed fretfully at her banana split, part of her attention focused on the meager size of the dessert (which she was sure had shrunk by at least fifty percent since she had been a teen-ager), the rest of it silently protesting the noise from across the street.

The Praying Mantis—she wondered how they came up with such a silly name—had opened only a month ago, and Leona's worst fears had been immediately justified. A few of the Neilsville High students had drifted in, but it quickly became obvious that the disco was going to be the headquarters for the youngsters from St. Francis Xavier's. Leona had visions of drug traffic—or worse. She was sure the opening of the Praying Mantis spelled the end of decent living in Neilsville.

"Isn't there a law against making that much noise?" Inez Nelson complained from the opposite side of the booth. Leona shook her head grimly.

"I checked, of course," she said. "It's zoned for commercial use. They can do whatever they want." Her tone implied that she was sure they were doing exactly that, and that "whatever they want" went far beyond blasting a jukebox at top volume. "I'm not sure we should allow the girls to go there," Leona continued. She glared out the window at the offending building, as if by simply staring at it she could make it disappear.

"Oh, I don't know," Inez Nelson said tentatively. "Things just aren't the same as they were when we were teen-agers. I suppose you have to bend with the wind. Times change."

"Do they?" Leona asked crossly. "Then why are we sitting here in the same drugstore we sat in twenty years ago? It's more than that, Inez. Sometimes I feel as if we've lost control of things."

Inez stirred her coffee silently, wishing she could deny the truth of what Leona had said. If she had ever been in control, that time was certainly over by now. Ever since Judy had come home from the hospital, Inez had felt like she was walking on eggs. Being manipulated. She knew it was wrong, knew she should be more forceful with her daughter, but she couldn't. She just couldn't. She was too frightened of what might happen. Particularly after last night. Inez knew she'd never forget the look on Harriet Morton's face as they led her out of the house to take her to the hospital.

Leona's right, she thought. We have lost control. She followed Leona's gaze and she, too, began conjuring up images of the bizarre things that must be going on inside the Praying Mantis. A few minutes later the noise became too much for them, and the women fled.

The truth was that not much at all was going on in the discotheque. The jukebox was blaring, but from inside the large room, the music seemed somewhat hollow and desperate.

A few of the teen-agers were dancing, but it was a desultory kind of dancing. For the most part, they were clustered around tables, sitting, the music vibrating against them, trying to forget that Karen Morton was no longer with them.

Except for Janet Connally, whose mother had insisted that she go home right after the services ended, the group of girls who had created the disturbance at the church were there. But they were no longer all together. Judy Nelson was sitting alone, taking in her surroundings unhappily.

It was sleazy, hastily thrown together, without the money to do it right. Rock posters covered the walls; a sensuously sweating Mick Jagger, apparently in a state of sustained orgasm, presided over a gallery of his second- and third-rate imitators.

A makeshift light panel had been tied into the jukebox, but instead of creating the psychedelic visual symphony that had been intended, the crude box could produce no more than an occasional flash of red or green. Because of the poor quality of the light show, another lighting system had been installed, consisting of several strings of outdoor Christmas lights that glowed eerily in the dimness. In the center of the room, slowly revolving, hung the immense papier-mâché insect for which the place was named. Had Leona Anderson seen the inside of the Praying Mantis, much of her worry would have been displaced by disgust, and she would have wondered why the kids wanted to be there in the first place. But it was, for the students of St. Francis Xavier's, the only game in town.

And so they were gathered, trying in their own way to pretend that everything was all right. It might have worked if Jim Mulvey had not been sitting alone at a table, a constant reminder of Karen Morton's absence.

Penny Anderson broke away from the group she had been standing with, and glanced around. She saw Judy Nelson sitting alone, and started across the room to join her. Before she had taken three steps, she realized that Jim Mulvey was also sitting by himself. On an impulse, Penny changed her course and approached Jim's table.

"Hi," she said. He looked up disinterestedly. "Okay if I sit down?" Without waiting for an answer, she slipped into the chair next to Jim. He glanced at her once more, not smiling, then turned his attention back to his Coke.

"I wanted to talk to you," Penny said softly. "About Karen." She waited for a reaction, and when there was none, she continued talking. "We're all going to miss her, you know. I mean, Judy and Janet and me. We've always been sort of a foursome, ever since we were little. Of course, in the last year or so—" Penny suddenly broke off. It had been in the last year or so that Karen had started dating Jim Mulvey.

Now Jim looked at her curiously. "What were you going to say?" he said bitterly. "Were you going to say that in the last year or so—*ever since she started going with me*—Karen changed?" Jim stared accusingly at Penny.

"N-no—" Penny stammered. "I wasn't going to say that at all."

"Yes, you were," Jim said flatly, leaving no room for argument. "Don't you think I know what's been going on? Don't you think I've heard the talk? Hell, I started some of it." He stared sourly into his Coke, and when he spoke again, Penny wasn't sure he was talking to her. "It's my fault," he said so quietly Penny could hardly hear him. "I never treated her the way she wanted to be treated. I never talked to her. I should have talked to her. If I had, none of this would ever have happened."

Penny reached out and touched his hand. He seemed so unhappy, so unsure of himself. Not at all like the Jim Mulvey she had grown up with. The cockiness, the self-confidence, had vanished.

"It isn't your fault," she said. Then, as if trying to convince herself, she added, "It isn't anyone's fault."

Jim's head snapped up, and he realized he'd been talking out loud. "Shut up," he said savagely. "Just shut up about her, all right?"

Penny felt herself blushing. She wanted to leave the table. But something held her, something told her to stay with Jim. She held his hand a little tighter.

"I just wanted to tell you how sorry I am," she said desperately. "I know you were crazy about her, and I know you'll miss her, too."

Now Jim looked at her, and saw the hurt in her eyes. "I'm sorry," he said. "I just don't want to talk about her. Not now. It's too soon. Maybe not ever." He looked into Penny's eyes, and thought he saw an invitation. "I've got to forget her."

"Then let's talk about something else," Penny offered.

"What else is there to talk about?" Jim shrugged. "Look around. It's like a morgue in here. All anybody's thinking about is Karen."

"I'm not."

He looked at her questioningly. "What are you thinking about?"

"You," Penny said. "How you aren't at all like I always thought you were. You're really very nice."

She felt Jim's hand respond under her own. The pressure sent a thrill through her, and she returned the squeeze.

"I like you, too," Jim said. He looked at her speculatively. Was she telling him what he thought she was telling him? "Why don't we get out of here?"

Penny started to refuse, but then she looked around the room. Judy Nelson was watching her, as were several of her other friends. What would they think, Penny wondered. What would they think if they saw me leave with Jim Mulvey? Particularly after what I said at lunch—my God, was it really only yesterday? They'd all heard her. They'd all heard her say she was going to take Jim away from Karen. Well, Karen was gone now, but why wait? If she left with him, wouldn't they think that Jim had been planning to break up with Karen anyway? Karen wouldn't care. She was dead.

"Where would we go?" Penny asked, stalling for time.

Jim shrugged. "I dunno. Not the drugstore. That place is really gross." Then he had an idea. "How about Bill Enders' cabin? I haven't seen Bill in awhile."

Penny thought it over. She barely knew Bill Enders. Bill was another of her mother's favorite gripes. The young man had built a cabin for himself about a year ago, and because he had long hair and lived alone, Leona Anderson had immediately labeled him a hippie and begun agitating against him all over Neilsville. It turned out Enders had paid cash for the land he'd built his house on, and kept a steady, if modest, balance in the bank. But he kept pretty much to himself, and as far as Penny knew, Jim Mulvey was the only person in town who knew him well enough to drop in on him. The prospect excited her.

"Isn't it a little late?" She half-hoped Jim would agree.

"Not for Bill. He's always up." Jim smiled at her reassuringly, wondering what her reaction would be when she found out Bill Enders wasn't at the cabin at all.

Penny made up her mind, and stood up. "Well, what are we waiting for?" As they left, Penny saw Judy Nelson beckoning to her.

"You're not leaving with Jim Mulvey, are you?" she whispered.

Penny, feeling terribly adventurous, did her best to look sophisticated. "We're just running out to say hello to Bill Enders," she said, loudly enough to be heard at all the tables in the area. Then, as Judy Nelson's eyes narrowed suspiciously, Penny took Jim Mulvey's arm and walked out of the Praying Mantis.

As they drove out of town a few minutes later, Penny thought she heard it—faintly in the distance, a sound that was becoming familiar to her. She put it out of her mind and turned her attention back to Jim.

But Penny was right; she *had* heard it. Somewhere in the night, an ambulance was wailing through town. The music stopped in the Praying Mantis, and everyone began looking around, trying to assess who was there, and who was not. When they realized what they were doing they became self-conscious, and a nervous buzz of conversation grew in the room as the siren slowly faded.

Penny looked apprehensively at the darkened cabin, tucked away in a tiny stand of cottonwood trees.

"He must have gone to bed," she said, feeling slightly relieved. All the way out from town, she had been wondering if this was a mistake. Now she relaxed. They would turn around and drive back to Neilsville. But Jim switched off the engine.

"Nah," he said. "Too early. He must have gone out for a while. Come on, I know where the key is. We can go in and wait for him to come back."

Penny wanted to ask him to take her home, but then she told herself that that was silly. She'd come this far, and she wasn't going to chicken out now. Besides, everyone at the disco knew where she'd gone, and who she'd gone with, and if she made Jim take her home, he'd be sure to spread it around. Penny could hear Judy Nelson's caustic remarks about people who talk big and don't follow through.

She got out of the car.

She looked around the cabin curiously, surprised at how neat and cozy it was. It was entirely made of wood, and Bill Enders had obviously known what he was doing. Even the furniture seemed to have been made by hand.

"It's nice," she said. "I always thought it was just a shack."

"That's what your mother wanted everyone to think," Jim commented. "Lemme see if Bill has any beer around." He went to the refrigerator, sure that it would be well stocked. It was. He took out two Olys, and handed one to Penny.

"I've never drunk beer before," she said hesitantly.

"No time like the present," Jim said. "I'll build a fire."

Penny hadn't realized how cold the night had gotten. She shivered. A fire would be nice.

Ten minutes later, she and Jim Mulvey were sitting cross-legged on the floor, the flames dancing on the hearth. But the beer was bitter.

"I don't like it," Penny said, setting the bottle down.

Jim grinned at her. "I'll fix you something else."

He went to the kitchen and surveyed the liquor stock. He settled on sloe gin, mixed with ginger ale. He took the drink back to the living room and handed it to Penny. "Try that."

Penny tasted it. "Sweet, but good. What's in it?" she asked.

"Mostly ginger ale, with a little grenadine," Jim lied. "They call it a Shirley Temple."

"Didn't she used to be in the movies?" Penny asked.

"I guess," Jim said. "About a hundred years ago."

Penny giggled, and took another swallow of the drink. She decided she liked it. She drained the glass and held it out to Jim. "Can I have another one?"

He fixed the second drink, and they sat in front of the fire, enjoying the warmth and the quiet. Penny was beginning to feel much better. She looked at Jim, and thought he was terribly handsome in the firelight.

"You're nice," she blurted. "I like you a lot."

Jim turned and gazed at her. "I like you, too." Then, after a pause, "Do you smoke?"

"Smoke?" Penny repeated blankly.

"You know. Grass."

"God, no!" Penny repeated blankly.

"Well, it's not that bad," Jim chuckled.

"It's bad enough," Penny countered.

"How do you know, if you haven't tried it?"

Penny thought it over. She was feeling relaxed—really good—and the idea of smoking some grass didn't seem nearly as shocking as it always had before.

"Why not?" she giggled. Then: "Do you have any?"

"I don't," Jim said, winking at her. "But Bill does."

He got up and went to one of the drawers that was built into the wall next to the fireplace. In a minute he was back, two joints in his hand. Penny reached to take one, but Jim held them out of her grasp.

"Not yet," he said, laughing. "One at a time. No sense wasting all that good smoke. Just a second, and I'll put on some music." He chose an Alice Cooper record, and put it on the stereo. Then he rejoined Penny on the floor, and lit one of the joints.

She coughed on the first drag, but Jim showed her how to do it. The second drag went into her lungs, and she held her breath. When she felt her lungs beginning to hurt, she let the air out.

"I don't feel anything," she said, a little surprised.

"You will," Jim promised her. "Take another hit."

This time she seemed to inhale endlessly before her lungs were full and then she thought she could hold her breath for an eternity. It felt good.

"I'm thirsty," she said, lazily stretching herself out in front of the fire.

"I'll fix you another," Jim said softly. "Finish the joint, and we'll light the other one when I get back."

When he came back into the room a few minutes later, her drink in his hand, his shirt was off.

"I always get hot when I smoke," he said. "Hope you don't mind."

Penny realized she was staring at his chest. She wondered what it would be like to touch Jim's skin. As if reading her mind, Jim lay down on the floor and put his head in her lap. Her hand fell naturally to his chest and she thought she could feel his heart beating. It was almost as if her fingertips were inside him.

They smoked the second joint and Penny watched the fire, listened to the music, and stroked Jim's chest.

"God, I'm hot," Jim moaned. Penny looked down at him, and saw him looking hungrily back at her. He reached up and put his hand behind her head. Then he pulled her forward, and kissed her.

It was like an electric shock. She felt his tongue push into her mouth, and suddenly she felt as though she was inside her own mouth, not only feeling the kiss but watching it, helping it. She sucked hungrily at Jim's tongue, wanting it deeper in her mouth.

Then she was lying on her back, and he was on top of her, his body pressing her against the floor. She could feel his hips moving. In the background the music kept time to Jim's movements. By the time his hand touched her breast, she was ready.

"Touch me," she moaned. "Oh, God, it feels so good."

Penny found herself groping for Jim, and she wasn't surprised when she found his jeans unzipped. She slid her hand inside his shorts and touched him.

"Please," she said. "Do it to me, Jim. Do it to me."

He kicked his jeans aside and began removing her clothes. She lay on the floor, the liquor and grass working inside her, dissolving her inhibitions. She felt the heat of the fire, and then the heat of Jim's body. She felt him entering her, felt him pressing against her. And then, painlessly, the membrane broke, and he plunged into her. She gave herself up to the ecstasy, only dimly aware of the sound of Jim's voice calling out near her ear.

"Karen," he cried. "Karen . . . Karen . . . Karen . . ."

She knew it was morning even before she opened her eyes. There was a grayness around her, and now she knew she wasn't at home.

She began to remember.

Even through the pounding headache, she could remember it all. The drink. It couldn't have been "mostly ginger ale." If it had been, she never would have agreed to try the grass.

And the rest of it. What they had done. She tried to force the images out of her mind, tried to tell herself that it hadn't happened, that what she was remembering was a dream, not a memory. She looked around.

Jim Mulvey, naked, lay next to her on the floor, one hand holding his groin, almost as if he were protecting himself. Penny stared at him for a moment, then leaped to her feet and scrambled into her clothes. She wanted to wake him, but first she wanted to cover him up. She didn't want him to wake up nude, and find her staring down at him. She went into the bedroom and pulled a quilt from the bed.

She took it back into the living room, and threw it over Jim. Then she began shaking him.

"Wake up," she said. "Please, Jim, wake up."

He stirred finally, and looked at her sleepily.

"What time is it?" He jumped up, grabbing the quilt just before it fell away from his body, and picked up his clothes. Then he scuttled into the bedroom.

"It's all right," he said a couple of minutes later as he emerged from the other room. "It's just a little after five. If we hurry, you'll be home before anyone even wakes up."

Penny didn't say anything, nothing at all. She followed him mutely to the car, got in, and huddled miserably in the corner of the seat as he drove her home.

"Stop here," she said suddenly. They were a block from her house. "If I get out here, at least no one will see you bringing me home. Then maybe I can convince them I was at Judy's all night."

Jim let her out, wanting to apologize for what had happened, but unable to find the words. He hadn't meant for the night to end that way, but he had just gotten too stoned. He hadn't known what he was doing. In fact, he had thought he was making love to Karen. But he didn't tell Penny any of it. Instead, he put the car in gear and drove away. He could understand why she didn't want her parents to see him, but he still resented it.

Penny hurried up the steps and into the house. Her mother, bleary-eyed, gazed at her steadily.

"Where have you been all night?" Leona Anderson demanded.

"At Judy's," Penny said. She wondered why her mother was looking at her so strangely; it wouldn't have been the first time she had stayed at Judy's overnight without telling her mother. Besides, her mother would have called the Nelsons, and Judy would have covered up for her somehow. And why was her mother still dressed? Hadn't she been to bed at all? Suddenly Penny was frightened.

"Something's happened, hasn't it?" she said.

Leona Anderson, her mouth set, nodded stiffly.

"Well, what is it?" Penny asked. "Mother, what is it?"

"I've been at the hospital all night," Leona said. "As a matter of fact, I just got home myself. Janet Connally tried to hang herself last night."

Penny stared at her mother for a second, then screamed.

She screamed again.

Something broke inside her, and she crumpled to the floor. Leona Anderson stared at her daughter, then her hands instinctively began working the beads she had taken to the hospital with her.

"Holy Mary, Mother of God, pray for us sinners . . ."

She broke off, unable to finish the prayer. But in her mind the words echoed.

". . . now, and at the hour of our death . . ."

## TWENTY-THREE

P ENNY ANDERSON'S FIRST THOUGHT WAS that it had all been a bad dream. But then she realized she wasn't in her bed; she was on the sofa in the living room, and her mother was staring down at her.

It wasn't a bad dream. It was real. It had all happened. Penny closed her eyes again, trying to shut it all out, but it wouldn't be shut out.

"Janet—" she said finally. "Is Janet going to be all right?"

"She'll be fine," Leona snapped. "Although what's going on in this town I don't know. Ever since that Mr. Balsam got here . . ." She trailed off. No sense going into that now, she reminded herself. "Do you want to tell me where you were all night?"

"I wasn't anywhere," Penny said. "I was just wandering around."

"No," Leona said definitely. "You weren't out 'wandering around.' You went somewhere with Jim Mulvey, and I want to know where."

"We were out at the lake, talking."

"All night? Don't try to fool me, Penelope Louise!"

"He was upset," Penny replied. "He wanted to talk about Karen, and he asked me if I'd go for a ride with him, and talk to him for a while."

"You expect me to believe that?" Leona demanded. "Jim Mulvey never talked for more than two minutes at a stretch in his life!" She glared at Penny, as if the truth would somehow be pulled out of her by sheer concentration. Penny stared at the floor.

It wasn't that she wanted to lie to her mother. She wanted to tell her mother the truth. In fact, she wanted to throw herself in her mother's arms and cry. But her mother wouldn't understand. Penny was sure of it. Her mother would be horrified by what she'd done, and start yelling at her. Penny couldn't let that happen; she was already too upset. She knew she'd fall apart completely if her mother started yelling at her. Shakily, she got up from the sofa.

"I'm going to take a bath, and go to bed," she announced. "I feel awful."

"I'll bet you do," Leona agreed. "And you can take a bath. But you're not going to bed, young lady. You're going to school."

Penny stared at her mother. School? The way she felt? No. She couldn't go. She wouldn't go. Not after last night. She needed a day by herself; a day to deal with what had happened. A day to forget. But she looked at her mother and knew it was no use. She was going to school.

Tiredly, she started up the stairs. Halfway up she heard her mother's voice again.

"When you get there," Leona said darkly, "don't bother to go to your first classes. Go to Monsignor's office. If you won't tell me what happened last night, you can tell him."

Penny froze on the stairs and listened for the words she didn't want to hear. They came.

"Monsignor will hear your confession."

Penny could feel people staring at her as she walked up Main Street. She tried to tell herself that they weren't staring at her, that she didn't look any different now than she had yesterday, or the day before, or the day before that. But she could feel the eyes on her, feel people wondering why she was on her way to school so late.

They *were* watching her, and wondering. Neilsville was getting worried. One of their girls was dead, and two others had tried to take their lives. And they were all from the Catholic school on the hill. What was going on up there? So they watched Penny Anderson as she self-consciously walked through town and started up the hill toward St. Francis Xavier's.

She noticed a chill in the air this morning, and glanced up at the leaden sky. Summer was definitely over, and the world seemed to be cloaked in the same gray shroud Penny felt herself suffocating in. She hurried up the steps and through the main door of the school.

Monsignor Vernon was waiting for her, seated at his desk, his fingers drumming impatiently. His lips tightened when he saw Penny Anderson framed in the doorway.

"Your mother has asked me to hear your confession," he said.

"Couldn't we talk here?" Penny countered. She knew she would have to tell the priest the truth in the confessional. Here, in the office, she could avoid it.

"Shall we go into the church?" Monsignor Vernon said, and Penny knew that he was not asking a question. Silently, she followed the priest out of the school and into the church.

When she was in the tiny confessional, the door latched firmly, Penny knelt and began praying. She heard the shutter open. The priest was waiting for her to begin.

The story came out slowly. But Monsignor Vernon prodded, and poked, dragging it from her detail by detail.

"Did you know it was going to happen?" the priest's voice asked.

"No," Penny replied.

"Are you sure?"

She tried to remember. "Not at first," she said hesitantly.

"But then you knew?"

"When he took his shirt off—"

"How did you feel?"

"I'm—I'm not sure. I wanted to—to—"

"To touch him?" the disembodied voice accused.

"Yes," Penny hissed. "Yes, I wanted to touch him."

"And you wanted him to touch you?"

"Yes," Penny wailed.

In the other half of the booth, Monsignor Vernon was sweating. It was sinful. What they did was repulsive and sinful. He could see them, the naked boy lying on top of her, her hands on his back, on his buttocks, then reaching around, touching him, touching him. He pictured her hands on the boy's organ, and his own hands began working. He could almost feel the hardness of the boy . . .

"Tell it to me," he urged her softly. "Tell me all of it."

Once more Penny went into the recital of her sins, and the priest felt the wrath of a vengeful God rise in him. A combination of excitement and revulsion. And then it was over. Monsignor Vernon felt a sudden release within himself. Now he would have to deal with the penitent who knelt quietly on the other side of the screen, waiting for him to speak.

He began the prayer of absolution, but was suddenly conscious of a stirring from Penny's side of the confessional. He broke off the prayer.

"Is there more?"

There was a slight hesitation, and then he heard Penny's voice.

"The penance, Father. What is the penance?"

In the dimness of the tiny booth, Monsignor Vernon smiled softly.

"You will know what the penance is," he whispered. "When the time comes, you will know what to do."

Then, as Penny wondered what he meant, Monsignor Vernon absolved her of all her sins.

Monsignor Vernon glanced at one of the hall clocks. "We're late," he said, increasing his stride. Penny almost had to run to keep up with him.

"Late for what?"

"Your class," the priest announced. "I'm conducting it today."

Penny stopped in her tracks, the one bright spot in her day ruined. "Mr. Balsam isn't here today?" she asked. She wondered if she could plead sickness, and go home; she had been looking forward to the psychology class as the one ray of hope: Mr. Balsam always seemed to know what was happening with the kids, and what to say to them. And today he wasn't there.

"He went to the hospital," Monsignor Vernon said placidly. "Janet Connally wanted to talk to him, and we thought it best that he go."

"I see," Penny said vaguely, though she didn't see at all. They walked the rest of the way to Room 16 in silence.

Penny hesitated at the door, and stared at the empty seats in the front row. Judy Nelson was there, but all the other seats were empty: Karen Morton's, Janet Connally's, and Jim Mulvey's. Where was Jim? she wondered. Home in bed, probably, she thought bitterly.

She started to slip into a vacant seat in the back of the room, but Judy Nelson was signaling to her, so she walked to the front and took the seat next to Judy.

"I had to tell," Judy whispered urgently. She was speaking so fast Penny could hardly follow her. "Right after you left with Jim, we heard about Janet. We all went over there, and your mother was already there, and when you weren't with us, and Jim wasn't with us, well—she just put it together. What could I say?" She looked eagerly at Penny. "What happened? Did you—" But before she could finish her question, Monsignor Vernon rapped on the desk and cleared his throat.

He gazed out over the room, taking note of the empty desks in the front row. He stared at them for a long time, long enough for the class to be certain what he was thinking. As the silence lengthened, the class began to squirm, and the questions in their minds showed on their faces.

Why is he here?

Where's Mr. Balsam?

What's he going to do?

Monsignor Vernon cleared his throat and the squirming suddenly stopped.

He spoke without preamble, offering no explanation for their teacher's absence. He made a simple announcement.

"Your assignment today will be to write a paper."

There was a rustling in Room 16. Maybe the hour wouldn't be so bad after all.

"A paper about death," Monsignor Vernon said. Suddenly the silence in the room was tangible. They stared at him, not sure they had heard him correctly. They had.

"Something is happening in this class," Monsignor Vernon went on, "and I don't know too much about it. So I want you, each of you, to tell me. You will spend the rest of this hour writing about death. Specifically, your own deaths."

Now the students looked terrified. The Monsignor continued.

"You are to look within yourselves. You will decide if there are any circumstances under which you would contemplate committing suicide. If you find that there are, you will describe those circumstances in your papers, and then attempt to reconcile your feelings with the Doctrines of the Church." He looked out over the class. "Your papers will be entirely confidential. No one will see them except me and Mr. Balsam. We will read them, evaluate them, and destroy them. They won't be graded, and they won't be recorded. But I think we might be able to get some valuable information about what has been happening to—some of you."

Suddenly everyone in the class began glancing at Judy Nelson. But Judy sat calmly in her seat, unaffected by what the priest had asked of them.

In the back of the room, Marilyn Crane tried to hold back her tears. To think of killing yourself was a mortal sin! But if it was a sin, surely a priest wouldn't ask you to do it, would he? Then Marilyn realized that the Monsignor had given them an opportunity: if she was honest with herself, she knew that she had thought about it but had always stopped herself. Now she had a chance to think it through, and think it through with a clear conscience. She silently blessed the priest for giving her the assignment, and set to work.

Penny Anderson couldn't think at all. She sat numbly in the front row, and stared at the Monsignor. How could he? With Karen dead and Janet in the hospital, how could he ask them to do such a thing?

Her head was still pounding from the night before, and she felt as though she hadn't slept in a week. She tried to force herself to concentrate. But all she could do was sit and stare at Monsignor Vernon.

And then she realized that he was beckoning to her, signaling her to come to him. She responded to the summons.

"Is something wrong?" the priest asked when she was next to the desk.

"I—I can't seem to concentrate," Penny stammered.

The priest smiled at her. "Perhaps you'd better work in the quiet-room," he said. "Maybe it would be easier for you if you were alone."

*But I don't want to be alone,* Penny's mind cried out. *I want to talk to someone. I want to talk to Mr. Balsam!* Aloud she said: "I'll try." Then she repeated it: "Really, I'll try!" She picked up her things and hurried out of Room 16.

On her way to the basement, where the quiet-room was, Penny hoped she'd find someone else already there. She didn't care who—anyone—just someone she could talk to for a while, to take her mind off herself, off last night, off everything. But the quiet-room was empty, and as Penny closed the door behind her she felt even worse than before.

Resolutely, she put her things down on one of the tables and took out a pen and some paper. She put her name neatly in the upper left-hand corner, and then printed the title of her paper.

### WHY SHOULD I KILL MYSELF?

Then, underneath, she wrote something else:

### WHY SHOULDN'T I?

Penny stared at the paper for a long time, and after a while the paper blurred in her vision. She began to see other images. She saw Jim Mulvey, his chest glistening in the firelight, his eyes inviting her. She saw herself, kneeling in front of him, tearing at his pants.

And then the image was gone, and Penny saw Karen Morton. She was wearing a white dress—it was her confirmation dress—and she was walking toward Penny. But something was wrong. Penny looked closer. Now she knew what was wrong—Karen was walking toward her from the grave! But Karen was happy; she was smiling; and waving to Penny. How could she be happy? She was dead. Dead! *Dead!* Penny repeated the word to herself over and over again. *Dead.* DEAD! DEAD-DEAD-DEAD-deaddeaddead. And suddenly the word didn't mean anything to her anymore. It was just a sound without any meaning at all. Karen wasn't deaddeaddead. No. Karen was happy. She was wearing her confirmation dress, and she was happy. Penny wanted to be with her . . .

Penny Anderson sat up suddenly, and looked around. Where was she? The quiet-room. Of course. She was in the quiet-room and she was supposed to be writing a paper. What had happened?

She looked at the clock: a few minutes after four o'clock. It must be broken.

But the second hand was moving steadily.

She left her things in the quiet-room and climbed up the stairs to the main floor. The clock on the main floor said the same thing. Seven minutes after four.

It was impossible, of course. She had been downstairs only a few minutes. Then she stopped, and listened. It was quiet. Too quiet. Not the busy quiet of a building full of students, but the awful, deserted silence that comes over a school in late afternoons and on weekends.

Somehow, Penny Anderson had lost most of the day. Shaken, she pushed quickly through the door of the girls' room. As she was washing her hands, she glanced at the mirror. What she saw horrified her.

Her eyes were puffy.

Her whole face seemed to have swollen.

She stared at herself, and began to feel sick at her stomach. Then, as if trying to blot out the image, her fist came up and smashed into the mirror. It shattered, and jagged pieces of glass crashed to the floor at her feet. Shocked, she stared at the mess around her, at the cut that was slowly beginning to ooze blood on her leg. And something clicked in her mind.

The penance.

Something about the penance.

*"You will know what the penance is."* That was what he had said. *"When the time comes, you will know what to do."*

Penny Anderson knew what to do.

She reached down and picked up the largest shard. Then she went back into the stall she had just came out of, and carefully latched the door behind her.

She took off her shoes and her pantyhose.

She sat on the plumbing above the toilet, and carefully put both feet in the toilet bowl.

She grasped the fragment of broken mirror and reached down.

The blood came slowly at first, then faster, running down her ankles into the bowl. She stared at the red water, then flushed the toilet. A moment later, the bowl refilled with clean water, but that, too, soon turned red.

Over and over again, Penny slashed at herself with the broken glass, lacerating her legs until the blood poured from them as from a tap. Then she let the glass fall to the floor.

She watched the blood flow into the toilet bowl, and when it again turned red, she reached down once more and pressed on the lever. She watched her life swirl down into the sewers, watched the clean water bubble into the bowl, watched her blood mix into it once more.

The fifth time she reached for the lever, she was too weak to press it. Instead she sat, resting her weight on one hand, watching the red fluid rise in the bowl. And she thought she heard music, somewhere in the background. It sounded like the nuns chanting vespers, but she knew it was too early for that. Or was it? It seemed to be getting darker.

She slipped from the toilet to the floor, and gave herself up to the darkness. She thought she saw a tunnel. At its end Karen Morton was waiting for her, still in her confirmation dress, beckoning to her. And in the background, the chanting continued, sending Penny onward.

In the room next to Room 16—not a room, really, but an oversized storeroom that had been converted into a makeshift laboratory—Marilyn Crane was patiently working with the white rat. She had set up a particularly difficult maze, with two routes through it—one shorter, but complicated, the other much longer, but much simpler. She was trying to determine if the rat would discover both routes, explore them, and then choose one. So far, the results had been inconclusive. The rat had made his way through the maze several times, but he seemed to take just as long by either route, and so far hadn't shown any preference for either.

Marilyn had made herself come to the laboratory that afternoon. Until two days ago she had enjoyed working with the rats. Now, every time she was with them, the image of the disemboweled creature loomed up in front of her, and she had to force herself to pick up the live animals. Gingerly, she reached down and picked up the wriggling creature.

I should have gone home, she thought. Why did I stay? But she knew why she'd stayed. It had been the essay for Monsignor Vernon that morning. What she'd written had frightened her, and she was afraid her fear showed. She didn't want her mother to ask her what had happened that day, so she'd decided to stay after school until she calmed down. It hadn't helped.

She was about to drop the rat back at the beginning of the maze when she felt it. Hot. Wet. Instantly she knew what had happened. Marilyn cried out in disgust and dropped the rat. It missed the maze entirely, hit the floor, and scuttled off into a corner, where it sat looking curiously at Marilyn. But Marilyn was staring at the yellow fluid that was running off her hand onto the floor.

The rat had—had *peed* on her!

Mortified, she ran out of the room and down the hall to the girls' room.

She knew something was wrong as soon as she opened the door. Glass all over the floor. She decided to ignore it, and began to pick her way carefully around it to use the other wash basin.

Then she saw the blood. At first, she thought it was just a drop, but then she realized it was a puddle of blood, oozing slowly toward the drain in the middle of the floor.

Almost against her will, her eyes followed the blood toward its source. It was coming from a closed stall.

"Is someone here?" Marilyn said softly, knowing there would be no answer. The silence only increased her fear. She pushed at the door. It didn't give.

She knelt down, carefully avoiding the glass and blood, and looked under the door.

Penny Anderson, her eyes open and vacant, stared back at her.

Marilyn felt the sickness rise.

Moving with a strange calm, she let herself into the end stall, bent down, and threw up into the toilet. Then, detached, wondering why she was behaving as she was, she waited for the sickness to subside, washed out her mouth, and left the girls' room. She returned to Room 16, gathered her things, and left the school.

The fresh air hit her like a bucket of water, and she knew what had happened. Penny had killed herself. But why was she so calm? Why wasn't she screaming? Why wasn't she running, calling for help? Maybe Penny was still alive. Maybe if she did something, they could still save Penny.

And then she realized that Penny wouldn't want her to do that, that Penny would want her to stay calm, and walk down the hill. And leave her alone.

Marilyn started down the steps, and away from the school. Suddenly it all seemed to be closing in on her, and she felt the pressure building in her, the pressure she had been fighting against for so long—the pressure to do what should be done, instead of what she wanted to do. Now she was going to do what she wanted to do. She was going to listen to the voices.

She was not going to tell anybody what she had seen in the restroom.

She passed the rectory, glancing at it as she passed. Then she stopped and looked more closely. Smoke was coming out of the chimney. It struck her as strange, since the afternoon was still warm. The evening would be cold, but not yet.

Then she heard the chanting. At first she thought it must be coming from the convent. Then she knew it wasn't. It was coming from the rectory.

And it was telling her the same things the voices inside her were telling her. She listened for a moment, then hurried down the hill.

## TWENTY-FOUR

**M**ARGO LOOKED SURREPTITIOUSLY ACROSS the table at Peter, trying to see him with his guard down, trying to decide whether he looked strained, or whether it was her imagination. He was concentrating on his food, unaware of her scrutiny.

"I'm not going to stay tonight," Margo said, breaking the silence that had reigned over the table since they had sat down for dinner. Peter looked up from his steak.

"Don't ask me why," she went on, anticipating the question. "I couldn't tell you. I just have a feeling I'm going to be needed at the hospital tonight."

"It's the atmosphere around here lately," Peter said, putting down his fork. "I've felt the same way all day, ever since I talked to Janet Connally."

"Can you tell me what she said, or is it confidential?" Margo wanted to know. She had already heard about Peter's visit with Janet from Dr. Shields, but she wanted to hear it again, first-hand, from Peter. If his story differed much from the one Dr. Shields had told her, it might help her make up her mind.

Peter looked at her wryly. "It's not confidential," he said. "As a matter of fact, I'd like to hear what you think of it. The whole day, not just the visit with Janet." He cast around in his mind, trying to decide where to start.

"There was a note in my box, just before the psych class. It was from Monsignor, and it told me to go to the hospital right away, that Janet wanted to talk to me. He said he'd take over my class, and I should leave as soon as I found the note. I stopped by his office to see if there were any details but he wasn't there. So I left . . ."

He walked into the hospital just after eleven, and asked for Janet Connally's room number. The nurse looked slightly annoyed; then, when he identified himself, her annoyance grew.

"Well, you certainly took long enough." She didn't seem to expect an answer, so Peter followed her silently down the hall. He was relieved when they passed the room Judy Nelson had been in, and turned into the next one. Janet was propped up on a pillow, watching television. As soon as she saw him she reached over and snapped the TV off.

"You certainly took long enough," she echoed the nurse. "I was beginning to think you weren't coming at all."

Peter sat down in the chair at the foot of the bed and looked at Janet in puzzlement. "The nurse said the same thing, that I 'certainly took long enough.' I came as soon as I got the message."

"It must be the school, then," Janet complained. "I called at seven-thirty this morning, and talked to Monsignor. He promised he'd give you the message as soon as you got there." She smiled sheepishly. "I really did a number on him, Mr. Balsam. I tried to make it sound like I was dying, and that if you didn't come instantly, terrible things were going to happen to me. But I guess he didn't believe me."

Or, more likely, chose to ignore it, Peter thought. He looked at Janet carefully, trying to determine if she was as well as she appeared to be.

Last night this girl had tried to hang herself.

Today she was the same as she had always seemed—happy, cheerful, with no apparent problems. Or were the problems just too well concealed for his eyes to see?

"I look too good, don't I?" Janet said. Her perceptiveness startled Balsam and made him wary.

"I don't know," he said evasively. "How do you feel?"

"No different than ever," Janet responded immediately. Then, realizing the answer could have a double meaning, she clarified it. "That means fine. I feel fine now, and I felt fine yesterday."

"Then why are you here?" Peter said, trying to approach the issue obliquely. Janet, in her straightforward way, hit it head on.

"Because I hung myself last night. Or tried to. I've been trying all morning to decide if an attempt counts. I mean, since I'm not dead or anything, do I say 'I hung myself,' or 'I *tried* to hang myself'?"

Peter bit his lip, suddenly nervous. She must be covering up something. She *had* to be. But what? He decided to be as forthright as she.

"Janet," he said somberly, "it isn't funny. You hung yourself—or if you want to be absolutely correct, 'hanged yourself'—last night. If your father hadn't gotten to you as quickly as he did, you'd be dead right now. As it is, you're lucky you didn't suffer any brain damage."

The grin vanished from Janet's face, and she shifted in the bed. When she spoke, the lightness had gone from her voice.

"I know it isn't funny," she said. "But right now it's the only way I can cope with it. If I don't make fun of it, I think I'll go crazy. I might be crazy anyway."

Peter Balsam's brows arched, and she took the expression as a question.

"That's why I called you. I suppose I should talk to Dr. Shields, but I just can't. He's nice, but I don't know him, and he doesn't know me. You've seen me every day this semester—"

"Which has barely begun," Peter broke in.

"All right, so it's barely begun. But you've seen me every day, and you know what I'm like. Or, anyway, better than Dr. Shields does. Dr. Shields is sure to think I'm some kind of a nut. I mean, what else can he think? Anybody'd have to be crazy to do what I did."

Peter decided to take a gamble. "Then by your own terms, you're crazy."

She stared at him for a moment, then nodded.

"I know. That's why I called you. You decide if I'm crazy."

"I'm not qualified," Peter protested.

"I don't care," Janet said. "You're the one I want to talk to. There isn't anybody else I can talk to. Don't you see? Dr. Shields has to think I'm crazy, and why shouldn't he? And everybody else—well, you know what it's like around here. Particularly at school. All they'll do is tell me I'm a sinner, and give me a penance. But I'm *not* a sinner."

Peter moved his chair closer to the bed and took Janet's hand. "All right," he said gently. "What happened?"

"First, I didn't try to kill myself."

"You didn't?"

"No, I didn't. Oh, yes, I *did,* I know, but I didn't *really.*" Her face twisted in frustration. "I'm sorry," she went on, forcing herself to relax. "I know none of this makes sense, but just listen to me, then you try to figure out what happened. I've tried, and I can't, and I'm scared. So please, help me?" For the first time since he'd gotten there, Peter Balsam saw the part of Janet Connally that was still a small child. He wanted to hold her and comfort her. "I'll listen," he said softly. "Tell me what happened."

"I keep telling you," Janet said. "I don't know what happened. Where shall I start?" Without waiting for an answer she went right on talking. "Everything was fine yesterday, or as fine as it could be, what with Karen and all. I don't know how I got caught up in what happened at church. In fact, I can barely remember it. We must have sounded like a bunch of Holy Rollers. Anyway, after it was over with, I went home with my parents, and we watched television for awhile. Then I went up to do my homework." She stopped talking. Peter waited patiently for her to resume the story. Finally he prompted her.

"And?"

She looked at him bleakly. "And that's when it happened. I was studying, and all of a sudden I got this crazy urge to hang myself. At first I told myself it was ridiculous, that there wasn't a reason in the world why I should want to kill myself. But I still wanted to. So I sat there for about an hour, and argued with myself. I mean, I literally argued with myself. But the feeling wouldn't go away."

"But why? There must have been some reason why you wanted to kill yourself."

"That's the part that makes me think I must be crazy. There wasn't any reason. Just this incredible urge to hang myself. And I did."

Balsam nodded gravely. "This may sound strange, but do you remember what it was like?"

"It wasn't *like* anything. I mean, there I was, getting a chair, and putting it under the chandelier in my room, and taking an extension cord, and tying it around my neck. And all the time wondering why I was doing it, and trying to make myself stop. But I couldn't."

"It must have been frightening."

"That's what I kept thinking, too. But it wasn't. All the time, there was just this strange sense of not being able to control myself. Like a puppet. It was just like someone was pulling strings, and I had to do whatever they wanted me to do." Her voice suddenly became bitter. "So I stood up on the chair, and tied the cord around my neck, and kicked the chair away." The blood drained from her face as she remembered it. "What if they hadn't been home? What if Mom and Dad had gone out last night?" Janet Connally shuddered, and fell silent.

Peter Balsam turned the story over in his mind. It all seemed preposterous, and if it had been anybody but Janet telling him, he would have been inclined to discount it. But not Janet. Her assessment of herself coincided exactly with his own, and the story had the ring of truth. Or of what Janet thought was the truth. Then her voice interrupted his thoughts.

"Mr. Balsam," she said, almost pleading, "am I crazy?"

"Do you feel crazy?" he countered.

"No."

"And you don't look crazy, and you don't sound crazy. Granted, the story sounds crazy, but you don't. So," he went on, more lightly, "I think we can assume that, since you don't feel like a duck, look like a duck, or sound like a duck, you probably aren't a duck."

"Probably," she said, repeating the qualifying word.

Peter Balsam shrugged. "Would you believe me if I said 'absolutely'?" He was pleased when she smiled again.

"No. And 'probably' is a lot better than I was doing by myself." Silence. Then: "Mr. Balsam, what am I going to do?" Again, the plaintive, childlike quality in the voice.

Balsam had been expecting the question. But when it came, he had no ready answer. All he could offer was some reassurance.

"Try not to worry," he said. "Just relax, try to stop worrying, and I'll go talk to Dr. Shields and see if I can convince him that you aren't quite ready for the looney bin yet." And talk to him about a few other things, he silently added to himself. He squeezed Janet's hand one last time, and stood up. "Do you need anything?"

Janet shook her head. She started to speak, stopped, then started again. "Mr. Balsam? Thanks for coming. I feel better just talking about it to someone."

"There's lots of people you can talk to about it," he said.

Janet smiled wanly. "I suppose so. But not around here." Then, as if to preclude any answer, she reached out and switched the television set back on. Peter Balsam stood in the doorway for a second or two longer, then turned and left the room.

He approached the nurses' station and waited for the nurse to finish with the chart she was working on. Finally, she looked up and put on a practiced smile.

"Can you tell me where Dr. Shields's office is?"

"I'd better show you." She stood up and led him down the hall. "You're the psychology teacher, aren't you?" Her voice stayed carefully neutral, and Peter wondered whether the question was hostile.

"Yes."

"And all these girls . . . they're in your class, aren't they?"

"I'm afraid they are."

The nurse smiled tightly. "Must be some class," she observed. Then, before Peter could respond, she was pointing to a door. "Dr. Shields's office is right through there." And she was gone. Peter watched her until she turned a corner and disappeared from view, then went into the reception room she had indicated, and tapped on the inner door, half-hoping Margo would come out. Instead, Dr. Shields himself opened the door.

"Excuse me," Peter said. "I don't know if you remember me. I'm—"

"Peter Balsam," Dr. Shields said, opening the door wide. "I've been expecting you." He held the door until Peter was inside the inner office, then closed it firmly. Instead of taking the chair behind the desk, he seated himself in one of the armchairs that flanked a small table, and gestured for Peter to take the other.

"Expecting me?" Balsam asked.

"Janet Connally. Ever since she was admitted she's been saying you were the only one she wanted to talk to. So this morning we gave in, and let her call you. I assumed that as a matter of—what shall we call it? professional courtesy?—you'd drop by to see me after you talked to her."

"I have a few questions of my own."

"I'll do my best," Dr. Shields said, observing Balsam behind a smile.

As Balsam related the conversation he'd had with Janet Connally, Dr. Shields found himself putting all his attention on what the girl had said. When Balsam finished the story, Shields's first question was, "Will she tell me the same story?"

Balsam nodded. "I told her I was going to try to convince you that she's not crazy."

"You don't think she is?"

"I don't."

"What about her story? Do you believe it?"

"I don't know," Balsam said carefully. "I guess I'd have to say that I do. In fact, that's what I wanted to talk to you about. The control thing. It sounded as though she thinks she's a victim of some kind of mind control." Peter's expression grew intense, and his voice took on a note of urgency. "Is it possible? I mean suppose, just suppose, that a group of people was trying to exercise its will on others. Without the others knowing what was happening. Could it be done?"

Why doesn't he say it? Dr. Shields wondered. Why doesn't he say he's thinking of the Society of St. Peter Martyr? Aloud he said:

"Who knows? I suppose anything's possible. But I'd say it's highly improbable. I don't think anything of the sort is going on."

"Something's going on," Peter stated.

"Of course it is," Dr. Shields agreed. "Answer this: Are they all friends? Judy Nelson? Karen Morton? Janet Connally?"

"Close friends. And there's one more in the group. A girl named Penny Anderson."

"Then it's pretty obvious what's happening," Dr. Shields said. "It's called a suicide contagion."

Peter Balsam had heard the term before, but wasn't sure what it meant. "A what?"

"Suicide contagion. Put simply, the urge to self-destruction passing from one person to another. It's not unusual, in fact. But it almost always happens in an institutional environment. Read 'hospital' for that. And it's almost always restricted to teen-aged girls. There's even a term for them— 'slashers.' In some places, it's gotten so bad that entire wards of teen-age girls have had to be put under physical restriction to keep them from cutting themselves."

Balsam's eyes widened in surprise. "But what causes it?"

"It's a hysterical condition," Dr. Shields explained. "As far as I know, though, it only occurs in hospitals, and the victims are always pretty unstable types to begin with." He paused, considering. "But what's happening up at St. Francis Xavier's sounds like a suicide contagion to me."

"But couldn't it be something else?" Peter Balsam felt himself grabbing at straws. "You said they were called slashers. That certainly fits Judy Nelson and Karen Morton. But what about Janet? She didn't cut herself."

Dr. Shields shrugged expressively. "I don't know. Until today, I hadn't even considered the possibility of a suicide contagion. Now, I have to. But mind control? I don't think so."

When he left the psychiatrist's office a few minutes later, Peter Balsam felt more alone than ever. Alone, and frightened . . .

"The whole thing sounds too bizarre to be believed," Margo said.

"It is too bizarre to be believed," Peter said, "but it's happening."

Margo fell silent, thinking. Dr. Shields had already told her Peter's story. But Dr. Shields had gone further, and Margo decided it was time to tell Peter about it.

"You should talk to Dr. Shields about the Society," she said. "Since he already knows about it."

"He knows about it? How?"

Suddenly Margo felt guilty, as if she had betrayed a trust. But she hadn't talked to the psychiatrist to betray Peter; only to gain some insight.

"I told him," she said. "I've been talking to him a lot lately, about you . . . about us."

"And about the Society?" It was almost an accusation.

"Of course about the Society. Peter, the Society has been a pretty big thing between us."

"How much did you tell him?" Peter felt embarrassed, as if a private part of him had been exposed for public scrutiny.

"Not much," Margo hastened to assure him. "As little as possible, really." She smiled at Peter wryly. "I guess I didn't want him to think we were both crazy."

"Is that what you think?"

"You know it isn't." Hurt edged Margo's voice and Peter was immediately sorry. Before he could apologize, the telephone rang.

"It's for you," Peter said a moment later. "Your boss. He sounds upset."

Margo took the receiver and carried on a one-sided conversation. Though she said very little, Peter knew something was wrong. Her complexion turned chalky. Finally, after what seemed an eternity, she hung up and turned to him.

"It can't be . . ." she began.

"What——?"

"Penny Anderson. They found her half an hour ago. Peter, she's dead."

"Oh, Jesus." Peter sank back into his chair, and buried his face in his hands. Then, forcing himself, he looked up at Margo again.

"How?"

"She—she cut herself. At the school. In the restroom." Margo was already gathering her things together. "I have to go to the hospital. Leona's there—she's in pretty bad shape—and Dr. Shields says there are other people there, too. All of them suffering from all kinds of strange symptoms. He says it's hysteria, and it seems like it's all over the place."

Peter pulled himself together. "I'll go with you."

"No!" Margo said the word too sharply, and immediately regretted it. Dr. Shields had warned her. Some of the people were saying the whole mess was Peter Balsam's fault; whatever she did, she mustn't let him come to the hospital with her. "I—I'd rather go by myself," Margo stammered.

"I see," Peter said, the situation suddenly becoming clear to him. "Yes, I suppose I should stay here." He looked mutely at Margo, and she wanted to go to him, hold him, stay with him.

Instead, she turned, and hurried out of his apartment.

* * *

Peter washed the dishes, then tried to read. He tried the television next, then turned it off and went back to his book. Finally he went to bed. But before he turned off the lights he made sure to lock and bolt the front door. Then, as an afterthought, and feeling silly, he moved a chair in front of the door as well.

Just before he turned off the lights, he wondered whether he'd taken the precautions to keep others out, or himself in. But he put the thought out of his mind, and went to bed.

He woke up the next morning more tired than he had been the night before. He felt restless, and sweaty, as if he'd been running all night. He'd had bad dreams. Dreams about the Society of St. Peter Martyr.

In the dreams he'd been back in the rectory, back with the priests, and they had been doing things to him. Things he didn't want to think about. He'd tried to keep it from happening but there were six of them, and only one of him, and they could do anything they wanted to. Anything. And they did.

He lay in bed, thinking about the dream, then decided to put it out of his mind. He rose from the bed, threw on a robe, and went into the living room.

The chair had been moved away from the door.

The chain hung loose.

The door was unlocked.

Peter tried to tell himself it wasn't true, that he must have done it himself, in one of the restless periods during the night. But he knew he didn't remember it. No, something else had happened.

Something unspeakable.

He went quickly to the bathroom and dropped the robe from his shoulders.

His back was covered with the strange red welts.

## TWENTY-FIVE

MARILYN CRANE HADN'T SLEPT ALL night. She covered a yawn as best she could and seated herself at the table. Her father didn't even glance up from his paper, but her mother surveyed her critically. Marilyn wondered what she'd done wrong now.

"Dressed for school?" Geraldine asked.

Marilyn looked at her curiously. Was today a holiday? She searched her mind rapidly. "Shouldn't I be?" For some reason she felt vaguely guilty.

"I don't see why," Geraldine Crane said a little too sharply. "You're not going."

"Of course I'm going to school," Marilyn protested.

Geraldine set down the frying pan she had been holding and faced her daughter.

"Not today," she said. "Not after what happened yesterday. Imagine that poor child lying there all afternoon. It must have been terrible." She clucked her tongue, her head bobbing sympathetically.

Terrible for whom? Marilyn wondered. Certainly not for Penny Anderson. Why did everyone worry so much about what happened to people when they were already dead? It wasn't as if Penny had been in pain. Penny's face appeared before her again, the eyes wide open, the features frozen. Penny had looked almost happy.

Marilyn kept her thoughts to herself. After all, nobody knew she had seen Penny.

"But I want to go to school."

Her father lowered his newspaper and looked at her curiously.

"I'd think you'd want to stay as far away from there as possible," he remarked. "Anyway, it doesn't matter. There isn't going to be any school today, at least not at St. Francis Xavier's. I don't know what they're doing at the public school. He shook the paper out again, prepared to drop the subject, but Marilyn didn't want to let it go.

"Just because of Penny?" The newspaper went down again, and at the stove Geraldine froze.

"*Just* because of Penny?" her father repeated, emphasizing the first word. "Marilyn, she killed herself."

It was the first time anyone had actually used those words, at least in front of her, and they echoed in her ears. "*Killed herself . . . killed herself . . . killed herself . . .*" Until that moment, it hadn't been real for her. Now it was. Penny had killed herself. By her own hand. Penny was *dead*. Marilyn looked from one of her parents to the other, then, wordlessly, left the table. A few seconds later they heard her tread on the stairs. Geraldine glanced toward the ceiling, as if her eyes could bore through the plaster and wood, and detect what was happening in the mind of the girl above. Then she shifted her gaze to her husband, whose interest was back on his newspaper.

"Bill," she said quietly, "something's wrong."

He looked up at her, faintly annoyed. "You're just catching on?"

Geraldine ignored the sarcastic tone. "I'm not just talking about Karen and Penny," she began.

"And Janet Connally, and the Nelson girl," her husband interjected.

"I'm talking about Marilyn," Geraldine said.

"There's nothing wrong with Marilyn." Bill's nose was buried in the paper again. "Just growing pains."

"I don't know," Geraldine protested. "I think it's something more."

"If something's bothering her, she'll tell us about it. Greta always did. Why should Marilyn be any different?"

Geraldine shook her head now, as if trying to jar loose a thought that was nagging at her. "They aren't the same. They're really quite different. And something's happening to Marilyn. Maybe I should talk to Monsignor about her."

Bill Crane turned the page of his newspaper. "Good idea. Why don't you do that?"

No one had told him school was canceled for the day. He had simply arrived at St. Francis Xavier's to find the place deserted. The sisters were nowhere to be seen. Monsignor Vernon, if he was around, wasn't in his office. Peter had started to check his mail, then changed his mind. What if there was a message there? A message from the Monsignor? Better not to check at all.

He hurried down the hill, aware of the strange silence that had fallen over Neilsville. Everywhere he looked, there were clusters of people, talking softly among themselves, and looking up now and then, suspiciously, as if by quick furtive glances they would be able to catch a glimpse of the evil in their midst.

Peter felt the glances piercing him. They were looking at him, and wondering. Nothing much had ever happened in Neilsville until he came along. But since he had arrived, things had started going bad. How long would it be before the entire town became infected with whatever it was that was infecting the girls from St. Francis Xavier's? The only thing they could pinpoint was the outsider. Peter Balsam. The stranger. Not to be trusted.

As he passed each group the silence deepened, and he could sense that he was the focus of it. Then, after he passed, the talk would begin again, the heads drawn more closely together, lips close to ears, but the eyes, always the eyes, following him as he made his way down Main Street.

As soon as he got to his apartment, he called Margo.

"Peter? Is that you?" He hadn't spoken, and was pleased at the anxiety in her voice. He tried to mask his fears about the night before.

"Want to go for a ride? I've got the day off."

"I didn't sleep all night—" Margo hesitated.

"Who did? But they canceled school, and I decided to go see the Bishop. I was going to borrow your car, but why don't you come with me?"

She almost refused, almost told him she was going to spend the day in bed. But she didn't.

"I'll pick you up in twenty minutes," she said. Then, as an afterthought: "Are you going to take the tape?"

"I—I don't know," Peter hedged. "I hadn't thought about it."

A silence, then Margo's voice, very confident.

"You don't have to tell him one of the voices is yours," she pointed out, pinpointing his hesitation. "The only voice that's recognizable is Monsignor Vernon's."

What she said was true, but still he hesitated, wishing there was some other way. He knew there wasn't. Without the tape, how could he expect the Bishop to believe him? He made up his mind.

"I'll be waiting," he said. "With the tape."

He hung up the phone, and opened the bottom drawer of the desk. He reached into the back of the drawer, groping for the tiny cassette. His fingers couldn't find it. He pulled the drawer out further, and felt again.

He was still searching when Margo arrived twenty minutes later. All the drawers had been emptied, and he was methodically going through their contents, though he knew it was useless. As soon as Margo saw what was happening, she knew.

"It's gone, isn't it?"

Peter nodded mutely.

"Was it hidden?"

Again, he nodded. "But no one searched for it. They knew exactly where it was." Margo's face clouded: was he accusing her?

"Only one person knew where the tape was," Peter went on. He looked at her with an anguish that tore at her. Whatever he was going through, he wasn't accusing her.

"Who?" She wasn't sure she wanted to know the answer.

"Me," Peter said bitterly. "I'm the only one who knew where that tape was. So I must have taken it myself."

He told her about the night before, about locking himself in and chaining the door. Then about putting a chair in front of the door, to be extra sure. Then about the dreams, the dream in which he had been at the rectory, been back with the Society.

"This morning the door was unlocked," he finished. "The chain was loose, the chair was back over there . . . And I was a mess."

Margo sank onto the sofa, despair washing over her like a wave.

"And you took them the tape?" she said softly. "Is that what happened?"

"What else could have happened?" Peter answered, spreading his hands in a gesture of frustration. "The only thing I had on them, and I gave it to them myself."

"Maybe you didn't," Margo said suddenly, standing up. "Maybe you just hid it somewhere else, and forgot." She began searching the room, methodically at first, but then more and more frantically, as Peter looked on. As suddenly as she had begun searching, she stopped. She looked at him, and for the first time Peter saw fear reflected in the depths of her eyes.

"It's no good, is it?" she said bleakly. "I won't find it here, will I?"

"No," Peter said softly. "I don't think you will." He went to her and put his arms around her. She stiffened, then let go, her arms curling around him, holding on to him.

"Oh, God, Peter, are they going to get you too?"

She believes me, he thought. At least she believes me. But he didn't have an answer for her question.

Father Duncan looked up at them and smiled.

"Mr. Balsam," he said. "What a pleasant surprise." But something in his face told Peter it wasn't pleasant at all. A surprise, yes. But not pleasant. He could almost see the young priest trying to sneak a look at the calendar on his desk, hoping he had not made a mistake, hoping his name was not there.

"It's all right," he said, trying to put him at his ease. "I don't have an appointment."

It was the right thing to say. Father Duncan relaxed in his chair, and his smile suddenly became genuine.

"Well, that's a relief. Usually people come in here without an appointment, demand to see His Eminence, then insist that they set up an appointment two weeks ago."

"Then I can't see him?"

"I didn't say that," the secretary grinned. "Honesty should be rewarded." He pressed the key on the intercom. "Mr. Balsam is here for his ten-o'clock appointment," he said smoothly. He winked at Peter, then included Margo in the wink. There was an ominous silence from the intercom, then the Bishop's voice crackled through.

"I don't see his name on my calendar," he barked.

"Really?" Father Duncan said smoothly. "My mistake; I must have forgotten. But we can't take that out on Mr. Balsam, can we?"

"Whom *can* we take it out on?" the Bishop's voice came back.

"Your next appointment," Father Duncan said. "It's Mrs. Chambers. She wants to arrange for you to give some spiritual guidance to her Girl Scouts."

"Little green trolls," the Bishop muttered. "All right, show Balsam in."

Margo settled herself in the secretary's office to wait, and Father Duncan ushered Peter into the inner office. The Bishop was on his feet, his hand out.

"Nice to see you again, young man, however unexpectedly." He tried to direct a severe look at Father Duncan and failed. "Any idea how long you can keep Mrs. Chambers at bay?"

"She won't wait more than twenty minutes," the secretary warned.

"Then let's count on at least an hour's chat, shall we? Sit down, Mr. Balsam, sit down." The Bishop waited until Father Duncan was out of the room, then turned twinkling eyes back to Peter.

"He's terrific," he said. "Always manages to get the people I want to see in, and keep the others out. But Mrs. Chambers won't be easy."

"I'm sorry," Peter apologized. "I should have made an appointment, but I didn't know I'd have any free time till just a couple of hours ago."

"Of course you should have, but it doesn't matter. I was going to have Father Duncan call you today anyway." The sparkle left his eyes. "What's going on in Neilsville?"

"That's what I want to talk to you about."

It took nearly thirty minutes for Peter to reconstruct the entire story for the Bishop. He tried to make the realities of the Society of St. Peter Martyr as palatable as possible, but the Bishop prodded him. "Out with it, young man. I'm not a prude, and I've been around."

Peter told him as much as he could remember, and everything he and

Margo had been able to piece together from the tape. The Bishop listened in silence.

"And you think the Society is connected with the suicides in Neilsville?"

"I do."

"It sounds pretty farfetched."

"I know it does. But what happened last night is pretty farfetched, too. I'm sure I wound up in the rectory last night, and I know I didn't want to go. I don't remember going, I don't remember being there, and I don't remember coming home again. But I'm sure that's where I was."

"And you think they got you there by using some kind of mind control." The Bishop turned it over in his mind. "Frankly, I don't think it's possible."

"I wouldn't have either, a few days ago. But when nothing makes any sense, you have to believe whatever the facts point to. Nothing else makes any sense at all—it's got to be some form of mind control or hypnotism . . . or something."

"You make it all sound rather sinister," the Bishop commented.

"It is sinister. Two girls are dead. Two more nearly died. At first I thought the Society was just a sick pastime for some unbalanced priests. But it isn't, Your Eminence. It's something else entirely. Monsignor Vernon believes he *is* Peter Martyr—his reincarnation. And they think I'm a reincarnation of St. Acerinus, a man named Piero da Balsama, the man who killed St. Peter Martyr. At first I thought it was harmless, but I don't think so any more. I think they're all very sick, and I think they've found some way to inflict their sickness on everyone else."

Bishop O'Malley leaned forward slightly.

"I wish I could agree with you," he said gravely, "but I'm afraid I can't. I talked to a—" He consulted a pad on his desk. "—Dr. Shields this morning."

"I know him."

"He thinks Neilsville is experiencing a suicide contagion."

"I know," Peter said shortly.

"Then you should also know that I agree with him," the Bishop said. "It is quite obvious to me that what's going on at St. Francis Xavier's is a hysterical phenomenon. And, quite frankly, it doesn't surprise me. Dr. Shields told me that the sort of thing we seem to be experiencing usually—almost without exception—occurs in mental hospitals." The Bishop paused, considering. "Unfortunately, in small towns, parochial schools can become very institutional. I think we're going to have to begin making some rather radical changes in the structure of the school."

"Will that include Monsignor Vernon's dismissal?" Peter asked. He supposed the question was rude, or at best impertinent, but he didn't care. He felt his stomach tighten when the Bishop shook his head.

"I don't see that I can go that far," he said gently. "Not right away, at least. It may become necessary if he refuses to go along with the changes I have in mind. But not now."

Peter stared at the Bishop. When he finally found his tongue, the words tumbled out.

"But he's a danger now! It's now that he's doing whatever it is he's doing! I had it all on the tape!"

"But you don't have the tape, do you?"

Peter could only shake his head.

The Bishop stood up. "I'm sorry Mr. Balsam—Peter. May I call you Peter?" Balsam nodded. "Peter, I just don't see that anyone in the world would believe the story you just told me. I don't believe it myself. I grant you that I don't think much of the Society of St. Peter Martyr, but all you've given me are a lot of impressions about things you can't even remember. After all, you could be wrong."

It was over. Peter walked numbly through Father Duncan's office, and Margo fell in step behind him.

"It didn't go well, did it?" she asked, knowing by his face that it had not. "What are you going to do?"

He didn't answer the question for a long time. Instead, as he drove back toward Neilsville, he watched the barren countryside, and remembered how foreign it had looked to him when he had come in on the train only a few weeks earlier. Now, it all seemed terribly familiar. Now the countryside around Neilsville looked every bit as bleak as Peter Balsam felt.

Beside him, Margo Henderson maintained the silence. She, too, watched the desert go by, and wondered if there would ever be anything else for her. She was getting tired of desert; she'd lived in it too long. She'd hoped Peter Balsam would take her out of it. Instead, he was getting caught by it.

As they approached the outskirts of Neilsville, he suddenly took her hand. "I know what I'm going to do." He said it so quietly she almost didn't realize what he was talking about. Then, remembering, she looked at him questioningly.

"I'm going to play my part," Peter said quietly. "I'm going to be St. Acerinus."

# BOOK FOUR

# ST. ACERINUS

# TWENTY-SIX

LEONA ANDERSON SAT IN HER LIVING room, staring vacantly ahead, trying to understand it. She had sat like that all day, wordlessly, not hearing the condolences of her friends.

She had listened to Monsignor Vernon that morning, heard him telling her why her daughter could not be buried in sanctified ground. She had known it, of course, but until the priest had come to tell her, she had not believed it.

"It's that teacher," she said bitterly, shattering the silence that had fallen over the room.

One of the women glanced at Leona, then away.

"It is," Leona insisted quietly. "They were all in his class, all of them. Judy and Karen, and Janet and—and—" she broke off, knowing that if she said her daughter's name she would lose control. She must not cry. Not yet. First, she must destroy Peter Balsam. "When I first met him I knew there was something wrong. And look what's happened to us." She looked desolately from one face to another.

"Leona, we don't know what's happening," one of the women said soothingly. Leona Anderson turned to the woman who had spoken, and a hardness came into her eyes.

"Don't we, Marie?" Then, remembering that only a few days ago Marie Connally had come close to going through what she was going through now, Leona spoke more softly: "But what if Janet had died? How would you feel then?"

Marie Connally smiled. "But she didn't die, and she isn't going to. She's home, and she's feeling fine. And that's largely because of Peter Balsam. I'm sorry, Leona, but if you want to attack Mr. Balsam, please don't do it in front of me."

"Think what you like," Leona said stiffly. "But mark my words. It isn't over yet. As long as Peter Balsam is in this town, it won't be over."

The object of Leona's bitterness emerged from the church into the darkness of night, and began making his way back down the hill.

Below him he watched the scattered lights of Neilsville glowing dimly in the night. It crossed his mind that the lights of Neilsville were as dim as his own faith. He had spent two hours in the church, seeking guidance and solace, and had found none. Instead, he had found himself.

A few minutes later he was on Main Street. But it was a different Main Street than the one he had walked up two hours earlier. Or he was different.

Now, as he felt the eyes of strangers on him, he met their glances, and smiled at them. They turned away, embarrassed. Once he heard a voice shouting at him from a doorway.

"Go away, teacher," a woman shouted. "Leave us in peace!"

Peter turned around to confront the source of the shout, but the woman was gone, faded back into the cloak of the evening.

In the middle of town, music throbbed from the Praying Mantis, and Peter found himself drawn to it. He paused at the door, then made up his mind. He pulled the door open, and stepped into the shabby discotheque.

In the flickering light the faces seemed gaunt and hollow and there was a heavy silence behind the blaring music. It was a moment before Peter realized that there were no girls in the room: the girls seemed to have disappeared from the face of the earth. He knew why. None of them would be allowed to go out tonight. They would all be home, their parents keeping a watchful eye on them.

Someone waved to Peter, and he started across the floor.

Sitting together at a table were Jim Mulvey, Lyle Crandall, and Jeff Bremmer. Without waiting for an invitation, Peter seated himself in the fourth chair at their table. All three boys looked at him. He could see fear in their eyes.

"It isn't all that bad," he said softly. "It's almost over now."

"What is?" Lyle Crandall asked. He looked curiously at the teacher, and thought the man looked different. It was the eyes. There was something about Mr. Balsam's eyes that had changed.

"The dying," Peter Balsam said. "It won't go on much longer. It can't."

Jeff Bremmer stared at him. "Mr. Balsam, what's going on?"

Peter smiled at the boy, a warm smile. "I wish I could tell you, Jeff."

"But you know, don't you?" Jeff said, more as a statement than as a question.

Balsam shrugged. "As much as anybody knows, I guess."

"It's my fault," Jim Mulvey said suddenly. Peter shifted in his chair to look squarely at the boy.

"Don't believe that," he said. "Don't ever believe that. Whoever's to blame, it isn't you. It isn't any of you. Children don't do things like what's being done here."

"But they do," Jeff Bremmer said softly. "My dad says it's called a suicide contagion, and it happens all the time."

"In mental hospitals," Balsam said. "That only happens in mental hospitals."

"Then what is it?" Lyle asked. All three boys were staring at Balsam.

"It's a game," Peter said, more to himself than to the boys. They looked at each other, puzzled.

"A game?" It was Jim Mulvey, and now he, too, saw that something had changed in their teacher. "What kind of a game?"

"A religious game, I suppose you might say." He was about to say something else, but he was interrupted.

The sound tore through the room like a knife, cutting through the music, through what little conversation was going on, through each of the people who heard it.

It was the siren, wailing through Neilsville.


"Oh, Jesus, not again."

No one knew who had spoken, and no one cared. It was the thought that had come to all of them, and all of them knew it was too late.

Somewhere in Neilsville, "again" had happened. As if an order had been given, all the people in the Praying Mantis moved out into the street, where they were swallowed up by the crowd that had emerged as if from nowhere in response to the eerie cry of the speeding ambulance.

Peter Balsam spoke to no one, and no one spoke to him. He made his way quickly through the crowd, and started once more up Cathedral Hill, moving faster as he climbed, until, by the time he reached the top, he was running.

He didn't stop till he reached the rectory.

He looked up.

Smoke was curling from the chimney. The sound of chanting drifted through the night.


Marie Connally was trying to hurry her husband as they walked home from the Andersons'.

"Can't you walk a little faster?" Marie asked, increasing her pace.

Dick Connally's arm tightened around his wife's shoulder. "There's nothing wrong. No need to hurry," he said with a conviction he didn't feel.

"But she's only been out of the hospital a day. I just don't like the idea of leaving her alone."

"She's not alone," Dick reminded her. "Your mother's with her."

"Well, I just don't like it. Janet should have us—"

She broke off as the sound of the siren reached them. They stopped on the sidewalk and stared at each other, listening. Then, as the siren grew steadily louder, they began running.

Lights blazed from their house.

The ambulance was parked in the driveway, its red lights still flashing.

"Stay back," someone called to them. "Don't go in!"

They ignored the warning.

Marie Connally's mother stood numbly at the foot of the stairs, her face pale, her whole body shaking. She stared hollowly at her daughter and son-in-law, then one hand reached toward them, grasping at them.

"I fell asleep," she muttered. "I was watching television, and I fell asleep." No one heard her: Marie and Dick were already halfway up the stairs.

And so they saw her again. It was like a recurring nightmare. She looked exactly the same, her limp body suspended from the fixture in the ceiling, an extension cord knotted around her neck.

Only this time it was too late. Her skin was bluish, and her eyes bulged. Her face, which had always been so pretty, was no longer recognizable.

From her wrists, blood was still dripping to the floor.

Marie Connally began screaming.

Her husband put his arms around her, and tried to pull her from the room. But it was no use; she remained rooted to the spot, staring at Janet, screaming.

She stayed that way for almost five minutes, until one of the paramedics prepared a shot and administered it to her.

The shot could stop the crying, but it could never erase the image. For the rest of her life, Marie Connally would live with the vision of her daughter hanging dead from a light cord.

Just before she fell under the deadening influence of the sedative, Marie Connally decided that Leona Anderson had been right.

It was Peter Balsam. It must have been. There could be no other answer.

In Neilsville that night, no one slept.

# TWENTY-SEVEN

THERE WAS AN UNCOMFORTABLE STILLNESS in the auditorium. It was as if they had been anesthetized and were waiting for the stimulant that would bring them awake again. When Monsignor Vernon moved to the lectern they looked at him expectantly; for years they had been trained to look to their religious superiors for guidance. Now, the teaching sisters of St. Francis Xavier's rustled their habits; all over the room beads were suddenly released from tight grips.

Monsignor Vernon looked from face to face, trying to gauge the mood of the sisters. With a few exceptions, they looked confused. Concerned, and confused. Sister Elizabeth, however, looked angry, as did Sister Kathleen. And Sister Marie, back from retreat, seemed to be entirely closed down, her face impassive, a glaze in her eyes that gave no clue as to what might be going on in her mind.

"I wish I could say 'good morning,' " Monsignor Vernon began gravely. "But there isn't very much good about this morning."

"Monsignor—" It was a hesitant voice from the back of the room, and the priest smiled at the elderly nun whose face seemed particularly drawn. She had been teaching at St. Francis Xavier's for nearly forty years, and the parents of most of the students had been students of hers. Leona Anderson, in fact, had named her daughter for the nun.

"Yes, Sister Penelope?"

"I—I—" the old sister faltered, trying not to cry. "It's just all so terrible. What's happening to us?"

"We don't know," Monsignor Vernon said calmly. "That's why I wanted all of you here this morning, to try to tell you what little we do know, and to decide what to do."

"Penny," Sister Penelope said, her voice breaking. "I need to know about Penny. She was always my favorite—always."

One of the other sisters reached out to pat Sister Penelope gently on the hand, and whisper a word or two in her ear.

"I wish I could tell you what happened," Monsignor said sorrowfully. "All we know is that she left her things in the quiet-room."

"What about Janet?"

Now Monsignor Vernon frowned slightly. "Again, we don't know exactly what happened. But Janet did leave a note."

A ripple passed through the room as the sisters looked at each other, murmuring among themselves. At last, there was something.

"She said she didn't know exactly why she was doing . . . what she did. She said she was having very strange feelings lately, feelings she didn't understand. It was almost like—and I'm quoting her now—'someone outside is making me want to kill myself.' "

The nuns looked at each other. None of it made any sense to them. They turned their attention back to the Monsignor.

"She went on to say that she was feeling more and more hopeless, and even though she really didn't want to kill herself, she was being forced to anyway. She asked to be forgiven for what she did."

"Forgiven?" Sister Elizabeth asked stiffly. "By whom?"

Monsignor Vernon's eyes met those of the nun, and a look of understanding passed between them: The Church is a rock and cannot be bent. "I don't know," the priest said softly. "Perhaps she forgot she would not be dying in a state of grace." Another murmur buzzed through the room as the nuns considered the state of Janet's soul. Monsignor Vernon let it go on for a moment, then cleared his throat to regain their attention.

"We don't know, of course, what is going on here. I confess I'm as baffled as any of you. And I also find I'm forced to go outside the Church for help."

"Outside the Church?" Sister Kathleen said in a manner that made her opinion clear: there could not possibly be any help outside the Church.

"I—we—are put in a very difficult situation," the priest said with unease. "My faith, of course, lies in the Church, and the Church places full responsibility for suicide on the person who commits it. And yet, we are faced with a unique situation. Three of our girls have died, and a fourth one has tried to kill herself. Can it be that each of these girls came to the same decision independently?" Though he had intended the question rhetorically, Sister Elizabeth had an answer.

"They were all friends," she said emphatically. "Close friends. Even since they were small, what one of those girls did, all of them did. That's why we have always tried to keep them apart."

"I'm aware of that, Sister," Monsignor Vernon said. "And I'm afraid that closeness is part of the problem. Dr. Shields—"

"Who?" It was Sister Penelope again.

"Dr. Shields," the priest repeated the name. "He's a psychiatrist at the hospital. And he tells me that, despite what the Church teaches, there is a phenomenon called suicide contagion."

Suddenly the nuns were frowning and staring at each other as Monsignor Vernon explained the term.

"But what can be done about it?" Sister Elizabeth demanded.

"I don't know. When it happens in a mental institution, the solution is easy. They simply put the girls under physical restraint until the hysteria that causes the syndrome passes. That, of course, is impossible in this situation. It simply isn't feasible to put all the girls in the school under physical restraint. Although," he added, "there have been times when I wished I could do exactly that."

An appreciative chuckle passed over the room, and some of the tension seemed to ease. Then Sister Kathleen made a small gesture.

"Monsignor?"

"Yes, Sister?"

"You've only mentioned girls. What about the boys?"

"According to Dr. Shields this sort of hysteria only affects adolescent girls. Our boys are quite safe."

"But what do we do?" one of the sisters asked.

Monsignor Vernon shrugged. "There isn't too much we can do. But," he warned, "we must stay calm. We must carry on as always. School will be in session tomorrow, and the parents of every child who isn't there will be contacted, and urged very strongly to keep their children in school."

"Are you sure that's wise?" It was Sister Marie, and it was the first time she had spoken that morning.

"It's the only thing we can do," Monsignor Vernon said. "If the children are here we can watch them. If they aren't . . ." The Monsignor's voice trailed off, as if the consequences he had been about to name were too dire to be articulated. "We must watch them," he repeated, "we must watch the girls." He paused, then added crisply, "If you notice anything out of the ordinary, anything at all, I want you to report it to me at once."

The sisters digested this, and wondered just what was to be considered "out of the ordinary." Lately, everything had begun to look out of the ordinary.

"Monsignor," Sister Marie asked suddenly, "why isn't Peter Balsam here?"

"I asked him to stay home today, and perhaps tomorrow as well. This whole thing has been very difficult for him, and it seemed to me that he needed some rest."

It was as if a dam had burst in the room. The sisters were suddenly talking animatedly among themselves, glancing at Monsignor Vernon every now and then, then whispering to each other once more. Only Sister Marie remained aloof from the buzzing. She sat almost isolated in the hubbub, her eyes fixed on Monsignor Vernon. She still wore that slightly glazed, unfathomable look. Then, as quickly as it had begun, the nuns' talk subsided. Sister Elizabeth stood. It was apparent she had become the spokesman for them all.

"Monsignor," she said, "we have some questions about Mr. Balsam. I'm not sure how to begin," she went on, though it was obvious that she certainly did know how to begin. "I'm afraid, though, that we all think there has to be some connection between Mr. Balsam and what's happening to the girls. Particularly in light of what Janet Connally said in her note. About someone putting thoughts into her head. Who else could it be but Mr. Balsam? Certainly, before he came, we never had any trouble like this. And before he came, those four girls were never in a class together. But now he's here, and the four girls were all in his class, and of course we all know what kind of class he teaches—" She paused significantly, as though the conclusion was inescapable; the psychology class was somehow responsible for the deaths of the girls. "—and it seems to us that the most obvious way to put a stop to all this . . . this madness is to put a stop to Mr. Balsam and his psychology class."

She sat down again, her expression telling the world that as far as she was concerned, the matter was closed. She, and the rest of the sisters, had placed Peter Balsam in the center of the horror around them, and it was now up to Monsignor Vernon to expel the offender from their midst.

"I can understand your concerns," he said carefully, trying to read the mood of the sisters as accurately as he could. He would have to tread lightly. "As a matter of fact, I share some of them. It certainly does seem strange that all this is happening to girls in one class, particularly a psychology class. But I think we have to be very careful not to judge—not to make quick decisions based more on feelings than on facts. Of course, I realize it must seem a bit strange to all of you, asking a man with Peter Balsam's background to instruct adolescent girls on the subject of psychology—"

"His background?" Sister Elizabeth was on her feet again. "What about his background?"

"Well, I just mean that all things considered, it strikes me as being a bit peculiar that Peter Balsam should be involved with so many girls killing themselves. Considering his history, I mean."

"What history?" Sister Elizabeth demanded. "What about his background? Monsignor, what are you talking about?"

The priest stared at them. "You mean, you didn't know?" he said, as if genuinely puzzled. "But I thought I'd told you long ago."

"Told us *what?*" Monsignor Vernon could see the swing of Sister Elizabeth's habit as her foot tapped impatiently beneath the heavy skirts.

"I'm sorry," he said contritely. "I thought you were all familiar with Peter Balsam's background. But I can see that you're not." He looked from one face to the next, as if trying to make up his mind whether to go on. He made his decision. "But since you aren't," he said, "I think it would be highly inappropriate of me to talk about him just now. Highly inappropriate." He turned, and a moment later had left the room. The nuns, left to themselves, huddled together, trying to decide what the priest had been talking about.

All but Sister Marie. Sister Marie remained in her seat, her eyes fixed on the door through which Monsignor Vernon had just passed.

Peter Balsam spent most of that day alone in his apartment. In the middle of the morning he had gone out, gone downtown, just because the walls had begun closing in on him. Downtown, it was worse. Downtown, Neilsville closed in on him.

They were staring at him openly now. There was no silence as he passed. Now, they raised their voices to be sure he heard what they were saying. Much of the talk was about Janet Connally:

"Why did they let her out of the hospital?"

"They thought she was all right. *He* said she was all right!" (A not very surreptitious look at Peter Balsam.)

"*He* went to see her, you know."

"And they let him? Well, I never!"

"Lord knows what he told her, but after that note she left—"

The talk that wasn't about Janet Connally was about him:

"Comes from Philadelphia—"

"Studied for the priesthood, but they threw him out—"

"You know, he's seeing Margo Henderson!"

"But she's *divorced*—"

"Ever since he came to Neilsville—"

That was the summation. Everywhere he went, Peter Balsam felt it bearing down on him. "Ever since he came to Neilsville—" The sentence was never finished, always left hanging to be completed by the listener. By noon he was back in his apartment, the door locked, the draperies drawn. He was beginning to feel like a caged animal, and he was sure he could sense them outside; the small-town people, passing by his building and looking at the closed-up apartment, and wondering what he was doing inside, what he might be planning in the darkness.

He had not been accused. He had not been tried.

But he had been judged, and found guilty.

Peter Balsam wanted to leave Neilsville, wanted to pack his clothes and flee. It would be easy. He could simply walk once more through the town, and go to the train station. There would be a train at six o'clock. Once, he went so far as to pull his suitcases down from the closet shelf and open them on the bed.

But he couldn't do it. Not this time. He'd run away before—from the priesthood, then from his marriage. Besides, this time there was more to think about than himself. There were the children. If he left, it would go on and on, and nobody would know how to stop it.

Nobody would even understand it. And why would they? It was simply too bizarre.

Too bizarre. The words rang in his head. It *was* too bizarre. There had to be something more. Something he was overlooking. In the middle of the afternoon, he went back to his books.

First the story of the saints. He reviewed it all, what little there was.

He read briefly over the paragraphs about Piero da Verona, the fanatical Dominican priest who had roamed Italy during the early years of the Inquisition, persecuting heretics and sinners, in the name of the True Faith and the Mother Church.

Then he came to the man whose name was so similar to his own—Piero da Balsama, the heretic who had finally been driven too far, and waited in ambush one night to crush Verona's head with a stone.

Not that the killing had accomplished anything, Balsam realized. The Medieval Church had elevated its murdered Inquisitor to the status of saint, named him St. Peter Martyr, and used his martyrdom to carry on the Inquisition. And apparently it had worked very nicely, for the murderer, poor Piero da Balsama, had repented, and joined an order himself. Eventually he had even joined his Inquisitor in the ranks of the saints.

Piero da Balsama had become St. Acerinus.

Was it all really happening again? Balsam wondered. Had his old friend Pete Vernon really come to believe that the two of them were the ancient saints in reincarnation?

He went over their histories in his mind. Certainly there were parallels beyond the simple coincidence of their names. Pete Vernon, since his elevation to Monsignor, had certainly taken on the sort of fanatical dedication to the Church that had been the hallmark of the Dominican Inquisitors.

And Peter Balsam had certainly undergone some profound doubts of his own faith, the sort of doubts that once, long ago, would have branded him a heretic. But that was long ago. In the modern Church, questioning such as his was common. Many Catholic theologians, Balsam knew, had proposed more radical ideas than he ever had. But not in Neilsville. With a chill that turned his body to ice, Balsam remembered the massive blackclad figure of the Monsignor standing in the gym, pointing at him; remembered the light in his eyes and the word he had used: *heretic.*

He remembered all the times he had tried to confront the priest, and all the times he had backed off in the face of the priest's hypnotic wrath.

Hypnotic.

It was like a light had been switched on, and the darkness cleared away. The word stood out in Balsam's mind, and images began to swirl around it.

The flickering candlelight.

The steady rhythms of the chanting.

The memory lapses, when time had been telescoped, and hours had been compressed into minutes.

The things Janet had told him: "I'm being forced to do things I don't want to do." "It's as if something's controlling me, making me do things."

It had to be a form of hypnosis, but a form that went beyond the normal.

Feverishly, Peter began going through his books; not the texts, but the odd volumes he had been collecting over the years, the flotsam and jetsam of parapsychology, psychic phenomena, and speculation.

He picked up a piece here, a bit there. It was like fitting together extra pieces from several jigsaw puzzles to form something new. And when he was finished, it made a certain kind of sense.

Monsignor Vernon had found a way to control minds.

In his fanaticism he had stumbled onto a method of using the combined concentration of several minds to inflict his will on others. And it was working.

The girls were dying.

But why? Peter Balsam spent the rest of the afternoon worrying at the problem, turning it over in his mind, trying to fathom the motivations of the priest.

He knew it had to do with the girls. But was it just the four girls who had been victimized so far, or would there be more?

And there was the problem of his own role. He tried to figure out how he fit into the scheme.

He was sure that he did. Too many times Monsignor Vernon had insisted that he was vital to the Society of St. Peter Martyr, although he certainly didn't share their fanatical opinions. It was something else. It had to be.

Something clicked in his mind. Something from his past, but way back in his past, when he had first come to the convent. There was something about one of the boys, something none of them were supposed to talk about.

Could it have been about Pete Vernon? His thoughts were interrupted by the telephone.

Margo's voice brought him out of his reverie, and he glanced at the clock. The day was gone.

"Want me to bring over some dinner?"

"Yes. And I want you to spend the night."

There was a silence. Margo thought she detected something different in Peter's voice, a sureness that she had never heard before.

"Are you all right?" she asked.

"I'm fine," Peter replied. "I finally put it all together, Margo. I know what's happening around here."

"Are you sure?"

"I'm positive. The only thing I don't know is why it's happening, but I'll find that out, too. And then I'll put an end to it all."

The confidence in his voice made up her mind for her. For the first time, Peter Balsam sounded as she had hoped he would sound.

"I'll bring some steaks. And my toothbrush."

While Peter Balsam and Margo Henderson ate dinner that night, and made love, and were happy together, Marilyn Crane found herself in turmoil. She tried to read, and she tried to watch television. Then she went up to her room, and tried to study. She couldn't concentrate.

She heard things in her mind. She heard a strange chanting, and voices calling to her. She imagined the voices were angels, and they wanted her to come to them.

She knew she couldn't. If the angels wanted her, they would have to come for her. She wished they would.

She listened to the angels call out to her.

She wanted to respond, wanted to heed their call.

But it was sinful, and Marilyn didn't want to sin. The Sorrowful Mother hated sin.

Marilyn Crane forced herself not to listen to the voices.

From the chimney on the roof of the rectory, smoke curled slowly into the sky.

No one in Neilsville noticed it. They were all at home, worrying about their children, and watching them.

## TWENTY-EIGHT

A SOMNOLENCE LAY OVER THE TOWN, AND it was centered on Cathedral Hill, where the buildings of the church, the school, and the convent had taken on the air of a fortress. People moved slowly, forcing themselves through the motions of the day, as if by keeping up the appearance of normality they could somehow achieve it.

They watched each other, all of them. In every class, lessons came to a sudden halt as the teachers found themselves studying the faces of their students, searching for a clue as to who would be next.

The students, too, watched each other, and gossiped together between classes. But with them, there was almost a sense of anticipation, an excitement, as if they were spectators at a macabre circus. With the confidence of youth, each of them was sure that whatever force was striking out at them would inevitably hit someone else. Who?

There was an unspoken consensus.

As she moved through the day, Marilyn Crane could feel it. As long as she could remember, she had felt people watching her, felt them talking about her, felt them snickering silently at her. Now, she was sure, they had decided she was next, and they were watching her more intently than ever.

It didn't matter where she went; she could feel the curious eyes on her, examining her as if she were an exotic insect. And it wasn't just her classmates, it was the Sisters, too. She heard the rustling of habits as the nuns began to keep a vigil over her. Every time she turned around one of them was there: a figure in black disappearing around a corner, or seeming to be busy with something else, or bending close to another black-garbed figure, whispering something into an invisible ear.

The days went by and her turmoil grew. As her emotions became more chaotic and her thoughts more confused, they knew. They knew, and they were waiting.

She began spending more time in church. She stopped eating lunch, preferring to spend the hour in the sanctuary, losing herself in the Madonna, silently crying out to the serene figure to help her.

She was rarely alone in the church; always there were two or three people scattered among the pews, each of them lost in his own meditations. Often they were the families of the girls who had already died, privately seeking solace for their loss, praying for understanding.

Peter Balsam, at his own insistence, had returned to the school after only one day's absence. But he had changed, and everyone noticed the change. They were watching him almost as closely as they were watching Marilyn Crane, and he knew why. Just as they thought Marilyn Crane would be the next victim, they thought he was responsible. Leona Anderson, in her grief, had done her work.

Everywhere he went the watching eyes, the hostile stares, of the people of Neilsville frightened him. The nuns, too, had changed, had hardened toward him. He had tried to find out why, but none of them would tell him. They merely stared at him, as if to say "you know better than we."

Except Sister Marie. She came to him the day he returned to St. Francis Xavier's, and offered to help him.

"Help?" he asked blankly. "Help with what?"

"Before I left, you wanted me to translate something for you. Or at least try."

Peter remembered. The tape. "I'm sorry," he said. "It's too late." Then: "Sister Marie, why did you leave?"

A small frown crossed her brow. "I don't know, really," she said. "Just one of Monsignor's quirks, I guess."

"Monsignor's?"

"He ordered me into retreat." Sister Marie's infectious grin suddenly lit up her face. "I don't think he likes me. I'm afraid I just don't take things seriously enough for him. Every time he thinks I'm getting out of hand—my words, not his—he sends me off to spend a few days in retreat. Believe me, if you'd ever had to maintain the Silence for three days, you'd come back feeling more serious about everything too."

Peter tried to remember exactly what Monsignor Vernon had told him about Sister Marie's sudden absence. No, there was no conflict between what the priest had told him and what the nun was telling him now.

"I'm sorry I had to go just then," he heard the nun saying. "Was it terribly important? Whatever it was you wanted me to translate?"

Peter shook his head briefly, and tried to smile. "I don't think so," he said. "I thought it was, but now I'm not sure. Anyway, it's too late."

"Peter," Sister Marie said slowly, as if having a difficult time making up her mind to speak. "What you wanted me to translate—did it have anything to do with—with what's been going on? The girls?"

"I thought it did. But now I'm not sure."

"Do you know what's going on?" Sister Marie asked bluntly.

"I think I do," Peter said uncertainly, wondering whether to take her into his confidence.

Sister Marie chewed her lower lip. When she looked at him again there wasn't a trace of her usual merriment left in her eyes.

"A lot of people here think—" She broke off, embarrassed.

"That I'm responsible for what's happened to the girls?"

She nodded.

"What do you think?" Peter said softly.

She stared at him, and Peter saw tears brimming in her eyes. "I—I don't know what to think," she blurted finally. Then she turned, and hurried away from him.

Sister Marie hadn't spoken to him since, nor had Peter sought her out.

Every day he was growing more exhausted. Only on the nights that Margo Henderson stayed with him did he let himself sleep, and there had only been two of those nights. When she wasn't with him, he stayed up, keeping himself awake with coffee, afraid to sleep alone. The exhaustion was showing in his eyes, and he knew it was not going unnoticed in Neilsville.

He knew Leona Anderson had gone to Monsignor Vernon, demanding that Peter be dismissed immediately; he knew that the priest had refused. But he didn't know why the Monsignor had refused—the chill between the two men had grown to the point where they rarely spoke now, and the obvious tension between them served only to give the town one more thing to whisper about.

Occasionally Balsam himself wondered why he stayed, but each day he told himself that this would be the day he would find a way to be alone in the rectory, to search the study for whatever might be there that would fit the last piece into his puzzle. If there was anything, he had decided, it would be in the study, for it was in the study that the horror took place. Then, when he knew why the horror was perpetrated, he would know how to stop it.

His only solace was Margo Henderson. They began to spend each evening together; each evening Peter would reiterate his theory to Margo. And she would listen.

But nothing was happening. Neilsville was quiet. The days were beginning to take on the dull sameness they had always had, and Margo found it a relief. The town was still restless, people were still talking, but the tension was easing.

Except that each evening Peter Balsam would tell her again that what they were going through was only a respite, that the horror would begin again.

"But how can you be so sure?" she demanded one night. "I mean, if anything's going to happen, why isn't it happening?"

"I don't know," Peter said doggedly. "But I know it isn't over yet. I won't be able to end it until I know why it's happening."

Margo looked at his pale complexion and haggard eyes. It was becoming an obsession with him. Their evenings weren't fun anymore; he was too wrapped up in a problem Margo was no longer sure even existed.

"Even if you find out, what makes you so sure you can do anything about it?" She tried to keep her voice level, but her own growing doubts about Peter came through.

"You don't believe me, do you?" Peter asked.

Margo saw no point in denying it. The doubts had been growing for days.

"I don't know," she said, compromising with herself. "I *want* to believe you, Peter. But it's all so—" She groped for the right word. "—so far-fetched. Peter, it just isn't rational."

"I never said it was," Peter countered.

"No, you didn't," Margo complained. "Maybe if you had tried to make the whole thing sound reasonable it would be easier. But you don't. You just insist that I believe you. You know, there really isn't any difference between you and Monsignor."

The words stung, and Peter winced. "I'm sorry you feel that way," he said stiffly.

"So am I," Margo said coldly. "But it's the way I feel, and I can't do anything about it."

Peter rose from his chair and went to the kitchen to fix himself a drink. As he pried the ice loose, and measured the liquor, he reflected on the fragility of the threads of faith. His faith in the Church had broken, and he had turned to himself. Now the carefully nurtured threads between himself and Margo had broken, too. Where could he turn now?

He returned to the living room.

Margo was gone.

Peter Balsam was alone.

It was on Tuesday that Peter Balsam overheard Marilyn Crane. He was sitting behind his desk in Room 16, trying to grade Latin exams. In the small room adjoining Room 16, Marilyn Crane and Jeff Bremmer were working with the rats. Peter had been vaguely aware of their conversation as they worked, but it wasn't until Marilyn suddenly began talking about the rats that Peter gave up trying to concentrate on his work and began listening to the two adolescents in the next room.

"They aren't any good anymore," Marilyn suddenly commented.

Jeff Bremmer glanced at her, annoyed first that he had been assigned to work on the experiment with Marilyn, and currently because now she was insisting on talking, instead of simply getting on with it.

"What's that supposed to mean?"

Marilyn ignored the implied rebuke.

"Look at them. They don't even try anymore. It doesn't matter what you do; they just plod along until they get through the maze. A few days ago, you could tell them apart. But not anymore. Now they're all alike. It's like their personalities are gone."

"They never had any personalities," Jeff said, his irritation growing. "They're just rats, for Christ's sake!"

Marilyn shot him a look. "You shouldn't talk that way."

"What way?"

"Swearing."

"Oh, Jesus," Jeff said deliberately.

Marilyn didn't hear him this time; her attention was back on the rats.

"Why do they do it?" she mused. "Why don't they just sit in a corner and wait it out? All they get for finding their way through the maze is a little piece of food, and they'd get that anyway."

"They don't know that," Jeff said, anxious to get back to work. "For all they know, if they sit down and do nothing, they'll starve to death."

Marilyn didn't seem to hear him. "Sometimes I feel just like them," she said. Her voice had taken on a dreamy quality, and Jeff was no longer sure if she was talking to him, or to herself. "Sometimes I feel like my life is just like that maze, and every time I figure out what I'm supposed to do, somebody changes the rules, and I have to start all over again."

In Room 16, Peter Balsam put down the exam he had been working on, and devoted his full attention to Marilyn.

"Why do I bother to do it?" she was saying. "Why don't I just quit? I mean, what could happen to me? I'm just like the rats." Her voice grew bitter. "They keep going, and I keep going, and they're all starting to seem alike, and I'm starting to seem like all the rest of them. It must have been the same for them. They must have felt just like I do, like someone else is running their lives for them. But they all gave in, and did what they were supposed to do. Except Judy. But she never does what she's supposed to do."

Jeff Bremmer had stopped working, and was gaping at Marilyn. She no longer seemed to be aware of his presence, or even of where she was. Though she was still staring down into the maze, her eyes had taken on a faraway look, and Jeff wasn't sure she even saw the rats. Her voice continued to drone through the sudden quiet that had fallen over the two rooms.

"Janet tried to fight it, too; she just wasn't as strong as Judy is. But she was stronger than me. If she couldn't hold out against him, how can I? And why should I? It would be a lot easier just to give in to him, and get it over with."

Jeff picked up on the word. "Him." She had said "him." He reached out and grabbed Marilyn's arm.

"Who?" he said. "Give in to who?"

Marilyn didn't respond for a second or two, but then her eyes focused on Jeff, and her body stiffened. She hadn't realized she'd been talking out loud. She'd been thinking. Only thinking. But Jeff had heard.

She shifted her gaze, and looked through the open door to Room 16. Mr. Balsam was staring at her too. Everything she'd been thinking—no, said—they'd heard. Now they'd think she was crazy. She had to get out. Get out of the room. Get out of the school.

She wrenched her arm free of Jeff's grasp, and bolted toward the door. As she passed through Room 16 her tears began to come, and she tried to force back the sob that was in her throat. She began to run, out of the room, down the hall.

Out.

She had to get out. By the time the wracking sob tore loose from her throat, Marilyn Crane was halfway down Cathedral Hill.

She hadn't even noticed the smoke curling up from the roof of the rectory. She was only aware of her own sobbing, and the noises in her head. The sounds. The awful, compelling sounds.

By the time Peter Balsam could react, she was gone. He hurried to the door of the room, but she had disappeared around the corner; all he could hear was the pounding of her feet. He went slowly back into Room 16. Jeff Bremmer was waiting for him.

"What did she mean?" Jeff asked. "It sounded like—"

"Never mind what it sounded like," Peter snapped. Immediately he regretted his tone; he hadn't been thinking when he spoke. He tried to ease the hurt that had sprung into Jeff's face.

"I'm sorry," he said. "I was worried about Marilyn."

"She's getting worse," Jeff commented.

"Worse? What do you mean, worse?"

Jeff fidgeted uncomfortably. Maybe he shouldn't have said that. "Well, she was always a little, you know, weird. But lately it's really gotten bad. I mean, most of the kids think——" He broke off, unwilling to condemn a peer in front of an adult, even if the peer was Marilyn Crane.

"Think what?" Peter asked. Then: "Never mind. I know what they think."

Jeff looked at his teacher curiously, remembering the word Marilyn had used. "Him." And then, when she had seen Mr. Balsam looking at her, she had run.

"You," Jeff said suddenly. "She was talking about you, wasn't she?"

"Me?" Balsam said blankly.

"When she was talking about giving in. She said something about giving in to 'him.' She was talking about you, wasn't she?"

"No," Peter said definitely. "She wasn't talking about me."

But there was something in his eyes, something in his face, that made Jeff doubt him. When he left the room, Jeff Bremmer was sure that whatever had happened to all the girls—what was happening now to Marilyn Crane—Mr. Balsam was to blame.

Peter Balsam sat alone in the room for several minutes, trying to decide what to do. Whatever he did, he would have to do it alone. There was no one left to turn to.

He made up his mind. He would call Marilyn's mother. He would warn her, tell her to watch out for Marilyn, to talk to her.

Peter gathered his things together, locked the uncorrected quizzes into his desk, and left the room. His mind was so occupied with trying to decide exactly what to say to Mrs. Crane that he passed the rectory without even looking up.

No one answered the telephone at the Cranes' home until nearly nine o'clock, and as the hour grew later, Peter became more and more worried. Maybe he was too late. Maybe something had already happened to Marilyn. But when the phone was finally answered, the voice speaking in his ear sounded normal.

"Yes?"

"Mrs. Crane?"

"Yes. Who is this?"

"We haven't met, Mrs. Crane. I'm one of Marilyn's teachers."

Geraldine Crane's impulse was to hang up. How dare he call her? Didn't he know what everyone was saying about him?

"Mrs. Crane, are you still there?"

"What do you want?" Geraldine asked coldly.

"I'm calling about Marilyn. Is she there?"

"Of course she's here. Where else would she be?"

"Mrs. Crane, I'm very worried about Marilyn. I think she may be in danger, and I don't know what to do."

"Danger?" Geraldine Crane held the receiver away from her ear and stared at it. What was the man talking about?

"She was working in the lab this afternoon, and I—well, I don't know how to put it exactly—"

"I suggest you put it the way it happened, whatever it was."

"Well, she was sort of talking to herself."

"Marilyn? Don't be ridiculous." Geraldine was finding the man more annoying every minute.

"I'm sorry, maybe I put it badly." He told her what he'd overheard, and what had happened after Marilyn realized she'd been talking out loud.

"I tried to go after her," Peter finished. "But by the time I got to the hall, she was gone."

"Well, I can assure you, she's quite all right now," Mrs. Crane said icily. "She came home this afternoon, and we all went out for dinner. Right now she's upstairs, doing her homework."

"Mrs. Crane, I know it sounds like a strange request, but I think you ought to spend some time with Marilyn. Talk to her. Try to find out what's bothering her."

Geraldine Crane lost her patience. "Mr. Balsam, apparently you don't know who you're talking to. I happen to be her mother. I talk to Marilyn every day. You spend perhaps one hour with her each day, and now you presume to tell me how to behave with my daughter. I know you claim to be a psychologist, but I have to tell you that I don't have much faith in that sort of thing. I never have, and after what's been happening in Neilsville since you arrived, I have even less. As far as I'm concerned, I think it might be best for everyone if you spent a lot less time meddling in the affairs of your students, and stuck entirely to your classes."

"Mrs. Crane—"

"Mr. Balsam, I'll appreciate it if you don't interrupt me. Marilyn isn't like any of the other children in Neilsville. She's always, since she was a baby, been somewhat withdrawn. I don't know why, but it's always been that way. So you see," she went on, her voice dripping with sarcasm, "your wonderful perceptions are no news to me. I'm aware that Marilyn has been upset lately, but why wouldn't she be? My Lord, Mr. Balsam, she's lost three of her best friends. I don't know if you're aware of it, but Marilyn was very close to those girls. She visited Judy Nelson in the hospital, and Karen Morton had Marilyn at her party. So of course she's upset. She's a normal teen-ager, Mr. Balsam, and I would think you'd understand that." Without waiting for a reply, Geraldine Crane firmly placed the receiver back in its cradle.

Peter Balsam stared at the dead phone in his hand, and wondered what to do. But there didn't seem to be anything left. He put on the coffee pot, and took one of the pills that helped him stay awake. It was going to be a long night.

Geraldine Crane sat seething for several minutes after she hung up on Peter Balsam, and congratulated herself on how well she'd handled the impudent teacher. Then, as her anger eased, she remembered what he'd said. Could he have been right? Was something bothering Marilyn?

Marilyn was on her bed, a book open in front of her. She looked up when her mother came into the room, but didn't close the book.

"Marilyn?" Geraldine's voice was tentative, as if she weren't quite sure how to approach her daughter.

"I'm studying, Mother." There was a flatness to Marilyn's voice.

"I just thought you might like to talk awhile."

"I don't. I talk too much. Can't you just leave me alone?" Marilyn turned her attention back to her book.

Geraldine stood helplessly at the door, wondering what she should do. Then, following the path of least resistance, she started out of the room.

"Marilyn? If you need to talk, I'm here."

"I know, Mother." But it was a dismissal, and Geraldine knew it. She left her daughter, and went back downstairs.

Marilyn got up and closed the door to her room. Why couldn't they leave her alone? All of them? It was Mr. Balsam on the telephone. She was sure of it. If it wasn't him, who else would have called and induced her mother to try to talk to her?

She couldn't talk to them. What could she talk to them about? The strange things she wanted to do to herself? They wouldn't understand. She didn't even understand it herself, so how could they?

Maybe they wanted her to be upset. Maybe it all was Mr. Balsam, or he was part of it, whatever it was. But it couldn't be him, could it?

She would pray. She would pray for guidance, and the Blessed Virgin would tell her what to do.

She began praying. She prayed all through the night. And all through the night, the voices howled in her mind, calling to her, chanting to her.

The night was long, but for Marilyn Crane it wasn't nearly long enough.

## TWENTY-NINE

PETER BALSAM WATCHED THE SUN COME UP, watched the black horizon turn first to a pearly gray, then to a pale rose as the first rays crept above the hills. The long night was over. He'd sat up through the endless hours, concentrating his depleted energy on resisting the strange impulses within him. Hour after hour, he had heard the chanting echoing in his mind, reaching out to him like invisible fingers, pulling at him, demanding that he leave his home and go— where?

He was sure he knew. He was sure the Society of St. Peter Martyr was reaching out to him, trying to draw him to the rectory, trying to ply its evil on him once again.

The telephone had rung several times during the night, its jarring clangor breaking into his intense concentration, sending waves of fear through him. He wouldn't answer, wouldn't leave the chair he clung to. Each time it rang, it seemed louder, and went on longer. The last call had been just before dawn, and went on endlessly, the steadily paced rhythm of the bell breaking in on him, rattling on his nerves, shaking him.

Now, as the sun rose over Neilsville, Peter Balsam dragged himself into the tiny bathroom. He stared at himself in the mirror, and wondered if the image he saw was truly himself, or if something else was being reflected there.

The eyes were rimmed in red from lack of sleep, and at the corners, crow's feet were beginning to show starkly against his pale skin. His whole face seemed to sag under the weariness he felt. He wondered how long he could go on.

Today, he decided. Today, somehow, he must find a way to get into the rectory, to search the study. Whatever he was looking for, it had to be there. If it wasn't, there was no hope at all.

He began dressing, fighting off the tiredness. An irrational idea grew in his mind, and he reached up to the highest shelf of his closet, and pulled a large box from the depths. He set it on the bed, and opened it. His monastic robes lay inside, relics from a more secure past. He put on the unfamiliar articles, one by one.

He knew the exhaustion was overtaking him, knew that he shouldn't be doing what he was doing. He tried to tell himself to take off the vestments, to put on his ordinary clothing. But his body wouldn't obey, and once again he heard the chanting voices reaching out to grasp his mind. Only now he had no more resources left. His fight was done. As the unspoken commands came into his mind, his body numbly obeyed.

In his black robes, a crucifix swinging from his waist, an exhausted Peter Balsam left his apartment and began walking toward Main Street.

Marilyn Crane, too, had fought against the voices through the long night, her beads clutched in her hands, counting out the decades over and over, praying for her soul. As the sun climbed into the sky above Neilsville, Marilyn put the rosary aside, and looked at her fingers. They had grown red during the night, and had swollen. Blisters showed where she had squeezed the beads, as if through pressure alone she could find strength. Her legs ached, and at first she could barely move. She sat on the edge of the bed, flexing first one knee, then the other. She tried to close out the chaos that still raged in her mind, and concentrated instead on the sounds of her family preparing for the day.

She heard her mother calling her, and forced herself to get up from the bed, and move through the door of her room, and down the stairs.

In the kitchen, her mother stared at her.

"You're not dressed," the voice accused. One more accusing voice. One more fragment of disapproval, adding itself to the confusion.

"I'm staying home today." Her voice was flat, drained by the long hours of whispered prayer.

"Don't be silly." Geraldine looked sharply at her younger daughter. "Are you sick?"

"No. Just tired."

"Well, I'm sorry. You shouldn't have studied so late. But that's your fault and no one else's. You'll go to school."

The words rang in Marilyn's mind as she slowly plodded up the stairs. "Your fault. Your fault. Your fault." Everything was her fault. Everything that went wrong was her fault. The chaos in her mind grew, and Marilyn Crane stopped thinking.

She dressed slowly, almost dreamily, and when she was finished, she gazed at herself in the mirror.

I'm pretty, she thought. I'm really very pretty.

She went downstairs, and presented herself to her mother. Geraldine surveyed her daughter critically.

"White?" she asked. "For school? That's a Sunday dress."

"But I want to wear it today."

Why not? Geraldine Crane asked herself. She looks so tired, and if it'll make her feel better, why not? She kissed her daughter on the cheek, and Marilyn left the house.

She walked slowly, almost unaware of her surroundings. Suddenly she felt at peace, and the voices in her head were no longer calling to her so stridently; now they were singing to her, caressing her spirit.

She got to Main Street, but instead of turning to start up the long hill to the school, she turned the other way, and began walking into Neilsville, her soft white skirt floating around her, the morning sun bathing her face.

Far ahead, as if at the end of a tunnel, she saw a shape moving toward her. She concentrated on the shape, and her focus seemed to narrow until she was no longer aware of anything else: only the dark shape coming slowly closer. Marilyn clutched her purse to her abdomen with one hand, and with the other once again began counting the decades of the rosary.

Peter Balsam trudged slowly up Main Street, vaguely aware that people were staring at him. He knew he must be an odd spectacle in his robes, his face unshaven, his eyes swollen and red. He wanted to go back, to go home and lock himself in once more. But it was too late. The chanting had a firm grasp on his mind now, and he could only keep walking, his pace steady, one foot carefully placed in front of the other.

Then, far ahead, he saw a figure in white coming toward him. He felt his pace pick up, and idly wondered why. The white figure wavered in front of him, and he realized that it wasn't the figure that wavered; it was himself. He steadied himself, pausing for a moment to regain his balance. Ahead of him the figure in white seemed to pause too.

Peter strained his eyes, trying to make out who it was. Then he knew.

It was Marilyn Crane.

She should have been going the same way he was going, up the hill, to the school. Instead, she was coming toward him.

Something was wrong. He forced his exhausted mind to begin functioning again. Marilyn was coming toward him, and something was wrong.

Now he tried consciously to hurry; his feet refused to obey him. But he had to get to her.

He raised his black-robed arm and waved.

Marilyn saw the dark shape coming closer, and then she saw the uplifted arm. It was beckoning to her. Beckoning, as the voices in her head had beckoned.

Suddenly she knew what the figure was.

Clothed in black, Death was coming for her.

She wanted to run, wanted to fling herself into the arms of the specter, and let him carry her away.

But there was something she had to do first. There was some act she had to commit, some symbolic gesture she was required to make to let the figure know that she was ready to accept Him.

Her right hand dropped the rosary beads, and the crucifix clattered to the sidewalk. Marilyn knelt, reached into her purse, her eyes fastened on the black figure before her. Her fingers closed on the package. The razor blades that had been with her for so long. She fumbled at them.

Peter stopped suddenly, realizing that Marilyn was no longer coming toward him. He saw the crucifix and beads fall to the sidewalk, and his hand went to his waist, his fingers tightening on his own rosary.

She was kneeling now, and had dropped her purse near her beads.

And then the redness began to flow from her wrist, and Peter knew what was happening. He began to run.

Marilyn watched the blood spurt from her left wrist, and quickly transferred the blade to her other hand. She began hacking clumsily at the arteries of her right wrist. Suddenly the blade met its mark; skin and flesh parted. She stared at the throbbing artery for a split second, then plunged the razor deep into it. A crimson fountain gushed forth, splashing against the white of her dress, and dribbling slowly to the pavement beneath her.

She looked up, away from the blood. She had been right. Death was coming for her now, hurrying toward her, and she must go to meet Him. She began running, her arms stretched out toward her approaching Death, the blood spewing from her wrists.

The truck was coming toward Main Street on First Street. For once, the light—Neilsville's only traffic light—was green. The driver pressed on the accelerator and the engine surged. He would make the light.

It happened so fast the driver had no time to respond.

From the left, a figure ran in front of the truck, a blur of red and blinding white. He moved his foot to the brake, but before the truck even began to slow he heard the dull thump, and the scream.

He brought the truck to a halt, and leaped from the cab. He threw up on the pavement.

Her head caught under the left front wheel, her neck broken, Marilyn Crane lay in a crimson heap. Only the blood, still being slowly pumped from her wrists, signified that she was still alive.

Peter Balsam saw it happen, saw Marilyn dashing across the street toward him, too intent on him to notice that the light was wrong, and that the truck was coming. If she saw it before it hit her, she gave no sign. She didn't try to veer away, she didn't try to stop.

She screamed once, but that was a reflex.

He never knew whether he paused, or whether he took in the scene as he ran. But suddenly he was beside her, on his knees, her blood soaking the heavy material of his robes.

Peter Balsam, his mind reeling, began praying over the broken and dying body of Marilyn Crane.

From out of his past, from somewhere in his memory, Peter began administering the Last Rites to Marilyn.

The crowd gathered slowly, until there was a solid mass of people surrounding Peter as he prayed for Marilyn's soul. The crowd was in shock, but finally one of them broke away and found a telephone.

A few moments later, the ambulance screamed through Neilsville.

In the rectory, Monsignor Vernon stared into the last coals of the dying fire. An intense satisfaction filled him, and he stood up. He moved to the window, drawing the curtain open to the sunlight. With the sunshine came the howl of the siren.

The priest smiled softly. At last, the long night was over.

He began to prepare for the day ahead.

## THIRTY

THE STORY WAS SWEEPING THROUGH NEILS-ville even before the ambulance had taken Marilyn Crane and Peter Balsam to the hospital.

Neilsville stopped functioning. For the first time, each one of them, as he heard the story, felt personally touched. Until that day they had talked, spoken in whispers, wondered about the girls who had died. But that day, they had seen it, watched from the sidewalks, from the windows, as the evil among them spilled out into the street. By noon, everyone in town had heard the story, and told it, and heard it again. For each of them it was as if they had seen it themselves; by afternoon each of them believed he had seen it.

School was canceled before it even began that day, and the Sisters retired to their private chapel to spend the day in prayer. The children went home, but on their way home they talked, and by the time they reached their homes, all of them were sure that they had seen Marilyn Crane die.

She was dead by the time the ambulance reached the hospital, but still, in the manner of hospitals, they tried to act as if she was not. They worked over her for nearly an hour, and all the time they worked, Peter Balsam sat numbly looking on, knowing they were not treating Marilyn, but treating themselves, avoiding by simple activity the truth of what had happened, what was happening.

Margo Henderson walked briskly into the emergency room, but when she saw why she had been called she came to an abrupt halt. She stared at the specter before her, not wanting to believe her eyes. But then the professionalism born of years in the hospital came to the fore, and she steeled herself. She approached Peter Balsam.

"Peter?" There was no answer, and she realized he was in shock. She repeated his name: "Peter."

"I have to end it," he murmured. "I have to end it." He kept repeating the phrase as Margo led him through the halls.

Dr. Shields gave him a shot, and he slowly came out of it. He gazed first at Margo, then at the doctor.

"She's dead," he said, neither asking a question nor stating a fact.

"What happened?" Dr. Shields asked gently. "Can you talk about it?"

"Nothing to talk about," Peter said thickly. "I have to end it, that's all."

"Peter, there's nothing for you to do," Margo said. Suddenly an image flashed in her mind, an image of the attractive young man she had met on the train such a short time ago. Could this haggard being, his bloody robe hanging limply from stooped shoulders, be the same young man?

No, she decided, it could not. Biting her lips to hold back her tears, she hurried from the room. Peter watched her go, and knew that this time she was gone forever. It didn't matter. The only thing that mattered was that he must end the horror. He tried to focus on the doctor.

"I have to sleep," he said. "Can you give me something to sleep? If I sleep, I'll be all right."

Dr. Shields nodded. "Why don't I admit you to the hospital?"

"They'll watch me?" Peter asked.

"Watch you?"

"While I sleep. They'll watch me while I sleep?"

Dr. Shields nodded.

"If they'll watch me," Peter said vaguely. "I can't sleep alone, you know."

Dr. Shields nodded understandingly, though he hadn't the vaguest idea of what the young man was talking about.

"I'll see to it," he promised.

Thirty minutes later Peter Balsam was asleep in Neilsville Memorial Hospital, a nurse sitting by his bed. She watched him for an hour, checking his breathing and his pulse. When she decided all was well with him, she silently left the room to go about her duties.

He woke to the sound of church bells pealing, and knew what it meant.

All over Neilsville the churches were holding special services. The people had asked for them, needing something to take their minds off the horror of the day, needing something to tell them that soon all would be well among them again.

Peter lay in his hospital bed, thinking that it was curious. The bells were sounding for Marilyn, all of them except St. Francis Xavier's. The bells of St. Francis Xavier were sounding as usual, calling the faithful to evening Mass. Usually, on a weeknight, attendance would be light. But not tonight, he was sure. Tonight they would all be there, praying guiltily for the soul of Marilyn Crane, knowing in their minds that they should not, that Marilyn was no longer worthy of their prayers, but praying for her nonetheless.

He glanced at the clock. Thirty minutes, he thought, and they'll all be in church. All of us, except those of us here, or in the grave.

All of us. He repeated the words to himself. All of us. Peter Balsam sat up in bed, the last vestiges of sleep falling away as his mind suddenly became alert. Now was the time. If ever there was going to be a time, it would be now.

He rose from his bed and shuffled into the tiny bathroom wedged economically between his room and the next. He splashed cold water on his face and looked in the mirror.

His eyes were better, and the crow's feet had faded. He needed a shave but it didn't matter. No one was going to see him anyway.

He found the bloodstained robes hanging in the closet. Loathing them, he put them on. Then he sat down to wait.

He waited until the bells died away, and silence fell over Neilsville. Then he left his room. Without speaking to anyone, Peter Balsam walked out of the hospital.

No one tried to stop him. Perhaps it was the strange figure he presented, barefoot, his bloodstained robes trailing the floor, his crucifix clutched tightly in his hand. The orderlies looked at the nurses, and the nurses looked at the resident, but none of them spoke. Dr. Shields had admitted him, but had said nothing about keeping him there. "Make sure he sleeps." That's what the doctor had ordered, and that's what they had done. Peter Balsam had slept, and now he was going home.

But he didn't go home. Instead he walked slowly up Cathedral Hill, listening to the sounds of the choirs that were raising their voices to God all over Neilsville. No one was in sight, but he could sense them around him, praying quietly in the churches.

He mounted the steps to the rectory, and let himself in the front door. He picked up the silver bell and shook it, then shook it again. Its tinkle echoed through the dimly lit house, and Peter knew he was alone. He walked quickly down the hall to the door of the study.

He paused there, suddenly frightened. He had to remind himself that the room on the other side of the door was empty, that there were no strange rituals being performed, that tonight no one was reaching out to draw him to this room. Tonight, he had come on his own.

He opened the door, and entered the small room. He found the light switch, and the room was filled with a yellow glow that seemed to change its configuration, washing away the gloom.

He began his search of the desk, opening and closing the drawers rapidly. He wasn't sure what he was looking for. He would recognize it when he saw it.

There was nothing in the desk, and he moved to a small filing cabinet that was built into one of the walls. He opened the top drawer, and began going through the files. Nothing.

Nothing in the second.

In the third, he found what he was looking for.

It was a large sealed envelope, wedged behind the last of the files. Peter pulled it from its hiding place, and tore open the envelope. A scrapbook. A scrapbook and a file folder. He opened the file folder.

On top was a single sheet of paper; on it was written a list of names. Five of them had been scratched out.

*Judy Nelson*
*Karen Morton*
*Penny Anderson*
*Janet Connally*
*Marilyn Crane*

At the end of the list, Judy Nelson's name appeared again, with no line through it.

Peter Balsam had found what he was looking for.

He slipped the file folder back in the envelope, and closed the drawer of the cabinet. He let himself out of the study, snapping the light off as he went, then, carrying the bulging envelope, walked out of the rectory into the fading light of evening.

For the first time in several days the dusk held no fear for Peter. This night he would complete the puzzle. This night would end the terror, both for him and for Neilsville.

As he hurried down the hill the bells of St. Francis Xavier began to peel once again. Mass was over.

In his apartment, Peter began going through the scrapbook. He leafed through the pages quickly. They were all more or less the same: filled with yellowed newspaper clippings, each clipping headlined in bold type:

GIRL SLAYS PARENTS, SELF
MODERN LIZZIE BORDEN WILL NEVER STAND TRIAL
CHILD WATCHES AS FAMILY DIES

There were nearly fifty clippings in the scrapbook, from brief articles less than a column long to major features spread over several pages. All of them were about the same crime, all of them were from the same time. Peter Balsam subtracted quickly. He would have been two or three at the time the crime took place.

He went back to the first page of the scrapbook, and began reading the articles carefully.

Most of them gave simply the bare facts:

A man and his wife had been found in bed, murdered. In the same room their daughter was discovered hanging from a light fixture. When the room was thoroughly searched, the couple's small son was found hiding in the closet of the bedroom, in shock.

The tabloids had spread the story over several pages, and it was in the clippings from the tabloids that Peter Balsam was able to glean the details of the bizarre crime.

The couple had been murdered while in the act of making love. Their daughter had walked in on them and hacked them to death with a cleaver. The weapon indicated premeditation. The motive was unclear. There was some speculation that the girl was reacting badly to her own misfortune—an autopsy had revealed that she was pregnant.

But what the tabloids played up most was the little boy—the little boy who was thought to have watched the entire thing from the closet, from the moment when his parents came into the room and began making love—not knowing they were being observed—to the moment when his sixteen-year-old sister brought the cleaver into the bedroom, hacked her parents to death, then hanged herself from the light fixture.

He had been in shock when he was found, and had been rushed to a hospital. There, it was discovered that the child had no living relatives. In the end he had been anonymously placed in a convent.

The convent was unnamed, but Balsam was sure he knew which one it was. What he had just read was the story that had been whispered about when he was a child. None of the children at the convent had known the facts. Now Peter Balsam knew them all.

He searched through the papers.

The name. Where was the name of the family?

The name was not given. Nowhere. In every story the names of everyone involved in the crime had been carefully deleted, as if whoever had compiled the scrapbook had wanted the story known, but the identities kept secret. Nor were the papers themselves identified. Each clipping had been carefully cut from its page.

In only one story was there even a clue. In one story, someone had slipped. The child's name was Peter.

Suddenly it all made sense. He had never gotten over the shock. It had festered in him all the time he was growing up, all the time he had studied for the priesthood. And then, sometime, not too long ago, the shock had caught up with him.

He had begun to hate adolescent girls. And why shouldn't he? Hadn't one of them taken his parents away from him? Taken his home away from him? Left him with nothing? If one of them could do that, why not all of them? His hatred had grown, had turned into an obsession.

And Peter Vernon—now Monsignor Vernon—had acted on his obsession. He had gathered together the forces at his disposal, and begun to strike back, taking revenge on the children his injured mind blamed for the loss of his parents.

Balsam leafed through the scrapbook. He could understand it, now, and for the first time he felt a trace of sympathy for the priest.

He wondered what to do with the scrapbook. Should he take it to the police? But what would they do? All right, so the Monsignor kept a scrapbook about a crime more than thirty years old. So what? If it was your family, wouldn't you have kept a scrapbook too? Those girls killed themselves, mister, and the fact that a priest's older sister did the same thing thirty years ago is just one of those coincidences.

The Bishop. He could take it to the Bishop. Even if the Bishop didn't believe the Monsignor had anything to do with the suicides, at least the scrapbook would prove that something had gone wrong in the Monsignor's early life, and that the priest should at least be carefully observed. The Bishop could order the Monsignor to undergo observation. From there, the psychiatrists could take over. It would all come out.

The door suddenly opened.

Monsignor Vernon stood framed in the door, a small smile playing around his lips; a smile that was betrayed by the burning fire in his eyes.

"I went to see you at the hospital," he said. "But you'd left."

"Yes, I did," Peter said blankly, his mind whirling.

"May I come in?" The burning eyes bored into Peter, and without waiting for an answer the priest entered the room and closed the door behind him.

"You found my scrapbook," he said softly. His eyes darted around the room, coming to rest on the open scrapbook on the desk.

"It was you we all talked about, wasn't it? When we were kids?"

"Yes, it was me," the priest said. "But I didn't know it, not until five years ago."

"Five years ago?"

"Someone sent me that scrapbook. I don't know who, and I don't know why. But it explained a lot to me. It made me see what I had to do."

"Do?" Peter Balsam felt his heart beat faster.

"I had to punish them. All of them."

"You mean the girls?"

"They're evil," the priest said. "They're evil with their minds, and with their bodies. The Lord wants me to punish them."

"I thought it was St. Peter Martyr," Balsam said softly.

"Of course you did. That's what I wanted you to think. And that's what

I wanted the members of the Society to think. It makes it much easier that way.''

"I see," said Peter. "The Society never had anything to do with religion, did it?"

"What is religion? It has to do with my religion, and with St. Peter Martyr's religion. But not with the religion of the Church. The Church has no religion any more. It has become weak. It tolerates."

"And you do not."

"I don't need to," the priest said. The fire in his eyes was raging now, and Peter Balsam was suddenly afraid. But he had to know.

"Me," he said. "Why did you need me?"

Monsignor Vernon smiled now.

"You think I'm insane, don't you?" he asked.

"Are you?"

"If I were, I wouldn't do what I've done."

The fear stabbed at Balsam again. "Done? What do you mean?"

"You," the priest said simply. "You've figured out everything else, but you haven't figured out your own part in it, have you?"

"I'm to be St. Acerinus," Peter said. "I'm supposed to kill you, and then repent. But I won't do it."

"No, you won't," the Monsignor said. "You've done everything else admirably, but I don't expect you to kill me. That was never part of the plan. That was the way it happened the first time. This time, St. Peter takes his revenge."

"I'm not sure I'm following you," Balsam said. It was all getting confused again. Did the priest really believe, after all, that he was St. Peter Martyr's reincarnation? And then the truth struck. Of course he did. He had to, or the guilt would be too much for him. If he weren't Peter Vernon—if he were St. Peter Martyr—then everything was different. He was punishing heretics and sinners, carrying on the work of the Lord, and protecting the Mother Church. He was no longer just Peter Vernon, insanely avenging the death of his parents.

"I'm going to kill you," Monsignor Vernon said in the silence.

Balsam stared at him. "You can't," he protested.

"Can't I?" The priest's eyes had grown cold. "What will happen if I do? They'll think it was suicide." He picked a letter opener off Peter Balsam's desk, and began twirling it in his hands as he talked.

"When they find you, what will they find? A young man, a psychologist, a teacher. Wearing monasic robes stained with blood."

The letter opener glittered as it reflected the light from the desk lamp. Peter Balsam blinked as the flashes of light struck his eyes.

"And who is this young man? His name is Peter. He grew up in a convent, after a tragedy in his youth." The priest touched the scrapbook with the point of the letter opener. "And he was a failure at nearly everything."

The letter opener glinted again. Peter Balsam watched it, unable to force his eyes away from the lamplight reflecting on the blade.

"His students have been dying, one by one," Monsignor Vernon's voice went on inexorably. "But has he been trying to help them? No. Instead, he's been busying himself by spreading preposterous tales about a simple religious study group. And he's been acting very strangely."

The light seemed to bounce off the blade directly into Peter's brain.

He felt the sleepiness overcoming him, felt the heaviness in his limbs that he knew marked the first stages of hypnosis.

He tried to fight it, tried to summon his last reserves of energy to rouse himself, to look away from the flashing light, and block out the voice of the priest. But he couldn't tear his eyes away from the blade; the voice was relentless.

"They'll find the scrapbook, of course, and they'll read about what happened to the little boy—the little boy Peter—who grew up and became a psychologist, and whose students began to kill themselves.

"They'll put it all together, Peter. They'll call your death a suicide. Your work is done, Peter. Mine is just beginning."

Peter saw the priest come toward him, the letter opener held almost carelessly in his right hand. Still the light flashed in his eyes. He told his body to do something, to move, to react, but there was nothing. His brain cried out in its weariness, but his body would not respond.

"Would you like to watch yourself die, Peter? It won't hurt, I promise you. There won't be any pain, Peter. No pain at all. The blade will simply slide into you, and it will all end."

The point of the letter opener was against his chest now, its tip lost in the folds of his robe. And still he watched it, his eyes drawn to the blade in fascination.

Is this how it ends, he wondered, staring at the polished blade. Is this what they felt—Karen and Penny and Janet and Marilyn? Did they see the shining metal, coming for them? He tried to rouse himself from the awful torpor that had claimed him. It was too late.

He felt a slight pressure, but Monsignor Vernon was right. It wasn't pain, not really. What he'd been feeling the last few days had been pain. This was release.

He gave himself up to it, and began praying silently for redemption.

Peter Balsam watched as the blade slid into his chest, but he felt nothing. Only a sense of anticipation, and a sense of gladness. For him, finally, the horror was truly over.

Ten minutes later Monsignor Vernon left Peter Balsam's apartment, and began walking back to the rectory. He took the side streets. No one saw him as he moved deliberately through Neilsville. Not that it would have mattered had he been seen; the tall authoritarian figure of the Monsignor was a familiar sight in Neilsville. They believed in him. They leaned on him.

# THIRTY-ONE

**T**HEY BURIED HIM A WEEK LATER, IN AN unmarked grave. They tried to reach his wife, but she had disappeared. They weren't sure that even if they found her, she would want him. Not after hearing what they would have to tell her.

In the manner of small towns, everyone in Neilsville knew where the grave was. And they went; the Catholics secretly, the others openly. They covered it with filth, as if by desecrating his grave they could wipe him out of their memories. Each day the filth was cleaned away, and each night it reappeared.

It took nearly a year, but eventually they forgot, or buried their memories deep in the backs of their minds. Peter Balsam's grave lay clean, unvisited, untended. For a while.

For Judy Nelson, that year was the most difficult of her life. She had always felt set apart from the town, but during that year it was worse than ever. Her friends were gone, and she was unable to make new ones. It was as if she was tainted; as if whatever had brushed against her, then attacked her friends, might still be in Neilsville, ready to strike again.

Judy was haunted by the memory of Marilyn Crane. Late at night, when she should have been sleeping, she would remember. She hadn't intended for the pranks to go as far as they had. She had only been teasing Marilyn. She hadn't meant for Marilyn to die. But Marilyn had died, and Judy knew that, whatever had happened to the other girls, with Marilyn it had been different. She, Judy, had driven her to her death. Her mind would not let her forget.

On the anniversary of Peter Balsam's death, the memory of Marilyn Crane loomed larger than ever in Judy's mind. She woke out of a sound sleep, and Marilyn was singing to her, calling her. She left her bed and moved to her closet. From the top shelf she removed the box that contained her confirmation dress. She opened the box and shook the dress out.

She put it on.

She left the house quietly, and walked through the streets of Neilsville. She entered the graveyard, and went to the spot where Marilyn Crane lay buried. She stood for a long time, staring down at the grave and praying.

Then, as the first gray of dawn showed in the eastern sky, Judy moved to Peter Balsam's grave. There, too, she stood for a long while, praying once more. As she prayed, the music—a sort of chanting—grew in her ears.

She began searching in the rubble around the grave until she found a piece of broken glass.

With the shard of glass she began to cut herself.

They found her late that morning. She was lying on Peter Balsam's grave, face down, her arms spread wide, as if trying to embrace the decaying remains that lay below. Pools of blood soaked the earth beneath her palms, and her rosary lay broken, the beads scattered in the mud where the headstone should have been.

They removed Peter Balsam's bones from the ground and burned them.

But it happened again, and yet again.

The people of Neilsville wondered, and were frightened.

They grew expectant, and each year, about the same time, they began watching their daughters, looking for a sign. But there was never a sign, never a clue. But each year, sometime in the fall, one of their children would be missed from her home. She would always be found in the same place, reaching out as if to embrace the empty grave.

And each year, in the rectory of the Church of St. Francis Xavier, the Society of St. Peter Martyr met.

Six priests, meeting in the glow of the firelight, praying to their patron saint.

On each of those nights, very late, the flames would begin to dance in a slow rhythm, and the voice would speak to them.

"Give praise unto the Lord, my servants. Strike down the heretics, and punish the sinners."

Each year the will of St. Peter Martyr was carried out, and the sins of the faithful were punished.

# CRY FOR THE STRANGERS

For my parents

# PROLOGUE

A CLAP OF THUNDER AWAKENED THE BOY, and he lay very still in his bed for a long time, wishing the storm would go away, yet, at the same time enjoying the excitement of it. As each flash of lightning briefly illuminated his bedroom, he began counting the seconds, waiting for the explosive roar of thunder. The storm bore down on the coast; the interval between the flash and the sound grew shorter.

When the moment separating sight and sound shrank to only seconds, and the boy knew the storm had reached the beach a mile away, he rose from his bed and began to dress.

A few minutes later he opened the door and stepped out into the driving rain. It slashed through his clothing, but he seemed not to notice. He began walking slowly away from his home, into the wrath of the storm.

He heard the roar of the surf when he was still a quarter of a mile from the beach. The rhythmic pounding of the waves, usually a soft, gentle sound, was amplified by the storm, its steady beat carried on the wind. The boy began to run toward the sound.

A sheet of lightning lit the sky as he left the road and turned onto the path that would take him through a narrow strip of forest to the beach beyond. The thunder crashed in his ears as the white light faded from his eyes: the storm was all around him.

He approached the beach slowly, almost with reverence. Just beyond the woods a mound of driftwood lay tangled on the beach, blocking his way. He worked his way over it carefully but steadily, his feet finding the familiar toeholds almost without guidance from his eyes.

He was about to clamber over the last immense log when the storm suddenly broke and a full moon illuminated the beach. As if by instinct, the boy dropped to his knees, crouching as he surveyed the strip of sand and rocks in front of him.

He was not alone on the beach.

Directly in front of him he could see shapes, dark figures of dancers writhing in the moonlight as if in some sort of ceremony. He watched them in fascination. Then he realized there was something else. Something vaguely disturbing.

As he watched his eye was caught by a movement near the dancers. Two other forms were moving in the moonlight—not gracefully, purposefully, as the dancers did, but struggling, rolling about in the sand as they fought the ropes that bound them hand and foot. The boy remembered the legends, the stories his grandmother had told him about the beach, and with the memories came an electric surge of fear. He was watching a storm dance, and he knew what would happen. He crouched lower, concealing himself behind the log.

The dancers continued their strange rhythms for a little longer, then suddenly stopped.

As the boy looked on, the dancers surrounded the bound figures who lay squirming at their feet—a man and a woman, he realized now.

They put the man into the pit first, then the woman beside him. They seemed to be weakened, for their struggles were feeble and their voices could not be heard above the surf.

The dancers put them in the pit so that they faced the sea.

And then the dancers began refilling the pit.

They did it carefully, relentlessly. No sand fell into the faces of the victims, nor did the shovels strike them. But as the minutes passed, the pit filled. In a little while there was nothing left above the surface except the silhouettes of the two heads against the foaming surf beyond.

The dancers stared briefly at the results of their work, then burst into loud laughter—laughter that carried above the surf and sounded in the boy's ears, driving out memory of the thunder and the roar of the sea.

As the tide began to rise the dancers started walking toward the woods, toward the boy.

The moon disappeared as quickly as it had come, and the driving rain began again. The macabre scene on the beach disappeared into the gloom, remaining only in the boy's memory, where it would stay forever.

Under cover of the storm the boy left his hiding place behind the log and scurried back into the woods. By the time the dancers from the beach had made their way through the driftwood barrier, he was almost home.

The tide was rising.


The boy woke up early the next morning and stretched in the warm coziness of his bed. The sun poured through his window in bright denial of the recent storm, and the child smiled happily as he looked out at the clear blue sky. It would be a good day for the beach.

The beach.

The night came back to him, a dark confusion of shapes and sounds. He remembered the storm, and waking up. He remembered counting the seconds between the flashes of lightning and the thunderclaps. But the rest was all fuzzy, like a dream.

He dimly recalled going down to the beach and seeing something.

Dancers, burying two people in the sand.

And the tide coming in.

The boy shook himself. It must have been a dream. It had to be.

He began listening for the sounds of morning. His father would be gone already, working the woods. His grandmother would be bustling around the kitchen, and his grandfather would be sitting at the kitchen table, drinking coffee and reading out loud to nobody in particular.

But this morning there was silence.

He lay in bed for a long time, listening. He told himself that if he listened long enough, the familiar sounds would begin, and the nightmare would fade from his mind.

The silence terrified him.

At last he rose and started to dress. But his clothes, the clothes he had neatly placed on the chair the evening before, were scattered on the floor this morning, and wet.

It hadn't been a dream after all.

He put on clean clothes, dressing slowly, hoping every second that the morning sounds would begin, that he would hear his grandmother clattering dishes in the sink and his grandfather's voice droning steadily in the background. But when he was fully dressed the silence still resonated through the house.

He went to the kitchen. The remains of his father's breakfast were still on the table. That was all right, then. But where were his grandparents?

He made his way up the stairs, calling out to them as he went. They must have overslept. That was it—they were still in bed, sound asleep.

Their room was empty.

The dream came back to him.

He left the house and began running toward the beach.

* * *

He paused at the edge of the woods and stared into the trees as if hoping that somehow he would be able to see through them to whatever lay waiting for him on the beach.

His face tightened with worry as he stepped into the woods. He almost turned back when he came to the driftwood barrier.

But he had to know.

He picked his way carefully through the tangle of logs, not so much because the way was unfamiliar, but because he wanted to prolong it, wanted to put off reaching the crescent of the sand.

Minutes later he climbed slowly over the last log and stood on the beach.

The storm had covered the beach with debris: kelp lay in tangled heaps everywhere, and a new crop of driftwood was scattered helter-skelter across the expanse of sand and rock.

The boy looked quickly around. Nothing unusual. His heart surged with relief and the worry on his face gave way to a grin. There would be good beachcombing this morning. With a little luck he might even find some glass floats lying in the seaweed.

Near the water he saw a huge mound of kelp and headed toward it. He walked eagerly at first, but as he approached the dark brown tangle, he slowed, his apprehension flooding back.

He began pulling at the tangle.

Either it was buried deep in the sand or it was caught on something.

He pulled harder.

The kelp gave way.

It hadn't been a dream. From under the kelp, still buried in the sand up to their necks, two faces stared grotesquely up at the child, their features contorted with fear, the eyes bulging open.

His grandparents.

The boy stared helplessly back at them, frozen, his mind whirling.

He could see in their faces how they must have died, waiting helplessly, watching the surf creep inexorably toward them, lapping at their faces, licking at them, then withdrawing to mount another attack. It must have been a slow death, and a terrifying one. They must have coughed and choked, holding their breaths and spitting out the brine, screaming, unheard, into the wind and rain.

The boy looked once more into the eyes of, first, his grandfather, then his grandmother. As he stared, grieving, into the finely planed, dark face of the old lady, he thought he heard something.

Softly at first, then louder.

"Cry . . ." the voice inside his head wailed. "Cry for them . . . and for me."

It was his grandmother's voice, but she was dead.

The boy screamed and turned away.

But he never forgot.

BOOK ONE

# CLARK'S HARBOR

# ONE

PETE SHELLING STARED OUT AT THE SEA, reading the swells like a map. Far off to the south the rest of the fleet was moving slowly toward the harbor, their running lights winking cheerfully in the night. Pete was tempted to alter his course and follow the fleet. He put the temptation down at once.

Following the fleet was not Shelling's way; it never had been, and wouldn't be now.

The wind freshened and Pete went aft to begin the back breaking task of hauling in his nets. Even with the power winch it was difficult work. He grimaced quietly, wishing he'd brought someone with him—he was getting too old to work alone, and the years were beginning to take their toll.

The nets began coming inexorably in, and he guided the thrashing fish into the hold, keeping the net neatly piled, ready to be reset. By the time he was finished, with the catch secure in the hold, Pete Shelling was alone on the sea.

The fleet was gone.

Once more he considered returning to harbor. He looked critically at the sea and remembered all the stories he'd heard about this part of the Pacific—about the sudden storms that plagued this stretch of the Washington coast, storms that seemed to come up out of nowhere, whipping the sea into a frenzy of wrath that could pick up a boat the size of *Sea Spray* and spin it across the surface like a top. But he had never seen such a storm—they seemed to be a thing of the past, probably an exaggeration, tales built into legend more by the active imaginations of generations of local fishermen than by the storms' actual ferocity.

Pete Shelling's eyes swept the horizon and he made his decision. He would reset the nets and take in one more catch before calling it a night. The tide would be at its fullest and he would have to fight the beginning ebb on his way back into the harbor, but that was all right. Pete Shelling was used to fighting.

Not that he'd intended to fight, not at first. Years ago, when he'd first decided to put his roots down in Clark's Harbor, he'd planned to take life easy, join the fishing community, and spend the rest of his years in affable companionship.

But it hadn't worked out that way.

Clark's Harbor hadn't welcomed him, and he'd spent fifteen years feeling like a stranger. He'd become a fisherman, but not part of the fleet. The rumors of good fishing never came to him, nor did the easy banter over beers at the Harbor Inn. Instead, the fishermen of Clark's Harbor merely tolerated Pete Shelling, and he learned to live with it. But it had hardened him, made him as obstinate as they. Now, when the fleet went in, he stayed, waiting for the last catch, the catch that would prove to them that no matter what they thought of him, he was better than they were.

He moved the boat north now and began slowly letting the nets out again, bringing the trawler around in a sweeping arc so that the current would carry the richest harvest into the submerged mesh. Then, when the nets were fully out, he dropped anchor and lit his pipe. One, maybe two pipefuls, and he would start the last haul of the night. The last and the longest.

He was knocking the dottle out of his pipe, about to check the position of the nets, when he realized something was wrong. The wind, which had been blowing steadily, suddenly shifted, gusting against the boat. The face of the water was different. The swell had been running steadily shoreward; now, it turned choppy, and grew in front of Shelling's eyes.

Pete moved aft, intent on hauling in the nets. He threw a switch and the winch began humming steadily. The nets snaked slowly in. He worked quickly, gathering in the net, guiding the thrashing fish into the hold.

The swell increased and the wind began tearing at his slicker. He increased the speed of the winch and stopped worrying about stowing the net: there would be plenty of time in the morning to straighten it out. The important thing now was to get the catch in and head for the harbor before the full force of the storm broke over him. Pete Shelling worked furiously, hauling on the net, kicking at the fish, racing the elements.

Moments later, the storm broke with a flash of lightning and a clap of thunder. For a brief second the wild coastline was silhouetted in white light.

Disaster struck as the roar of the thunder died away. The humming of the winch stopped and the nets suddenly reversed themselves, pouring back into the sea. Pete Shelling cursed loudly, realized the danger, and tried to leap aside.

But it was too late. A coil of net seemed to leap up at him, wrap itself around his foot, and twist. The fisherman was thrown violently from his feet and felt himself being pulled overboard. He grabbed at the gunwhale, held on for a split second, then was torn loose by the weight of the sea tugging mightily at the net. Before he could scream the cold water closed over his head.

Time seemed to slow down for him, and he resisted the panic building in him, struggling against the almost overpowering urge to thrash toward the surface. Instead, he forced himself still deeper, straining to reach the entangled foot. He opened his eyes, then closed them again immediately—there was nothing to see in the blackness. He felt the loop around his ankle and, with a terrible twist and thrust, managed to work it free. Now he began fighting his way upward.

He felt the net tangling his arms imprisoning him. He kicked harder, and suddenly his head broke the surface. He gasped desperately, sucking the icy air deep into his lungs, and sank back into the sea, the net pulling at him, his kicks barely holding up against its weight.

He tried to untangle his arms from the grasping cords, but soon had to give it up and use his arms to force his way once more to the surface. This time, as he broke free of the water, he opened his eyes and saw his boat. The net was still feeding swiftly over the side, the winch spinning free.

Shelling sank once more below the surface. The net was all around him now and he no longer had room to kick. He thrashed his arms, but with his legs bound and useless in the grip of the heavy mesh, his struggles did no good.

Pete Shelling knew he was going to die.

Fear rose up in his gorge. He forced it back. Slowly, methodically, he began letting air out of his bursting lungs. He felt himself losing his buoyancy, and for an instant his fear left him. As soon as he breathed air in, the buoyancy would return. Then he remembered that there was no air to breathe. Only water.

He steeled himself to suck the sea into his lungs, and was mildly surprised to find that he couldn't do it. His muscles steadfastly refused to obey the messages he sent them. His throat closed. He began to feel himself dying.

When at last he relaxed and the sea found its way in, Pete Shelling changed his mind. He wouldn't die. He would fight back. The sea would not defeat him.

He thrashed again, thrashed wildly against the entangling net, his weakening arms struggling against the bonds.

Then suddenly, almost miraculously, he broke the surface. But it was too late. His eyes searched wildly for help, but there was no one. He tried to scream, but was too choked with salt water for any sound to emerge. He sank back below the surface.

As Pete Shelling died, he tried to analyze the strange vision that was his last glimpse of the world. A boat. There seemed to be a boat. Not his own *Sea Spray,* but a smaller one. And a face. A dark face, almost like an Indian. But it couldn't have been, of course. He was alone on the sea, alone in a storm that had blown up from nowhere. He was dying alone. There was nothing——only the last desperate hope of a drowning man.

The sea drowned the hope, and the man.

When sunrise came, hours later, *Sea Spray* floated peacefully on a calm sea, her nets spread around her like the tired skirts of an exhausted woman who has stayed too late and danced too long.

Pete Shelling had long since disappeared. The *Sea Spray,* alone in the ocean, seemed to mourn him.

## TWO

**B**RAD RANDALL GLANCED AT HIS WATCH and saw that his stomach and the instrument on his wrist were, as usual, perfectly synchronized.

"Lunchtime?" his wife asked, reading his mind.

"I can go another half hour, but then I'll get grouchy," Brad said. "Any place around here look promising?"

Elaine reached for the map that lay neatly folded on the dashboard. "Unfortunately, they don't put anything on road maps except the names of the towns," she said dryly. "No evaluations." She glanced at the map briefly, then looked out the window. "God, Brad, it's so beautiful out here."

They were driving south on Route 101 along the west coast of the Olympic Peninsula. For the last hour, ever since they had passed Crescent Lake, the road had wound through lush green forests, choked with underbrush so dense that Elaine had several times wondered aloud how anyone could have cut through it to build the highway. Then the forest had given way to beach, and just as they had arrived at the coast the cloud cover had broken. To their right the Pacific Ocean lay sparkling in the late morning sun, a stiff breeze frosting it with whitecaps. To the left the dense forest rose steeply to the towering heights of the Olympic Range, standing as a proud barrier between the ocean to the west and Puget Sound to the east.

"Let's stop," Elaine said suddenly. "Please? Just for a few minutes?"

Brad paused, considering, then looked once more at his watch. "Okay, but remember: just a few minutes. And remember that there is no more room in the trunk for driftwood."

He veered the car off the road and came to a stop, then turned his full attention to the beach. It was, indeed, beautiful. Between the road and the sand the ever-present tangle of driftwood formed a silvery barrier that promised hidden treasures for the persistent beachcomber. And Elaine Randall was persistent. Before Brad had even made his way around the car she was clambering over the driftwood, poking here and there, picking up pieces of flotsam, evaluating them against the memory of things she had already collected, then discarding them in the hope of finding something better in the next nook. Brad watched with amusement; during their two weeks on the peninsula Elaine had filled and emptied the trunk of their car at least three times—throwing away yesterday's "perfect" piece of driftwood in favor of today's, which would in turn be discarded tomorrow.

He began making his way toward her, knowing from experience that his help would be required to haul her finds back to the car. He was only a few yards from her when Elaine gave a whoop of victory.

"I found one!" she cried. "I finally found one!" She held a sparkling blue object aloft and Brad knew immediately that it was one of the Japanese fishing floats she had sworn to find before going home.

"Great," he called. "Now can we have lunch?"

If she heard him she gave no sign—she was totally engrossed in examining the float, as if looking for the flaw that ought to be there; to find a perfect one was almost too much good luck. But it *was* perfect. Elaine looked happily up at her husband as he settled next to her on the log.

"It's not even chipped," she said softly. She held it up to the light and watched the dancing refraction of the sun through the blue glass. "It's an omen," she declared.

"An omen?"

She grinned impishly. "Of course. It means we're going to find the right place today."

"We'd better," Brad said gloomily. "If we don't, we're in trouble. There aren't many more places left to look."

Elaine stood up decisively. "Come on," she said. "Back to the car with you. I'm going to look at the map, and I'll bet the first place I pick will be exactly what we've been looking for."

In the car Elaine carefully packed the sparkling blue globe in her purse, then picked up the map.

"Clark's Harbor," she announced.

"Clark's Harbor?" Brad repeated. "Where is it?"

"About twenty miles south."

Brad shrugged. "It'll do for lunch." He started the engine, put the car in gear, then pressed the accelerator. Beside him, Elaine settled confidently in her seat.

"You seem awfully sure," Brad said. "And you're thinking about more than a place for lunch."

"I am."

"Mind telling me why?"

"I told you—the float is an omen. Besides, it sounds right. 'I'm in Clark's Harbor writing a book.' It sounds very professional. And of course you're going to write a very professional book."

"I wonder," Brad mused with a sudden sense of misgiving. "Am I making a big mistake? I mean, taking a whole year off just to write a book that might not even sell—"

"Of course it will sell," Elaine declared. "Millions of people will gobble it up."

"A book on bio-rhythms?"

"All right," she said, unconcerned. "So it'll only be hundreds of thousands."

"Tens of tens, more likely," Brad said darkly.

Elaine laughed and patted his knee. "Even if it doesn't sell at all, who cares? We can afford the year off, and I can't imagine a better place to spend the time than out here. So even if the book is only an excuse to spend a few months at the beach—which it isn't, of course—" she added quickly, "it's still worth it."

"And what about my patients?"

"What about them?" Elaine said airily. "Their neuroses will keep, with Bill Carpenter looking out for them. He may not be the psychiatrist you are, but he's not going to kill your patients."

Brad lapsed into silence. Elaine was right. It was a comfortable silence, the kind of silence that comes only between people who love and understand each other, a silence born, not from lack of anything to say, but rather from a lack of necessity to say anything at all.

They had been combing the peninsula for two weeks, looking for the right town in which to spend the year Brad estimated it would take him to complete his book. But there had been something wrong with every town they had seen—too commercial or too shabby, too self-consciously quaint or too self-satisfied. Today, Brad knew, they would either find the right town or give up the search, for if they continued on, they would be into the unrelieved dullness of Aberdeen and Hoquiam, having made a complete circuit of the peninsula. Maybe Elaine's right, Brad thought. Maybe Clark's Harbor is the right place. He rolled the name of the town around in his mind. Clark's Harbor. Clark's Harbor. It had a nice lilt to it, like an old New England fishing village.

"It's right up ahead," Elaine said softly, breaking the silence.

Brad realized he hadn't been paying much attention to the road, driving more by habit than by concentration. Now he saw they were in the outskirts of a town.

It didn't seem to be a large town, which was fine, and it seemed to be well tended, which was even better. The houses were scattered along the road, frame houses, some neatly painted, others weathered to a silver patina by the sea wind. But even the older structures stood firmly upright, solidly built to withstand the elements.

They drove down a slight incline into the heart of Clark's Harbor. It was little more than a village. There was a side street running perpendicular to the highway, and Brad made a right turn onto it. The incline steepened and they dropped quickly into the center of the village. The street ended at a wharf. Brad brought the car to a stop and he and Elaine looked curiously around.

"It looks like something out of New England," Elaine said softly, echoing Brad's thought. "I love it."

And it did look like a picture-postcard New England town. The buildings that clustered along the waterfront were all of a type: neat clapboards, brightly painted, with manicured gardens flowering gaily in the spring air. Set apart, grandly aloof from the rest, was an old Victorian building, its lawn and garden neatly bounded by a white picket fence. A hand-lettered sign proclaimed it the Harbor Inn.

There were several people on the streets, enough so the town seemed busy but not frantic. One or two glanced at the Randalls' car, but with no particular interest. No one stopped to stare; no one gestured or commented. Brad frowned slightly, feeling a strange lack of curiosity in the people who had glanced at them so disinterestedly. Always sensitive to her husband, Elaine looked quickly at him, concern clouding her face.

"Is something wrong?" she asked.

"I don't know," Brad said. Then he grinned at her. "What do you say we get something to eat?"

Rebecca Palmer had noticed the strange car passing by as she was about to go into Blake's Dry Goods, but she was preoccupied with other things. Right now she was more concerned with her shopping than with who might have arrived in Clark's Harbor. The dark green Volvo had seemed somehow familiar, though. Wishful thinking; she pushed it out of her mind.

She pulled a cart from the row that stood waiting just inside the front door and began wheeling it slowly through the aisles, stopping to look at a display of china that struck her as being in particularly bad taste, even for dime-store dinnerware. Shaking her head sadly at the garish pink and blue pansies that paraded helplessly around the perimeter of the plates, she moved on, picking up an item here and there and depositing it in the basket of the cart.

The crash came as she was pausing in front of a rack of inexpensive dresses. She whirled around and saw George Blake hurrying toward the china display. Satisfied that the accident had had nothing to do with her, Rebecca turned back to the rack and continued her search for a dress that would set off her almost ethereal prettiness. Rebecca had a fragile look to her, and it was difficult for her to find clothing that didn't overwhelm her. She was about to give up her search when she heard Mr. Blake behind her.

"You're going to have to pay for that stuff." His voice was gruff, as if he was expecting to be contradicted. Rebecca turned and looked shyly at him.

"I beg your pardon?"

"The china," Blake said accusingly. "You're going to have to pay for the things you broke."

"But I didn't have anything to do with that," Rebecca explained. "I was standing right here, looking at the dresses."

"I saw you looking at the china," Blake said evenly.

Rebecca frowned unhappily. "But that was five or ten minutes ago. And I didn't even touch it."

Blake's face darkened, and Rebecca almost recoiled from the man's unconcealed hostility.

"Don't lie to me, Mrs. Palmer. You must have knocked the stack over. There isn't anybody here but you and me."

Rebecca glanced quickly around and saw that he was right. Except for her and the proprietor, the store was empty.

"But I didn't have anything to do with it," she insisted helplessly. "I told you, I wasn't anywhere near that table."

Blake just stared at her.

"Don't know why you want to say something like that," he said finally. "Ever since you and your family got here, we've all known there was something funny about you. Now I guess I know what it is—you're a liar."

"I am not!" Rebecca flared. "If I'd done it, I'd admit it, and pay for the damage. But I didn't do anything."

"All right," Blake replied. "I'll take your word for it. But if you don't mind, I'll just put all that stuff in your basket back on the shelves."

"You'll do *what?*"

"I don't want you shopping here anymore," Blake said. "I suppose you have a right to be in Clark's Harbor, but that doesn't mean I have to sell to you. From now on take your business somewhere else."

Rebecca Palmer bit her lip and forced herself not to burst into tears. What is it, she asked herself. What is it about this town? But she knew there was no point in asking Blake, less point in arguing with him.

Silently, Rebecca left the dry goods store, wondering how she would explain the incident to her husband and how he would react to it. Not well, she was sure. Glen Palmer controlled his artist's temperament well, but sometimes he blew. This, she was sure, would make him blow.

"There's a café," Elaine Randall said, pointing. The restaurant was on the second floor of a two-story building, above a tavern. The Randalls had to pass through the tavern to go upstairs, and Brad glanced around when his eyes had adjusted to the gloom. The bar was nearly empty—only a couple of old men sitting at a scarred oak table, a checkerboard and a pitcher of beer between them. He grinned his approval to Elaine and followed her upstairs.

The café, in contrast to the bar, was nearly full. There was one empty table by the window, and the Randalls headed for it. Brad scanned the menu, deciding on a crab salad without really considering the options, then put the menu aside in favor of his favorite hobby: people watching.

A few minutes later a waitress appeared and took their order. When she was done, Elaine placed the menu back in its holder behind the napkins and folded her hands.

"Well?"

"Well, what?"

"Tell me who's here."

"Not much to tell, really," Brad said. "It looks to me like mostly fishermen—"

"Very astute of you," Elaine broke in, "considering there's a wharf right outside the window."

"Also some housewives and shopkeepers," Brad continued, ignoring the gibe. "And one person I can't figure out."

"Where?" Elaine asked, glancing around. "Never mind—it has to be that man sitting by himself over there. I see what you mean."

"Really? What do I mean?"

"He's different from the rest of them," Elaine said. "He looks like he doesn't quite fit in, and knows it."

Brad nodded and glanced once more at the man they were talking about. It was his clothes, Brad decided, and something about his face. Like a number of the men they'd seen, this one wore jeans and a faded work shirt, but somehow he wore them differently. It was the fit of them. They fit too well. And the face. What was it about the face? Then it hit Brad: the man had recently shaved off a beard, leaving a pallor where the lower part of his face had been protected from the sun. And something else hit Brad: a sense of recognition. He was almost sure he knew the man.

Before he could ask Elaine about it their food arrived and the Randalls began eating, though every now and then Brad's glance moved curiously to the man whose clothes fit and who had just cut off his beard. The man kept his eyes on his plate and ate steadily, not rushing, but wasting no time. Once he signaled for more coffee. The waitress poured it willingly but didn't stop to chat for a few seconds as she did with everyone else in the café. When the man finished his meal, he dug into his pocket, dropped some money on the table, and started to leave. But as he moved toward the stairs his eyes suddenly met Brad's, and he stopped short. A grin lit his face and he moved quickly across the room, his hand extended in greeting.

"Dr. Randall? Is it really you?"

Brad recognized him then and stood up. "Glen Palmer! For Christ's sake! I've been sitting here all along, sure I recognized you, but I couldn't place you."

"It's the beard," Glen Palmer answered. "I shaved it off when we moved out here."

"Sit down. This is my wife, Elaine. Honey, this is Glen Palmer, the father of Robby Palmer."

Elaine's brow furrowed with puzzlement, then cleared as she extended a hand in greeting. "Of course," she said, smiling. "How is he? Brad tells me there was some kind of miracle."

"That's the only word to describe it," Palmer agreed as he sat down. Brad looked at him expectantly, wanting to bombard Palmer with questions but reluctant to embarrass the man.

Robby Palmer, Glen's nine-year-old son, had been under Brad Randall's care for nearly three years, a victim of hyperkinesis. It had been a particularly severe case. The first time he had seen the child, Robby was six years old, and unable to sit still for more than a second or two, talking constantly, compulsively, his hands and feet always moving, sometimes only nervously, but more often destructively. Brad had quickly learned to remove all breakable things from his office when Robby Palmer was coming. A small boy with an angel's face and a "devil" within. There was something inside him, some malfunction in his nervous system, that kept him moving, relentlessly, exhaustingly, sometimes frighteningly. The child had been subject to sudden fits of senseless rage, and it had been during these fits that his violence would surface, his small hands darting out to seize the closest objects—any objects—and hurl them at the nearest window, wall, or person. Brad had a memory, one he would not soon forget, of two pieces of Steuben crystal, his two favorites, bought when he could ill afford them, that had been smashed irreparably one afternoon by a mildly upset Robby Palmer, who had then stared at the splinters of glass, puzzled, as if he wondered what had happened to them. There had been no evidence of remorse in the child, no fear of punishment. Only a second's detached coldness, as if the shattered figurines had nothing to do with himself, before the compulsive nervous motion took hold again.

One day, a few months ago, Robby Palmer had stopped coming to see Brad Randall, and Brad had never understood why. When he had tried to talk to the Palmers about it they had only said there was a miracle and left it at that. Silently, Brad Randall wondered if Clark's Harbor had anything to do with that miracle. Now Glen told him.

"You won't believe it," he was saying. "The change in Robby is absolutely incredible. Ever since we brought him out here. He's calm, Dr. Randall. He's still active, but it isn't like it used to be. Now he's like other children."

"But what caused it?" Brad asked.

Glen Palmer shrugged. "I haven't any idea. We came out here on a camping trip and stopped just north of town, at a place called Sod Beach. And Robby calmed down. Just like that," he said, snapping his fingers. "And he stayed calm as long as we were on the beach. So we moved out here."

"It doesn't make any sense," Brad mused.

"Maybe not," Palmer agreed. "But we don't question it. Whatever demons were in him, they're gone now. Gone forever."

Brad's fingers drummed softly on the table top as he turned Glen's statement over in his mind, trying to figure out what could have cured Robby's disorder. It had been a problem case too long, and Brad was always skeptical of "miracles." "I wonder if I could see him?" he asked.

"Why not?" Glen agreed amiably. "He always liked you."

"Tell that to my receptionist," Brad chuckled. The receptionist had lived in terror of Robby's visits to the office, and often made up reasons not to be there when the child arrived.

Glen glanced up at the clock on the wall. "Tell you what," he said, "why don't you come out to our place this evening or tomorrow morning? Are you staying in town?"

"I guess we might as well," Elaine said uncertainly, knowing Brad would want to. "Is there a decent place?"

"The Harbor Inn, down on the waterfront," Glen said. "It's the only place." He stood up. "Look, I've got a lot to do this afternoon. See you later, okay?"

"Sure," Brad said. Before he could say anything else Glen Palmer hurried away from their table and disappeared through the door.

"That was sudden," Elaine commented.

"It was, wasn't it?" Brad agreed. Then he noticed that as soon as Palmer left a buzz of conversation had started among the remaining patrons of the café.

"Well," a woman at the next table said a bit too loudly to her lunch partner. "At least he's shaved off that awful beard."

"Not that it matters," the other woman replied. "He still doesn't fit in around here."

"You'd think he'd get the message," the first woman said. "Everybody else like them has caught on right away and left us in peace."

"My Joe offered to buy that building of theirs just yesterday," the second woman said. "And do you know what Glen Palmer told him? He told him it wasn't for sale. Joe told him he'd better sell while he could, before he ruined it completely, but Palmer told him he wasn't ruining it— he was remodeling it."

"Into an art gallery," the first woman sniffed. "What makes him think he can make a living with an art gallery in Clark's Harbor? And that wife of his—makes pottery that looks like mud pies and thinks people will actually buy it!"

The conversation continued to buzz around them. From the few words Brad could catch, he knew they were all talking about the same person— Glen Palmer. Everyone, apparently, talked *about* him. No one had talked *to* him.

"Maybe I was wrong," Brad heard Elaine say. She also was listening to the comments from the other tables.

" 'New England,' you said." Brad gave her a wry smile. "Sounds to me like you were right on target. These people don't seem to like strangers any more than villagers do anywhere else."

"It's kind of scary, isn't it?" Elaine asked.

Brad shrugged. "I don't know. I think it's more or less to be expected. We'll probably get the same treatment no matter where we go. But it's just a matter of time. People have to get used to you, particularly in places like this. I'll bet a lot of people in this town rarely see someone they don't know. When they do they get suspicious."

Elaine fell silent and continued eating her lunch. The psychiatrist in Brad was enjoying himself, finding the hostile attitudes of the locals "interesting," and she wasn't sure she approved. But, she quickly reminded herself, you knew when you married him that he was a psychiatrist; you have nothing to complain about. She concentrated on looking out the window and did her best to ignore the chatter going on around her.

It wasn't until they were finishing their coffee that Brad spoke again.

"I think we should look around."

"I'm not so sure . . ." Elaine began.

Brad tried to reassure her. "Honey, any small town is going to be the same, and if we're going to live in a place like this for a year, we're going to have to tolerate some hostility and suspicion at first. It goes with the territory: if you want to be in a small town, you have to put up with small town attitudes."

He paid the check and they left the café. Downstairs, in the tavern, Brad saw that the checker game seemed not to have progressed at all. One of the old men stared intently at the board, the other out the window. If either of them noticed the Randalls neither gave a sign.

"Let's look around the wharf," Brad suggested, as they came out into the sunlight.

Most of the slips were empty, but five or six fishing boats were still tied up, with men working on them, repairing nets, tinkering with engines, inspecting equipment. They walked the length of the wharf, pausing to inspect each boat as they passed it. No one spoke to them, and once, when Brad offered a tentative "hello," there was no response.

"They don't talk much, do they?" Elaine observed as they neared the end of the pier.

"Odd, isn't it?" Brad replied. "Apparently the image of the happy fisherman hasn't reached Clark's Harbor yet." He glanced around as if unsure what to do next. "Shall we go for a ride?"

Before Elaine could answer him there was a blast of a siren and a police car pulled up to the wharf. From the driver's side a barrel-chested man of about sixty emerged, then circled the car to open the door for a heavyset woman. She got out of the car, one hand clutching the police officer's arm, the other holding onto a crumpled handkerchief.

All activity on the wharf came to a halt as the men on the boats stared at the new arrivals.

"Something wrong, Chief?" a voice called.

"Something's always wrong when Harney Whalen comes to the wharf," another voice shouted.

Police Chief Harney Whalen didn't acknowledge the second voice, but chose instead to answer the first.

"Don't know," he called out. "Miriam Shelling here can't seem to find Pete. Any of you guys seen him?"

There were negative murmurings among the fishermen, and they began leaving their boats to gather around the chief. Miriam Shelling still clung to Whalen and dabbed at her eyes with her handkerchief.

"He went out last night," she said, looking from one of the men to another, then another, her eyes never resting for long on any single face. "He said he'd be back about four o'clock this morning, but he never came in."

One of the fishermen nodded in agreement. "Yeah, he was right behind me when I went out last night, but he didn't come back in when I did. He's probably found a school and wants to get all he can."

Miriam Shelling shook her head. "He wouldn't do that," she insisted. "He'd know I'd be worried. He'd at least have called me on the radio."

The men exchanged glances among themselves. Harney Whalen looked uncomfortable, as if he was wondering what to do next, when the silence was broken by the blast of an air horn. Everyone turned toward the harbor, where a small launch was speeding toward the wharf. Miriam Shelling's fingers tightened on the police chief's arm.

The launch pulled up into one of the empty slips and a line was tossed out, caught, and tied to a cleat. A man leaped from the small boat, his face pale. He looked quickly around, his eyes coming to rest on Harney Whalen.

"Are you a policeman?"

"I'm the chief," Whalen said. "Something the matter?"

The man nodded. "I found a boat drifting out there. When I hailed it there wasn't any response, so I went aboard. The boat was deserted."

"Where is it?" Whalen asked.

"It's anchored about a mile north, maybe three hundred yards out," the man said. "It's called the *Sea Spray*."

"That's Pete's boat," Miriam Shelling cried. The man stared at her for a moment, then pulled Whalen a few feet away. When he spoke again his voice dropped low.

"Its nets were out," he said softly. "I decided to pull them in. And they weren't empty."

Whalen glanced quickly at Miriam, then back to the stranger.

"A body?"

The man nodded. "I brought it back with me."

Whalen moved to the launch and stepped down into it. The fishermen crowded around as Whalen pulled back the tarpaulin that lay bundled in the stern. Pete Shelling's vacant eyes stared up at them.

Ten yards away the Randalls watched as the fishermen reacted to the death. They stared mutely down into the boat, then one by one began drifting away, as if somehow embarrassed to be in the presence of death. They passed Miriam Shelling silently, offering her neither a word nor a gesture of comfort. When they were gone and only Harney Whalen and the owner of the launch remained, Miriam finally stepped forward and peered down at her husband. She froze for a moment, then wailed his name and threw herself into Harney Whalen's arms. He held her for a moment, then spoke quietly to the man who had brought Pete Shelling home. Finally he led Miriam Shelling from the wharf, helped her back into the police car, and drove her away.

"My God," Elaine breathed softly. "How awful."

Brad nodded, his eyes still fixed on the wharf. Elaine grasped his arm. "Let's get out of here," she said. "Please?"

Brad seemed not to hear her. "Did you notice?" he asked. "It was almost as if nothing had happened. They didn't speak to her, they didn't speak to each other, they didn't ask any questions, they didn't even seem surprised. It was almost as if they were expecting it."

"What?" Elaine asked blankly.

"The fishermen. They didn't react to that man's death at all. It was almost as if they were expecting it, or it didn't have anything to do with them—or something. But what happened to him could happen to any of them."

Elaine looked carefully at her husband. She knew what was coming. She tried to head it off.

"Let's leave, Brad," she said. "Please? I don't like Clark's Harbor." But it was too late, and she knew it.

"It's fascinating," Brad went on. "Those men didn't react like normal people at all. Not at all." He took Elaine's hand and squeezed it.

"Come on," he said, "let's find that inn."

"We're staying?" Elaine asked.

"Of course." Brad grinned. "What else?"

Elaine felt a twist of fear deep in her stomach and forced it away, telling herself it was unreasonable. But deep inside, the fear remained, unreasonable or not.

Far out on the horizon, a storm was gathering.

# THREE

THE HARBOR INN, ITS VICTORIAN FAÇADE painted a fresh white with sky-blue trim, perched almost defiantly in the center of a neatly tended lawn. It gazed suspiciously out over the water, as if it expected the sea to snatch it away at any second. From a room on the second floor Elaine Randall stared at the sea in unconscious imitation of the inn. She listened to the wind whistle under the eaves of the old building and marveled that the fishing boats, secured against the growing storm, rode so easily in the choppy water of the bay. As rain began to splash against the window she turned to her husband.

"I suppose it will do for one night," she said doubtfully, glancing around the room. Brad grinned at her.

"You love it and you know you love it," he chuckled. "If it hadn't been for that drowning, you'd be happy as a clam."

Elaine sat down heavily in the slipcovered wing chair that filled one corner of the small room and tried to analyze her feelings. She knew Brad was right: if they hadn't been on the wharf when that man's body had been brought it, she would now be raving about the room, raving about the town, and excitedly planning to spend a year here. But the fisherman's death had drained her enthusiasm, and now she looked bleakly at the antique furnishings of the equally antique inn and found herself unable to muster any positive thoughts at all.

"It's run-down," she said sourly.

"It isn't at all," Brad countered. "All things considered, it's remarkably well kept up."

"If you like this sort of thing."

"Which you do," Brad said emphatically. "Look at that washstand. Not a chip in the marble anywhere, and if that oak isn't hand rubbed, I'll eat it for dinner."

Elaine examined the washstand closely and had to admit that Brad was right—it was a genuine antique and it was flawless. Forcing her negative feelings aside, she made herself look at the room once again. She had to concede that it was charming. There was no trace of standard hotel furnishings, nothing to indicate it was anything but the cozy bedroom of a private home. The double bed sported what was obviously a handmade quilt, and all the furniture was good sturdy oak. Not fancy, but warm and functional.

"All right," Elaine gave in. "It *is* nice, and it's exactly the sort of thing I love. I just wish it weren't in Clark's Harbor."

"But if it weren't in Clark's Harbor it wouldn't exist, would it?" Brad reasoned.

"You're not going to trap me into *that* old argument. Besides, you know perfectly well what I'm talking about. You're just trying to be ornery."

"Me?" Brad said with exaggerated innocence. "Would I do a thing like that?"

"Yes, you would," Elaine replied, trying to keep her voice severe. "But I won't fall for it. If I did, in another minute you'd have me all turned around and I'd be begging you to let us stay here at least for a few days. But I don't want to stay. I want to go back to Seattle, and I want to go in the morning."

"Yes, ma'am," her husband said, clicking his heels and saluting. He smiled at his wife and wondered how serious she was—and how much arguing he was going to have to do to convince her to stay in Clark's Harbor for a while. He decided to approach the problem obliquely. He began untying his shoes.

"I've been thinking about Robby Palmer," he said neutrally.

Elaine caught on immediately. "The book," she said. "You've decided to write your book about him, haven't you?"

"I don't know," Brad countered. "I'd like to find out what happened to him, though. The kind of disorder he has doesn't just clear up as Glen said it did. It just doesn't happen."

"But if it did?" Elaine asked.

"Then it's worth knowing about. My God, if there's something out here, something about the area, that affects children like Robby, and helps them, then the world should know about it."

"What would you call the book? *Paradise Found?*"

"Well, a book about Robby Palmer might have a wider appeal than a book about bio-rhythms," Brad said defensively.

"Why don't you write about both?" Elaine offered. "Get both audiences?" She began laughing at her own joke, but stopped when she saw the look on Brad's face. "Did I say something?" she asked warily.

"I don't know," Brad said. He kicked his shoes off, then tossed his socks after them. He stretched out on the bed and opened his arms invitingly. Elaine moved from the chair to the bed and snuggled close to him. His arms pressed her against his chest; one hand stroked the back of her neck softly. The patter of rain against the window became a steady drumming. And he knew he was about to win: they would not be going home in the morning.

"Do you really hate it here all that much?" he asked after a moment.

Elaine wriggled sensuously and nuzzled Brad's neck, then once more tried to sort out her feelings.

"I suppose it was mostly that body," she said finally, shuddering slightly at the memory. "I keep telling myself that the same thing could happen anywhere—I mean, fishermen drown all the time, don't they?—but I keep seeing that face, all blue and bloated, and I'm afraid that I'll always associate that memory with Clark's Harbor." She paused and felt Brad stir. "You want to stay here, don't you?"

"Well, it's certainly the prettiest place we've seen so far, and it seems perfect for what we want. It's isolated and it's small and there isn't much chance that we'll get so caught up in the social whirl that I won't get any writing done."

"Social whirl, indeed," Elaine chuckled. "I'll bet that boils down to an ice-cream social at the church once a month. But I don't know, Brad. I keep telling myself to forget about that man, but even when I do, there's something about this place. Something that just doesn't seem right. I suppose it's partly the way Glen Palmer was treated in the café this afternoon."

"We've already been through that," Brad pointed out.

"I know and I agree with you. There's bound to be some of that sort of thing anywhere we go. But I just have a bad feeling about the whole place. Maybe it's this storm." As if on cue, a flash of lightning illuminated the room and the drumming of the rain was momentarily drowned out by a crash of thunder. Elaine, who usually liked storms, winced.

"Or maybe it's your woman's intuition?"

"If you want to call it that."

"Well, I like it here," Brad said decisively. "I think the whole place is fascinating. The people intrigue me. I suppose they interest me professionally. They seem sort of detached, if you know what I mean, as if they live together but they don't really care about each other. It's an interesting phenomenon, almost a contradiction in terms. A small, close-knit village, probably inbred as hell, yet no one seems to have any emotional involvement with anyone else. At least not on the surface. They probably cover a lot."

"Maybe it's just that nobody liked the poor man who drowned," Elaine suggested.

"Maybe so," Brad agreed. "But I think it's something else, something deeper." He broke off and the two of them nestled together on the bed listening to the storm. Outside, the wind was building, and the inn was beginning to creak softly.

"I even love the weather," Brad said softly. "It makes me want to make love."

Elaine pulled away from her husband and stood up. A moment later her skirt dropped to the floor, followed by her blouse. She stood naked in front of Brad and arched her back, her breasts jutting forward. She smiled softly down at him.

"One nice thing about a storm," she whispered, "is that you can never hear what's going on in the next room."

Then she slipped into bed.

Two miles out of Clark's Harbor, at the north end of a crescent of sand that was called Sod Beach, a single soft light glowed in the darkness from inside a tiny cabin. Too weak to illuminate even the corners of the room, it barely penetrated the dense black woods that nearly surrounded the structure. Rebecca Palmer, peering at the dishes she was washing in the dimness of the lantern light, cursed quietly to herself—nearly whispering so that her words would not be audible. But her son's ears were sharper than she thought.

"Daddy!" Robby Palmer cried out with all the puritanical fervor of his nine-and-a-half years, "Mommy said a bad word!"

Glen glanced up from the game he was playing with his daughter and regarded his son seriously. "Well, I suppose we'll have to do something about that, won't we?" he observed mildly. Robby bobbed his head in agreement, but before he could say anything more his little sister's voice interrupted.

"Which one?" she demanded. "The one that means poop?"

Robby looked at her scornfully. "Not that one, Missy. Everyone says that one. She said the one that means screw."

Missy turned to her father, her seven-year-old face alive with curiosity. "I don't know that one. Which one is that?"

"Never mind," Glen said gently, then turned his attention to his wife. "What's wrong, honey?"

Rebecca bit her lip, stilling her sudden urge to cry. "Oh, nothing, I suppose. I just wish we had electricity out here. I can't even see if these dishes are clean."

"What's to worry about?" Glen said lightly. "If you can't tell if they're clean, we certainly won't be able to tell if they're dirty, will we?" Then, sensing that his attempt at humor was a mistake, he got to his feet and moved closer to Rebecca. Robby took his sister by the hand and led her into the tiny room that served as their bedroom. With the children gone, Glen drew his wife into his arms and held her close.

"It's rough, isn't it?" he said. Her face pressed against his chest, Rebecca nodded. For a moment she thought she was going to lose control and let her tears flow, but she decided to curse instead.

"Fuck it all," she said softly. "Fuck it all." Then, feeling a little better, she pulled away from Glen and grinned uncertainly. "I'm sorry," she said. "I'll be fine—really I will. I seem to be able to handle the big things—it's always some dumb *little* thing that sets me off, like kerosene lanterns that don't give off as much light as a forty watt bulb. Not that we'd have any electricity tonight even if we had electricity," she added as a flash of lightning illuminated the room and the immediate clap of thunder flushed the children from the bedroom. Missy climbed into her father's arms, while Robby stood in the doorway, his arms clasped tightly around a wriggling black-and-white spaniel. Glen felt a surge of relief at the appearance of the children, the relief that comes when a moment of tension is suddenly broken. He knew the break was only temporary, that the pressures that were building in both of them would have to be defused. But he had no idea how.

The Palmers had been in Clark's Harbor only five months, but the months had not been easy. At first Glen and Rebecca had told each other that the coldness they felt from the town was only natural, that things would warm up for them. But Clark's Harbor remained cold, unwelcoming, and many times they had thought of leaving.

If it hadn't been for Robby they probably would have left.

Robby had never been an easy child. From the time he was a year old, Glen and Rebecca had realized that he was "different." But only in the last three years had they truly begun to understand that Robby was not just "different," not just precocious as they had assumed. He was, in fact, ill, and the older he got, the worse his illness became. Slowly, insidiously, Robby's hyperkinesis had begun destroying all of them. Glen found himself increasingly unable to work, unable to concentrate, unable to create. And nearly all Rebecca's time was taken up by what she had come to think of as "tending" Robby. She could hardly call it raising him, not even call it supervising him. It was cleaning up after him, trying to anticipate him, struggling to stay ahead of him. Each year Rebecca had become more tired, more irritable, more desperate.

Only Missy had been unaffected.

Missy, two years younger than her brother, had always remained calm, had learned early to take care of herself, knowing somehow that her brother had special needs that she did not have.

Then they had come to Clark's Harbor.

When Glen had first suggested that a vacation might help them all, Rebecca had resisted, certain it would be no vacation at all, but only more of the same—Robby constantly talking, constantly moving, poking at his sister, demanding things, becoming suddenly violent. But Glen had prevailed. They had left Seattle and driven out to the peninsula, camping on the beaches. Finally they had come to the crescent of beach just north of Clark's Harbor and pitched their tent.

There, the miracle had happened.

Neither one of them had noticed it at first. It was Missy who brought it to their attention. "Something's wrong with Robby," she said one afternoon.

Rebecca dropped the pair of jeans she was scrubbing, and ran out to the beach. She saw Robby playing near the surf line, building a sand castle, patiently building up the walls and parapets, digging the moats, and constructing drainage systems against the incoming tide. Rebecca watched, stunned, for a minute, then called to Glen.

"Look," she said when he appeared on the beach.

Glen looked. "So?" he asked. "What's so special about a kid building a sand castle?"

"It's Robby," Rebecca said softly. "And he hasn't torn it down."

It was true. Something had dispelled Robby's frenetic restlessness. He sat quietly in the sand building his castle. They waited for the moment when he would suddenly jump to his feet, kick the structure all over the beach, and begin screaming and crying, venting his frustrations on whatever—whoever—was closest. But it didn't happen. He continued working on the castle until it was built to his satisfaction, then looked up and, seeing his parents, waved to them.

"Look what I built," he called. Glen and Rebecca, with Missy trailing behind, solemnly inspected Robby's work. At first they didn't know what to make of it, so used were they to his habit of starting something, then wrecking it and moving immediately on to something else. And yet there it was, a maze of walls and moats, stretching almost fifteen feet along the beach.

"He's been working on it all morning," Missy said proudly.

"The tide will wash it all away," Glen pointed out, more to soften the inevitable blow than to disparage the work.

"That's okay," Robby said. "I can build another one further up." He took his sister by the hand and started down the beach, walking slowly so that his stride matched Missy's shorter steps. Glen and Rebecca watched them go, wondering what had happened, and waited for the terror to surface again.

But it didn't, not once in the five days they spent on the beach, which they found out was called Sod Beach. It didn't appear until they left Sod Beach and started back to Seattle. It started in the car the morning after they began the trip south. Robby became his familiar nervous self, fidgeting, teasing his sister, needing constant stimulation, interested in nothing.

Back in Seattle they told Brad Randall what had happened on Sod Beach, but he had no explanation. A fluke, he said, a coincidence. But Glen and Rebecca couldn't accept that. All they knew was that on Sod Beach their son had been a normal nine-year-old boy. And so, during one long night of talk, they decided to leave Seattle. They would take the few thousand dollars Rebecca had inherited from her grandmother and move to Clark's Harbor. There they would open a small art gallery, and with a little luck they would be able to make a living.

But the luck hadn't come. They had quickly discovered that Clark's Harbor was not the least bit interested in them or their plans. They had succeeded in buying the cabin on Sod Beach and making a down payment on a building which they were in the process of converting into a gallery. But the conversion was slow. Materials Glen needed never seemed to be in stock; deliveries seemed to take forever. Twice Glen had hired local men to help him with the work, but he had quickly discovered that the locals, either through inexperience or malice, were more a hindrance than a help.

Robby, though, was flourishing. The hyperkinesis that had plagued him throughout his short life had vanished as soon as they moved into the cabin on Sod Beach and showed no signs of recurring. Glen glanced at his son. He was sitting cross-legged on the floor, playing quietly with his dog while Missy watched. If it hadn't been for Robby, Glen and Rebecca would have left Clark's Harbor. But for him they stayed.

"Did something happen today?" Glen suddenly asked Rebecca.

She nodded. "I wasn't going to tell you about it, but I suppose I might as well. It was weird."

She told him about the incident at Blake's Dry Goods, while Glen listened to the strange story in silence. When she was finished, he shrugged.

"So we don't shop at Blake's anymore," he said. "All things considered, I don't suppose it'll make much difference."

"It'll be a damned nuisance," Rebecca snapped. Seeing Glen flinch, she was immediately sorry. "Well, I suppose worse things could have happened. And I suppose they will."

Glen was about to reply when Robby suddenly came into the room. Sensing that the boy was about to ask a question about what had happened to his mother that day, and not wanting to have to explain, Glen decided to divert him.

"Guess who I saw today?"

Robby looked at him curiously. "Who?"

"Dr. Randall."

"Who?" Robby asked blankly.

Rebecca's response was more positive. "Dr. Randall? Why didn't you tell me? Where was he? Is he still in town?"

"One at a time," Glen protested. "He and his wife are on vacation and they happened to be at the café when I went in for lunch. They're staying at the inn, and I told them to stop by tonight or tomorrow."

"Company . . ." Rebecca breathed, then glanced quickly around the tiny room, wondering what the Randalls would think of it. Robby was still gazing at his father.

"Who's Dr. Randall?" he asked again.

Behind him Missy's voice piped up. "Oh, Robby, he was your doctor. Don't you remember?"

"No."

"You never remember *anything*," Missy taunted him.

"You'll remember him in the morning," Glen said, putting a quick end to the budding argument. "I think it's time you two were in bed."

"It's too early," Robby objected automatically.

"You don't know what time it is," Rebecca said.

"Well, whatever time it is, it's too early," Robby insisted. "We always stay up later than this."

"Not tonight, you don't," Glen said. "Come on, both of you."

He picked his daughter up and took his son by the hand. A moment later they were all in the tiny bedroom the two shared. Glen helped them into their pajamas, then tucked them into the bunk beds, Robby on top and Missy below. He had started to kiss them good-night when Missy spoke.

"Daddy, can we have a light on in here?"

"A light? Since when do you need a light?"

"Just for tonight," Missy begged. "I don't like the storm."

"It's only wind and thunder and lightning, darling. It won't hurt you."

"Then what about Snooker?" Robby put in. "Can't he sleep with us tonight?"

Snooker, the small black-and-white spaniel, stood in the doorway, his tail wagging hopefully, his soulful brown eyes pleading. Glen almost gave in, then changed his mind.

"No," he said firmly. "He can't. You know very well that dogs belong outside, not inside."

"But he'll get all wet," Missy argued.

"He'll survive. He sleeps under the house anyway."

Before the children could argue any more, Glen kissed them both and picked up the lantern. "See you both in the morning," he said, then pulled the door closed behind him.

He put a protesting Snooker outside, then sat down next to Rebecca, slipping an arm around her.

"Don't let it get to you," he said softly. "By tomorrow old Blake will have forgotten all about his damned dishes."

"Hmm? Oh, I wasn't worried about that. It's Robby."

"Robby?"

"How could he have forgotten Dr. Randall?"

"Children do that."

"But, my God, Glen, he spent two or three hours a week with Randall for almost three years."

"Then he's blocked it." Glen shrugged. "What's so mysterious about that?"

"I didn't say it was mysterious," Rebecca said. "It just seems . . . odd, I guess."

They fell silent then and sat quietly in front of the fire, listening to the wind and the pounding of the surf.

"I do love it here," Rebecca said after a while. "Even when I think I can't make it through another day, all I have to do is listen to that surf and I know everything's going to be all right." She snuggled closer. "It is, isn't it?"

"Of course it is," Glen said. "It just takes a little time."

A few moments later, as Glen and Rebecca were about to go to bed, a small voice summoned them to the bedroom. Missy sat bolt upright in the lower bunk while Robby peered dolefully down at her from the upper.

"I told her not to call you," Robby said importantly.

"I heard something outside," Missy declared, ignoring her brother.

"What did you hear, darling?" Rebecca asked gently.

"I'm not sure, but it was something."

"Sort of a rustling sound?"

The little girl's head bobbed eagerly.

"It was probably just a branch rubbing against the house," Glen said reassuringly.

"Or old Snooker looking for something," Robby added.

"It was something else," Missy insisted. "Something's out there."

Glen went to the small window and pulled the makeshift drapery aside. Beyond the glass the darkness was almost palpable, but he made a great show of looking first in one direction, then another. At last he dropped the curtain back into place, and turned to his daughter, who was watching him anxiously from the bunk. "Nothing there."

Missy looked unconvinced. "Can I sleep with you and Mommy tonight?"

"Oh, don't be such a baby," Robby said scornfully. Missy cowered under the quilt at her brother's reproach. But Rebecca leaned over the tiny face, and kissed it gently.

"It's all right, sweetheart," she murmured. "There's nothing outside, and Mommy and Daddy will be right in the next room. If you get frightened, you just call us and we'll be right here."

She straightened, winked at her son, and left the room. After kissing each of his children once more, Glen followed his wife.

"Are you asleep?" Robby whispered.

"No." Missy's voice seemed to echo in the darkness.

A flash of lightning lit the room, followed immediately by a thunderclap.

"I wish it would stop," Missy complained.

"I like it," Robby replied. "It makes me feel good." There was a silence, then the little boy spoke again. "Let's go outside and find Snooker."

Missy crept out of bed and went to the window, straining to see in the blackness. "It's raining. We'll get soaked."

"We can put on our slickers."

"I don't think Snooker's out there," Missy said doubtfully.

"Yes he is. Daddy says he sleeps under the house."

Robby climbed down from the top bunk and crouched next to his sister. "It'll be fun," he said. "It'll be an adventure."

"I don't like adventures."

"Fraidy cat."

"I'm not either!"

"Then come outside with me." Robby was pulling on his clothes. After watching him for a few seconds, Missy, too, began dressing.

"What if Mommy and Daddy hear us?" she asked as Robby opened the window.

"They won't," Robby replied with the assurance of his nine-and-one-half years. He began climbing over the sill. A moment later the children were outside, huddled against the cabin wall, trying to shelter themselves from the rain and wind.

"Snooker?" Robby called softly. "Come here, Snooker."

They waited, expecting the spaniel to come bounding out of the darkness, wagging his tail and lapping their faces.

He didn't come.

The two children looked at each other, unsure what to do next. Robby made the decision.

"We'd better go find him."

"It's too dark," Missy complained.

"No it isn't. Come on." Robby started through the trees toward the beach. Hesitantly, Missy followed him.

As soon as he was clear of the woods, the force of the wind and rain hit Robby full in the face, filling him with a strange sense of exhilaration. He began running through the storm, listening to the roaring surf, calling out into the night. Behind him, her small feet pounding the packed sand, Missy ran as hard as she could to keep up with her brother. Though she could barely see him, she could follow the sound of his voice as he called out for the recalcitrant dog.

"Snooker! Snoooooooker!!"

Suddenly Robby stopped running and Missy caught up with him. "Did you find him?"

"Shh!"

Missy lapsed into silence, and stared at her brother. "What's wrong?" she whispered.

"Listen!"

She listened as hard as she could, but at first all she heard was the wind and the surf. Then there was something else.

A crackling sound, like twigs breaking.

"Someone's here," she whispered.

A dark figure, indistinct in the blackness, moved out of the woods and began coming across the beach toward them.

"Daddy?" Missy piped in a tiny voice, then fell silent as she realized that it was not her father. She moved closer to Robby, taking his hand in hers and squeezing it tight. "What'll we do?"

"I don't know," Robby whispered. He was frightened, but he was determined not to let his sister know it. "Who's there?" he said in his bravest voice.

The shadowy figure stopped moving toward them, then a voice, old and unsteady, came across the sand.

"Who's that yourself, standing out in the rain?"

"Robby Palmer," Robby said automatically.

"Well, don't just stand there! Come over here where I can see you."

Robby, pulling Missy with him, started toward the man, his fear vanishing. "Who are you?"

"Mac Riley." The old man was in front of them now, his leathery features more distinct. "What are you doing out here?"

"Looking for our dog," Robby replied. "He's supposed to sleep under the house, but he isn't there."

"Well, if he's smart he isn't on the beach either," Riley said. "This isn't a good beach to be on. Not on a night like this."

"Then why are you here?" Missy asked.

"Just keeping an eye on things," Riley said mysteriously. The rain suddenly stopped and Riley looked up toward the sky. "Well, I'll be damned," he said softly. "They must be working overtime tonight."

"Who?"

Riley reached out and rumpled Robby's wet hair.

"The ghosts. This beach is full of them."

The two children drew closer together and glanced around warily.

"There's no such thing as ghosts," Missy said.

"Spirits, then," Riley corrected himself. "And don't say there's no such thing. Just because you haven't seen something, don't believe it doesn't exist."

"Have you ever seen them?" Robby asked.

"Many times," Riley said. "And always on nights like this, when the tide's high, and the wind's blowing. That's when they come out here and do what they have to do."

"What do they do?" Robby demanded.

The old man gazed at the two children, then lifted his eyes and stared out at the angry sea.

"They kill," he said softly. "They kill the unwary stranger."

Robby and Missy looked at each other, spoke no words, but simultaneously bolted and began racing for home, the wind clutching at them, the surf pounding in their ears.

Mac Riley, standing still on the beach, watched them until they disappeared into the night, then turned and started back into the woods.

Behind him, on the beach, something moved.

Something indistinct, something almost formless in the blackness.

# FOUR

ELAINE RANDALL WOKE EARLY THE FOL-
lowing morning, momentarily disoriented. She lay quietly in bed next to her husband, staring at the ceiling, waiting for the confusion to pass. The blast of an airhorn jolted her into reality and she remembered where she was. Next to her Brad stirred in his sleep, turned over, and resumed his light snoring. Elaine, fully awake now, left the bed and went to the window.

The storm had passed on to the east and in the sparkling clear morning light Clark's Harbor seemed to beckon to her. She watched a small trawler chug slowly away from the wharf, then, remembering the storm of the previous night, decided to do some early morning beachcombing. She dressed quickly, resisting her impulse to wake Brad, and slipped from the room. As she passed the desk the same little man who had checked them in the afternoon before smiled brightly at her and bobbed his head in greeting. Elaine returned the smile, then walked briskly through the front door into the fresh salt air. She shivered, and drew her sweater more closely around her.

The street was deserted. Elaine hurried across it, then walked along the sea wall to the pier. For a moment she was tempted to explore the wharf, but the memory of the dead fisherman flooded back to her and she chose instead to clamber down the short flight of stairs that would put her on the beach. It wasn't until she had walked a hundred yards along the sand that she realized she was in the wrong place for beachcombing: the harbor was too well protected for much to have washed up. She strode purposefully toward the north point of the bay, enjoying the soft lapping sound of the water and the increasing warmth of the morning sun. Above her a cloudless sky matched the blue of the ocean, and the breeze barely frosted the surface of the water with foam.

She rounded the point and found herself on a rocky beach mounded with driftwood. She picked her way slowly over the uneven ground, stopping now and then to poke at a likely looking chunk of wood, each time half-expecting to find one of the incredibly blue glass balls. Each time she was disappointed—but only briefly: the search was half the fun.

Forty minutes later she came to another point. Beyond it, to the north, the rocky landscape changed radically. Warmed by her discovery, Elaine stood looking out over a magnificent unspoiled beach. It was a long, wide crescent of sand, broken in two places by creeks wandering across the beach on their way to the sea. At the far end of the crescent, almost hidden in the woods, she could barely distinguish a tiny cabin tucked neatly away among the trees. Much closer, and in stark contrast to the distant cabin, a ramshackle old house stood on the sand, its wood siding silvered by the wind and salt. It had the lonely empty look of abandonment, and Elaine had an urge to explore. Only her city dweller's sense of impropriety kept her from acting on her curiosity. She made a mental note to tell Brad about the old house. His sense of what was proper, and what was not, allowed him to do things she would never do. Perhaps if she hinted broadly enough he would insist on coming back to do a little snooping.

She began walking along the beach, poking into the mounds of kelp that had been washed up by the tide. Every now and then she stooped, picked up a rock or a shell, examined it, then dropped it back to the sand. Finally she gave up the search of the surf line, and made her way to the omnipresent mound of driftwood that lay above the high tide line, forming a barrier between the beach and the woods beyond. She clambered carefully over the logs, her eyes darting from nook to cranny, hoping to discover hidden treasure, but finding instead only rusted beer cans, old tires, and pieces of fishnet.

When she was halfway up the beach she sat down on a log to watch the sea. The morning surf had a soft look to it and she was able to count seven separate ranks of breakers, testifying to the gentle slope that extended from the beach far out toward the horizon. She watched the surf for a long time, listened to its rhythmic throbbing, and realized that her trepidation of the night before had all but vanished. The silent serenity of the deserted beach enveloped her, and she found herself fantasizing about what it would be like to live here, spending her days wandering the beach while Brad wrote. She began to picture herself trying her hand at watercolors, then laughed out loud at her sudden desire to take up painting seascapes. The sound of the breakers swallowed up her solitary laughter. That pleased her too. She could talk to herself for hours on end out here and never have to worry about being overheard. She experimented with it for a couple of minutes, then lapsed back into silence and continued her lazy examination of the beach.

At first she wasn't sure she was seeing anything at all, but the more she stared, the more certain she was that there was something buried in the sand. It was no more than a slight rise in the flatness of the beach that she dismissed as a natural contour caused by the surf. But the more she stared at it, the more conscious she became that except for that single spot the beach was pancake flat. She found a stick and began walking toward the slight hump in the sand.

It was about midway between the driftwood barrier and the surf line, and as she approached it, it almost disappeared. Had the sun been any higher, the bright light would have effectively flattened the bulge—a small mound two or three feet across—and she never would have seen it. She stared down at it for a moment, hesitating, then jabbed at it with her stick.

The stick went easily into the sand for an inch or two, then stopped. She pushed, and the stick sunk in a little deeper, then sprang back when she released the pressure. Whatever it was, it wasn't hard.

She began scraping the sand away, first with the stick, then with her hands. Her fingers touched something. Something soft, like fur. A seal, she told herself, I've found a dead seal. She picked up the stick again, and began digging in earnest.

It wasn't until the tail emerged that Elaine knew what she had found. A dog, not a seal. Her first impulse was to leave it alone. If it had been a seal, she probably would have. Her curiosity would have been satisfied and she would have been content to leave it where it lay, for nature to take its course. But a dog was something else. A dog was someone's pet. Somewhere, someone was going to miss this animal. Perhaps, she told herself, it isn't quite dead. She continued digging.

Minutes later the corpse was exposed. Elaine stared down at it, afraid she was going to be sick. It looked so pitiful, lying limply in the sand, its coat matted with slime. She knew immediately that it had been dead for several hours, but still she felt impelled to make sure. With the stick, she prodded at the dead animal. The body moved, but the head did not. She prodded at the head, then, and it moved around at an unnatural angle. With a shudder Elaine realized that its neck was broken. She dropped the stick and glanced wildly around, looking for help. The beach was still deserted. She looked back to the dog, and wished she hadn't. Its eyes were open, and the dead eyes stared up at her as if pleading for her to do something. But all she could do was rebury it. Using the stick, she did the job as quickly as she could. Then she began running blindly back down the beach, hoping that the image of the dead creature would leave her as she left the place where she had found it.

Brad was standing at the desk chatting with the manager when Elaine burst through the door of the Harbor Inn. His smile disappeared when he saw his wife's strained look. He followed her up the stairs to their room.

"What happened?" he asked. "You look like you've seen a ghost."

"I found something on the beach," Elaine said tightly. "I think I'm going to be sick." She sat heavily on the bed and her hands moved instinctively to her stomach, as if trying to stop the heaving there. Looking at her ashen face, Brad felt his own stomach tighten. He sat down beside her, slipping his arm around her.

"What was it?" he asked softly.

"A dog," Elaine said, choking. "A poor little dog. It was buried in the sand."

Brad's brow knotted in puzzlement. "Buried? What do you mean?"

Elaine leaped to her feet and stared furiously down at her husband. "Buried! I mean it was dead and it was buried! Its neck was broken and whoever did it buried the poor thing in the sand! Brad, let's get out of here. I hate this place. I want to go home."

Brad took her hand and pulled her back down on the bed beside him. "Now calm down," he said, "and tell me what happened. And don't dramatize it. Just tell me what you found."

Elaine breathed deeply, composing herself, then told him what had happened. When she was finished, Brad shrugged. "That doesn't sound so horrible," he commented.

"Well, it *was* horrible. You weren't there. You didn't see it."

"No, I wasn't," Brad said reasonably. "But how can you be so sure that someone killed it, then buried it in the sand?"

"What else could have happened?" Elaine demanded.

"There was a storm last night, right?"

Elaine nodded mutely.

"Well, didn't it occur to you that the dog could have been playing on the beach and been hit by a chunk of driftwood? That could certainly break its neck. And then the surf does the rest, burying it in the sand. It seems to me that if someone maliciously killed a dog the beach is the last place he would have buried it. The surf could easily have exposed it. If you're going to bury a dog you bury it where it will stay buried, don't you?"

Suddenly Elaine felt foolish. She smiled sheepishly at Brad. "Why did you marry me?" she asked. "Don't you get sick of me overreacting to everything?"

"Not really. It makes a nice balance, since I tend to underreact." He smiled mischievously. "Maybe that's what makes me a good shrink. I hear the most incredible tales from my patients and never react to them at all. Want to hear some?"

"I certainly don't," Elaine said, blushing deeply. "Didn't you ever hear about the confidentiality between doctors and patients?"

"That's for courts, not for wives," Brad said easily. "Come on, let's go get some breakfast."

A few minutes later, as they passed through the lobby, the manager asked them if they'd be checking out that morning. Elaine started to tell him that they would, but Brad squeezed her hand.

"We'll be here a few more days," he said. He avoided Elaine's eyes as she stared at him accusingly. "I want to take a look at Robby Palmer," he muttered. But Elaine was sure it was more than that.

An hour later, after she had eaten, Elaine began to feel better. The sun still shone brightly and Clark's Harbor, basking in the brilliance, once more seemed as charming as it had when they had discovered it the day before. The images of the dead fisherman and the broken corpse of the dog faded from her mind, and Elaine began to wonder if it might not be fun to spend a year here. After all, she told herself, fishermen do drown, but they don't drown every day. It was just a coincidence.

Rebecca Palmer parked the battered minibus in front of the building her husband was remodeling and hurried inside. For a second she thought the place was deserted, but then a pounding from the back room told her that Glen was there, and working. She called out to him.

"I'm back here." His voice suggested that he wasn't going to come out, so she moved quickly around the half-finished display case, and stepped into an alcove that would eventually be an office.

"This son-of-a-bitch doesn't want to fit," Glen said with a grin. He struck the offending shelf once more, then tossed the hammer aside.

"If you'd measure before you cut, it might help," Rebecca pointed out. She picked up the hammer, knocked the shelf loose, measured first the board, and then the space it was supposed to fit in, then the board once more. She set the board on a pair of sawhorses, picked up a skillsaw, and neatly removed an eighth of an inch from one end of the plank. Seconds later it sat securely and steadily in place. Glen gazed at his wife admiringly.

"I didn't know you could do that."

"You never asked. Maybe from now on you should take care of the house and I'll do the remodeling."

"That would give Clark's Harbor something to talk about, wouldn't it? Want some coffee?" Without waiting for a reply, Glen poured them each a cup, then winked at Rebecca. "Perked with genuine electricity," he teased. "By the way, your latest batch of pottery came out without a single crack. One of these days, with a little luck, I'll get this place in shape to start selling some of it."

"You'd better. I have a whole new batch in the van. Give me a hand with it, will you?"

They transferred the unfired pottery to the shelves around the kiln, then put the finished pieces from the night before carefully aside.

"Now all I have to do is collect Snooker and I can get back home to work," Rebecca said when they were done.

"Snooker?"

"Didn't you bring him in with you this morning?" Rebecca asked.

"I didn't see him at all this morning," Glen replied.

"That's funny. When he didn't show up for his breakfast I assumed you'd brought him with you."

"Did you try calling him?"

"Of course. Not that it ever does any good. Well, I suppose he'll show up when he's good and ready. But I hope he's ready by this afternoon or the kids are going to be upset. I told them you had him." Rebecca shrugged. "It was either that or let them search the beach instead of going to school."

"Searching the beach might have been more educational," Glen said.

"Oh, come on, the school isn't that bad. Maybe it isn't as good as the one in Seattle, but at least both kids can go to the same school."

"And get hassled by the same kids."

Rebecca looked exasperated, and Glen was immediately sorry he had started in on the school. "I guess I'm the one who's paranoid today, huh?"

Rebecca smiled, relieved that there wasn't going to be an argument. "I wonder what will happen if Clark's Harbor ever gets to both of us on the same day?"

"We'll get over it," Glen said. "After all, it may be rough here, but it's not as rough as it was when Robby was sick. Whatever this place deals out to us, it's worth it, just to see Robby turning into a normal boy."

"It is, isn't it?" Rebecca smiled. "And it's beautiful here on days like today. I'm not sorry we came, Glen, really I'm not. And things are going to be fine as soon as this place is finished and open for business. But the first five hundred in profits goes to put electricity into the cabin, right?"

"Right. That should take about five years, the way I figure it."

Before Rebecca could respond, they heard the door of the gallery open and close, then a voice called out tentatively.

"Hello?"

Rebecca and Glen exchanged a look as they moved to the front room. Visitors to the gallery were rare. This one was totally unexpected.

Miriam Shelling stood just inside the front door, her hands behind her, clutching at the knob. Her hair hung limply around her face and there was a wildness in her eyes that almost frightened Rebecca.

"Mrs. Shelling," she said quickly. "How nice to see you. I'm so sorry about—"

Before she could complete the sentence, Miriam Shelling interrupted her.

"I came to warn you," she said harshly. "They're going to get you, just like they got Pete. It may take them awhile, but in the end they'll get you. You mark my words!" She glanced rapidly from Rebecca to Glen and back again. Then she lifted one arm and pointed a finger at them.

"Mark my words!" she repeated. A moment later she was gone.

"Jesus," Glen breathed. "What was that all about?"

Rebecca's eyes were still on the doorway where the distraught woman had stood. It was a few seconds before she answered.

"And we think we have it bad," she said at last. "We should count our blessings, Glen. We don't have any electricity and we feel a bit lonely, but we have each other. Mrs. Shelling doesn't have anything now."

"She looked a little crazy," Glen said.

"Why wouldn't she?" Rebecca flared. "What's the poor woman going to do with her husband gone?"

Glen chose not to answer the question. "What do you suppose she meant—'they got him'? Does she think someone killed Pete? And they'll get us too? She must be crazy."

"She's probably just upset," Rebecca said with compassion. "People say funny things when something like that happens to them. And it must have been horrible for her, being right there on the wharf when they brought him in."

"But why would she come here?" Glen wondered. "Why would she come and tell us something like that?"

"Who knows?" Rebecca shrugged. But she wished she did know.

Miriam Shelling walked purposefully along the sidewalk, muttering to herself, seeing nothing. The few people who saw her coming stepped aside, but it would have been difficult to tell if it was out of fear or respect for her grief. She didn't pause until she reached the tiny town hall that housed the police department. She marched up the steps and into the building, coming to a halt only when she was in front of Harney Whalen's desk.

"What are you going to do?" she demanded.

Harney Whalen stood up and stepped around the desk, holding out a hand to Miriam. She ignored it and stood rooted to the floor.

"Miriam," Whalen said. He saw the wildness in her eyes. He glanced quickly around, but he was alone with the upset woman. "Let me get you a chair," he offered.

She seemed not to hear him. "What are you going to do?" she demanded once more.

Whalen decided the best course was to act as if everything was all right. He retreated behind his desk again and sat down. Then he looked up at Miriam Shelling. "I'm not sure what you mean," he said quietly.

"Pete. I mean Pete. What are you going to do about finding the people who killed him?"

A memory stirred in Harney Whalen and a tiny shiver crept up his spine, settling in the back of his neck. There had been another woman, long ago, who had said these same words. *Who killed him?* Then, a few days later . . . He forced the memory away.

"No one killed Pete, Miriam," he said firmly. "It was an accident. He fell overboard and got caught in his nets."

"He was killed."

Harney shook his head sorrowfully, partly for the woman in front of him, and partly for the difficulty she was going to cause him. "There isn't any evidence of that, Miriam. I went over his boat myself yesterday afternoon. Chip Connor and I spent almost two hours on the *Sea Spray*. If there had been anything there we would have found it."

"What about the man who brought him in?"

"He's a lawyer from Aberdeen. Last night, when Pete drowned, he was home in bed. Believe me, we checked that out first thing."

When Miriam showed no signs of moving, Harney decided to try to explain what must have happened to her husband.

"Miriam, you've lived here for fifteen years," he began. "You know what it's like out there. Fishermen drown all the time. We've been damned lucky more of ours haven't been lost, but our boys tend to be careful. All of them but Pete grew up here, and they know better than to go out alone. The storms come up fast and they're mean. Pete knew that too. He should never have gone out by himself. It was an accident, Miriam, and that's all there is to it."

"That's all you have to say?" Miriam said dully. "You're not going to do anything?"

"I don't know what else I can do, Miriam. Pete was by himself out there and nobody saw what happened."

"Somebody saw it," Miriam said quietly. "Somebody was out there when it happened."

"Who?" Whalen inquired mildly.

"It's your job to find out."

"I've done what I can, Miriam. I've talked to everybody in the fleet and they all say the same thing. They went out together and they came back together. All of them except Pete. He stayed out alone when the fleet came in. The storm was already brewing and he should have come in with the rest of them. But he didn't. That's all there is to it. It's over."

"It's not over," Miriam said, her voice rising dangerously. "I know it's not over." For a moment Harney Whalen was afraid she was going to go to pieces. But she merely turned and left his office. He watched her go. He was still watching when his deputy, Chip Connor, came in.

"What was that all about?" Chip asked.

"I'm not sure," Harney replied. "Miriam seems to think what happened to Pete wasn't an accident."

Chip frowned. "What does she expect us to do?"

"Search me." Whalen shrugged. "We did everything we could yesterday." Then he scratched his head. "Say, Chip, when I was down on the wharf yesterday there were a couple of strangers down there. Looked like city people."

"So?"

"So I don't know," Whalen said testily. "But do me a favor, will you? Go over to the inn and ask Merle if they're still here, and if they are, how long they're planning to stay."

Chip looked puzzled. "What business is it of ours?"

Harney Whalen glared at his deputy. "Someone died here, Chip, and there's strangers in town. Don't you think we ought to find out why they're here?"

Chip Connor started to argue with his chief, but one glance at Whalen's expression changed his mind. When Harn Whalen set his jaw like that, there was no arguing.

Feeling somewhat foolish, he set off to talk to the proprietor of the Harbor Inn.

# FIVE

"**M**ORNING, MERLE."
He recognized Chip Connor's voice immediately, but Merle Glind still jumped slightly, nearly knocking his thick-lensed glasses from their precarious perch on his tiny nose. One hand flew up to smooth what was left of his hair, and he tried to cover his embarrassment at his own nervousness with a broad smile. The effect, unfortunately, was ruined by his inability to complete the smile. His lips twitched spasmodically for a second, and Chip waited patiently for the odd little man to compose himself.

"Is something wrong?" Merle asked. His rabbity eyes flicked around the hotel lobby as if he expected to find a crime being committed under his very nose.

"Nothing like that," Chip said easily, wishing he could put Merle at his ease. But as long as Chip could remember, Merle Glind had remained unchanged, fussing around the inn day and night, inspecting each seldom-used room as if it were the Presidential suite of a major hotel, going over and over the receipts as if hoping to find evidence of embezzlement, and constantly poking his head into the door of the bar—his major source of income—to count the customers. When Chip was a boy, Merle had always been glad to see him, but ever since he had become Harn Whalen's deputy three years ago, Merle had begun to show signs of acute nervousness whenever Chip appeared at the Harbor Inn. Chip supposed it was simply a natural wariness of the police, amplified by Merle's natural nervousness and not modified in the least by the fact the innkeeper had known Chip Connor since the day he was born.

"Well, there's nothing going on here," Merle hastened to assure him. "Nothing at all. Nothing ever goes on here. Sometimes I wonder why I even keep the place open. Gives me something to do, I suppose. Thirty-five years I've had this place, and I'll have it till I die." He glanced around the spotless lobby with unconcealed pride and Chip felt called upon to make a reassuring comment.

"Place looks nice," he said. "Who polishes the spittoons?"

"I do," Merle said promptly, holding up a can of Brasso he mysteriously produced from somewhere behind the counter. "Can't trust anybody else—they'd scratch the brass. Nothing as bad for a hotel's reputation as scratched brass. That and dirty linen. And I don't mind saying that in thirty-five years I've never yet rented a room with dirty linen. Old, maybe, but not dirty," he finished with a weak attempt at humor. Chip laughed appreciatively.

"What's the occupancy?"

"Twenty percent," Merle responded proudly. Then, honesty prodding him, he added, "One room occupied, four empty."

"Who's the customer?" Chip said casually.

"Harney want to know?" Merle's eyes narrowed immediately.

"You know Harn," Chip replied. "Keeps an eye on everything. But this time he has a reason. Something about Pete Shelling."

Merle clucked sympathetically, then realized the import of what Chip had just said.

"Harney doesn't think——" he began, then broke off, not wanting even to voice the awful thought. Visions of the hotel's ruined reputation danced in his head.

"Harney doesn't think anything," Chip said, reading the little man's mind. "It's just that Miriam Shelling was in this morning claiming that Pete was murdered. Harney's just doing his job, checking out everything."

Relieved, Merle Glind pushed the register across the counter, turning it so that it faced Chip. It wasn't anything unusual, he told himself. Whenever there were guests at the hotel either Chip or Harn stopped by to check them out. No reason to be nervous, no reason at all. Still, he felt anxious, and peered at Chip as the deputy examined the latest entry in the register.

"Randall," Chip read the entry out loud, "Dr. and Mrs. Bradford, from Seattle." He looked up at Merle. "Vacationing?"

"I don't ask questions like that," Merle said pompously, though Chip knew that he did. Then, lowering his voice: "I did notice they had quite a bit of luggage though, so I suppose they're on some kind of trip."

"Staying long?"

"A couple of days. He told me this morning."

"Says he's a doctor. I wonder what kind of doctor?"

"Well, I'm sure I don't know," Merle said. "But I suppose I could find out. Do you think it's important?" he added eagerly.

"I doubt it," Chip gave a short laugh. "But you know Harney. Doesn't matter if it's worth knowing or not, Harn wants to know it. Think you could find out a couple of things for me?"

"I can try, that's all I can do."

"Well, if you can find out what kind of doctor Randall is and why they chose Clark's Harbor, let us know, okay?" He winked at Glind, pushed the register back across the counter, and left the inn.

Chip drove slowly through Clark's Harbor, looking for nothing in particular, since nothing was likely to happen. Eventually he found himself approaching the tiny schoolhouse that had served the town for three generations.

He pulled the car to a stop and sat watching the children playing in the small yard next to the building. He recognized all of them and knew most of them very well. He, himself, had gone to school with their parents.

His eyes fell on two children who stood apart from the rest, a little boy and his younger sister. He knew who they were—the newcomers, the Palmer children. And he knew why they were standing apart—they had not yet been accepted by the rest of the children of Clark's Harbor.

Chip wondered how long it would take before Robby and Missy Palmer would be part of the crowd. The rest of the year? Part of next year? Longer?

The children, he knew, were no different from their parents. If anything, they were worse.

If their parents didn't like strangers the children would hate them.

If their parents made remarks about the Palmers, the children would taunt the Palmers' children.

There was nothing Chip could do about it. Indeed, Chip didn't even worry about it. He started the engine and drove away.

In the schoolyard Robby Palmer watched the police car disappear into the distance and wondered why it had stopped. He knew Missy, too, had been watching, but before he could make any comment, he heard his name being called.

"Robby! Little baby Robby!" The voice was taunting, hurting. Before Robby even turned around he knew who it was.

Jimmy Phipps. Jimmy was bigger than Robby, a year older, but Robby and he were in the same grade. Jimmy had made it clear from Robby's first day at school that he thought the younger boy should be in a lower grade—and that he would make Robby's life miserable. Now, when Robby turned, he saw Jimmy Phipps standing a few feet away, glowering at him.

"You want to fight?" Jimmy challenged him.

Robby shook his head, saying nothing.

"You're chicken," Jimmy said.

"He is not!" Missy snapped, leaping to her brother's defense.

"Don't say anything, Missy," Robby told his sister. "Just act like he isn't there."

Jimmy Phipps reddened. "Your daddy's a queer," he shouted.

Robby wasn't sure what the word meant but felt called upon to deny the charge.

"My daddy's an artist!" he declared.

"And my dad says all artists are queers," Jimmy replied. "My dad says your parents are commies and bums and you should go back where you came from."

Robby glared at the bigger boy, his eyes blazing with anger. He knew he shouldn't swing at him—his parents wouldn't approve. But how else could he defend himself from Jimmy Phipps's taunts? He took a step forward and saw three other boys line themselves up behind Jimmy.

"Get him, Jimmy," Joe Taylor urged. "Rub his face in the dirt."

"I don't want to fight," Robby said in a final effort to avoid a fracas.

"That's 'cause you're chicken!" Jimmy cried. His friends urging him on, he leaped on Robby, his fists pummeling the smaller boy.

Robby fought back and managed, somehow, to get on top of Jimmy, but then the other boys crowded in, grabbing Robby and holding him while Jimmy Phipps recovered himself.

"Let go of him!" Missy screamed. "You let go of my brother!"

She aimed a kick at one of the boys, but Robby stopped her, telling her to stay out of it. Then he jerked suddenly, struggled free, and threw a punch at Joe Taylor. Joe's nose started to bleed immediately and he ran off toward the schoolhouse, howling in pain and clutching his injured face. The other boys looked on in surprise. Jimmy Phipps, about to leap on Robby again, stopped and stared, suddenly unsure of himself. Robby, though small, apparently packed a wallop.

"You leave me alone," Robby said. "And you take back what you said."

"All right," Jimmy Phipps said. "You're not chicken. But your daddy's still a commie queer. My dad says so."

Robby jumped on the bigger boy, but the fight was suddenly stopped when their teacher appeared, grabbing each of the boys by the shoulder and separating them by pure force.

"That will be enough," she said. "What's this all about?"

"It's Robby's fault, Miss Peters! He gave Joe Taylor a bloody nose and jumped on Jimmy Phipps!"

Miss Peters had been teaching at the Clark's Harbor school for thirty years. She was sure there was more to the story than that, but she had learned long ago that getting the whole truth out of half a dozen ten-year-olds is harder than undoing the Gordian Knot. The most effective way to deal with a situation like this was to listen to no one at all.

"I don't care what happened," she said. "Robby, your clothes are filthy and it looks like you're going to have a black eye. Go home for the rest of the day." Jimmy Phipps grinned maliciously but Miss Peters put a quick end to his triumph.

"As for you, James, you can spend this afternoon cleaning the school, and the rest of you can help him!" She took Missy by the hand and started back inside.

Robby stood glowering at his tormentors for a moment, then started toward the schoolyard gate. Behind him, Jimmy Phipps couldn't resist a parting shot.

"We'll get you for this!" he shouted. "You'll wish you never came to Clark's Harbor!"

Robby Palmer, his eye beginning to swell, burst into tears and began running home.

Rebecca gave the pottery wheel a final kick, gently molded the clay between the fingers of her right hand and the palm of the left, then wiped the dampness from her hands while the wheel coasted to a stop. She surveyed her work with a critical eye. The rim of the vase should be a little thinner, perhaps a shade more fluted. Then, with a sigh, she decided to leave well enough alone. Heavy, chunky pottery was her style—the fact that it was easier for her to execute was a bonus—and why take a risk she didn't have to take? She brushed a strand of long dark hair away from one eye, then carefully removed the nearly finished vase from the wheel.

She left the old tool shed that had been converted into a makeshift pottery and walked slowly toward the cabin to check on her bread dough. To her right the beach arched invitingly away to the south, white sands glistening, and for a moment she was tempted to go off beachcombing, looking for items that could eventually be sold in the gallery. But somehow it didn't seem fair to abandon herself to the beach while Glen was cooped up in the gallery, struggling with two-by-fours that refused to bend themselves to his desires. Which was strange, she reflected, considering that he could do anything at all with wood-carving tools. In fact, Rebecca considered Glen to be a better wood sculptor than painter, but she would never tell him so. Yet when it came to a simple thing like measuring and cutting a shelf, he was a dead loss. She smiled to herself as she pictured the finished gallery, its shelves all slightly lopsided. No, she decided, Glen's sense of artistry would make the gallery look right, no matter how ill-fitting everything might be.

With one last longing look at the beach, she made herself continue on into the cabin. She surveyed the bread dough dolefully. In fairness to Glen, there were things she wasn't very good at either, bread making among them. The dough, which should have risen by now, sat stolidly where she had left it. It seemed, if anything, to have shrunk. She poked at it, hoping to set off some small, magical trigger inside, that would start it swelling up to what it should be. Instead, it resisted the pressure of her finger and looked as if it resented the intrusion. Rebecca contemplated alternate uses for the whitish mass, since it was obvious that it was never going to burst forth from the oven, a mouth-watering, golden-brown, prize-winning loaf. Finally, since she could think of nothing better, she simply dumped the mass of dough onto a cookie sheet, shoved it into the oven, and threw another piece of wood into the ancient stove, hoping for the best.

She was about to move on to another of her endless tasks when she heard Robby's voice. She wasn't sure it was his at first, but as it grew louder she had a sudden feeling of panic.

"Mommy, Mommy!" The child's voice came through the woods. And again: "Mommy! Mommy!"

Dear God, Rebecca thought, it's starting up again. He's done something awful at school and they don't want him back, and now what are we going to do? With a shock she realized how near the surface the old fears, the fears she had lived with for so many years, were. She thought she had buried them. Since they had come here Robby had been so well, she believed she'd put them aside forever. Now, as Robby's cries drew closer, Rebecca struggled to control herself. She had never been good at dealing with her son's violent outbursts. She could feel the terror rising inside her. Dear God! Why wasn't Glen here?

"Mommy!"

Rebecca dashed out of the cabin just in time to see Robby emerge from the woods. Fear clutching at her, she saw that his nose was bleeding and his clothes were a mess. Then he was upon her, his arms wrapped around her, his head buried in her stomach. He was crying.

"It's all right," she said. "It's all right. Mommy's here, and everything's going to be fine." God, she prayed silently, please let everything be fine. Please . . .

Still sobbing, Robby let himself be led into the cabin. Rebecca braced herself for trouble as she began cleaning him up, but Robby sat quietly while she washed his face. Most of her fear left her: it wasn't the hyperkinesis then. It was something else. But what? He should be at school, not home, bloody and crying.

"What happened, Robby?" she said when the bleeding had stopped and most of the smudges had been removed from his face.

"I had a fight," Robby said sullenly.

"A fight?"

Robby nodded.

"What was it about?"

"You and Daddy."

"Me and Daddy? What about us?"

"They were calling you names and saying we shouldn't have come here." He looked beseechingly at his mother. "Why didn't we stay in Seattle?"

"You were sick there."

"I was? I don't remember."

Rebecca smiled at her son and hugged him. "It's just as well you don't remember," she said. "You weren't very happy when you were sick, and neither were Daddy or Missy or I."

Robby frowned. "But we're not very happy here, are we?"

"We're happier here than anyplace else," Rebecca whispered. "And things will get better. Just don't listen to them when they say things about you."

"But they weren't saying anything about *me*," Robby said. "They were saying things about you and Daddy."

"Well, it's the same thing. Now I want you to promise me you won't fight anymore."

"But what if they beat up on me again?"

"If you won't fight back they won't do much to you. It won't be any fun for them and they'll leave you alone."

"But they'll think I'm chicken and they won't play with me."

Rebecca suddenly found herself wondering if she was getting old, for she had no answer for Robby's statement. What he had said was true, but in her adulthood she had forgotten the level on which children think. She decided to drop the entire subject and let Glen deal with it when he got home.

"I don't suppose there's any point in my suggesting you go back to school this afternoon, is there?" she said.

"I won't go," Robby said flatly. He decided not to mention that he'd been sent home.

She surveyed the bruises on his face critically, then relented. "Do you feel up to helping me out or would you rather play on the beach?"

"I'd rather play on the beach," came Robby's prompt reply.

"Somehow I thought you would." Rebecca grinned. "But here's the rules."

"Aw, Mom!"

"No, 'aw, Moms,' thank you very much. Either listen to the rules and obey them, or stay here and help me." Robby's expression told her he'd listen to the rules. "Stay within a hundred feet of the house. And just so you can't claim you don't know what a hundred feet is, see that big tree?" She pointed to an immense cedar that dominated the strip of forest beyond the beach. Robby nodded solemnly. "That's a hundred feet away. Don't go past that tree. Also, stay out of the driftwood. You could slip and break your leg."

"Aw, Mom . . ." But the protest faded at Rebecca's upraised finger. "And stay out of the water. Okay?"

"Okay."

"And make sure you come if I call you."

She stood in the doorway and watched her son scamper out onto the beach. Once more Rebecca marveled at the fact that she could let him play alone now without having to worry constantly about what he might be up to.

Happily, Rebecca returned to her chores.

Brad Randall parked in front of the inn, turned off the engine, then slapped his forehead as he remembered.

"Damn," he said. "We forgot all about it!"

"All about what?" Elaine asked. They had spent the entire day poking around Clark's Harbor and she couldn't imagine what they might have missed.

"The Palmers. We said we'd drop in on them."

"Well, it's too late now," Elaine replied, glancing at the sinking sun. "Besides, he was probably just being polite. I mean, it's not as if they're old friends. We hardly know them."

"But I do want to see Robby again," Brad said. "If there's really been a miraculous cure, I want to see it for myself."

"Maybe you can see him tomorrow," Elaine suggested. "Right now I'm bushed."

"I did sort of run you ragged, didn't I?" Brad chuckled. "But what do you think? I mean, what do you really think?"

"I don't know." Elaine was pensive. "It's beautiful, it really is, and if it hadn't been for that poor man yesterday and that dog this morning, I'd be all for it. But I just don't know."

"It was coincidence, honey," Brad argued. "The same thing could have happened anywhere."

"But they happened here," Elaine said stubbornly, "and I'm sorry, but I can't get them out of my mind." Then she relented a little. Clark's Harbor *was* beautiful, and she knew Brad had fallen in love with it. "Let's sleep on it, shall we?"

They got out of the car and walked to the hotel gate. Elaine paused, staring up at the building. "I still say it's on the wrong coast," she said. "And not just the hotel. The whole town. It's so neat and so tidy and so settled looking. Not like most of the towns on the peninsula that sort of fade in, sprawl, then fade out again. This place seems to have cut a niche for itself in the forest and huddled there. As though it knows its bounds and isn't about to step over them."

Brad smiled. "Maybe that's what appeals to me," he said, "I guess it strikes a chord in me somewhere. I like it."

They strolled across the lawn arm-in-arm and went into the hotel. Behind his counter, Merle Glind bobbed his head at them.

"Have a nice day?"

"Fine," Brad answered. "Pretty town you have here. Beautiful."

"We like it," Glind responded. There was a pause, and Brad started toward the stairs.

"You folks on vacation?" Merle suddenly asked.

Brad turned. "In a way. Actually we're looking for someplace to live for a while."

"We already got a doctor," Merle said hastily. "Doc Phelps. Been here for years."

"Well, I wouldn't be any threat to him. I'm not that kind of doctor and I wasn't planning to practice anyway. Frankly, I doubt there'd be much call for my kind of doctoring out here."

"Well, if you're not going to work, what are you going to do?" Merle Glind didn't try to disguise the suspicion in his voice. As far as he was concerned anyone under seventy-five who didn't do an honest day's work was a shirker.

"I thought I'd try to write a book," Brad said easily.

Merle's frown deepened. "A book? What kind of a book?"

Brad started to explain but before he could get a word in Elaine had cut him off. "A technical book," she said. "The kind nobody reads, except maybe a few other psychiatrists."

If he'd known his wife any less well Brad would have been hurt. Instead, he gave her an admiring wink. Elaine had just rescued him from a long explanation of the subject of his book and the inevitable, endless questions about bio-rhythms. "It seemed to me this might be the perfect place to write it," he said now. "Lots of peace and quiet."

"I don't know," Merle said pensively. "Seems to me you'd be better off up in Pacific Beach or Moclips or one of those places. That's where the artists hang out."

"Right." Brad grinned. "And party and drink and do all the things they shouldn't do if they want to get any work done. But Clark's Harbor doesn't look like that kind of town."

"It's not," Glind said emphatically. "We're working folk here and we mind our business, most of us. It's a quiet town and we like to keep it that way."

Elaine sighed to herself. With every word the odd little man spoke Brad's resolve to move to Clark's Harbor would strengthen. His next words proved her right.

"I've been looking around today. Not too many houses on the market, are there?"

"Nope," Merle said. "Not a one, and not likely to be. Most of the houses here get passed on from one generation to the next. The Harbor isn't like so many little towns. Our children stay right here, most of them."

"What about renting? Are there any houses for rent?"

Merle appeared to think for a minute, and Brad wasn't sure whether he was running his mind over the town or trying to decide how to evade the question.

Merle, for his part, decided to duck the issue entirely. "Only one that I know of belongs to the police chief, Harney Whalen. Don't know if it's for rent, though. You'd have to talk to Harn about that."

"Does anybody live in it now?" Brad pressed.

"Not so far as I know. If he's got people out there Harn hasn't told me. But then, it wouldn't be any of my business, would it?"

Realizing he was unlikely to get any information out of the old man, Brad dropped the subject. "Got any recommendations for dinner?" he asked. Merle smiled eagerly.

"Right through the door. Best food and drink in town. Drinks sixty cents a shot and the freshest seafood you can get. Cook gets it right off the boats every day." When he saw Elaine peering into the empty dining room and bar, he added: "Won't be anyone in there yet, of course, but just wait till later. Place'll be packed. Absolutely packed."

"Maybe we'd better make reservations," Elaine wondered aloud.

"Oh, no need for that," Merle said. "No need at all. I'll make sure there's a table for you. What time do you want to eat?"

"Seven? Seven thirty?"

Merle Glind wrote himself a hasty note and smiled up at the Randalls. "There you are. All taken care of, see? No need for reservations at all—just leave it to me."

Two minutes later, in their room, Elaine threw herself onto the bed and burst into laughter. "I don't believe it," she cried. "He's too perfect. Do you know, Brad, I think he actually didn't realize he was taking a reservation? It's incredible!"

Brad lay down on the bed beside his wife and kissed her gently. "Now what do you think?" he asked.

"I think we have enough time before dinner," Elaine replied. She began unbuttoning Brad's shirt. . . .

Merle Glind sat nervously at his desk and his eyes kept flicking to the stairway as he dialed the phone. It rang twice, then was answered. Briefly, he filled Harney Whalen in on what he'd found out about the Randalls. When he was done there was a silence before the police chief spoke.

"So they're planning to stay awhile, are they? Well, maybe they will, and then again, maybe they won't. Thanks Merle, you've been a big help."

Merle Glind, feeling pleased with himself, put the receiver back on the cradle, then went into the dining room, where he put a small sign on one of the tables. "Reserved," the sign said.

# SIX

HARNEY WHALEN GLANCED AT THE clock, drummed his fingers nervously on the worn oak surface of his desk, then rose and paced to the window, where he stood staring down the street, as if his stares could hurry the arrival of Chip Connor. His deputy was late, and that was unusual. Anything unusual worried Harn Whalen, and too many unusual things were happening in Clark's Harbor the last couple of days. First Pete Shelling (nothing more than an unfortunate accident, of course), and now these Randall people, acting like they wanted to move to the Harbor. Now *that* was upsetting.

Harney moved away from the window and unconsciously flexed his still-solid body, patting his firm belly with the palm of his right hand. Then he reseated himself at his desk, pulled the meager file on Pete Shelling to a spot in front of him, and read it once more. He was still reading it, scowling, when Chip Connor finally appeared.

"Thought you'd decided to take the evening off," Harney observed as he glanced at Chip.

"Just having a little dinner," Chip replied mildly. "Anything doing?"

"Not really, except I had a call from Merle Glind a few minutes ago." Chip's brow arched curiously as he waited for the chief to continue. "Seems they think they'd like to settle down here for a while," Harney said.

"They?"

"That guy Randall and his wife at the inn."

Chip frowned. That spelled trouble. As long as he'd known Harn Whalen, which was all of his life, Harn had had an aversion to strangers, a distrust that sometimes seemed to go beyond the natural feelings of most of the Harborites. Chip supposed it was not really so strange. Harn knew everyone in town—he was related to half of them, including Chip—and his knowledge of them made his job much easier. He knew them all inside out—who were the troublemakers, who were the drunks, and what was the best way to handle everybody. But strangers were an unknown quantity, and Harn Whalen didn't like unknown quantities. Strangers upset the balance of the town. For a while no one reacted the way he was supposed to react, and that made Harn Whalen's life more difficult. And then there were the outsiders themselves to deal with. For Harn, that was the hardest part. Among his own people he was fine, but introduce him to a stranger and he'd clam right up. He'd watch them warily, from a distance, as if he half-expected them to do something to him. It had been that way with the Shellings for a long time after Pete and Miriam arrived in Clark's Harbor. It had taken Harney nearly five years just to offer them a nod of greeting. Chip supposed he understood though. He felt much the same way himself. By the time he was as old as Harney, and as set in his ways, he'd probably have all the same reactions as the chief. But Harn was up to something now; that was for sure.

"What do they want here?" Chip said finally.

"Merle says the guy's planning to write some kind of book and thinks this is a good place to do it."

"Well," Chip mused, "you've got to admit it's quiet here."

"And that's the way I like it," Harney said. "Won't stay quiet, though, if the place fills up with city folk. They always bring their noise with them. Like Palmer and his wife."

"They haven't been much trouble," Chip suggested.

"Pounding all day?" Whalen countered.

"Well, you can't remodel a building without some pounding."

Whalen grunted in reluctant assent. It was true, but that didn't mean he had to like it. He decided to shift gears. "Don't know what he thinks he'll accomplish by opening an art gallery here," he grumbled. "Nobody's going to buy his junk."

"Then he won't be here long, will he?" Chip grinned. "I'd think you'd be down there every day helping out. After all, the sooner he gets the place open, the sooner he'll go broke, right?"

Harney looked sourly at his deputy but couldn't help smiling.

"You're too sharp for me, Chip. Too sharp by a long shot. So tell me, what'll we do about the Randalls? I'm just not sure I can stomach another set of strangers right now. They upset me. And don't give me any lectures about how I can't keep the town the same forever—maybe I can't, but as long as I'm chief of police, I'll damn well try."

"What are they going to do about a place to live?"

"Merle told them to come and talk to me."

"Then it's easy," Chip suggested. "Just tell them the old house isn't for rent."

"I told that to the Palmers but it didn't stop them. They just talked old Mrs. Pruitt into selling them that crummy cabin at the other end of the beach. If she'd have talked to me first, I'd have bought the cabin myself, but she didn't. No, I think the best thing to do is just try to talk them out of the whole idea. If that doesn't work, I'll rent the old Baron place to them. A month on Sod Beach in that wreck ought to change their minds for them."

"You're a devious old man, Harn," Chip said with a smile.

"Not devious at all," Whalen said. "I just don't like strangers. Now, why don't you get to work on Pete Shelling? The file's right here."

"What's to work on?"

"Search me." Harney shrugged. "As far as I'm concerned it was just an accident, but I figure if Miriam Shelling should come walking in here again, it wouldn't hurt at all to be 'working on the case,' if you know what I mean."

Chip laughed out loud. "*Now* tell me you aren't devious."

"The old dog knows some old tricks, that's all," Harney said with a wink. A moment later he was gone and Chip Connor was alone in the tiny police station.

Glen Palmer watched the police chief drive past the gallery and started to wave, as he did every day. But suddenly he changed his mind and his hand dropped back to his side, the gesture uncompleted. What was the point? Whalen never returned the greeting, never even so much as glanced his way. Glen wasn't sure if it was conscious rudeness or if the man was merely preoccupied, but he knew he resented it. The chief's coldness seemed symbolic of the attitude of the whole town. Glen had come to believe that if he could only win the chief's approval, his acceptance in Clark's Harbor would begin. But so far he had been unable to make a single dent in Whalen's shield of hostility. All in good time, he told himself for the hundredth time, all in good time.

That was also the attitude he was trying to take about the gallery itself, but it was more difficult every day. He glanced around at the front room. Tomorrow he would begin spending all his time on the display area. The office could wait, but the display area could not. If he could finish it in the next couple of weeks they could open for business by Memorial Day—and the hell with what the office looked like.

It would be a pretty gallery, Glen was sure. The rough-hewn plank paneling would show off his primitive painting style to its best advantage, and his sculptures, finely finished and glowing with their hand-rubbed patina, would provide a nice contrast. Reluctantly, he decided to swallow his pride and ask Rebecca to pitch in. With a wry chuckle he admitted to himself that her help would speed the work fivefold at least. He should have done it weeks ago but his ego had prevented it. And now another afternoon was gone with not enough done. Time to call it a day. He put his tools away, locked up the building, and climbed into the ancient Chevy that served as the Palmers' second car. It refused to start.

"Damn," he said aloud. He twisted the key again and listened to the angry grinding of the starter. Three tries later he got out of the car and raised the hood to stare at the engine. But he knew even less about motors than he did about carpentry. He slammed the hood down again and, with the blind faith characteristic of people who know nothing about cars, got in and tried the starter once more. Again the grinding noise, but weaker this time. Glen decided to give it up before he ruined the battery as well.

He searched his mind. Pruitt's gas station would be closed by now. He considered searching out Bill Pruitt and talking him into taking a look at the car. No good. Pruitt had never been particularly friendly, less so after his mother had sold the Palmers their cabin—no doubt against Bill's advice. Glen was sure that even if the owner of the town's sole service station could be persuaded to do something with the car, the bill would be padded because of the late hour. He'd leave the Chevy where it was and walk home. He could take care of it in the morning.

He walked along the road at first, thinking of trying his luck at hitchhiking, but soon put that idea aside: he was enjoying the walk and the exercise was relaxing, so he left the road and cut through the forest to the ocean, emerging from the woods at the south end of Sod Beach, near the old house he and Rebecca had originally tried to rent. Now he was glad Harney Whalen had refused to rent to him: though the house was larger than the Palmers' cabin, it stood exposed on the beach, unprotected by the sheltering forest that nearly surrounded the tiny home he and his family occupied. And it had that awful look of abandonment, a look he hadn't recognized the first time he had seen the place. Then it had seemed picturesque; now he found it forbidding.

He skirted the house quickly and made his way down to the surf line, where the sand was packed hard and walking was easy. In the distance he was pleased to see the faint glow of the lantern in his window, just beginning to contrast with the fading light of the evening. Smoke curled from both chimneys of the cabin and he wondered what Rebecca was fixing for dinner.

He almost passed Miriam Shelling without seeing her, and probably would have if she hadn't waved to him. At her movement he veered away from the lapping water to angle across the beach.

"Hello," he said as he approached her, smiling tentatively.

Miriam stared at him for a long time, not speaking. Glen was about to turn away from her when she raised her hand again and made a vague gesture.

"You didn't believe me, did you?"

It was an accusation. Glen hedged, studying her. "I'm not sure what you mean," he said. The odd glaze was gone from her eyes; now she seemed to be nothing more than a tired middle-aged woman.

"Today," she said, "when I came into your—what do you call it?"

"The gallery?"

Miriam nodded. "The gallery," she repeated dully. "You should have believed me."

Glen watched the woman carefully, trying to fathom what might be going on in her mind. She seemed much more in control of herself now than she had earlier. But you never knew with people like her.

"What are you doing out here?" he asked.

"Waiting."

"Waiting? For me?"

"Maybe. I don't know. I'm just waiting. Something's going to happen, and I'm waiting for it."

"But why here?" Glen pressed.

"I don't know," Miriam said slowly. "It just seemed like a good place to wait." Suddenly her eyes were filled with anxiety as she looked up at Glen. "It's all right, isn't it? You don't mind if I wait here?"

"No, of course I don't mind. I don't own the beach. But it will be getting cold soon."

"A storm's coming," Miriam Shelling said softly. "A big one. Well, it doesn't matter anymore. It can't hurt Pete now."

"But what about you?" Glen asked gently. He wondered if he ought to invite Mrs. Shelling home with him, then thought of the children. He didn't want them hearing any of this ominous nonsense she kept muttering.

"I'll go home soon," she said. "I guess I can wait there just as well as here. You go on now—I'll be all right."

Glen started away but turned back when he heard Miriam Shelling calling to him.

"Young man? You be careful, you hear? It's going to be a big storm."

Glen smiled at her and waved. "I'll be all right," he called. He walked on and didn't look back again till he was near the cabin. When he did finally turn, Miriam Shelling was gone. Glen felt an odd sense of relief, as if a momentary threat had passed. He went into the cabin as the last of the sunlight faded from the beach.

"I didn't hear you drive up," Rebecca said as Glen came in.

"I didn't drive—I walked."

Rebecca felt a sinking sensation as the meager balance in their checking account flashed in front of her eyes. "What happened to the car?" she asked.

"I wish I knew. It wouldn't start, and you know how I am with cars. I thought about walking over to see if I could find Bill Pruitt but he charges double after six."

Rebecca was about to press him for details when the children came tumbling out of their tiny bedroom, Missy demanding to be picked up and Robby saying, "Look at me! Look at me!"

Glen swung his daughter off the floor, then looked at his son. He set Missy back down and knelt next to Robby.

"What happened to you?" He asked the question of Robby but his eyes went immediately to Rebecca.

"He was defending our honor," Rebecca began, but Robby cut in.

"I had a fight," he said in a rush. "Four guys ganged up on me and I got a black eye, but I won. Did you bring Snooker home?"

Glen glanced at Rebecca but she shrugged helplessly. "No, I didn't," he said. "He must be off on a hunting expedition."

"He's never stayed away all day," Robby said accusingly.

"Well, he must be getting adventurous, just like his master," Glen replied. "But he'll be back, you'll see. Just wait until morning."

"He's not coming back," Missy said softly. She looked ready to cry. "He's not ever coming back."

"He is too," Robby shot back.

"Of course he's coming back, Missy," Rebecca said. "Why wouldn't he?"

"I don't know," Missy said, her eyes brimming with tears. "But he's not coming back, and I miss him." The tears overflowed and she fled to the bedroom, where she flung herself on her bunk. Rebecca looked helplessly at Glen, then went after her daughter. Robby stared at his father.

"He is coming back, isn't he?" he asked plaintively.

"Of course he is, son; of course he is," Glen said. But he suddenly had the sinking feeling that the dog was not going to return.

After dinner they put the children to bed, then Glen threw another log on the fire. Rebecca watched him but didn't speak until he had finished poking at the blaze and sat down again.

"Glen, what's wrong?"

"I don't know. Little things, I guess. The car and the gallery and now Snooker. I think Missy's right. I don't think he's coming back."

"Don't be silly. What could have happened to him? Of course he'll be back."

"There's something else too."

Rebecca suddenly stiffened. Whatever he was about to say, it was going to be important. She could tell by the look in his eyes.

"I saw Miriam Shelling tonight."

Rebecca relaxed. "Did she come back to the gallery?"

"She was on the beach when I came home. Sitting on a piece of driftwood, staring out at the sea."

"Lots of people do that," Rebecca said. She rummaged through her sewing box, searching for a button. "I do that myself and so do you. It's one of the joys of living out here."

"She said she was waiting for something. It was weird."

"Waiting for what?"

"I don't know. I'm not sure she knew herself. But she said a big storm was coming and told me to be careful."

"That makes sense," Rebecca said. "Did she say anything else?"

"No." There was a long pause, then: "Maybe we ought to give it up."

Rebecca put down her sewing and stared at Glen. "Now you are sounding like I did yesterday. But you'll get over it, just like I did." Then she chuckled softly. "You know what? While you were busily getting yourself into a funk today, I was getting out of mine. I decided I really love this place. I love living near the water and the forest, I love the peace and quiet, and I love what's happening to my children, especially Robby. So you might as well get yourself into a better frame of mind, my love, because I've decided that no matter what happens, I'm going to see things through right here. And so are you."

Glen Palmer looked at his wife with loving eyes and thanked God for her strength. As long as I have her, he thought, I'll be fine. As long as I have her.

And then a premonition struck him, and he knew that he wouldn't always have Rebecca, wouldn't have her nearly long enough. He rose from his chair, crossed the small room, and knelt by his wife. He put his arms around her and held her tightly and tried to keep from crying. Rebecca, unaware of the emotions that were surging through her husband, continued sewing.

Harney Whalen stretched, snapped the television set on, then wandered over to the window before he sat down to watch the nine o'clock movie. His house, the house he had been born in and had grown up in and would undoubtedly die in, sat on a knoll that commanded a beautiful view of Clark's Harbor and the ocean beyond. He watched the lights of the town as they twinkled on around the bay, then looked up at the starless night sky. A layer of clouds had closed in and the feel of the air told him that another storm was brewing. Harney hated the storms and sometimes wondered why he stayed on the peninsula. But it was home, and even though he'd never appreciated the weather, he'd learned to live with it. Still, he began his usual round of the house, checking that all the windows were tightly closed against whatever might be coming in from the sea.

His grandfather had built the house, and he'd built it well. It had stood against the Northeasters for more than a century, and its joints were as snug as ever, its foundation maintaining a perfect level. Only the roof ever demanded Harney's attention, and that only rarely. He wandered from room to room, not really seeing the furnishings that filled them but feeling their comforting presence, and wondering idly what it would be like to be one of those people who spent their lives like gypsies, wandering from one residence to another, never really putting down roots anywhere. Well, it wasn't for him. He liked knowing that his past was always around him. Even though he lived by himself in the house now, he wasn't really alone—his family was all around him and he never felt lonesome here.

He made a sandwich, then opened a can of beer to wash it down with. By the time he returned to the living room, the movie had begun, and he sat down to munch his sandwich contentedly and enjoy the film.

Sometime during a barrage of commercials he felt the uneasiness begin, and he glanced around the room as if half-expecting someone to be there. He noticed then that the wind had come up and left his chair to go again to the window. It had been raining and the water on the glass made the lights of Clark's Harbor appear streaked and blurred. Harney Whalen shook his head and returned to his chair in front of the television set.

He tried to concentrate on the movie, but more and more he found himself listening to the wind as it grasped at the house. Each time he realized he didn't know what was happening on the television screen, he snapped himself alert and forced his attention back to it.

The storm grew.

Just before the end of the movie Harney Whalen felt a nerve in his cheek begin to twitch and wondered if he was going to have one of what he called his "spells." A moment later, as he was about to put the last bite of his sandwich into his mouth, his face suddenly contorted into an ugly grimace and his hands began twitching spasmodically. The scrap of sandwich fell to the floor beside his chair, and Harney Whalen stood up.

Robby and Missy lay awake in their bunks, listening to the rain splash against the window.

"You want to go look for him, don't you?" Missy suddenly whispered in the darkness, a note almost of reproach coloring her voice.

"Who?" Robby asked.

"Snooker."

"He's out there, isn't he?"

"Could we find him?"

"Sure," Robby said with an assurance he didn't feel.

"But what about the ghosts?"

"There isn't any such thing." Robby climbed down from the top bunk and sat on his sister's bed. "You didn't believe that old man, did you?"

Missy squirmed and avoided looking at her brother. "Why would he lie?"

"Grown-ups lie to children all the time, to make us do what they want us to."

Missy looked fearfully at her brother. She wished he wouldn't say things like that. "Let's go to sleep."

Robby ignored her and started dressing. Missy watched him for a moment, then she, too, began pulling her clothes on, all the time wishing she were still in bed. But when Robby opened the window and crept out, Missy followed him.

As soon as they were on the beach Missy thought she saw something, but it was too dark to be sure. It was a shape, large and dark against the heaving ocean, that seemed to be moving near the surf line, dancing almost, but without a pattern. She clutched Robby's hand.

"Look," she whispered.

Robby peered into the darkness. "What is it? I don't see anything."

"Over there," Missy hissed. "Right near the water." She pushed up against Robby, squeezing his hand so hard it hurt.

"Let go," Robby commanded, but the pressure remained.

"Let's go into the woods," Missy begged. "It'll be safer there."

Robby hesitated, then decided to go along with his sister; if Snooker was anywhere around, he was likely to be in the woods. They were creeping over the barrier of driftwood when Missy suddenly yanked on Robby's arm.

"Something's happening," she whispered. "Let's hide!"

Robby stiffened, then made himself look around, but there was nothing. Only the blackness of the night and the noise of the wind and surf, building on each other into a steady roar. Still, when Missy tugged on his arm again, he let himself be pulled down into the shelter of a log.

A few yards away Miriam Shelling stirred slightly, a strange sensation forcing itself into her consciousness. Her fingers were tingling and her hair seemed to stand on end, as if charged with static electricity. She stared blankly into the night, her confused mind trying to match the eerie feeling with the terrifying images she saw on the beach. Strangers, strangers with odd, dead-looking eyes, their faces frozen in silent agony, their arms raised, their hands reaching, clutching at something Miriam couldn't see.

She rose and began walking across the beach, drawn to the eerie tableau by a force beyond her control.

Missy peered fearfully over the top of the log, her eyes wide and unblinking.

There were several shapes on the beach now, but they were all indistinct—all except one, which moved outward toward the ocean slowly, steadily. Missy wanted to call out into the darkness, to disturb the strange scene that seemed to be unfolding silently in the maelstrom of noise that filled the night. But she couldn't find her voice, couldn't bring herself to cry out. Instead, transfixed, she watched as the strange forms, the forms that seemed to glow against the dark backdrop of sea and sky, circled slowly around the other shape, the distinct shape, the shape she knew was human.

They closed on the human figure, circling ever more tightly, until Missy could no longer tell one from another. When the single figure finally disappeared, Missy came to life, fear overwhelming her. She reached out to clutch Robby's hand.

Robby was gone.

Panicked, Missy forced herself to look back out at the beach once more. The beach was empty.

Where only a moment before the night had been filled with activity, with frightening shapes moving about in the dimness, now there were only blackness and scudding clouds.

Terrified, Missy ran for home.

When she got there Robby was in his bunk, sleeping peacefully.

On Sod Beach, the rising tide washed the sand from the corpse of the dog, and moments later a wave, whipped abnormally large by the wind, swept Snooker's remains out to sea.

By then the children were both in bed, though Missy was not asleep, and Miriam Shelling had disappeared from the beach.

## SEVEN

**M**ERLE GLIND GLANCED NERVOUSLY AT Brad and Elaine Randall as they came down the stairs the next morning and busied himself with the previous day's receipts. It was the fifth time he had checked them through. As soon as they passed his desk, his eyes left the ledgers and followed the Randalls out the front door.

"Did you get the feeling Mr. Glind wasn't too pleased to see us?" Elaine asked Brad as they descended from the porch.

"Maybe he had a bad night," Brad suggested.

"I don't think he approves of us," Elaine said, squeezing Brad's arm. "And I suspect he won't be the only one. I mean, after all, planning to spend a whole year just writing a book? It *is* scandalous." She sighed dramatically, sucked in the fresh morning air, and looked around. "Shall we go to the café? I'm hungry."

"I vote for the police station," Brad replied. "If there really is a house for rent we might as well get started—from what Glind had to say yesterday it might take all day just to talk what's his name into renting it to us."

"His name is Whalen, darling, and if I were you I'd remember it. He looks like a real red-neck to me, a small town dictator, and you won't win any points with him by not being able to remember his name."

They walked along the waterfront, then turned up the hill on Harbor Road. A few minutes later they had found the tiny police station.

"You'd be the Randalls?" the police chief said without standing up. Brad and Elaine exchanged a quick glance, then advanced into the room. Harney Whalen looked as if he'd been expecting them.

"Brad Randall, and this is my wife, Elaine." Brad was careful not to preface his name with his title. But it was soon apparent that there were few secrets in Clark's Harbor.

"Dr. Randall, isn't it?" Harney said mildly. "They tell me you're a psychiatrist." He neither invited the Randalls to sit down nor told them who "they" might be.

Brad immediately decided there was more to Whalen than a mere "small town dictator." He clearly knew something about manipulating people and putting himself in a position of strength. Well, two could play that game. "You don't mind if we sit down, do you?" he asked mildly, seating himself before Whalen had a chance to reply. Elaine, taking his cue, took a chair close to Brad.

Whalen surveyed them for a minute, feeling somehow slighted. He wasn't sure exactly what had happened, but he suspected he had lost the upper hand. The feeling annoyed him. "What can I do for you folks this morning?" he asked, though he knew perfectly well why they were there.

"They told us you have a house for rent," Brad said. He took a certain malicious pleasure in using the same vague "they" that the police chief had used on him, but Elaine shot him a look that told him to stop being cute and get on with it.

"That depends," Whalen said. "I might, and I might not. I think maybe I'd like to talk to you a little bit first."

"That's why we're here," Brad said with a smile. "We like the town."

"Can't say I blame you," Whalen replied. "I like Clark's Harbor myself. I was born here. So were my parents. My grandparents helped found the Harbor, back when it was a lumbering town. Still a little lumbering going on, but the big company closed years ago. Now it's mostly fishing. You fish?" Brad shook his head. "Too bad," the chief went on. "If you don't fish there isn't much else to do. You live in Seattle?" he suddenly asked, shifting the subject abruptly.

"Seward Park," Elaine answered. When the chief looked blank, she explained. "It's on the lake, at the south end."

"Sounds nice," Whalen commented neutrally. Then, eyes narrowed: "Why do you want to leave?"

"We don't, not permanently. I've been kicking around an idea for a book for quite a while, though, and in Seattle I just never seem to get to it. You know how it is—if it's not one thing it's another. I finally decided that if I'm ever going to get the damned thing written, I'd have to get out of town for awhile."

"Why Clark's Harbor?" the chief probed. "Seems to me there's a lot of better places for you than this. Pacific Beach or Moclips, or up to Port Townsend maybe."

Elaine smiled at the chief cordially, but she was growing annoyed by all his questions. If he has a house to rent why doesn't he just say so, she thought. Why the cross-examination? It's as though he doesn't want us here, the same as Mr. Glind. Being unwanted was a new experience for Elaine. Suddenly she was determined—almost as determined as Brad—to settle in Clark's Harbor and *make* these people accept her. Carefully keeping her annoyance concealed, she spoke warmly.

"But those are exactly the sorts of places we *don't* want to be," she said. "What we need is someplace quiet where Brad can concentrate. I don't know about Pacific Beach, but Port Townsend has entirely too many people who spend all their time having parties and talking about the books they're *going* to write. Brad wants to avoid all that and get the book written."

"Well, you people seem to know what you want," Harney said when she was finished. He smiled thinly. "Ever been on the peninsula during the winter?"

The Randalls shook their heads.

"It's cold," Whalen said simply. "Not a nice kind of cold like you get inland. It's a damp cold and it cuts right through you. And it rains all the time—practically every day. Not much to do during the winter, either— you can walk on the beach, but not for very long. Too cold. There's no golf course and no movies and only one television channel. And I might as well tell you, we Harborites aren't very friendly. Always been that way, likely always will be. We stick close together—most of us are related one way or another—and we don't take kindly to strangers. As far as we're concerned, if you weren't born here you're a stranger."

"Are you telling us not to come to Clark's Harbor?" Elaine asked.

"Nope. Only telling you what the town's like. You can make your own decision about whether you want to come. But I don't want you coming to me six months down the road and saying I didn't tell you this or I should have told you that. I believe in playing fair, and I believe people should know what they're getting into."

"Then you do have a house for rent?" Brad asked.

"If you can call it a house," Harney said, shrugging his shoulders.

"Tell us about it."

"It's out on Sod Beach. Been empty for quite a while." He smiled tightly at Elaine. "Ever cooked on a wood stove?"

She hadn't, but wasn't about to admit it to Whalen. "I can manage," she said softly, and prayed that Brad wouldn't laugh out loud. He didn't.

"You'll have to," Whalen said flatly. "The place has no gas or electricity."

"Running water?" Brad inquired.

"That it has, but only cold. Hot water you'd have to boil on the stove. As for heat, there's a big fireplace in the living room and a smaller one in the master bedroom. Nothing in the upstairs, but it doesn't get too bad since the stairs act like a chimney."

"You don't make it sound very inviting," Elaine admitted. In her mind's eye she pictured the old house she'd seen on the beach the day before, almost sure that was the one the police chief was describing. "How long has it been since anybody's lived there?"

"Nearly a year," Whalen replied. "As a matter of fact, most of their stuff's still there."

"Still there?" Brad repeated. "What do you mean?"

"They skipped out," Whalen said. "They got behind on the rent and one day I went out to tell them to pay up or go elsewhere, but they'd already gone. Took their clothes and their car but left everything else and never came back. So there's some furniture there. If you want the place I suppose you could use it. Don't think you'll want it though."

"Really?" Elaine said, trying to keep the sarcasm out of her voice but not entirely succeeding. "Why? Is it haunted?"

"Some people think so. It's the beach, I imagine."

"What about the beach?"

"It didn't used to be called Sod Beach. That just sort of came into being by accident. Used to be called the Sands of Death years ago. Then the maps shortened it to S.O.D., and that eventually got turned into Sod Beach."

"The Sands of Death," Brad said softly. "I'll bet there's a story about that."

Whalen nodded. "It was the old Klickashaw name for the beach. Can't remember what the Indian words were, if I ever knew. It don't matter anyhow. What matters is why they called the beach the Sands of Death. The Klickashaws had a wonderful custom—makes a hell of a good story for scaring kids with. It seems they had a cult—they called themselves Storm Dancers—that used to use the beach for executions."

"Executions?" Elaine echoed the word hollowly, not sure she really wanted to hear the tale.

"The story goes that the Klickashaws didn't like strangers any more than we do now. But they dealt with them a little bit different than we do. We at least tolerate 'em if we don't exactly make 'em welcome. The Indians didn't."

"You mean they took them out on the beach and killed them?" Brad asked.

"Not exactly. They took them out to the beach and let the sea kill them."

"I'm not sure I understand," Elaine said softly.

"They buried them in the sand," Harney Whalen said. His voice had become almost toneless, as though he was repeating the tale by rote. "They'd wait till low tide, then put their victims in a pit, and cover them with sand until only their heads were left showing. Then they'd wait for the tide to come in."

"My God," Elaine breathed. She could picture it in her mind—the terrified victims waiting for death, watching the surf's relentless advance, feeling the salt water lap at them, then slowly begin to wash over them; she could almost hear them gasping for air during the increasingly short intervals between the waves, and finally, inexorably . . . She forced the horrifying image from her mind and shuddered. "It's horrible," she said.

But Brad didn't appear to hear her. His eyes were fixed on the iron-haired police chief. "I don't see what that has to do with people not staying in your house on the beach," he said.

Whalen's smile was grim. "The legend has it, those people are still buried in the sand out there and that their ghosts sometimes wander the beach at night. To warn strangers about the beach," he added, leaning back in his chair to stare at the ceiling for a while before he spoke again. "Don't know if there's any truth to it, but I do know nobody ever stays in that house for long."

"Which might have something to do with the lack of amenities, right?" Brad said.

"Might," Whalen agreed.

"When can we see the house?" Brad asked. There was little point in further discussion. They would look at the house; either it would be suitable or it wouldn't.

"If you really want to look at it I suppose we could go out there right now. Frankly, I don't think you'll like it."

"Why don't you let us decide that?" Elaine said, forcing her voice to be cheerful. "We might like it a lot more than you think."

Before Whalen could respond to this the telephone rang. He plucked the receiver up.

"Chief Whalen," he said. Then he listened for a moment. Both Brad and Elaine were sure that his face turned slightly pale. "Oh, Jesus," he said softly. "Where is she?" There was another silence, then Whalen spoke again. "Okay, I'll get out there as fast as I can." He dropped the phone back on the hook and stood up. "It'll have to wait," he said. "Something's come up."

"Something serious?" Brad asked.

Whalen frowned, started to say something, then seemed to change his mind. "Nothing that concerns you," he said, almost curtly. Brad and Elaine got to their feet.

"Maybe later this afternoon——?" Brad began.

But Whalen was already on his way out the door. The Randalls followed him to his car. For a second Brad thought he had forgotten them, but as he started the motor Whalen suddenly stuck his head out the window. "Tell you what," he said. "Meet me out at the house, about three. Merle Glind at the inn can tell you how to get there." He gunned the engine, flipped the siren on, and took off with a resentful screech from the tires. The Randalls stood alone on the sidewalk, watching the car speed away.

"Well," Brad said when Whalen was out of sight. "What do you think about that?"

"He burned me up," Elaine said, glancing over her shoulder to make sure no one but Brad was close enough to hear. "My God, Brad, he acted like the whole town is some kind of private preserve. Like nobody has a right to live here unless his great-grandparents were born here."

"Kind of got your hackles up, did it?" Brad grinned.

"Damn right it did. I'll cook on that damned wood stove of his for the rest of my life if I have to, just to let him know he can't always have things the way he wants them."

"You might hate the house," Brad cautioned her.

She smiled at him almost maliciously. "Do you want me to describe it to you, or would you rather be surprised?"

"What are you talking about?"

"The house. I've seen it. I'm sure it's on the beach I was on yesterday, where I found the dead dog."

"You're kidding."

"No, I'm not. I walked right by it. It has to be the one. It was the only house on the beach and it looked as though no one had lived in it for years."

"What's it like?"

"I think a realtor would describe it as 'a picturesque beach charmer, perfect for the handyman, needs work, easy terms.' "

"Doesn't sound too promising."

"Mr. Whalen certainly didn't lie to us, I'll say that much."

They walked back to the inn. They would have a leisurely lunch, then walk up the beach to meet Harney Whalen at the old house. But when they reached the hotel they found Merle Glind in a state of extreme excitement.

"Isn't it terrible?" he asked them. When they looked totally blank, he plunged on. "Of course you haven't heard. It wouldn't mean anything to you anyway, would it?"

"What wouldn't?" Brad asked. "What happened?"

It was as if a door had slammed shut. The moment Brad asked the question, Merle Glind went rigid. His eyes narrowed and his mouth closed in a tight, thin-lipped line. Finally, he spoke. "It's none of your business," he said. "You take my advice, you go back where you belong."

Then, unable to resist, he told them.

Rebecca Palmer finished cleaning up the mess from breakfast and took the pan of dirty water outside to empty it onto the tiny cedar tree she had planted near the pottery shed. She examined the fragile-looking plant carefully, pleased to see that the makeshift fence she had rigged up around it seemed to be working—the little cedar showed no new signs of having served as dessert for the neighborhood deer. She was about to go back into the cabin when she heard the first faint sounds of the siren. At first she wasn't sure what it was, but as it grew louder she frowned a little. A fire truck? An ambulance? It was louder now, headed in her direction—but there was nothing out here except their own cabin. Deciding it must be Harney Whalen after a speeding car that hadn't had the sense to slow down as it passed through the Clark's Harbor speed zone, she went on into the cabin. But when the siren stopped abruptly a few seconds later and she thought she heard sounds of shouting, she went back outside.

There *were* voices coming from the woods now. She thought she could hear someone calling out, "Over this way," but she wasn't sure.

Rebecca took off her apron, tossed it onto a chair just inside the door, and strode out onto the beach. When she thought she was close to the place where the shouting had been going on, she picked her way carefully over the driftwood barrier and headed into the woods. A minute later she wished she'd followed the road.

The ground was nearly covered with ferns and salal, and everywhere she stepped there seemed to be an ancient, crumbling log buried in the undergrowth. She stopped after a while and strained her ears, trying to pick up the sounds of the voices that had drifted so plainly over the beach. Finally she called out.

"Hello? Is anybody out here?"

"Over here," a voice came back. "Who's that?"

"Rebecca Palmer."

"Stay away," the voice called. "Go back to the house and stay there. Someone will come over in a little while."

Rebecca paused, debating what she should do. It didn't take her long to make up her mind. She plunged onward toward the anonymous voice, annoyed at being told what to do on what she was almost sure was her own property.

After a few seconds she thought she could make out a flash of movement off to the left. Whatever was happening, it was definitely happening on the Palmers' land.

"Who's there?" she called.

"It's me, Mrs. Palmer," the voice came back, "Chief Whalen. Just go back home and I'll send someone down as soon as I can."

The hell I will, Rebecca thought. If something's going on, I have a right to know what it is. She'd be damned if Harney Whalen was going to tell her what to do. She pressed on through the tangle of undergrowth and suddenly broke through into a small clearing. Harney Whalen and Chip Connor and a man Rebecca didn't recognize stood in the clearing, looking upward. Automatically, Rebecca's eyes followed theirs. Suddenly she wished she had done what Whalen had told her to.

Rebecca began screaming.

"Oh, God," Whalen muttered under his breath. Then, aloud, he said, "Take care of her, will you Chip? Get her out of here." He pulled his eyes away from Rebecca, and looked once more up into the trees. . . .

# EIGHT

MIRIAM SHELLING'S BODY HUNG LIMPLY ten feet above the ground. Her eyes bulged grotesquely from her blackened face, and her tongue hung loosely from her mouth. The rancid smell of human excrement drifted on the breeze—Miriam had evacuated her bowels at the moment her neck had snapped.

A small group of people stared uncomprehendingly up at her, their stupor unbroken by Rebecca Palmer's screams. At the order from the chief,

Chip Connor separated himself from the group and went to Rebecca, leading her away by the same route as she had come.

"Oh, God," Rebecca repeated over and over again. "What happened to her? What happened to her? Last night——" she broke off suddenly, but Chip prompted her.

"What about last night?" he asked. They emerged from the forest and Chip helped her over the pile of driftwood, then gently guided her toward the cabin.

"Nothing," Rebecca said. For some reason she didn't want to tell the deputy that her husband had seen, even talked with, Miriam Shelling on the beach the evening before. She remained silent as they walked.

"Will you be all right?" Chip asked when they were inside the cabin.

"I'll be fine," Rebecca replied weakly. "Well, not fine exactly, but you go ahead and do what you have to do. I'll take care of myself."

Chip looked at Rebecca carefully, wondering if what she had seen could have put her into a state of shock; then, realizing that he probably wouldn't recognize shock if he saw it, he decided to go back to the clearing. When Doc Phelps arrived, Chip would have him come over and check on Mrs. Palmer. Patting her gently on the hand and assuring her that everything would be all right, Chip started back to the small clearing.

Rebecca watched him go, strangling back a sob. As soon as he disappeared from sight she wished she'd told him that she wasn't all right. She shivered a little, and put on a sweater even though the day was bright and warm, then built up the banked fire until it blazed hotly.

She said she was waiting for something, Glen had said last night. She was sitting on a piece of driftwood, and she was waiting for something. Suddenly Rebecca had a vision of Miriam Shelling sitting quietly, watching the beach, waiting for Death to come and take her to her husband. But why the beach, Rebecca wondered. Why out here?

In the clearing, Harney Whalen was wondering the same thing. He was remembering the previous day, too, when Miriam Shelling had appeared in his office demanding that he do something. She had been upset—very upset. He searched his mind, trying to remember every detail of what she had said, trying to find something—anything—that should have warned him that she was about to do something drastic. But there was nothing. She had only been demanding that he find whoever had killed her husband. And then, a sudden hunch coming into his mind, he left the clearing and beat his way through the woods to the beach. He looked out across the expanse of sand, then glanced north and south, taking a quick bearing. His hunch was right— Miriam had chosen a spot almost directly onshore from the place Pete Shelling had gotten caught in his own nets. Wondering if it meant anything or was merely a coincidence, he retreated back to the clearing. Doctor Phelps was waiting for him.

"Why hasn't she been taken down?" the old doctor demanded. He stared accusingly at Whalen over the rims of his glasses.

"I wanted to wait for you," Whalen said, trying not to feel defensive. But the doctor, eighty-six years old and still going strong, had treated

Harney Whalen when the police chief was a child and never let him forget that as far as he was concerned, Whalen was a child still.

"Well, it's pretty obvious she's dead, isn't it?" Phelps said sourly. "Am I supposed to climb up there myself to see what happened?"

Whalen was about to begin climbing the tree himself when Chip Connor reappeared.

"Chip? Think you can get her down?"

Chip forced himself to stare up into the tree once more, though his stomach rebelled every time his eyes fell on Miriam's face. He examined the branches carefully.

"No problem," he said out loud. Privately he wondered how he was going to be able to lower the body to the ground without—he broke off the thought without completing it and started up the tree. The climb was easy—the branches almost formed a ladder. A minute later he was level with the branch from which Miriam hung. Though it was invisible from below, a neat coil of rope lay in the fork of the tree. Carefully, Chip examined the knot from which Miriam was suspended, though a glance had told him how to get her down. All that held Miriam to the tree was a double slip knot, the kind children make in a string when they first discover how to knit it into a rope. He picked up the coil of rope and dropped it down. Then he made his way back to the ground.

"Give me a hand, will you, Harn?" he asked. He took hold of the rope that now dangled from the tree and yanked on it. He felt a double jerk as the knot gave way. Then, with the chief helping him, he gently lowered the corpse out of the tree.

Doctor Phelps examined her slowly, first cutting the rope away from Miriam Shelling's neck, then going over the body carefully, adjusting his glasses every few seconds as they slid down his nose. Finally he stood up, shrugged, and shook his head sadly.

"Why do they do it?" he muttered, almost under his breath.

"Suicide." Harney Whalen made the question a statement.

"Looks like it," Phelps agreed. "But damned strange if you ask me."

"Strange? What do you mean?"

"Not sure," the doctor said. "Seems like I remember something like this before. A fisherman dying and his wife hanging herself a few days later. It's these damned storms."

Whalen looked at the old doctor and Phelps smiled self-consciously. "Didn't know the weather affects people?" he said. Without waiting for a reply, he went on: "Well, it does. There's winds some places—down south, and in Switzerland and a couple of other places. They make people do funny things." He paused significantly. "And we've got these damned storms. Whip up out of nowhere, blow like hell, then they're gone. Vanished. They don't show up inland, they don't show up north or south. Just here. Makes you wonder, doesn't it?"

"No," Whalen said flatly. "It doesn't. What makes me wonder, is why she chose Glen Palmer's property to kill herself on. If she did."

"She did, Harn, she did," Phelps assured him. "Can't put this one on anybody. Not Palmer, not anybody."

"Maybe not," Whalen growled. "But I can try."

The old doctor stared at Whalen in puzzlement, then started toward his car. There was nothing further he could do. Behind him he heard Whalen begin giving orders for photographs to be taken and the body removed. But he was sure Whalen was not thinking about the orders he was giving. He was thinking about something else. Phelps wished he knew what it was.

They had barely spoken during lunch. As he finished his coffee and poured the last of a bottle of wine into his glass, Brad decided to face the issue.

"It's bothering you, isn't it?" he asked abruptly, sure that Elaine would know what he was talking about.

"Shouldn't it?" Elaine snapped. "We've been here two days and two people and a dog have died."

"You don't know how long the dog had been dead," Brad said.

"Then let's stick to the people."

"All right. How many people do you think die in Seattle every day? Or didn't you know that Seattle has the second highest suicide rate on the coast?"

"I know," Elaine said darkly, resenting her husband's logic.

"Then I should think you'd be wanting to pick up and move out. I'll bet the rate here is considerably lower than it is in Seattle. And frankly, I'm not terribly surprised by what happened."

Elaine looked sharply at Brad. "You aren't?"

"Think what it must have been like for her. Her husband was a fisherman—probably no insurance, and certainly no retirement fund with widow's benefits. He probably didn't even have any Social Security. Now, what is there for a woman in her position? Welfare? Small town people are very prideful about things like that."

"She could have sold the boat," Elaine said doggedly. "My God, Brad, women are widowed every day, but they don't kill themselves over it." She drained her wineglass, then set it down and sighed. "Oh, come on," she said tiredly. "Doesn't it all seem just a little strange to you?"

"Of course it does. But you have to be reasonable. It would have happened whether we'd been here or not. Two days earlier or two days later, and we never would have known about it. You're acting as though it's some kind of—I don't know—omen or something. And that's nonsense."

"Is it?" Elaine said softly. "Is it, really? I wish I could believe that, but there's something about this place that gives me the willies." She stood up suddenly. "Let's get out of here. Maybe the sunshine will help."

Brad paid the check and they made their way out of the café and down the stairs. In the tavern the same elderly men were playing checkers, as they had been the day before yesterday. Neither of them looked up at the Randalls.

"Let's walk up the beach," Elaine said. "Maybe by the time we get to the house Whalen will be there. If he isn't, I suspect we can get in by ourselves—it didn't look capable of being locked."

They retraced the path Elaine had taken the previous morning, but to Elaine it all looked different now. The sun had warmed the afternoon air, and the crackle of the morning freshness had long since gone. As they made their way across the point that separated the harbor from the beaches, Brad inhaled the scent of salt water mixed with pine. "Not like Seattle," he commented.

"There's nothing wrong with the air in Seattle," Elaine said defensively.

"I didn't say there was," Brad grinned at her. "All I said was that this isn't like the air in Seattle, and it isn't. Is it?"

Elaine, sorry she'd snapped at him, took his hand. "No," she said, "it isn't, and I'm being a ninny again. I'll stop it, I promise." She felt Brad squeeze her hand and returned the slight pressure. Then she saw a flash of movement and pointed. "Brad, look!" she cried. "What is it?"

A small creature, about the size of a weasel, sat perfectly still, one foot on a rock, staring at them, its tiny nose twitching with curiosity.

"It's an otter," Brad said.

"A sea otter? This far north?"

"I don't know. It's some type of otter though. Look, there's another!"

The Randalls sat down on a piece of driftwood, and the two small animals looked them over carefully. After what seemed to Elaine like an eternity, first one, then the other returned to its business of scraping at the pebbles on the beach, searching for food. As soon as the pair began its search, four smaller ones suddenly appeared as if they had received a message from their parents that all was well.

"Aren't they darling!" Elaine exclaimed. At the sudden sound the four pups disappeared and the parents once again turned their attention to the two humans. Then they, too, disappeared.

"Moral:" Brad said, "never talk in the presence of otters."

"But I couldn't help it," Elaine protested. "They're wonderful. Do you suppose they live here?"

"They probably have a Winnebago parked on the road and just stopped for lunch," Brad said dryly. Elaine swung at him playfully.

"Oh, stop it! Come on, let's see if we can find them."

Her vague feeling of unease—what she called the willies—was gone as she set off after the otters, picking her way carefully over the rocky beach. She knew it was no use, but she kept going, hoping for one more glimpse of the enchanting creatures before they disappeared into the forest. It was too late; the otters might as well have been plucked from the face of the earth. She stopped and waited for Brad.

"They're gone," she sighed.

"You'll see them again," Brad assured her. "If they're not on this beach they're probably on Sod Beach. It's the next one, isn't it?"

Elaine nodded and pointed. "Just beyond that point. If you want we can cut through the woods."

"Let's stick to the beach," Brad said. "That way I can get a view of the whole thing all at once."

"Sort of a general overview?" Elaine asked, but she was smiling.

"If you want to put it that way," Brad said with a grin.

They rounded the point and Brad stopped so suddenly Elaine almost bumped into him. "My God, it's beautiful, isn't it?" She came abreast of him and they stood together surveying the crescent that was Sod Beach. The sky was cloudless and the deep blue water and the intensely green forest were separated by a strip of sand that glistened in the brilliant sunlight, highlighted by the silvery stripe of driftwood sparkling next to the woods. The breakers, eight ranks of them, washed gently in, as if caressing the beach. Brad slipped his arm around Elaine's shoulders and pulled her close to him. With his free arm, he pointed.

"And that, I take it, is the house?"

Elaine's head moved almost imperceptibly in assent. For one brief moment she wished she could deny it, and instead say something that would take them forever away from Clark's Harbor and this beautiful beach with its bizarre past. For an instant she thought she could see the victims of the Sands of Death buried to the neck, their pitiful wailings lost in the sea wind and the roar of the surf that would soon claim them as its own. Then the vision was gone. Only the weathered house remained on the beach and, far off at the opposite end, the tiny cabin.

"Well, we won't have many neighbors, will we?" Brad said finally, and Elaine had a sinking sensation in her stomach. Brad had already made up his mind. She pulled free of his encircling arm and started moving up the beach.

"Come on," she said. "We might as well see what it's like." Brad trotted silently after her, ignoring the negative tone in her voice.

They had walked once around the house when Harney Whalen arrived, appearing suddenly out of the woods.

"Didn't think you folks were here yet," he called to them. "There wasn't any car out on the road."

"We walked along the beach," Brad replied, extending his hand to the approaching police chief. Whalen ignored the gesture, instead mounting the steps to the porch and fishing in his pocket for keys.

"It's not in very good shape. I haven't even had it cleaned since the last people . . . left."

Brad and Elaine exchanged a look at his slight hesitation, but neither one of them commented on it.

"The place seems to be sound enough," Brad remarked as Harney opened the front door.

"All the old houses are sound," Whalen responded. "We knew how to build them back then."

"How old is it?"

"Must be about fifty or sixty. If you want I suppose I could figure it out exactly. Don't see any point in it, though." His tone said clearly to Brad, Don't bother me with foolish questions.

But Elaine plunged in. "Did your family build it?" she asked. Whalen looked at her sharply, then his face cleared.

"Might say we did; might say we didn't. We sold the land the house is on and my grandfather helped build the house, then we bought it back when the Barons . . . left." Again there was the slight hesitation, and again the Randalls exchanged a look. Brad wondered how much more there was to the story and why the chief didn't want to tell them all of it. Then he looked around and realized that Whalen hadn't been kidding when he said the place hadn't been cleaned.

If it hadn't been for the layer of dust covering everything, Brad would have sworn the house was inhabited. Magazines and newspapers lay open on the chairs and floor, and the remains of a candle, burned to the bottom, sat bleakly on a table. There wasn't much furniture—only a sofa and two chairs—and what there was had obviously been obtained secondhand.

"They left in a hurry, didn't they?" Brad asked.

"Like I told you, skipped right out on me," Whalen said. Then, before Brad could comment further, he began telling them about the house.

"That's a double fireplace over there. The other side opens in the kitchen, and between the two of them the downstairs stays pretty warm. There's a bedroom through that door that I suppose you'd want to use, unless you've got kids. If you do, I'd put them in there, just in case of fire. It's a lot easier to get out of the first floor than the second."

"We don't have children," Elaine said, and stuck her head in the bedroom. It was a large room, facing the beach, and one wall was partly brick. She heard Whalen behind her explaining.

"The brick's part of the fireplace. The whole house is built around the fireplaces. You'd be surprised how much heat comes through those bricks, especially if you keep fires going in both rooms. Don't know why they don't build houses like that anymore—with all the talk about energy, you'd think they'd want to. But no, they build them with the fireplaces on an outside wall, and you can kiss the heat good-bye.

"If you go through there," he went on, "there's the bathroom—that opens into the kitchen as well. It's not so convenient for guests, but for whoever's living here it works just fine."

Elaine followed his directions and found herself in a small and incredibly grimy bathroom. She went through it and into the kitchen, where she stared at the forbiddingly large and ungainly wood stove. It seemed to challenge her, and she glared at it, silently telling the stove that come what may, she would learn to make it behave. But she wasn't too sure.

The kitchen was as filthy as the bathroom. The pots and pans used for the preparation of what had apparently been the last tenants' final meal were still stacked unwashed in the sink. Elaine swallowed hard, wondering if she would be expected to clean up the mess in the event they rented the place, and pushed on into the dining room.

The table was set, and at each place there was the remains of a half-eaten meal. The food had long since decayed, but from the looks of things it was an abandoned dinner. In the center of the table an ancient glass kerosene lamp stood, and Elaine could see that it was empty: whoever had lived here must have gotten up in the middle of dinner and left without even putting the lamp out. The lamp—God knew how much later—had simply burned itself out.

She was about to ask Whalen what had happened—why his tenants had "skipped out" in the middle of dinner—when she became aware that Brad was already talking to the police chief.

"How much would you want if you were to sell the place?" he was asking. Elaine felt her stomach sink again, and was relieved to hear Whalen's reply.

"It's not for sale," he said in a tone that left no room for argument. "It was a mistake when my grandfather sold the land in the first place. I won't repeat that mistake."

"You're going to pass it on to your children?"

"I never married," Harney replied. "Got lots of family, though. Most of the town is related to me one way or another. I wouldn't be surprised if my deputy wound up with this place—he's some kind of nephew."

"Well, let's talk about a lease, then," Brad said.

"Why don't we look at the upstairs?" Elaine interrupted.

Whalen shrugged and pointed the way toward the staircase that separated the living room from the dining room. He stayed downstairs as Brad followed Elaine to the second floor.

As soon as they were alone Elaine turned to her husband. "My God, Brad, it's a mess," she began.

Brad laughed. "Of course it's a mess, and I'll bet we can get it cheap. But picture it cleaned up. It's sound as a dollar and the location is perfect. Peace, quiet, and an unbeatable view. All it needs is a coat of paint on the inside and it'll be wonderful."

"But there's no electricity," Elaine protested.

"Well, you've always said you longed for the simple life," Brad teased.

Elaine wasn't amused. "Not this simple," she said, frowning. Then, at the look of deep disappointment on her husband's face, she relented. "Brad, it'll be so much work, you won't get anything done on your book for weeks!"

"I can think while I paint," Brad said. "It won't be like Seattle, where I have to keep my mind on my work every minute. And chopping wood is good exercise. I could stand to lose a few pounds." He patted his flat firm stomach with the confidence of a man who hadn't gained an ounce in ten years.

"If I have to cook on that stove, you'll lose more than a few pounds."

"You can learn," Brad said, and there was a pleading tone to his voice that Elaine had rarely heard in the twelve years of their marriage.

"You really want it, don't you?" she asked quietly, looking deep into his eyes.

He nodded. "I love it," he said. "I don't know exactly why, but I have a feeling about it. It's as though the whole place is calling out to me. Elaine, if I'm going to be able to write that book at all, I'm going to do it here."

She gave in, as she always did. If Brad wanted it that badly, she would learn to live with it. "All right," she said, smiling with a confidence she didn't feel. "We might as well have a look around up here and see how bad it is."

"You mean it?" Brad asked eagerly. And seeing the look on his face, Elaine realized that she did mean it. Her smile turned genuine.

"Come on, Randall, let's see how much work it's going to take to make this place livable."

\* \* \*

Harney Whalen was not waiting for them downstairs.

They found him on the beach in front of the house, his eyes fixed on the horizon. When they followed his gaze Brad and Elaine saw nothing but the sea and the sky, meeting darkly in a low bank of fog that seemed to be hanging barely within their vision.

"Mr. Whalen?" Brad said softly. There was no response from the police chief. "Mr. Whalen?" Brad repeated, louder this time. Whalen swung slowly around to look at them, his hands clenched into fists, the knuckles white with apparent strain.

"Are you all right?" Elaine asked. Whalen nodded curtly.

"We want the house," Brad said.

"No, you don't. And it doesn't matter anyhow, 'cause I won't sell it."

There was an intensity in his voice that Elaine found disturbing. But Brad ignored it. "We want to lease it," he said.

Whalen seemed to turn the matter over in his mind, then slowly unclenched his fist and put a hand inside his jacket.

"This is the lease. Take it or leave it."

Brad glanced at the lease, noting the rent—two hundred dollars a month—and ignoring most of the body of the agreement. It was a standard form, already filled out. Elaine handed him a pen and he quickly signed both copies, returning one to Whalen, keeping the other. Whalen took the signed lease disinterestedly, replaced it in his inner pocket, then suddenly pointed north. "See that cabin up there? Almost hidden in the trees? Those are your nearest neighbors. The Palmers." He stared at the distant cabin for a long time, then turned back to the Randalls. "The Palmers are strangers here too," he said darkly. Then he stalked off toward the woods.

Brad and Elaine watched him go, then started back south toward the Harbor and the inn.

"You know something?" Brad said after a long silence. "I'm not sure he even knows we leased the place. It was like he was in some kind of a trance."

Elaine nodded thoughtfully. "That was the impression I got too. Well, it's too late now. He signed it. The place is ours."

She turned back for a final look at the old house. For an instant she thought she saw something at the window—a face, but not really a face. More like a shadow.

She decided she was imagining things.

# NINE

THE DINING ROOM OF THE HARBOR INN was quiet that evening; Brad and Elaine Randall dined in isolation. The same small card sat on their table that had been there the previous evening, but there seemed to be no reason for its presence—only one other table was filled. The rest, set and waiting, remained deserted. A few people sat at the bar, but their conversation was minimal, and what there was, was whispered in low tones impossible to overhear.

"If you stretch your ear any further, you'll fall off your chair," Elaine finally said. Neither of them had spoken for minutes. It was as though the Randalls had almost unconsciously matched the silence that shrouded the room. Now her words seemed to bounce off the walls, and Elaine glanced around to see if anyone had overheard her. Apparently no one had—the other table of diners appeared to be engrossed in their steamed crab, the drinkers continued to stare morosely into their glasses.

"I can't figure it out," Brad said as he surveyed the quiet room. "I'd have expected the place to be full tonight, alive with people gossiping about—what was her name?"

"Miriam Shelling," Elaine supplied.

"Mrs. Shelling, yes. But from what little I've been able to hear, no one seems the least bit interested in her or what happened to her."

Just then Merle Glind bustled up to them, recommending the blueberry pie for dessert. Brad declined, but while Elaine struggled with herself, torn between her weight and her desires, he decided to pump the little hotel proprietor.

"Kind of quiet in here tonight, isn't it?"

Glind's head moved spasmodically and he took a quick inventory of the room, his expression testifying to a sudden fear that something must have gone wrong. When nothing looked amiss he turned back to Brad.

"About the same as usual," he said nervously. "About the same as usual."

"I'd have thought you'd have a good crowd tonight, all things considered," Brad ventured carefully.

"All things considered?" the little man repeated. "All what things?"

"Well, it just seems to me that people would be wanting to talk tonight."

"What about?" Glind asked blankly.

"Mrs. Shelling?" Brad suggested. "I mean, isn't it a little unusual to have a woman commit suicide here?"

"Why, I don't know," Glind said vaguely, appearing to turn the matter over in his mind. "But now that you mention it, I suppose it is." There was a long pause, then Glind spoke again. "Not that it's any of our concern, of course."

Elaine frowned slightly and gazed at the strange man. "I should think it would be everyone's concern," she said softly. "I always thought that in towns like this everyone looked after everyone else."

"We do," Glind replied. "But the Shellings weren't really part of the town."

"I thought they lived here." Brad's voice was flat, as if he were merely prompting a statement he knew was inevitable.

"Oh, they lived here, but they were newcomers. They didn't really belong."

"Newcomers? How long had they lived here?"

Glind shrugged as if it was of no consequence. "Fifteen, twenty years. Not long." The Randalls gazed at each other across the table, silently exchanging a thought. *How long does it take? How long, before you're a part of Clark's Harbor?* Their unspoken exchange was broken by Merle Glind's forced cheer.

"What about that pie? I guarantee it myself!"

Elaine jumped a little, as if she had been lost somewhere, and without thinking she accepted Glind's offer. He scurried away. When they were alone Brad and Elaine smiled weakly at each other.

"Fifteen or twenty years," Elaine said wryly. "Somehow I'd been thinking in terms of a couple of lonely months and then the Welcome Wagon suddenly appearing."

"Look at it this way: what would you have in common with most of these people anyway? We've always been pretty self-sufficient—"

"Pretty self-sufficient is one thing," Elaine interrupted. "Being pariahs is absolutely another."

"I wouldn't worry too much about it," Brad reassured her as the pie arrived. "somewhere in Clark's Harbor there's got to be someone who'll welcome us. It's just a matter of finding them."

Elaine bit into the pie and was pleased to find that it met her expectations. Then a thought hit her. "The Palmers!" she exclaimed.

Brad understood at once. "Of course," he said, smiling. Then he dropped his voice a little in a surprisingly good imitation of Harney Whalen's morbid bass tones. "They're strangers here, you know!"

Elaine laughed and eagerly finished her pie.

"It doesn't concern us!" Glen Palmer said for the fourth time. He tried to smile, but the hollow, sunken look in his wife's eyes frightened him.

"How can you say that?" Rebecca shot back. "She was found on our land, Glen." When he didn't respond she pressed harder. "That clearing *is* on our property, isn't it?"

"Yes, I suppose it is," Glen admitted reluctantly. "But it still doesn't concern us."

"What about the children? Suppose they'd been the ones to find her,

Glen. Just suppose that on their way to school Robby and Missy had decided to cut through the woods and found her?''

She could see that her point was being lost on her husband and she searched desperately for a way to make him understand.

''You can't imagine what it was like,'' she went on limply. ''You just can't imagine it.'' She was about to describe the grisly scene for him once more when she heard the children coming in.

''What *what* was like?'' Robby demanded. Rebecca stretched her arms out to her son but Robby backed away and moved to his father's side. His child's mind knew something was wrong between his parents, and he was instinctively drawn to his father. ''You mean Mrs. Shelling?'' he guessed.

''How did you know about her?'' Rebecca gasped.

Robby's face broke into a grin. ''Jimmy Phipps went home for lunch and his mother told him all about it. Did you really see her?''

For a split second Rebecca considered denying it. But she and Glen had always been truthful with their children. Now, though it might cause her pain—indeed, it was sure to—she felt she had to discuss what had happened with Robby. ''Yes,'' she said slowly, ''I did.''

Robby's eyes widened. ''Did she really crap her pants?'' he demanded. Rebecca winced, but Glen had to suppress a grin.

''It's something that happens to people when they die, dear,'' Rebecca said gently.

''What did she look like? Jimmy Phipps said her face was all blue and her tongue was hanging out.''

Rebecca, remembering, had to fight to control a contracting stomach. ''It doesn't matter what she looked like, Robby,'' she said almost desperately.

Robby's mind worked at the problem, trying to decipher why the appearance of the body didn't matter. It had certainly mattered to Jimmy Phipps. He turned to his father, as if the problem was one only a man could solve.

''What happened to her?'' he asked gravely.

''She was very unhappy, Robby, and she just decided she didn't want to live anymore. Can you understand that?''

Robby nodded gravely. ''I feel like that sometimes, but then the storms come and I feel better.''

''Oh, Robby,'' Rebecca cried. She knelt by her son and drew him closer to her. ''You mustn't ever feel that way. Not ever! Why, what would we do without you?''

A small frown knit Robby's brow and he disentangled himself from his mother. ''It hardly ever happens,'' he said impatiently. ''And anyway, it isn't such a bad feeling. In a way it's kind of exciting.'' Then, before his parents could pursue the subject any further, he posed another question. ''Did Mrs. Shelling do a bad thing? I mean, if she didn't want to live anymore, why should she have to?''

Rebecca and Glen exchanged a glance, and Glen knew it was going to be left up to him to answer his son's question.

''It just isn't the best thing to do,'' he said carefully. ''If you have a problem, it's much better to try to find a way to solve it. Dying doesn't do any good at all, for anyone.''

The answer seemed to satisfy the boy. He shrugged, then gazed up at his father. ''Can I go look for Snooker?''

''No!'' Rebecca snapped without thinking. Suddenly the idea of her son out on the beach, the beach on which Miriam Shelling had spent her last hours, terrified her. ''It's too late,'' she said hurriedly, trying to take the sting out of her words as Robby recoiled. ''You should both be in bed.''

''I'll go out in a little while and have a look,'' Glen promised his son. But for the first time since they had come in Missy spoke.

''You won't find him,'' she said. ''He's gone and we aren't ever going to see him again.''

''You keep saying that,'' Robby said. ''But you don't know.''

''I do too know,'' Missy shot back, her voice rising.

Rebecca almost intervened, but suddenly a quarrel between her children seemed a welcome respite from the strain she had been feeling all day. ''Why don't you two take your fight into the bedroom?'' she suggested.

The children stared at their mother, shocked into silence by her failure to try to mediate between them. A moment later, warming to their argument, they tumbled off to the tiny bedroom.

As soon as they were gone Rebecca turned to Glen. ''And I don't want you going out there either,'' she said.

''I don't see that there's much choice now,'' Glen said with a shrug. ''I already promised Robby and I can't really back out of it. Besides, we've been walking on the beach at night for months. You know as well as I do that it's perfectly safe.''

''That was before last night,'' Rebecca said, shuddering. ''It's all different now.''

''It is not different, Rebecca,'' Glen said, placing his hands on her shoulders and forcing her to look at him. ''Miriam Shelling's problems had nothing to do with us, and it has nothing to do with us that she killed herself out here.'' He laughed, but there was no mirth in the sound. ''Well, at least now we know what she was waiting for.'' He began putting on his coat.

''Please?'' Rebecca pleaded. ''At least wait until I've calmed down.'' Glen tossed his coat aside, sat down on the couch next to his wife, and drew her near him. In the bedroom, the argument subsided. For a while, the tiny cabin was quiet.

''Let's go for a walk,'' Brad suggested as he and Elaine stepped out of the dining room. ''It's gorgeous tonight—no storm and a full moon.'' He grinned suggestively. ''And we haven't been romantic on a beach in years.''

Elaine started to protest but changed her mind before an expression of doubt even clouded her face. She had been silly enough for a while; it was time to start acting like an adult. ''Best idea you've come up with since we got here,'' she said with a wink. ''I'll go up and get our coats.''

A few minutes later they were on the beach, and as she watched the moonlight glisten on the water, Elaine was glad she'd put aside her trepidations. The steady rhythm of the surf, soft tonight in the stillness, soothed her. She took Brad's hand.

"Let's walk up to the house," she said. "I'll bet it's beautiful in the moonlight."

They walked slowly, enjoying the night-quiet. When they came to the rocky stretch just before Sod Beach, they moved with particular care, hoping for a glimpse of the otter family. But there was nothing except a sudden clattering sound from somewhere overhead. They looked up in time to see the silhouette of an owl as it left the branch of a tree, swooping low, then beating its way up to cruise over the beach.

"We won't see the otters tonight," Brad commented. "They'll have packed the pups off somewhere."

"He's so big," Elaine said as the owl disappeared. "His wingspan must be six feet."

"Gives him lots of glide. That way his prey doesn't have any warning before he dives."

They rounded the point and Sod Beach suddenly lay before them, its vibrant colors flattened by the darkness to dramatic shades of black and white. The sand seemed to gleam with a fluorescence of its own in the silvered light, and the bank of driftwood lining the length of the beach glowed whitely. In the midst of the pale expanse of sand, the old house stood, dark-shadowed, aloof from the eerie moonlight that bathed its surroundings.

"It's like a fantasy," Elaine whispered. "I've never seen anything so beautiful."

Brad said nothing but pulled his wife close to him. They stood for a long time, trying to comprehend the almost unearthly beauty of the place and listening to the soft music of the gentle surf. Finally they walked out onto the beach, leaving a double row of footprints neatly embedded in the otherwise unmarred smooth damp sand.

They circled the house, but widely, as if unwilling to come close enough to discover the flaws in the ancient structure. Neither of them suggested going in, certain that the tired remains of the last tenancy would pull them away from the magic of the night. Instead, after completing their survey of their new home, they continued walking up the beach until, by mutual but unspoken consent, they settled themselves on the sand, leaning against one of the massive driftwood stumps.

"I take it all back," Elaine said. "This place is paradise."

Brad reached in his coat pocket and pulled a pipe and some tobacco from its depths. He stuffed the pipe, lit it, put the tobacco back in his pocket, and stared out to sea.

"I've been thinking," he said. "I'm going to change the thrust of the book."

Elaine stirred against him, then settled in closer. "What made you think of that?"

"Lots of things. This place. Robby Palmer."

"Robby Palmer?" Elaine sat up, looking sharply at her husband. "That's a hell of a change, from bio-rhythms to Robby Palmer!"

"Not necessarily. There's something about this place, something that affects everybody here one way or another. Who knows? It might have something to do with bio-rhythms. And if I can find out, it would make a great book. Particularly if I can use Robby Palmer to tie it all together. Think of it: a place—this place—where something seems to screw people up. People like Miriam Shelling, and maybe Harney Whalen. But for Robby, who was already screwed up, whatever it is that's here straightens him out."

"How lucky for you that Robby just happens to live up the beach," Elaine said sarcastically.

Brad ignored the gibe. "It could be a very valuable book," he said. "In more ways than one."

"You mean a best seller?"

"Not *just* a best seller. Something worthwhile too. And if I could make a lot of money from a book . . ." His voice trailed off and he left the thought hanging.

"Well, I still don't like the idea, but do what you want." Elaine's arms slipped around Brad and she hugged him tightly. "You always do."

"That doesn't make me sound very nice," Brad said softly.

Elaine smiled in the darkness, knowing Brad would feel the smile even if he didn't see it. "I didn't mean it that way. I just meant that in the end you usually do what you want to do. It's usually the right thing to do and I don't have any objections to it, but it's still true."

"You know what you are?"

"What?" Elaine asked.

"A hopelessly unliberated woman."

"You found me out," Elaine replied. "But don't tell anybody about it—it's not very fashionable."

"Fashionable enough for me," Brad whispered. His hand slid inside her coat and began caressing her breast. "Everything about you is fashionable enough for me." He nuzzled her, then whispered in her ear. "When was the last time we made love on a beach?"

"We never did," Elaine whispered back. "But there's a first time for everything." Her fingers began fumbling with his belt, and she felt the hardness in his trousers. She wriggled in the sand, and pulled him over on top of her. . . .

"I think we ought to go look for him again," Robby Palmer whispered to his sister.

"He isn't out there," Missy whispered back. "He's gone and we're never going to see him again." She turned over in the lower bunk and buried her head in the pillow.

"He isn't either," Robby insisted. "He's probably caught in a trap in the woods or something." He slid down from the upper bunk and poked at Missy. "Are you asleep?"

"Stop that," Missy complained, wriggling down under the covers. "I'll call Mother."

"If you do I won't take you with me."

Missy sat up and peered at her brother. "I won't go out there again," she whispered. Robby shrugged. "It's too dark," Missy said, glancing at the curtained window.

"It is not," Robby countered. "The moon's out and it's shining on the water. Look."

Reluctantly, Missy left her bed and peeked out the window. A deep shadow hung just outside the cabin, but through the trees she could see the silvery light playing on the water.

"We should stay in bed," she decided.

"Well, you can stay in bed if you want," Robby said, pulling his jeans on. "I'm going out to find Snooker."

Missy crept back into bed and pulled the covers up under her chin. She watched with wide eyes as Robby finished dressing. Then he carefully opened the window and climbed out. As soon as he was gone Missy jumped out of bed and ran to the window. Her brother was nowhere in sight. She wished he hadn't gone out. Not after last night. She stayed at the window for a minute, then made up her mind.

Rebecca looked up from her knitting as her daughter appeared in the doorway of the tiny bedroom.

"Can't sleep, darling?" she asked.

"Robby's gone," Missy said. "He went out to look for Snooker. I told him not to, but he went anyway."

Rebecca felt a stab of fear in her heart and turned to Glen. He was already on his feet, pulling his windbreaker on.

"When did he leave?"

"Just now," Missy said, her eyes bright as she watched her father dash to the front door. "He's all right, Daddy," she called, but Glen was gone. Rebecca put her knitting aside and gathered Missy into her arms.

"Of course he is," she said softly, "of course he is." But inside, she wasn't sure.

Robby dashed around the corner of the house and into the woods. As soon as he was gone his sister would tell on him. Girls were like that, he thought, wishing he had a brother instead of a sister. Then he forgot about Missy and concentrated on making his way through the woods. He followed the path that would lead him out to the main road but turned off to the right before he got to the highway. He knew this path would take him through the woods, but he wasn't sure where it would come out. And it all looked different at night, even with the moonlight. There were shadows everywhere—shadows that completely blotted out the path and made the trees seem bigger and more forbidding than they were in the daytime.

When he heard his father's voice calling him a few minutes later, he almost went back, then changed his mind. Missy would laugh at him. He hurried along the path, trying to see, but stumbling every few steps as his toe caught on roots that lay hidden in the darkness. Then he came to a clearing and stopped.

Something inside him told him that this was the spot where Mrs. Shelling had hanged herself. He stared around, searching the trees, trying to determine which branch she might have used. A sudden sound startled him, then an enormous shadow swept across the clearing. A bird, Robby told himself. It's just a bird. But he left the clearing and continued along the path. Behind him he thought he could hear his father's footsteps, following him. He walked faster. Then he began running.

Brad and Elaine Randall lay in each other's arms, enjoying the closeness they always felt after making love.

"That was nice," Elaine murmured. "Am I wicked for thinking sex is always better outdoors?"

"Not wicked," Brad replied. "Just sensuous."

Elaine poked him and he poked her back. They began tickling each other, rolling in the sand and giggling, until Elaine suddenly stopped and lay still.

"Did you hear something?"

"Just the surf."

"No, something else. A shout."

Brad listened for a moment but could hear nothing but the crashing of the surf. Suddenly a shadow fell over them and Brad looked up. A cloud had covered the face of the moon and the night grew darker.

"I don't hear anything," he began, but Elaine cut him off.

"Shh." She listened intently, then spoke again. "There's something there," she whispered. "I hear something in the woods." She pulled her coat tight around her and stood up.

"Don't be silly," Brad said. "It's nothing, just some animal." But his eyes went to the forest, peering into its blackness. Then he heard it: the crackling of twigs. He got to his feet, pulling Elaine up next to him, an arm protectively around her shoulders. He heard a shout from far up the beach and the crackling sound again. Closer. It seemed to be in the woods directly in front of him.

"Who's there?" he called.

Silence.

"Who is it?" Brad called again. The sounds began again, louder now, and heading right toward them. He moved Elaine behind him, so that who-ever—whatever—was coming out of the woods would face him first.

The cloud that had covered the moon drifted on, and the beach was once more bathed in an eerie glow. Looking at him from the other side of the pile of driftwood was a small and very worried face.

"It's all right," Brad said softly. "Come on over here."

Robby Palmer, his terror easing, began scrambling through the drift-wood. Whoever these people were, he would be safer with them. He had not felt safe in the woods. Not safe at all.

# TEN

**R**OBBY HESITATED AT TOP OF THE MOUND OF driftwood, suddenly unsure of himself. For a second he was tempted to take off, not back into the woods, but up the beach toward the soft glow that emanated from the window of the cabin. When Elaine suddenly stepped out from behind Brad, Robby made up his mind.

"I'm looking for my dog," he said shyly.

"Isn't it a little late for that?" Brad asked. "Most nine-year-olds are home in bed."

Robby cocked his head inquisitively. "How did you know how old I am?"

"Now how could I forget something like that?" Brad said. Then his brow furrowed. "Don't you recognize me?"

Robby shook his head.

"I'm Dr. Randall, from Seattle. You really don't remember me?"

"Are you the doctor I went to when I was sick?"

"That's right."

"I don't really remember being sick either."

Before Brad could pursue the subject, Elaine went to Robby and knelt beside him.

"Do your parents know where you are?"

"I think so," Robby replied. "I think I heard my father calling me a little while ago."

"Did you answer him?"

Robby shook his head. "It might not have been my father," he said. "It might have been somebody else."

"Who?" Brad asked.

"I—I'm not sure," Robby stammered.

"Well, I think we'd better get you home. I'll bet your parents are worried sick about you."

"But I have to find my dog," Robby protested. "He's been gone two nights now and Daddy won't go look for him." Robby looked to be on the verge of tears and Elaine put her arms around him. She was suddenly sure that the dog she had found on the beach had been his. "There, there," she soothed him. "Don't you worry about anything. He's probably wandered off somewhere, but he'll come home."

"Missy says he won't," Robby said flatly. "She wouldn't help me look for Snooker either, because she says he's gone."

Before either of the Randalls could determine the meaning of this odd statement, they heard a call from the forest.

"Robby? Robby!"

"Over here!" Brad shouted. "On the beach!"

A moment later Glen Palmer broke out of the forest at almost the same spot where Robby had appeared a few minutes earlier.

"Dr. Randall! What are you doing out here? You haven't seen Robby around—" He broke off as he saw his son and climbed swiftly over onto the beach. "Robby! I've been looking for you!"

"I was trying to find Snooker," Robby wailed. "You said you were going to look for him but you weren't, so I—" He ran to his father and buried his face against him. Glen held him for a moment, looking helplessly at the Randalls, then disentangled himself from his son. He knelt down and met the boy's tear-filled eyes.

"I was going to come out and look for him but your mother needed me," he explained. "We were talking, and as soon as we finished, I'd have come out looking."

Robby peered doubtfully at his father, wanting to believe him, and Glen shifted his own gaze to Brad Randall.

"You haven't seen a dog out here, have you?" he asked doubtfully. Elaine's eyes darted to the child, and she bit her lip.

"We've only been here a few minutes ourselves," she said, evading the question entirely. She'd tell Palmer the bad news when the boy was out of hearing. "We wanted to see what the place looked like at night."

Glen looked puzzled. "Sod Beach?"

"The house," Elaine explained. "We rented the old house today." She gestured in the direction of the dilapidated structure, but Glen's puzzlement only seemed to deepen.

"Whalen rented it to you?" he asked. He shook his head. "Well, I'll be damned."

"He didn't seem too eager but he gave in," Brad said with a chuckle. The chuckle faded as he remembered the police chief's odd behavior just before the lease was signed, but he didn't mention it to Glen.

"He wouldn't rent it to me at all," Glen said almost bitterly. Then he brightened. "Say, why don't you walk up the beach with me? Rebecca's waiting for me—all upset about Robby—and I'd better get back. Besides, you promised to stop by yesterday and then you didn't. Rebecca hasn't said anything but I think she's disappointed. Frankly she doesn't have many people to talk to out here."

"Of course," Elaine said immediately. "We should have stopped today but we've just been so busy. I mean, coming to a decision like the one we just made takes all your concentration. But it was rude of us, wasn't it?" She took Glen's arm and started up the beach, leaving Brad to walk with Robby. Brad, sensing immediately that his wife was going to tell Glen about the dog, kept Robby occupied. And while he kept the boy busy, he observed him.

The change in Robby was as dramatic as Glen had described it. Not a trace remained of the frenetic, anguished child Brad Randall remembered so vividly. Instead, he found himself walking along the beach with a remarkably normal nine-year-old boy, a child who was obviously active, but not overactive; who talked easily, readily, but not with the frenzied pace he had constantly displayed only months before. As they walked Brad found his puzzlement at the change deepening, found himself wondering exactly what could have happened to Robby Palmer, or what might still be happening to him. The boy was almost *too* normal. Brad found it vaguely disturbing. . . .

When she was sure they were out of earshot of her husband and Glen Palmer's son, Elaine suddenly turned to Glen. "Was your dog black-and-white, sort of a spaniel?"

"You've seen him?" Glen asked eagerly.

"I think so," Elaine replied, her voice somber. "Yesterday morning I took a walk on the beach. I found a dead dog, buried in the sand. It was medium-sized, black with whitish patches."

"That sounds like Snooker," Glen said. "He was a mutt, but there was a lot of springer spaniel in him." He paused for a moment, then: "You say he was buried in the sand?"

"Not very deep. The sea might have done it, I suppose, but I'm not sure. His neck was broken."

Glen stopped and turned to face Elaine. "Broken? What do you mean?"

"I'm not sure," Elaine said unhappily. "He didn't seem to have any other injuries, but his neck was broken. Brad said he could have been hit by a piece of driftwood that was coming in on the surf the night before. . . ." She trailed off, thinking the story sounded hollow. As if he read her mind, Glen shook his head.

"Doesn't sound very plausible, does it?"

"I didn't think so," Elaine said. "I suppose I should have told you before, but I didn't want to, not in front of Robby."

"Of course not," Glen agreed. "I'll wait a day or so—maybe try to find the kids a new puppy—then tell them. Or maybe I won't tell them at all. I'll just find them another dog and that'll take their minds off Snooker."

Robby and Brad caught up with them in the trees in front of the Palmers' cabin, and as they approached, Glen called to his wife.

"Rebecca? Come on out here—we've got company!"

Rebecca appeared at the door and, seeing her son, immediately swept him into her arms. Robby wriggled, protesting that he was fine, and finally Rebecca let him go, straightened up, and looked with surprise at Brad and Elaine.

"You remember Dr. Randall, of course," Glen said. "This is his wife, Elaine. I found them on the beach near the old Baron house. They've leased it and we're going to be neighbors, so I brought them home for a glass of wine."

"Come in," Rebecca urged them. "It's not nearly as big as the house you got, but there's room for everyone." She led Brad and Elaine into the small main room and pressed them to take the two chairs usually reserved for her and Glen. "Let me get Robby settled in bed. Glen, why don't you open the wine?'' She disappeared into the tiny bedroom, and while Glen poured four glasses of wine Elaine and Brad inspected the cabin, Brad curiously, and Elaine carefully. By the time Rebecca reappeared Elaine was ready.

"Can you really cook on that stove?'' she asked, making the question almost a challenge.

Rebecca looked blank for a second, then burst into laughter.

"It isn't nearly as difficult as it looks,'' she said. "Come here and I'll show you what happens.'' She bent over the stove with Elaine, demonstrating how the various vents worked and how to control the fire so that the burners would operate at various levels of heat.

"The main trick is to keep the fire fairly small so that you can move it around and control it. Otherwise the thing gets so hot you can't even get close to it. But if your husband is anything like mine,'' she finished, "you won't have any problem—there won't ever be enough wood to build a really big fire.''

Elaine shook her head doubtfully. "I don't know,'' she said. "Something tells me we're going to be eating out a lot.''

"We can't,'' Rebecca said. "And even if we could, we wouldn't. Much as I hate to admit it, I've gotten to the point where I actually enjoy cooking on this thing. The worst part of living on the beach is bathing.''

"My God,'' Elaine breathed, closing her eyes as if to shut out a hideous vision. "I hadn't even thought about that!''

"You'll learn to *dream* about it,'' Rebecca laughed.

Elaine turned to her husband. "Did you hear that, Brad?''

"I heard.'' Brad looked unconcerned. "And I know perfectly well that I'm capable of getting myself spotless in one small pan of hot water. And after I've bathed in it, I can shave in it.''

Elaine gaped at him. "You? You're the one who loves to use up all the hot water with twenty-minute showers.''

"If it's available, why not?'' Brad countered. "But loving to do it and having to do it are two different things. Just give me a couple of quarts of hot water—I'll be fine.''

"Good,'' Elaine said sarcastically. "Then you can boil a gallon at a time and I'll use what's left.''

"Before we get too involved in the glories of primitive living,'' Glen interrupted, "I have a question. How on earth did you get Harney Whalen to rent you the old Baron house? We tried, and he absolutely refused.''

"Maybe he didn't want to rent to someone with children,'' Elaine suggested.

"That old house?'' Rebecca said. "I don't mean to sound negative— God knows it's a lot better than this—but still, it isn't a place children can do much damage to.''

"It was something else,'' Glen said. "I'm still not sure exactly what it was. I thought it had something to do with us personally at first, but then I changed my mind. I figured he just didn't want to rent the house at all, especially to strangers. I guess I was wrong.''

"I'm not so sure,'' Brad said pensively. "He wasn't eager to rent to us either. When he finally did he was acting strange, almost as though he was thinking about something else entirely."

"That *is* strange," Rebecca commented.

"This whole place is strange," Brad offered. "I think I'll write a book about it."

"A book?" Glen looked at Brad critically, then shook his head. "Nope. You don't look like a writer."

"I'm not," Brad said. "But I've been kicking around an idea for a book for a long time. Now seems like a good time to do it, and Sod Beach seems like a good place. So here we are."

"Just like that?" Rebecca asked.

"Well, not quite," Elaine replied. "We have to go back to Seattle and close up our house. But I should think we'll be moving out here in a couple of weeks."

"Two weeks," Rebecca said, almost under her breath. "I can make it that long." She hadn't intended to speak out loud, but everyone in the room heard her. Glen looked embarrassed, but Brad decided to probe.

"I'm not sure what that means," he said with a tentative smile that he hoped would put Rebecca at her ease.

Rebecca flushed a deep red and tried to recover herself. "Nothing, really," she began. Then she changed her mind. "Yes, I do mean something by it," she said. "It's damned lonely out here and sometimes I'm frightened. You have no idea how glad I am that you're going to be living just down the beach. I know it may sound strange since I barely know you, but sometimes this place gets to me. Now I won't be the only one."

"The only one?" Elaine repeated Rebecca's last words.

"The only stranger here," Rebecca said. Then she looked from Brad to Elaine, her expression almost panicky. "You *are* strangers here, aren't you? You don't have relatives in Clark's Harbor?"

"I see," Elaine said, leaning back and relaxing. She smiled at Rebecca. "No, we don't know a soul here except you, and we're not related to anybody, and," she added in a rush, "I know exactly what you're talking about. It's not easy to be a stranger in Clark's Harbor, is it?"

"It's terrible," Rebecca said softly. "Sometimes I've wanted to just pick up and leave."

"Why haven't you?" Elaine asked.

"Lots of reasons," Rebecca said vaguely. "We've got most of our money tied up here—not that there's very much of it. If we were to leave now we wouldn't have anything left."

"And, of course, there's Robby," Glen added quietly.

Rebecca looked almost embarrassed but Brad picked the subject of Robby up with apparent eagerness. "The change in him is almost unbelievable. In fact, if I hadn't see him myself, I wouldn't have believed you. And you don't have any idea what caused it?"

"Not the slightest." Glen shrugged. "But we aren't about to question it either. As long as Robby stays the way he is now, we'll stay in Clark's Harbor, come what may."

"How bad has it been?" Elaine asked. "Or am I prying?"

"You're not prying at all," Rebecca said emphatically. "In fact, maybe it would be good for us to talk about it, just to hear what someone else thinks. Sometimes we think we're paranoid about Clark's Harbor. But frankly, I hate to subject you to it—it's so depressing." She picked up the bottle of wine and refilled everyone's glass.

"Oh, come on," Elaine said. "If nothing else at least it'll let us know what we're in for."

Softly, almost as if she were ashamed, Rebecca explained how they had come to feel that the whole town was somehow united against them. "But there's never anything you can put your finger on," Glen finished. "Every time something goes wrong there's always a reasonable explanation. Except that I always have the unreasonable feeling that if I weren't a stranger here none of it would ever have gone wrong at all. And then, of course, there was this morning."

"This morning?" Elaine thought a moment. "Oh, you mean Mrs. Shelling?"

Glen nodded and Rebecca's face tightened.

"Did you know her?" Brad probed.

"Not really," Glen said. "I ran into her last night on the beach. Apparently just before she did it."

"Just before she did it?" Elaine echoed. "You don't mean—?"

"It happened on our property," Glen said. "Our land goes back into the woods to the road, then parallels the road for a hundred feet or so. Miriam Shelling hanged herself from one of our trees."

"Oh, God," Elaine said softly. "I'm so sorry. Rebecca—it must have been terrible for you."

"I keep seeing her," Rebecca whispered. "Every time I close my eyes I keep seeing her. And the kids—what if one of them had seen her?"

"But it wasn't anything to do with you," Brad said.

"Wasn't it?" Rebecca's face was bleak. "I keep wondering. We talked to Miriam yesterday. She came to the gallery and started ranting at us. We thought she was just upset—"

"Obviously she was," Brad pointed out.

"She kept saying 'they' got her husband and 'they' were going to get us too. And then last night—" Rebecca broke off her sentence and fought to keep from bursting into tears. While she struggled to hold herself together, her husband spoke.

"So you can see, it hasn't been easy." He laughed self-consciously. "Some welcome we're giving you, huh? Really makes you want to settle down here, doesn't it?"

"Actually, yes, it does," Brad said. The Palmers stared at him. "You mentioned paranoia, and I'm not sure you were so far off base. You two have been living in pretty much of a vacuum out here as far as I can tell. Odd things happen in vacuums. Things get blown all out of proportion. Things that would seem small in ordinary circumstances suddenly seem terribly important. And the longer it goes on, the worse it all seems to get. But the key word is 'seems.' How bad are things, really? Are you going to be able to open the gallery before you run out of money?"

"It looks like it, but I'm not sure how we've managed."

"You want me to tell you? By working steadily along, dealing with whatever has happened. Actually, everything has gone pretty much according to plan, hasn't it?"

"Well, I'd hoped to have the gallery open by now——"

"Hoped," Brad pounced. "But what had you *planned* on?"

Glen grinned sheepishly. "Actually, if you get right down to it, I'm a little bit ahead of schedule. I allowed a lot of time for clumsiness."

"So what's really gotten to you is the attitude you've run into, or more accurately, what you *think* you've run into."

"Oh, come on, Brad, be fair," Elaine cried. "You know damned well what Clark's Harbor is like for strangers. You can read it all over the place. And you heard as well as I did what those people were saying about Glen the first day we were in town."

"They were talking?" Glen said, unable to keep the bitterness out of his voice. Elaine looked away, wishing she hadn't spoken so quickly.

"Well, that's something new," he went on. "When I'm around it's like everyone's been struck dumb. What were they saying?"

"Oh, just the typical small town stuff about artists," Elaine said, forcing a lightness she didn't feel into her voice. But Rebecca would not let the subject drop.

"It must have been more than that," she said gently. "Otherwise you wouldn't have remembered it."

"Well, the gist of the conversation—if you can call it that, since it was mostly just backbiting—was that no one in town seems to be glad you're here," Elaine told them. "But *I'm* glad you're here," she went on, "for the same reasons you're glad we're coming. Maybe we can take the curse off the place for each other." Elaine caught herself and glanced from one face to the other. "Sorry about that. I'm beginning to sound like Miriam Shelling, aren't I?"

"Don't worry about it," Rebecca said. "Suddenly, with some people around and a couple of glasses of wine, I think I'm beginning to see some reason again. But an hour ago I wasn't. Is there any more wine in that bottle?"

Glen poured them each another round, then went out to find another log for the fireplace.

"I really am glad you're going to be here," Rebecca said while he was gone. "I had no idea how dependent I'd become on people till we moved up here and all of a sudden there wasn't anyone to talk to. Sometimes I've thought I was going out of my mind, and I think Glen's felt the same way. We've been holding on for so long now, telling each other it's going to get better. But until tonight I didn't believe it. Now I do." She grinned suddenly. "I hope I don't get to be a nuisance—I suspect I'll be running up and down the beach every five minutes at first, just making sure you're really there."

"You'd better be," Elaine replied. "If you're not I'll have to do all the running, just to find out how to survive without electricity."

"Why don't you talk to Whalen about putting some in?" Glen said, returning in time to hear the last. "It shouldn't cost much from where you are—the main line runs out almost as far as your house."

"Not worth it," Brad said. "And even if it were I doubt Whalen would go for it. For some reason he seems to be rooted in the past. He made a big deal out of telling us the old Indian story about the Sands of Death."

"That's not so funny, considering what happened last night," Elaine pointed out.

"Except that Mrs. Shelling killed herself," Brad said. "No one else was involved, and she certainly wasn't buried on the beach in the style of the story Whalen told us."

*No, but the dog was,* Elaine thought suddenly. She said nothing, standing up instead: sending Brad a signal that it was time for them to leave.

A few minutes later they started the long walk back down the beach.

Glen and Rebecca watched them go until they were only shadows in the moonlight. Then they closed the cabin door and put their arms around each other.

"Things are going to get better now, aren't they?" Rebecca whispered.

"Yes, honey, I think they are," Glen said softly. He didn't tell Rebecca about the strange feeling he had gotten while he was out getting the log: *the strange feeling of being watched.* . . .

## ELEVEN

"WELL, THAT'S THAT," ELAINE SAID AS she closed the last suitcase and snapped the latches into place. She began her final inspection of the room, pulling each of the drawers open, then moved on into the bathroom. "Damn," Brad heard her say.

"The hair dryer?" he called.

"What else?" Elaine replied, returning to the room with the offending object in her hand. She stared glumly at the suitcase on the bed, mentally rearranging it so that the cumbersome dryer would fit. "Maybe I'll just throw it on the back seat," she speculated. She tossed the hair dryer onto the bed and dropped heavily into one of the chairs, glancing around the room as if she expected some other item she had overlooked to appear suddenly from her new vantage point.

"You were right," she said suddenly. "This *is* a nice room. In a way I hate to leave it."

"We'll be back."

"Yes, but not here." She sighed and got to her feet, reaching for the coat Brad was holding. "Do I need this today?" She looked doubtfully out the window; the sun was shining brightly and the harbor lay softly blue below her.

"It's a bit snappy out," Brad said. He picked up the dryer. "What about it? The back seat?"

Elaine scowled at him playfully and reopened the suitcase.

"As if you didn't know." She quickly reorganized the suitcase, mostly a matter of stuffing several of Brad's shirts further into a corner, and crammed the dryer in. It was a struggle but the suitcase closed.

"How come the dryer always winds up ruining *my* clothes?"

"Yours are cheaper, and besides, you don't care how you look," Elaine teased. "Come on, let's get it over with."

Each of them picked up two suitcases and they left the room, its door standing open, to make their way down stairs. Merle Glind looked up when he saw them coming but didn't offer to help them with the luggage.

"Checking out?" he inquired.

"No, actually we're just moving our luggage around," Brad replied, but the sarcasm was lost on the little innkeeper. He set the luggage down and tossed the key onto the desk. Glind picked it up and examined it carefully, then pulled their bill from a bin on his desk, matched the room number to the number on the bill, and began adding it up. Brad suppressed a smile as he noted that their bill had been the only one in the bin, and wondered what Glind would have done if the numbers had failed to match. He handed Glind a credit card, which was inspected minutely, then signed the voucher when it was presented to him. He wasn't surprised when Glind carefully compared the signature on the voucher with the one on the back of the card. Finally Glind returned the plastic card and smiled brightly.

"Hear you folks rented the old Baron house," he said.

"That's right," Brad said neutrally as he slipped his credit card back into his wallet.

"Not much of a house," Merle remarked. "No electricity. I wouldn't be surprised if the roof leaks."

"Well, we'll be living mostly on the first floor anyway, so I don't expect a few leaks will bother us."

Merle stared hard at Brad, then decided he was being kidded. He chuckled self-consciously. "I suppose you folks know what you're doing," he said, "but if I were you, I'd think twice, then think twice again before I moved out there."

"You mean the legend?"

Glind shrugged. "Who knows? But Harney Whalen believes in the legend, and he's part Indian."

"The police chief?" Elaine asked unbelievingly. "He certainly doesn't look it!"

"Take another look," Merle replied. "If you know, it shows up right away. Anyway, he thinks there's something to the legend. That's why he doesn't like to rent the house out there. Fact is, I'm surprised he rented it to you."

"Well, he didn't seem too eager," Brad said.

"Don't imagine he was. And if I were you I'd have let him discourage me. That's a bad place out there—no mistaking it."

Elaine suddenly felt angry, and her eyes narrowed.

"Exactly what do you mean?" she demanded.

Her tone seemed to frighten the nervous little man and he retreated a step back from the counter. "N-nothing, really," he stammered. "It's just the stories. You must have heard the stories."

"We've heard them," Brad said levelly, "and frankly, we don't put any stock in them."

Glind's eyes suddenly clouded over and he almost glared at them. "Well, that's up to you," he said stiffly. "For your sake I hope you're right." But his tone told them that his hope was faint. Brad and Elaine picked up their suitcases and left the Harbor Inn.

"That really burns me up," Elaine grumbled as they carefully fit the suitcases into the car. "It's almost as though he was trying to scare us off."

"That's exactly what he was trying to do," Brad said, slamming the trunk closed. He heard something crack inside and ignored it. "But it won't work, will it?" He smiled confidently at his wife, knowing her instinctive reaction to Glind's tactics would be to prove the odd little man wrong.

"No, it won't," Elaine said defiantly as she got into the car. She waited until Brad was behind the wheel before she spoke again. "The way I feel now, I wish you'd been able to talk Whalen into selling the place to us!"

"That's my girl!" Brad said happily, reaching over to pat her on the leg. Suddenly Elaine stared suspiciously at him, her eyes narrowing and a tiny smile playing around her mouth. "Did you put him up to that? Just to bring me around?"

"Absolutely not," Brad said sincerely, staring straight ahead through the windshield. Then he turned and grinned at her. "But if I'd thought of it I would have!"

"Bastard!" Elaine said, laughing suddenly. Then: "Hey, let's stop and see Glen Palmer before we leave, just to say good-bye."

"I'd already planned on it," Brad said easily. He turned the corner and headed up Harbor Road toward the main road. A few minutes later they pulled up in front of the gallery.

Brad and Elaine were standing in front of the gallery, trying to picture what it might look like when it was finished, when Rebecca Palmer appeared at the front door.

"I was hoping you two would show up," she said happily. "That's why I came in this morning. A little bird told me you might stop on your way back to Seattle. Come on in—I've got coffee going."

She led them into the gallery. A moment later Glen appeared from the back room.

"Rebecca's little bird was right, I see. Well, what do you think?" The Randalls looked around as Glen led them through the room, explaining what would eventually be where, trying to build a visual image for them with his words. He was only half-successful, but Brad and Elaine admired the work anyway. Glen looked just a little crestfallen.

"You can't see it, can you?"

"Just because I can't see it doesn't mean it isn't there," Elaine protested. "Let me see it again when it's finished. Did you say there's some coffee?"

"Some beer too," Glen offered. "Come on back and see what I got this morning."

In the back room, standing on its hind legs and whimpering plaintively, a tiny puppy peered at them from the confines of a small carton.

"Oh, he's adorable!" Elaine cried, sweeping the puppy into her arms and cuddling it. "Where did you find him?"

"I didn't," Glen said. "He found us. He was sitting out front this morning when we arrived."

"But he can't be more than eight weeks old," Elaine protested. "What would a puppy that young be doing wandering around at night?"

"Search me," Glen said. "I asked a couple of people about him this morning but no one seems to know where he might have come from. Bill Pruitt down at the gas station said sometimes people from Aberdeen or Hoquiam come up here and dump puppies instead of having them put to sleep. I figure if nobody comes looking for him today, he's ours."

Elaine carefully put the puppy back in its box. Immediately it began trying to scramble out again, its tiny tail wagging furiously.

"Was Snooker's neck really broken?" Rebecca suddenly asked. Elaine looked at her sharply and bit her lip.

"Glen told you?"

Rebecca nodded mutely.

"Well, then there isn't any use lying about it, is there?" She smiled weakly. "I'm sorry. When I found him I had no idea he was your dog."

"What did you do with him?"

"I left him where he was," Elaine said gently. "I didn't know what else to do."

"Well, there isn't anything to be done now, is there?"

"There wasn't anything to be done when I found him, Rebecca. He'd been dead for hours, I'm sure."

"I know," Rebecca replied. "But it just seems too coincidental, Snooker getting his neck broken and then Mrs. Shelling——" She let the sentence hang, then pulled herself together and tried to smile. "I'm sorry," she said. "These things have just gotten to me. I'll be so glad when you're back, Elaine. All of a sudden I just don't like the idea of being out at Sod Beach all by myself."

"That's nonsense," Elaine said with a certainty she didn't feel. "It's a beautiful beach and you've been very happy there. It's absolutely silly to let this get to you."

"I know," Rebecca said. "And if it were just one thing—even if the one thing was Miriam Shelling—I think I'd be all right. But two things? It just seems spooky."

"Another minute and you're going to start sounding like Merle Glind," Brad said.

"Merle?" Glen said the name sharply and Brad's attention was drawn away from Rebecca. "What did he have to say?"

"Not much, really," Brad answered. "Some nonsense about what a mistake we're making moving out to the beach. Without really saying it, he managed to imply that there's something to that legend of Whalen's. Say, did you know that Whalen's part Indian?"

"Not me," Rebecca said. "But now that you mention it, I suppose he does have that look."

Outside, a car pulled up and the group suddenly fell silent, waiting for the door to open. When it didn't Rebecca got up and went to look out. "Well, speak of the devil," she said. Frowning slightly, Glen joined his wife. Outside, Harney Whalen was standing next to the Randalls' car, one foot on the bumper, writing in what appeared to be a citation book. "What the hell is he up to?" Glen muttered. He started for the front door but was stopped by Brad's voice.

"I'll take care of it, Glen. It's my car he's got his foot on." He went to the door and stepped outside. "Good morning," he said cheerfully. The police chief didn't respond.

"Something wrong?" Brad asked. Whalen glanced up at him, then finished writing and tore a page from the book. He handed it to Brad.

"Parking ticket," he said evenly, his eyes boring into Brad's.

Brad grinned crookedly. "A parking ticket?" he repeated vacantly. "What are you talking about?"

"Car's parked illegally," Whalen stated. Brad glanced around, looking for a sign that would tell him he had broken the law. There was none.

"It isn't posted," he said.

"It's not illegal to park here, Randall," the chief said. "It's the way you parked. Rear end of the car is over the pavement."

Brad walked around the car. The edge of the pavement, indistinct in the dust, appeared to be no more than an inch or two under the side of the Volvo. Suddenly he knew what was going on. "I'm sorry," he said easily. "Very careless of me. How much is this going to cost?"

"Ten dollars," Whalen said. His face wore what appeared to be an insolent smile, as if he were waiting for Brad to protest the citation. Instead, Brad simply reached for his wallet, pulled out a ten-dollar bill, and handed it to the chief together with the citation.

"I assume I can pay you?" he asked politely.

"No problem," the chief said, pocketing both the citation and the money.

"I'll need a receipt for that," Brad said.

The police chief glared at him for a second, then moved to his patrol car. He sat behind the wheel and scribbled a receipt, then returned to the spot where Brad waited for him.

"Be more careful next time," he said, handing the receipt to Brad. He turned and started back to the black-and-white.

"Chief Whalen?" Brad called. The policeman turned and stared at him. "If you think you can scare me off with a phony parking ticket, you're wrong," Brad said quietly. "It's going to take a lot more than that to keep me out of Clark's Harbor."

Harney Whalen pulled at his lower lip and seemed to turn something over in his mind. When he finally spoke his voice was just as quiet as Brad Randall's had been.

"Dr. Randall, I don't give phony tickets. Your car is parked illegally, so I cited it. If I wanted to keep you out of Clark's Harbor, believe me, I could. I tried to tell you what things are like here. Now, you want to come out here or you want to stay away, that's your business. But don't come to me looking for trouble—you're likely to get it. Do I make myself clear?"

Brad suddenly felt foolish. Perhaps he'd been mistaken and the ticket hadn't been the harassment he'd assumed it was. And yet it had to be—the violation, if indeed it was a violation, was so trivial. He decided to drop the matter, at least for the moment.

"Perfectly clear," he said. "If I was out of order I apologize."

The chief nodded curtly and wordlessly, got into his car, and drove away. Brad watched him go, then went back into the Palmers' gallery.

"What was that all about?" Elaine asked. "Was he giving us a ticket?"

"He gave us one and I paid it," Brad said pensively.

"What for?" It was Rebecca, a look of concern on her face.

"Apparently I parked illegally. It seems the right rear corner of the car is an inch or two over the pavement."

"And he cited you for that?" Glen was outraged. "That's ridiculous!"

"I thought so too, but I didn't push it. No sense getting off on the wrong foot."

"Sometimes I don't think there's a right foot," Glen said bitterly. There was a silence, and Rebecca moved to him and took his hand.

Elaine looked down at her watch. "It's time to get going," she said softly. "It'll take us at least three hours to get home."

Rebecca suddenly put her arms around Elaine and hugged her. "Don't change your mind," she whispered.

"Not a chance," Elaine assured her. "This town's got my dander up now." She pulled away from Rebecca. "Give us a week, more or less, and we'll be back. Okay?"

Rebecca nodded. "I feel silly," she said. "But all of a sudden things seem like they're going to be fine. Hurry back."

"We will," Brad said. "And I expect to find this place finished by then. If it's not I'll have to pitch in and do it myself."

"I'll hold you to that," Glen promised him. He and Rebecca walked with the Randalls to their car, then watched them drive away.

"I hate to see them go," Rebecca said. "What if they change their minds and don't come back?"

"They'll be back," Glen told her. "Now come on in and forget about them for a while. There's lots of work to be done and a puppy to be taken care of."

Together, the Palmers went back into the gallery.

* * *

"What are you thinking about?" Brad asked as they drove away from the gallery.

"Nothing much," Elaine said, not sure she wanted to share her thoughts with Brad. She was afraid she was being silly. She didn't fool her husband.

"Worried again?" he guessed.

"I suppose so. Maybe we jumped in too fast. I mean, a house at the beach is one thing, but without electricity and in a town that doesn't seem to want us?"

"It isn't the whole town," Brad pointed out. "It's only Harney Whalen and Merle Glind. There are also Glen and Rebecca, who want us very much."

Elaine lapsed back into silence. Resolutely, she put her thoughts aside. But as they drove further and further away from Clark's Harbor, the thoughts kept coming back: *And they're strangers,* she thought. *Strangers, just like us. And just like the Shellings.*

Harney Whalen waited until the Randalls' car was completely out of sight before he pulled out from behind the billboard and headed back into town. As he made the turn onto Harbor Road he glanced at the Palmers' gallery with annoyance and wished once more that they had taken him up on his offer to buy them out. Then, with the offending gallery behind him, he looked out over the town. *His* town. He had a proprietary feeling about Clark's Harbor, a feeling he nurtured. Now it lay before him, peaceful and serene in the morning sun.

He pulled up in front of the tiny town hall and ambled into his office. Chip Connor was already there, enjoying a steaming cup of coffee. When Harney came in Chip immediately poured a cup for his boss.

"Well, they're gone," Harney said.

"Gone? Who?"

"The Randalls. Left just now."

"But they'll be back," Chip pointed out.

"Maybe," Harney drawled. "Maybe not." He sat down and put his feet up on his desk. "Beautiful day, isn't it, Chip?"

"For now," the deputy commented. "But a storm's coming. A big one."

"I know," Whalen replied. "I can feel it in my bones."

Harney Whalen smiled and savored his cup of coffee and waited for the storm.

# BOOK TWO

# NIGHT WAVES

## TWELVE

THE REVEREND LUCAS PEMBROKE PEERED over the tops of his half-glasses at the sparse crowd that had gathered in the tiny Methodist church and tried to blame the poor attendance on the weather. It had been raining almost steadily for the last five days—ever since Miriam and Pete Shelling had been buried—and the Reverend Pembroke wanted to believe that it was the weather that was keeping people away. Only a few, the bored and the curious, had showed up at the burial. Lucas had hoped that more would turn out for this service. It seemed almost useless for him to have driven all the way up from Hoquiam just to hold a service for two people he hardly knew in front of an audience of less than ten. Perhaps, he reflected, if the bodies were here . . . He let the thought die and chastised himself for its uncharitability.

No, it was something else, something he had been acutely aware of ever since he had added Clark's Harbor to his circuit. He had felt it from the first: a standoffishness among his congregation that he had never completely overcome. It was as if they felt that though they ought to have a pastor for their church, still, an outsider was an outsider and not to be completely accepted. Lucas Pembroke had thought he had come to grips with the situation in Clark's Harbor, but the deaths of Pete and Mirian Shelling had hit him hard. Of all his congregation they had been the only ones who had ever really let him know they appreciated his weekly trips to the Harbor, perhaps because they, too, had never felt particularly welcome here. He missed the Shellings, so he had decided to hold a service to say farewell to them. Apparently not many people in Clark's Harbor shared his feelings.

Merle Glind was there, of course, but Lucas was sure that Glind's presence was due more to his innate snoopiness than to any feelings for Pete and Miriam. Glind sat in the fourth pew, about halfway between the door and the chancel, and his small, nearly bald head kept swiveling around as he noted who was there and who wasn't.

Other than Glind, only three fishermen and Harney Whalen represented the town at the service. But in the front pew, off to one side, Rebecca and Glen Palmer sat with their children, strangely out of place. They had never been in the church before, and Lucas wondered what had brought them here today. He glanced at the clock he had placed above the door of the church to remind him of the time when his tendency to ramble on too long got the best of him, and decided he had delayed long enough.

He began the service.

An hour later the small assemblage filed out of the church. Harney Whalen was the first to leave, and Pembroke noticed that the police chief seemed to be in a hurry. He hadn't stopped to chat, even for a minute or two. Merle Glind paused briefly to pump Lucas's hand, then, mumbling that he had to get back to the inn, bustled off. As soon as he was gone, Rebecca Palmer stepped up to him.

"It was a very nice service, Mr. Pembroke," she said shyly.

"I'm glad you came." Pembroke's response was warm. "So few did, and it always hurts me when people stay away from a funeral. I suppose I can understand it but it always makes me feel lonely. I didn't know you knew the Shellings," he added, making it almost a question.

"We didn't, really," Glen answered. "Actually, I don't think I ever spoke to Mr. Shelling. But I talked to Mrs. Shelling the night she died, and we just felt that we should come."

Lucas Pembroke shook his head sympathetically. "It must have been very difficult for you," he said to Rebecca. "If there's anything I can do . . ."

"I'm fine now," Rebecca assured him. "Really I am. Your service helped. I know it sounds strange, but I thought if we came it might help me stop thinking about it. And I think it will."

"Come back again," Lucas urged. "I mean for the regular services, of course. We don't have a large congregation and I hate to preach to an empty church. Makes me feel unimportant, I suppose," he joked.

The Palmers assured him that they would, but the minister was sure they wouldn't. He couldn't really say he blamed them. They were undoubtedly feeling the same chill he had felt when he first came to the Harbor, and he suspected they would continue to keep pretty much to themselves. He watched them leave the church, then turned his attention to the three fishermen.

The youngest of them, Tad Corey, was one of Pembroke's regular parishioners. "Tad," Lucas said warmly. "It was good of you to come. Although I must say I'm surprised."

"It wasn't my idea, Reverend," Tad Corey said genially. "I told Mac Riley here, that there were better things to do than spend the day in church, but he wouldn't listen." There was no malice in Corey's voice, and he winked at the pastor as he said it. Lucas Pembroke chuckled appreciatively and turned his attention to the oldest of the three fishermen.

"I don't see you very often, Mr. Riley," he observed.

The old man, his eyes almost lost in the wrinkles of his weathered face, didn't seem to hear Pembroke. Instead, his attention was centered on Missy and Robby Palmer, who stood a few feet away staring curiously at the fisherman. Pembroke sensed a silent interchange taking place between the ancient fisherman and the two children, a shared experience that they were now remembering, and keeping to themselves.

Riley broke the moment and smiled at the minister.

"Not likely to see me here often either," he rasped. "After seventy years of fishing these waters I know too much of too many things. There are things going on here. Things you don't know anything about."

"Well, I'm glad to see you made it today," Lucas Pembroke said uneasily, wondering what Riley was trying to tell him.

"Pete Shelling was a good fisherman," the old man continued, and Pembroke was grateful to be back on familiar ground. "Never knew his wife very well but I knew Pete. It's a shame, that's what it is. A crying shame."

"Well, accidents do happen," Lucas said consolingly.

"Yes," Riley agreed tartly. "But not often," He turned away from the pastor and started to leave the church. When he was a few paces away he called, without turning around: "You boys planning to waste the whole day?"

Tad Corey and the third fisherman, Clem Ledbetter, exchanged a quick glance, bade the pastor good-bye, and hurried after Riley. Lucas Pembroke watched them go, then went back into the church. He began tidying up the few hymnals that had been used during the service and wondered what to do with the flowers he had brought with him for the occasion. He considered using them again on Sunday, then quickly, almost spitefully, rejected the idea—he didn't think the people of Clark's Harbor would appreciate the gesture. But if he took them home to Hoquiam, his landlady would be thrilled. She might even fix a decent dinner.

Harney Whalen walked into his office and settled in the chair behind his desk. He shuffled through some papers, but Chip Connor wasn't fooled. Something was on Harn's mind.

"Kind of quiet, aren't you?" Whalen finally asked.

"Nothing to say. All quiet." He paused a moment, then decided to goad his chief. "Quiet as a funeral," he added.

Harney looked up at him then, and leaned back in the chair. "Is that supposed to be a hint?"

"I guess so," Chip said mildly. "How was it?"

"A funeral's a funeral," Whalen said. "First time I've ever been to a double one with no bodies, though."

"Lots of people?"

"Not really. Old Man Riley."

"Granddad? That doesn't surprise me." Chip grinned. "Sometimes I think he has a fixation about funerals. Like if he skips one the next one will be his. I suppose Tad and Clem were with him?"

"Yup. Those three and me, and four other people. Bet you can't guess who the other four were."

Chip turned it over in his mind. From the way Whalen said it, it must not have been anyone he was likely to think of. Then it came to him.

"Not the Palmers?" he asked.

"Right on the money," Harney said. "Now you tell me. Why would the Palmers be at that funeral? Hell, hardly anybody was there and everybody in town knew the Shellings better than the Palmers did. So why'd they turn up?"

"How should I know?" Chip asked. "Why did they?"

"Good question," Whalen said sarcastically. "Guess who's going to find out the answer?"

"I see," Chip said heavily, standing up. "You want me to go on over there and have a little talk with Palmer?"

"Right?" Whalen replied. "No rush, though. Anytime before tomorrow will be fine."

He watched his deputy leave and wondered how Chip would handle the situation; wondered, indeed, why he even wanted Glen Palmer questioned. Doc Phelps had said Miriam Shelling killed herself. But Harney Whalen didn't believe it. There was something more—something else happening, and Harney was sure that it involved the Palmers. It was just a hunch, but Harney Whalen trusted his hunches.

The Palmers walked the few blocks to the service station, paid an inflated repair bill without comment, and drove back to Sod Beach in silence. The silence was respected even by the children, who seemed to know that for the moment they should be quiet. Glen turned the Chevy off the main road and they bumped over the last hundred yards into the clearing where their cabin stood.

"Can we go out on the beach now?" Robby begged as he and Missy scrambled out of the back seat.

"Don't you think you ought to go to school?" Rebecca suggested.

"Aw, it's after lunchtime already." Robby's face crumbled and Rebecca softened immediately.

"Well, I don't suppose one day will hurt you," she said. "Why don't you let Scooter out before he ruins the house completely?" Before she had finished the words Missy and Robby were racing to the door of the cabin. A moment later the tiny puppy tumbled happily out to chase the children. Glen and Rebecca watched the scene until the trio disappeared around a corner toward the beach, then went inside.

"Damn that dog," Rebecca said as she saw the pile in the middle of the rug. They had given up trying to confine the puppy to a box after the first day, when he had earned his name by chewing a hole through every box they had put him in, then scooting under the nearest piece of furniture, waiting for someone to chase him. Also, the name was close enough to that of the disappeared Snooker that the puppy would respond even when the children slipped and called him by their previous pet's name. All in all, the puppy had worked out very well, and the Palmers had been spared the task of telling the children what had happened to the spaniel: since Scooter's arrival, they both seemed to have forgotten the black-and-white mutt. The only problem was Scooter's recalcitrance at learning the basics of being housebroken. Rebecca found a scrap of newspaper and gingerly picked up the pile, took it outside, and dumped it into the garbage can.

"Want to go out on the beach?" she asked Glen when she came back in. "The sun's about to break through and you know how I feel about the children being out there by themselves."

Glen looked at his wife speculatively. This was the first time she had let them play on the beach at all since the day Miriam Shelling had died. He decided to approach the subject obliquely.

"Are you glad we went to the service?" he asked.

Rebecca seemed surprised by the question. "Well, of course I'm glad we went. I was the one who insisted we go, remember?" Then she suddenly realized what he was getting at. Instinctively, she started for the door, then stopped herself.

"It really is over, isn't it?" she said.

"It was over as soon as it happened, darling," Glen said gently. "But you needed that service just to tell you so."

"I know," Rebecca replied. "And I don't mind telling you that I feel pretty silly about it now, but it really shook me up."

"Well, at least the kids have the beach again. I don't know about you, but I was beginning to go a little crazy with them and that puppy underfoot all the time." He opened the ice box. "Tell you what. Let's make some sandwiches and have a picnic on the beach. I'll forget about going back to the gallery and you forget about whatever you were going to do this afternoon, and we'll have a little wake for the Shellings, just the four of us."

"We're not Irish," Rebecca protested.

"We can pretend." Glen grinned. "Besides, you know as well as I do that those kids are going to have a million questions. So we might as well make a party out of answering them."

For the first time in days Rebecca's depression suddenly lifted and she realized she was once again happy to be at the beach. She hugged Glen and kissed him firmly.

"What's that about?" he said after he returned the kiss.

"Nothing in particular. Just to let you know that I appreciate having such a wonderful husband." She looked out the window just in time to see the clouds break and the sun pour through. The leaden-gray sea suddenly turned a deep blue, and the green of the forest sprang to life. "The storm's over," she said. "I can hardly believe it."

"I wouldn't believe it if I were you," Glen said. "According to the old-timers I've heard talking around town, the last few days have just been a prelude. The real storm's been sitting out there waiting to come in."

Rebecca made a face at her husband. "Well, aren't you just the prophet of doom?"

"Only repeating what I heard."

"And do you believe everything you hear?" Rebecca teased. "Come on, let's make hay while the sun shines!"

Clem Ledbetter set aside the net he was working on and shook a cigarette from a crumpled package he fished from his pants pocket.

"What do you think?" he said to no one in particular as he lit the cigarette and took a deep drag on it.

"You gonna work or smoke?" Tad Corey asked. "I know you can't do both."

"I was thinking about Miriam Shelling," Clem said, ignoring Tad. "It just don't make any sense to me."

"Lots of things don't make sense." Mac Riley set aside his work and pulled out his pipe. As he carefully packed it from an ancient sealskin tobacco pouch, he peered at Clem. "What is it in particular?"

"Miriam Shelling. It just don't make sense, her killing herself. She just wasn't the kind of woman to do something like that."

"What makes you such an expert?" Corey asked. "You and her closer than you let on?"

"Shit, no. It's just that she didn't seem like the type, that's all. Me and Alice knew Pete and Miriam as well as anybody around here and if you ask me, the whole thing doesn't make any sense."

"Pete Shelling was a fool," Tad Corey said vehemently. "Anybody who stays out alone like that is a fool."

"That may be," Clem said. "But Pete was a good fisherman and you know it. He ran a good boat—I never once saw *Sea Spray* but what everything wasn't in order. Not like some people I could name whose boats look like pigsties."

Tad refused to rise to the bait. "Kept his boat too neat if you ask me," he said.

"Maybe so," Clem said doggedly. "But someone who kept his boat as neat as Pete Shelling did just isn't likely to let himself get caught in his own nets. And Miriam—well, she knew what she was getting into when she married Pete. Any woman who marries a fisherman knows. So when something like that happens they don't go out and kill themselves."

"Well, what's done is over with," Tad replied. "I don't know why we're wasting time talking about it. Pete Shelling never did fit in around here, and I for one don't give a damn about it one way or another. As for Miriam, well, Harn Whalen says she killed herself, and that's that."

"Is it?" Mac Riley's quavering voice inquired. "I wonder."

He'd set his pipe down as he listened to the two younger men talk, but now he picked it up and relit it. He puffed on it for a few minutes. Clem and Tad had begun to suspect that the old man had drifted off in his own mind when he suddenly started speaking again.

"I remember something that happened a long time ago, not so very long after you two were born. There were a couple of people here, a man and his wife. Don't know where they came from—fact is, I might never have known—but anyway, he was a fisherman. And one day I found his boat drifting off Sod Beach, just about where that feller found Pete Shelling's boat. He was caught in his nets, just like Pete Shelling."

"So?" Tad Corey asked. "I don't see what's so strange about that. The currents off that beach get pretty wild sometimes, and it isn't that hard to lose control of your nets if you don't know what you're doing. So two people die there the same way in forty years. I don't see how that means anything. If it were two people in a month, say, or maybe even a year, that'd be one thing. But forty years? Shit, Riley, the only thing that surprises me is that there haven't been more."

"You didn't let me finish my story," the old man said patiently. "A couple of days after I found that man his wife died."

"Died?" Tad asked. "What happened to her?"

"Hanged herself," Riley said quietly. "I ain't going to say it was from the same tree as Miriam Shelling used, but you can believe me when I tell you it wasn't far from it."

The two younger men stared at the old man, and there was a long silence. Finally Clem spoke.

"Were they sure it was suicide?"

"Nobody had any reason to doubt it," Riley said. "But if you ask me, what happened to them and what happened to the Shellings is a little bit too close for comfort."

"But it doesn't make any sense," Clem Ledbetter said softly.

"Doesn't it?" Riley mused. "I wonder. I just wonder."

Tad and Clem exchanged a worried glance, but Riley caught it.

"You think I'm a senile old man, don't you?" he asked them. "Well, I may be, and then again, I may not be. But I can tell you one thing. That sea out there, she's like a living thing, she is. And she has a personality all her own. The Indians knew that and they respected her. The Indians believed that a spirit lives in the sea and that she has to be appeased."

"That's bullshit," Corey said.

"You think so? Well, maybe you're right. But what the Indians said makes a lot of sense when you think about it. We get a lot from the sea, but what do we ever put back? Not much of anything. It's not that way with, say, farming. Farmers take a lot out of the soil, but they put a lot back in too. Well, the Indians thought the same thing was true of the sea. You had to offer it something in return for all it gave you. And they did. Out there on what they used to call the Sands of Death."

"I've heard the stories," Clem said.

"About what they used to do to strangers out there? Sure, everyone's heard those stories. But there are other stories, stories that aren't talked about so much.''

"For instance?" Clem asked.

"When I was a little boy, I remember my father telling me the old Klickashaw customs. One of 'em had to do with fishermen that died at sea. The Indians didn't believe in accidents. Not a'tall. If somebody died there was always a reason, likely an offended spirit. The story was that if a fisherman died, it meant the spirit of the sea was angry.''

"What did they do?"

"They made a sacrifice," Riley said quietly. "They took the wife of the fisherman out to the Sands of Death and offered her to the sea. Usually they hanged her in the woods out there, but sometimes they just strangled her or broke her neck and left her on the beach.''

"Jesus," Clem breathed softly.

The old man smoked his pipe for a while and stared out at the calm sea. "Makes you wonder, doesn't it?" he said finally. "I hadn't thought about that story for years, not until Miriam Shelling died. But I wonder. I just wonder if maybe the Indians didn't know some things we don't know. We live off the sea here, and what do we do in return? Dump our garbage in. I suppose we can't blame the sea if she wants something more every now and then.''

"You mean you believe those old Indian stories?" Tad gasped.

Riley looked sharply at the younger man. "Got no reason not to," he said. "And a lot of reasons to believe them. I've been living with the sea for most of a century now and one thing I've learned. Never underestimate her. You may think you've got her by the tail but you haven't. Any time she wants to, that ocean can pick herself up and smash you down.

"At night, usually," he went on, more softly now. "You have to be particularly careful of her at night. She can be smooth as glass, and you almost fall asleep. But that's what she wants. She wants you to relax. Then all it takes is one good wave and it's over. She's got you. Just like she got Pete Shelling, and that other fisherman so long ago.''

"And their wives too?" Tad scoffed.

"That's the beach," Riley replied. "And it's just as dangerous as the ocean, particularly at night when the tide's high and the wind's blowing. The Indians used to call them the night waves. It was when the night waves were coming in that they made their sacrifices. . . .''

He trailed off and there was a long silence while Corey and Ledbetter digested what Riley had told him.

"Do you really believe all that?" Ledbetter finally asked.

"I do," Riley said. "And if you live long enough, you'll believe in it too." As if to signal an end to the conversation, Riley tamped out his pipe, put it back in his pocket, and stood up. "What do you say we call it a day?"

Clem and Tad stowed the nets and the three men left the wharf, heading for the tavern for an afternoon drink. When they had gotten their glasses and settled at a table, Tad Corey suddenly spotted Harney Whalen.

"Hey, Harn," he called. "Come over here a minute."

The chief approached their table and pulled up a chair.

"You're part Indian, aren't you?" Tad asked him. Whalen nodded.

"Well, Riley here has just been telling us some old Indian legends."

Whalen studied the old man and seemed to consider his words carefully. "What were you telling them about?" he asked.

"The night waves," Riley replied. "And how dangerous they are."

Harney Whalen fell silent and appeared to be thinking. Then he smiled at Corey and Ledbetter.

"I know about the night waves," he said. "And you can relax. The night waves are only dangerous to strangers. And we're not strangers, are we?"

# THIRTEEN

CHIP CONNOR WAS UP EARLY THE NEXT morning after a night of fitful sleep disturbed by dreams in which he saw the faces of the Shellings staring at him, their dead eyes accusing him. The dreams made no sense. Each time they woke him he had lain in bed breathing hard, watching the shadow play on the ceiling until he drifted off into another nightmare. Finally, as the sun came up he had left his bed and put on a pot of coffee, then sat by the window sipping his coffee and trying to figure out what his dreams had meant. But he came to no answers—they were simply dreams.

At nine, he decided it was time to start the day. He dressed slowly, almost reluctantly. He put on his uniform, knotting the necktie carefully, and surveyed himself in the mirror. He grinned self-consciously as he realized that his dark, almost brooding good looks combined perfectly with the uniform to make him look almost a caricature of a recruitment-poster cop.

He drove more slowly than usual as he made his way toward the village, but it wasn't until he neared the Harbor Road turnoff and saw the Palmers' gallery that he realized why he had been feeling strange all morning. He pulled off the highway and sat in his car for a few minutes thinking.

He had been relieved yesterday afternoon when he found the gallery locked and Glen Palmer apparently gone for the day. He had considered driving out to Sod Beach but had quickly dismissed the idea, telling himself that he had tried to follow Whalen's orders but had been unable to locate Palmer. He had known, of course, the real reason he hadn't driven on out to the beach. He wasn't looking forward to questioning Palmer. In fact, he was dreading it. But now, seeing the door to the gallery standing open and an array of paintings propped neatly against the front of the building, he knew he could not put it off. Harn would be on him first thing this morning, wanting to know what Glen Palmer had had to say, and Chip wasn't about to report that he had been unable to locate Palmer.

He got out of the car, slammed the door moodily, and started toward the gallery. Suddenly a picture caught his eye and he paused to look at it. It was an oil painting of the old Baron house out on Sod Beach, and at first Chip was unable to figure out exactly what it was that had caught his attention. Then he realized it was something about the house itself. A shadow behind one of the windows, a shadow that came from within the house, as if someone were standing just out of sight but the artist had somehow captured the essence of his presence. For a second Chip was almost sure that he could make out the figure, and felt a shudder of recognition, but when he looked more closely, it was just a shadow.

He examined the rest of the paintings. They were good. Unconsciously he loosened his tie as he went into the gallery.

Glen Palmer glanced up from the display case he was staining and felt a wave of hostility pass through him as he recognized Chip Connor. He stood up and tried to smile.

"Don't tell me I've broken the law now," he said.

"Not as far as I know," Chip replied. "I was just looking at the pictures. Are they yours?"

"Every single one of them, unless you'd like to buy one. In that case it would be yours."

"I meant did you paint them?" Chip said self-consciously.

"Yes, I did."

"That one of the old Baron house . . ." Chip began. He wasn't sure how to put his question, so he let it drop.

"It's two hundred dollars," Glen said. "Including the frame."

"Too much for me," Chip said ruefully. "But there's something about it. This might sound dumb, but who's in the house?"

Glen suddenly smiled and felt some of his initial hostility drain away. "You noticed that? You've got a sharp eye."

Chip ignored the compliment and repeated the question. "When I first glanced at the picture I thought I recognized the person in it, but when I looked more closely, there isn't anybody. Only a shadow. I was just wondering who you had in mind when you put the shadow in."

Glen looked appraisingly at Chip and wondered what had prompted the question. He remembered painting the picture several weeks earlier, remembered thinking it was almost finished when suddenly he had, almost without thinking, put the shadow in the window. After he'd done it he'd realized that it belonged there. He still wasn't sure why.

"What makes you ask?" he countered.

Chip shrugged uncomfortably. He was making a fool of himself. "I don't know. It's just that I thought—well, for a second I thought it was Harn. Harney Whalen."

Glen frowned slightly, then his expression cleared. "Well, that seems natural enough. It's his house, isn't it? But I didn't have anyone in mind. I guess it's whoever you want it to be."

Chip shifted his weight and wondered how to come to the point of his visit—the point that Harney Whalen had ordered. He decided to stall for a while.

"Are you selling much?"

"Nothing so far. But this is the first day I've displayed anything and it's still early. I should think hordes of customers will be stampeding in any minute now."

"Not much traffic this time of year," Chip commented. "And most people don't stop here anyway."

"It should pick up next month. I just thought I'd put some things out in case someone drove by. And it worked," he said, brightening. "You stopped."

Chip nodded and again shifted his weight. Glen was suddenly very sure that Chip had not stopped because of the pictures—there was something else. He decided to wait it out and let Chip make the first move.

"Well, if there's nothing else I can do for you I'll get back to work." He turned his back on the deputy and picked up his brush, acutely aware that Chip didn't move.

"Mr. Palmer," Chip said, "I have to ask you some questions."

Glen put his brush down again. "About what?"

"You were at the service for the Shellings yesterday," Chip said.

"So?"

"I didn't know you were that close to them."

"I don't think that makes any difference. Is it against the law to go to a funeral?"

"No, of course not," Chip said hastily. "I just . . . Oh, shit!"

Glen Palmer's eyes narrowed, and Chip could feel the hostility coming from them almost as if it were a physical force. "Look, Mr. Palmer, I'm only following orders. Harn asked me to come over here and talk to you, so here I am. But I'm not even sure what I should be asking you."

"Maybe you should tell Whalen that if he wants to talk to me he should do it himself."

"Now wait a minute," Connor said. "If Harney Whalen wants some questions answered, it doesn't matter if he asks them or if I ask them." Suddenly he was angry at Palmer. "So why don't you just tell me why you and your family were at that funeral, and we can get this over with."

Glen felt his own anger swell. "Because there's no reason on earth why I should," he said. "As long as my family and I obey the law, what we do and where we go is none of your affair, none of Harney Whalen's affair, none of Clark's Harbor's affair, understand?"

"I understand, Mr. Palmer," Chip said levelly, controlling his rage. "But there are a few things *you* should understand. You moved here. We didn't come to you. You don't fit in here, and I think everyone in town, you included, knows it. Now if you want to cooperate with us, I'm sure we'll cooperate with you. But it seems like you've got a bad attitude. All I did was come in to ask a few questions and you're acting like you're on trial or something!"

"How do I know I'm not?" Glen shot back. "You want to know how I feel? I feel like ever since my family and I got here we've been on trial for something. No, that's wrong. We've been found guilty and there hasn't even been any trial. I didn't come here with a chip on my shoulder, Connor, but I'm sure getting one. I don't appreciate having my wife accused of breaking up the merchandise down at Blake's, or having my son ganged up on at school. I don't appreciate the fact that every time I order something at the lumberyard it takes weeks to get it, and when I do get it it's usually damaged. And I sure don't appreciate having the police come to see me simply because I attended a memorial service for a woman who killed herself on my property! Now maybe if this town had been taking a different attitude toward me over the last few months, I might feel a little different. But frankly, Connor, unless you can give me a damned good reason why I should answer your questions, you can take your damn questions and shove them up Harney Whalen's ass.''

Chip Connor turned a deep scarlet. His hand began clenching into a fist. Glen thought for a moment that the deputy was going to hit him, and he prepared himself to fight back. But then Connor's hand relaxed and the blood began draining from his face. He was breathing hard, though his moment of fury had passed.

"I'm only trying to do my job," he said softly. "If Harn asks me to do something, I do it."

"Did he ask you to talk to everybody who was at the Shellings' funeral?"

"No, of course not," Chip said. "Only you."

"Why? What am I suspected of? My God, Connor, he died in a fishing accident and she killed herself! I just can't see why Whalen's so interested in my motives."

"It's just Harney," Connor said patiently. "You have to understand. He takes everything that happens in this town very personally. He wants to know why things happen, and the only way he can know that is by knowing everybody."

"Then he should come and talk to me himself," Glen insisted.

Chip Connor shook his head and wondered why Glen Palmer couldn't seem to grasp what he was saying. He decided to try one more time. "Look, Harney doesn't like strangers—he doesn't like to talk to them, he doesn't like to deal with them, he doesn't even want to be around them. So he sent me. All he wants to know is why you were at the Shellings' funeral. Is it really so much to ask?" He held up his hand against Glen's imminent protest and kept talking. "And don't start in about what right I have to ask you the questions. I'm sure I don't have a legal leg to stand on. But please, try to remember where you are and who I am. I'm just the deputy in a small town, and I really don't want to make any trouble for you or anybody else. Is it such a big secret, anyway?"

Glen Palmer was quiet for a minute. Finally, he decided that Chip Connor was right. He didn't have anything to hide, and he was beginning to sound paranoid. He grinned sheepishly.

"Well, if you really want to know, it wasn't even my idea. It was my wife's—Rebecca's. Ever since she saw Mrs. Shelling—you know—"

"I know," Chip said. "I took her home, remember?"

"Yes, of course." Glen threw him a small smile, then went on. "Well, anyway, Rebecca was very upset. She couldn't seem to get it out of her mind. And she thought if we went to the funeral it might put an end to the whole thing for her, if you know what I mean."

"I think so," Chip said, nodding. "That's it?"

"That's it," Glen said. He chuckled softly. "I sure kicked up a hell of a fuss over nothing, didn't I?"

"Seems like it," Chip agreed. The two men remained silent for a while, then Chip spoke again. "Mind if I ask a question?"

"Do I have to answer it?"

"Not if you don't want to."

"Shoot."

"Would you mind telling me why you kicked up such a fuss? Why don't you try giving *us* a chance?"

"It seems to me the town could give us a chance too."

"I think we are," Connor said. "We aren't the friendliest people in the world, but we're not so bad either. It's sort of a trade-off. We get used to you and you get used to us." He turned to go. "I'd better get on down and report to Harn. But he's never going to believe that I spent nearly an hour here and all I have to report is that you went to the service because your wife wanted to."

"Tell him you beat the information out of me with a rubber hose," Glen said. "Or wouldn't he believe that either?"

"Not a chance. He always says that when they passed out the meanness in the family I was standing behind the door."

"The family?" Glen asked. "Are you and Whalen related?"

"Sure. He's sort of an uncle. His mother was my grandmother's sister on my father's side. That's where we get our Indian blood. The sisters were half-breeds. Of course nobody would call them that now, but that's what they were always called around here."

"They must have had it rough," Glen commented.

"I imagine they did," Chip mused. "For that matter, I guess it wasn't always easy for Harney, either. You see? You and your family aren't the only ones who have it rough around here."

They walked to the front of the gallery together. Outside, Chip paused once more to look at the painting.

"I like the picture, but I sure wouldn't want to live in that house," he said.

"Don't tell me it's haunted," Glen laughed.

"No, it's broken-down," Chip replied. "Are those people really going to live out there?"

"The Randalls? They sure are. He's going to write a book, and we're looking forward to having some neighbors. We won't be the only strangers in town for a change."

Chip got into his car, slammed the door, and rolled the window down. He stuck his hand out the open window.

"Well, good luck. Frankly, I don't think you're ever going to make a nickel on your gallery, but I hope I'm wrong. I think you made a big mistake in choosing Clark's Harbor to try something like this."

"Well, we didn't really have much choice in the matter," Glen said, taking Chip's hand and shaking it firmly. "Sorry I gave you such a rough time."

"If it's the worst time we ever have we're both in good shape," Chip replied. Then he started the engine and a moment later pulled onto the highway, made a neat U-turn, and headed for town. Glen watched until he'd disappeared, then went back into the gallery.

As he continued staining the display case he'd been working on, he thought over the conversation with Connor and decided that maybe he'd been wrong. Maybe he *was* paranoid and the town wasn't really out to get him. But then Miriam Shelling's words came back to him, ringing in his ears.

*"They're going to get you! Just like they got Pete. . . . They'll get you too!"*

## FOURTEEN

THE FOLDER ON THE DEATHS OF PETE AND Miriam Shelling lay open on the desk in front of him, but Harney Whalen wasn't reading. By now he knew the contents of the folder—could repeat them verbatim, if necesary. Still, none of it made sense. Despite Miriam's insistence to the contrary, Whalen was still sure Pete's death had been an accident. But Miriam Shelling's was something else.

*Somebody strangled her.*

The words crawled up from the depths of Whalen's mind, tormenting his sense of order. Suicide fit for Miriam Shelling; murder didn't. Even so, those three words kept coming to him. *Somebody strangled her.* But Whalen could find no reasonable motive for someone to want to kill Miriam Shelling. So he went back once more, as he had periodically over the last several days, to considering unreasonable motives. And, as always, the name Glen Palmer popped into his head.

He glanced at the clock, then at his watch, annoyed that Chip Connor had not yet come in this morning. He was about to phone him when Chip suddenly appeared in the doorway.

"You keep banking hours?" Harney growled.

"Sorry," Chip said quickly. Something was eating at Whalen this morning. "Talking to Palmer took longer than I expected."

Whalen's brows rose skeptically. "I thought you were going to take care of that yesterday."

"I tried," Chip explained. "But the gallery was closed, and when I drove out to the Palmers' nobody was home." Chip excused himself for the small lie: after all, there was a good possibility the Palmers hadn't been home the previous afternoon. Whalen seemed satisfied. He looked at Chip expectantly.

"You want to tell me what you found out?"

"Not much of anything. His wife wanted to go to the funeral, so they went. That's all there was to it."

Whalen stared at Chip. "How long did you talk to him?"

"An hour, maybe a little longer," Chip said uncomfortably.

"And all you found out was that his wife wanted to go to the funeral, so they went?" Whalen's voice dripped sarcasm and Chip winced.

"I found out some other things, too, but they don't have anything to do with the funeral." He decided to try to shift the conversation a little. "Frankly, Harn, I don't see what's so important about that funeral. Why are you so concerned about who was there?"

"Because I don't think Miriam Shelling committed suicide," Whalen said flatly. Chip gaped at him, and Whalen grinned, pleased that he had disturbed his deputy's normal calm.

"I don't understand—" Chip began, then fell silent as Whalen made an impatient gesture.

"There's nothing to understand," the chief snapped. "It's nothing but a hunch. But over the years I've learned to pay attention to my hunches, and right now my hunch tells me that there's more to Miriam Shelling's death than a simple suicide."

"And you think Glen Palmer had something to do with it?"

Whalen leaned back in his chair and swiveled it around to gaze out the window as he talked. "When you live in a town all your life you get so you know the people. You know what they'll do and what they won't do. As far as I know, nobody in town would kill Miriam Shelling. So it has to be a stranger. Palmer's a stranger."

Chip felt baffled: it didn't make sense—none of it made sense. As if he had heard Chip's unspoken thought, Whalen began explaining:

"He was the last person to talk to her. She was saying strange things. Probably acting crazy, like she was when she came in here the day before, and she scared him. Hell, maybe she even attacked him. How the hell do I know? But it happened on his property, and he was the last person to talk to her, and I can't see that anybody else in town would do something like that."

"But that certainly doesn't mean Glen Palmer did it," Chip protested. "It doesn't even mean that *anybody* did it!" Now he spoke his earlier thought out loud. "It doesn't make any sense."

"No, and if you'll notice, I haven't charged him with anything, have I? I didn't say it makes sense, Chip. Hell, I didn't even say he did it. All I said is that if Miriam was murdered, a stranger did it. Palmer's a stranger, and he could have done it."

"So what are you going to do?" Chip asked, confused by Whalen's logic, but curious.

"Same thing you're going to do. Keep my ears open, my mouth shut, and my eye on Glen Palmer."

"I don't know," Chip said, shaking his head doubtfully. "I just don't think Palmer could have done it. He just doesn't seem to me like the type who would do a thing like that."

"But you don't *know*," Whalen replied. "And until we do know I think Palmer's a damned good suspect."

Chip wanted to protest that there was no need for any suspect at all, but Whalen was too caught up in his "hunch" to be dissuaded now. So instead of protesting he tried to defend Glen Palmer.

"I think we ought to be a little bit careful of him," Chip said reluctantly.

"Careful? What do you mean?"

"He's pretty upset right now. In fact, he almost refused to answer my questions. Claimed I didn't have any right to ask them."

Harney Whalen's face paled and his hands twitched slightly. "Did he now?" he growled. "And what did you have to say to that?"

"I told him I didn't have any right to question him but that I thought he ought to cooperate with me. With us," he corrected himself. Then his face twisted into a wry grimace. "That's when he suggested maybe the town could cooperate with him. His gallery hasn't been going very well."

"Nobody ever thought it would. He's mad because nobody's buying his junk?"

"No," Chip said mildly. "He just thinks that everybody in town's been trying to make it difficult for him. Thinks people are holding up on deliveries and delivering bad goods—that sort of thing."

"Tough," Whalen replied. "Everything takes time out here, and everybody gets damaged goods now and then. What makes him think he's special?"

"He doesn't think he's special," Chip said. He could feel his patience wearing thin and wondered why Harn was so hostile toward Palmer. "Anyway, he's almost got the place finished. In fact, he's displaying some of his stuff outside the building this morning. You ought to go take a look. Some of it isn't half-bad. In fact, there's a picture of the old Baron place that I bet you'd like."

But Harney Whalen was no longer listening. He was glaring at Chip. "Did I say something wrong?" Chip asked.

"He's displaying his merchandise outside?" Whalen said.

"Yeah," Chip replied, wondering what could be wrong. "He's got maybe fifteen or twenty canvases lined up against the building so you can see them as you drive by."

"And you didn't cite him?" Whalen demanded.

"Cite him?" Chip was totally baffled now. "For what, for Christ's sake?"

"Peddling," Whalen snapped. "We have an ordinance here against peddling without a license. If he's displaying stuff outside he's peddling."

"Oh, come on," Chip said. "That's ridiculous. Even if there is such an ordinance, when did we ever enforce it?"

"That's not the point," Whalen said stubbornly.

"Well, it seems to me that if you're going to enforce it against Glen Palmer, you'd better be ready to enforce it against anybody in town who violates it, because I'll bet Palmer will start watching."

"Yeah, I'll bet he just would at that," Whalen agreed. Then a slow smile came over his face. "So I won't cite him. But I'll get those pictures off the highway, just the same."

Chip frowned and stared suspiciously at the chief. "What are you going to do?"

"Come along and find out."

Something inside Chip told him that whatever Whalen was planning, it wasn't something he wanted any part of. He shook his head. "No thanks. I'll hang around here."

"Suit yourself," Whalen said. "But if you change your mind, drive on up to the highway in about ten minutes. Just pull off the road and wait." He put on his hat, glanced at himself in the mirror on the inside of the door, and left. A moment later Chip saw him leave the building and get into the police car.

Chip picked up the file on Whalen's desk, glanced at it, then closed it and put it in the file cabinet, locking the drawer after he slid it shut. He wandered around the office for several minutes, looking for something to do.

"Ah, shit," he muttered to himself finally. He put his own hat on, closed the office door behind him, and went to his car. A few seconds later he was on his way up Harbor Road. When he got to the intersection with the highway, he pulled off the road, parked where he would have a good view of the Palmers' gallery, and waited.

He didn't have to wait long. In the distance behind him, Chip heard the faint wailing of the siren on Harn Whalen's car. As it grew louder he began to think that Whalen must be pursuing a speeder. The car would be coming into sight any minute.

But no speeding car appeared. Instead, the wail only increased, and suddenly Chip saw the police car roar around the bend, lights flashing, siren screaming. As the car charged into the stretch of straight roadway, it seemed to accelerate, and Chip tore his eyes away from it to look ahead, almost expecting to see Whalen's prey disappear around the next curve. But all he saw was Glen Palmer coming out of the gallery, a puzzled look on his face.

Chip realized then what was about to happen. He leaned on his own horn, hoping to warn Glen, but it was too late. Whalen, in the speeding black-and-white, roared by him, and the sound of Chip's horn was drowned in the shriek of the siren. Then, just as he was about to pass the gallery, Whalen swerved to the right, slightly off the pavement.

Glen Palmer jumped back before he realized that the car had not been aimed at him. Indeed, he wasn't even sure that it had been aimed at all, the swerve had been so slight and so quick. But the right tires of the police car hit a long, narrow puddle, and the muddy water cascaded over Glen, soaking him to the skin. Almost before he realized what had happened he thought of the pictures.

They lay in the mud, most of them knocked over by the force of the cascading water. Without even looking at them, Glen was sure they were ruined. He stared at them, rooted to the spot, seeing weeks of work destroyed in an instant.

He was still standing there when Chip Connor raced by him and began grabbing the paintings, snatching them out of the mud, taking them inside the gallery, then coming back for more.

"Well, for Christ's sake, don't just stand there," Chip cried. "Help me get these things inside."

Harney Whalen glanced in the rearview mirror just in time to see the last of the cascading water pour over the pictures, then put his eyes back on the road. He moved his foot from the accelerator to the brake, slowing the speeding squad car enough to keep it on the road as he went into the curve that would cut the gallery off from his view. He left the siren on for a moment, enjoying the wailing sound that poured from the roof of the car, then reached up to snap it off: Palmer had gotten the message. Not, Whalen reflected, that he really cared—if he hadn't, Whalen could always repeat the performance.

Close to Sod Beach, he decided to stop and have a look at the Baron house. He turned the police car into the nearly invisible lane that cut through the woods toward the beach and parked it when he could drive no farther.

From outside the house looked no different than it had ever looked, and Whalen didn't bother to inspect the porch that ran almost all the way around it. Instead he let himself in through the kitchen door, closing the door behind him.

He made a mental note to hire a couple of the local kids to clean the place up. It wouldn't cost much to have the rotting garbage removed and the dishes washed and put away. If the sink wasn't scoured, the ancient wood stove not cleaned, and the floor still badly stained, it wouldn't matter— nobody was living there, and Whalen had no intention of having anybody live there.

A faint memory stirred at the back of his mind. Something about the Randalls. They had wanted to rent the place but he had refused.

Again the faint stirring. Whalen shook his head, trying to catch the elusive memory, then dismissed it. He *had* refused to rent the house to them. He was sure of it.

He wandered through the lower floor and picked up a stray sweater that lay haphazardly on one of the worn-looking chairs. Then he saw a fire neatly laid in the fireplace and felt vaguely annoyed. Before he could define his annoyance a chill suddenly came over him and he impulsively lit the fire. The chill stayed with him. He pulled one of the old chairs close to the hearth and sat in it, huddling his bulk far back in the chair. As the fire blazed into life and began to spread its warmth through the room, a light rain began to fall, streaking the windows of the old house and blurring the view of the ocean.

Harney Whalen sat alone, watching the flames and listening to the rain. He could feel a storm building.

* * *

Glen Palmer stood up, tossed the muddy rag into a corner, and surveyed the painting carefully.

"Well, it isn't ruined anyway," he said. The seventeen canvases were scattered over the floor of the gallery, and Chip Connor knelt by one—the one of the Baron house on Sod Beach—carefully wiping away the flecks of mud that clung to its frame. There were streaks of brown across the surface where he had clumsily tried to blot up the muddy water. "Let me do that," Glen said. "It isn't nearly as fragile as it looks."

"Sorry," Chip mumbled. "I was only trying to help . . ."

"You already helped," Glen said. "If you hadn't been there I probably would have stood there like a dummy all day." He glanced up at Chip and thought he saw a flash of embarrassment on the young deputy's face. He concentrated his attention on the picture in front of him then, and tried to keep his voice level. "What the hell was that all about, Connor?"

"I guess Harney must have lost control of the car for a second," Chip offered. He knew it wasn't true, knew he should tell Palmer what had happened: that Harney Whalen had deliberately tried to destroy the paintings. And yet, he knew he wouldn't. Harney Whalen was his boss and his uncle. He'd grown up with Whalen, and trusted him. He didn't understand why Harn had done what he'd done, but Chip knew he wouldn't tell Palmer the truth about it. Yet even as he told Glen Palmer the lie he was sure that Palmer knew. He wondered what would happen if the artist pushed him.

For his own part, Glen Palmer forced himself to keep working steadily on the canvas. Connor was lying. He had an urge to turn on the deputy and force the truth out of him, but he had, that morning, established some kind of truce with Connor and he didn't want to disturb it. So he concentrated on cleaning away the ugly stains on the painting, and forced himself to calm down. When he was sure he could face Chip Connor with a steady expression he stood up, turned, and offered his hand.

"Well, I guess it doesn't matter exactly what happened, does it? It's over and there isn't much either one of us can do now."

Chip felt a knot of tension in his stomach suddenly relax, a knot he hadn't even realized was there. He had a sudden urge to tell Palmer the truth and opened his mouth. But he couldn't say the words. Instead his mouth worked a moment, then closed again. He took Palmer's extended hand and shook it.

"Are they all ruined?" he asked.

Glen forced a smile and tried to reassure the deputy with a lie of his own. "I don't think it's so bad. Oil paints are pretty waterproof. The damage would have been a lot worse if I'd had the pictures facing the wall. The water would have hit the bare canvas, and it would have been a hell of a mess." He glanced at his watch. "Jesus, did you know we've been working for almost an hour? What do you say we have some lunch?"

"Lunch?" Chip repeated the word tonelessly, as if it had no meaning.

"Yes, lunch. You know, a sandwich and a beer? I have some in the back if you're hungry."

"I don't think—" Chip began, but Glen cut him off.

"Look, it's the least I can do. Unless there's something you have to do."

Chip chuckled. "Most of my job is just sitting around the station keeping Harn company. Except on weekends, when we usually have to break up a fight or two. Otherwise, not much ever happens around here."

"So you might as well have a sandwich and a beer," Glen urged. Then: "If you don't stay I'll just spend the rest of the day getting pissed off at your boss."

"Well, I guess I couldn't blame you," Chip said, his smile fading into an expression of concern. "I know it was an accident, but still—"

"So do Whalen a favor and keep a citizen from getting mad at him. Besides, I could use the company."

Chip started to refuse, then changed his mind. There was a quality to Glen's voice that reached inside him, and he realized that it was the same quality he'd heard in Harn Whalen's voice now and then—not often, but on nights when Whalen seemed to be lonely and wanted Chip to hang around late, not because he had anything on his mind, but because he needed company.

"Let me pull the car up," he said. "So I'll be able to hear the radio if Harn calls me."

Chip spent most of the afternoon at the gallery. He and Glen split the lunch that Rebecca had packed and polished off the best part of a six-pack.

As he ate, Chip wandered around the gallery asking questions about the remodeling.

"Deciding what to do was easy," Glen said. They were standing under a large window that Glen was cutting. It was an odd shape, but it appeared to fit into the space Glen had allocated for it. "For instance, that window. It was just a matter of extending the line from that beam over there, carrying the ledge over the door on across, and then duplicating the pitch of the roof. Bingo—an interesting window that seems to have been part of the original design." He grinned ruefully. "The only problem is, I can't figure out how I'm going to keep the roof up. I cut a support post out to make the window."

"No problem," Chip said. "Cut another foot off the support, then build a lintel between the posts to support the one you cut. That way you have plenty of support for the roof and it doesn't ruin the shape of the window."

Glen studied the wall for a minute, then shook his head. "You'd better show me," he said finally. "I can see what I want as an artist, but as a carpenter I'm pretty much of a loss."

Chip found a ladder, dragged it over, and climbed up, explaining as he did so. Then, seeing the baffled look still on Glen's face, he climbed down and stripped off the jacket of his uniform.

"Got a saw? It won't take me more than an hour to put it in for you."

For a while Glen tried to help, but soon realized the deputy didn't need any help. He went back to the soiled pictures and began the tedious work of cleaning the stains from them. He moved slowly and methodically, using tiny brushes, picks, pieces of straw, anything he could find to lift off the bits of mud without disturbing the colors beneath. The cleaning went better than he had hoped; only a few of the canvases would even need a touch-up. By the time he had repaired the worst of the damage Chip had finished the lintel and was in the process of pulling down the shelves Glen had worked so hard to put up.

"What are you doing?" Glen cried. "Those things took me almost a week to build."

Chip nonchalantly continued to pry the shelves loose from the wall. "Were you planning to use these shelves?"

"They're display shelves for my wife's pottery."

"Didn't you ever hear of a toggle bolt? These nails will hold the shelves up, but the shelves won't hold anything. Look."

He grabbed one of them with his left hand and pulled it off the wall. "What's your wife going to say when all her pottery falls on the floor? Have you got any toggle bolts?"

"I don't think so."

"I'll run down to Blake's and pick some up. Do you have an account there?"

Glen gaped at the deputy. "An account? Are you serious? Didn't I tell you this morning what happened to my wife down there?"

Chip suddenly looked embarrassed, and Glen wished he'd kept his mouth shut. He dug into his pocket and pulled out his wallet.

"Will this be enough?" he asked, handing Chip a five-dollar bill.

"That'll be plenty," Chip said. "Why don't you finish pulling those shelves down while I'm gone." He picked up his coat and started for the door, but Glen stopped him.

"Chip?"

The deputy stopped at the door and turned around.

"I don't know exactly why you're doing all this for me, but thanks."

Again Chip looked embarrassed, but then he grinned. "Well, if we're going to have an art gallery in town we might as well have one that won't fall down the first week." His face reddened slightly. "Besides, I guess I sort of owe it to you." Before Glen could reply Chip pulled the door open and stepped out into the rain.

Neither Glen nor Chip noticed that all afternoon the police radio in Chip's car had remained silent.

The light rain that had been falling all afternoon grew heavier as the storm moved relentlessly toward the coast; the wind picked up, and the tide turned. Sod Beach took on a foreboding gloom, and Robby and Missy, their slickers already dripping wet, started toward the forest.

"We should go home," Missy complained. "It's cold and the rain's starting to come down my neck."

"We're going home," Robby explained. "We're going to take the path through the woods, so we won't get soaked."

"I'd rather go along the beach," Missy sulked. "I don't like the woods. Or we could go into the old house and wait for the rain to stop."

"The rain isn't going to stop." Robby grabbed his sister by the hand and began leading her toward the woods. "Besides, we aren't supposed to go anywhere near that house. Mommy says empty houses can be dangerous."

"It isn't empty," Missy replied. "There's someone there. There's been someone there all afternoon."

Robby stopped and turned to the little girl. "That's dumb," he said. "Nobody lives there. Besides, how would you know if someone was there?"

"I just know," Missy insisted.

Robby glanced at the old house, bleak and forbidding in the failing light, then pulled at Missy once more.

"Come on. If we aren't home pretty soon, Daddy will come looking for us." He started picking his way over the driftwood, looking back every few seconds to make sure Missy was behind him. Missy, more afraid of being left behind than of the woods, scrambled after him.

## FIFTEEN

MAX HORTON GLANCED AT THE THREAT-ening sky, then adjusted the helm a few degrees starboard, compensating for the drift of the wind that buffeted the trawler.

"Jeff!" He waited a few seconds, then called again, louder. "Jeff, get your ass up here!"

His brother's head appeared from below. "What's up?"

"This storm's going to be a real son-of-a-bitch. Take over up here while I figure out where's the best place to put in."

Jeff took over the helm and Max went below to pore over a chart. He switched on the Loran unit he'd installed a month earlier, then pinpointed their exact location on the chart that was permanently mounted on the bulkhead. They could probably make it to Grays Harbor, but it would be tricky. If the storm built at the rate it had been going for the last hour there was a good chance they'd be trying to batter their way into port through a full gale. He looked for something closer and found it. A minute later he was back at the wheel.

"Ever heard of Clark's Harbor?" he asked Jeff.

Jeff thought a minute, then nodded. "It's a little place—just a village. They've got a wharf though."

"Well, I think we'd better head there. We could probably make it on down to Grays Harbor, but I don't like the feel of things." He pulled *Osprey* around to port and felt the roll change into a pitch as the boat responded to the rudder. The pitch was long and slow with both the wind and the sea at their stern, and Max chewed his lip tensely as he tried to gauge how much time he had before he'd have to bring the boat around, throw out a sea anchor, and ride it out.

"I told you we shouldn't have come this far south," Jeff muttered.

"Huh?"

"I said, I told you we should have stayed up north. We've heard the stories about the freak storms down here. This isn't any big surprise!"

"It isn't any big disaster either," Max replied. "We've got the wind and the tide working for us, and we can make Clark's Harbor in thirty minutes. Is there any coffee down there?" He jerked one thumb toward the galley, then quickly replaced his hand on the wheel as *Osprey* began drifting off course. Jeff disappeared and returned with a steaming mug, which he placed in a gimbaled holder near Max's right hand. Then he lit two cigarettes and handed one to his brother. Max took the cigarette and grinned.

"Scared, kid?"

Jeff grinned back at Max, feeling no resentment at being called "kid." Max had always called him that, but he had always used the term fondly, not patronizingly, and Jeff had never objected, even though both of them were now nearing thirty.

The trawler, a commercial fisherman, was their joint property, but Jeff always thought of it as Max's boat. Max was the captain—always had been and always would be—and Jeff was a contented mate.

There was a two-year difference in their ages, but they had always been more like friends than brothers, even when they were children. Wherever Max had gone he had taken Jeff with him, not because their parents made him do it, but because he liked Jeff. If Max's friends objected to the "kid" tagging along, they were no longer his friends.

They had bought *Osprey* four years ago, when Max was twenty-five and Jeff twenty-three. Jeff had been very worried the first year, sure that the immense loan would sink them even if the sea didn't. But the sea had been kind to them, and it looked as though the loan would be paid off by the end of the current season—all they really needed was four or five more really good catches, and Max seemed to have a nose for fish.

It was Max's nose that had brought them here today. The rest of the fleet that worked out of Port Angeles had stayed safely in the Strait, but Max had gotten up that morning and announced that he "smelled" a school of tuna to the south. They would go after it and spend the night in Grays Harbor before heading back north the following day.

He had been right. The hold was filled with tuna, and all had gone according to plan. Except for the storm. It had come upon them suddenly, as if from nowhere, giving them no time to complete the run south.

Now they were moving steadily if sluggishly through the heaving sea. A constant stream of rain mixed with salt spray battered against the windows of the wheelhouse, but Max held his course by compass, only occasionally glancing out into the gathering darkness. After some twenty minutes had passed in silence, he spoke.

"I'm going to have to send you outside."

Jeff checked the buttons on his slicker and put on his rain hat.

"What am I looking for?"

"Chart shows some rocks in the mouth of the harbor. They should be well off the port bow, but keep a lookout. No sense piling this thing up when it's almost paid for."

Jeff left the wheelhouse and felt the wind buffet him. He clung to the lifelines strung along the length of the boat and made his way slowly forward until he was in the bow pulpit. He strained to see through the fading afternoon light, and his stomach knotted as he thought of what might happen if he failed to see the rocks.

And then they were there, sticking jaggedly above the surface, fingers of granite reaching up to grasp the unwary. Jeff waved frantically, but even before he made the gesture, he felt *Osprey* swinging slightly to starboard: Max must have seen the rocks at almost the same instant he had. He watched the water swirling and eddying around the reef as they swept past; then, when the danger had disappeared beyond the stern, he returned to the wheelhouse.

Max was finishing his coffee, one hand relaxing on the wheel, grinning cheerfully.

"You could have given them a little more room," Jeff commented.

"A miss is as good as a mile," Max replied. "Want to take her in?"

"You're doing fine. I'll get ready to tie up."

A few minutes later, as the trawler crept into a vacant slip, Jeff jumped from the deck to the wharf and began securing the lines. On board, Max cut the engines.

Jeff had just finished tying the boat up when he became conscious of someone standing nearby watching him. He straightened up and nodded a greeting. "Some storm," he offered.

"You planning to spend the night here?" Mac Riley said.

"On board," Jeff replied.

"Storm's going to get a lot worse before it gets better," Riley said dourly. "Don't think you can do it."

"Do it? Do what?"

"Spend the night on that boat. We got a regulation against that here. Too dangerous."

Max came out of the wheelhouse in time to hear the last, and jumped from the deck to join Jeff on the wharf.

"What do you mean, too dangerous?" he challenged. "You've got a good harbor here."

"Didn't say you don't," Riley responded, unperturbed. "But in a storm like this anything can happen. So you won't sleep on your boat."

Max stared at the old man, annoyed. "I could take her out in the middle of the harbor and drop anchor."

"You could just scuttle her right here too, but I don't think you will."

Max looked over his shoulder and saw the windwhipped whitecaps that covered the small bay. All around him, securely moored though they were, the other boats rocked and groaned restlessly, complaining at their captivity.

"You got any suggestions?"

"The inn's right up there," Riley said, jerking a thumb shoreward.

Jeff and Max exchanged a look and nodded in unspoken agreement.

While Max prepared the boat for the night, battening her down against the storm, Jeff and Riley started toward shore, the wind and spray whipping at their backs. As they hurried toward the Harbor Inn, a bolt of lightning flashed out of the sky and the roar of thunder rolled in from the angry sea.

The lobby of the inn was deserted, but when Jeff banged impatiently on the bell that sat on the counter Merle Glind appeared at the dining-room door. He blinked rapidly and stared at Jeff over the rims of his glasses.

"Something I can do for you?" he piped anxiously.

"A room," Jeff said. "I need a room for the night."

Merle bobbed his head, and scuttled around the end of the counter, flipped open the reservation book, and studied it intently. Then he peered up at the young man and frowned.

"I've got a room," he announced victoriously, as if he had had to search for a highly unlikely cancellation. "Just one night?"

"Depends on how long the storm lasts," Jeff explained. "My brother and I were heading for Grays Harbor, but it got so bad we put in here. If it blows over tonight we'll head out tomorrow."

Merle Glind pushed the register toward him, collected his money, and handed him a key.

"No baggage?"

"We're not on vacation," Jeff said. "All we need is a place to sleep."

Glind nodded amiably and watched the fisherman go up the stairs. Then he returned to the dining room and climbed onto the barstool he had been occupying when the bell had interrupted him.

"Guests?" Chip Connor asked.

"Couple of fishermen coming in out of the rain," Merle said. He peered out the window, seeing nothing but the reflected lights of the dining room wavering in the rivulets of water that ran down the glass. "Can't say I blame them. Not fit for man nor beast out there tonight." He frowned slightly. "One of them's still out there."

Chip slid off his own stool, and dropped two dollars onto the bar. "Order me another, will you? I'd better give Harn a call. You know how he is."

"Use the phone behind the bar," Glind said. "Save yourself a dime."

Chip suppressed a grin and didn't tell Merle that he had never intended to use any other phone. He went to the end of the bar and fished the phone off the shelf below it. First he dialed the police station. When there was no answer there, he called Harnay Whalen at home. He let the phone ring ten times, then dropped it back on the hook.

"Well, I tried," he said, picking up the fresh drink that waited for him. "At least I tried." Then, remembering what Harn had had to say to him that morning when he reported not having gotten much information out of Glen Palmer, Chip made a mental note to try to reach the chief later.

"So that's what happened," Glen Palmer said. He had just finished telling Rebecca about the strange sequence of events that day—first Chip Connor's questioning and the near fight, then Whalen's deliberate attempt to ruin the paintings, and finally Chip's help at the gallery all afternoon.

"First I thought he was just trying to cover Whalen's ass," he mused. "He wouldn't admit Whalen did it on purpose, and I figured he hung around for a while just to calm me down, but now I don't know. If I hadn't called a halt I think he'd still be there, tearing apart everything I've done and doing it all over again." He grinned, remembering. "You should have seen him. It was like what I'd done was a personal affront, but he never said a word. Just kept fixing things. I have a feeling I haven't seen the last of him. Oh, and we now have a charge account at Blake's."

When Rebecca made no reply Glen came out of his reverie and studied his wife. Her brow was knitted into a frown. She seemed to be listening to something, but Glen was sure it wasn't him.

"Rebecca?"

She jumped a little and smiled at him self-consciously. "I'm sorry," she said. "I wasn't listening." Then, with an apologetic smile, she murmured, "It's the storm, I guess. I'm still a little nervous. It seems like whenever there's a storm out here something terrible happens."

"Now that isn't true and you know it," Glen protested. He was feeling very good and wasn't about to let his wife spoil it.

"I know," Rebecca agreed ruefully. "I suppose I'll get over it. But there's something else too."

"Something else?" Glen's voice took on an anxious tone, and he wondered what she hadn't told him.

"It's Missy. She says there was someone in the old house this afternoon. The Randalls' house."

"How did she know?"

"Search me," Rebecca said, shrugging helplessly. "Robby says they weren't anywhere near the place, but Missy insists that someone was inside the house."

Glen frowned, then called the children. They came out of their bedroom, Robby carrying Scooter. The puppy squirmed in his arms, and when Robby finally set him down he hurled himself at Glen, scrambling clumsily into his lap and licking his face.

"What's this I hear about someone being in the Randalls' house?" Glen asked as he struggled to contain the puppy.

"I didn't say anyone was there," Robby said self-righteously. "Missy said someone was there, but she was wrong."

"I wasn't either," Missy said hotly. Her tiny face screwed up and she looked as though she was about to cry. "I said Snooker wasn't coming back too, and he didn't, did he?" she demanded, as if it would provide proof of her honesty.

"No, he didn't," Glen said patiently. "And I'm not saying no one was in the Randalls' house today. I only want to know how you knew someone was there."

Missy, mollified by what her father had said, turned the matter over in her mind. When she finally spoke her face looked perplexed. "I don't know how I know," she said. "I just know."

"You don't know," Robby said scornfully.

"Now, Robby, don't say that," Glen objected. "She might have seen something, or heard something, and has just forgotten about it."

"Smoke," Missy said suddenly. "I saw smoke coming out of the chimney."

"You didn't either," Robby argued. "Smoke's the same color as clouds, and you wouldn't have seen it even if there was any."

Missy started to argue but Rebecca cut them both off.

"That's enough. Now take Scooter back into your room and get ready for bed."

"Can he stay inside again tonight?" Robby demanded. It was a request he had made every night since the arrival of the puppy, and it had always been granted, partly because of what had happened to Snooker, and partly because Scooter was so tiny and appealing that neither Rebecca nor Glen had had the heart to make him stay outside. Now Rebecca nodded her head in resignation.

"Just make sure he stays in his box. I don't want him messing up the blankets."

"He's almost housebroken," Robby said eagerly, hoping he could gain a little ground in his campaign to make the dog a bedmate. Unfortunately Scooter chose that moment to squat in the middle of the floor and form a puddle under his belly. Neither Glen nor Rebecca could contain the urge to giggle, and Robby, realizing he and Scooter had lost the argument, snatched the puppy up and scolded it severely. Scooter lapped wetly at Robby's face.

"Get him out of here," Rebecca cried. Laughing, she shooed her children and their pet back to their room and wiped the mess off the floor. As she finished she realized Glen was putting on his raincoat.

"Where are you going?"

"I think I'll take a walk down the beach and have a look at the Randalls' place. If there *is* someone there, I'll report it to Chip Connor."

"In this rain?" Rebecca protested. "Honey, you'll be soaked to the skin—it's pouring out there, and the wind's nearly tearing the roof off."

"Does that mean you don't want to come with me?" Glen asked innocently. Rebecca glared at him.

"That means I don't want you to go at all."

Glen gave her a quick hug and kissed her on the nose. "Well, I'm going and that's that. If we're ever away, I hope the Randalls will keep an eye on this place. It seems to me that the least I can do is keep an eye on theirs. And if Missy thinks she saw someone—"

"She didn't say she saw anyone."

"Well, she saw smoke."

"She said that tonight," Rebecca argued. "She didn't say anything about it this afternoon. I think she was just trying to convince us that someone was there. I probably put the idea into her head myself when I said she might have seen something."

"But she might have seen smoke," Glen countered, "and if she did I want to know what's going on."

Rebecca sighed, knowing further argument was useless. "All right, but be careful. Please?"

"Nothing to worry about," Glen reassured her. "I'll be back in half an hour, probably sooner."

A moment later he was gone. Rebecca strained to see him from the window as he went out into the night. But the storm swallowed him up, and she was left to wait alone and worry.

## SIXTEEN

**M**AX HORTON SURVEYED THE CABIN OF the trawler, making a final inspection before going ashore. He'd been working steadily for half an hour, though he could have finished the job of putting the boat to rights in ten minutes. He'd been dawdling, making the work last, enjoying his solitude, enjoying the boat. But now the job was done and he could no longer delay joining his brother at the inn. A slight smile crossed his face as he anticipated the warm glow that a hot brandy and water would bring.

Then he heard a sound. It was faint, nearly drowned out by the storm raging in from the sea, and indistinct. But it sounded like a hatch cover being dropped into place.

A sense of impending danger made Max's spine tingle, and he moved quickly to the hatchway.

He was only seconds too late.

*Osprey* was adrift.

It was already too far from the wharf for Max to attempt a jump, and even if it had been closer, the water was too rough. Then, as a bolt of lightning lashed out of the sky, Max saw the figure on the wharf. It stood perfectly still, hands on hips, head thrown back as if in laughter. The screaming wind drowned out any sounds and the effect of the silent, maniacal laughter chilled Max.

The brilliance of the lightning faded away as the crash of thunder shook the pitching trawler. Max ducked back into the wheelhouse, fumbling in his pocket for his keys. He jammed the ignition key in its lock, twisted it violently, and pressed the starter of the port engine.

Nothing happened.

He pressed the other starter. Again nothing.

He glanced out the window in time to see the wharf disappear into the darkness, and realized the boat was riding the turning tide. He was being drawn toward the mouth of the harbor—and the waiting rocks.

He jabbed at the recalcitrant starter buttons once more, then threw the switch that would drop the main anchor. When it too failed to respond, he left the wheelhouse and moved as swiftly as he could to the stern. He kicked open the anchor locker on the deck and hurled the anchor over the side.

Then he watched as ten feet of line played out and the frayed end of the line disappeared into the blackness of the water.

Something had done its job well.

Max yanked open the hatch cover over the engine compartment and dropped nimbly into the space between the two big Chrysler engines. At first glance everything seemed to be normal, but as he flashed his light over the immense machines he noticed something.

The wiring.

The new wiring that he and Jeff had installed only a week ago had changed. The insulation was gone, burned off as if it had been hugely overloaded, or struck by lightning. The copper wiring, pitted and looking worn, gleamed dully in the glow of his flashlight.

He scrambled out of the engine compartment and replaced the hatch cover. He returned to the wheelhouse and tried to assess the situation. Only then did he realize he was trembling with frustration and rage. He groped in his pockets, pulled a crumpled pack of cigarettes out, and lit one. He sat quietly at the helm and dragged deeply on his cigarette, forcing himself to calm down, analyze the situation, then do whatever had to be done to save the ship. Once more an image of the fingers of rock looming out of the mouth of the harbor came into his mind. . . .

Glen Palmer approached the old Baron house cautiously. He had intended to walk along the beach and arrive at the house from the seaward side, but the storm had quickly driven him into the comparative shelter of the woods. He had walked quickly, though the sodden ground had sucked at his shoes. The wind screaming in the treetops above him had chilled his spirit as the rain, funneling through the dense foliage, had chilled his body.

Finally he had found the path that would take him back to the beach— the same path his children had used that afternoon—and he had broken out of the woods only forty feet from the house. The house itself blended almost perfectly with the blackness of the night, and only occasional flashes of lightning revealed that it still stood, a silent sentinel on the beach, testimony to the long-disappeared people who had built it. No light seeped from its dark windows, no clue as to what might lie within escaped its walls. As he made his way around it, Glen shivered, less from the cold than from the deathly stillness that seemed to emanate from the house.

He paused when he found the kitchen door unlocked, sure that something was wrong. Then he entered the kitchen, flashing his light from one corner to another, illuminating first a wall, then the sink, next the icebox, and finally the door to the dining room. He didn't call out, not out of a fear of alerting anyone who might be inside, but because of deep certainty that the house was empty.

He went confidently into the dining room, again flashed the light briefly around, then moved on to the living room. It was then he knew that someone had been there.

It was at least ten degrees warmer here, and the air was drier—the mustiness of the house had been dispelled in the living room, and the slightly sweet, yet acrid smell of a wood fire lingered. He went to the fireplace and snapped the flashlight off. In the sudden blackness the dull red of a banked fire glowed dimly. Glen put out a foot and kicked the remains of the fire. The thin layer of dead ash fell away and the fire leaped into life. Glen frowned at it and shook his head, wondering whether Missy really had seen the smoke that must have been curling from the chimney only a couple of hours ago. Or had it only been a lucky guess?

He moved slowly through the rest of the house, examining everything more carefully. There was no sign of vandalism, no sign that anything had been disturbed at all. Whoever had been here had apparently borne the house no ill will; even the fire seemed to have been tended to.

Glen returned to the living room. The fire had built itself up to a steady blaze. He looked around for a poker, intending to break it down again, but found nothing. He sank into the chair facing the hearth and wondered if it would be safe to leave. But as he listened to the raging storm, he decided to wait awhile, at least until the fire burned down. It would give the storm time to spend itself, and himself time to dry out and warm up. He got up and went to the window that faced north, flashed his light steadily five times, then returned to the chair in front of the fire. If Rebecca was watching she would know he was all right.

On the fishing trawler, Max Horton returned to the engine compartment for a more thorough investigation. There was an off chance that what damage had been done could be repaired and Max could get at least one of the engines going. A close examination dashed his hopes, and he returned to the deck. He cast the beam of the flashlight ahead and immediately realized that the boat had drifted around and was now proceeding stern first. He grabbed a large bucket and ran to the bow, where he tied the bucket to one of the mooring lines. He threw the primitive sea anchor overboard, hoping the current would catch it with enough strength to pull the trawler around. Then he began to consider the advisability of abandoning the boat.

The wind seemed not to be slackening at all—if anything, its intensity was increasing, and it was an onshore wind. If he could rig a sail on the dinghy he just might make it back to safety. But if the sail failed to work the ebbing tide would carry him out to sea. It was this possiblity that made up his mind for him.

If he stayed on the trawler and the sea anchor held, there was a good chance he could ride out the storm, providing he missed the rocks at the mouth of the harbor. But in the dinghy he would have no chance. True, the wind might carry him shoreward, but the combination of wind and tide would surely capsize him. If that happened he would be unconscious in ten minutes, dead in twenty. In daylight he might have risked it, counting on someone to come to his rescue. But at night, in the storm, he would be on his own. He decided to stay with the boat.

As he came to his decision another flash of lightning rent the sky and he tried to get his bearings. The sea anchor had worked, and the trawler was now riding with the tide, her bow into the wind. Far ahead, Max thought he could barely make out the jagged points of the reef, and he told himself that with a little luck he would clear them on the starboard side. He returned to the wheelhouse and lit another cigarette. All he could do was wait.

Harney Whalen parked his car in front of his house and hurried up the steps to the front door, pushing it open, then closing it behind him before he turned on the lights. His uniform was soaking wet; he felt cold clear through to his bones. And his heart was pounding.

He stripped off his dripping clothes and put on a robe, then turned up the heat, lit a fire in the fireplace, and mixed himself a strong brandy and water. He slugged the drink down, mixed another, then went to the bathroom. As the hot water streamed over him and the chill slowly dissipated, his pulse slowed, and by the time he stepped out of the shower, dried himself, and settled down in front of the fire to sip his second drink he felt much better. But he still wasn't entirely sure what had happened.

He remembered being out at Sod Beach, sitting in front of the fire, enjoying the rain and the solitude. He had listened to the storm bear down on the coast, even gotten up once to watch the thunderheads gather before moving in to lash out at Clark's Harbor. He had built up the fire then and settled back into the chair, and begun to daydream. But he must have fallen asleep, or had one of his "spells," for the next thing he remembered he was in his car, driving home. And try as he would, he couldn't account for his uniform being soaked through: the car had been parked only ten or twenty yards from the Baron house. Surely his clothes wouldn't have gotten that wet even if he had crawled the distance.

An image flickered in his mind for a split second, then disappeared: he thought he saw himself on the beach, walking in the storm, staring out to sea. And there was something else, something just beyond his vision. Shapes, familiar shapes, and they were calling to him. But everything was confused, and Whalen couldn't decide whether he'd had a flash of an old memory or whether it was simply his imagination.

He mixed a third drink, weaker this time, and pondered the advisability of discussing the "spells" with Doc Phelps. But Phelps would insist on giving him a complete examination, and Harn wasn't sure he wanted to go through that. You never knew what the doctors might find, and Harn was only a couple of years from retirement. No sense rocking the boat . . .

The ringing of the telephone broke his train of thought.

"Whalen," he said automatically as he picked up the receiver.

"Harn? Where've you been?" Chip Connor's voice sounded almost accusatory, and Whalen scowled.

"Out," he said flatly. There was a slight pause, and Harney felt better as Chip's sudden discomfort projected itself over the telephone line.

"I've been trying to get you all evening," Chip said, his voice conciliatory now. "Thought you'd want to know a couple of fishermen checked into the inn."

"Fishermen?" Whalen repeated.

"Couple guys from up to Port Angeles. Merle says they were heading to Grays Harbor but the storm drove them in here."

Whalen shrugged indifferently. "They have any trouble?" he asked.

"Trouble? No, not that I know of. I just thought you'd want to know they were here."

"Okay," Harn said. "Thanks for calling." He was about to hang up when he suddenly thought of something else. "Chip?"

"Yeah?"

"Anything happen today?"

"Nothing at all," Chip told him. "Quiet as a tomb."

"How'd you like what I did to Palmer?"

There was a silence, and for a moment Harn wasn't sure Chip had heard him. He was about to repeat his question when his deputy spoke.

"I'm trying to act like it was an accident, Harn," Chip said hesitantly.

"It wasn't," Harn growled.

"No, I guess it wasn't." There was another silence, longer than the previous one, as each man waited for the other to speak. Chip weakened first. "I told Palmer it was an accident, Chief."

"I wish you hadn't," Whalen said. "I wish you'd just let him worry."

Chip decided to let the matter drop. "Well, I'll see you in the morning," he said.

"Yeah," Whalen said shortly. "See you in the morning." He dropped the receiver back on its cradle, picked up his drink, and went to the window. He stared out at the storm, not quite seeing it, and his brow furrowed into a deep scowl. All in all, he decided, it had been a rotten day. And the worst of it was, there were parts of it he couldn't even remember. Then he chuckled hollowly to himself, thinking that it didn't much matter—the parts he couldn't remember probably weren't worth remembering anyway.

Jeff Horton glanced at his watch, then went to the window of his hotel room. He tried to make out the wharf a hundred yards away, but the storm was impenetrable. He looked once more at his watch. He had been in the room for nearly forty-five minutes; Max shouldn't have taken more than ten to batten down the boat.

He turned from the window, pulled on his slicker, and left the room. He stopped downstairs and glanced at the bar, but Max wasn't there. Only Merle Glind, perched on a stool, chattering amiably to a young policeman next to him. Jeff went out into the storm.

Even on the wharf the fury of the storm blinded him, and he moved slowly, peering up at each boat as he came abreast of it. Then he came to the empty slip.

The storm forgotten, Jeff stared at the gap which he was sure had been occupied by *Osprey*. He told himself he was wrong, that they had moored the trawler farther out. He broke into a run, struggling against the gale, and made his way to the end of the wharf. There were no other empty slips, and no sign of *Osprey*. He was about to turn back and walk the wharf once more when the night again came alive with lightning, a blue-white sheet that illuminated the whole horizon. The flash pulled his eyes seaward. Far out in the harbor, nearing its mouth, was the silhouette of a boat.

There was no question in Jeff's mind. The boat was *Osprey,* and she was headed directly for the rocks. The white light faded back into blackness, but Jeff stayed rooted to the dock, his eyes straining to pierce the darkness, his mind crying out for another flash of lightning to let him see that the boat had swept past the beckoning fingers of stone. The seconds crept by.

Max Horton was staring numbly out the windshield of the wheelhouse when the sheet of lightning tore the curtain of darkness from his eyes and he realized instantly that the boat was going on the rocks. They loomed dead ahead, only yards away, the sea swirling around them, churning itself into foam as it battered at the ancient barrier.

The imminent peril jerked him out of the lethargy he had sunk into during the past thirty minutes, and he grabbed a life jacket, securing it around his waist. Then he left the wheelhouse and began preparing the dinghy for launching. He pulled its cover free and released the lines that secured it to the davits, then began lowering it into the turbulent sea as it swung free.

He was too late.

The tiny dinghy hit the water and was immediately caught in the eddying currents around the reef. It swamped, then settled into the water, only its gunwales still above the surface.

Finally *Osprey* too became entangled in the furious currents, and her stern swung around. Broadside, she hurled herself onto the rocks, shuddering as her planking split amidships. She settled in the water, groaning and complaining, as the sea pressed in upon her, grinding her against the rocks, tearing her to pieces.

Beneath the surface one of the fuel tanks collapsed under the pressure, and suddenly the hull filled with fumes.

Seconds later, *Osprey* exploded.

Max Horton was blown overboard by the force of the explosion, briefly stunned by the icy water, but began swimming as soon as he came to the surface. It was only a gesture—the tide took him, pulled him away from what might have been the security of the rocks. As soon as he realized what was happening he stopped swimming and rolled over on his back, to watch his trawler go up in flames. He felt the cold begin to grip him, felt the lethargy sink in.

And then the wreck began to fade from his vision. At first he thought it was because he was drifting out on the tide, but then he knew it was something else. Silently, he apologized to Jeff for what had happened, then gave in to the sea. His eyes closed and the storm suddenly was no longer threatening. Now it was lulling him, rocking him gently to sleep. He looked forward to the sleep, though he knew he would never wake up. . . .

The ball of fire rising from the sea didn't register on Jeff immediately. It wasn't until the roar of the explosion hit him seconds later that he realized what had happened. By then the flames had become a fiery beacon in the mouth of the harbor, an inferno of glowing red intertwined with veins of oily black smoke. Then the other fuel tank blew and a second ball of fire rose into the night sky. Jeff Horton, his mind numb with shock, began crying softly, his tears mixing with the rain and salt spray.

Glen Palmer didn't see the first explosion, but when the shock wave hit the old house on the beach he leaped to his feet and ran to a window. He saw the red glow immediately and was staring at it when the second explosion ripped through the night. He grabbed his flashlight and charged out of the house, running along the beach toward the wharf. It wasn't until he'd reached the small point that separated Sod Beach from the short stretch of rocky coast that he realized the explosion had not been at the wharf. It was out in the harbor, far out. And then he knew. A boat had gone on the rocks.

He dashed across the long sand spit that formed the northern arm of the bay and arrived at the wharf just as Merle Glind and Chip Connor stepped out onto the porch of the inn. He started toward them, but as he glanced out the length of the wharf to the fire far beyond, he realized someone was there.

Framed against the inferno, the black silhouette of a man stood quietly, almost sadly, staring out to sea. Glen Palmer changed his mind. Instead of going to the inn, he hurried out onto the wharf.

From his window Harney Whalen gazed out on the fire burning brightly in the harbor.

"Son-of-a-bitch," he said softly to himself. "Somebody's sure got themselves in a peck of trouble tonight."

He went to his bedroom, shed his robe, and began dressing in a clean uniform. He didn't hurry—he'd lived in Clark's Harbor long enough to know that no matter what had happened out there, there wasn't much he could do about it tonight. Not tonight, and not tomorrow.

Not until the storm broke.

Sometimes it seemed to Harney Whalen that in Clark's Harbor the storms never broke.

He was about to leave the house when the telephone rang. He didn't bother to go back. He already knew why it was ringing.

# SEVENTEEN

GLEN PALMER REACHED OUT AND touched Jeff Horton on the shoulder. Jeff turned, and Glen recoiled slightly from the vacant look in the young man's eyes and the dazed expression that had wiped all traces of emotion from his face.

"What happened?" he asked gently.

Jeff blinked twice and his mouth worked spasmodically. "My brother—" he said. "Max—the boat . . ." The reality of it seemed to hit him then like a physical force, and he sank slowly to his knees and buried his face in his hands. His shoulders shook with the sobs that wracked his body.

Glen bit his lip nervously, uncertain what to do. He thought he probably should go to the inn and ask Merle Glind to report what had happened, but he didn't want to leave the grieving young man alone. Then he heard the sound of running feet pounding on the wharf. There was no need to go to the inn.

He knelt next to Jeff and squeezed his shoulder.

"Is it your boat out there?"

Jeff nodded, unable to speak.

"And your brother . . . ?"

Jeff looked up then, and the slackness in his face had been replaced by a grimace of confusion and pain.

"He was only going to batten down and grab a couple of charts—" Jeff tried to explain. "He said he'd be right back. But he didn't come back—" Sobs overtook him and he leaned heavily against Glen, his body heaving.

"Glen?" The voice was tentative, and Glen looked up to see Chip Connor standing over him. "I thought it was you. What the hell's going on?"

Glen shook his head. "I don't know. I just got here myself."

"I told Merle to call Harn Whalen," Chip said. Then he too knelt beside Jeff Horton. "That your boat out there, buddy?"

Jeff nodded miserably. Chip gazed out into the night. The fire was dying down; the driving rain and wind would put it out in a matter of minutes. "Let's get over to the inn," he said softly. "No point in staying here."

Supporting Jeff Horton between them, Chip and Glen started back along the wharf. After a few steps Jeff seemed to come to his senses a little and was able to walk unaided. Every few steps he would stop, turn, and gaze out at the blaze for a few seconds. Then, finally, he turned to look and saw only the blackness of the night. The fire was out; *Osprey* had disappeared. Jeff didn't look back again.

Merle Glind bustled up to the trio as they entered the inn. "I called Harney," he chirped breathlessly. "There wasn't any answer."

"Don't worry about it," Chip told him. "He probably saw the fire from up on the hill and left by the time you called. Why don't you give this guy a slug of brandy—he looks like he could use it."

Jeff was slumped in a chair. The bright light of the inn revealed an ashen face, the stubble of a day-old beard, and red-rimmed eyes that made him seem old and broken. The vacant stare Glen had noticed when he first found Jeff had returned, and once more his face had gone slack.

"I think we'd better call a doctor," Glen said. "I think he's in shock."

"Call Phelps," Chip said.

Glen quickly made the call and was returning to the lobby when Harney Whalen lumbered through the door. Whalen glanced around, sizing up the situation, then approached his deputy.

"What the hell's going on?" he asked, echoing Chip's question of only a few minutes ago. "Is everybody all right?"

"We don't know yet," Chip replied. "I was in the bar with Merle, having a couple drinks, when we heard the explosion. I thought it was thunder but then we saw the fire. Merle called you and I went down to the wharf. Glen Palmer was there with this guy." He nodded toward Jeff Horton, who sat staring at the floor, his hands clutching the glass of brandy Merle Glind had brought from the bar. If he was aware of the conversation between the chief and his deputy, he gave no sign. Whalen's eyes narrowed slightly as he looked Jeff over, then he approached the young man.

"You want to tell me what happened?" he asked. His voice held neither hostility nor concern; it was his professional voice, the voice he habitually used before he had made up his mind.

"I don't know what happened," Jeff said absently. He still stared at the floor.

"My deputy tells me you were out on the wharf when that boat blew up."

Jeff nodded and sipped his drink.

"Mind telling me what you were doing out there?"

Jeff frowned a little, as if trying to remember. "I was looking for my brother . . . I was looking for Max . . ." he trailed off, then suddenly took a long swallow of brandy, and set the empty glass down. Whalen sat down next to him.

"Why don't you start at the beginning?"

"There isn't anything to tell," Jeff said slowly, making an effort to keep himself under control. "I was up in our room waiting for Max. He was going to secure the boat for the night—he shouldn't have been more than ten minutes. After forty-five minutes I looked for him in the bar over there, then went down to the wharf. The boat was gone. I didn't believe it at first, but then there was a bolt of sheet lightning and the whole harbor lit up. And I saw *Osprey*. She was heading out of the harbor, right toward the rocks—"

He broke off, seeing the explosion once more, hearing the dull booming sound, watching the trawler burn. He struggled with himself and regained the composure that had nearly collapsed. "I have to go out there," he said dully. "I have to go out and look for Max."

"You aren't going anywhere tonight, son, and neither is anyone else," Whalen said emphatically. "No sense having two boats piled up on those rocks."

Doc Phelps arrived then, and immediately began examining Jeff Horton. While he bent over the young man, Whalen turned his attention to Merle Glind.

"Who is he?" he asked Glind quietly.

"His name's Jeff Horton," Glind said. "He checked in about five thirty, six o'clock. He's from Port Angeles." Glind frowned, as if remembering something. "Didn't Chip call you? I was sure he did."

"He called me," Whalen said patiently. "But that didn't mean this was one of the same guys he told me about. Did you hear what Horton just told me?"

Glind bobbed his head. "Not that I was eavesdropping, mind you. You know me, Harney—I'd never try to listen in on something that's none of my business. But he is a guest in my hotel and I figured—" Before he could continue, Whalen cut him off.

"Merle, it's all right. All I want to know is if you can verify any of his story."

Glind thought hard and finally nodded. "I can verify the time he went out. I was sitting with Chip and I was facing the door. I saw him stick his head in and look around. Then he went out and about five minutes later, maybe less, the explosion happened. He couldn't have had anything to do with it, Harn. There wasn't enough time. It'd take any boat a lot longer than that to get from the wharf to the rocks."

"You don't say," Whalen said, scowling at the little man. Merle flushed and his glance darted toward the bar.

"I'd better be getting back to business," Glind said anxiously. "Likely to be a lot of customers in here tonight. Not every night we have excitement like this." Rubbing his hands together in anticipation of the cash he expected to see flowing over the bar this evening, he hurried away. Whalen watched him go and shook his head sadly, pitying the fussy little fellow who tried so hard to fit in—and failed so miserably. But Whalen forgave him his shortcomings: he and Merle Glind had grown up together.

He was about to ask Dr. Phelps about Jeff Horton's condition when Chip Connor waved to him. He and Glen Palmer had been talking near the registration counter. Whalen looked inquiringly at Chip.

"Do you need me for anything?" Chip asked him. "If you don't, I thought I'd run Glen home. He's afraid his wife will be worrying about him."

"Well, she's just going to have to worry awhile longer, I'm afraid," Whalen said, his voice hard, uncompromising. "I have a few questions to ask you, Palmer."

Glen started to argue, then changed his mind. An argument would only make Whalen determined to keep him even longer. Instead, he turned to Chip.

"I know it's a hell of a thing to ask, but do you think you could run out there anyway, just to let her know I'm all right?"

"No problem," Chip said. "Unless Harn has something pressing he wants me to take care of." He turned to the chief, and Whalen chewed his lip, thinking. Finally he nodded curtly.

"All right, but don't be gone all night. I'm going to need you later."

"I'll be back in half an hour," he promised. He went to the bar, and returned a minute later with his raincoat. "Anything special you want me to tell her?" he asked Glen. Glen shook his head.

"Just tell her what's happened and not to worry. Tell her I'll be home when I get there."

Chip nodded and went out into the storm. Glen waited until he was gone, then went over to Whalen, who was talking to Dr. Phelps.

"Shall we get started?" he asked as amiably as he could. "I'd just as soon not be here all night. It's been a long day."

"I'll bet it has," Whalen replied. "It's likely to be a lot longer before it's over. Why don't you have a seat. I'll get to you when I get to you."

"Is it all right if I wait in the bar?" Glen asked.

"Suit yourself. Just don't try to leave the hotel."

Glen chose to ignore the veiled threat, and nodded briefly. He ordered a beer and prepared to drink it slowly. He was going to have a long wait.

Rebecca Palmer sat by the fireplace and tried to concentrate on her knitting, but she was unable to complete more than a stitch or two before she set her work aside and went to the window once more, straining to see beyond the wet blackness of the rain and the wind.

It had been almost an hour and a half since Glen had left the cabin, and he should have been back at least an hour ago. She had stayed by the window after he left, and fifteen minutes later had seen his flashlight, dim but distinct, going steadily on and off. She had relaxed then and waited for him to return, sure she had read his signal correctly. But then—she wasn't sure how much later—she had heard the explosion and run to the window to see the ball of fire far beyond the beach. There had been a second explosion, a second fireball, and a blaze out at sea.

Since then, nothing.

Innumerable trips to the window.

Impulses to go out on the beach and search for Glen.

Attempts to concentrate on her knitting.

And a continually growing fear.

Something had happened. She didn't know why, but she was sure the explosions at sea had something to do with Glen's protracted absence. But what?

It was the not knowing that was the worst. If only they had a telephone. If only the storm weren't so bad. If only the children were old enough to stay by themselves. But there was no phone, the storm showed no signs of abating, and the children could not be left alone. Even the puppy was too young to serve as a guardian.

She was about to go to the window again when she thought she heard a car door slam. She froze where she was, listening intently. Then came the knock at the door.

Rebecca felt her heart begin to pound as she went to the door, but before she reached out to pull it open, something in her mind rang a warning bell.

"Who is it?" she called softly, not wanting to wake the children.

"Chip Connor," came the reply. Rebecca threw open the door and stared up at the deputy, her fear growing.

"What is it?" she cried. "What's happened?"

"Nothing's happened, Mrs. Palmer. Well, nothing's happened to Glen, anyway. May I come in?"

Rebecca felt the tension she had been under suddenly release; her knees felt weak. "Of course," she said, stepping back to make room for the deputy. She closed the door after him, then went to the fire. She poked it, then turned to Chip.

"What's happened? Where's Glen?"

"He's fine, Mrs. Palmer. He asked me to come out here and tell you he's all right. He'll be back as soon as he can." He saw the look of bewilderment on Rebecca's face and decided he'd better explain things. Fast. "There was an accident. We still don't know exactly what happened," he began, but Rebecca cut him off.

"An accident?" she said dazedly. "What kind of accident? Was it that fire? I saw a fire out in the water. Was that it?"

Chip nodded. "That's it. A boat that was tied up in the harbor for the night wound up on the rocks in the mouth of the harbor. It blew up."

"My God," Rebecca breathed. "Was anyone hurt?"

"Someone may have been on the boat. We don't know for sure yet. Anyway, when I got to the wharf Glen was already there. He saw as much of what happened as anybody. So Whalen asked him to stick around for a while." Chip saw no point in telling Rebecca that her husband had been ordered to stay at the scene, not invited.

"Thank God," Rebecca sighed. "You don't have any idea of how worried I was. He should have been back, and then I saw those awful explosions, and—" she stopped talking when she saw the expression on Chip's face.

"You mean he wasn't here when the explosions happened?" he asked.

"No, of course not," Rebecca said. "Didn't he tell you?"

"He didn't tell me much of anything," Chip replied. "Where was he?"

"He'd gone down the beach to check on the old house—the one the Randalls are going to move into. Missy—our daughter—thought there was someone in the house this afternoon, so Glen went down to check on it. He must have seen the explosions from there and gone to the wharf."

"How long was he gone? Before the explosions, I mean?"

"I'm not sure," Rebecca began. Then she realized what Chip was getting at. "My God, you don't think Glen had anything to do with those explosions, do you?"

"Of course not," Chip said immediately. "But I want you to tell me exactly what happened." He got out a notebook and a pencil, then saw the look of fear in Rebecca's eyes, the same fear he had seen in Glen's eyes earlier. He smiled at her reassuringly. "Mrs. Palmer, you don't have to answer any of my questions if you don't want to. But I hope you will. I want to put down in this notebook, right now, everything you can remember about what you and Glen talked about, why he went out, what time he went out—everything. I'm absolutely sure that everything you tell me will match up exactly with what Glen tells Harn Whalen. And then I'll be able to back him up, because I'll have the same story from you before you and Glen could possibly have talked to each other."

Rebecca turned it over in her mind and tried to figure out what Glen would want her to do. She remembered Glen talking about this man, telling her he'd spent most of the day helping him—helping *them*. Now here he was, volunteering to help them again. Or was he? She gazed into his eyes, trying to read his motives.

His eyes were clear.

"My name's Rebecca," she said softly. "Glen told me about what you did today. I want to thank you."

Chip flushed and kept his eyes on the pad. "It's okay," he said. "I had a good time doing it." Then he looked up at her. "What about the questions? Will you answer them?"

"Of course," Rebecca said. "Where shall we start?"

The third beer was sitting untouched in front of Glen when Harney Whalen stepped through the door to the bar and called him.

"Palmer, you want to come in here now?"

Glen slid off his stool, and went into the lobby. Dr. Phelps had left, after concluding that Jeff Horton was suffering from a mild case of shock that would pass before morning. The doctor had assured Whalen that there was nothing about the young fisherman's condition that would make it inadvisable for Harn to question him, and Whalen was in the final stages of doing just that. As Glen appeared in the lobby he looked up.

"I want you and Horton here to come down to the station. We might just as well fill out the official reports tonight, while everything's still fresh in your memories."

Glen grinned wryly, and said, "I'm not sure anything's still fresh in my memory. I've been drinking beer for almost an hour." Then he glanced around the room and his grin faded. "Where's Connor?"

"He hasn't come back yet," Whalen informed him. "You ready?"

Glen shrugged, as if to imply that he had no choice, then followed Jeff Horton and Harn Whalen to Whalen's black-and-white. Minutes later they were in the police station.

"Okay, Palmer," Whalen said without preamble, "let's have it."

"Have what?" Glen asked. "I'm afraid you've kept me around all night for nothing. I don't have any idea what happened."

"Maybe you'd like to tell me about how you happened to be on the wharf?"

"I saw the explosions and ran to the harbor. Then I saw this fellow at the end of the dock. I went out to see if he needed any help. That's all there was to it."

Whalen studied him through narrowed eyes for a few seconds. "You sure must run fast. The wharf's a long way from your house."

"I wasn't at home," Glen said, offering no more information.

"Why don't you tell me just where you were?" Whalen growled.

"Actually I was in your house, at the other end of Sod Beach from mine. From there it isn't very far to the wharf. Just around the point, across the rocky beach and the sandbar."

Whalen's fingers drummed on the desk. He seemed to be turning something over in his mind.

"How did you happen to be the only one who went out on the wharf? Merle and Chip were both outside, but they didn't go out on the dock."

"They probably didn't see any reason to go. From where they were standing they wouldn't have been able to see Jeff. I only saw him because he happened to be between me and the fire. If I hadn't, I would have gone to the inn. But I saw him, so I went out on the wharf."

"What the hell were you doing in my house?" Whalen said suddenly, changing the subject of the conversation so violently that for a second Glen drew a blank. Then he recovered himself.

"You might say I was doing you a favor," he said, controlling his anger. Who the hell did Whalen think he was? "My daughter thought someone was in the house this afternoon, and I thought I ought to check up. Or don't you care who goes in and out of your own property?"

"What I care about or don't care about is my own damned business, mister. Understand? Next time you think someone might have been in that house you tell me about it. Don't go snooping around on your own."

Glen felt his fury almost choking him but he held it back. "Fine," he said tightly. "But in case you're interested, which apparently you're not, someone was in that house today. And he hadn't been gone long when I arrived. There was a fire still burning in the fireplace. It had been banked, but not for long."

"You're right," Whalen said easily. "I was in the house this afternoon." Then he jerked a thumb at Jeff Horton. "You ever see him before tonight?"

"No."

"What about you, Horton? You ever see this guy before?"

"I already told you, Chief, I've never seen anybody around here before tonight. Not you, not him, not anybody. Now, for God's sake, aren't you going to do anything about my brother?"

"And I've already told you," Whalen mimicked him, "there's nothing we can do about your brother. If he was on that boat he died when it blew. If he went overboard he didn't last more than twenty minutes in the water. In ten minutes a man passes out, out there. In ten more minutes he's dead. So you'd better hope that your brother was never on that boat. And that seems pretty unlikely, since you claim the boat was headed directly for the rocks."

"What the hell are you saying?" Jeff cried.

"I'm saying that unless one of you two is lying, it looks to me like your brother got on that boat and deliberately piled himself up."

"That's a fucking lie!" Jeff yelled. "He was securing the boat for the night. Max would never do anything like that. Never!"

A slow smile came over Whalen's face. "What are you saying then? That someone killed him? Cut the boat loose? Steered it out onto that reef?"

"Something like that," Jeff replied. "I don't know why, and I don't know who, but it was something like that. But we won't know anything about it until we go out there, will we?"

"No," Whalen agreed, "we won't. Meantime, Horton, I think maybe you'd better plan on sticking around to answer some more questions. You too, Palmer."

Glen's fury finally exploded. "Are you out of your mind?" he yelled at the police chief. "You tell me right now, Whalen, am I under arrest or not?"

"You're not," Whalen said mildly, almost enjoying the other man's rage. "Not yet."

"And I damned well won't be," Palmer declared. "I had no motive, I wasn't there. Hell, I don't even know what kind of a boat it was. Dammit, Whalen, all I did was try to help out." He stalked out of the police station, half-expecting Whalen to stop him. But he didn't.

Instead, when they were alone, Whalen turned to Jeff Horton.

"I don't like what happened here tonight," he said softly, almost menacingly. "I don't like it at all. I intend to find out what happened though, and I intend to see to it that it never happens again. And once I've found out I'll expect you to get out of Clark's Harbor. I don't like strangers. They bring trouble. You've brought trouble, and your friend Palmer's brought trouble. So hang around only as long as I tell you to. Then get out. Understand?"

Jeff Horton, still numbed from the shock of what had happened, nodded mutely and told himself he wasn't hearing what he thought he had just heard. As he walked slowly back to the hotel, Jeff cursed the storm that had brought him to Clark's Harbor, cursed Clark's Harbor, and cursed Harney Whalen.

His impulse was to leave. He had no baggage, nothing. He could simply check out of the inn, walk up to the main highway, and thumb a ride north. But he knew he couldn't.

He had to stay in Clark's Harbor.

He had to find Max.

As the storm slashed rain in his face, Jeff tried to tell himself that he would find his brother, that Max would be all right.

His guts told him he was wrong. His guts told him Max was not all right; nothing would ever be all right again.

Glen Palmer was still almost shaking with rage when he left the police station. He began walking toward the harbor before he stopped to think it out. He wondered if Rebecca might drive in to pick him up, but decided she wouldn't—she didn't like leaving the children by themselves. Then he remembered Chip Connor. The deputy still hadn't returned, but if Glen followed the road Chip might pass him and give him a lift. He turned around and began walking up Harbor Road. He had just reached the intersection with the main highway when a pair of headlights appeared from the north. Glen stepped out into the road and waved. The car pulled up beside him.

"Climb in," Chip called. "I'm so late now a few more minutes won't matter. Is Harn mad at me?"

Gratefully Glen got into the car, and as Chip made the U-turn that would take them back north, he asked the deputy for a cigarette.

"I quit a couple of years ago," he said as he lit it. "But after what just happened, I think I'm going to start again."

Chip glanced at him, then his eyes went back to the road.

"If you want to cuss Whalen out," he said, "could you wait until you're home and I'm gone?"

"What does that mean?" Glen asked.

"Ah, shit, I don't know," Chip said. Then he grinned crookedly at Glen. "You know, it would have been a lot easier for you tonight if you hadn't gone out playing good citizen."

"Rebecca told you where I was?"

"I asked her. And don't worry, I told her she didn't have to answer any questions."

"But why did you even ask any?"

"Just in case," Chip said. He turned off the highway into the narrow drive that led to the Palmers' cabin. He pulled up as close to the little house as he could but didn't turn off the engine. "I'm not coming in. I'd better get back to town and see what Harn's got." He paused. Glen had started to get out of the car when Chip spoke again. "Glen?" Glen turned back to the deputy. "I'm not sure how to say this, but I like you and I like your wife. That's why I didn't want to hear you cuss Harney out. I know what must have happened down there, and I have a feeling it isn't over yet." He paused, suddenly unsure of himself, then plunged on. "That's why I wanted to get Rebecca's story before you talked to her. Look, try to keep cool, okay? Harney can be hard to deal with, particularly if he doesn't know you. But he's fair. I know you don't think so, but he is. Or anyway, he tries to be," Chip added, remembering the spattered paintings that morning.

Glen took a deep breath, then let it out in an even deeper sigh. "I don't know," he said finally. Then he chuckled hollowly. "But I guess I have no choice." He extended his hand to the deputy. "I'll sit tight and we'll see what happens. Thanks for the ride. And everything else too."

The two men shook hands and Glen got out of the car. The rain had let up a little, and Glen waited until Chip had disappeared into the night before he went in.

Rebecca was waiting for him. She threw her arms around him, and hugged him tightly.

"What's happening? Dear God, Glen, what's happening here?"

"I don't know," Glen whispered gently. "But whatever it is, it doesn't have anything to do with us. Nothing at all."

He wished he was as certain of that as he had tried to sound. But something was happening, and he could feel himself and his family getting caught up in it. Without telling Rebecca, he decided to call Brad Randall in the morning.

In the tiny bedroom adjoining the main room of the cabin, Missy and Robby lay in their bunks, neither of them asleep. Robby's eyes were closed, but Missy was wide-eyed, staring at the bed above her. When she spoke her voice sounded hollow in the darkness.

"Are you all right?" she whispered.

There was a moment's silence, then Robby's voice drifted back to her. "I think so. But I've been feeling funny for a long time."

"I know," Missy said. "I had a dream." Her voice faltered, then went on. "It was scary. And I don't think I was asleep."

Robby crept down from the upper bunk and crouched by his sister. "What was it?"

"I'm not sure," the little girl said shyly. "I thought you were in it, but you seemed big. Real big, And not like you."

Robby frowned and waited for Missy to continue. When she remained silent he asked a question.

"Was I . . . all right? Or was I sick again?"

"You were . . ." Missy began, but broke off when she couldn't find the right words. She started again. "You were making things happen. You made a boat sink and you laughed. At least I think it was you. Maybe it wasn't," she added hopefully.

Robby shook his head in the darkness. "I don't remember anything," he said vaguely. "I couldn't sleep and I wanted to go outside."

"Why didn't you?" Missy asked.

"You would have told Mom and Dad," Robby said matter-of-factly. He climbed back up into the top bunk.

Again there was a silence, and the two children listened to the storm howling outside.

"I wish it would stop," Missy said quietly.

"I do too," Robby agreed.

Suddenly, without any warning, the rain stopped and the wind died.

Silence fell over Sod Beach.

# STORM DANCERS

# EIGHTEEN

**E**LAINE RANDALL WAS STARING DISCONSO-
lately at the dishes stacked on the kitchen counter. There seemed to
be so many of them, now that they had been taken out of the
cupboard, that she couldn't decide whether to pack them in a box to
be taken to Clark's Harbor or to haul them down to the large storeroom in
the basement where most of their personal effects were going to be stored
while they were gone. Finally she evaded the issue entirely by turning her
attention to the pots and pans. Those were easy—the old, battered ones
went with them, the good ones stayed behind. She was about to begin
packing what seemed to her like the ninety-fifth box when the telephone
rang. Gratefully, she straightened up and reached for the phone.

"I'll get it," Brad called from the living room, where he was filling
cartons with books.

"Some people get all the breaks," Elaine muttered loudly enough so she was sure Brad heard her.

"Hello?" Brad said automatically as he picked up the receiver.

"Brad? Is that you? It's Glen Palmer."

"Hi!" Brad exclaimed warmly. "What's up?"

There was a slight hesitation, then Glen's voice came over the line once more, but almost haltingly.

"Look, are you people still planning to move out here?"

"Imminently," Brad replied. "I'm packing books and Elaine's working on the kitchen. Sort of a last vestige of sexism, you might say." When the joke elicited no response, not even the faintest chuckle, Brad frowned slightly. "Is something wrong out there?"

"I don't know," Glen replied slowly. "A boat cracked up on the rocks out here last night."

"Last night? But it was calm and clear last night."

"Not in Clark's Harbor, it wasn't. We had a hell of a storm."

Brad's brows rose in puzzlement, but then he shrugged. "Well, anybody who goes out in 'a hell of a storm' deserves to go on the rocks," he said complacently.

"Except that nobody knows how the boat got there. Your landlord seems to think I had something to do with it."

"You? What gave him that idea?"

"I don't know. I don't know anything anymore." There was a silence, then Glen's voice went on, hesitantly, almost apologetically. "That's why I called you. Everything seems crazy out here and I didn't have anyone else to talk to. How long before you'll be coming out?"

"Not long," Brad said. "Today, in fact."

"Today?" There was an eagerness in Glen's voice that Brad found disturbing.

"We're packing up the last of our stuff. The truck should be here around noon. I'd say we should be there somewhere around four, maybe five o'clock."

"Well, I guess I won't crack up by then," Glen said, but his voice shook slightly. "I hate to tell you this, Brad, but something horrible is going on out here."

"You make it sound like some kind of conspiracy," Brad said, his curiosity whetted. "You sure you're not letting your imagination get the best of you?"

"I don't know," Glen said. "How many times have I said that? Look, do me a favor, will you? Come see me this afternoon or this evening? If I'm not at the gallery I'll be at home."

"I'd planned on it anyway," Brad assured him. "And look, don't get yourself too upset. Whatever's happening, I'm sure there's a reasonable explanation."

"Well, I'm glad you're sure. All right, no sense running this call up any higher. See you later."

As Brad said good-bye he realized Elaine was standing in the archway that separated the living room from the dining room, a curious expression on her face.

"What's going on? Who was that?"

"Glen Palmer."

"What did he want?"

"I'm not really sure," Brad mused. "He's all upset about something. A boat went on the rocks last night and Glen seems to think Harney Whalen wants to blame it on him."

"I didn't know Glen even had a boat."

"It wasn't his boat apparently." He shrugged, and began packing books again. "I told him we'd be out there this afternoon, so he didn't go into the details. But he sure sounded upset."

Elaine stayed where she was and watched Brad work. Then she moved to the living-room window and stared out at Seward Park and the lake beyond. "I wonder if we're making a mistake," she said, not turning around.

"A mistake?" Brad's voice sounded concerned. Elaine faced him, letting him see the worry on her face.

"It just seems to me that maybe we shouldn't go out there. I mean, there really isn't any reason why you can't write here, is there? Certainly our view is as good as the view from the beach, and you don't have to be bothered with interruptions. A lot of people manage to live like hermits in the middle of the city. Why can't we?"

"I suppose we could," Brad replied. "But I don't want to. Besides, maybe something *is* going on out there."

"If there is I don't want any part of it," Elaine said with a shudder.

"Well, I do. Who knows? Maybe I'll get a best seller out of this whole deal."

"Or maybe you'll just get a lot of trouble," Elaine said. But she realized that there was going to be no argument. Brad's mind was made up, and that was that. So she winked at him, tried to put her trepidations out of her mind, and went back to her packing.

She finished in the kitchen at the same time Brad sealed the last carton of books. As if on cue the truck that would move them to Clark's Harbor pulled into the driveway.

Jeff Horton stayed in bed as long as he could that morning, but by ten o'clock he decided it was futile and got up. It had been a night of fitful sleep disturbed by visions of the fire, and through most of the small hours he had lain awake, trying to accept what had happened, trying to find an explanation. But there was none.

Max had been securing the boat. That was all.

He wouldn't have taken her out. Not alone, and cetainly not in a storm.

But he must have been on the boat or he would have come to the inn.

If he was on the boat, why did it go on the rocks? Why didn't he start the engines?

There was only one logical answer to that: the engines had been tampered with. But by whom? And why? They were strangers here; they knew no one. So no one here would have any reason to sabotage the boat.

None of it made any sense, but it had cost Jeff dearly. His brother was gone, his boat was gone, and he felt helpless.

Several times during the night he had gone to the window and tried to peer through the darkness, tried to make himself see *Osprey* still tied up at the wharf, floating peacefully in the now-calm harbor. But when morning came Jeff avoided the window, postponing the moment when he would have to face the bleak truth of the empty slip at the dock.

Merle Glind peered at him dolefully when he went downstairs, as if he were an unwelcome reminder of something better forgotten, and Jeff hurried out of the inn without speaking to the little man. He paused on the porch and forced himself to look out over the harbor.

Far in the distance the mass of rocks protruded from the calm surface of the sea, looking harmless in the morning sunlight.

There was no sign of the fishing trawler that had gutted itself on them only hours ago.

Seeing the naked rocks, Jeff felt a surge of hope. Then his eyes went to the wharf, and there was the empty slip, silent testimony to the disappearance of *Osprey*. Jeff walked slowly down to the pier, to the spot where the trawler should have been moored. He stood there for a long time, as if trying by the force of his will alone to make the trawler reappear. Then he heard a voice behind him.

"She's gone, son," Mac Riley said softly. Jeff turned around and faced the old man.

"I warned you," Riley said, his voice gentle and without a trace of malice. "It's not safe, not when the storms are up."

"It wasn't the storm," Jeff said. "I don't care how bad that storm was, those lines didn't give way. Someone threw them."

Riley didn't argue. Instead, his eyes drifted away from Jeff, out to the mouth of the harbor. "Sort of seems like the wreck should still be there, doesn't it?" he mused. Before Jeff could make any reply, the old man continued, "That's the way she is, the sea. Sometimes she throws ships up on the rocks, then leaves them there for years, almost like she's trying to warn you. But not here. Here she takes things, and she keeps them. Reckon that'll be the way with your boat. Wouldn't be surprised if nothing ever turns up."

"There's always wreckage," Jeff said. "It'll turn up somewhere."

"If I were you I'd just go away and forget all about it," Riley said. "Ain't nothing you can do about it, son. Clark's Harbor ain't like other places. Things work different here."

"That's just what the police chief said last night," Jeff said angrily. "What do you mean, things work different here?"

"Just that. It's the sea, and the beach. The Indians knew all about it, and they thought this was a holy place. I suppose we do too. Strangers have to be careful here. If you don't know what you're doing, bad things happen. Well, I guess you know about that, don't you?"

"All I know," Jeff said doggedly, "is that my boat's wrecked and my brother's missing."

"He's dead, son. If he was on that boat he's dead." There was no malice in Riley's voice; it was simply a statement of fact.

"If his body turns up then he's dead," Jeff replied. "As long as there's no body he isn't dead."

"Suit yourself," Riley said. "But if I were you I'd just head on back to wherever you came from and start over again. And stay away from Clark's Harbor."

He reached out and patted Jeff on the shoulder, but Jeff drew angrily away.

"I'm going to find out what happened," he said.

"Maybe you will, son," Riley said placidly. "But I wouldn't count on that. Best thing to do is learn to live with it, like all the rest of us."

"I can't," Jeff said almost inaudibly. "I have to know what happened to my brother."

"Sometimes it's better not to know," Riley replied. "But I guess you can't understand that, can you?"

"No, I can't."

"You will, son. Someday, maybe not very far down the road, you'll understand."

The old man patted him on the shoulder once more and started back toward shore. Then he turned, and Jeff thought he was going to say something else, but he seemed to change his mind. Wordlessly, he continued on his way.

Jeff stayed on the wharf awhile longer, then began walking south along the narrow strip of beach that bordered the harbor. Somewhere, parts of *Osprey* must have been washed ashore. If he was lucky, one of those parts might offer some clue.

The storm of the night before had left a layer of silt on the beach, washed down from the forest above. Wet and thick, it clung to Jeff's boots as he trod slowly out to the end of the southern arm of the harbor. Nowhere did he find even a trace of wreckage. He hadn't really expected to. If there was going to be anything it would probably be north, taken out by the ebbing tide, then carried up the coast on the current. But from the end of the point he would have a good view of the rocks. Perhaps something would be visible from there that couldn't be seen from the wharf.

There was nothing, only the black and glistening crags of granite, clearly visible and unthreatening in the calm sea. Nowhere was there a sign of the damage they had wreaked the night before, nowhere a scrap of the boat that had broken up on them.

Jeff lingered on the point for a while, almost as if his proximity to the scene of the disaster would somehow help him to determine what had happened. But the reef merely mocked him, taunting him with its look of innocence.

After thirty minutes he turned away and started back along the beach.

He didn't go out to the end of the sand spit at the north end of the harbor. Instead he followed the worn path that cut across it to the rock-strewn cove beyond. Jeff explored the small beach carefully, inspecting pieces of driftwood that appeared to have been brought to shore the night before, his eyes carefully searching for any familiar object, any broken piece of flotsam that might be part of the vanished trawler. Again there was nothing.

Finally he rounded the point and stood at the southernmost tip of Sod Beach. For the first time his eyes stopped searching the shore at his feet and took in the beauty of the spot. It seemed incongruous to him that something as magnificent as this could be here, in the middle of such deadly surround-ings. The beach lay bathed in sunlight, and the surf, free to wash the shore here, had cleaned away the silt that covered the harbor sands. Only a haphaz-ard scattering of driftwood gave evidence of the storm that had battered the coast the night before, and even that, strewn evenly over the beach, only enhanced the beauty and peace of the place.

Jeff began walking the beach, no longer really looking for wreckage from *Osprey*. The splendor of the white sands had overcome him, and for the moment he forgot about the previous night and let its serenity wash over him. He picked up a small stone and threw it expertly at one of the logs that lay along the tide line, then laughed out loud as the tiny brown shape of a baby otter sprang out from behind it, peered vacantly at him for a moment, and began scurrying toward the woods.

He began running, and the running felt good, felt free. He could feel the tension he had been under releasing itself as he ran and pushed himself harder. When he felt his breath grow short and his heart begin to pound, he slowed to a trot, then gave it up entirely and sat panting on a log, facing the surf.

He had been staring at the object floating in the water for several seconds before he even realized he was watching it. It was about thirty yards out and nearly submerged; all that showed above the surface was a grayish mass, gleaming wetly in the sunlight. At first Jeff thought it was a piece of driftwood, but as the surf carried it slowly shoreward he realized it was something else. It looked like canvas. Jeff stood and advanced toward the water, straining for a better view of it, sure that it was from *Osprey*.

The object washed back and forth, but finally a large breaker rolled in, caught it up, and threw it forward. Jeff dashed into the surf, his outstretched hands reaching to grasp it.

He had a firm grip on it before he realized it was Max.

The body, limp and grayish, was suspended under the sodden life pre-server. Without thinking, Jeff grasped his brother under the arms and pulled him up onto the beach, far beyond the reach of the surf, and lay him gently on his back.

He wrestled with the straps of the life jacket, tugging at swollen strips of material, forcing them loose. Then he cast the preserver aside and pressed violently on Max's chest. A stream of water gushed from between the lips of the corpse, and there was a faint gurgling sound as the water was replaced by air when Jeff released the pressure.

Feverishly, he worked over his brother's body. He knew Max was dead, yet his mind refused to accept the fact. Over and over he applied pressure to the torso, but after the first efforts no more water appeared. Max lay limp and unresponding on the sand.

Jeff gave it up finally and crouched on his haunches next to his brother, staring down into the open, unseeing eyes. When he could stand it no longer he gently closed the eyelids. For the rest of his life he would live with the memory of Max's eyes, staring up at him from the sand, almost reproachful.

Jeff began to cry, his sobs shaking him, his tears flowing freely. And then, a few minutes later, it was over.

Jeff Horton picked up his brother's body, cradling it in his arms, and began to walk back down Sod Beach, back toward Clark's Harbor.

A few minutes later the beach was empty once more, except for the gulls wheeling overhead and the baby otter playing in the driftwood. All was peaceful.

But far out to sea, beyond the horizon, the clouds began to gather and the wind began to blow. Another storm was coming to life.

## NINETEEN

"HOW MUCH FARTHER?" ELAINE ASKED. "Five miles? Ten? Something like that," Brad answered. "Please note that it isn't raining."

"Noted," Elaine said. By rights they should have run into the storm that had battered Clark's Harbor the night before, and Elaine had made a bet with Brad that they would make the entire drive out to Clark's Harbor in a downpour. But as they swung around Olympia and started west, they encountered nothing but clear skies, and for the last two hours they had been enjoying the warmth of a spring sun. A ground layer of mist lay in the valleys, intertwined with the ferns and salal that blanketed the area in a spectrum of greens, broken by the brown trunks of the giant cedars and the silvery whiteness of budding aspens. Here and there a rhododendron was bursting with color, the sunlight flashing in the raindrops caught in its petals.

"You want to pay off now or wait till we get there?"

"I'll wait," Elaine said complacently. "You never know when it might cloud up. If there's even a drop of rain while we're unloading, I win."

Brad glanced up at the clear blue sky, and grinned. "I can't lose." He glanced in the rearview mirror, as he had every few minutes for the last three and a half hours, checking to make sure the truck was still following behind them. "I can't believe how much stuff they jam in those trucks," he commented.

"I can't believe how much stuff we're dragging with us," Elaine replied archly. "The house out here *is* furnished as I recall."

Brad shrugged indifferently but couldn't keep himself from flushing slightly. As the movers had begun loading Brad had begun adding things to the load. His desk and chair had been first, followed by an ancient leather-upholstered club chair that Elaine had claimed would fit in perfectly since it was nearly as dilapidated as the furniture already in the house on Sod Beach.

When he had started to add the television and stereo console, Elaine had drawn the line, reminding him that there was no electricity in their new home.

Finally they had been ready to go; the truck was almost full and the storage room in the basement almost empty. But, as Brad kept insisting, at least they were getting their money's worth out of the truck.

They swung around a bend in the road. They were almost in Clark's Harbor. Ahead of them they could see the intersection with Harbor Road and, just beyond, Glen Palmer's gallery.

"Are we stopping at the gallery?" Elaine asked as Brad began slowing the car.

"I thought I'd stop off at the police station first and pick up the key," Brad replied. "Then you can ride on out to the house in the truck and supervise the unloading while I talk to Glen."

"The hell you will," Elaine protested. "If you think I'm going to try to get all that junk into the house by myself, you're crazy! Besides, I want to see Glen too!"

"All right, all right," Brad said. He completed the turn and they started down the gentle incline into the village. "Well, whatever's going on, it certainly looks peaceful enough."

Elaine couldn't disagree; Clark's Harbor, basking in the sunlight, lay clustered peacefully around the harbor, its brightly painted buildings sparkling against the backdrop of blue sky and water. Once again Elaine was reminded of a New England fishing village, an image enhanced by the small fleet that was neatly moored at the wharf.

They pulled up in front of the police station and Brad told the truck driver to find someplace to park the truck for a few minutes without blocking traffic. Then he and Elaine went inside.

They found Harney Whalen in his office talking on the telephone. He looked up, stared at them in apparent surprise, then returned to his telephone call. Elaine lit a cigarette and occupied herself by peering uncomfortably out the window. But Brad made no attempt to conceal the fact that he was listening to Whalen's end of the conversation.

"I'm telling you," Whalen was saying, "there isn't any point in your coming up here. It was an accident, nothing more. There's nothing to investigate. Not even a trace of wreckage has washed up. Only the body."

He listened then, his eyes on the ceiling, almost closed, as if whatever he was hearing was hardly worth listening to.

"Listen," he said finally, apparently interrupting whoever was on the other end of the line. "I looked the body over, and Doc Phelps looked the body over. Now, I'm no expert, but Phelps is. And we both agree the guy drowned. Looks like the guy went overboard when the boat cracked up. Hell, nobody can last long in the water this time of year.''

He seemed about to say more but fell silent again, and Brad assumed that whoever he was talking to was objecting to something Whalen had said.

"Well, anyway, I'm gonna ship the body up to Port Angeles tomorrow. The guy's brother's hanging around getting on everyone's nerves, and I've just about had it with the whole thing. So if you want to do anything—look at the body or something—you'd better do it today.''

Just then the door to the police station opened and a young man Brad didn't recognize came in. Whoever he was, he was not a native of Clark's Harbor. He seemed very upset—his face was flushed and his eyes flashed with anger. He glanced at Brad and Elaine, then turned his attention to the police chief, who was still on the phone. As he listened, Harney Whalen watched the young man pace the small room impatiently. In his mind Brad put it all together and decided this was the brother of the dead man, and that he had stumbled into the "something horrible" Glen Palmer had been talking about on the phone that morning.

"All right, all right," Whalen said at last. "I'll wait till you get here." He slammed the receiver down and stared balefully at the young man.

"What is it now, Horton?" he said levelly.

Jeff Horton stopped pacing and stood squarely in front of Whalen's desk, glaring at the police chief.

"Who the hell do you think you are?" he demanded.

"I think I'm the police chief here," Whalen said easily, enjoying the young man's discomfiture. "What of it?"

"That gives you the right to decide what's to be done with my brother's body?"

"You heard?"

"I heard. And I'd like to know why you didn't tell me you were releasing it. I can get it home myself.''

"Fine," Whalen replied, getting to his feet. "I just thought I'd save you the trouble.''

"Save me the trouble!" Jeff exclaimed. His face turned scarlet and his fists began working spasmodically. "I don't need anybody to save me any trouble. I need someone to help me find out what happened to Max." Then, as suddenly as his face had turned scarlet, it drained of color and became an ashen gray. Brad stood up and moved to the young man's side.

"Sit down," he said gently but firmly. When Jeff started to resist, Brad took his arm. "If you don't sit down, you're going to pass out," he said. He pushed Jeff into the chair he had just vacated and made him put his head between his knees. "If you start feeling like you're going to be sick, lie down on the floor. You'll feel foolish but it's better than throwing up. Now breathe deeply.''

Brad turned his attention to Whalen. "What's going on?" he asked.

"It's between him and me," Whalen declared. "It doesn't have anything to do with you.''

"I'm a doctor and this fellow's not in the best shape. I'm just wondering why.''

"And I'm telling you it's none of your concern," Whalen snapped.

"Whose concern should it be?" Jeff said, sitting up again. He looked at Brad. "Who are you?"

"Brad Randall," Brad said, extending his right hand. "I'm a doctor from Seattle. I take it it's your brother who died?"

Jeff nodded. "This guy keeps claiming it was an accident but I don't believe it. And now he's made plans to ship Max home and he didn't even tell me about it."

"Max, I assume, is your brother. Mind telling me your name?"

"Jeff. Jeff Horton."

"Fine, Jeff. Now, what happened?"

But before Jeff could tell him, Harney Whalen interrupted. "This your office all of a sudden, Dr. Randall?" he said unpleasantly. " 'Cause you're sure acting like it is."

Brad bit his lip. "Sorry," he said. "It isn't any of my business, of course. But Jeff seems pretty upset, and dealing with people who are upset happens to be my specialty." When Jeff looked at him quizzically, Brad winked. "I'm a psychiatrist."

Elaine stood up suddenly, and the movement caught Brad's attention, exactly as she had intended.

"Why don't I take Jeff out for a cup of coffee while you settle our business with the chief?" she suggested. "All right?"

Brad knew immediately his wife was trying to defuse the situation. He smiled at her gratefully. "If you don't mind," he said, knowing she didn't; knowing, in fact, that she had taken the situation in hand.

"Of course I don't mind." She turned to Whalen and smiled at him. "Is there anything I'll need to know about the house right away?"

Whalen shook his head slowly, glancing from one of the Randalls to the other and back again. But before he could speak Elaine plunged on.

"Fine. Then we'll see you in a few minutes," she told Brad. She took Jeff Horton by the arm and pulled him to his feet. Jeff, looking baffled, offered no resistance as she led him from the office.

"Do you have the keys?" she heard Brad asking Whalen as she walked down the corridor. She silently congratulated herself. Maybe the wrong member of their family was the psychiatrist.

"It hasn't been easy for you, has it?" Elaine asked Jeff. They were sitting in the café, drinking their second cup of coffee, and Jeff had told Elaine what had happened.

"That's putting it mildly," Jeff said bitterly. "The worst of it is, I'm not going to be able to hang around here any longer, and the minute I leave that police chief is going to drop the whole thing. Hell, he almost has already."

"It might really have been an accident," Elaine offered.

"If it were anyone but Max, I'd agree. But Max was one of those people who just doesn't have accidents. He was always methodical, always careful. He always said there's no such thing as an accident. Like the other night, when the storm caught up with us? Anyone else would have tried to make it down to Grays Harbor, and if they hadn't made it, it would have been called an accident. But Max would have called it damned foolishness and blamed it on the skipper.''

"And he would have been right," Elaine agreed.

"For all the good it did him. Anyway, *Osprey* couldn't have slipped her moorings by accident. Somebody cast her lines off the dock, but I can't get that police chief to do anything about it. It's like he just doesn't care.''

"I don't think he does," Elaine said softly. Before Jeff could ask what she meant she changed the subject. "What are you going to do now?''

"Go back up north, I guess, and start over. But without Max it isn't going to be easy.''

"Can't you stay here awhile?''

"I'm broke. I can pay for one more night at the hotel and that's it. But I want to stay and find out what happened to Max." He looked deeply into Elaine's eyes and his voice took on an intensity that almost frightened her.

"Somebody killed Max, Mrs. Randall. I don't know who, but somebody killed him. I have to find out why.''

Elaine studied the young man opposite her and tried to weigh what he had said. Still in shock, she thought, and badly shaken up. Yet what he had said made sense. If his brother had been as careful as Jeff claimed—and she had no reason to doubt it—then it seemed unlikely that the trawler's getting loose had been an accident. And if it wasn't an accident . . .

"Look," she said suddenly. "If it's that important for you to stay around here for a while, you can stay with us. It's primitive, but it's free.''

"With you?" Jeff seemed totally bewildered. "But you don't even know me.''

Elaine smiled warmly at him. "If you hadn't said that I might have been worried. Anyway, that makes us even: you don't know us, either. Believe me, after a couple of days we'll know each other very, very well. The house we rented isn't big and it doesn't have any electricity. I'm told the plumbing works but I'll believe it when I see it. There's a couple of bedrooms upstairs, guest rooms, and you might as well be the first guest." Before Jeff could reply Elaine glanced at her watch and stood up. "Come on, we've been here long enough. If Brad isn't through with Mr. Whalen yet, something's gone wrong. And the movers must think we've died.''

"Movers?''

"I told you we were just moving in. That was a sort of a lie, really. We haven't moved in yet. As a matter of fact, we just got to town half an hour ago.''

Taking Jeff by the arm, she led him out the door.

They almost bumped into Brad as they turned the corner onto Main Street, and Elaine knew by the look on his face that something was wrong. "What's happened?" she asked.

Brad stared at her blankly for a moment, then chuckled hollowly. "You won't believe it," he said. "Whalen didn't remember renting the house to us.''

"Didn't remember? Are you serious?''

Brad nodded. "That's why he looked so surprised when we walked into his office. He thought we were gone for good. I had to show him the lease before he'd give me the keys to the house. I guess we were right when we thought he was in some kind of trance the day he showed us the place." He saw Elaine turn slightly pale and decided now was not the time to pursue the subject. Instead, he made himself smile genially at Jeff Horton. "I assume Elaine invited you to stay with us?"

"If it's all right with you, Dr. Randall."

"My name's Brad, and of course it's all right with me. If she hadn't invited you I would have. We'd better get going though, or the movers are going to dump our stuff in the street. Whalen'll lead us out there, just to make sure the place is all right."

As if on cue, Harney Whalen emerged from the police station and stared balefully at the three of them. When he spoke his words were obviously directed at Jeff.

"I thought you'd be on your way by now."

"I'm not going anywhere," Jeff said softly. "Not till I find out what happened to my brother."

Whalen's tongue worked at his left cheek as he thought it over. "Still staying at the hotel?" he asked finally.

"He'll be staying with us," Elaine said flatly, as if to end the discussion.

"That so?" Whalen said. "Well, I guess it's none of my business, is it. You want to follow me?"

"Sure," Brad replied. He turned and signaled the movers, who were lounging against the fender of their truck half a block away. They ground their cigarettes out and climbed into the cab. "We'll be right behind you," Brad called to Whalen, who was already in his police car. Whalen's hand, black-gloved, waved an acknowledgment, but he didn't speak. Instead he simply started his engine and pulled away from the curb, his face expressionless as he passed them. The Randalls, with Jeff Horton, followed. Behind them, the moving truck closed the gap.

Harney Whalen drove the black-and-white slowly and kept his eyes steadily on the road. But he was driving automatically, guiding the car almost by instinct. His mind was in turmoil.

Jeff Horton wasn't going to go home.

Instead he was going to stay in Clark's Harbor, stirring up trouble.

And the Randalls. Where had they come from? He searched his mind, trying to remember having signed a lease.

His mind was blank. He remembered showing them the house, but as for a lease—nothing. Absolutely nothing.

More trouble.

Harney Whalen didn't like trouble. He wondered what he should do about it.

And he wondered why strangers kept coming to Clark's Harbor. It had never been a good place for strangers.

Never had been, and never would be.

# TWENTY

T HE PROCESSION MADE AN ODD SPECTA-
cle as it moved out of Clark's Harbor, the black-and-white police car
leading the way with Harney Whalen at the wheel, his eyes fixed
firmly on the road in front of him, an odd look on his face: a look
that would have told anyone who happened to see it that Whalen's mind was
far away. Behind him were the Randalls, with Jeff Horton in the back seat.
Elaine made sporadic attempts at conversation, but all three of them were
preoccupied with their own thoughts, and they soon fell silent. The small
moving truck brought up the rear.

It's almost like some bizarre funeral cortege, Elaine was thinking. She
glanced out the side window of the car and saw several people standing on
the sidewalk, having left whatever they had been doing to watch the newcomers make their arrival. Their faces seemed to Elaine to be impassive, as if
the arrival of the Randalls would have no effect on them whatsoever—
something to be observed that would not change their lives. And yet, as she
absorbed their strange impassivity, Elaine began to feel as if there was
something else, some fear that they were trying to cover up. She glanced
quickly at Brad, but he was concentrating on the road, unaware of the
watching faces on the sidewalks. Then they turned up Harbor Road, leaving
the village behind.

The procession headed north on the highway, passed Glen Palmer's
gallery, and quickly disappeared around the bend that would take them close
to the coastline. Harney Whalen increased his speed, and the car and truck
behind him accelerated. They were cruising at the speed limit when Whalen
suddenly noticed the two children in the road ahead. For a few seconds he
kept up his speed, bearing down on Robby and Missy Palmer, the car
hurtling forward straight toward them. Whalen felt himself freeze at the
wheel, unable to move. Then, as the gap between himself and the children
quickly closed, he forced his right foot off the accelerator, hit the brake,
swerved, and leaned on the horn.

Missy scrambled off the pavement into the ditch almost before the sound
of the horn split the air. But Robby remained in the road, turning slowly to
stare at the oncoming car as if he didn't recognize that he was in danger.

"Robby!" Missy screamed. And then the horn was followed by the
shrieking of tires being ripped loose from their grip on the pavement as the
police car began to fishtail. Finally Robby moved.

It was a lazy movement, slow and methodical.

He stepped casually out of the path of the speeding police car, then watched idly as it skidded in a full circle, left the pavement, and came to rest on the opposite side of the street. As soon as it stopped Harney Whalen leaped from the driver's seat and started toward Robby.

Brad Randall was already bringing his car to a halt almost on the spot where the children had been. He hadn't seen anything until Whalen's brake lights had flashed on, the sound of the horn had hit him, and the police car had gone into its skid. Only at the last instant had he seen Missy leap off the road, then Robby moved slowly away from the path of the car.

"My God," he said as he brought his own car to a stop. "He damn near ran them down. Didn't he see them?"

"He must have," Elaine said. She paused a second and a strange note crept into her voice. "Those are the Palmers' children! Are they all right?"

Before Brad could answer, Elaine had scrambled out of the car and knelt beside Missy. The little girl was sobbing, and Elaine gathered her into her arms.

"It's all right. Everything's okay. Nobody's hurt."

"He did it on purpose," Missy sobbed. "He tried to run over us."

"No," Elaine purred soothingly. "Nobody did that. Nobody would want to run over you."

Then Harney Whalen was there, standing over her, his face pale, his hands shaking. "What the hell were you kids doing?" he demanded.

Elaine pulled the sobbing Missy closer to her and stared up at Whalen, her brows knitted into a scowl of anger.

"Didn't you see them?" she demanded. "They must have been right in front of you." She looked quickly around, searching for Brad, needing his support. Then she saw him crouched down next to Robby, checking the boy over. "Is he all right?" she called.

"He's fine," Brad replied. "Not a scratch on him. Just scared."

"I'm not scared," Robby replied.

"If you aren't you should be," Brad said, tousling the boy's hair. "Didn't anybody ever tell you not to walk in the street?" Then he turned to Whalen.

"Didn't you see them?" he asked, echoing Elaine's question.

"It happened so fast," Whalen said. "All of a sudden there they were."

"You must have seen them in plenty of time," Brad protested.

Whalen stiffened and glared at Brad. "Well, I didn't," he said. "But I saw them soon enough. Nobody got hurt; nobody except me even got shaken up. So that's that, isn't it?"

"Is your car okay?" Brad asked.

"It's fine," Whalen assured him. "The shoulder's almost level on that side." He started moving toward the car, but Brad stopped him.

"Don't you think we should offer the kids a ride home?"

Whalen glanced from Missy to Robby, then back to Missy.

"How about it? You two want a ride in the police car?"

Robby's face brightened immediately but Missy frowned.

"No," she said with finality.

"We can take you home," Elaine offered.

"That's all right," Missy said. "We can walk."

"Are you sure?" Elaine looked anxiously at the little girl, almost as if she thought the child should be unable to walk. Missy unconsciously pulled away from her. "We're not supposed to ride with strangers," she said carefully.

"We're not strangers," Elaine countered. Missy looked at her thoughtfully, then shook her head.

"We don't want to," she said. Her lip began to quiver, as if she were about to begin crying again.

Elaine stood up, shrugged, and sighed. "Well, if you're sure you're all right . . ." she began. She looked helplessly at Brad, but he was staying out of the situation, faintly amused by his wife's efforts with the children. Whalen, accepting Missy's decision as final, returned to his car and began maneuvering the vehicle back onto the road.

Reluctantly, Elaine followed Brad back to their car, where Jeff Horton was still sitting in the back seat. Twice she looked back at the children, but they didn't move. Robby was watching the police car, but Missy seemed not to be watching anything. It was almost as if she were waiting for something, but Elaine hadn't a clue as to what it might be. She got into the passenger seat next to Brad just as Harney Whalen finished turning the police car around. A minute later the procession was once more under way.

"He wanted to run over us," Missy said to Robby as the two cars and the truck disappeared from view.

"He didn't either," Robby replied. He glared at his sister, wishing she weren't so stubborn. "How come you didn't let us ride in the police car?"

"I don't like that man. He wants to hurt us."

"That's dumb. Why would he want to hurt us?"

"I don't know," Missy said petulantly. "But he does."

Robby decided not to argue the point. "Well, we could have ridden with the Randalls."

"Mommy and Daddy don't want us to ride with strangers."

"They aren't strangers. He used to be my doctor, and they're moving into the house on the beach."

"Well, I don't know them," Missy insisted. "So they're strangers." Then she looked at her brother quizzically. "How come you stayed in the street?"

"I didn't," Robby replied.

"Yes, you did. I yelled at you, and you just stood there."

Robby scratched his head thoughtfully. "I don't really remember it," he said. "It happened too fast. Anyway, I got out of the way, didn't I? I didn't just jump like a scared rabbit like some people did. Let's cut through the woods and go home by the beach," he suggested.

"I don't want to," Missy objected. "I don't like the beach."

"You never want to do anything," Robby said scornfully. "If you don't want to go by the beach, you can stay on the road by yourself."

Missy's eyes widened with indignation. "You can't leave me here. Mommy says we're supposed to stay together."

"But she didn't say we're always supposed to do what you want. Come on.'' He started across the road, but Missy stayed where she was. When he got to the other side, Robby turned around and glared at his sister.

"Are you coming, or not?"

Missy felt torn. She didn't want to go through the woods, didn't want to walk on the beach. For some reason the beach scared her, even though she knew it didn't scare Robby. Most of all, though, she didn't want to walk home by herself.

She wondered what her mother's reaction would be if she showed up by herself. Mommy might punish Robby for leaving her alone, but she also might punish Missy for not staying with her brother. She made up her mind, on the theory that being a little bit scared was better than being punished.

"Oh, all right," she said, and hurried across the highway to catch up with Robby, who was already hunting for a path into the forest.

Harney Whalen pulled as far up the narrow driveway as he could and still leave room for the Randalls and the truck to get in ahead of him. He switched off the engine but didn't leave the car immediately.

He was still bothered by what had happened. He had tried to act as if it had been the children who had been careless. But he knew they hadn't been.

He knew that he had seen them in plenty of time.

He had frozen at the wheel.

He had nearly killed them both.

And he didn't know why.

For a moment it had been very much like the few seconds before he went into one of his spells. Time seemed almost to stand still, and something happened to his muscles—he lost control of them, as if his body were a thing apart from himself, operating under its own volition.

But always before it had been all right: usually he was alone when something like that happened. Alone, where no one could get hurt.

This afternoon two children had almost been killed. He decided it was time to have the talk with Doc Phelps that he had been postponing for so long.

The decision made, he got out of the police car and walked over to the Randalls, who were waiting for him together with Jeff Horton.

"Something wrong?" Brad Randall asked him.

"I'm okay. Just thought I heard something in the engine."

Without further words, he led the way along the path that took them out of the forest and through the tangle of driftwood. He opened the kitchen door, surprised that it wasn't locked, then handed the key to Brad.

"There's only the one key," he said. "It fits both doors, and I have the only copy. If you want another one you'll have to get Blake to cut it for you."

"I doubt we'll ever lock the place," Brad said.

"Suit yourselves," Whalen said noncommittally. "City people always seem to think they're a lot safer in the country than in town. But there's nuts all over the place." His eyes went to Jeff Horton, and Jeff felt himself flush with anger, but he kept silent.

Whalen led them through the house, halfheartedly apologizing for the mess, but not offering to have it cleaned up. "Sometimes I think I ought to just tear the place down," he muttered.

"Why don't you?" Brad asked. Harney looked surprised, and Brad realized the chief hadn't intended to speak out loud.

"I don't know," Whalen mused. "Just never get around to it, I guess. Or maybe I just don't want to. I come out here every now and then. Gets me out of the house." He started to leave, then stopped and turned back to face the Randalls once more.

"I'm going to tell you folks something," he said heavily. "Clark's Harbor is an inbred town. We're all related to each other, and we don't take kindly to strangers. And it isn't just that we're not friendly. It's something else—whenever strangers come to town the whole place seems to get sort of out of whack, if you know what I mean. So don't expect things to be any good for you here. They won't be."

"Well, if we don't go looking for trouble, I can't see that it's going to come looking for us," Brad said.

"Can't you?" Whalen replied. "Better ask around, Randall. What about Horton here? He and his brother came and trouble found them in a few hours. With the Shellings it took fifteen years, but trouble found them too. And there's your friends the Palmers. They damned near had a peck of trouble just about an hour ago. Well, nothing I can say will convince you." He glanced at his watch. "Better be getting back to town. There isn't any more I can do here. The place is all yours. Rent's due on the first of every month."

Then he was gone.

"That bastard," Elaine said almost under her breath.

"Is that any way to talk about your landlord?" Brad asked. Then he chuckled. "I think he enjoys playing the voice of doom."

Jeff Horton shook his head. "I agree with your wife," he said. "He's a bastard."

Before the discussion could go any farther, a burly form appeared in the kitchen door.

"You people want this stuff unloaded, or do we take it back to Seattle?"

From their hiding place in the woods, Robby and Missy watched Brad leave the house. They had been watching everything, watching the movers haul carton after carton into the old house, watching them leave. Now Brad was leaving too.

"I thought he was going to live here," Missy said plaintively. "That's what you said."

"Well, who says he's not?" Robby asked. "He's probably just going into town for something. Why don't we go say hello to Mrs. Randall?"

"I don't want to," Miss complained. "I don't like that house."

"You always say that," Robby pointed out. "What's wrong with it?"

"I don't know. Bad things happen there. They happen all over this beach. I want to go home."

"So go home."

"Come with me."

"I don't want to. I like the beach."

"It's late," Missy pointed out. "Mommy's going to be mad at us."

"Oh, she isn't either," Robby replied. But despite his brave words, he wasn't sure that Missy wasn't right; his mother had been acting very strange lately and Robby couldn't figure out why. Ever since that woman had killed herself, his mother had seemed worried. He gave in to his sister.

"All right," he said. "Come on."

He started out of the woods but again Missy stopped him.

"Let's go through the woods for a while."

"Why?"

"This is the part of the beach where that man washed up," Missy said.

"How do you know?"

"I just *know,* that's all!"

"You don't either," Robby said angrily.

"I do too!" Missy insisted. She began walking away from her brother. "You can go that way if you want, but I'm going through the forest."

Robby decided his sister was a royal pain, but he followed her anyway, obeying his mother's edict that the two of them should stick together. A few minutes later Missy clutched his hand.

"What's wrong?" Robby asked wearily.

"I'm scared. Let's run." She tugged at Robby's arm and almost involuntarily he began running with Missy. When they were near the cabin Missy suddenly stopped.

"It's all right now," she said. "I'm not scared anymore."

"That's because we're almost home," Robby pointed out. Missy looked up, and sure enough, there was the cabin, just visible through the trees. As they walked the last few yards to the house, Missy took Robby's hand and squeezed it hard.

"Let's not go on the beach anymore," she pleaded softly.

Robby looked at her curiously, but said nothing.

Brad pulled up in front of the gallery and made sure he wasn't parked on the pavement, remembering the ticket Harney Whalen had written him the last time he had been here. Then he went to the gallery door and stuck his head in.

"Glen? You here?"

"In back," Glen called.

As he made his way to the rear of the building Brad looked around, surprised at the progress that had been made. He was even more surprised to find that Glen wasn't alone in the back room.

"You mean you finally got some help?" he asked.

Glen straightened up from the drafting table where he was working on some sketches and grinned.

"Did you meet Chip Connor when you were out here?" he asked.

The deputy put aside the saw he was holding and extended his hand to Brad. "Glad to meet you," he said with a smile. "You must be Dr. Randall."

"Brad," Brad corrected him. He gazed quizzically at Chip. "Are you on duty?"

"Not for the last hour," Chip said. "But if anybody in town wants to charge me with neglecting my duties, they could probably make it stick."

Now Brad's gaze shifted to Glen, and when he spoke he sounded genuinely puzzled.

"I don't quite understand," he said. "When you called this morning you sounded horrible. I expected to find you huddled in a corner or worse, not happily at work with the deputy sheriff." He glanced at Chip. "You *are* Whalen's deputy, aren't you?"

"Also his nephew, more or less," Chip said. As Brad shifted uncomfortably Chip's smile faded. "You want to talk to Glen alone?"

"That's up to Glen," Brad countered.

"It's all right," Glen said. "Chip knows what's been going on. As a matter of fact, he's been helping me out with more than just this."

Brad looked at the nearly finished gallery. "It certainly seems to be coming along," he said. "Now why don't you fill me in on whatever else has been going on?"

Glen opened three cans of beer and they sat down, making themselves as comfortable as possible on the makeshift furniture. Brad listened quietly as Glen and Chip explained what had happened over the last few days, and Harney Whalen's unreasonable insinuations that Glen was somehow involved in the death of Max Horton, and possibly even Miriam Shelling's. When he was done Brad shook his head sadly.

"I don't understand that man," he said. "At first I thought he simply didn't like strangers. But I'm beginning to think it's something else. Something much more complicated—"

"More complicated?" Chip asked. "What do you mean?"

Brad didn't answer, didn't even seem to hear what Chip had asked. Instead he asked Glen an apparently irrelevant question.

"What about Robby?"

"Robby? What's he got to do with all this?"

"I don't know," Brad said, trying to sound casual. "But we know something's happened to him out here, and now things are happening to other people too."

Glen's eyes narrowed as he recognized the implication. "Are you trying to say you think Robby's involved in whatever's happening?"

"I'm not trying to say anything," Brad replied. "But things that seem to be unrelated often aren't. I think I better have a look at Robby."

The three men fell silent. Suddenly there was nothing to say.

## TWENTY-ONE

CHIP CONNOR SAT AT THE BAR OF THE Harbor Inn that evening sipping slowly on a beer, trying to sort out his thoughts. He was confused and upset; things seemed to him to be getting far too complicated. He drained the beer, slammed the empty glass down on the bar, and called for another one. Merle Glind appeared next to him.

"You want a little company?" he asked, rubbing his hands together. Chip smiled at the little man.

"Sure. Let me buy you a beer."

Glind scrambled onto the stool next to Chip. He carefully added a dash of salt to the beer he had drawn, tasted it, and nodded happily.

"Nothing finishes off the day like a good salty beer," he chirped. Then he looked at Chip inquisitively. "You want to tell me what's on your mind?"

"I'm not sure anything is," Chip replied evasively.

But Merle Glind was not to be put off. "It's written all over your face. I know—I can tell. Now why don't you tell me about it?"

"There's not much to tell," Chip said uncomfortably. "It's just a bunch of things, all added together. I guess I'm worried about Harn."

"Harn? Harn Whalen?" Merle Glind's voice was filled with disbelief, as if it were incomprehensible to him that anyone could be worried about the police chief.

"That's what I said," Chip repeated sourly, but Glind seemed not to hear.

"Why, I just can't imagine that," he clucked. "There isn't anything wrong with him, is there?"

Chip shrugged, almost indifferently. "Not that I know of," he said slowly. "It's just a lot of little things."

"What kind of little things?" The innkeeper's eyes glistened with anticipation, and Chip Connor suddenly decided he didn't want to confide in Glind.

"Nothing I can put my finger on," he said. He finished the beer that had just been put in front of him and stood up. "I think I'll go for a walk. I'm probably just nervous."

"It's starting to rain out there," Glind pointed out, his lips pursing and his brows knitting as he realized he wasn't going to find out what was on Chip's mind.

"It's always starting to rain out here," Chip replied. "Or if it isn't starting, it's stopping. See you later." He tossed a couple of dollar bills on the bar and grinned as Merle scooped them up. Then he patted Glind on the shoulder and left.

It was a light rain, the misty kind of rain that makes the air smell fresh and doesn't require an umbrella. It felt cold on Chip's face, and he liked the feeling. It was almost like sea spray, but softer, gentler, almost caressing.

He started for the wharf, thinking he might check the moorings on the boats, but as he stepped out onto the pier he realized someone was already there: a small light bobbed in the darkness.

"Hello?" Chip called. The bobbing light swung around. Chip instinctively raised a hand to cover his eyes as the light blinded him.

"Chip? That you?" Chip recognized the reedy voice immediately.

"Granddad?"

"Well, it's not the bogeyman, if that's what you were expecting."

Chip hurried out onto the wharf. "What are you doing out here in the rain? You'll catch pneumonia."

"If I were going to catch pneumonia I'd have caught it years ago," Mac Riley groused. "I'm checking the boats."

Chip chuckled. "That's what I was going to do."

"Well, it's done. Everything's secure, tight as a drum." Then he frowned at Chip. "How come you were going to check? You don't usually do that."

"I was at the inn and I felt like taking a walk—"

"Something on your mind?" Riley interrupted.

"I'm not sure."

"Of course you're sure," Riley snapped. "Give me a ride home and let's talk about it. I've got some scotch that I've been saving just for a night like tonight."

"What's so special about tonight?" Chip asked.

"You. I don't get to see you as much as I'd like. Well, that's grandsons for you. Only come around when they have a problem. I can sit around jawing with Tad Corey and Clem Ledbetter all day and it doesn't do me any good at all. They think I'm a senile old man."

"You?" Chip laughed out loud. "The day you get senile will be the day you die."

"Thanks a lot," the old man said dryly. "You wanting to stand here in the rain all night, or do we get going?"

They returned to the inn, where Chip's car was parked, and drove the few blocks to Mac Riley's house in silence. "You ought to sell the house or buy a car," Chip remarked as they went into the large Victorian house that Riley had built for his bride more than sixty years earlier.

"I'm too old," Riley complained. "Can't get a driver's license, and can't learn to live anyplace else. Besides, I don't feel lonely here. Your grandmother's in this house."

As Chip's brows rose in skepticism, Riley snorted at him.

"I don't mean a ghost, or anything like that," he said impatiently. "It's just memories. When you get to be my age you'll know what I'm talking about. Every room in this house has memories for me. Your grandmother, your mother, even you. But mostly your grandmother.''

They were in the tiny sitting room just off the entry hall, and Chip looked at the portrait of his grandmother that hung over the fireplace.

"She looks a lot like Harney Whalen," he commented.

"Why shouldn't she?" Riley countered. "She was his aunt."

"I know. But for some reason I never think of it that way. I always think of Harn as kissing kin, rather than blood kin."

"Around here there ain't much difference," Riley said. He found the bottle of scotch, poured two tumblers full—no ice, no water—and handed one of them to Chip.

"That who's on your mind? Harn Whalen?"

Chip nodded and sipped at the scotch, feeling it burn as it trickled down his throat. "I'm worried about him," he said. He was thoughtful for several minutes. Then he explained, "It's a lot of little things. But mostly it's the way he feels about strangers."

"We all feel that way," Riley said. "It goes back a long time."

"But there doesn't seem to be any reason for it."

"Maybe not now," Riley replied. "But there are reasons all right. Tell me what's going on with Harney."

"He's been going after Glen Palmer."

"Palmer? I didn't know you even knew the man."

"I didn't up until a few days ago," Chip said. "The day after Miriam and Pete Shelling's funeral."

Riley nodded briefly. "I was there, with Corey and Ledbetter. Other than us and Harn Whalen, the Palmers were the only ones who came."

"That's what Harney said. He made me go out and talk to Palmer. He wanted to know why Glen was there."

"That doesn't seem unreasonable," the old man said. "Did you find out?"

"Sure. It wasn't any secret really, except Glen didn't think it was any of our business."

"In a town this size everything is everybody's business," Riley chuckled.

"Anyway," Chip went on, "Glen told me why he and his family went to the funeral, and I told Harney. Then he did something I just can't account for at all. He tried to wreck most of Glen's work."

"Wreck it? What do you mean?"

Chip told his grandfather what had happened. "I felt rotten about it," he finished. "I stayed around and gave Glen a hand, and he's really a nice guy. I've been spending quite a bit of time with him. It's funny—he can draw anything, but put a saw in his hand and it's all over." He smiled at his grandfather. "Wait'll you see that gallery. With him designing it and me building it, it's really going to be something."

"You getting paid for it?" Riley inquired.

Chip squirmed. "Not exactly," he said. "Glen doesn't have any money right now. But I'm still getting paid. I'm finding out a lot of things I never knew about before. Nothing terribly important, I guess, but it's the first time in my life I've ever really gotten to know anyone who wasn't born right here. And the more I get to know Glen, the less I understand Harney's attitude. If he'd just take the time to get to know him too, I don't think he'd be so down on him.''

"I wouldn't bet on it," Riley said.

"Well, I can understand him being suspicious of strangers, but it's getting out of hand. He won't do anything to find out what happened to that guy Horton, except that he seemed to think Glen had something to do with it—God only knows why—and the whole thing's getting to me. I keep telling myself it's only my imagination, but it seems to be getting worse. I'm thinking of quitting my job.''

Riley frowned and studied his grandson. Finally he appeared to make up his mind about something.

"Maybe I'd better tell you a little about Harney," he said. "Life hasn't been too easy for him, and most of the rough times were caused by strangers. It was a long time ago, but things like what happened to Harney when he was a boy stay with a man. And sometimes the old memories are stronger than the new ones, if you know what I mean." He leaned forward confidentially. "Don't tell anybody, but sometimes I can remember things that happened sixty, seventy years ago better than I can recollect things that happened last month.''

He handed his glass to Chip and asked him to refill it. While the younger man did, Riley's gaze drifted away, focused somewhere beyond the room and the rainy night. When Chip gave him the full glass, his eyes seemed to be almost closed. But as he took the glass, he began talking.

"When Harney was a boy he lived with his grandparents. His mother— your grandmother's sister—died birthing Harn, and his father took off a little after that. He came back, but he was never quite the same. So it wound up that Harn's grandparents took care of them both. Anyway, Harn's grandaddy owned a whole lot of land around here, most of it forest. He never did much with it, just sort of sat on it, but eventually some of the big lumbering boys from Seattle came out here and tried to buy it.

"Old Man Whalen wouldn't sell, so then they tried to get him to lease the timber rights to them. That didn't work either, and it looked for a while like that would be the end of it. But then something happened.''

The old man stopped talking and his eyes closed once more. For a few seconds Chip thought his grandfather had fallen asleep, but then Riley's eyes blinked open and he stared at Chip.

"I'm not sure I ought to tell you the story—it happened a long time ago and it isn't very pleasant. But it might help you to understand why Harn feels the way he does about strangers.''

"Go on," Chip urged him.

"Well, it was a night very much like this one," Riley began. "There was a storm brewing, but when Harney—he was only seven or eight at the time—went to bed, it hadn't really hit the coast yet. Then, late at night, it came in, blowing like crazy.

"Nobody ever found out exactly what happened that night, but during the storm there were terrible things done. It was the next morning that all hell broke loose. Harney woke up and the house was empty. He looked around for his grandparents but they weren't there. So he started searching for them." Riley closed his eyes, visualizing the scene as he talked. "He found them on the beach. Sod Beach, about halfway between where the houses are now. Neither of them was there back then—the beach was just a beach. Anyway, Harn went out there and at first he didn't see them. But they were there: buried in the sand up to their necks, drowned. It was just like the old Klickashaw stories, but that time it wasn't a story. It was Harn's grandparents. I saw them myself a little while later. The whole town went out there before they even dug the Whalens up. Awful. Their eyes were all bugged out, and their faces were blue. And the expressions—you wouldn't have believed it."

"Jesus," Chip said softly. "Did they find out who did it?"

"Nah," Riley said. Disgust edged his voice. "Everybody had suspicions, of course, and what happened after that didn't help any."

"Something else happened?"

"About a week after the funeral, Harney's dad gave in and signed a lease with the lumber people. The old man wouldn't, but Harney's dad did. And then he leased the beach to that guy Baron, who built the house out there that Harney owns now."

"How'd Harney get it?"

"He grew up," Riley said flatly. "He just waited around. The lease wasn't a long one—only about ten or fifteen years—but by the time it was up his dad had died too and Harney owned the land. He just refused to renew the lease. Baron was mad—real mad. Claimed there'd been an unwritten agreement, some kinda option, I think. But Harn got some fancy lawyer from Olympia to go to work on that. Anyway, he ended the lease, and that was it for Baron. He stayed around for a while and tried to fish, but that didn't work either. Got himself drowned, he did. Nobody around here gave a shit—they all thought he'd been in on killing Old Man Whalen and his wife." The old man chuckled then. "Funny how I always think of him as Old Man Whalen—he must have been twenty years younger than I am now when he died."

He stopped talking for a few minutes, then grinned at his grandson. "Funny thing. I was telling Tad and Clem about Baron the other day, but I couldn't remember his name then. I know it as well as I know my own but it just slipped right on away. Anyway, like I told Tad and Clem, same thing happened to Baron's wife as happened to Miriam Shelling. Hung herself in the woods. Might even have been the same tree for all I know."

Chip stared at his grandfather. "She hanged herself? After her husband drowned?"

"Yup. Just like Pete and Miriam. Funny how things like that happen. I guess the guy who said history repeats itself wasn't so far off, was he?"

"Funny Harney didn't tell me about it," Chip commented.

Riley made an impatient gesture. "Why would he? What happened to the Barons was thirty-five, forty years ago, long before you were even born.

Anyway, that's why Harney hates strangers so much. A couple of them killed his grandparents, even if no one ever proved it.''

Chip swirled the half-inch of scotch that still remained in his glass and stared thoughtfully up at the portrait of his grandmother. Her dark face had a stoic, almost impassive look, as if life had been hard for her but she had survived it. As he studied the portrait Chip realized that the resemblance between her and her nephew, Harney Whalen, was not so much a physical thing at all. It was the look. The look of impassivity.

Chip began to understand Harney Whalen, and his sense of worry deepened.

Missy Palmer lay in bed asleep, her hands clenched into small fists, her face twisted into an expression of fear. The rain pattered on the roof, and Missy began to toss in the bed. At the sound of a twig snapping outside, her eyes flew open.

She was suddenly wide awake, the memory of her nightmare still fresh in her mind.

"Robby?" she whispered.

No sound came from the bunk above.

Missy lay still, her heart thumping loudly in her ears. Then she thought she heard something. A snapping sound, like a branch breaking.

Her eyes went to the window and the thumping of her heart grew louder.

*Was there something at the window? Something watching her?*

Her dream came back to her. In it the . . . something at the window was chasing her. She was on the beach with Robby, and it was chasing both of them. They ran into the woods, trying to hide, but it followed them, looming closer and closer. Her legs wouldn't move anymore. Try as she would, she couldn't run. Her feet were stuck in something, something gooey, that sucked at her, trying to pull her down.

Then she fell, and suddenly the shape was above her, towering over her, reaching for her.

She screamed.

She felt her mother's arms go around her and began sobbing, clinging to Rebecca.

"There, there," Rebecca soothed her. "It's all right. It was a dream, that's all. You had a dream."

"But there was someone here," Missy sobbed. "He was trying to get us. Robby and I were running from him but he was after us. And then I fell . . ." She dissolved once more into her sobbing, and Rebecca stroked her hair softly.

Robby, awakened by the scream, hung over the top bunk, a look of curiosity on his sleepy face.

"What's wrong?" he asked groggily.

"Nothing," Rebecca assured him. "Missy had a nightmare, that's all. Go back to sleep."

Robby's head disappeared as Glen came into the doorway.

"Is she all right?" he asked anxiously.

"She's fine," Rebecca told him. "Just a bad dream."

Missy's head stirred in her mother's lap. "It wasn't a dream," she cried. "It was real. He was here. I saw him outside the window."

"Who did you see, darling?" Glen asked.

"A man," Missy said. "But I couldn't see his face."

"You were dreaming," Rebecca said. "There isn't anyone out there."

"Yes there is," Missy insisted.

"I'll have a look," Glen said.

He threw a raincoat on over his pajamas and opened the door of the cabin, shining his flashlight around the surrounding forest. There was nothing.

Then, as he was about to close the door, Scooter dashed between his feet, his tiny tail wagging furiously, barking as loudly as his puppy voice would allow. Glen reached down and scooped him up.

"It's all right," he said to the puppy, scratching its belly. "Nothing's out there."

Scooter, soothed by the scratching, stopped barking.

But Missy kept on crying.

Two miles away, while the wind rose to a vicious howl, the back door of Glen Palmer's gallery flew open. The horror began.

## TWENTY-TWO

EARLY THE FOLLOWING MORNING GLEN Palmer put on his slicker, opened the cabin door, and let Scooter out. The puppy scuttled around the corner, and when Glen followed, he found the dog sniffing under the window of the children's room. He squatted down, picked up the wriggling puppy, and carefully examined the ground. There was a slight depression, obscured by the still-falling rain, that might have been a footprint.

Or it might not.

Glen frowned a little and tried to find another, similar depression, but the ground was rough, soggy, and covered with pine needles.

"Well, if anything was there, it isn't now," he muttered to Scooter, then set the puppy down again. Scooter, having lost interest in whatever he had been sniffing at, trotted happily off into the woods, looking back every few seconds to make sure he hadn't lost sight of Glen. Clumsily he lifted a leg next to a bush, then ran back to the front door, where he began yapping to be let in.

As Glen followed the puppy into the house, Rebecca looked curiously at him from the stove, where she was frying eggs.

"Find anything?"

"What makes you think I was looking for anything?"

"You were. Was there anything to find?"

"Not without a liberal dose of imagination. There's a dent in the ground outside the kids' window, and I suppose I could claim it's a footprint if I wanted to, but I don't think anybody'd believe me. I certainly wouldn't."

Rebecca put down the spatula she was holding and began setting the table. "You want to get the kids going?" she asked.

"Let them sleep a few more minutes. I'll take them in when I go and drop them at school."

"What's the rush this morning?"

"There isn't any really. Except that Chip might show up and I don't want to miss him."

"I like him."

"So do I," Glen grinned. "I especially like the way he works. We'll have the place open by the end of the week. And I'm going to give him that painting."

"Painting? Which one?"

"The one of the old house where the Randalls live. He really likes it. It seems like the least I can do."

They fell silent, but it wasn't a comfortable silence.

"Something's bothering you," Glen said at last. Rebecca nodded.

"I keep having a feeling something's happened, or is about to happen."

Glen laughed. "Maybe you'd better go see Brad Randall along with Robby."

"Robby?" Rebecca said blankly. "What about Robby?"

"Nothing, really," Glen replied, trying to pass it off. "He just asked me if he could look Robby over. I think he wants to try to figure out what happened to him when we came up here. But if you ask me, he's wasting his time." Then his voice grew more serious. "What about you? This feeling you have?"

"Oh, it's probably nothing," Rebecca said, though her tone belied the statement. "Just nerves, I guess." She paused a moment, then: "When was the last time Missy had a nightmare?"

Glen frowned, trying to remember. Then he saw what Rebecca was getting at. "Never, I guess. But that doesn't prove anything."

"Except that she said someone was outside last night and you found a footprint."

"I found something that *might* have been a footprint," Glen corrected her. "Let's not make a mountain out of a molehill. One nightmare doesn't mean anything."

"But she thought she saw someone outside before, remember?"

"That happens to all kids. They have vivid imaginations. You know that as well as I do."

Rebecca sighed. "I suppose so," she said reluctantly. "But I still have this feeling.'' Then she forced a smile. ''I suppose I'll get over it. Why don't you get the kids out of bed?''

Glen dropped the children off at the tiny Clark's Harbor school an hour later, then went on to the gallery. He knew something was wrong as soon as he opened the door.

The display cases, finished only the day before, had been smashed. All the glass was shattered, and the framing had been torn apart and scattered around the room. The shelves, securely anchored to the walls by Chip Connor only a few days before, had been ripped down.

The back room was even worse. The shelves on which Rebecca's pottery had been stored were empty; the pottery itself was on the floor, heaped against one wall, every piece smashed beyond recognition.

And the paintings.

They were still in their frames, but they too had been destroyed, viciously slashed. Every canvas was in tatters, made even more grotesque by the undamaged frames.

Glen stared at the wreckage, first in disbelief, then in grief, and finally in rage. He felt the anger surge through him, felt a towering indignation take possession of him. He turned away from the wreckage, walked through the main gallery and out the front door. Without pausing at his car, he started walking into the village, staring straight ahead.

Fifteen minutes later he stalked into the police station.

Chip Connor looked up when he heard the door open. At the look on Glen's face, his greeting died on his lips and he stood up.

''The gallery—'' Glen began. Then he choked on his own words and stopped. He stood quivering in front of Chip, trying to control himself, trying to force himself neither to scream nor to cry. He breathed deeply, sucking air into his constricted lungs, then let it out in an immense sigh.

''Someone broke into the gallery last night,'' he said at last. ''They wrecked it.''

''Come on.'' Chip grabbed his hat and started out of the office.

''Where are you going?'' Glen demanded.

''I want to see it,'' Chip said. There was an icy quality in his voice that Glen had never heard before.

''Not yet,'' Glen said. ''Let me sit down a minute.'' He felt suddenly weak, and let himself sink into a chair. ''Do you have any coffee around here? Or maybe even a drink?''

The coldness immediately left Chip's manner. He closed the office door, poured Glen some coffee from the huge percolator that was always ready, and sat down at the desk again.

''Sorry,'' he said. ''I guess that wasn't very professional of me. What happened?''

''I don't know. I walked in and the place was wrecked. Both rooms. And Rebecca's pottery. And my paintings.''

''Shit,'' Chip cursed softly. ''How bad is it?''

''The pottery and the paintings are completely ruined. As for the gallery, you'll know better than I. Frankly, I didn't take time to really look. I walked down here as soon as I saw what had happened.''

"You walked?"

"I was so mad I could hardly see straight, and I didn't even think about getting into the car. If I had, I probably would have run it into a tree." Then he frowned slightly. "Where's Whalen?"

"Not here. He's over to Doc Phelps' this morning."

"Well, I'm just as glad he isn't here," Glen said wearily. "I probably would have blown it completely if I'd had to talk to him. Is there more coffee there?"

"Help yourself." He waited, chewing thoughtfully on his lips, while Glen refilled his cup. When Glen was seated once more, Chip spoke again. "Can I ask you a question?" he said.

"Sure," Glen said tonelessly.

"Did you come over here to report what happened, or to yell at Harney Whalen?"

The question caught Glen by surprise and he had to think about it. "I don't honestly know," he said finally. "Both, I guess. I had to report it, of course, but I was going to to vent some anger on Whalen too." He smiled weakly. "I guess it's just as well he isn't here."

"I guess so," Chip agreed. "You about ready to go over to the gallery? I'll make out a report there, and we can decide what to do next."

"Do? What's there to do? Everything's ruined."

"Maybe," Chip agreed. "Maybe not. Let's go find out."

"Holy Christ," Chip said as the two of them entered the gallery. "It looks like someone let a bear loose in here."

He pulled out his notebook and began writing down a description of the damage. When he was finished in the front room he went into the back and repeated the process.

"They came in here," he said, starting at the back door. It hung grotesquely, one hinge completely torn loose from the frame.

He made a few more notes, then put the notebook away. Glen was staring at the shreds of the paintings, his face expressionless.

"Is there any way to repair them?" Chip asked.

Glen shook his head. "You can fix a small tear sometimes, but nothing like this," he said tonelessly.

Chip couldn't bear the look in Glen's eyes. "I don't know if it'll do any good," he said, "since there doesn't seem to be anything to sell. But we can fix the gallery."

"It's all broken up," Glen said dully.

"Not that bad. We'll have to get new glass, but the cases can be put back together again." He smiled briefly, then added, "It isn't as if the shelves haven't been torn off the walls before."

"It will just happen again," Glen pointed out.

"Not if we put in an alarm system. And not if we find out who did it."

"Oh, come on, Chip. We're not going to find out who did it, and you know it."

"We might," Chip said. Then he decided he might as well be honest. "No, you're right, we probably won't. Hell, we don't even know *why* they did it."

"I guess you know what I think," Glen said.

"Can I make a suggestion?" Chip asked, deliberately ignoring Glen's comment. Without waiting for an answer, he went on. "Take the day off. Go home and tell Rebecca what happened, then decide what the two of you want to do. We'll start cleaning up tomorrow. I'm off duty."

"Okay. The mess has to be cleaned up anyway." Glen's face clouded as a memory came back to him. "Rebecca said something was going to happen," he said. "Just this morning, when we got up. She said something's happened or is about to happen. I guess she was right."

They had walked from the back room into the gallery, but suddenly Glen returned to the workroom. A minute later he was back.

"They didn't get everything," he said triumphantly. "There was one picture I put away and they didn't find it."

Chip looked curiously at him as Glen turned the picture he held. It was the canvas depicting Sod Beach and the weathered old house with the strange presence in the window.

"I'm glad it was this one," Glen said. "I put it away because I was saving it. But you'd better take it now, Chip. It might not be around much longer."

"Take it? What are you talking about?"

"I was going to give it to you the day we finished the gallery," Glen explained. "So I put it away, just so I couldn't be tempted to sell it. But I think you'd better take it now, just in case."

"I can't take it," Chip protested. "My God, it's all you've got left."

But when they left the gallery a few minutes later, Chip was carrying the painting and planning where to hang it.

Harney Whalen sat in Dr. Phelps' cluttered office, and described what had happened the previous afternoon. Phelps listened patiently. When Harney finished he shrugged his shoulders.

"I don't see why you came to me," he said. "You froze at the wheel for a couple of seconds. Everybody does that now and then."

"But it's more than that, Doc." Harney hesitated. "I have spells."

"Spells? What do you mean, spells? Sounds like a little old lady's symptom."

"It's the only way I can describe them. It's almost like blacking out for a while, I guess. They don't happen very often, or at least I don't think they do, but when they start my hands start to twitch and I feel funny. Then there's nothing until I wake up."

Phelps frowned. "When was the last time you had one?"

"Last night," Whalen admitted. "I was watching television and I felt it coming on. I don't remember anything until this morning. I was in bed, but I don't remember going to bed."

"Hmm," Phelps said noncommittally. "Well, we'd better look you over." He took Whalen's blood pressure and pulse, tested his reflexes, and went over him with a stethoscope. Then he took a blood sample and had Whalen produce a urine sample as well.

"I'll have to send these down to a lab in Aberdeen, but we should find out if there's anything there in a couple of days. Apart from the 'spells' how do you feel?"

"Fine. Same as ever. When have I ever been sick?"

Phelps nodded. "Well, everything looks normal so far. If nothing turns up in the samples, how would you feel about going into a hospital for a couple of days?"

"Forget it," Whalen said. "I've got too much to do."

Phelps rolled his eyes. "Oh, come on, Harn. You and I are the most underworked people in town. Or we were until recently."

"It's the strangers," Whalen murmured. "Every time strangers come we have trouble."

"You mean the Palmers?" Phelps asked.

"Them and the new ones. Randall's the name. They moved into my old house out at the beach."

Now Phelps's interest was definitely piqued. "The Baron house? I thought you weren't going to rent it anymore."

Whalen smiled bitterly. "I wasn't. But it seems I did." He frowned, searching for the best way to explain what had happened. "I guess I had one of my spells while I was showing the place to Randall and his wife. Anyway, they showed up with a signed lease, and I don't remember signing it." He stood up, and began buttoning his shirt. "Well, what about it? Am I going to live?"

"As far as I can tell," Phelps said slowly. "But what you just said bothers me. I have a good mind to send you to Aberdeen right now."

Whalen shook his head. "Not a chance. If you can't find anything wrong, that's that. Never been in a hospital. I don't intend to start now."

"Suit yourself," Phelps said. "But if you won't follow my advice, don't ask me what's wrong with you."

"Maybe nothing's wrong with me," Whalen said amiably. "Maybe I'm just getting old."

"Maybe so," Phelps replied tartly. "And maybe something *is* wrong with you and you just don't want to know about it."

"What you don't know can't hurt you."

"Can't help you either," Phelps countered. "And what about other people? You might hurt someone—you almost did yesterday."

"But I didn't," Whalen reminded him. "And I won't."

As Harney Whalen left his office Dr. Phelps wished he were as confident as Whalen seemed to be. But he wasn't. The idea of Harney Whalen having "spells" worried him. It worried him very much.

Glen Palmer arrived home to find the cabin deserted. A note from Rebecca said she had gone down to the Randalls' to see if she could give them a hand. He could fix his own lunch or come and get her. Since it was still early Glen decided to walk down the beach.

The leaden sky showed no signs of clearing; the sky to the west was almost black, and near the horizon storm clouds were scudding back and forth, swirling among themselves as if grouping for an attack on the coast. The light rain that had been coming down all night and all morning still fell softly, soaking into the beach immediately, leaving the sand close-packed and solid. The tide was far out, and the level beach, exposed far beyond its normal width, glistened wetly.

Glen walked out toward the surf line, then turned south, moving slowly, almost reluctantly. He was trying to decide how to break the news to Rebecca and what her response would be.

She would give up and demand that they leave Clark's Harbor. Or she would be angry. Or prepared for a fight, ready to do anything to show that she could not be frightened off. The last, he thought, would be typical of Rebecca.

He was wrong. Rebecca saw him coming when he was still fifty yards from the old house on the beach and went out to meet him.

"It happened, didn't it?" she asked softly.

Glen looked up, startled. He hadn't seen her coming—he'd been staring at the sand at his feet, preoccupied. He nodded mutely.

"What was it?"

"The gallery's been vandalized," Glen told her.

"Vandalized? You mean someone broke in?"

"They broke in, they wrecked the gallery, they smashed all your pottery, and they shredded all but one of my canvases."

"Which one?" Rebecca asked irrelevantly, and Glen realized that she was shutting out what he had said. Of all the possible reactions, this was one Glen hadn't considered.

"The one I gave Chip," he said softly. Rebecca turned slowly and gazed at the old house that was the subject of Glen's only surviving canvas.

"Somehow that seems right," she commented. Then she slipped her arm through Glen's and stared up into his trouble eyes. "Let's not worry about it now. Not this minute anyway. If I have to decide what to do right now I'll make the wrong decision. So let's wait, all right? We'll talk it over with Brad and Elaine, then pretend nothing's happened for the rest of the day. And tonight when we're in bed we'll make up our minds."

Glen pulled her closer and kissed her softly. "If we decide in bed I know what we'll do: we'll stick it out here. When we're in bed anything seems possible."

"Then so be it," Rebecca murmured. "But let's not talk about it right now, all right?"

The chaos in the Randalls' house was only slightly more orderly than that in the gallery, and Glen tried to sound cheerful as he made the comparison. But as he listened to Glen's story of what had happened the night before Brad wondered if Robby had stayed in bed last night: Glen's description of the gallery sounded all too much like the havoc the boy had been known to create in the past. So when Robby and Missy arrived, scrambling over the driftwood on their way home from school, Brad quickly found an excuse to take Robby for a long walk on the beach.

"Pretty out here, isn't it?" he said casually when they were out of earshot of the house. Robby nodded noncommittally.

"Your dad tells me you love it out here," Brad prodded gently.

"It's all right. But I like it best when it rains."

"Why's that?"

Robby turned the question over in his mind. Nobody had ever asked him that before, and he hadn't ever thought about it. Now, with the openness of childhood, he began thinking out loud. "I guess I feel excited when the storms come up," he said slowly. "But it's a funny kind of excited. Not like Christmas, or my birthday, when I know something good's going to happen. It's more like a feeling in my body. I get sort of tingly, and sometimes it's hard to move. But it's not a bad feeling—it's more like it's what's supposed to happen. It's exciting and relaxing all at the same time. Sometimes when I'm out in the storms I feel like lying down on the ground and letting the rain fall all over me."

"You go out in the storms?" Brad tried to keep his voice casual but there was a note of concern in it that Robby detected immediately. He stared up at Brad, his eyes large and frightened.

"Don't tell Mom and Dad," he begged. "They wouldn't like it. They'd think I was still sick, but I'm not. The storms make me well."

"I won't tell anyone," Brad reassured the boy. "But I'd like to know what happens when you go out in the storms."

"Nothing, really. Missy thinks she sees things when we're out together, but nothing ever happens. Sometimes I go by myself, but sometimes Missy comes with me," he explained, though Brad hadn't voiced the question that was in his mind. "But Missy never wants to go and I always have to talk her into it. She's a scaredy-cat."

"What about the night I met you on the beach? Missy wasn't with you then."

"I was looking for Snooker and Missy wouldn't come. She said he was gone and wasn't coming back and there wasn't any use looking for him." Robby looked dejected. "I guess she was right," he said softly, as if the admission hurt him.

"Do you ever see anyone else when you're out in the storms?"

Robby thought about it and decided that the only time he'd actually *seen* anyone was a few weeks earlier. "We met Old Man Riley once. He told us stories about the Indians, and how they used to kill people on the beach and hold ceremonies and all kinds of stuff. But that's all."

They walked in silence for a while as Brad tried to make sense out of what Robby had said. It seemed, on the surface, as if nothing particularly unusual was happening. And yet, Brad was sure there was something else just beneath the surface. He decided to ask one more question.

"Aren't you ever frightened when you're out by yourself and the storms are blowing?"

Robby Palmer looked bewildered. "No," he finally said. "Why should I? I belong here." Then, before Brad could absorb what he had said or question him about the previous night, Robby turned and began running back to the house. Brad watched him go and wondered what he had meant.

Wasn't Robby, like the rest of his family, a stranger here? How could he "belong"?

As soon as Brad returned to the house Glen drew him aside, his expression a mixture of curiosity and concern. "Well?" he asked expectantly.

"I don't know," Brad said slowly, wishing he could come up with an easy explanation for the events that were ensnaring Clark's Harbor. "It has something to do with the storms. Robby says they 'excite' him. And if they excite him they must do the same to other people. Only they don't calm the other people down. The storms must turn them into monsters instead."

Brad didn't tell Glen what Robby had said about Missy. For the moment, he decided, he would keep it to himself. At least until he had a chance to talk to Missy directly.

As the afternoon light began to fade Dr. Bradford Randall stared out over the Pacific Ocean and tried to keep the dogs of fear that were nibbling at the edges of his consciousness at bay.

There was an explanation for what was happening around him. He could find it.

But even if he found it he wasn't sure he could do anything about it. He remembered the old adage: everybody talks about the weather, but nobody does anything about it.

Maybe there was nothing that *could* be done about it.

## TWENTY-THREE

ELAINE RANDALL HADN'T SLEPT WELL. She was uneasy in their new surroundings, but there was something more—what Brad had told them the night before. It hadn't sounded logical. And yet she knew that weather could affect people. Ionization, the Santa Ana winds, that sort of thing. But here, in Clark's Harbor? It may not have made sense, but it was frightening. So she had lain awake most of the night, listening to the steady roar of the surf. And thinking.

Twice she had gotten up, both times without disturbing Brad, and stared out at the beach. It was clear and she had seen the Big Dipper glowing brightly in the black sky. A half-moon had turned the beach a burnished pewter tone.

Near dawn she had finally drifted into a fitful sleep.

Now she was up, battling with the recalcitrant wood stove, poking at the remains of a dead fire. Rebecca had showed her how to bank the fire last night, but Elaine wasn't sure it had worked. She grasped a poker in her right hand. A small bellows sat on top of the stove, ready for her to use in the unlikely event a spark should appear. She jabbed viciously at the largest chunk of wood remaining in the firebox, and was surprised when it broke in two and exposed its glowing interior.

She crammed a wad of newspaper into the firebox, picked up the bellows, and began frantically pumping. She heard Brad come into the kitchen but was too intent on getting the fire going to offer more than a muttered "good morning."

Brad watched her for a few minutes, then took the bellows out of her hands.

"You're working too hard," he said. "You'll blow the fire out as fast as you feed it. Do it slowly." He worked the bellows easily and a moment later a tiny flame leaped to life, igniting the paper. Brad put the bellows aside and tossed some chips of wood onto the tiny blaze, then some kindling. The fire grew steadily.

"Nothing to it," he announced.

"Beginner's luck," Elaine said. "It was all set to go when you took over. Hand me the coffee."

She carefully measured out the coffee, then placed the basket inside the aluminum percolator that stood waiting on the stove. "I could learn to do without coffee at this rate," she complained. "Any idea how long it's supposed to perk, assuming it ever starts?"

"Till it's done," Brad replied just as there was a knock at the kitchen door, followed by a voice.

"Anybody home?" It was Rebecca Palmer, and she didn't wait for a reply before coming in. She was carrying a thermos.

"I thought you might be able to use this," she said cheerfully. "The first couple of days we were here I couldn't get the coffee to perk at all." She pulled the top off the thermos and the room filled with the aroma of fresh, strong coffee. Elaine poured three cups and immediately took a sip from one of them.

"I may live," she sighed. Then she looked questioningly at Rebecca. "Did you see Jeff?"

"Jeff? Isn't he here?"

"I thought I heard him go out just before I got up," Elaine replied. "I think he was going out to look for wreckage."

"He's not on the beach," Rebecca said.

"Probably went the other way," Brad suggested. "But I don't think he'll find anything."

Chip Connor found Harney at his desk, sourly going over the report Chip had left there the night before. The chief looked up at him and pushed the file aside.

"You expect me to do anything about that?" he asked.

"It's our job," Chip pointed out.

"Anything stolen?"

"Not as far as Glen could tell. But you should see the place," Chip added. "It's a mess."

"Well, that's the way things go sometimes," Whalen said, unconcerned. "If nothing was stolen then what's the big deal?"

"You mean you aren't going to do anything?" Chip couldn't believe what he was hearing.

"No," Whalen said heavily, "I'm not."

Chip's eyes narrowed angrily. "I don't know what's going on with you, Harn. It seems like lately you just don't give a damn what goes on around here."

"I don't give a damn about what happens to outsiders," Whalen corrected. "And I have my reasons."

"I know about your reasons," Chip replied. "Granddad told me all about it. But the past is the past, Harney. All that happened years ago. Things change."

"Some things change. Some don't. Some things can be forgiven, and some can't. I haven't forgotten what happened to my grandparents. Never will. And as far as I'm concerned, I don't want any outsiders hanging around this town. They're dangerous."

"It seems to me that this town's more dangerous for them than they are for us," Chip countered.

"That's the way things are here." A hatred came into Whalen's voice, a tone that Chip had never heard before. "When my grandparents first came here it was dangerous for them. The Indians didn't like what was going on and they did their damnedest to get rid of all the whites. But my grandparents hung on and they learned to live here. My daddy even married a girl who was part Indian, but I guess you know about that, don't you?"

Chip nodded, wondering what Whalen was getting at.

"Well, the Indians went away after a while, up north, and left us alone. But they always said the place would be no good for strangers. And it hasn't been. The lumbermen tried to come in here, but it wasn't any good for them."

"That was your doing," Chip said. "First your grandfather's, then yours."

"I didn't renew a lease, that's all," Whalen said mildly. "But they should have gone away then. They didn't. They tried to stay and fish. And it didn't work."

"I heard," Chip said dully.

"Well, it's been that way ever since," Whalen said. "Every now and then strangers come, and they always bring trouble. But it's just like the Indians said. The trouble always flies back in their faces. And you know something, Chip? There's not a damned thing we can do about it."

"You don't even try."

"Not anymore, no," Whalen agreed. "I used to but it never did any good. So I live with it. Can't say it bothers me particularly." He picked up the folder containing Chip's report on the vandalism at Glen Palmer's gallery. "So don't expect me to do anything about this. I won't find anything—anybody could have done it and there's nothing to look for. If I were you I'd forget it. You just tell Palmer, if he wants to stay in Clark's Harbor, he'd better expect things like this."

Chip nodded his head absently and started to leave. But before he got to the door he remembered something and turned back.

"Did you see Doc Phelps yesterday?"

"Yeah." Whalen said the word tonelessly, as if there were nothing more to add, but Chip pressed him.

"Is anything wrong?"

"Nothing he could find. I just didn't feel very well the other night, so I decided to have him take a look. Must have been indigestion."

Whalen wondered briefly why he was lying to Chip, why he didn't want to tell Chip about his "spells," then decided it was just none of Chip's business. Besides, the spells weren't serious. If Phelps couldn't find out what was causing them there wasn't any point in talking about them.

"Well, if you need me call me on the radio. I'm going to give Glen Palmer a hand today, but I'll leave the radio open."

Whalen scowled at his deputy. "I don't suppose it's any of my business what you do on your days off, but I think you're wasting your time. You get involved with Palmer and you'll get in trouble."

"I don't see how," Chip said, annoyed at Whalen.

"That's the way it happens, that's all," Harney said flatly. He pulled a file from the top drawer of his desk, and opened it, as if to dismiss Chip.

But as the door to his office closed behind his deputy, Harney Whalen looked up from the file he had been pretending to be reading. His eyes fastened vacantly on the closed door but he didn't really see it. Instead he saw Chip's face, but it was not quite the face he knew so well. There was something different about the face Harney Whalen visualized.

Something strange.

That was it, he thought to himself.

Chip's become a stranger to me.

Then he put the thought aside and returned to the file in front of him.

"Want a beer?" Glen asked as Brad came through the front door. He and Chip were leaning against one of the display cases admiring their work. The mess was gone, the shelves were back up, and all but one of the display cases had been repaired.

"I thought you said it was destroyed," Brad said, puzzled.

"I guess it wasn't as bad as I thought," Glen replied a little sheepishly. "Not that I could have fixed it myself, of course."

"He's been fussing around, getting in the way all day," Chip said. "I told him to go out and paint a picture but he wouldn't."

"Well, if you can get along without him I'll drag him down to the library with me."

"The library?" Chip asked. "What's at the library?"

Brad glanced at Glen and Glen nodded his head. "If he doesn't think I'm crazy," he said, "he's not likely to think you are." He turned to Chip. "Brad has a theory about what's going on around here."

"It has to do with the storms," Brad said. "They seem to affect Glen's son and I'm wondering if they might be affecting somebody else too."

Chip frowned, puzzled. "I don't get it."

"I'm not sure I do either," Brad said. "But it just seems as though too many 'accidents' have happened out here. I'm just trying to find out if they really are accidents."

"You mean the drownings?" Chip asked.

"Not just the drownings," Glen answered. "There's also what happened here, and Miriam Shelling, and my dog. It all just seems like too much."

"I don't know what you think you'll find out," Chip said. "Harney Whalen sure doesn't seem too interested."

"What does he think is going on?" Glen asked carefully. He'd learned to be careful with Chip on the subject of Whalen.

"He seems to think it's some kind of fate, or an old Klickashaw curse or something. He says whenever strangers come to Clark's Harbor trouble comes with them, but that it always turns back on them."

"Makes things simple anyway," Brad commented.

"Yeah," Chip said, a little uncomfortably. He glanced around the gallery and set his empty beer can down. "Tell you what," he suggested to Glen. "If Brad wants you to help him, why don't we call it a day? I'll go down to Blake's and pick up what we need to finish this off and we'll do it tomorrow."

The sky had turned black by the time they locked up the gallery, and Chip glanced at the western horizon. "Looks like a storm's getting ready to hit." The three men shuddered, keenly aware of what a storm could mean in Clark's Harbor.

Jeff Horton had spent the entire day walking the beach, tramping north aimlessly, telling himself he was looking for wreckage from *Osprey* when in fact he was trying to sort out the pieces of what had happened.

He had been awake all night, and several times he had heard someone else downstairs, also awake. Twice he had been tempted to go down and tap at the Randalls' bedroom door, just for the company. But it wasn't company he needed. He needed to understand what was happening.

He had left the house early in the morning, telling no one where he was going—he was sure the Randalls would understand, and besides, he wasn't sure where he *was* going. Or what he was looking for.

He knew that storms could kill people, but they did it simply, straightforwardly. They came down on you if you were at sea, tossed you around, terrified you, then, if the spirit moved them, hurled a gigantic wave at you and crushed you.

If you were on land you were safer, though a storm could still smash your house, drop an electrical line on you, or cut you down with a bolt of lightning. But could a storm make someone cast a boat adrift? Could it send someone into an art gallery to destroy its contents? Could it hang a woman from the branch of a tree in the middle of the woods? All Jeff Horton's sensibilities told him it could not. And yet, as the wind began to blow and the dark clouds began to lower over the horizon, he turned south and started back toward Clark's Harbor. The surf began to build and the tide began flooding in, the storm on its heels.

\*   \*   \*

Missy and Robby were on Sod Beach when the storm struck the coast. As the first drops of rain fell Missy gave up her search for a perfect sand dollar and called out to her brother.

"It's starting to rain."

"So what?" Robby said, not looking up from the patch of sand he was carefully searching. So far he had found five undamaged shells, and Missy none, and he was sure she was just trying to spoil his fun. Besides, the beginnings of the storm made the beach exciting. He glanced up at the clouds, then grinned happily at the sight of the churning surf. He was only vaguely aware of Missy's complaining voice.

"I want to go *home,*" she insisted. "I don't want to stay out here and get soaked!"

"Nobody's home," Robby pointed out. "Dad's still at work and Mom's down at Dr. Randall's."

"Then let's go there," Missy begged. "We can go through the woods." She started across the beach, determined not to look back, not to give her brother a chance to cajole her into staying on the unprotected sand. She wanted to turn around when she got to the reef of driftwood that lay at the high water line but was afraid to, afraid that if Robby wasn't coming along behind her she would give in and go back toward the angry sea and the growing storm. Not until she was safely into the forest did she risk a look.

Robby was no longer on the beach. Missy had a moment of panic, then decided that her brother was teasing her, trying to scare her. Well, she wouldn't be frightened. And she wouldn't go running around looking for him, the way he wanted her to. She would stay right where she was, in the safety of the forest, and watch. Sooner or later, Robby would come looking for her. . . .

Jeff Horton arrived at the north end of Sod Beach in a shadowy half-light, a dark gray dusk made heavy by the now-raging storm. The beach looked deserted, but as Jeff passed the Palmers' cabin he paused, a curious sense of apprehension sweeping over him. When he began walking again he had an urge to run but fought it off, telling himself there was no danger, nothing to be afraid of; he only had a few hundred yards to go before he would be comfortably inside the Randalls' house.

But as he moved through the storm Jeff began to feel an odd sensation: the lightning flashing around him seemed to slow him down, drain his energy. He wanted to run but found he could only walk, and with each step his stride became slower.

He tried to force himself to hurry but it did no good. And as his pace slowed he came to the realization that he was no longer alone on the beach. Something else was there, something terrifying. Something that had come out of the storm. . . .

From her vantage point in the meager shelter of the forest Missy could barely make out the shape moving steadily down the beach. At first she thought it must be Robby, but then she realized it was too big. It was too dark for her to recognize who it might be; indeed, as the light faded into darkness the figure began to disappear entirely. But as night closed around her the full force of the storm struck, and the beach was lit up by sudden flashes of lightning. Each time the beach became momentarily visible, Missy looked fearfully around for her brother. He was nowhere to be seen.

A few minutes later she lost her courage and crept away into the woods when the white flash of pent-up electricity suddenly revealed not one, but two figures on the beach. They were close together, and as she watched they suddenly merged. . . .

Jeff Horton felt the attack before it came. The hair on the back of his neck tingled and stood on end, and his feeling of apprehension changed suddenly into a sense of danger. He was turning to face whatever enemy was behind him when he felt the massive arm slide around his neck and a force on the back of his head pushing forward. He felt his windpipe close under the pressure of the opposing forces and began to struggle, his arms flailing in the rain. Once he got a grip on his unseen assailant, but his hands, slick with wetness, slid loose. Before he could break free he began to lose consciousness. His last memory was of a sound, a cracking noise from just below his head. He wondered what it might have been, but before he could find an answer the blackness closed in on him and he relaxed. Seconds later he lay alone on the beach, the rain pounding down on him, the surf licking at him like a beast sniffing at its fallen prey.

Missy ran along the trail through the woods, her heart pounding, her small voice crying out to her brother. And then he was there, standing on the trail ahead of her, waiting for her.

"I was looking for you," Robby said softly. "How come you hid?"

Missy stopped running and stared at her brother, her breath coming in great heaves. She tried to speak through her gasps of exhaustion and fear but couldn't. She sat heavily on a log and began crying. Perplexed, Robby sat beside her and put his arm around her.

"I—I saw something," Missy stammered. "I was waiting for you, but you didn't come, and I saw something. On the beach—there was someone on the beach, and then someone else—and I—oh, Robby, let's go *home,*" she wailed.

Robby took her hand and pulled her to her feet. "You didn't see anything," he assured her. "It's too dark." He began leading her along the path, his step sure, his pace fast. The excitement of the storm swept over him. He wished it would never end.

At nine o'clock that evening the librarian at the tiny Clark's Harbor public library—two rooms in the town hall—tapped Brad Randall on the shoulder. Brad stopped writing in the notebook he had nearly filled in the five hours he and Glen had been working and looked up.

"It's closing time." The gray-haired woman whispered, though there was no one else in the area. "You'll have to come back on Monday."

"That's all right," Brad said. "I'm almost finished." He smiled at the woman ruefully. "I hope we haven't put you through too much."

"Oh, it's all right," the librarian assured him. "Most days I just sit here. It's nice to have something to do now and then. Though what you want with all those papers is beyond me, I'm sure."

"Just checking some things out," Brad said mildly. "Sort of a research project on the history of the town."

"Not much history," the librarian sniffed. "We live and die and that's about it."

"That's what I'm interested in," Brad said mysteriously. The librarian's eyes widened, but before she could ask any questions Glen Palmer came in from the other room.

"That does it," he said. "We've gone as far back as the records go."

"That's all right. We've got enough information, I think."

As Brad and Glen left, the librarian began putting away all the old newspapers they had gone through. She was puzzled. She made a mental note to talk to Merle Glind about it. If something was happening he would surely know what it was.

The storm had closed in and rain was coming down in sheets as Glen and Brad made a dash for Brad's car. As they started toward the main highway the wind, blowing at close to gale force, pulled at the Volvo, and Brad had trouble keeping it on the road.

"Why don't we leave your minibus at the gallery?" he suggested as they turned onto the highway. Glen shook his head.

"Not in weather like this. If there's anything to your theory, this is the kind of night that something could happen to it."

Brad chuckled appreciatively, and pulled as close to the ancient Volkswagen van as he could get. "You want to stop at our place on the way? I wouldn't be surprised if Rebecca and the kids aren't there, keeping Elaine company."

"Fine," Glen replied. "See you there."

They found Rebecca and Elaine in the living room. The two women rose to greet them with worried faces.

"It's all right," Brad assured them. "We're here and we're safe. You don't have to look like tragedy struck."

His grin failed to wipe the frowns from their faces and they glanced at each other nervously. It was Elaine who spoke.

"The children came in a while ago," she said quietly. "About half an hour after the storm struck. Missy thought she saw something on the beach, but she isn't sure what."

"Where are they?" Brad asked.

"We put them to bed," Rebecca explained. "They were soaked and Missy was frightened."

*Missy thinks she sees things.* Robby's words echoed in Brad's mind but he decided not to say anything. Not yet anyway.

"Did you find anything at the library?" Elaine asked softly, almost hesitantly.

Brad nodded. "Something's going on all right," he said. "We went through a lot of papers this evening. Every time something's happened out here, there's been a storm blowing. And it's funny, it seems as though the worse the storm is, the worse the things that happen." He was warming to his subject now, oblivious of the stricken look on his wife's face. "For instance," he went on, "did you know the Shellings weren't the first case of a couple dying here?"

"What do you mean?" Rebecca asked, suddenly pale.

"The people who built this house died the same way," Glen said quietly. "Baron fell off his fishing boat and got caught in his own nets. A few days later, Mrs. Baron hanged herself. It happened during a three-day storm."

"I wish you hadn't told me that," Elaine said softly. "Things like that scare me." Brad moved to put his arm around her shoulder but she pulled away suddenly as a thought struck her. "Where's Jeff?"

Glen and Brad looked at each other blankly. "Jeff? He wasn't with us. We haven't seen him all day . . ." Glen's voice trailed off as he realized what he had just said. Jeff must have been on the beach.

And a storm was blowing.

A bad storm.

He grabbed his coat and began putting it back on. "Let's get going," he said to Brad. He picked up a flashlight from the dining-room table and was gone, disappearing into the blackness. The wind-driven rain quickly blotted out even the faint glow from his light.

# TWENTY-FOUR

T HEY ALMOST STUMBLED OVER JEFF.
The young fisherman was lying in the sand, and if they hadn't been walking at the water's edge they would have missed him entirely.

"Oh, Jesus," Glen whispered as Brad's light played over Jeff's face. The mouth was twisted in a grimace of pain. Dead, Glen thought. Oh, my God, he's dead. But then his eyelids fluttered and Glen fell to his knees, touching Jeff's arm. The eyes opened.

Jeff's mouth began to work, but no sound came out. His eyes closed again, tightly this time, as he winced in pain.

Brad wanted to move him, to pull him further up the beach so the surf couldn't get at him, but as he played the flashlight over Jeff's body he realized something was terribly wrong.

Jeff's head lay at a strange angle. His neck was broken.

That Jeff was alive at all was a miracle.

Then Jeff's eyelids fluttered again and once more he tried to speak. Glen leaned down, close to Jeff's lips.

"What is it, Jeff? What happened?"

Jeff tried hard but no sound would come out of him. He used the last of his strength to take a deep breath, then made a desperate effort to speak. But before the words could be formed the breath turned into a soul-shaking rattle and was expelled in a long, slow sigh.

Jeff Horton, like his brother, lay dead on Sod Beach.

Elaine Randall paced between the kitchen and the living room, pausing every few seconds to stare futilely into the blackness of the night. Several times she forced herself to sit down in front of the fire, but it was useless. A moment later she was on her feet again, her nerves jangling, a knot of fear twisting her stomach.

Her eyes flicked around the room and she wondered briefly what she was looking for. Then she knew.

The float.

The glistening blue glass ball she had found on the beach—how long ago? It seemed like years, though it had been only weeks.

She picked the sphere up from its place on the mantel, and stared into its depths.

It was no longer beautiful.

What she had thought of as an omen for good now seemed evil to her. She turned it over in her hands, wondering what to do with it.

She decided to return it to the sea.

Without giving herself time to change her mind, Elaine put on her pea coat and hurried out of the house. She moved directly across the beach, and when she neared the surf line she stopped. She looked at the float once more, curiously, then raised her arm and hurled it into the pounding waves. As it left her hand Elaine felt a tingling—almost electric—in her arm. Suddenly terrified, she turned and fled back into the house.

Glen Palmer lurched unsteadily through the kitchen door, his face pale and his hands trembling.

Elaine stood at the stove stirring a pan of hot cider. As soon as she saw Glen she knew.

"You found him, didn't you?" she whispered.

Glen nodded mutely and sank into a chair at the kitchen table, cradling his head in his hands.

*Missy saw it,* Elaine thought. *She saw it happen.* She touched Glen gently on the shoulder. "Just sit here. I'll get Rebecca." She frowned. "Where's Brad?"

"He went to town," Glen muttered. "He went to report what we found." Elaine, not yet wanting to hear exactly what they had found, went to the living room and gestured Rebecca to the kitchen. "I'll check on the kids," she whispered. Rebecca hurried toward the kitchen as Elaine stepped into the room where Missy and Robby were occupying her bed.

Robby was sleeping quietly but Missy was wide awake.

"Where's Daddy?" she asked.

"He'll be in in a little while," Elaine whispered. "He had to go out on the beach."

The little girl seemed to shrink before her eyes. "He shouldn't have done that," she whispered. "The beach is a bad place."

Missy's words sent a shiver up Elaine's spine but she said nothing. Instead she merely tucked Missy in and kissed her on the forehead. "Now go back to sleep. I want to be able to send your daddy in to kiss you, not scold you for staying awake. All right?"

Missy made no reply, but her eyes closed tightly and she squirmed further into the bed.

*Did she really see it?* Elaine asked herself. *Dear God, I hope not.*

She carefully checked the window, then pulled the door closed behind her. A moment later she was in the kitchen, listening as Glen tonelessly told them what had happened on the beach.

Merle Glind was pouring a third beer for Chip Connor when the telephone tucked away at the end of the bar suddenly began ringing.

"They never let you alone," Merle clucked, setting the half-empty bottle on the bar next to Chip's glass. "If it isn't one thing it's another."

Chip grinned as Merle bustled down to the telephone, but his smile faded when the fussy little man held the receiver up and called out to him.

"It's for you but I don't know who it is."

"Hello?" Chip said into the phone a moment later.

"Chip? It's Brad Randall. Are you still sober?"

"I'm on my third beer," Chip replied. "What's happened?"

"Jeff Horton. Glen and I found him on the beach a little while ago. He's dead."

"Shit!" Chip said. Then: "Did you call Harn?"

There was a slight pause before Brad spoke again. "I decided to call you instead," he said almost hesitantly.

"All right," Chip said. "Where's the body?"

"Still on the beach. We didn't want to move it."

"Okay, I'll be right out." Then he paused and frowned slightly. "Where are you?"

"Pruitt's gas station. It was the nearest telephone. You want me to wait here for you?"

"No, I can meet you at your place. I'll have to call Harney and tell him what's happened."

"I know," Brad said. "If I hadn't been able to find you I'd have called him myself."

"Okay," Chip grunted. "Go on back home. I'll get there as soon as I can." Almost as an afterthought, he added, "Is Glen all right?"

"A little shock but he should be out of it by the time you get there."

"Will he be able to answer questions?"

Now there was a long silence, and when Brad finally answered his voice was guarded. "It depends on what kind of questions. That's why I called you instead of Whalen, Chip."

Chip bit his lip thoughtfully and wondered what would happen if he simply handled it himself and didn't notify Harney until morning. He'd get his ass chewed, that's what would happen, he decided. "I have to call him," he told Brad. "He's the chief."

"I know," Brad said tiredly. "All right. See you."

Chip replaced the receiver on the phone under the bar and wasn't surprised when he found Merle Glind hovering behind him, his eyes wide and curious.

"What is it?" he asked. "What's happened?"

"Jeff Horton. He's out on Sod Beach, dead."

"Mercy!" Glind said. Then he clucked his tongue, his head wagging sympathetically. "I knew he should have gone. I just knew it."

But Chip wasn't listening. He had the phone in his hand once more, and was dialing Harney Whalen's number. On the tenth ring, just as Chip was about to give up, Whalen's voice came onto the line.

"Did I get you out of bed?" Chip asked.

"No," Whalen replied, his voice sounding a little vague. "I was watching television. I guess I must have dozed off."

"Well, you'd better get down to Sod Beach right away. Jeff Horton's out there and he's dead." There was a silence and Chip wasn't sure the chief had heard him. Then, as he was about to repeat himself, Whalen's voice grated over the line.

"I warned the son-of-a-bitch," he said. "Nobody can say I didn't warn him. Take care of it, will you, Chip?"

The phone went dead in Chip's hand. Harney had hung up on him.

By midnight it was all over. Chip Connor and Brad Randall had brought Jeff Horton's body in out of the storm. It lay in the dining room, covered by a blanket, until an ambulance could be summoned to take it away. Rebecca and Elaine, chilled by the closeness of death, avoided the dining room as if whatever had killed Jeff might still be lurking there.

Chip hovered near while Brad examined the body, going over it quickly but expertly. When he was finished he drew the blanket over Jeff's face and spoke quietly to Chip.

"His neck's broken. That's all I can find. Of course a full autopsy will have to be done, but that's not my business. And I doubt they'll find anything else. It's almost incredible that he was still alive when Glen found him."

"Why?"

"The way his neck was bent. He should have been dead just a minute or two after his neck was broken."

"Then how did he stay alive?"

Brad shook his head doubtfully. "I'm not sure. Pure will, probably. His windpipe must have stayed open, but his spinal column is a mess."

"Did Glen's touching him have anything to do with him dying?"

"It might have but he'd have died anyway. If anything, all Glen did was put him out of his misery. There was no way he could have survived what happened."

"What did happen?" Chip asked. "Can you tell?"

"From the bruises on the back of the neck, it looks like someone hit him with something—hard enough to crush the bones in his neck—then jerked on his head to make sure the job was done."

"Christ," Chip groaned, feeling a little sick at his stomach. "Why would anyone want to do that?"

"I wish I knew." He looked curiously at Chip. "Isn't Whalen coming out?"

"No. He told me to take care of it for him. I guess he still isn't feeling well."

"What do you mean?"

"He took yesterday off," Chip said. "When I talked to him this morning he said something about indigestion. I guess it must have hit him again tonight."

"Indigestion?" Brad repeated. "He doesn't seem the type. He looks strong as an ox."

"He is," Chip agreed. "But he's sixty-eight years old, even though he doesn't look it."

"Sixty-eight? I'd have thought he was in his late fifties."

"Nope. He'll be sixty-nine in August."

Brad shook his head admiringly. "I should look that good when I'm his age," he said, but his mind was no longer on Whalen's appearance. It was his age that Brad had focused on. Something about his age that made some kind of connection. But before he could sort it out the ambulance arrived, and by the time they had finished attending to Jeff Horton's body the elusive connection had slipped away.

Brad closed the kitchen door against the rain as the ambulance disappeared into the storm. "You still on duty, or can I offer you a drink?"

"I'd better not," Chip replied. "I have to get down to the station and write up this report so Harney will have it in the morning." He closed his notebook and prepared to leave. Then, just as he was about to open the door, he turned to Brad. He had one last question.

"Brad, do you have any idea what's going on out here? What's causing all this mess?"

Brad shook his head sorrowfully. "I wish I did. All I can tell you is that I think it has something to do with the storms."

"The storms?" Chip repeated. "But we've always had storms."

"I know," Brad said softly. "And it seems like you've always had a mess too."

Chip stared at him, then tried to laugh it off. "Maybe it's the Indians. God knows they did terrible things out here." Then he put on his hat and disappeared into the blackness outside.

## TWENTY-FIVE

THE STORM HAD NOT LET UP BY MORNING. As Brad and Glen drove into Clark's Harbor the rain buffeted the car, flooding the windshield faster than the wipers could clear it away.

"I've never seen anything like this," Glen commented. "I thought the worst storms hit during the winter."

"You never know," Brad said as they pulled up in front of the town hall. "Sometimes I think they gave the Pacific the wrong name. This one looks as though it could blow for days."

Several people lounging in the lobby looked up as they came in, examining them with speculative expressions. Something new in Clark's Harbor, Brad thought with some irony. Ignoring the inquisitive stares, they hurried down the hall to the police station.

Harney Whalen glared balefully at Glen as they came into his office. Before either of them could say anything, Whalen set the tone of the conversation.

"Seems like every time there's trouble around here you're right in the middle of it, doesn't it, Palmer?"

Glen felt the first pangs of anger form a knot in his stomach and silently reminded himself that losing his temper wouldn't accomplish anything.

"It seems like every time there's trouble it happens on Sod Beach," he countered.

Harney Whalen snorted and tossed a folder toward Glen and Brad. "You want to look that over and tell me if it's accurate?"

Glen scanned the report, then handed it to Brad. When both of them had read it, Brad returned it to Whalen.

"That's about it," Brad said.

"You want to tell me about it?" Whalen asked Glen, ignoring Brad.

"There's nothing to tell. We went out looking for Jeff and we found him. He died almost immediately."

"Why were you looking for him?" The curiosity in Whalen's voice was almost lost in the hostility. "He's a grown man—*was* a grown man."

"It was getting late—there was a storm blowing in. We just didn't like the idea of him being out in it," Glen replied.

"I think it was something else," Whalen said coldly.

"Something else? What?"

"I think you killed him," Whalen said. "Maybe one of you, maybe the other, maybe both. But I sure as hell don't believe the two of you just went for a walk on the beach and found a dying man. Something makes men die and it's usually other men.''

Brad and Glen gaped at the police chief, unable to comprehend what they were hearing. Brad recovered first.

"I'd be careful what I said if I were you, Whalen."

"Would you?" The sneer in Harney Whalen's voice hung in the air, a challenge. But before either of them could take it up Whalen went on. "How about this? The two of you were at the library last night, right? Well, let's suppose that while you were gone Horton wasn't staying home taking care of your wives like a good guest. Let's suppose he was just taking care of them. And you two walked in on it." He eyed first Glen, then Brad, looking for a reaction.

Glen Palmer stood quivering with rage, staring out the window at the downpour, saying nothing. But Brad Randall returned Whalen's icy look, and when he spoke it was with a calmness that Whalen hadn't expected.

"Are you charging us?" he asked calmly.

"I haven't decided yet," Whalen growled.

"Then we're leaving," Brad said quietly. "Come on, Glen." He turned and forced Glen to turn with him. Before they reached the door Whalen's voice stopped them.

"I'm not through with you yet."

Brad turned back to face the police chief. When he spoke his voice was every bit as cold as Whalen's had been.

"Aren't you? I think you are, Whalen. You aren't questioning us at all. You're accusing us. Now I'm not a lawyer, but I know damned well, and I suspect you know it too, that there's no way you can talk to us if we don't want to talk to you. Not without a lawyer here anyway."

Once more he started for the door with Glen behind him. This time Harney Whalen didn't try to stop them. He simply watched them go, hating them, wishing they had never come to Clark's Harbor, wishing they would leave him and his town in peace.

His fury and frustration mounting, Whalen put on his overcoat and rain hat and stalked out of his office. As he passed through the door of the police station, the loiterers quickly scattered, reading his ugly mood.

He started toward the wharf, unsure of where he was going or why. When he got to the wharf he turned north and began walking up the beach. The tide had peaked and was on its way out, and as he walked in the rain, the wind licking at him, his anger seemed to recede.

He walked the beach all morning and well into the afternoon.

He walked alone, silently.

As he walked, the storm swelled.

Robby and Missy sat on the floor of their tiny bedroom, a checkerboard between them. Robby stared sullenly at the board. No matter what he did, Missy was going to jump his last man and win the third straight game.

"I don't want to play anymore," he said.

"You have to move," Missy replied.

"I don't either. I can concede."

"Move," Missy insisted. "I want to jump you."

"You win anyway," Robby said. He stood up and went to look out the window. "Let's go outside," he said suddenly. From the floor Missy stared at him, her eyes wide with fear.

"We can't do that. Mommy said we have to stay in today. It's raining."

"I like it when it rains."

"I don't. Not when it rains like this. Bad things happen."

"Oh, come on," Robby urged her. "It's not even six o'clock. We can climb out the window, like I did last time. We'll go down to the Randalls' and come back with Daddy."

"I don't think we should."

"Scaredy-cat."

"That's right!" Missy exclaimed. "And you should be too!" Her mouth quivered, partly from fear but more from embarrassment at having admitted her fear.

"Well, I'm not afraid. I like it out there!" Robby pulled their raincoats out of the closet and began putting his on.

"I'm not going," Missy insisted.

"Who cares?" Robby asked with a show of unconcern. "I'll go by myself."

"I'm going to tell," Missy challenged, her eyes narrowing.

"If you do I'll beat you up," Robby threatened.

"You won't either."

Robby pulled on his boots. "Are you coming or not?"

"No," Missy said.

"All right for you then." He opened the window and clambered out. As soon as he was gone Missy ran to the window, pulled it shut, and latched it. Then she went into the other room, where Rebecca was sitting in front of the fire, knitting.

"Robby went outside," she said.

"Outside? What do you mean, he went outside?"

"He put on his raincoat and climbed out the window," Missy explained.

Rebecca dropped her knitting and ran to the tiny bedroom, hoping her daughter was playing a joke on her.

"Robby? Robby, where are you?"

"I *told* you, he went outside," Missy insisted.

Rebecca ran to the door, pulled it open, and started to step outside, but the storm drove her back in. She shielded her face and tried to see into the growing darkness.

"Robby? Robby!" she called. "Robby, come back here." But the wind and the pounding surf of the cresting tide drowned her words.

She thought desperately, wondering what to do, and immediately knew she would have to go find him. If only Glen were here, she thought. If only he hadn't gone down to the Randalls'. But he had. She would have to find Robby alone.

"I'll go get him," she told Missy. "You stay here."

"By myself?" Missy asked. She looked terrified.

"I'll only be gone a few minutes," Rebecca assured her. "Only until I find Robby."

"I don't want to stay by myself," Missy wailed. "I want to go too."

Rebecca tried to think it out but she was too upset. Her instincts told her to make Missy stay by herself, but the thought of having both her children alone frightened her even more than the idea of taking Missy with her.

"All right," she said. "Put on your raincoat and your boots, but hurry!"

Missy darted into the bedroom and came back with the coat and boots that Robby had already pulled from the closet. Rebecca pulled her own coat on, then helped Missy. A minute later, clutching a flashlight with one hand and Missy with the other, Rebecca left the cabin. A sudden gusting of the storm snuffed out the lantern just before she closed the door.

The wind whipped at her and drove the pounding rain through every small gap in her raincoat. Before they were a hundred feet from the house, both Rebecca and Missy were soaked to the skin.

"I want to go home," Missy wailed.

"We have to find Robby," Rebecca shouted. "Which way did he go?"

"He said he was going out on the beach." Missy was running now to keep up with Rebecca.

They stayed as close to the high-water line as they could, hurrying down the beach. The flashlight was almost useless, its beam refracting madly in the downpour, shattering into a thousand pinpoints of light that illuminated nothing, but made the darkness seem even blacker than it was.

Suddenly Missy stopped and yanked at her mother's hand.

"Someone's here," she said.

Rebecca flashed the light around with a shaking hand. "Robby?" she called. "Roobbeeeee!"

She turned so that her back was to the wind and called out again. There was no answer, but she suddenly felt the sharp sting of an electrical shock as a bolt of lightning flashed out of the sky and grounded itself in the nearby forest. And, she was sure, there was something behind her: an unfamiliar presence.

A presence she knew was not her son.

She dropped Missy's hand.

"Run, Missy! Run as fast as you can."

And then, as she watched Missy dash off into the darkness, she felt something slide around her neck.

It was an arm, a strong arm, and it was choking her. She tried to scream but her voice wouldn't respond. She tried to batter at the arm with the flashlight, but the pressure on her neck only increased.

*No,* she thought. *Not like this. Please, God, no . . .*

Missy ran into the darkness, not knowing which way she was going. She only knew she was going away.

Away from her mother.

Away from whoever was with her mother.

Then she stumbled and fell into the sand, crying out into the darkness.

"Missy? Is that you?" She couldn't see who was calling to her but she recognized the voice.

"Robby? Where are you?"

"Over here. Come on."

She scrambled toward his voice and found herself blocked by a log.

"Climb over," Robby urged.

Then she was beside him, crouched down behind the log, peering over the top of it into the darkness. In the distance the beam of the flashlight danced crazily, then suddenly fell to the ground and went out.

"What's happening?" Robby asked.

"It's Mommy," Missy sobbed. "Someone's out there—"

A bolt of lightning split the darkness, and the two children saw their mother. She was on her knees and there was a shape behind her, looming over her, holding her neck, forcing her head forward . . .

A shiver of excitement made Robby tremble, and he could feel every muscle in his body tense with anticipation.

The light faded from the sky and the roar of thunder rolled over them, drowning the scream that was welling from Missy's throat. It was as if the storm was clutching at Robby, immobilizing him.

"Let's go home, Missy," Robby whispered. He forced himself to take his sobbing sister by the hand and lead her into the woods. Then, as the beach disappeared from their view, he began running, pulling Missy behind him.

Rebecca's struggles grew weaker. She was blacking out. Time began to stretch for her, and she thought she could feel her blood desperately trying to suck oxygen from her strangled lungs.

Then she heard a crack, sharp, close to her ear, and she realized she could no longer move. It was as if she had lost all contact with her body.

My neck, she thought curiously. My neck is broken.

A second later Rebecca Palmer lay dead on Sod Beach.

# TWENTY-SIX

THE COLEMAN LANTERN ON THE DINING-room table began to fade, and Glen Palmer reached out to pump it up just as the bolt of lightning that had illuminated Rebecca's death a hundred yards away also flooded the Randalls' house with light. Reflexively, Glen snatched his hand away from the lantern, then chuckled. Brad Randall looked up from the chart he was poring over.

"Maybe we should give it up for today," Brad said. "I don't know about you but my eyes are getting tired. I'm not used to lantern light."

They had been at it all afternoon, charting the various events that had occurred in Clark's Harbor, from the deaths of Pete and Miriam Shelling all the way back to the frighteningly similar demise of Frank and Myrtle Baron years earlier. Over the years there had been several fatalities in the area, usually in the vicinity of Sod Beach, always on stormy nights when the coast was battered by high winds. And as far as they could tell, most of the victims, if not all, had been strangers to Clark's Harbor. Strangers who had come to the Harbor for various reasons and intended to settle there.

"It's like the Indian legends," Glen commented as they stared at the charts. "It's almost as if the beach itself doesn't want strangers here—as if it waits, gathers its forces, then strikes out at people."

"Which makes a nice story," Brad said archly. "But I don't believe it for a minute. There's another explanation but I'm damned if I know how to go about finding it."

Glen thought a moment. "What about Robby?" he asked.

"Robby?"

"You said that the beach affects him. If that's true, couldn't it affect someone else too?"

Brad smiled wryly. "Sure. But it doesn't help the problem. Until I know *how* the beach affects Robby, how can I figure out who else might be affected? So far I don't have the slightest idea what the common denominator might be."

Elaine appeared in the doorway. "Getting anywhere?" She looked drawn and tired.

"I wish we were," Brad said. "But so far it's nothing but dead ends. Apparently the storms are killing people, which is, of course, ridiculous."

"What about Missy? Hasn't anybody talked to her?"

The two men stared blankly at Elaine, wondering what she was talking about. A memory suddenly flashed into Brad's mind, a memory of Robby, talking to him on the beach.

*"Missy thinks she sees things."*

Did Elaine know something about that too?

"What about Missy?" he asked quietly. The tone of his voice, the seriousness with which he asked the question, frightened Glen, but Elaine's answer frightened him even more.

"I think Missy saw Jeff Horton get killed," she said. There was a flatness to her voice that somehow emphasized her words. "I haven't talked to her but she said something last night. I—I told her that her daddy had gone out on the beach, and she said, 'He shouldn't have done that. Bad things happen there.' That's all she said, but I got the strangest feeling that she'd seen what happened to Jeff, or at least had seen *something.*"

Glen sat in stunned silence, but Brad was nodding thoughtfully. "Robby told me awhile ago that Missy thinks she sees things on the beach," he murmured.

Glen suddenly found his voice. "Things?" he asked, his word edged with hysteria. "What kind of things?"

"He didn't say," Brad replied quietly. "I was going to talk to her about it but then everything started happening, and . . ." his voice trailed off, his words sounding hollow.

Glen stood up and pulled on his coat.

"Then we'll talk to her now. I'll go get Rebecca and bring her and the kids back here."

Brad glanced out into the blackness of the storm. "You want me to drive you? It's getting pretty dark out there."

"No thanks," Glen replied. "I'll walk along the beach. It doesn't look so bad out there now." He finished buttoning his coat and opened the door. The wind caught it and slammed it back against the kitchen wall.

"Sure you don't want me to drive you?"

Glen grinned crookedly. "You mean because of last night? They say if you fall off a horse the best thing to do is get right back up and ride him again. If I don't walk the beach tonight I never will."

He pulled the door closed behind him and disappeared into the rain.

Glen leaned forward into the wind, his right hand clutching the collar of his coat in a useless attempt to keep the rain out. His left hand, plunged deep in his coat pocket, was balled into a fist, and he kept his eyes squinted tightly against the stinging rain.

He made his way slowly, keeping close to the surf line, keeping his head down, watching the sand at his feet. Every few seconds he looked up, searching the darkness for the soft glow that should be coming from the cabin windows. Then, as the glow failed to appear out of the darkness, he began to worry and picked up his pace.

When he had walked nearly a hundred yards and felt the cabin should be clearly visible, he stopped and stared into the darkness, as if by concentrating hard enough he could force the dim light of the kerosene lanterns to appear in front of him. But still there was only blackness, and his concern turned to fear.

He began to run, no longer watching his steps, but straining his eyes to find the cabin, the cabin where Rebecca and the children would be waiting for him.

He tripped, sprawling headlong into the sand, his right hand only partially breaking his fall, his left hand, suddenly entangled in his pocket, useless.

He tasted brackish salt water in his mouth and felt the abrasive scraping of sand on his face. As he thrashed around, wiping his mouth on his sleeve and trying to get his left hand free, his foot hit something.

Something soft.

He felt the numbness begin in his mind—the same numbness that had fallen over him last night. He moved slowly, almost reluctantly.

He touched Rebecca gently, caressing her face. Even though she was still warm, he knew she was dead.

Her head, cradled in the sand, lay at the same unnatural angle as had Jeff Horton's the night before.

It was as if his mind refused to accept it at first. Glen crouched beside her, rocking slowly back and forth, no longer feeling the wind, the rain funneling unheeded down his collar.

"Rebecca," he said softly. Then he repeated her name. "Rebecca."

The pain hit him, washing over him with all the unexpected intensity of a tidal wave, and he threw himself onto her, wrapping her in his arms, sobbing on her breast.

"Rebecca," he moaned. "Oh, God, Rebecca, don't leave me."

She lay limply in his arms, her head rolling gently from side to side, her unseeing eyes staring up into the night sky.

Glen's pain changed from the wracking misery of the moment of discovery into a dull ache, an ache he was sure he would bear for the rest of his life.

Why had Rebecca been on the beach at all?

He thought of the children.

*Where were the children?*

He should look for them. They must have left the cabin, and Rebecca must have gone to look for them; she would never have left them alone, not Rebecca.

He stood up and looked uncertainly toward the forest, a black shadow set deep in the darkness of the night. If they were out here they would be in the woods.

But he couldn't leave Rebecca, couldn't leave her lying cold in the rain and the wind, the surf lapping at her feet. Before he went looking for his children he would have to attend to his wife.

He picked her up and began carrying her toward the cabin, his fogged mind wondering with each step at his need to care for the dead before tending to the living.

Where Rebecca had lain, there was now nothing but sand—and the darkly glistening form of a blue glass fisherman's float.

When he got to the cabin he paused, something preventing him from going inside. At first he wasn't sure what it was, but after a moment he knew.

The cabin wasn't empty.

There was nothing about it that told him it was occupied, only an intangible feeling. Though there was no sound, he was sure his children were there.

He laid Rebecca's body gently on the porch, then opened the door.

"Robby? Missy? It's Daddy."

He heard a scrambling sound, and then the children threw themselves on him.

"Daddy, Daddy," Missy sobbed. "Something awful happened."

Glen sank to his knees and drew the children close. "I'm sorry, Daddy, I'm sorry," Robby kept repeating, over and over.

"There's nothing for you to be sorry about," Glen told his son. "Nothing that happened is your fault. Nothing at all."

"But I went out," Robby insisted. "I wanted to go outside, so I did. And Mommy and Missy came to look for me, and then—then—" he choked on his words and began sobbing helplessly.

"We were on the beach," Missy said. "Something grabbed Mommy, and Mommy told me to run, and I did, and—and—"

"Hush," Glen whispered. "You don't have to tell me about it now. I have to take care of Mommy, and I want you to do something for me."

He disentangled himself from the children and lit the small lantern that should have been lighting Rebecca's work as she waited for him to come home, but instead had remained cold and dark as night fell over the beach. As the flame flickered to life the room seemed to warm slightly, and Robby and Missy began to calm down.

"Robby, I want you to take Missy into your bedroom. Put some clean clothes in a bag. For both of you. Can you do that?"

Robby nodded gravely.

"All right. Then wait for me. In the bedroom. Don't come out until I come for you, all right?"

"Are you going somewhere?" Missy asked, her eyes wide and her mouth quivering.

"No, darling, of course not. I'll be right here."

Missy started to ask another question, but Robby grabbed her hand and began pulling her toward their tiny bedroom. "Come on," he said.

"Stop pulling," Missy cried. "Daddy, make him stop."

"Don't pull her, Robby," Glen said. "And you stay in there with your brother," he instructed Missy.

As soon as the door separating their room from the main part of the cabin was closed, Glen opened the sofa bed he and Rebecca had shared and pulled one of the blankets off it. Then he carefully reclosed the bed and went back to the front porch.

He moved Rebecca to the end of the porch farthest from the door and carefully wrapped her in the blanket. When he was finished he went back to the front door, then turned to survey his work. If he got the children across the porch fast enough, they wouldn't notice that something was lying there only a few feet away. Struggling to maintain his self-control, Glen went back into the cabin.

Robby and Missy were sitting quietly on the edge of the lower bunk, their faces serious, their hands folded in their laps. Between them was a brown bag stuffed with clothing.

"Mommy's dead, isn't she?" Robby asked.

"Yes, she is," Glen said steadily.

"Why?" It was Missy, and her face looked more curious than anything else. Glen realized for the first time that Rebecca's death had no meaning for them yet. While it was painful beyond bearing for him, for his children it was still an abstract event.

"I don't know," he said gently. "Sometimes things like this happen."

"Do we have to go away?" Robby asked.

"Go away?"

"Is that why I put our clothes in the bag? Because we have to go away?"

"I'm going to take you down to stay with Brad and Elaine tonight," Glen said. "I'll stay there too, but I have to do some things tonight and I don't want to leave you alone."

"Are we going now?" Missy asked.

"Right now," Glen replied, forcing himself to smile. "Now it's pouring rain outside, so I want you two to see who can get to the car first, all right?"

The two children nodded eagerly.

"I'll open the door, and you two race. The first one to the car gets a surprise."

"What is it?" Robby demanded.

"If I told you it wouldn't be a surprise anymore, would it?"

He led them into the other room and made them stay back from the door while he opened it. Tears were streaming down his face.

"On your mark. Get set. Go!" he cried, and the children, intent only on the race, streaked through the door and across the porch, vying to be the first to reach the ancient VW van. Glen picked up their bag of clothing, closed the door, and followed them.

"Oh, Jesus," Brad Randall moaned as he opened the door for Glen Palmer and the children. The look in Glen's eyes and the tear-streaked faces of the children told him something terrible had happened. He could guess what.

Hearing his words from the living room, Elaine hurried in to find out what had gone wrong.

"Glen? Is something wrong?" She looked first at Glen, then at the children, and she too knew immediately. She knelt down and gathered the children into her arms. They clung to her, almost tentatively, then Missy, followed by Robby, broke into tears and buried their faces against her. As she held the children she looked up into Glen Palmer's drained face.

"I'm sorry," she said. "I'm so sorry . . ."

Glen swallowed and forced himself to stay coherent. "Can you . . . can you . . . ?" He couldn't finish the sentence, but Elaine understood.

"I'll take care of them. Brad, go with him. Help him."

Brad had been silently standing by but he suddenly came to life, grabbing for his coat. A moment later the two men disappeared into the night.

Elaine steered the children into the living room and settled them on the sofa. Then, before she did anything else, she quickly went through the house, checking all the windows, making sure they were closed and locked. Finally she bolted the doors, rattling each to be sure it was secure.

When she returned to the living room Missy was staring into the fire, lost in some small world of her own devising. But as Elaine sank down beside her the little girl took one of her hands, squeezed it, and smiled up at her.

"It's going to be all right," she said. "Really it is."

For some reason that Elaine never understood, Missy's words made her cry.

Glen and Brad carried Rebecca into the cabin and laid her on the floor. While Glen poked at the dying fire, wishing he could bring life back to Rebecca as easily as he could the coals, Brad began a quick examination.

It didn't take him long. By the time the fire was blazing he had finished.

"She was strangled," he said. "And her neck's broken."

"Oh, God," Glen said, shuddering. "It must have been terrible for her."

"That's something we don't know," Brad replied quietly. "I like to think the body has ways of dealing with things like this. We know we go into shock immediately when something happens to us suddenly and unexpectedly. I should think it would be the same with dying. Some automatic mechanism takes over and makes us comfortable. Anyway, that's the way it should be. But we'll never know, will we?"

"How long has she been dead?" Glen asked.

"Not long. An hour. Maybe two at the most."

"If only I hadn't stayed so long," Glen said. "If only I'd left a little earlier. Just a few minutes maybe——"

"Don't," Brad said. "Don't start that or you'll wind up blaming yourself for what happened. And you aren't to blame."

"I brought her here," Glen said.

"And it could as easily have been you out there tonight," Brad said roughly. "Now come on. We'd better get into town."

Glen looked around the little room.

"I hate to leave her here, all alone . . . ."

"No. You're coming with me. I'm not leaving you with her. Not tonight, not here. Put on your coat."

They were about to leave when they suddenly heard a sound from the children's room.

A small sound, barely a whimper.

Then, as they were about to investigate, Scooter, his small tail tucked between his legs, crept out into the living room.

He stopped, peered vacantly up at the two of them; then his tail began to wag and he stumbled clumsily toward Glen. Glen stooped, picked the puppy up, and scratched its belly. By the time they were in the car Scooter was fast asleep.

Chip Connor was alone in the police station when Brad and Glen arrived.

"It's Rebecca," Brad said.

The muscles in Chip's face tightened and he sank back into the chair behind Harney Whalen's desk.

"Is she dead?"

"Yes."

"Where?"

"On the beach."

"Shit." Then: "I'll have to call Harn."

"I know," said Brad. "But before you do I should tell you that I'm not going to let Glen talk to him tonight. As a doctor I'm putting him under my care."

"Of course," Chip said. "I don't think anyone would expect anything else."

"Don't you?" Brad said mildly, almost tiredly. "I wish I could share your thought."

If Chip even heard what Brad said he gave no sign. Instead he called Harney Whalen and quickly reported what had happened.

"I'll meet you out at the Palmers'," he said as he finished. Then he hung up the phone and looked at Glen, who had not yet spoken.

"Glen, can I ask you something, as a friend?"

"Sure," Glen said dully.

"Did you do it?"

Brad was about make an angry reply but Glen put a hand on his arm, stopping him.

"No, Chip, I didn't." The two men stared into each other's eyes, and finally Chip stood up and came around the desk.

"Try to take it easy, Glen. I'll find him for you, so help me." Then he turned to Brad.

"Can you give him a pill? To make him sleep?"

Brad frowned slightly. "I'm not sure he needs one."

"Well, if it won't hurt him give him one, will you?" There was a pause, then Chip shook his head sadly. "You were right about what you said before. Harney does want to talk to him."

"I've just changed my mind," Brad said. "What this man needs more than anything else is a good night's sleep."

But it wasn't a good night's sleep. Before dawn Glen Palmer woke up and reached for Rebecca.

She wasn't there. She would never be there again.

Quietly, Glen Palmer began to cry.

## TWENTY-SEVEN

THERE WAS A QUALITY IN THE AIR THE following morning, a numbing chill that lay over Clark's Harbor like an invisible fog, shrouding the town.

The people of the village went about their business, tending their shops and boats, greeting each other as they always had. When they spoke of Rebecca Palmer, and of Jeff Horton, it was not with the worried clucking of tongues and expressions of concern that might have been expected, but rather with the knowing looks, the almost lewdly arched eyebrows of people who have finally witnessed that which they had known would come to pass.

When Glen Palmer arrived at the police station in midmorning, he was not stared at, not subjected to the hostile glares he had been expecting. Nor were there any expressions of sympathy at the loss of his wife. Rather—and to Glen even more frightening—it was as if nothing had changed, as if what had happened to him was not a part of Clark's Harbor at all, not an event that touched the lives of the Harborites.

Only when he was inside the police station, inside Harney Whalen's office, did reality intrude on the sense of surrealism that surrounded him.

Harney Whalen sat impassively at his desk, staring at Glen.

"Are you ready to talk about it now?" The words were more a challenge than a question. Glen braced himself. He knew what was coming.

In the old house on Sod Beach Elaine Randall did her best to keep Missy and Robby occupied, to keep them from dwelling on the loss of their mother. After Glen left the house, insisting on going alone to see Whalen, the children had wanted to go out on the beach.

Elaine had refused, not so much out of fear that anything would happen to them, but out of her own inability to face the beach that day.

She was not sure she would ever again be able to enjoy the beauty of the crescent of sand. For her it was permanently soiled.

Around noon she set the children to work on a jigsaw puzzle, then went to the kitchen to fix lunch.

"Keep an eye on them, will you, honey?" she asked Brad as she passed through the dining room. Brad glanced up from the charts he was poring over.

"Hmm?"

"The kids," Elaine replied. "Keep an eye on them for me while I put lunch together."

"Sure," Brad muttered, and went back to work. Elaine smiled softly to herself and continued into the kitchen. The house could fall down around him without his noticing. She poked halfheartedly at the fire in the ancient stove and decided a cold lunch would do just fine.

Fifteen minutes went by, then Robby appeared in the kitchen.

"When are we having lunch?"

"In about two minutes. Are your hands clean?"

Robby solemnly inspected his hands, then held them up to Elaine for approval. She looked them over carefully and nodded.

"Okay. Take these into the dining room and see if you can get Brad to make room for us." She handed the little boy a tray of sandwiches, then followed him a few minutes later with napkins, silver, and a jar of pickles. The table, she noted, had miraculously been cleared, and Missy and Robby sat flanking Brad, all of them patiently awaiting her arrival.

"Isn't Daddy coming?" Missy asked as Elaine sat down.

"He'll be back as soon as he can get here," Elaine explained.

"Can I save my sandwich for him?"

"What'll you eat?"

"I'm not hungry," Missy said softly. "I'll just drink some milk."

"I'm sure your—" Elaine began, then stopped short. She had been about to say "mother," but quickly changed it. "—father would want you to eat your lunch," she finished.

"No, he wouldn't," Missy assured her.

"He would too," Robby said. "He'd say the same thing Mother would say—'you eat what's put in front of you!' Even if it *is* liverwurst," he added almost under his breath. He determinedly bit into his sandwich, and a moment later Missy did the same. The children munched in silence for a moment, then Robby put the remains of his sandwich down and looked quizzically at Elaine.

"Are we going to have to go away?"

"Go away? What do you mean?"

"Are we going to have to move away, after what happened to Mommy?"

"Well, I don't know," Elaine replied carefully. "That depends on your father, I suppose."

"Do you want to move away?" Brad asked. Robby shook his head emphatically but it was Missy who spoke.

"Yes! I hate it here! Mr. Riley told us a long time ago that there are ghosts on the beach, and he's right. I've seen them. They killed Mommy and they killed Mr. Horton and they'll kill everybody else too."

Elaine half-rose from her chair, intent on calming the child, but Brad signaled her to stay where she was. "Ghosts? What kind of ghosts."

"Indians," Missy said sulkily. "Mr. Riley told us they used to kill people on the beach, and sometimes they come back and do it some more. And I've seen them. I saw them the day Mr. Riley told us about them, and I saw them the night Mr. Horton got killed, and I saw them last night." As she spoke the last words Missy fled sobbing from the table. Elaine immediately followed her.

Robby seemed unperturbed by Missy's outburst. He picked his sandwich up again, took a big bite, and munched on it thoughtfully. Brad watched the boy eat, sure that he was turning something over in his mind. He was right, for Robby suddenly put the sandwich down again.

"Maybe she really does see things," Robby suggested hesitantly.

"Could be," Brad offered.

"I mean, the beach is a weird place during the storms."

"Oh?" Brad could feel something coming and wanted it to come from Robby undisturbed, uninfluenced by his own feelings.

"I like the storms," Robby went on, "but it's funny. I can't really remember what happens when I'm on the beach. It used to be fun, before all the bad things started happening. It was like I was all alone in the world, and it felt good. Even though it was raining real hard, I didn't feel it. I didn't feel anything, except inside myself." His brows knotted in sudden puzzlement.

"What is it?" Brad prompted him.

"It's funny," Robby said. "I can remember how I felt but I can't remember what I did. I mean, I can't remember going anyplace or doing anything, but I guess I must have." His voice dropped, and he seemed about to cry. "I wish I hadn't gone out last night. If I hadn't nothing would have happened."

"Robby," Brad assured him, "it isn't your fault."

But Robby looked unconvinced.

* * *

Glen Palmer came back to the Randalls' in the middle of the afternoon, but when Brad asked him how the talk with Whalen had gone he was uncommunicative.

"I'm going to go up to the cabin," he said. "Is it all right if I leave the kids here?"

"Of course," Elaine agreed, watching him worriedly. "But wouldn't you like one of us to go with you?"

"I'd rather go by myself. I have some thinking to do and I think I can do it best there."

Brad nodded understandingly and accompanied Glen to the door. When he was sure they were out of range of the children he put his hand on Glen's shoulder and spoke softly.

"If it's any comfort, I don't think that whoever killed Rebecca and Jeff knew what they were doing."

Glen paled slightly and stared blankly at Brad.

"I had a talk with Robby a little while ago," Brad explained. "He doesn't remember what he did on the beach last night. He only remembers feeling good."

"What does that mean?" Glen asked dully.

"Well, whatever happens to Robby must be happening to someone else. But with the opposite effect: Robby feels good, someone else goes crazy. He probably doesn't even know what he's doing. Jeff and Rebecca just happened to be there." In his own mind Brad had dismissed Missy's story as childish imagination, not worth mentioning.

"Oh, God," Glen groaned. "It all seems so—so futile!"

"I know," Brad replied sympathetically. "But we'll find out what's happening, and we'll stop it."

"I wonder," Glen said. "I wonder if it really even matters anymore." He started out onto the beach but Brad called him back.

"Try to get back before dark, will you? Let's not have anything else happening."

"Okay," Glen agreed. Then he turned and started up the beach, his shoulders slumped, his steps slow, uncertain. A few moments later, he disappeared around the corner of the house, and Brad stopped watching. While Glen walked and thought, Brad would work.

Chip Connor arrived at the Randalls' at five thirty that afternoon and hesitated nervously before knocking at the front door. When Elaine opened it a few seconds later she found Chip twisting his hat in his hands and looking very upset.

"Chip!" she said warmly. "Come in."

"Thanks," Chip replied automatically. "Is your husband here?"

"Yes, of course," Elaine said, her smile fading. "Is something wrong?"

"I'm not sure. But I need to talk to Brad."

"He's in the dining room. Come on."

Brad was at the dining-room table surrounded by stacks of books as he searched for an explanation for the madness around him. He looked up distractedly when he heard Elaine come into the room, then put his book aside when he realized who was with her.

"What brings you out here? If you're looking for Glen I think he's up at his place."

"I need to talk to you." Chip sank into one of the chairs around the table and Elaine quickly left the room, sensing that whatever Chip had to say, he wanted to say it only to Brad. When she was gone Brad gave Chip a searching look.

"What is it? Has something else happened?"

"I don't know," Chip said unhappily. "In fact, I'm not even sure I should be here. But I had to talk to someone and you were the only person I could think of."

"What is it?" Brad urged him again. "Is it about Glen?"

"Only indirectly," Chip replied. "I guess mostly it's Harn—Harney Whalen."

"What about him?"

"I'm not sure," Chip said, squirming in the chair. Then, almost as if to change the subject, he said, "Did Glen tell you about what happened today?"

"No. He came in a couple of hours ago, but went right out again. He said he had some thinking to do."

"I'll bet he did," Chip said. "I wish I knew what he was thinking."

"Well, you might go ask him," Brad suggested dryly. "You two seem to get along pretty well."

"Maybe I will after a while," Chip agreed. A silence fell over the two men.

"You said you wanted to talk about Whalen," Brad said at last.

Chip nodded glumly. "I think something's gone wrong with him."

"How do you mean, wrong? You mean physically?"

"I wish it were that simple," Chip hedged.

Brad's fingers drummed on the table and he decided to wait Chip out, let him get to the point any way he wanted to. He wasn't surprised when Chip suddenly stood up and started pacing the room.

"Something's been nagging at me for quite a while now," he said finally. "Harn's attitude, I guess you might say."

"You mean the way he feels about outsiders?"

"That's it," Chip agreed. "But up until today I've always been able to convince myself that it wasn't anything particularly serious—that it was sort of a quirk in his personality."

"But something happened today that changed your mind?"

"Glen Palmer. He came in to tell Harn what happened last night."

"And—?"

"And Harn didn't give him a chance. Instead he told Glen what happened."

"I'm not sure what you mean."

"It was crazy," Chip said. "I've been thinking about it ever since and the only word I come up with is crazy. Harn didn't ask Glen any questions at all. Instead he accused Glen of killing Rebecca himself."

"Just like that?" Brad asked.

"Close enough so that it doesn't make any difference what the exact words were. He must've spent most of the night last night dreaming up a story about how Glen found Rebecca and Jeff Horton making love and killed Jeff, then Rebecca. Apparently you're out of it," he added, smiling humorlessly. Brad ignored the comment.

"What did Glen have to say?"

"What could he say? He said it was ridiculous but Harn wasn't even interested in hearing what happened last night. He just kept after Glen, repeating his idea over and over, as if he were trying to convince Glen. I think he wanted Glen to confess."

"I hope he didn't."

"Of course not," Chip said. "And even if he had it wouldn't have made any difference. The way Harney was acting, any court I've ever heard of would disqualify the whole thing."

"But why? Why would he want to put the whole thing on Glen?"

"I don't think it has anything to do with Glen personally," Chip said. "For a while I thought it did, but I talked to my grandfather a few days ago, and he told me some things that made me wonder."

"What sort of things?"

"Stories. Stories about things that happened around here a long time ago. Long before I was even born. For instance, he told me why Harn hates strangers so much."

"You want to tell me?"

"It's a pretty ugly story." He paused a moment, then swallowed. When he spoke again, his voice was strained.

"Harney watched his grandparents being murdered when he was a little boy."

Brad's eyes widened. "Say that again, please?"

"When Harn was a little boy—maybe seven, eight years old—his grandparents were murdered on the beach. Harney watched it happen."

"Holy Christ," Brad muttered. "Who did it?"

"Nothing was ever proven but everyone seemed to think it was a group of people who were interested in lumbering the area. Maybe even the man who built this house."

"Baron? I thought he was a fisherman. He died by getting caught in his own fishing nets."

"Just like Pete Shelling," Chip agreed. "But he only became a fisherman after Harn canceled his lumbering lease. Anyway, whoever killed Harn's grandparents, they were strangers, and Harn's hated strangers ever since. Only now it's getting out of hand."

"What can I do?" Brad asked.

"I was wondering if maybe you could talk to him," Chip replied.

"Me? Haven't you forgotten something? I'm a stranger here too, and yesterday he as much as accused me of murder. What makes you think Whalen would talk to me?"

"I don't know," Chip said nervously. "I just thought maybe if you could go down there—maybe to talk about something being wrong with the house—and sort of draw him out. Maybe you could tell if he's all right or not."

Brad turned the idea over in his mind, wondering if it could possibly work. If the chief were obsessive, as Chip seemed to think, Whalen certainly wouldn't open up to him. But on the other hand, his refusal to talk just might tell him something too.

"Well, I suppose I could try," he agreed without much conviction. "But I can't promise you anything. Don't expect me to go down and talk to him for five minutes, then be able to tell you if he's sane or not. It just isn't that simple. Besides, he'll probably throw me out of his office."

"But you'd be able to tell if he's reasonable or not, wouldn't you?"

"I can tell you that right now. I don't think Whalen's reasonable, and I never have. But what I think doesn't constitute either a medical or a legal opinion. All it means is that as far as I can tell he's a rigid person with some pretty strong prejudices. That doesn't make him crazy. All it makes him is difficult."

"But what about Glen? What about what Harney's doing to him?"

"So far he hasn't done anything except make a lot of wild accusations. And he hasn't even done that on the record. I mean, he hasn't charged Glen with anything. Or has he?"

Chip shook his head. "No. But I think he's going to."

"Do you? I don't. I don't think Whalen has the vaguest idea of what's going on, and he certainly doesn't have anything to use against Glen Palmer, or anybody else. And I'll tell you something else—I don't think he's ever going to make sense out of this mess. I'm not sure there *is* any sense. All I know is that the storms around here do something to Robby Palmer, and my best guess is that they're doing something to someone else as well."

Something stirred in Chip's mind—a connection only half-made, but he was sure it was an important connection.

"What happens to Robby?"

"I'm not sure exactly," Brad confessed. He made a gesture encompassing the books around him. "I've been trying to find something similar, but so far there isn't anything. Even Robby isn't sure what happens to him. The storms excite him but he doesn't remember what he does during them."

The connection clicked home in Chip's mind. Whalen's visit to Doc Phelps. Was it really indigestion? And other things, little things. The day he had worked with Glen, undisturbed. It had been stormy that day and Whalen had never called him. And that night the Hortons' boat had gone on the rocks. He searched his mind frantically, trying to remember where Harney Whalen had been each time something had gone wrong in Clark's Harbor. And he couldn't remember. All he knew was that usually Harney had been home. Except . . . who knew if he was at home or somewhere else?

Chip made up his mind to have a talk with Doc Phelps. Then, and only then, would he talk to Brad Randall. After all, Randall was a stranger, and Harney Whalen was his uncle.

In Clark's Harbor the natives stuck together.

# TWENTY-EIGHT

THE LEADEN SKIES OVER THE OLYMPIC Peninsula were dropping a soft mist on the small graveyard that overlooked Clark's Harbor, but there were no umbrellas raised above the heads of the tiny group of people who watched as Rebecca Palmer was laid to rest.

Lucas Pembroke closed the bible and began reciting the prayers for Rebecca's soul from memory, his eyes closed not only in reverence, but so that no one would see the sorrow he was feeling for Rebecca.

"Ashes to ashes, dust to dust . . . ."

As the words droned automatically from his lips the minister wondered how much longer he would continue to come to Clark's Harbor, how much longer he would be able to tolerate the coldness that emanated from the village, how much longer, and how many more deaths, it would take before he turned his back on the little settlement nestled by the harbor.

Glen Palmer, holding Missy and Robby close, stood bare-headed in the rain, with Brad and Elaine Randall flanking him. They stood at the end of the open grave, and as the coffin was slowly lowered into the pit Missy began sobbing quietly. Elaine immediately knelt beside the child and gathered her into her arms. Robby, his face frozen in stoic acceptance, watched impassively, but as the coffin disappeared from his view a tear welled in his eye, overflowed, and ran unnoticed down his cheek.

A few yards away, his hands fingering his gloves nervously, Chip Connor stood with his grandfather, Mac Riley. Every few seconds Chip glanced at Glen, nodding slightly, as if to encourage his friend. The gesture went unheeded. Glen's eyes remained fastened on his wife's casket, his features a study in confusion and anguish.

At the fringe of the group, not really a part of it but observing everything, Merle Glind and the village librarian stood clucking together under the protection of a newspaper, their inquisitive eyes darting from face to face, filing away the reactions of everyone there for future discussion and reference.

As the Reverend Pembroke finished his prayers and picked up a clod of earth to sprinkle over the casket, he noticed a flash of movement in the trees beyond the graveyard. But when he looked more carefully, hoping to see who—or what—was there, there was nothing. Pembroke bit his lip, crushed the lump of earth, and dropped it into the grave.

It was like pulling a trigger. Missy Palmer, her quiet tears suddenly bursting forth into loud sobs, clung to Elaine Randall; and Robby, his hand tightening in his father's, suddenly looked up.

"I—I—" he began, but his words were choked off as he began to tremble and sob. Glen quickly sank to the ground beside him and held him.

"It's all right, son," he whispered. "Everything's going to be all right."

Then he scooped up a handful of damp earth, put it in Robby's hand, and led him to the edge of the grave. Together, father and son bade farewell to Rebecca.


"I'm so sorry, Glen," Chip said softly when it was over. "If there's anything I can do—anything at all—"

"Find out who did it," Glen pleaded. "Just find out who killed her."

Chip glanced quickly at Brad, who just as quickly shook his head slightly. Neither of them had yet told Glen of Brad's suspicion, and this was not the time to do it.

"We're working on it," Chip assured him.

"Thanks for coming," Glen said then. "I can't really say I expected you to be here. Not after what Whalen put me through yesterday."

"What Harney thinks is up to Harney," Chip replied. "I asked you what happened Sunday night and you told me. I haven't had any reason to change my mind."

There was a sudden silence and Elaine picked Missy up, then tried to smile cheerfully. "Why don't we all go out to our place," she suggested. "I'm not sure what we have but I'll scrape up something."

Mac Riley, his ancient sensibilities serving him well, took up the suggestion immediately.

"You figure out how to make that old stove go yet?"

"I'm working on it but it still gets to me."

"Nothing to it," Riley quavered. He began leading Elaine away from the graveside, sure that the others would follow. "I been using one of those things all my life, and the trick's in the wood. You got to have small pieces, and lots of different kinds. Some of 'em burn hotter than others. Once you know what's going to burn how, it's a lead-pipe cinch."

Moments later they had reached the cars. The cortege drove slowly away from the graveyard, leaving Rebecca Palmer at peace under the protection of the earth. Glen Palmer glanced back once and for a split second almost envied Rebecca. For her, the horror was truly over.

He wondered if it would ever be over for him.


The gathering at the Randalls' was a quiet one. Chip had begged off almost immediately, pleading business in town. While Elaine wrestled with the stove, encouraged only a little by Mac Riley's advice, Glen and Brad stood nervously in the kitchen, trying to explain to the old man what they thought might be happening.

Riley listened patiently as they told him about the strange effect the beach and the storms had on Robby, and how they had come to the conclusion that Robby was not the only one to be affected by the storms. When they finished Riley scratched his head thoughtfully and turned the whole matter over in his mind.

"Well, I just don't know," he said at last. "Sounds to me like craziness, but then this beach has always been full of craziness. Maybe that's what all the old legends were about." Then he shook his head. "Afraid I can't buy it though. I'm too old for these newfangled ideas. If you ask me it's the sea. The sea and the past. They always catch up with you in the end. No way to get around it."

"You think the sea is breaking people's necks?" Brad asked incredulously. Riley peered at him sadly.

"Could be," he said. "Or it could be the Indians. Some say they're still here, out on the beach."

"If they were we'd have seen them," Glen objected.

"Maybe you would, maybe you wouldn't." Riley's ancient voice crackled. "Only a few people can see the spirits, and even them that can, can't always."

Brad decided to play along with the old man. "Missy seems to think she sees things on the beach."

"Wouldn't surprise me a bit," Riley replied calmly. "Children have better eyes for things like that."

"And better ears for old men's stories?"

"Think what you like. Someday you'll know the truth." He glanced over the window. "Rain's starting up again. Big storm coming," he observed.

Involuntarily, the Randalls and Glen Palmer shuddered.

Chip Connor spent the afternoon with Harney Whalen. It was a difficult time for both of them: Chip tried to pretend that all was as it had always been between them, but Whalen was not fooled. Finally, in midafternoon, he accused Chip of staring at him and demanded to know what was wrong.

"Nothing," Chip assured him. "Nothing at all. I'm just a little worried about you."

"About me? I should think you'd be worried about your pal Glen Palmer. He's the one who's gotten himself in a peck of trouble."

Chip ignored the gibe, wanting to steer the conversation as far from Glen Palmer as possible. "I was just wondering how you're feeling," he said solicitously. "You look a little off color."

"I'm fine," Whalen growled. "Nothing wrong with me that won't be cured by a little peace and quiet around here." There was a pause, then Whalen went on. "Tell you what—why don't you take off for a couple of hours, then come back around dinnertime, and spell me for a while."

Chip couldn't think of a good reason not to, so he left the police station—reluctantly—and went looking for Doc Phelps. He found him at the inn, sitting on the stool Chip usually occupied, a half-empty beer in front of him. He started to get up when Chip came in, but Chip waved him back onto the stool.

"Order one for me and I'll fill yours up," he said cheerfully, sliding onto the stool next to Phelps.

"What about me?" Merle Glind piped eagerly from the stool on the other side of Phelps.

"You could buy your own just once," Chip teased. "But what the hell. Might as well be a big spender."

The beers were drawn and set up in front of them when Phelps asked about Harney Whalen.

"Whalen?" Chip said carefully. "What about him?"

"Well, I ordered him to come in for some tests, but he hasn't showed up. I guess he must be feeling better."

"What kind of tests?" Chip asked, trying to keep the eagerness out of his voice.

"Oh, just some things I'd like checked out," the doctor replied cautiously. "He hasn't been feeling too well, you know."

"Told me it's just indigestion."

"Indigestion?" Dr. Phelps gave the word a sarcastic twist that riveted Chip's attention. "Damnedest kind of indigestion I ever heard of. Most people remember indigestion."

Chip felt his heartbeat skip and a knot of anticipation form in his stomach.

"You mean he's having memory problems? Like blackouts?"

"That's what he told me," Phelps said. "Wanted me to keep it to myself, and I suppose I ought to. But if he isn't going to obey doctor's orders, seems to me something ought to be done."

Chip didn't hear what Phelps had just said—his mind was racing.

"Doc, tell me about the blackouts. It might be important. Very important."

Phelps frowned at the young man and tugged at his lower lip. He didn't like these kids trying to push him around.

"Well, I don't know," he hesitated. "Seems to me like I've already broken Harn's confidence—"

"The hell with Harn's confidence," Chip snapped. "Dr. Phelps, I *have* to know what you know about those blackouts."

"Well, I don't really know much at all," Phelps grumbled. He still resented being ordered to talk by Chip, and yet there was a note of urgency in the young deputy's voice that struck a chord in the doctor. "He didn't really tell me much. Mostly he was upset about something that happened the other day while he was driving out to Sod Beach. It was the day those new people moved in—the Randalls?—and I guess Harn was taking them out to their house. Anyway, he froze at the wheel, I guess, and almost ran over those two kids who live out there."

"Robby and Missy? The Palmer kids?"

"Those'd be the ones," the doctor agreed. "Anyway, it upset Harney enough so he came to see me. Told me he'd been having what he calls spells. His hands start twitching, and then he doesn't remember anything for an hour or so."

"Do you know what's causing it?" Chip asked anxiously.

"Haven't any idea at all," Phelps shrugged. "I wanted him to go down to Aberdeen for some tests, but you know Harn—stubborn as a mule!"

"And you didn't try to make him?" Chip demanded unbelievingly. "For Christ's sake, Doc, he might have killed somebody!"

"But he didn't, did he?" Phelps said blandly.

"Didn't he?" Chip muttered. "I wonder."

He slid off the barstool and headed back to the police station, intent on confronting the police chief. But when he got to the station, Harney Whalen's office was empty.

Chip glanced around the office and saw that Whalen's raincoat still hung from the coat tree in the corner. Wherever he had gone, and for whatever purpose, he hadn't bothered to take his coat with him.

The storm outside, so gentle this morning, was raging.

And it was getting dark. Tonight high tide would be an hour after dusk.

As dusk began to fall Elaine took Missy and Robby into the downstairs bedroom and began putting them to bed. The storm had increased, and the sound of rain battering against the window seemed menacing to Elaine, but she was careful not to communicate her feelings to the children. As she tucked them into the big bed Missy suddenly put her arms around her neck.

"Do we have to sleep here?" she whispered. "Can't we sleep at home?"

"Just for tonight, dear," Elaine said. "But don't you worry. We'll all be in the next room. Your father, and me, and Brad. Everything's going to be fine."

"No, it isn't," Missy said, her voice tiny and frightened. "Nothing's ever going to be fine. I know it isn't."

Elaine hugged the child reassuringly and kissed her on the forehead. Then she kissed Robby too and picked up the lantern by the bed.

"If you need anything you just call me," she told them. Then she pulled the door closed behind her as she left the room.

They lay in bed, listening to the rain beat against the window. For a long time they were quiet, but then Missy stirred.

"Are you asleep?"

"No. Are you?"

"No." Missy paused a moment, then: "I miss Mommy. I want to go home. I don't like this house."

"It's just a house," Robby said disdainfully. "It isn't any different than any other house, except that it's better than ours."

"It's creepy," Missy insisted.

"Oh, go to sleep," Robby said impatiently. He turned over and closed his eyes and tried to pretend that he was sleeping. But he heard the sounds of the rain and the wind and the building surf of the flowing tide. The sounds seemed to be calling him, and try as he would, he couldn't ignore them.

"If you really want to, we can go home," he whispered.

Missy stirred next to him, and he knew she'd heard him.

"Could we go through the woods?" she whispered.

"All right," Robby agreed. The beach would be better, he thought, but the woods would be all right. At least he'd be near the storm. . . .

A few moments later Robby raised the window and the two children crept out into the night.

## TWENTY-NINE

HARNEY WHALEN SAT BEHIND THE WHEEL of the patrol car, his knuckles white with tension, his face beginning to twitch spasmodically. The windshield wipers, almost useless against the driving rain, beat rhythmically back and forth in front of his eyes, but if he saw them, he gave no sign. He was watching the road in front of him, and there was an intensity in his look that would have frightened anyone who saw it. But he was alone, driving north toward Sod Beach.

As he approached the beach he began to hear voices in his mind, voices from his childhood, calling to him.

Floating in the darkness ahead of him, just beyond the windshield, he thought he saw faces—his grandmother was there, her face twisted in fear, her eyes reflecting the panic of a trapped animal. She seemed to be trying to call out to Harn, but her voice was lost in the howling tempest—all that came through was the faint sound of laughter, a laughter that mocked Harney, taunted him, made the chaos in his mind coalesce into hatred.

He turned the car into a narrow side road halfway up Sod Beach and picked his way carefully through the mud until the forest closed in on him, blocking him. He turned off the headlights, then the engine, and sat in the darkness, the rain pounding on the car, the wind whistling around him, and the roar of the pounding surf rolling over him, calling to him. Beckoning him.

Listening only to the voices within him, unmindful of reality, Harney Whalen suddenly opened the car door and stepped out into the storm. A moment later the police car stood lonely and abandoned in the forest.

Harney Whalen had disappeared into the night.

When the pounding on the front door began Brad Randall's first impulse was one of fear—the sudden, gripping fear that always accompanies an unexpected sound in the night. But when he heard a voice calling from outside, his fear dissipated and he hurried to the door.

"I can't find him," Chip Connor cried as he came in out of the storm. "He's gone, and I think it's going to happen again!"

"Can't find who?" Brad asked. "For Christ's sake, calm down! You're not making sense."

"It's Harney Whalen," Chip gasped. "I'm sure of it. He's been sick lately, then he got mad at me today. So I went and found Doc Phelps." Chip dropped into a chair and tried to catch his breath.

"Phelps?" Glen asked. "What the hell does he have to do with anything?"

"He told me about Harn," Chip said. "He told me that Harn's been having blackouts."

"Blackouts?" Brad repeated. "What kind of blackouts?"

"The same kind Robby has. He doesn't pass out—he just can't remember what he was doing. As soon as Phelps told me that I went back to the station, but he was gone. His raincoat's still there but he's not."

"Maybe he went home," Glen suggested, though he was sure it wasn't true.

"That's the first place I went," Chip said. "He's not there. So I figured I'd better come out here and warn you. If what you think is true, he's probably prowling around the beach somewhere."

"My God," Elaine moaned. "Is the house locked up?"

"It's been locked up all evening," Brad said.

"I'm going to check anyway." She picked up a lantern and started toward the dining room, intent on circling the main floor.

"We've got to find him," Chip said as soon as Elaine was out of the room.

"Maybe not," Brad replied. "As long as we're all here there isn't much chance that Whalen will find anyone on the beach. Not tonight."

As if to confirm what he said, a bolt of lightning struck, briefly illuminating the room, then the clap of thunder shook the old house, rattling the windows.

As the thunder died the sudden void was filled by Elaine Randall's scream of horror. A second later she appeared at the bedroom door. "They're gone," she cried, her face pale and her voice strangled. "The children are gone."

Glen Palmer started for the bedroom and Elaine stepped aside to let him pass. He looked frantically around the icy room, then went to the open window, the cold, wind-driven rain stinging his face.

"Please," he prayed silently. "Leave me my children."

When he returned to the living room, Chip and Brad were waiting for him, their coats on, flashlights in their hands. Next to the fireplace, Mac Riley stood uncertainly.

"I think I should go too," he said. "I've known Harney since he was a baby. If something's happening to him . . ."

"No, Grandpa," Chip replied. "Stay here. You can't move as fast as you used to, and Mrs. Randall shouldn't be left alone."

"Please," she begged. "Please stay with me. If I have to wait by myself I'll go out of my mind. I know I will." Sobbing softly, she sank into a chair. Brad started toward her, but Mac Riley held up his hand.

"Go on," he said. "Find the children. We'll be all right, I promise you."

As Chip, Brad, and Glen went out into the night, Mac Riley poked at the fire, then began one more circuit of the house, checking the doors and windows. When he came back to the living room he tried to comfort Elaine.

"They'll find the kids," he said softly. "Don't you worry."

But inside, the old man was worried.

## THIRTY

THE MAELSTROM CRASHED AROUND THEM, the high keening of the wind screaming in the treetops providing an eerie counterpoint to the roar of the surf as the tide came to full flood. The beach had shrunk to a narrow ribbon of sand between the roiling sea and the tangle of driftwood that creaked and shifted in the storm.

"I can't see anything," Missy cried out, clinging to her brother's hand, stumbling blindly along after him as he moved quickly through the night.

If he heard her Robby gave no sign. The excitement of the beach was upon him, and his senses took in the wildness of the elements, absorbing the unleashed energy of the tempest. His body was filling with a strange exultation, exciting him, yet at the same time calming him. It was a feeling he didn't quite understand, but he accepted it and was grateful for it.

Missy stopped suddenly and Robby nearly lost his footing as she jerked on his hand.

"Something's here," Missy whispered, pulling close to Robby and putting her lips to his ear. "I can feel it."

"Nothing's here," Robby said. "Only us."

"Yes there is," Missy insisted. "Something's in the woods looking for us. Let's go back. Please?"

"We can't go back," Robby told her. "Not anymore."

He started forward again, pulling Missy with him, and she began sobbing, her terror overcoming her. As they moved along the beach she began to see shapes, strange glowing figures, moving along beside her, in front of her, behind her, coming closer, reaching out for her.

She began screaming.

Harney Whalen crouched behind the pile of driftwood that separated the beach from the forest and listened to the sounds in his head. The laughter was getting louder and the screams of his grandmother seemed to be fading away.

There was a flash of lightning and he saw two figures coming toward him across the beach. They were small figures but he knew who they were.

They were strangers.

Strangers had killed his grandparents while he had helplessly watched.

He wanted to run, wanted to go away and hide, as he had done so many years ago.

But he couldn't. He felt something gripping him, forcing him to stay where he was. He turned and there was someone beside him in the night. His grandmother, her strong, chiseled features gleaming in the night, her dark eyes flashing, was beside him.

While the rain slashed at him and the wind tore through his clothes, chilling him, she whispered to him, her words echoing against the pounding of the surf.

*Don't run away. Avenge. Avenge.*

Harney waited behind the log, waited for them to come near.

He crouched lower, huddled in upon himself, and listened to the words of the old Klickashaw at his side. She spoke to him of ancient wrongs. . . .

On the beach Robby and Missy, the wind whirling around them, hurried along, unaware of the danger waiting for them in the forest.


Far down the beach, Chip Connor, Brad Randall, and Glen Palmer hurried through the storm, their flashlights playing over the sand, nearly useless in the rain.

"We'll never find them," Brad called out, raising his voice against the wind. "Not if we stay together. Let's spread out."

"You take the surf line," Chip yelled. "Glen, stay in the middle of the beach. I'll go up by the forest. And call for them. They might hear and it will let us keep track of each other. I don't think we should get too far apart."

They spread out, and the three dots of light scattered themselves across the beach, visible for only a few yards but lighting the way for the searchers. They began calling out the children's names.


Robby began pulling Missy toward the forest but she hung back, her terrified eyes seeing nothing but the strange figures closing in around her, reaching for her. A faint sound drifted through the night, nearly lost in the storm. Missy pulled Robby to a halt.

"Someone's calling us. I can hear my name."

Robby glared at his sister, tugging on her arm. "We have to go into the woods. We'll be safe there," he hissed.

Once more the faint sounds echoed through the night: *"Missy . . . Robby!"*

The children crouched uncertainly in the sand, straining to hear better, but it was useless. The wind increased, howling in from the ocean, carrying the acrid smell of salt water with it.

They began climbing over the pile of driftwood.

* * *

Harney Whalen also heard the voices calling. But stronger in his mind was his grandmother's voice, whispering to him, urging him on, reassuring him.

*We are with you. We will help you. You are a child of the storm. You belong to us.*

He stood up, facing the storm, and exultation swept through him. His grandmother cried out to him. *Vengeance! Vengeance!*

The lightning flashed.

The instant of electric brightness seemed to last an eternity, and the three figures froze, staring at each other across the driftwood.

And Missy knew.

"It's him," she screamed. "He's here, Robby. He's going to kill us."

Harney Whalen didn't hear the words Missy cried out—only the sound. He peered malevolently at the two figures, seeing not two small and frightened children, but two faceless figures from the past, two unidentifiable forms, laughing at him, laughing at what they had done to his grandparents.

He had to destroy them.

He started over the driftwood.

The two children, suddenly coming to life, began running up the beach.

The lightning faded and the roll of thunder began.

"I see them," Brad cried as the night closed around him once more. "North. They're north of us, right near the woods."

On either side of him, the pinpoints of light that were Chip and Glen suddenly began bobbing in the darkness as all three of them broke into a run. Then they began hearing Missy's frightened cries, leading them through the night.

The children tore through the night, hearing the pounding of feet behind them. Then Robby stumbled and fell, and Missy tumbled on top of him.

Harney Whalen, his breath coming in fitful gasps, caught up with them, towering over them, glowering down upon them like a furious giant.

Missy saw him first and her eyes widened in terror as she screamed out into the night. Then she felt a hand clamp over her mouth and her scream was cut off.

Robby scrambled free from the tangle of limbs, but his mind was confused and nothing was making any sense to him. He moved aside, staring helplessly at his struggling sister, then began to scream.

"My God, he's got them," Glen shouted as he heard first Missy's choked-off scream of terror, then Robby's mindless howling in the night. The three men were running together now, shining their lights into the darkness, praying that they would get to the children before it was too late.

And then they found them. Chip Connor hurled himself onto Harney Whalen's back, grabbing the chief by the neck. Whalen let go of Missy and began struggling with Chip, desperately fighting off his unseen assailant.

Glen grabbed Missy and held the sobbing child close to him, stroking her head, patting her, trying to calm her. Then Robby too flung himself onto Glen, and the three of them held each other, unmindful of what was happening around them.

Brad stood helplessly, wanting to come to Chip's aid but unsure if it would do any good. Then, before he could make up his mind, Whalen broke free of Chip's grasp and ran.

Chip started to follow him, but Whalen disappeared into the darkness. "Which way did he go?" Chip cried. "I can't find him."

"Toward the water," Brad called.

They began running, Brad shining his light ahead, the wind clutching at them.

And then they saw him.

Harney Whalen was in the surf, wading out to sea.

Chip started in after him, but Brad stopped, holding his light steadily on the retreating figure of the police chief.

"Let him go," Brad called.

Chip stopped, instinctively obeying the command.

As the two men watched, an immense wave swept in from the sea, breaking over Harney Whalen's head.

He struggled against the force of the water for a moment, his arms waving ineffectually in the air.

Then he was gone, taken by the sea.

Chip walked slowly back to where Brad stood, still playing the light over the spot where Harney Whalen had vanished.

"Why did you stop me?" Chip asked softly.

"It's better this way," Brad answered. "This way we know it ends."

Then they turned away from the sea and started back toward Glen Palmer.

Behind them the tide turned and began to ebb.

An hour later the storm broke.

Sod Beach was quiet.

# EPILOGUE

"IT'S OVER," CHIP CONNOR SAID AS HE walked into the Randalls' living room.

Brad and Elaine looked at him expectantly, but Glen Palmer didn't seem to care.

Two weeks had passed, two weeks during which the strange story of Harney Whalen had passed through Clark's Harbor in whispers, two weeks during which the people of the village had come to accept what had happened.

Today it had been finished. The coroner's inquest had been held. It had been a strange inquest.

There were few facts to be discussed. Much time had been spent on speculation, on trying to decide exactly what had happened to the police chief.

In the end it had been decided that Harney Whalen had died a suicide. Nothing was said about the other deaths in Clark's Harbor, the deaths that dotted its history like a pox. But outside the inquest the people talked, and wondered, and clucked their tongues in sympathy.

Sympathy for those who had died—and for Whalen, who apparently had killed them.

"They want me to take over Harney's job," Chip said when he had finished telling them the results of the inquest.

"Are you going to?" Brad asked.

"I don't know," Chip said uneasily. "It makes sense, I suppose, but I don't know if I want the job."

"You'd be good at it," Glen Palmer offered.

"That's not what worries me," Chip replied. "It's the memories. Too many memories. I'd probably do too many things differently from Harn."

"Would that be so bad?" Elaine asked.

Chip shook his head. "That's what I don't know. Harn wasn't all bad. For a long time he ran things very well. If it all hadn't gone wrong for him  . . ." He let the thought go, then turned to Brad. "What happened?" he asked. "Isn't there any explanation?"

"A theory," Brad said. "But I'll never be able to prove it. There was a connection between Robby and Harney Whalen."

"I don't understand—" Chip began, but Brad stopped him.

"I'm not sure I do either. It has to do with bio-rhythms, and bio-rhythms are elusive things. We know they affect us, but we don't know why. For that matter, we aren't even sure what they are. Everyone has a set pattern of rhythms that begins the day he's born, and the pattern only repeats itself every fifty-eight years and sixty-seven days. As it happens, that's exactly how much older Whalen was than Robby. Both of them, apparently, had a bio-rhythmic pattern that's affected by the storms out here. For Robby the effect is good. For Whalen—well, coupled with the trauma he had when he was a boy, the effect was disastrous."

Chip stared at the psychiatrist. "How come you didn't think of that before?" he demanded. "If you knew something like that could happen, Harn could have been—"

Again Brad cut him off. "I'm sorry, Chip," he said gently. "There's nothing that could have been done. In fact, I don't even know if my theory is right. All it is is a theory, but it fits the facts. And with bio-rhythms that's most of the story. You can't predict what's *going* to happen, but they often explain what *did* happen. You might call them a good tool for hindsight," he added wryly.

*But what about the future,* he wondered to himself. His eyes wandered to the window, and came to rest on Robby Palmer. The boy was walking slowly along the beach, studying the sand at his feet.

Again the words came into Brad's mind. *What about the future?* With Harney Whalen gone, what would the beach hold for Robby?

As if reading Brad's mind, Chip Connor suddenly stood up. "I think I'll go for a walk," he said, almost too casually. "One thing about this beach—it was always a good place to think." As he pulled on his coat, Chip gazed out at the calmness of Sod Beach. On the horizon, as often was the case, a storm seemed to be building, but it no longer posed a threat, no longer induced a fear of something horrible about to happen . . .

And yet, far down the beach, he could see Robby Palmer, standing still now, staring at the darkening horizon, his puppy frisking at his feet.

A chill crept through Chip's body, and he buttoned his coat snug around his neck.

He left the old house and started north, not stopping until he reached the point where Harney Whalen had disappeared into the surf.

Chip's eyes scanned the sea, unconsciously searching for the police chief's body.

It had never been found, never washed up on the sand, either here or on the beaches to the north and south, all of which had been patrolled regularly.

Chip turned away from the sea and started toward the woods. As he made his way to the top of the driftwood tangle the wind began to blow.

Two weeks ago the blowing of the wind would have frightened him.

He sat on a huge silvery log and tried to sort things out in his mind, tried to separate his memories—tried to categorize them, keeping the good memories and discarding the bad ones.

He wanted to create two Harney Whalens: the one he had known so well, the one he had grown up respecting and admiring; and the other one, the recent one, the Harney Whalen whose mind had been twisted, partly by his ancient memories, but also apparently by the same elements that had twisted the log on which Chip sat. Maybe, Chip reflected, his grandfather was right—maybe it was the sea that got to Harney.

As the sun began to go down and the wind blew harder, Chip shivered. He watched the sand dance across the beach, driven on the wind.

He saw something, something that had been buried on the beach but that was being revealed by the storm.

Curious, he climbed down from the driftwood and uncovered the object.

He recognized it instantly. It was Scooter, Missy and Robby Palmer's tiny puppy.

It was still warm.

Its neck had been wrung.

As the storm broke upon him, Chip turned to the woods, suddenly frightened. Carrying the tiny body of the puppy, Chip once again climbed the driftwood, but this time he crossed it and went into the woods.

Robby Palmer felt the first drops of rain splash on his face and was glad. He'd been waiting for the storm all afternoon and now it was here.

With the storm would come the excitement.

And with the excitement would come the shapes and the voices.

He hadn't told anybody about the things he saw on the beach now. He was sure they wouldn't believe him—none of them except Missy, but they hadn't believed her, either.

He still wasn't sure exactly who the people on the beach were, or why they were there.

Usually they danced strange dances that always ended with them burying someone on the beach—someone who didn't belong. But it didn't frighten Robby because he knew he belonged. He was part of the beach and the beach loved him.

It was the strangers who didn't belong.

The strangers who came and took the beach from the people who belonged and betrayed them.

As the storm grew the dance began, and Robby watched it from the forest. Then the voices began, telling him to join the dance.

But he didn't know how.

*You will know,* the voices said.

Robby suddenly became aware of a figure making its way over the driftwood.

*Betrayal,* the voices whispered. *Betrayal.*

The figure came closer, and the voices whispered again.

*Vengeance. Vengeance.*

Robby didn't quite understand the word, but he knew what to do.

He picked up a heavy stick and crept behind a tree.

He waited, and listened to the voices.

The full force of the tempest broke over the coast, lashing at the tree as the tide surged forth, marching before the thunderheads like a harbinger of death.

As the surf crested, Robby Palmer, his eyes seeing nothing of the storm, emerged from the forest to pick his way carefully over the bleached bones of driftwood littering the beach.

He was among them now, and as their ceremony came to its climax the storm dancers reached out to him, sang to him, pled with him to join them in their cry for the strangers.

Uncertainly at first, but then with a sense of all things being right, Robby Palmer gave himself up to them.

# ABOUT THE AUTHOR

John Saul has written 19 novels offering millions and millions of readers uncounted thrills and chills of all kinds. Born in Pasadena, California on February 25, 1942 and raised in Whittier, he attended several colleges but never obtained a degree.

With the huge success of his first book, *Suffer the Children,* John began his prolific career of writing bestselling terror and suspense. His books include, *The God Project, Brainchild, Hellfire, Creature, The Homing* and more. An actor and playwright, his plays have been produced in Los Angeles and Seattle. John has served on numerous boards and panels and is the winner of the *Life Time Achievement Award* from the Northwest Writers Conference. A veteran of publicity, he has made over four hundred radio and television appearances and has been featured in over five hundred newspapers and magazine articles.

John lives part-time in the Pacific Northwest, both in Seattle and the San Juan Islands. He also maintains a residence on Maui, Hawaii. He currently enjoys motor homing and boating. He is an avid bridge player, and loves to cook.

His newest novel is *Black Lightning.*

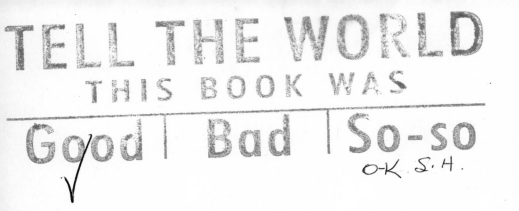

# TELL THE WORLD
## THIS BOOK WAS

| Good | Bad | So-so |
|------|-----|-------|
| ✓ | | O-K. S. H. |